THE GREAT SHORT NOVELS OF HENRY JAMES

THE GREAT SHORT NOVELS OF HENRY JAMES

EDITED WITH AN INTRODUCTION & COMMENTS BY

PHILIP RAHV

Carroll & Graf Publishers, inc.
New York

Introduction and commentary published through arrangement with Mrs. Philip Rahv.

First Carroll & Graf edition, 1986

Carroll & Graf Publishers, Inc.
260 Fifth Avenue
New York, NY 10001

ISBN: 0-88184-247-8

Manufactured in the United States of America

CONTENTS

A BIOGRAPHICAL INTRODUCTION

THE REPUTATION of Henry James has grown immeasurably since his death in 1916, and he is now generally regarded by discriminating readers as America's greatest novelist and a master of modern prose belonging to the company of Proust and Joyce. He is among the two or three American writers of the nineteenth century who were able to invent and put to creative use the imaginative methods of the twentieth century. And it is precisely because of the modernity of his gifts that his contemporaries failed to appraise him at his true worth.

The fact that James lived most of his adult life in England has made for a certain prejudice against him in his own country. The majority of critics, however, have long recognized the connection between his literary art and his quality as an archetypal American, a personality of historic rank and classic temper. Edmund Wilson has said that it is America which really gets the better of it in Henry James; and T. S. Eliot has observed that the soil of James's origin imparted a flavor which, paradoxically enough, was "improved and given its chance, not worked off" by his expatriation. The truth is that his quarrel with his native land was a lover's quarrel, as he himself defined it in one of his earliest writings.

In the Jamesian fiction you find a large group of American characters who stand in a vital and crucial relation to the national life. Very few figures created by our novelists are as significant from a national point of view as James's "passionate pilgrim," who enters the deep and dark and rich hive of Europe, driven by the desire to appropriate the fruits of civilization. It is at once the tragedy and humor of his case that he wants to be cut in on European experience without paying the price of sacrificing his new-world innocence. This drama has many variations, particularly as relating to the career of the "international" American girl—a type James invented and made real in a series of narratives and whom he elevated from her early modest beginnings in characters like Daisy Miller and Mary Garland to the golden display of such later heroines as Milly Theale and Maggie Verver. In the last great novels this heroine is endowed with the prerogatives of a princess and pictured as "the heiress of all the ages." A pure American product, she is filled with the wonderful belief that the world belongs to her and she is the best there is. She exists in no other literature and it is inconceivable that she should. But it is only by projecting her against a foreign background, by placing her in the center of "Europe's lighted and decorated stage," that James was able to bring out her latent "greatness."

The sense of Europe as a spiritual resource and as a literary theme was acquired by James in early childhood. Born in New York City on April 15, 1843, he was taken abroad at the age of two and again at the age of twelve, when for nearly five years the family traveled and the children attended schools in Paris, London, Bonn and Geneva. William, the elder brother by fifteen months, was vexed by the irregularities of their education; whereas Henry, an indifferent scholar, his faculties being all of the imagination and sensibility, was supremely content. From the very first the charm and color of history constituted an obsessive interest. Those formative years are depicted in the autobiographical volume *A Small Boy and Others* as shaping the pattern of all he was ever to want from life—"just to *be* somewhere . . . and somehow to receive an impression or an accession, feel a relation or a vibration." Everywhere he saw "so much," his eye making out "arrangements of things hanging together with the romantic rightness that had the force of a revelation." The picture composed itself into the characteristic Jamesian vision—the vision of Europe as a "sublime synthesis."

Yet it was impossible for James to identify himself wholly with the Old World, and through all the years he remained the spectator from across the sea. Identification would have meant missing the thousand and one ironies of the transatlantic relation and giving up his role as the "fond analyst" of the American psyche in its exposure to European conditions. It was on the perception of *differences* that his genius was nourished; and at the age of twenty-nine, when well on his way to discovering his major theme, he wrote: "It's a complex fate being an American, and one of the responsibilities it entails is fighting against a superstitious valuation of Europe."

The James family was remarkable for its intellectual vitality, inwardness and good faith. The father, Henry James, Sr., was a friend of the men of letters and philosophers of his age and himself a brilliant though somewhat eccentric writer on moral and theological subjects, a cosmic optimist, a disciple of Swedenborg and a radical democrat; and the elder son, William, displayed his dialectical prowess at an early age. The paternal grandfather had made a fortune in Albany, enabling his heirs to cast aside all neat practicalities in favor of the cultivation of individuality and the arts of life. In two generations they were never known "to be guilty of a stroke of business." It was difficult, however, to adjust a life of moneyed leisure to the demands of a society in which as yet "business alone was respectable." Thus the James children often came home in a state of acute embarrassment because of their inability to appease their inquiring schoolmates with a "presentable account" of their parent. Their constant appeal to him was, "What shall we tell them you *are*?"—an appeal to which he patiently replied: "Say I'm a philosopher, say I'm a seeker of truth, say I'm a lover of my kind, say I'm an author of books if you like; or, best of all, say I'm a student." Then there was the sad and mystifying example of a whole set of uncles and cousins who appeared to find no other use for inherited ease except to go to the bad with it. Under the circumstances Europe inevitably figured for the James family as a prime resource, for it seemed that leisure could be made to "pay" only where a social order existed which permitted people not to be "hurled straight, with the momentum of rising, upon an office or a store."

But in the long run the father always came back to the idea that America was superior to "those countries" after all, and in 1860 the family returned from abroad to settle in Newport. It was there that the Civil War broke upon them; the two younger brothers—Wilky and Bob—joined the struggle, but Henry was incapacitated by an accident suffered while helping to put out a fire. In later years he referred to it as "a horrid even if obscure hurt . . . the effects of which were to draw themselves out incalculably and intolerably." It became for him an "inexhaustible interest"; and as a psychoanalytic writer has recently attempted to prove, there can be little doubt that this accident, in all its psychic ramifications, is the essential clue to certain obscure tendencies in the private and literary experience of Henry James about which his biographers and critics have occasionally speculated but never cleared up in a satisfactory manner. Perhaps it is this "obscure hurt" which chiefly accounts for the fact that he never married.

At that time his brother William was already engaged in scientific work at Harvard, and Henry joined him there in 1862 to attend lectures at the Law School. The study of law petered out soon enough, but in the atmosphere of Boston and Cambridge it became possible to develop literary plans. He formed a lifelong friendship with W. D. Howells, with whom he discussed endlessly the craft of fiction; other friends were C. E. Norton and J. R. Lowell. As the latter was on the staff of *The North American Review* and Howells was assistant editor of the *Atlantic Monthly*, it was in those periodicals, as well as in *The Nation* and the *Galaxy*, that James's first stories and reviews appeared. The impressions of New England absorbed during the sixties he later put to good use in several narratives, the best of which is *The Bostonians* (1886), a novel that signally failed to please the residents of Back Bay. Europe he had not visited since boyhood, and he went to England in the spring of 1869, the famous springtime celebrated in the autobiographical volumes, when he was taken by the Nortons to see George Eliot, Ruskin, Rossetti, Tennyson and other distinguished persons—a series of meetings remembered as "a positive fairytale f privilege." The honorific language is characteristic of James, nd the unwary reader may well miss the note of irony it coneals—the irony of "the brooding monster . . . born to discriminate *tout propos*," who enjoyed dissecting the great no less than the mall. In *Notes of a Son and Brother* there is a richly humorous ccount of the visit to Tennyson. The bard presented a shaggy nd disconcertingly non-Tennysonian appearance and recited *Locksey Hall* in a manner that "took even more out of his verse than e had put in."

In his fiction of the early seventies James had come close to lefining his theme of the American in Europe, particularly in such tories as *Madame de Mauves, The Madonna of the Future* and *The Passionate Pilgrim*. The latter is the title story of his first book, ublished in 1875, the year he went to live permanently in Europe. Making his home in Paris, he was soon admitted into the briliant circle of Flaubert, Zola, Maupassant, Daudet and Turgenev. Their combined example served to reinforce his own conviction hat the art of literature was the most rigorous discipline coneivable and a complete fate in itself. Those writers, however, were n the main concerned with their own tradition, holding the opinions of a vague lonely American to be of little account; and James was generally indisposed to like French fashions in living. In July 1876 he was writing to William that he was done with the French forever: "Easy and smooth-flowing as life is in Paris, I would throw it over tomorrow for an even very small chance to plant myself for a while in England." A few months later, having taken up his post of observation in "the place where there is most in the world to observe," he was settled in London for good.

That James made a success of his life in England is established by the one test that really counts—the test of creative achievement. Thus during his initial five years in London, besides a large number of shorter pieces and the critical biography of Hawthorne, he wrote *Daisy Miller, An International Episode, The Europeans, Confidence, Washington Square,* and *The Portrait of a Lady*, the novel with which the fiction of his early manner is brought to a masterly close. James believed that it takes an old civilization to set a novelist in motion, that it takes manners, customs, usages, habits, forms of a settled and realized character. Now whatever the measure of general truth in his idea, the fact is that it reflected his own intense need, which if frustrated would surely have resulted in the warping of his genius. He was a man given to moods of depression and anxiety, and omens of disaster always had the advantage of his imagination; yet in all matters relating to his work he was a tower of strength. Above all he knew how to take care of his genius and this knowledge made of him the one salient example in our literature of a novelist who, not exhausted by the youthful assertion of power, learned how to sustain his gifts and grow to full maturity. He understood that for the artist there can be no second chance. It was truly his own case that he described in the short story *The Middle Years*, in which the artist-hero cries out at the end: "It *is* glory—to have been tested, to have had our little quality, and cast our little spell. . . . A second chance—*that's* the delusion. There never was to be but one. We work in the dark—we do what we can—we give what we have. Our doubt is our passion, and our passion is our task. The rest is the madness of art."

As James progressed in his work toward the ever more complex effects of his later period, he found that the public would not stay with him and that the popular success of *Daisy Miller* and *The Portrait of a Lady* was not to be repeated. It is generally thought that this is what induced him, in the early nineties, to try his hand as a playwright. After several years he gave up the attempt as a failure, but from his theatrical experience he brought back to his novels a sharper sense of economy in writing and an extraordinary aptitude for framing fictional situations in a scenic and dramatic manner. In 1897, as he left London to set up a permanent residence at Lamb House, near Rye, Sussex, he was in the midst of his greatest and most productive period; and between 1898 and 1904 he brought out several volumes of stories as well as the consummate novels of his late maturity—*The Wings of the Dove, The Ambassadors* and *The Golden Bowl.* Toward the end of 1904, when he was more than sixty years old, he undertook a visit to America which lasted ten months—months crowded with observations and impressions. *The American Scene* (1907) is the record of that visit.

It was in late middle age and afterward that he developed that strong and portentous personality of which his friends have written at such great length in their memoirs. Ford Madox Ford remembered him as the most masterful man he had ever met, in whose presence he not infrequently felt "something like awe."—"His skin was dark, his eyes very clear cut, his brow domed and bare. His eyes were singularly penetrating, dark and a little prominent. On their account he was regarded by the neighborhood poor as having the qualities of a Wise Man—a sorcerer." Edith Wharton describes him in her autobiography as having lost in those years the look of a "bearded Penseroso" conveyed by Sargent's well-known drawing; the beardless face revealed in all its sculptural beauty the "noble Roman mask and big dramatic mouth." And all who knew him remembered his talk—highly ceremonious, proceeding by elaborate pauses and Ciceronian periods, and full of fantastically subtle jesting—the kind of talk that at once astounded and hugely amused his interlocutors. It was personal relations rather than ideas that he mostly liked to discuss. He took a great interest in the young writers of his time, and among them he was on particularly good terms with Hugh Walpole, Compton Mackenzie, H. G. Wells, Joseph Conrad, Stephen Crane and Rupert Brooke.

The outbreak of the First World War was a prodigious experience to James. His feeling was that the stakes were enormous, and, laying aside his work, he threw himself into various activities bearing on the war effort. It was largely because of his impatience with America's dilatory policy in adopting the cause of the Allies, and also as a means of declaring his solidarity with the people in whose midst he had lived for so long, that he became a naturalized British subject in 1915. Edith Wharton thought that the war was his death-blow. After two years of it he could no longer endure to watch the slaughter.—"It was the gesture of Agamemnon, covering his face with his cloak before the unbearable." He died on February 28, 1916. "So here it is at last, the distinguished thing!" he is reported to have exclaimed as he suffered his first stroke.

PHILIP RAHV.

Madame de Mauves

Madame de Mauves

MADAME DE MAUVES, written in the summer of 1873, is the story of the ruinous marriage of an American girl, Euphemia Cleve, to a French aristocrat of low morals. James was living in an old inn at Homburg in the Taunus hills when he was "visited," as he recalled in a later preface, by the "gentle Euphemia," a type "experimentally international" who muffled her charming head in the lightest, finest, vaguest tissue of romance. . . ." In accounting for her the young James made great progress in tracing out the complex design of the theme so peculiarly his own—the theme of the "international situation." In point of technique as well this tale stands out as James's best work of the early seventies. It differs from his other stories of that period (*A Passionate Pilgrim, Eugene Pickering*, etc.) in being told mostly through the impressions of the hero, thus doing away both with the loose approach of the "omniscient author" and the equally loose approach of a narrator somewhat awkwardly situated outside the action. The change is all in the direction of greater dramatic effect, of maintaining the reader and the character whose function it is "to find things out" on the same plane of gradual revelation.

Since the early months of 1872 James had been living in Europe, and, to judge by a letter to W. D. Howells dated at the time of the composition of *Madame de Mauves,* he had once again fallen into a mood of anxious uncertainty as to the fate of the American who takes Europe as "hard" as he had been taking it. Perhaps it was a mistake, after all, to put so much stock in the Old World, which persisted in keeping one at arm's length despite all one's best efforts. To Howells he wrote of the desolation of exile and of the sacrifices exacted by "this arrogant old Europe which so little befriends us." And a few months later he was writing in the same vein to Grace Norton, remarking that one stood to America in a much less "factitious and artificial relation" than to Europe.—"It would seem that in our great unendowed, unfurnished, unentertained and unentertaining continent, where we all sit sniffing, as it were, the very earth of our foundations, we ought to have leisure to turn out something from the very heart of simple human nature."

The situation of *Madame de Mauves* is central to the experience of the Jamesian Americans in Europe. It is the situation, as its author once summed it up, of "some insidiously beguiled and betrayed, some cruelly wronged compatriot" who suffers at the hands of persons "pretending to represent the highest possible civilization and to be of an order in every way superior to his own." James was always identifying his native land with innocence and "simple human nature," an idea which his European critics have not found it easy to swallow. One such critic, an Englishman, has explained it as the psychological twist by means of which James was able to work off the guilt of his expatriation. This may be true in a way, but the more important fact is that his attitude of moral aggression toward Europe is the typical and classic attitude of his countrymen.

As for the "gentle Euphemia," the interesting question for the latter-day commentator is whether it is actually she or her French husband whose behavior is more akin to "simple human nature." The Baron's failings are transparent enough; it is his wife's epical virtue, rather, that the modern reader might well consider as lacking in simplicity and naturalness. For the closest she seems to come to emotional, even orgastic satisfaction, is in that scene on the terrace at Saint-Germain when in the heat of her paradoxical "passion" she renounces every prospect of love and happiness. And the last sentence of the narrative is sufficiently ambiguous to suggest that even Bernard Longmore, her renounced lover, had begun to suspect that his lady's goodness is of such immense proportions as to exclude her altogether from the chances of love.

Longmore is a cold fish, too, patently belonging to James's long line of sad and uncertain young men whose ideal frustration so "splendidly" confirms their delicacy of feeling. The truth is that James reserved the rewards of experience for his American young women. He repeatedly confessed that in the role of men of action his compatriots were beyond him; it is their sisters, with their ardent imaginations and truly Emersonian self-reliance, that he understood perfectly and learned to conduct through the "beautiful difficulties" of their transatlantic romances. The character of Euphemia, however, is but an initial sketch representing only one side of the Jamesian young woman—the side that makes for the difficulties rather than for the rewards.

Baron de Mauves is quite as characteristically a Jamesian figure as Longmore and Euphemia. The very image of the long-standing American suspicion of immorality in foreigners, this type appears in the early fictions in a more or less conventional guise. But his successors are gradually freed from the encumbrances of melodrama; and in such late novels as *The Wings of the Dove* and *The Golden Bowl* he emerges as a person of grace and intelligence whose evil acts spring inevitably from the situation in which he finds himself. The same process of refinement is to be observed in James's picture of the French milieu. In *Madame de Mauves* the picture is of a kind that a Frenchman would surely resent as another instance of Anglo-Saxon presumption. If we are to know, however, what James made of his career, that picture should be compared to the vision of Paris in *The Ambassadors,* written thirty years later. For in that work the style and charm of the great city are rendered in colors so exquisite as to convert the novel into a supreme tribute to French civilization.

I

THE VIEW from the terrace at Saint-Germain-en-Laye is immense and famous. Paris lies spread before you in dusky vastness, domed and fortified, glittering here and there through her light vapors, and girdled with her silver Seine. Behind you is a park of stately symmetry, and behind that a forest, where you may lounge through turfy avenues and light-checkered glades, and quite forget that you are within half an hour of the boulevards. One afternoon, however, in mid-spring, some five years ago, a young man seated on the terrace had chosen not to forget this. His eyes were fixed in idle wistfulness on the mighty human hive before him. He was fond of rural things, and he had come to Saint-Germain a week before to meet the spring half-way; but though he could boast of a six months' acquaintance with the great city, he never looked at it from his present standpoint without a feeling of painfully unsatisfied curiosity. There were moments when it seemed to him that not to be there just then was to miss some thrilling chapter of experience. And yet his winter's experience had been rather fruitless, and he had closed the book almost with a yawn. Though not in the least a cynic, he was what one may call a disappointed observer; and he never chose the right-hand road without beginning to suspect after an hour's wayfaring that the left would have been the interesting one. He now had a dozen minds to go to Paris for the evening, to dine at the Café Brébant, and to repair afterwards to the Gymnase and listen to the latest exposition of the duties of the injured husband. He would probably have risen to execute this project, if he had not observed a little girl who, wandering along the terrace, had suddenly stopped short and begun to gaze at him with round-eyed frankness. For a moment he was simply amused, for the child's face denoted helpless wonderment; the next he was agreeably surprised. "Why, this is my friend Maggie," he said; "I see you have not forgotten me."

Maggie, after a short parley, was induced to seal her remembrance with a kiss. Invited then to explain her appearance at Saint-Germain, she embarked on a recital in which the general, according to the infantine method, was so fatally sacrificed to the particular, that Longmore looked about him for a superior source of information. He found it in Maggie's mamma, who was seated with another lady at the opposite end of the terrace; so, taking the child by the hand, he led her back to her companions.

Maggie's mamma was a young American lady, as you would immediately have perceived, with a pretty and friendly face and an expensive spring toilet. She greeted Longmore with surprised cordiality, mentioned his name to her friend, and bade him bring a chair and sit with them. The other lady, who, though equally young and perhaps even prettier, was dressed more soberly, remained silent, stroking the hair of the little girl, whom she had drawn against her knee. She had never heard of Longmore, but she now perceived that her companion had crossed the ocean with him, had met him afterwards in travelling, and (having left her husband in Wall Street) was indebted to him for various small services.

Maggie's mamma turned from time to time and smiled at her friend with an air of invitation; the latter smiled back, and continued gracefully to say nothing.

For ten minutes Longmore felt a revival of interest in his interlocutors; then (as riddles are more amusing than commonplaces) it gave way to curiosity about her friend. His eyes wondered; her volubility was less suggestive than the latter's silence.

The stranger was perhaps not obviously a beauty nor obviously an American, but essentially both, on a closer scrutiny. She was slight and fair, and, though naturally pale, delicately flushed, apparently with recent excitement. What chiefly struck Longmore in her face was the union of a pair of beautifully gentle, almost languid gray eyes, with a mouth peculiarly expressive and firm. Her forehead was a trifle more expansive than belongs to classic types, and her thick brown hair was dressed out of the fashion, which was just then very ugly. Her throat and bust were slender, but all the more in harmony with certain rapid, charming movements of the head, which she had a way of throwing back every now and then, with an air of attention and a sidelong glance from her dove-like eyes. She seemed at once alert and indifferent, contemplative and restless; and Longmore very soon discovered that if she was not a brilliant beauty, she was at least an extremely interesting one. This very impression made him magnanimous. He perceived that he had interrupted a confidential conversation, and he judged it discreet to withdraw, having first learned from Maggie's mamma —Mrs. Draper—that she was to take the six-o'clock train back to Paris. He promised to meet her at the station.

He kept his appointment, and Mrs. Draper arrived betimes, accompanied by her friend. The latter, however, made her farewells at the door and drove away again, giving Longmore time only to raise his hat. "Who is she?" he asked with visible ardor, as he brought Mrs. Draper her tickets.

"Come and see me to-morrow at the Hôtel de l'Empire," she answered, "and I will tell you all about her." The force of this offer in making him punctual at the Hôtel de l'Empire Longmore doubtless never exactly measured; and it was perhaps well that he did not, for he found his friend, who was on the point of leaving Paris, so distracted by procrastinating milliners and perjured lingères that she had no wits left for disinterested narrative. "You must find Saint-Germain dreadfully dull," she said, as he was going. "Why won't you come with me to London?"

"Introduce me to Madame de Mauves," he answered, "and Saint-Germain will satisfy me." All he had learned was the lady's name and residence.

"Ah! she, poor woman, will not make Saint-Germain cheerful for you. She's very unhappy."

Longmore's further inquiries were arrested by the arrival of a young lady with a bandbox; but he went away with the promise of a note of introduction, to be immediately despatched to him at Saint-Germain.

He waited a week, but the note never came; and he declared that it was not for Mrs. Draper to complain of her milliner's treachery. He lounged on the terrace and walked in the forest, studied suburban street life, and made a languid attempt to investigate the records of the court of the exiled Stuarts; but he spent most of his time in wondering where Madame de Mauves lived, and whether she never walked on the terrace. Sometimes, he finally discovered; for one afternoon toward dusk he perceived her leaning against the parapet, alone. In his momentary hesitation to approach her, it seemed to him that there was almost a shade of trepidation; but his curiosity was not diminished by the consciousness of this result of a quarter of an hour's acquaintance. She immediately recognized him on his drawing near, with the manner of a person unaccustomed to encounter a confusing variety of faces. Her dress, her expression, were the same as before; her charm was there, like that of sweet music on a second hearing. She soon made conversation easy by asking him for news of Mrs. Draper. Longmore told her that he was daily expecting news, and, after a pause, mentioned the promised note of introduction.

"It seems less necessary now," he said—"for me, at least. But for you—I should have liked you to know the flattering things Mrs. Draper would probably have said about me."

"If it arrives at last," she answered, "you must come and see me and bring it. If it doesn't, you must come without it."

Then, as she continued to linger in spite of the thickening twilight, she explained that she was waiting for her husband, who was to arrive in the train from Paris, and who often passed along the terrace on his way home. Longmore well remembered that Mrs. Draper had pronounced her unhappy, and he found it convenient to suppose that this same husband made her so. Edified by his six months in Paris—"What else is possible," he asked himself, "for a sweet American girl who marries an unclean Frenchman?"

But this tender expectancy of her lord's return undermined his hypothesis, and it received a further check from the gentle eagerness with which she turned and greeted an approaching figure. Longmore beheld in the fading light a stoutish gentleman, on the fair side of forty, in a high light hat, whose countenance, indistinct against the sky, was adorned by a fantastically pointed mustache. M. de Mauves saluted his wife with punctilious gallantry, and having bowed to Longmore, asked her several questions in French. Before taking his proffered arm to walk to their carriage, which was in waiting at the terrace gate, she introduced our hero as a friend of Mrs. Draper, and a fellow-countryman, whom she hoped to see at home. M. de Mauves responded briefly, but civilly, in very fair English, and led his wife away.

Longmore watched him as he went, twisting his picturesque mustache, with a feeling of irritation which he certainly would have been at a loss to account for. The only conceivable cause was the light which M. de Mauves's good English cast upon his own bad French. For reasons involved apparently in the very structure of his being, Longmore found himself unable to speak the language tolerably. He admired and enjoyed it, but the very genius of awkwardness controlled his phraseology. But he reflected with satisfaction that Madame de Mauves and he had a common idiom, and his vexation was effectually dispelled by his finding on his table that evening a letter from Mrs. Draper. It enclosed a short, formal missive to Madame de Mauves, but the epistle itself was copious and confidential. She had deferred writing till she reached London, where for a week, of course, she had found other amusements.

"I think it is these distracting Englishwomen," she wrote, "with their green barege gowns and their white-stitched boots, who have reminded me in self-defense of my graceful friend at Saint-Germain and my promise to introduce you to her. I believe I told you that she was unhappy, and I wondered afterwards whether I had not been guilty of a breach of confidence. But you would have found it out for yourself, and besides, she told me no secrets. She declared she was the happiest creature in the world, and then, poor thing, she burst into tears, and I prayed to be delivered from such happiness. It's the miserable story of an American girl, born to be neither a slave nor a toy, marrying a profligate Frenchman, who believes that a woman must be one or the other. The silliest American woman is too good for the best foreigner, and the poorest of us have moral needs a Frenchman can't appreciate. She was romantic and wilful, and thought Americans were vulgar. Matrimonial felicity perhaps *is* vulgar; but I think nowadays she wishes she were a little less elegant. M. de Mauves cared, of course, for nothing but her money, which he's spending royally on his *menus plaisirs*. I hope you appreciate the compliment I pay you when I recommend you to go and console an unhappy wife. I have never given a man such a proof of esteem, and if you were to disappoint me I should renounce the world. Prove to Madame de Mauves that an American friend may mingle admiration and respect better than a French husband. She avoids society and lives quite alone, seeing no one but a horrible French sister-in-law. Do let me hear that you have drawn some of the sadness from that desperate smile of hers. Make her smile with a good conscience."

These zealous admonitions left Longmore slightly disturbed. He found himself on the edge of a domestic tragedy from which he instinctively recoiled. To call upon Madame de Mauves with his present knowledge seemed a sort of fishing in troubled waters. He was a modest man, and yet he asked himself whether the effect of his attentions might not be to add to her tribulation. A flattering sense of unwonted opportunity, however, made him, with the lapse of time, more confident,—possibly more reckless. It seemed a very inspiring idea to draw the sadness from his fair countrywoman's smile, and at least he hoped to persuade her that there was such a thing as an agreeable American. He immediately called upon her.

II

SHE had been placed for her education, fourteen years before, in a Parisian convent, by a widowed mamma, fonder of Homburg and Nice than of letting out tucks in the frocks of a vigorously growing daughter. Here, besides various elegant accomplishments,—the art of wearing a train, of composing a bouquet, of presenting a cup of tea,—she acquired a certain turn of the imagination which might have passed for a sign of precocious worldliness. She dreamed of marrying a title,—not for the pleasure of hearing herself called Mme. la Vicomtesse (for which it seemed to her that she should never greatly care), but because she had a romantic belief that the best birth is the guaranty of an ideal delicacy of feeling. Romances are rarely shaped in such perfect good faith, and Euphemia's excuse was in the radical purity of her imagination. She was profoundly incorruptible, and she cherished this pernicious conceit as if it had been a dogma revealed by a white-winged angel. Even after experience had given her a hundred rude hints, she found it easier to believe in fables, when they had a certain nobleness of meaning, than in well-attested but sordid facts. She believed that a gentleman with a long pedigree must be of necessity a very fine fellow, and that the consciousness of a picturesque family tradition imparts an exquisite tone to the character. *Noblesse oblige*, she thought, as regards yourself, and insures, as regards your wife. She had never spoken to a nobleman in her life, and these convictions were but a matter of transcendent theory. They were the fruit, in part, of the perusal of various ultramontane works of fiction—the only ones admitted to the convent library—in which the hero was always a legitimist vicomte who fought duels by the dozen, but went twice a month to confession; and in part of the perfumed gossip of her companions, many of them *filles de haut lieu*, who in the convent garden, after Sundays at home, depicted their brothers and cousins as Prince Charmings and young Paladins. Euphemia listened and said nothing; she shrouded her visions of matrimony under a coronet in religious mystery. She was not of that type of young lady who is easily induced to declare that her husband must be six feet high and a little near-sighted, part his hair in the middle, and have amber lights in his beard. To her companions she seemed to have a very pallid fancy; and even the fact that she was a sprig of the transatlantic democracy never sufficiently explained her apathy on social questions. She had a mental image of that son of the Crusaders who was to suffer her to adore him, but like many an artist who has produced a masterpiece of idealization, she shrank from exposing it to public criticism. It was the portrait of a gentleman rather ugly than handsome, and rather poor than rich. But his ugliness was to be nobly expressive, and his poverty delicately proud. Euphemia had a fortune of her own, which, at the proper time, after fixing on her in eloquent silence those fine eyes which were to soften the feudal severity of his visage, he was to accept with a world of stifled protestations. One condition alone she was to make,—that his blood should be of the very finest strain. On this she would stake her happiness.

It so chanced that circumstances were to give convincing color to this primitive logic.

Though little of a talker, Euphemia was an ardent listener, and there were moments when she fairly hung upon the lips of Mademoiselle Marie de Mauves. Her intimacy with this chosen schoolmate was, like most intimacies, based on their points of difference. Mademoiselle de Mauves was very positive, very shrewd, very ironical, very French,—everything that Euphemia felt herself unpardonable in not being. During her Sundays *en ville* she had examined the world and judged it, and she imparted her impressions to our attentive heroine with an agreeable mixture of enthusiasm and scepticism. She was moreover a handsome and well-grown person, on whom Euphemia's ribbons and trinkets had a trick of looking better than on their slender proprietress. She had, finally, the supreme merit of being a rigorous example of the virtue of exalted birth, having, as she did, ancestors honorably mentioned by Joinville and Commines, and a stately grandmother with a hooked nose, who came up with her after the holidays from a veritable *castel* in Auvergne. It seemed to Euphemia that these attributes made her friend more at home in the world than if she had been the daughter of even the most prosperous grocer. A certain aristocratic impudence Mademoiselle de Mauves abundantly possessed, and her raids among her friend's finery were quite in the spirit of her baronial ancestors in the twelfth century,—a spirit which Euphemia considered but a large way of understanding friendship,—a freedom from small deference to the world's opinions which would sooner or later justify itself in acts of surprising magnanimity. Mademoiselle de Mauves perhaps enjoyed but slightly that easy attitude toward society which Euphemia envied her. She proved herself later in life such an accomplished schemer that her sense of having further heights to scale must have awakened early. Our heroine's ribbons and trinkets had much to do with the other's sisterly patronage, and her appealing pliancy of character even more; but the concluding motive of Marie's writing to her grand-mamma to invite Euphemia for a three weeks' holiday to the *castel* in Auvergne, involved altogether superior considerations. Mademoiselle de Mauves was indeed at this time seventeen years of age, and presumably capable of general views; and Euphemia, who was hardly less, was a very well-grown subject for experiment, besides being pretty enough almost to pre-assure success. It is a proof of the sincerity of Euphemia's aspirations that the *castel* was not a shock to her faith. It was neither a cheerful nor a luxurious abode, but the young girl found it as delightful as a play. It had battered towers and an empty moat, a rusty drawbridge and a court paved with crooked, grass-grown slabs, over which the antique coach-wheels of the old lady with the hooked nose seemed to awaken the echoes of the seventeenth century. Euphemia was not frightened out of her dream; she had the pleasure of seeing it assume the consistency of a flattering presentiment. She had a taste for old servants, old anecdotes, old furniture, faded household colors, and sweetly stale odors,—musty treasures in which the Château de Mauves abounded. She made a dozen sketches in water-colors, after her conventual pattern; but sentimentally, as one may say, she was forever sketching with a freer hand.

Old Madame de Mauves had nothing severe but her nose, and she seemed to Euphemia, as indeed she was, a graciously venerable relic of a historic order of things. She took a great fancy to the young American, who was ready to sit all day at her feet and listen to anecdotes of the *bon temps* and quotations from the family chronicles. Madame de Mauves was a very honest old woman, and uttered her thoughts with antique plainness. One day, after pushing back Euphemia's shining locks and blinking at her with some tenderness from under her spectacles, she declared, with an energetic shake of the head, that she didn't know what to make of her. And in answer to the young girl's startled blush,—"I should like to advise you," she said, "but you seem to me so all of a piece that I am afraid that if I advise you, I shall spoil you. It's easy to see that you're not one of us. I don't know whether you're better, but you seem to me to listen to the murmur of your own young spirit, rather than to the voice from behind the confessional or to the whisper of opportunity. Young girls, in my day, when they were stupid, were very docile, but when they were clever, were very sly. You're clever enough, I imagine, and yet if I guessed all your secrets at this moment, is there one I should have to frown at? I can tell you a wickeder one than any you have discovered for yourself. If you expect to live in France, and you want to be happy, don't listen too hard to that little voice I just spoke of,—the voice that is neither the curé's nor the world's. You'll fancy it saying things that it won't help your case to hear. They'll make you sad, and when you're sad you'll grow plain, and when you're plain you'll grow bitter, and when you're bitter you'll be very disagreeable. I was brought up to think that a woman's first duty was to please, and the happiest women I've known have been the ones who performed this duty faithfully. As you're not a Catholic, I suppose you can't be a dévote; and if you don't take life as a fifty years' mass, the only way to take it is as a game of skill. Listen: not to lose, you must,—I don't say cheat; but don't be too sure your neighbor won't, and don't be shocked out of your self-possession if he does. Don't lose, my dear; I beseech you, don't lose. Be neither suspicious nor credulous; but if you find your neighbor peeping, don't cry out, but very politely wait your own chance. I've had my *revanche* more than once in my day, but I'm not sure that the sweetest I could take against life as a whole would be to have your blessed innocence profit by my experience."

This was rather awful advice, but Euphemia understood it too little to be either edified or frightened. She sat listening to it very much as she would have listened to the speeches of an old lady in a comedy, whose diction should picturesquely correspond to the pattern of her mantilla and the fashion of her headdress. Her indifference was doubly dangerous, for Madame de Mauves spoke at the prompting of coming events, and her words were the result of a somewhat troubled conscience,—a conscience which told her at once that Euphemia was too tender a victim to be sacrificed to an ambition, and that the prosperity of her house was too precious a heritage to be sacrificed to a scruple. The prosperity in question had suffered repeated and grievous breaches, and the house of De Mauves had been pervaded by the cold comfort of an establishment in which people were obliged to balance dinner-table allusions to feudal ancestors against the absence of side dishes; a state of things the more regrettable as the family was now mainly represented by a gentleman whose appetite was large, and who justly maintained that its historic glories were not established by underfed heroes.

Three days after Euphemia's arrival, Richard de Mauves came down from Paris to pay his respects to his grandmother, and treated our heroine to her first encounter with a gentilhomme in the flesh. On coming in he kissed his grandmother's hand, with a smile which caused her to draw it away with dignity, and set Euphemia, who was standing by, wondering what had happened between them. Her unanswered wonder was but the beginning of a life of bitter perplexity, but the reader is free to know that the smile of M. de Mauves was a reply to a certain postscript affixed by the old lady to a letter promptly addressed to him by her granddaughter, after Euphemia had been admitted to justify the latter's promises. Mademoiselle de Mauves brought her letter to her grandmother for approval, but obtained no more than was expressed in a frigid nod.

The old lady watched her with a sombre glance as she proceeded to seal the letter, and suddenly bade her open it again and bring her a pen.

"Your sister's flatteries are all nonsense," she wrote; "the young lady is far too good for you, *mauvais sujet*. If you have a conscience you'll not come and take possession of an angel of innocence."

The young girl, who had read these lines, made up a little face as she redirected the letter; but she laid down her pen with a confident nod, which might have seemed to mean that, to the best of her belief, her brother had not a conscience.

"If you meant what you said," the young man whispered to his grandmother on the first opportunity, "it would have been simpler not to let her send the letter!"

It was perhaps because she was wounded by this cynical insinuation, that Madame de Mauves remained in her own apartment during a greater part of Euphemia's stay, so that the latter's angelic innocence was left entirely to the Baron's mercy. It suffered no worse mischance, however, than to be prompted to intenser communion with itself. M. de Mauves was the hero of the young girl's romance made real, and so completely accordant with this creature of her imagination, that she felt afraid of him, very much as she would have been of a supernatural apparition. He was thirty-five years old,—young enough to suggest possibilities of ardent activity, and old enough to have formed opinions which a simple woman might deem it an intellectual privilege to listen to. He was perhaps a trifle handsomer than Euphemia's rather grim, Quixotic ideal, but a very few days reconciled her to his good looks, as they would have reconciled her to his ugliness. He was quiet, grave, and eminently distinguished. He spoke little, but his speeches, without being sententious, had a certain nobleness of tone which caused them to re-echo in the young girl's ears at the end of the day. He paid her very little direct attention, but his chance words—if he only asked her if she objected to his cigarette—were accompanied by a smile of extraordinary kindness.

It happened that shortly after his arrival, riding an unruly horse, which Euphemia with shy admiration had watched him mount in the castle yard, he was thrown with a violence which, without disparaging his skill, made him for a fortnight an interesting invalid, lounging in the library with a bandaged knee. To beguile his confinement, Euphemia was repeatedly induced to sing to him, which she did with a little natural tremor in her voice, which might have passed for an exquisite refinement of art. He never overwhelmed her with compliments, but he listened with unwandering attention, remembered all her melodies, and sat humming them to himself. While his imprisonment lasted, indeed, he passed hours in her company, and made her feel not unlike some unfriended artist who has suddenly gained the opportunity to devote a fortnight to the study of a great model. Euphemia studied with noiseless diligence what she supposed to be the "character" of M. de Mauves, and the more she looked the more fine lights and shades she seemed to behold in this masterpiece of nature. M. de Mauves's character indeed, whether from a sense of being generously scrutinized, or for reasons which bid graceful defiance to analysis, had never been so amiable; it seemed really to reflect the purity of Euphemia's interpretation of it. There had been nothing especially to admire in the state of mind in which he left Paris,—a hard determination to marry a young girl whose charms might or might not justify his sister's account of them, but who was mistress, at the worst, of a couple of hundred thousand francs a year. He had not counted out sentiment; if she pleased him, so much the better; but he had left a meagre margin for it, and he would hardly have admitted that so excellent a match could be improved by it. He was a placid sceptic, and it was a singular fate for a man who believed in nothing to be so tenderly believed in. What his original faith had been he could hardly have told you; for as he came back to his childhood's home to mend his fortunes by pretending to fall in love, he was a thoroughly perverted creature, and overlaid with more corruptions than a summer day's questioning of his conscience would have released him from. Ten years' pursuit of pleasure, which a bureau full of unpaid bills was all he had to show for, had pretty well stifled the natural lad, whose violent will and generous temper might have been shaped by other circumstances to a result which a romantic imagination might fairly accept as a late-blooming flower of hereditary honor. The Baron's violence had been subdued, and he had learned to be irreproachably polite; but he had lost the edge of his generosity, and his politeness, which in the long run society paid for, was hardly more than a form of luxurious egotism, like his fondness for cambric handkerchiefs, lavender gloves, and other fopperies by which shopkeepers remained out of pocket. In after years he was terribly polite to his wife. He had formed himself, as the phrase was, and the form prescribed to him by the society into which his birth and his tastes introduced him was marked by some peculiar features. That which mainly concerns us is its classification of the fairer half of humanity as objects not essentially different—say from the light gloves one soils in an evening and throws away. To do M. de Mauves justice, he had in the course of time encountered such plentiful evidence of this pliant, glove-like quality in the feminine character, that idealism naturally seemed to him a losing game.

Euphemia, as he lay on his sofa, seemed by no means a refutation; she simply reminded him that very young women are generally innocent, and that this, on the whole, was the most charming stage of their development. Her innocence inspired him with profound respect, and it seemed to him that if he shortly became her husband it would be exposed to a danger the less. Old Madame de Mauves, who flattered herself that in this whole matter she was being laudably rigid, might have learned a lesson from his gallant consideration. For a fortnight the Baron was almost a blushing boy again. He watched from behind the "Figaro," and admired, and held his tongue. He was not in the least disposed toward a flirtation; he had no desire to trouble the waters he proposed to transfuse into the golden cup of matrimony. Sometimes a word, a look, a movement of Euphemia's, gave him the oddest sense of being, or of seeming at least, almost bashful; for she had a way of not dropping her eyes, according to the mysterious virginal mechanism, of not fluttering out of the room when she found him there alone, of treating him rather as a benignant than as a pernicious influence,—a radiant frankness of demeanor, in fine, in spite of an evident natural reserve, which it seemed equally graceless not to make the subject of a compliment and indelicate not to take for granted. In this way there was wrought in the Baron's mind a vague, unwonted resonance of soft impressions, as we may call it, which indicated the transmutation of "sentiment" from a contingency into a fact. His imagination enjoyed it; he was very fond of music, and this reminded him of some of the best he had ever heard. In spite of the bore of being laid up with a lame knee, he was in a better humor than he had known for months; he lay smoking cigarettes and listening to the nightingales, with the comfortable smile of one of his country neighbors whose big ox should have taken the prize at a fair. Every now and then, with an impatient suspicion of the resemblance, he declared that he was pitifully *bête;* but he was under a charm which braved even the supreme penalty of seeming ridiculous. One morning he had half an hour's tête-à-tête with his grandmother's confessor, a soft-voiced old abbé, whom, for reasons of her own, Madame de Mauves had suddenly summoned, and had left waiting in the drawing-room while she rearranged her curls. His reverence, going up to the old lady, assured her that M. le Baron was in a most edifying state of mind, and a promising subject for the operation of grace. This was a pious interpretation of the Baron's momentary good-humor. He had always lazily wondered what priests were good for, and he now remembered, with a sense of especial obligation to the abbé, that they were excellent for marrying people.

A day or two after this he left off his bandages, and tried to walk. He made his way into the garden and hobbled successfully along one of the alleys; but in the midst of his progress he was seized with a spasm of pain which forced him to stop and call for help. In an instant Euphemia came tripping along the path and offered him her arm with the frankest solicitude.

"Not to the house," he said, taking it; "farther on, to the bosquet." This choice was prompted by her having immediately confessed that she had seen him leave the house, had feared an accident, and had followed him on tiptoe.

"Why didn't you join me?" he had asked, giving her a look in which admiration was no longer disguised, and yet felt itself half at the mercy of her replying that a *jeune fille* should not be seen following a gentleman. But it drew a breath which filled its lungs for a long time afterward, when she replied simply that if she had overtaken him he might have accepted her arm out of politeness, whereas she wished to have the pleasure of seeing him walk alone.

The bosquet was covered with an odorous tangle of blossoming vines, and a nightingale overhead was shaking out love-notes with a profuseness which made the Baron consider his own conduct the perfection of propriety.

"In America," he said, "I have always heard that when a man wishes to marry a young girl, he offers himself simply, face to face, without any ceremony,—without parents, and uncles, and cousins sitting round in a circle."

"Why, I believe so," said Euphemia, staring, and too surprised to be alarmed.

"Very well, then," said the Baron, "suppose our bosquet here to be American. I offer you my hand, à l'Américaine. It will make me intensely happy to have you accept it."

Whether Euphemia's acceptance was in the American manner is more than I can say; I incline to think that for fluttering, grateful, trustful, softly-amazed young hearts, there is only one manner all over the world.

That evening, in the little turret chamber which it was her happiness to inhabit, she wrote a dutiful letter to her mamma, and had just sealed it when she was sent for by Madame de Mauves. She found this ancient lady seated in her boudoir, in a lavender satin gown, with all her candles lighted, as if to celebrate her grandson's betrothal. "Are you very happy?" Madame de Mauves demanded, making Euphemia sit down before her.

"I'm almost afraid to say so," said the young girl, "lest I should wake myself up."

"May you never wake up, *belle enfant,*" said the old lady, solemnly. "This is the first marriage ever made in our family in this way,—by a Baron de Mauves proposing to a young girl in an arbor, like Jeannot and Jeannette. It has not been our way of doing things, and people may say it wants frankness. My grandson tells me he considers it the perfection of frankness. Very good. I'm a very old woman, and if your differences should ever be as frank as your agreement, I shouldn't like to see them. But I should be sorry to die and think you were going to be unhappy. You can't be, beyond a certain point; because, though in this world the Lord sometimes makes light of our expectations, he never altogether ignores our deserts. But you're very young and innocent, and easy to deceive. There never was a man in the world—among the saints themselves—as good as you believe the Baron. But he's a *galant homme* and a gentleman, and I've been talking to him tonight. To you I want to say this,—that you're to forget the worldly rubbish I talked the other day about frivolous women being happy. It's not the kind of happiness that would suit you. Whatever befalls you, promise me this: to be yourself. The Baron de Mauves will be none the worse for it. Yourself, understand, in spite of everything,—

bad precepts and bad examples, bad usage even. Be persistently and patiently yourself, and a De Mauves will do you justice!"

Euphemia remembered this speech in after years, and more than once, wearily closing her eyes, she seemed to see the old woman sitting upright in her faded finery and smiling grimly, like one of the Fates who sees the wheel of fortune turning up her favorite event. But at the moment it seemed to her simply to have the proper gravity of the occasion; this was the way, she supposed, in which lucky young girls were addressed on their engagement by wise old women of quality.

At her convent, to which she immediately returned, she found a letter from her mother, which shocked her far more than the remarks of Madame de Mauves. Who were these people, Mrs. Cleve demanded, who had presumed to talk to her daughter of marriage without asking her leave? Questionable gentlefolk, plainly; the best French people never did such things. Euphemia would return straightway to her convent, shut herself up, and await her own arrival.

It took Mrs. Cleve three weeks to travel from Nice to Paris, and during this time the young girl had no communication with her lover beyond accepting a bouquet of violets, marked with his initials and left by a female friend. "I've not brought you up with such devoted care," she declared to her daughter at their first interview, "to marry a penniless Frenchman. I will take you straight home, and you will please to forget M. de Mauves."

Mrs. Cleve received that evening at her hotel a visit from the Baron which mitigated her wrath, but failed to modify her decision. He had very good manners, but she was sure he had horrible morals; and Mrs. Cleve, who had been a very good-natured censor on her own account, felt a genuine spiritual need to sacrifice her daughter to propriety. She belonged to that large class of Americans who make light of America in familiar discourse, but are startled back into a sense of moral responsibility when they find Europeans taking them at their word. "I know the type, my dear," she said to her daughter with a sagacious nod. "He'll not beat you; sometimes you'll wish he would."

Euphemia remained solemnly silent; for the only answer she felt capable of making her mother was that her mind was too small a measure of things, and that the Baron's "type" was one which it took some mystical illumination to appreciate. A person who confounded him with the common throng of her watering-place acquaintance was not a person to argue with. It seemed to Euphemia that she had no cause to plead; her cause was in the Lord's hands and her lover's.

M. de Mauves had been irritated and mortified by Mrs. Cleve's opposition, and hardly knew how to handle an adversary who failed to perceive that a De Mauves of necessity gave more than he received. But he had obtained information on his return to Paris which exalted the uses of humility. Euphemia's fortune, wonderful to say, was greater than its fame, and in view of such a prize, even a De Mauves could afford to take a snubbing.

The young man's tact, his deference, his urbane insistence, won a concession from Mrs. Cleve. The engagement was to be suspended and her daughter was to return home, be brought out and receive the homage she was entitled to, and which would but too surely take a form dangerous to the Baron's suit. They were to exchange neither letters, nor mementos, nor messages; but if at the end of two years Euphemia had refused offers enough to attest the permanence of her attachment, he should receive an invitation to address her again.

This decision was promulgated in the presence of the parties interested. The Baron bore himself gallantly, and looked at the young girl, expecting some tender protestation. But she only looked at him silently in return, neither weeping, nor smiling, nor putting out her hand. On this they separated; but as the Baron walked away, he declared to himself that, in spite of the confounded two years, he was a very happy fellow,—to have a fiancée who, to several millions of francs, added such strangely beautiful eyes.

How many offers Euphemia refused but scantily concerns us,—and how the Baron wore his two years away. He found that he needed pastimes, and, as pastimes were expensive, he added heavily to the list of debts to be cancelled by Euphemia's millions. Sometimes, in the thick of what he had once called pleasure with a keener conviction than now, he put to himself the case of their failing him after all; and then he remembered that last mute assurance of her eyes, and drew a long breath of such confidence as he felt in nothing else in the world save his own punctuality in an affair of honor.

At last, one morning, he took the express to Havre with a letter of Mrs. Cleve's in his pocket, and ten days later made his bow to mother and daughter in New York. His stay was brief, and he was apparently unable to bring himself to view what Euphemia's uncle, Mr. Butterworth, who gave her away at the altar, called our great experiment in democratic self-government in a serious light. He smiled at everything, and seemed to regard the New World as a colossal *plaisanterie*. It is true that a perpetual smile was the most natural expression of countenance for a man about to marry Euphemia Cleve.

III

LONGMORE's first visit seemed to open to him so large an opportunity for tranquil enjoyment, that he very soon paid a second, and, at the end of a fortnight, had spent a great many hours in the little drawing-room which Madame de Mauves rarely quitted except to drive or walk in the forest. She lived in an old-fashioned pavilion, between a high-walled court and an excessively artificial garden, beyond whose enclosure you saw a long line of tree-tops. Longmore liked the garden, and in the mild afternoons used to move his chair through the open window to the little terrace which overlooked it, while his hostess sat just within. After a while she came out and wandered through the narrow alleys and beside the thin-spouting fountain, and last introduced him to a little gate in the garden wall, opening upon a lane which led into the forest. Hitherward, more than once, she wandered with him, bareheaded and meaning to go but twenty rods, but always strolling good-naturedly farther, and often taking a generous walk. They discovered a vast deal to talk about, and to the pleasure of finding the hours tread inaudibly away, Longmore was able to add the satisfaction of suspecting that he was a "resource" for Madame de Mauves. He had made her acquaintance with the sense, not altogether comfortable, that she was a woman with a painful secret, and that seeking her acquaintance would be like visiting at a house where there was an invalid who could bear no noise. But he very soon perceived that her sorrow, since sorrow it was, was not an aggressive one; that it was not fond of attitudes and ceremonies, and that her earnest wish was to forget it. He felt that even if Mrs. Draper had not told him she was unhappy, he would have guessed it; and yet he could hardly have pointed to his evidence. It was chiefly negative,—she never alluded to her husband. Beyond this it seemed to him simply that her whole being was pitched on a lower key than harmonious Nature meant; she was like a powerful singer who had lost her high notes. She never drooped nor sighed nor looked unutterable things; she indulged in no dusky sarcasms against fate; she had, in short, none of the coquetry of unhappiness. But Longmore was sure that her gentle gayety was the result of strenuous effort, and that she was trying to interest herself in his thoughts to escape from her own. It she had wished to irritate his curiosity and lead him to take her confidence by storm, nothing could have served her purpose better than this ingenuous reserve. He declared to himself that there was a rare magnanimity in such ardent self-effacement, and that but one woman in ten thousand was capable of merging an intensely personal grief in thankless outward contemplation. Madame de Mauves, he instinctively felt, was not sweeping the horizon for a compensation or a consoler; she had suffered a personal deception which had disgusted her with persons. She was not striving to balance her sorrow with some strongly flavored joy; for the present, she was trying to live with it, peaceably, reputably, and without scandal,—turning the key on it occasionally, as you would on a companion liable to attacks of insanity. Longmore was a man of fine senses and of an active imagination, whose leading-strings had never been slipped. He began to regard his hostess as a figure haunted by a shadow which was somehow her intenser, more authentic self. This hovering mystery came to have for him an extraordinary charm. Her delicate beauty acquired to his eye the serious cast of certain blank-browed Greek statues, and sometimes, when his imagination, more than his ear, detected a vague tremor in the tone in which she attempted to make a friendly question seem to have behind it none of the hollow resonance of absent-mindedness, his marvelling eyes gave her an answer more eloquent, though much less to the point, than the one she demanded.

She gave him indeed much to wonder about, and, in his ignorance, he formed a dozen experimental theories upon the history of her marriage. She had married for love and staked her whole soul on it; of that he was convinced. She had not married a Frenchman to be near Paris and her base of supplies of millinery; he was sure she had seen conjugal happiness in a light of which her present life, with its conveniences for shopping and its moral aridity, was the absolute negation. But by what extraordinary process of the heart—through what mysterious intermission of that moral instinct which may keep pace with the heart, even when that organ is making unprecedented time—had she fixed her affections on an arrogantly frivolous Frenchman? Longmore needed no telling; he knew M. de Mauves was frivolous; it was stamped on his eyes, his nose, his mouth, his carriage. For French women Longmore had but a scanty kindness, or at least (what with him was very much the same thing) but a scanty gallantry; they all seemed to belong to the type of a certain fine lady to whom he had ventured to present a letter of introduction, and whom, directly after his first visit to her, he had set down in his note-book as "metallic." Why should Madame de Mauves have chosen a French woman's lot,—she whose character had a perfume which doesn't belong to even the brightest metals? He asked her one day frankly if it had cost her nothing to transplant herself,—if she was not oppressed with a sense of irreconcilable difference from "all these people." She was silent awhile, and he fancied that she was hesitating as to whether she should resent so unceremonious an allusion to her husband. He almost wished she would; it would seem a proof that her deep reserve of sorrow had a limit.

"I almost grew up here," she said at last, "and it was here for me that those dreams of the future took shape that we all have when we cease to be very young. As matters stand, one may be very American and yet arrange it with one's conscience to live in Europe. My imagination perhaps—I had a little when I was younger—helped me to think I should find happiness here. And after all, for a woman, what does it signify? This is not America, perhaps, about me, but it's quite as little France. France is out there, beyond the garden, in the town, in the forest; but here, close about me, in my room and"—she paused a moment—"in my mind, it's a nameless country of my own. It's not her country," she added, "that makes a woman happy or unhappy."

Madame Clairin, Euphemia's sister-in-law, might have been supposed to have undertaken the graceful task of making Longmore ashamed of his uncivil jottings about her sex and nation. Mademoiselle de Mauves, bringing example to the confirmation of precept, had made a remunerative match and sacrificed her name to the millions of a prosperous and aspiring wholesale druggist,—a gentleman liberal enough to consider his fortune a moderate price for being towed into circles unpervaded by pharmaceutic odors. His system, possibly, was sound, but his own application of it was unfortunate. M. Clairin's head was turned by his good luck. Having secured an aristocratic wife, he adopted an aristocratic vice and began to gamble at the Bourse. In an evil hour he lost heavily and staked heavily to recover himself. But he overtook his loss only by a greater one. Then he let everything go,—his wits, his courage, his probity,—everything that had made him what his ridiculous marriage had so promptly unmade. He walked up the Rue Vivienne one day with his hands in his empty pockets, and stood for half an hour staring confusedly up and down the glittering boulevard. People brushed against him, and half a dozen carriages almost ran over him, until at last a policeman, who had been watching him for some time, took him by the arm and led him gently away. He looked at the man's cocked hat and sword with tears in his eyes; he hoped he was going to interpret to him the wrath of Heaven,—to execute the penalty of his dead-weight of self-abhorrence. But the sergent de ville only stationed him in the embrasure of a door, out of harm's way, and walked away to supervise a financial contest between an old lady and a cabman. Poor M. Clairin had only been married a year, but he had had time to measure the lofty spirit of a De Mauves. When night had fallen, he repaired to the house of a friend and asked for a night's lodging; and as his friend, who was simply his old head book-keeper and lived in a small way, was put to some trouble to accommodate him,—"You must excuse me," Clairin said, "but I can't go home. I'm afraid of my wife!" Toward morning he blew his brains out. His widow turned the remnants of his property to better account than could have been expected, and wore the very handsomest mourning. It was for this latter reason, perhaps, that she was obliged to retrench at other points and accept a temporary home under her brother's roof.

Fortune had played Madame Clairin a terrible trick, but had found an adversary and not a victim. Though quite without beauty, she had always had what is called the grand air, and her air from this time forward was grander than ever. As she trailed about in her sable furbelows, tossing back her well-dressed head, and holding up her vigilant eye-glass, she seemed to be sweeping the whole field of society and asking herself where she should pluck her revenge. Suddenly she espied it, ready made to her hand, in poor Longmore's wealth and amiability. American dollars and American complaisance had made her brother's fortune; why shouldn't they make hers? She overestimated Longmore's wealth and misinterpreted his amiability; for she was sure that a man could not be so contented without being rich, nor so unassuming without being weak. He encountered her advances with a formal politeness which covered a great deal of unflattering discomposure. She made him feel acutely uncomfortable; and though he was at a loss to conceive how he could be an object of interest to a shrewd Parisienne, he had an indefinable sense of being enclosed in a magnetic circle, like the victim of an incantation. If Madame Clairin could have fathomed his Puritanic soul, she would have laid by her wand and her book and admitted that he was an impossible subject. She gave him a kind of moral chill, and he never mentally alluded to her save as that dreadful woman,—that terrible woman. He did justice to her grand air, but for his pleasure he preferred the small air of Madame de Mauves; and he never made her his bow, after standing frigidly passive for five minutes to one of her gracious overtures to intimacy, without feeling a peculiar desire to ramble away into the forest, fling himself down on the warm grass, and, staring up at the blue sky, forget that there were any women in nature who didn't please like the swaying tree-tops. One day, on his arrival, she met him in the court and told him that her sister-in-law was shut up with a headache, and that his visit must be for her. He followed her into the drawing-room with the best grace at his command, and sat twirling his hat for half an hour. Suddenly he understood her; the caressing cadence of her voice was a distinct invitation to solicit the incomparable honor of her hand. He blushed to the roots of his hair and jumped up with uncontrollable alacrity; then, dropping a glance at Madame Clairin, who sat watching him with hard eyes over the edge of her smile, as it were, perceived on her brow a flash of unforgiving wrath. It was not becoming, but his eyes lingered a moment, for it seemed to illuminate her character. What he saw there frightened him, and he felt himself murmuring, "Poor Madame de Mauves!" His departure was abrupt, and this time he really went into the forest and lay down on the grass.

After this he admired Madame de Mauves more than ever; she seemed a brighter figure, dogged by a darker shadow. At the end of a month he received a letter from a friend with whom he had arranged a tour through the Low Countries, reminding him of his promise to meet him promptly at Brussels. It was only after his answer was posted that he fully measured the zeal with which he had declared that the journey must either be deferred or abandoned,—that he could not possibly leave Saint-Germain. He took a walk in the forest, and asked himself if this was irrevocably true. If it was, surely his duty was to march straight home and pack his trunk. Poor Webster, who, he knew, had counted ardently on this excursion, was an excellent fellow; six weeks ago he would have gone through fire and water to join Webster. It had never been in his books to throw overboard a friend whom he had loved for ten years for a married woman whom for six weeks he had—admired. It was certainly beyond question that he was lingering at Saint-Germain because this admirable married woman was there; but in the midst of all this admiration what had become of prudence? This was the conduct of a man prepared to fall utterly in love. If she was as unhappy as he believed, the love of such a man would help her very little more than his indifference; if she was less so, she needed no help and could dispense with his friendly offices. He was sure, moreover, that if she knew he was staying on her account, she would be extremely annoyed. But this very feeling had much to do with making it hard to go; her displeasure would only enhance the gentle stoicism which touched him to the heart. At moments, indeed, he assured himself that to linger was simply impertinent; it was indelicate to make a daily study of such a shrinking grief. But inclination answered that some day her self-support would fail, and he had a vision of this admirable creature calling vainly for help. He would be her friend, to any length; it was unworthy of both of them to think about consequences. But he was a friend who carried about with him a muttering resentment that he had not known her five years earlier, and a brooding hostility to those who had anticipated him. It seemed one of fortune's most mocking strokes, that she should be surrounded by persons whose only merit was that they threw the charm of her character into radiant relief.

Longmore's growing irritation made it more and more difficult for him to see any other merit than this in the Baron de Mauves. And yet, disinterestedly, it would have been hard to give a name to the portentous vices which such an estimate implied, and there were times when our hero was almost persuaded against his finer judgment that he was really the most considerate of husbands, and that his wife liked melancholy for melancholy's sake. His manners were perfect, his urbanity was unbounded, and he seemed never to address her but, sentimentally speaking, hat in hand. His tone to Longmore (as the latter was perfectly aware) was that of a man of the world to a man not quite of the world; but what it lacked in deference it made up in easy friendliness. "I can't thank you enough for having overcome my wife's shyness," he more than once declared. "If we left her to do as she pleased, she would bury herself alive. Come often, and bring some one else. She'll have nothing to do with my friends, but perhaps she'll accept yours."

The Baron made these speeches with a remorseless placidity very amazing to our hero, who had an innocent belief that a man's head may point out to him the shortcomings of his heart and make him ashamed of them. He could not fancy him capable both of neglecting his wife and taking an almost humorous view of her suffering. Longmore had, at any rate, an exasperating sense that the Baron thought rather less of his wife than more, for that very same fine difference of nature which so deeply stirred his own sympathies. He was rarely present during Longmore's visits, and made a daily journey to Paris, where he had "business," as he once mentioned,—not in the least with a tone of apology. When he appeared, it was late in the evening, and with an imperturbable air of being on the best of terms with every one and everything, which was peculiarly annoying if you happened to have a tacit quarrel with him. If he was a good fellow, he was surely a good fellow spoiled. Something he had, however, which Longmore vaguely envied—a kind of superb positiveness—a manner rounded and polished by the traditions of centuries—an amenity exercised for his own sake and not his neighbors'—which seemed the result of something better than a good conscience—of a vigorous and unscrupulous temperament. The Baron was plainly not a moral man, and poor Longmore, who was, would have been glad to learn the secret of his luxurious serenity. What was it that enabled him, without being a monster with visibly cloven feet, exhaling brimstone, to misprize so cruelly a lovely wife, and to walk about the world with a smile under his mustache? It was the essential grossness of his imagination, which had nevertheless helped him to turn so many neat compliments. He could be very polite, and he could doubtless be supremely impertinent; but he was as unable to draw a moral inference of the finer strain, as a school-boy who has been playing truant for a week to solve a problem in algebra. It was ten to one he didn't know his wife was unhappy; he and his brilliant sister had doubtless agreed to consider their companion a Puritanical little person, of meagre aspirations and slender accomplishments, contented with looking at Paris from the terrace, and, as an especial treat, having a countryman very much like herself to supply her with homely transatlantic gossip. M. de Mauves was tired of his companion: he relished a higher flavor in female society. She was too modest, too simple, too delicate; she had too few arts, too little coquetry, too much charity. M. de Mauves, some day, lighting a cigar, had probably decided she was stupid. It was the same sort of taste, Longmore moralized, as the taste for Gérôme in painting and for M. Gustave Flaubert in literature. The Baron was a pagan and his wife was a Christian, and between them, accordingly, was a gulf. He was by race and instinct a *grand seigneur*. Longmore had often heard of this distinguished social type, and was properly grateful for an opportunity to examine it closely. It had certainly a picturesque boldness of outline, but it was fed from spiritual sources so remote from those of which he felt the living gush in his own soul, that he found himself gazing at it, in irreconcilable antipathy, across a dim historic mist. "I'm a modern *bourgeois*," he said, "and not perhaps so good a judge of how far a pretty woman's tongue may go at supper without prejudice to her reputation. But I've not met one of the sweetest of women without recognizing her and discovering that a certain sort of character offers better entertainment than Thérésa's songs, sung by a dissipated duchess. Wit for wit, I think mine carries me further." It was easy indeed to perceive that, as became a *grand seigneur,* M. de Mauves had a stock of rigid notions. He would not especially have desired, perhaps, that his wife should compete in amateur operettas with the duchesses in question, chiefly of recent origin; but he held that a gentleman may take his amusement where he finds it, that he is quite at liberty not to find it at home; and that the wife of a De Mauves who should hang her head and have red eyes, and allow herself to make any other response to officious condolence than that her husband's amusements were his own affair, would have forfeited every claim to having her fingertips bowed over and kissed. And yet in spite of these sound principles, Longmore fancied that the Baron was more irritated than gratified by his wife's irreproachable reserve. Did it dimly occur to him that it was self-control and not self-effacement? She was a model to all the inferior matrons of his line, past and to come, and an occasional "scene" from her at a convenient moment would have something reassuring,—would attest her stupidity a trifle more forcibly than her inscrutable tranquillity.

Longmore would have given much to know the principle of her submissiveness, and he tried more than once, but with rather awkward timidity, to sound the mystery. She seemed to him to have been long resisting the force of cruel evidence, and, though she had succumbed to it at last, to have denied herself the right to complain, because if faith was gone her heroic generosity remained. He believed even that she was capable of reproaching herself with having expected too much, and of trying to persuade herself out of her bitterness by saying that her hopes had been illusions and that this was simply—life. "I hate tragedy," she once said to him; "I have a really pusillanimous dread of moral suffering. I believe that—without base concessions—there is always some way of escaping from it. I had almost rather never smile all my life than have a single violent explosion of grief." She lived evidently in nervous apprehension of being fatally convinced,—of seeing to the end of her deception. Longmore, when he thought of this, felt an immense longing to offer her something of which she could be as sure as of the sun in heaven.

IV

His friend Webster lost no time in accusing him of the basest infidelity, and asking him what he found at Saint-Germain to prefer to Van Eyck and Memling, Rubens and Rembrandt. A day or two after the receipt of Webster's letter, he took a walk with Madame de Mauves in the forest. They sat down on a fallen log, and she began to arrange into a bouquet the anemones and violets she had gathered. "I have a letter," he said at last, "from a friend whom I some time ago promised to join at Brussels. The time has come,—it has passed. It finds me terribly unwilling to leave Saint-Germain."

She looked up with the candid interest which she always displayed in his affairs, but with no disposition, apparently, to make a personal application of his words. "Saint-Germain is pleasant enough," she said; "but are you doing yourself justice? Won't you regret in future days that instead of travelling and seeing cities and monuments and museums and improving your mind, you sat here—for instance—on a log, pulling my flowers to pieces?"

"What I shall regret in future days," he answered after some hesitation, "is that I should have sat here and not spoken the truth on the matter. I am fond of museums and monuments and of improving my mind, and I'm particularly fond of my friend Webster. But I can't bring myself to leave Saint-Germain without asking you a question. You must forgive me if it's unfortunate, and be assured that curiosity was never more respectful. Are you really as unhappy as I imagine you to be?"

She had evidently not expected his question, and she greeted it with a startled blush. "If I strike you as unhappy," she said, "I have been a poorer friend to you than I wished to be."

"I, perhaps, have been a better friend of yours than you have supposed. I've admired your reserve, your courage, your studied gayety. But I have felt the existence of something beneath them that was more *you*—more you as I wished to know you—than they were; something that I have believed to be a constant sorrow."

She listened with great gravity, but without an air of offence, and he felt that while he had been timorously calculating the last consequences of friendship, she had placidly accepted them. "You surprise me," she said slowly, and her blush still lingered. "But to refuse to answer you would confirm an impression which is evidently already too strong. An unhappiness that one can sit comfortably talking about, is an unhappiness with distinct limitations. If I were examined before a board of commissioners for investigating the felicity of mankind, I'm sure I should be pronounced a very fortunate woman."

There was something delightfully gentle to him in her tone, and its softness seemed to deepen as she continued: "But let me add, with all gratitude for your sympathy, that it's my own affair altogether. It needn't disturb you, Mr. Longmore, for I have often found myself in your company a very contented person."

"You're a wonderful woman," he said, "and I admire you as I never have admired any one. You're wiser than anything I, for one, can say to you; and what I ask of you is not to let me advise or console you, but simply thank you for letting me know you." He had intended no such outburst as this, but his voice rang loud, and he felt a kind of unfamiliar joy as he uttered it.

She shook her head with some impatience. "Let us be friends,—as I supposed we were going to be,—without protestations and fine words. To have you making bows to my wisdom,—that would be real wretchedness. I can dispense with your admiration better than the Flemish painters can,—better than Van Eyck and Rubens, in spite of all their worshippers. Go join your friend,—see everything, enjoy everything, learn everything, and write me an excellent letter, brimming over with your impressions. I'm extremely fond of the Dutch painters," she added with a slight faltering of the voice, which Longmore had noticed once before, and which he had interpreted as the sudden weariness of a spirit self-condemned to play a part.

"I don't believe you care about the Dutch painters at all," he said with an unhesitating laugh. "But I shall certainly write you a letter."

She rose and turned homeward, thoughtfully rearranging her flowers as she walked. Little was said; Longmore was asking himself, with a tremor in the unspoken words, whether all this meant simply that he was in love. He looked at the rooks wheeling against the golden-hued sky, between the tree-tops, but not at his companion, whose personal presence seemed lost in the felicity she had created. Madame de Mauves was silent and grave, because she was painfully disappointed. A sentimental friendship she had not desired; her scheme had been to pass with Longmore as a placid creature with a good deal of leisure which she was disposed to devote to profitable conversation of an impersonal sort. She liked him extremely, and felt that there was something in him to which, when she made up her girlish mind that a needy French baron was the ripest fruit of time, she had done very scanty justice. They went through the little gate in the garden wall and approached the house. On the terrace Madame Clairin was entertaining a friend,—a little elderly gentleman with a white mustache, and an order in his button-hole. Madame de Mauves chose to pass round the house into the court; whereupon her sister-in-law, greeting Longmore with a commanding nod, lifted her eye-glass and stared at them as they went by. Longmore heard the little old gentleman uttering some old-fashioned epigram about "la vieille galanterie Française," and then, by a sudden impulse, he looked at Madame de Mauves and wondered what she was doing in such a world. She stopped before the house, without asking him to come in. "I hope," she said, "you'll consider my advice, and waste no more time at Saint-Germain."

For an instant there rose to his lips some faded compliment about his time not being wasted, but it expired before the simple sincerity of her look. She stood there as gently serious as the angel of disinterestedness, and Longmore felt as if he should insult her by treating her words as a bait for flattery. "I shall start in a day or two," he answered, "but I won't promise you not to come back."

"I hope not," she said simply. "I expect to be here a long time."

"I shall come and say good by," he rejoined; on which she nodded with a smile, and went in.

He turned away, and walked slowly homeward by the terrace. It seemed to him that to leave her thus, for a gain on which she herself insisted, was to know her better and admire her more. But he was in a vague ferment of feeling which her evasion of his question half an hour before had done more to deepen than to allay. Suddenly, on the terrace, he encountered M. de Mauves, who was leaning against the parapet finishing a cigar. The Baron, who, he fancied, had an air of peculiar affability, offered him his fair, plump hand. Longmore stopped; he felt a sudden angry desire to cry out to him that he had the loveliest wife in the world; that he ought to be ashamed of himself not to know it; and that for all his shrewdness he had never looked into the depths of her eyes. The Baron, we know, considered that he had; but there was something in Euphemia's eyes now that was not there five years before. They talked for a while about various things, and M. de Mauves gave a humorous account of his visit to America. His tone was not soothing to Longmore's excited sensibilities. He seemed to consider the country a gigantic joke, and his urbanity only went so far as to admit that it was not a bad one. Longmore was not, by habit, an aggressive apologist for our institutions; but the Baron's narrative confirmed his worst impressions of French superficiality. He had understood nothing, he had felt nothing, he had learned nothing; and our hero, glancing askance at his aristocratic profile, declared that if the chief merit of a long pedigree was to leave one so vaingloriously stupid, he thanked his stars that the Longmores had emerged from obscurity in the present century, in the person of an enterprising lumber merchant. M. de Mauves dwelt of course on that prime oddity of ours,—the liberty allowed to young girls; and related the history of his researches into the "opportunities" it presented to French noblemen,—researches in which, during a fortnight's stay, he seemed to have spent many agreeable hours. "I am bound to admit," he said, "that in every case I was disarmed by the extreme candor of the young lady, and that they took care of themselves to better purpose than I have seen some mammas in France take care of them." Longmore greeted this handsome concession with the grimmest of smiles, and damned his impertinent patronage.

Mentioning at last that he was about to leave Saint-Germain, he was surprised, without exactly being flattered, by the Baron's quickened attention. "I'm very sorry," the latter cried. "I hoped we had you for the summer." Longmore murmured something civil, and wondered why M. de Mauves should care whether he stayed or went. "You were a diversion to Madame de Mauves," the Baron added. "I assure you I mentally blessed your visits."

"They were a great pleasure to me," Longmore said gravely. "Some day I expect to come back."

"Pray do," and the Baron laid his hand urgently on his arm. "You see I have confidence in you!" Longmore was silent for a moment, and the Baron puffed his cigar reflectively and watched the smoke. "Madame de Mauves," he said at last, "is a rather singular person."

Longmore shifted his position, and wondered whether he was going to "explain" Madame de Mauves.

"Being as you are her fellow-countryman," the Baron went on, "I don't mind speaking frankly. She's just a little morbid,—the most charming woman in the world, as you see, but a little fanciful, —a little *exaltée*. Now you see she has taken this extraordinary fancy for solitude. I can't get her to go anywhere,—to see any one. When my friends present themselves she's polite, but she's freezing. She doesn't do herself justice, and I expect every day to hear two or three of them say to me, 'Your wife's *jolie à croquer*: what a pity she hasn't a little *esprit*.' You must have found out that she has really a great deal. But to tell the whole truth, what she needs is to forget herself. She sits alone for hours poring over her English books and looking at life through that terrible brown fog which they always seem to me to fling over the world. I doubt if your English authors," the Baron continued, with a serenity which Longmore afterwards characterized as sublime, "are very sound reading for young married women. I don't pretend to know much about them; but I remember that, not long after our marriage, Madame de Mauves undertook to read me one day a certain Wordsworth,—a poet highly esteemed, it appears, *chez vous*. It seemed to me that she took me by the nape of the neck and forced my head for half an hour over a basin of *soupe aux choux,* and that one ought to ventilate the drawing-room before any one called. But I suppose you know him, —*ce génie là.* I think my wife never forgave me, and that it was a real shock to her to find she had married a man who had very much the same taste in literature as in cookery. But you're a man of general culture," said the Baron, turning to Longmore and fixing his eyes on the seal on his watch-guard. "You can talk about everything, and I'm sure you like Alfred de Musset as well as Wordsworth. Talk to her about everything, Alfred de Musset included. Bah! I forgot you're going. Come back then as soon as possible and talk about your travels. If Madame de Mauves too would travel for a couple of months, it would do her good. It would enlarge her horizon,"—and M. de Mauves made a series of short nervous jerks with his stick in the air,—"it would wake up her imagination. She's too rigid, you know,—it would show her that one may bend a trifle without breaking." He paused a moment and gave two or three vigorous puffs. Then turning to his companion again, with a little nod and a confidential smile:—"I hope you admire my candor. I wouldn't say all this to one of *us.*"

Evening was coming on, and the lingering light seemed to float in the air in faintly golden motes. Longmore stood gazing at these luminous particles; he could almost have fancied them a swarm of humming insects, murmuring as a refrain, "She has a great deal of *esprit,*—she has a great deal of *esprit.*" "Yes, she has a great deal," he said mechanically, turning to the Baron. M. de Mauves glanced at him sharply, as if to ask what the deuce he was talking about. "She has a great deal of intelligence," said Longmore, deliberately, "a great deal of beauty, a great many virtues."

M. de Mauves busied himself for a moment in lighting another cigar, and when he had finished, with a return of his confidential smile, "I suspect you of thinking," he said, "that I don't do my wife justice. Take care,—take care, young man; that's a dangerous assumption. In general, a man always does his wife justice. More than justice," cried the Baron with a laugh,—"that we keep for the wives of other men!"

Longmore afterwards remembered it in favor of the Baron's grace of address that he had not measured at this moment the dusky abyss over which it hovered. But a sort of deepening subterranean echo lingered on his spiritual ear. For the present his keenest sensation was a desire to get away and cry aloud that M. de Mauves was an arrogant fool. He bade him an abrupt good-night, which must serve also, he said, as good by.

"Decidedly, then, you go?" said M. de Mauves, almost peremptorily.

"Decidedly."

"Of course you'll come and say good by to Madame de Mauves." His tone implied that the omission would be most uncivil; but there seemed to Longmore something so ludicrous in his taking a lesson in consideration from M. de Mauves, that he burst into a laugh. The Baron frowned, like a man for whom it was a new and most unpleasant sensation to be perplexed. "You're a queer fellow," he murmured, as Longmore turned away, not foreseeing that he would think him a very queer fellow indeed before he had done with him. Longmore sat down to dinner at his hotel with his usual good intentions; but as he was lifting his first glass of wine to his lips, he suddenly fell to musing and set down his wine untasted. His revery lasted long, and when he emerged from it, his fish was cold; but this mattered little, for his appetite was gone. That evening he packed his trunk with a kind of indignant energy. This was so effective that the operation was accomplished before bedtime, and as he was not in the least sleepy, he devoted the interval to writing two letters; one was a short note to Madame de Mauves, which he intrusted to a servant, to be delivered the next morning. He had found it best, he said, to leave Saint-Germain immediately, but he expected to be back in Paris in the early autumn. The other letter was the result of his having remembered a day or two before that he had not yet complied with Mrs. Draper's injunction to give her an account of his impressions of her friend. The present occasion seemed propitious, and he wrote half a dozen pages. His tone, however, was grave, and Mrs. Draper, on receiving them, was slightly disappointed,—she would have preferred a stronger flavor of rhapsody. But what chiefly concerns us is the concluding sentences.

"The only time she ever spoke to me of her marriage," he wrote, "she intimated that it had been a perfect love-match. With all abatements, I suppose most marriages are; but in her case this would mean more, I think, than in that of most women; for her love was an absolute idealization. She believed her husband was a hero of rose-colored romance, and he turns out to be not even a hero of very sad-colored reality. For some time now she has been sounding her mistake, but I don't believe she has touched the bottom of it yet. She strikes me as a person who is begging off from full knowledge,—who has struck a truce with painful truth, and is trying awhile the experiment of living with closed eyes. In the dark she tries to see again the gilding on her idol. Illusion of course is illusion, and one must always pay for it; but there is something truly tragical in seeing an earthly penalty levied on such divine folly as this. As for M. de Mauves, he's a Frenchman to his fingers' ends; and I confess I should dislike him for this if he were a much better man. He can't forgive his wife for having married him too sentimentally and loved him too well; for in some uncorrupted corner of his being he feels, I suppose, that as she saw him, so he ought to have been. It's a perpetual vexation to him that a little American bourgeoise should have fancied him a finer fellow than he is, or than he at all wants to be. He hasn't a glimmering of real acquaintance with his wife; he can't understand the stream of passion flowing so clear and still. To tell the truth, I hardly can myself; but when I see the spectacle I can admire it furiously. M. de Mauves, at any rate, would like to have the comfort of feeling that his wife was as corruptible as himself; and you'll hardly believe me when I tell you that he goes about intimating to gentlemen whom he deems worthy of the knowledge, that it would be a convenience to him to have them make love to her."

V

On reaching Paris, Longmore straightway purchased a Murray's "Belgium," to help himself to believe that he would start on the morrow for Brussels; but when the morrow came, it occurred to him that, by way of preparation, he ought to acquaint himself more intimately with the Flemish painters in the Louvre. This took a whole morning, but it did little to hasten his departure. He had abruptly left Saint-Germain, because it seemed to him that respect for Madame de Mauves demanded that he should allow her husband no reason to suppose that he had understood him; but now that he had satisfied this immediate need of delicacy, he found himself thinking more and more ardently of Euphemia. It was a poor expression of ardor to be lingering irresolutely on the deserted boulevards, but he detested the idea of leaving Saint-Germain five hundred miles behind him. He felt very foolish, nevertheless, and wandered about nervously, promising himself to take the next train; but a dozen trains started, and Longmore was still in Paris. This sentimental tumult was more than he had bargained for, and, as he looked in the shop windows, he wondered whether it was a "passion." He had never been fond of the word, and had grown up with a kind of horror of what it represented. He had hoped that when he fell in love, he should do it with an excellent conscience, with no greater agitation than a mild general glow of satisfaction. But here was a sentiment compounded of pity and anger, as well as admiration, and bristling with scruples and doubts. He had come abroad to enjoy the Flemish painters and all others; but what fair-tressed saint of Van Eyck or Memling was so appealing a figure as Madame de Mauves? His restless steps carried him at last out of the long villa-bordered avenue which leads to the Bois de Boulogne.

Summer had fairly begun, and the drive beside the lake was empty, but there were various loungers on the benches and chairs, and the great café had an air of animation. Longmore's walk had given him an appetite, and he went into the establishment and demanded a dinner, remarking for the hundredth time, as he observed the smart little tables disposed in the open air, how much better they ordered this matter in France.

"Will monsieur dine in the garden, or in the salon?" asked the waiter. Longmore chose the garden; and observing that a great vine of June roses was trained over the wall of the house, placed himself at a table near by, where the best of dinners was served him on the whitest of linen, in the most shining of porcelain. It so happened that his table was near a window, and that as he sat he could look into a corner of the salon. So it was that his attention rested on a lady seated just within the window, which was open, face to face apparently to a companion who was concealed by the curtain. She was a very pretty woman, and Longmore looked at her as often as was consistent with good manners. After a while he even began to wonder who she was, and to suspect that she was one of those ladies whom it is no breach of good manners to look at as often as you like. Longmore, too, if he had been so disposed, would have been the more free to give her all his attention, that her own was fixed upon the person opposite to her. She was what the French call a *belle brune,* and though our hero, who had rather a conservative taste in such matters, had no great relish for her bold outlines and even bolder coloring, he could not help admiring her expression of basking contentment.

She was evidently very happy, and her happiness gave her an air of innocence. The talk of her friend, whoever he was, abundantly suited her humor, for she sat listening to him with a broad, lazy smile, and interrupted him occasionally, while she crunched her bonbons, with a murmured response, presumably as broad, which seemed to deepen his eloquence. She drank a great deal of champagne and ate an immense number of strawberries, and was plainly altogether a person with an impartial relish for strawberries, champagne, and what she would have called *bêtises*.

They had half finished dinner when Longmore sat down, and he was still in his place when they rose. She had hung her bonnet on a nail above her chair, and her companion passed round the table to take it down for her. As he did so, she bent her head to look at a wine stain on her dress, and in the movement exposed the greater part of the back of a very handsome neck. The gentleman observed it, and observed also, apparently, that the room beyond them was empty; that he stood within eyeshot of Longmore he failed to observe. He stooped suddenly and imprinted a gallant kiss on the fair expanse. Longmore then recognized M. de Mauves. The recipient of this vigorous tribute put on her bonnet, using his flushed smile as a mirror, and in a moment they passed through the garden, on their way to their carriage.

Then, for the first time, M. de Mauves perceived Longmore. He measured with a rapid glance the young man's relation to the open window, and checked himself in the impulse to stop and speak to him. He contented himself with bowing with great gravity as he opened the gate for his companion.

That evening Longmore made a railway journey, but not to Brussels. He had effectually ceased to care about Brussels; the only thing he now cared about was Madame de Mauves. The atmosphere of his mind had had a sudden clearing up; pity and anger were still throbbing there, but they had space to rage at their pleasure, for doubts and scruples had abruptly departed. It was little, he felt, that he could interpose between her resignation and the unsparing harshness of her position; but that little, if it involved the sacrifice of everything that bound him to the tranquil past it seemed to him that he could offer her with a rapture which at last made reflection a woefully halting substitute for faith. Nothing in his tranquil past had given such a zest to consciousness as the sense of tending with all his being to a single aim which bore him company on his journey to Saint-Germain. How to justify his return, how to explain his ardor, troubled him little. He was not sure, even, that he wished to be understood; he wished only to feel that it was by no fault of his that Madame de Mauves was alone with the ugliness of fate. He was conscious of no distinct desire to "make love" to her; if he could have uttered the essence of his longing, he would have said that he wished her to remember that in a world colored gray to her vision by disappointment, there was one vividly honest man. She might certainly have remembered it, however, without his coming back to remind her; and it is not to be denied that, as he packed his valise that evening, he wished immensely to hear the sound of her voice.

He waited the next day till his usual hour of calling,—the late afternoon; but he learned at the door that Madame de Mauves was not at home. The servant offered the information that she was walking in the forest. Longmore went through the garden and out of the little door into the lane, and, after half an hour's vain exploration, saw her coming toward him at the end of a green bypath. As he appeared, she stopped for a moment, as if to turn aside; then recognizing him, she slowly advanced, and he was soon shaking hands with her.

"Nothing has happened," she said, looking at him fixedly. "You're not ill?"

"Nothing, except that when I got to Paris I found how fond I had grown of Saint-Germain."

She neither smiled nor looked flattered; it seemed indeed to Longmore that she was annoyed. But he was uncertain, for he immediately perceived that in his absence the whole character of her face had altered. It told him that something momentous had happened. It was no longer self-contained melancholy that he read in her eyes, but grief and agitation which had lately struggled with that passionate love of peace of which she had spoken to him, and forced it to know that deep experience is never peaceful. She was pale, and she had evidently been shedding tears. He felt his heart beating hard; he seemed now to know her secrets. She continued to look at him with a contracted brow, as if his return had given her a sense of responsibility too great to be disguised by a commonplace welcome. For some moments, as he turned and walked beside her, neither spoke; then abruptly,—"Tell me truly, Mr. Longmore," she said, "why you have come back."

He turned and looked at her with an air which startled her into a certainty of what she had feared. "Because I've learned the real answer to the question I asked you the other day. You're not happy,—you're too good to be happy on the terms offered you. Madame de Mauves," he went on with a gesture which protested against a gesture of her own, "I can't be happy if you're not. I don't care for anything so long as I see such a depth of unconquerable sadness in your eyes. I found during three dreary days in Paris that the thing in the world I most care for is this daily privilege of seeing you. I know it's absolutely brutal to tell you I admire you; it's an insult to you to treat you as if you had complained to me or appealed to me. But such a friendship as I waked up to there"—and he tossed his head toward the distant city—"is a potent force, I assure you; and when forces are compressed they explode. But if you had told me every trouble in your heart, it would have mattered little; I couldn't say more than I must say now,—that if that in life from which you've hoped most has given you least, *my* devoted respect will refuse no service and betray no trust."

She had begun to make marks in the earth with the point of her parasol; but she stopped and listened to him in perfect immobility. Rather, her immobility was not perfect; for when he stopped speaking a faint flush had stolen into her cheek. It told Longmore that she was moved, and his first perceiving it was the happiest instant of his life. She raised her eyes at last, and looked at him with what at first seemed a pleading dread of excessive emotion.

"Thank you—thank you!" she said, calmly enough; but the next moment her own emotion overcame her calmness, and she burst into tears. Her tears vanished as quickly as they came, but they did Longmore a world of good. He had always felt indefinably afraid of her; her being had somehow seemed fed by a deeper faith and a stronger will than his own; but her half-dozen smothered sobs showed him the bottom of her heart, and assured him that she was weak enough to be grateful.

"Excuse me," she said; "I'm too nervous to listen to you. I believe I could have faced an enemy to-day, but I can't endure a friend."

"You're killing yourself with stoicism,—that's my belief," he cried. "Listen to a friend for his own sake, if not for yours. I have never ventured to offer you an atom of compassion, and you can't accuse yourself of an abuse of charity."

She looked about her with a kind of weary confusion which promised a reluctant attention. But suddenly perceiving by the wayside the fallen log on which they had rested a few evenings before, she went and sat down on it in impatient resignation, and looked at Longmore, as he stood silent, watching her, with a glance which seemed to urge that, if she was charitable now, he must be very wise.

"Something came to my knowledge yesterday," he said as he sat down beside her, "which gave me a supreme sense of your moral isolation. You are truth itself, and there is no truth about you. You believe in purity and duty and dignity, and you live in a world in which they are daily belied. I sometimes ask myself with a kind of rage how you ever came into such a world,—and why the perversity of fate never let me know you before."

"I like my 'world' no better than you do, and it was not for its own sake I came into it. But what particular group of people is worth pinning one's faith upon? I confess it sometimes seems to me that men and women are very poor creatures. I suppose I'm romantic. I have a most unfortunate taste for poetic fitness. Life is hard prose, which one must learn to read contentedly. I believe I once thought that all the prose was in America, which was very foolish. What I thought, what I believed, what I expected, when I was an ignorant girl, fatally addicted to falling in love with my own theories, is more than I can begin to tell you now. Sometimes, when I remember certain impulses, certain illusions of those days, they take away my breath, and I wonder my bedazzled visions didn't lead me into troubles greater than any I have now to lament. I had a conviction which you would probably smile at if I were to attempt to express it to you. It was a singular form for passionate faith to take, but it had all of the sweetness and the ardor of passionate faith. It led me to take a great step, and it lies behind me now in the distance like a shadow melting slowly in the light of experience. It has faded, but it has not vanished. Some feelings, I am sure, die only with ourselves; some illusions are as much the condition of our life as our heart-beats. They say that life itself is an illusion,—that this world is a shadow of which the reality is yet to come. Life is all of a piece, then, and there is no shame in being miserably human. As for my 'isolation,' it doesn't greatly matter; it's the fault, in part, of my obstinacy. There have been times when I have been frantically distressed, and, to tell you the truth, wretchedly homesick, because my maid—a jewel of a maid—lied to me with every second breath. There have been moments when I have wished I was the daughter of a poor New England minister, living in a little white house under a couple of elms, and doing all the housework."

She had begun to speak slowly, with an air of effort; but she went on quickly, as if talking were a relief. "My marriage introduced me to people and things which seemed to me at first very strange and then very horrible, and then, to tell the truth, very contemptible. At first I expended a great deal of sorrow and dismay and pity on it all; but there soon came a time when I began to wonder whether it was worth one's tears. If I could tell you the eternal friendships I've seen broken, the inconsolable woes consoled, the jealousies and vanities leading off the dance, you would agree with me that tempers like yours and mine can understand neither such losses nor such compensations. A year ago, while I was in the country, a friend of mine was in despair at the infidelity of her husband; she wrote me a most tragical letter, and on my return to Paris I went immediately to see her. A week had elapsed, and, as I had seen stranger things, I thought she might have recovered her spirits. Not at all; she was still in despair,—but at what? At the conduct, the abandoned, shameless conduct of Mme. de T. You'll imagine, of course, that Mme. de T. was the lady whom my friend's husband preferred to his wife. Far from it; he had never seen her. Who, then, was Mme. de T.? Mme. de T. was cruelly devoted to M. de V. And who was M. de V.? M. de V.—in two words, my friend was cultivating two jealousies at once. I hardly know what I said to her; something, at any rate, that she found unpardonable, for she quite gave me up. Shortly afterward my husband proposed we should cease to live in Paris, and I gladly assented, for I believe I was falling into a state of mind that made me a detestable companion. I should have preferred to go quite into the country, into Auvergne, where my husband has a place. But to him Paris, in some degree, is necessary, and Saint-Germain has been a sort of compromise."

"A sort of compromise!" Longmore repeated. "That's your whole life."

"It's the life of many people, of most people of quiet tastes, and it is certainly better than acute distress. One is at loss theoretically to defend a compromise; but if I found a poor creature clinging to one from day to day, I should think it poor friendship to make him lose his hold." Madame de Mauves had no sooner uttered these words than she smiled faintly, as if to mitigate their personal application.

"Heaven forbid," said Longmore, "that one should do that unless one has something better to offer. And yet I am haunted by a vision of a life in which you should have found no compromises, for they are a perversion of natures that tend only to goodness and rectitude. As I see it, you should have found happiness serene, profound, complete; a *femme de chambre* not a jewel perhaps, but warranted to tell but one fib a day; a society possibly rather provincial, but (in spite of your poor opinion of mankind) a good deal of solid virtue; jealousies and vanities very tame, and no particular iniquities and adulteries. A husband," he added after a moment,—"a husband of your own faith and race and spiritual substance, who would have loved you well."

She rose to her feet, shaking her head. "You are very kind to go to the expense of visions for me. Visions are vain things; we must make the best of the reality."

"And yet," said Longmore, provoked by what seemed the very wantonness of her patience, "the reality, if I'm not mistaken, has very recently taken a shape that keenly tests your philosophy."

She seemed on the point of replying that his sympathy was too zealous; but a couple of impatient tears in his eyes proved that it was founded on a devotion to which it was impossible not to defer. "Philosophy?" she said. "I have none. Thank Heaven!" she cried, with vehemence, "I have none. I believe, Mr. Longmore," she added in a moment, "that I have nothing on earth but a conscience,—it's a good time to tell you so,—nothing but a dogged, clinging, inexpugnable conscience. Does that prove me to be indeed of your faith and race, and have you one for which you can say as much? I don't say it in vanity, for I believe that if my conscience will prevent me from doing anything very base, it will effectually prevent me from doing anything very fine."

"I am delighted to hear it," cried Longmore. "We are made for each other. It's very certain I too shall never do anything fine. And yet I have fancied that in my case this inexpugnable organ you so eloquently describe might be blinded and gagged awhile, in a fine cause, if not turned out of doors. In yours," he went on with the same appealing irony, "is it absolutely invincible?"

But her fancy made no concession to his sarcasm. "Don't laugh at your conscience," she answered gravely; "that's the only blasphemy I know."

She had hardly spoken when she turned suddenly at an unexpected sound, and at the same moment Longmore heard a footstep in an adjacent by-path which crossed their own at a short distance from where they stood.

"It's M. de Mauves," said Euphemia directly, and moved slowly forward. Longmore, wondering how she knew it, had overtaken her by the time her husband advanced into sight. A solitary walk in the forest was a pastime to which M. de Mauves was not addicted, but he seemed on this occasion to have resorted to it with some equanimity. He was smoking a fragrant cigar, and his thumb was thrust into the armhole of his waistcoat, with an air of contemplative serenity. He stopped short with surprise on seeing his wife and her companion, and Longmore considered his surprise impertinent. He glanced rapidly from one to the other, fixed Longmore's eye sharply for a single instant, and then lifted his hat with formal politeness.

"I was not aware," he said, turning to Madame de Mauves, "that I might congratulate you on the return of monsieur."

"You should have known it," she answered gravely, "if I had expected Mr. Longmore's return."

She had become very pale, and Longmore felt that this was a first meeting after a stormy parting. "My return was unexpected to myself," he said. "I came last evening."

M. de Mauves smiled with extreme urbanity. "It's needless for me to welcome you. Madame de Mauves knows the duties of hospitality." And with another bow he continued his walk.

Madame de Mauves and her companion returned slowly home, with few words, but, on Longmore's part at least, many thoughts. The Baron's appearance had given him an angry chill; it was a dusky cloud reabsorbing the light which had begun to shine between himself and his companion.

He watched Euphemia narrowly as they went, and wondered what she had last had to suffer. Her husband's presence had checked her frankness, but nothing indicated that she had accepted the insulting meaning of his words. Matters were evidently at a crisis between them, and Longmore wondered vainly what it was on Euphemia's part that prevented an absolute rupture. What did she suspect?—how much did she know? To what was she resigned?—how much had she forgiven? How, above all, did she reconcile with knowledge, or with suspicion, that ineradicable tenderness of which she had just now all but assured him? "She has loved him once," Longmore said with a sinking of the heart, "and with her to love once is to commit one's being forever. Her husband thinks her too rigid! What would a poet call it?"

He relapsed with a kind of aching impotence into the sense of her being somehow beyond him, unattainable, immeasurable by his own fretful spirit. Suddenly he gave three passionate switches in the air with his cane, which made Madame de Mauves look round. She could hardly have guessed that they meant that where ambition was so vain, it was an innocent compensation to plunge into worship.

Madame de Mauves found in her drawing-room the little elderly Frenchman, M. de Chalumeau, whom Longmore had observed a few days before on the terrace. On this occasion, too, Madame Clairin was entertaining him, but as his sister-in-law came in she surrendered her post and addressed herself to our hero. Longmore, at thirty, was still an ingenuous youth, and there was something in this lady's large coquetry which had the power of making him blush. He was surprised at finding he had not absolutely forfeited her favor by his deportment at their last interview, and a suspicion of her meaning to approach him on another line completed his uneasiness.

"So you've returned from Brussels," she said, "by way of the forest."

"I've not been to Brussels. I returned yesterday from Paris by the only way,—by the train."

Madame Clairin stared and laughed. "I've never known a young man to be so fond of Saint-Germain. They generally declare it's horribly dull."

"That's not very polite to you," said Longmore, who was vexed at his blushes, and determined not to be abashed.

"Ah, what am I?" demanded Madame Clairin, swinging open her fan. "I'm the dullest thing here. They've not had your success with my sister-in-law."

"It would have been very easy to have it. Madame de Mauves is kindness itself."

"To her own countrymen!"

Longmore remained silent; he hated the talk. Madame Clairin looked at him a moment, and then turned her head and surveyed Euphemia, to whom M. de Chalumeau was serving up another epigram, which she was receiving with a slight droop of the head and her eyes absently wandering through the window. "Don't pretend to tell me," she murmured suddenly, "that you're not in love with that pretty woman."

"Allons donc!" cried Longmore, in the best French he had ever uttered. He rose the next minute, and took a hasty farewell.

VI

HE ALLOWED several days to pass without going back; it seemed delicate not to appear to regard his friend's frankness during their last interview as a general invitation. This cost him a great effort, for hopeless passions are not the most deferential; and he had, moreover, a constant fear, that if, as he believed, the hour of supreme "explanations" had come, the magic of her magnanimity might convert M. de Mauves. Vicious men, it was abundantly recorded, had been so converted as to be acceptable to God, and the something divine in Euphemia's temper would sanctify any means she should choose to employ. Her means, he kept repeating, were no business of his, and the essence of his admiration ought to be to respect her freedom; but he felt as if he should turn away into a world out of which most of the joy had departed, if her freedom, after all, should spare him only a murmured "Thank you."

When he called again he found to his vexation that he was to run the gantlet of Madame Clairin's officious hospitality. It was one of the first mornings of perfect summer, and the drawing-room, through the open windows, was flooded with a sweet confusion of odors and bird-notes which filled him with the hope that Madame de Mauves would come out and spend half the day in the forest. But Madame Clairin, with her hair not yet dressed, emerged like a brassy discord in a maze of melody.

At the same moment the servant returned with Euphemia's regrets; she was indisposed and unable to see Mr. Longmore. The young man knew that he looked disappointed, and that Madame Clairin was observing him, and this consciousness impelled her to give him a glance of almost aggressive frigidity. This was apparently what she desired. She wished to throw him off his balance, and, if he was not mistaken, she had the means.

"Put down your hat, Mr. Longmore," she said, "and be polite for once. You were not at all polite the other day when I asked you that friendly question about the state of your heart."

"I have no heart—to talk about," said Longmore, uncompromisingly.

"As well say you've none at all. I advise you to cultivate a little eloquence; you may have use for it. That was not an idle question of mine; I don't ask idle questions. For a couple of months now that you've been coming and going among us, it seems to me that you have had very few to answer of any sort."

"I have certainly been very well treated," said Longmore.

Madame Clairin was silent a moment, and then—"Have you never felt disposed to ask any?" she demanded.

Her look, her tone, were so charged with roundabout meanings that it seemed to Longmore as if even to understand her would savor of dishonest complicity. "What is it you have to tell me?" he asked, frowning and blushing.

Madame Clairin flushed. It is rather hard, when you come bearing yourself very much as the sibyl when she came to the Roman king, to be treated as something worse than a vulgar gossip. "I might tell you, Mr. Longmore," she said, "that you have as bad a *ton* as any young man I ever met. Where have you lived,—what are your ideas? I wish to call your attention to a fact which it takes some delicacy to touch upon. You have noticed, I supposed, that my sister-in-law is not the happiest woman in the world."

Longmore assented with a gesture.

Madame Clairin looked slightly disappointed at his want of

enthusiasm. Nevertheless—"You have formed, I suppose," she continued, "your conjectures on the causes of her—dissatisfaction."

"Conjecture has been superfluous. I have seen the causes—or at least a specimen of them—with my own eyes."

"I know perfectly what you mean. My brother, in a single word, is in love with another woman. I don't judge him; I don't judge my sister-in-law. I permit myself to say that in her position I would have managed otherwise. I would have kept my husband's affection, or I would have frankly done without it, before this. But my sister is an odd compound; I don't profess to understand her. Therefore it is, in a measure, that I appeal to you, her fellow-countryman. Of course you'll be surprised at my way of looking at the matter, and I admit that it's a way in use only among people whose family traditions compel them to take a superior view of things." Madame Clairin paused, and Longmore wondered where her family traditions were going to lead her.

"Listen," she went on. "There has never been a De Mauves who has not given his wife the right to be jealous. We know our history for ages back, and the fact is established. It's a shame if you like, but it's something to have a shame with such a pedigree. The De Mauves are real Frenchmen, and their wives—I may say it—have been worthy of them. You may see all their portraits in our Château de Mauves; every one of them an 'injured' beauty, but not one of them hanging her head. Not one of them had the bad taste to be jealous, and yet not one in a dozen was guilty of an escapade,—not one of them was talked about. There's good sense for you! How they managed—go and look at the dusky, faded canvases and pastels, and ask. They were femmes d'esprit. When they had a headache, they put on a little rouge and came to supper as usual; and when they had a heart-ache, they put a little rouge on their hearts. These are fine traditions, and it doesn't seem to me fair that a little American bourgeoise should come in and interrupt them, and should hang her photograph, with her obstinate little *air penché,* in the gallery of our shrewd fine ladies. A De Mauves must be a De Mauves. When she married my brother, I don't suppose she took him for a member of a *societé de bonnes œuvres.* I don't say we're right; who is right? But we're as history has made us, and if any one is to change, it had better be Madame de Mauves herself." Again Madame Clairin paused and opened and closed her fan. "Let her conform!" she said, with amazing audacity.

Longmore's reply was ambiguous; he simply said, "Ah!"

Madame Clairin's pious retrospect had apparently imparted an honest zeal to her indignation. "For a long time," she continued, "my sister has been taking the attitude of an injured woman, affecting a disgust with the world, and shutting herself up to read the 'Imitation.' I've never remarked on her conduct, but I've quite lost patience with it. When a woman with her prettiness lets her husband wander, she deserves her fate. I don't wish you to agree with me—on the contrary; but I call such a woman a goose. She must have bored him to death. What has passed between them for many months needn't concern us; what provocation my sister has had—monstrous, if you wish—what ennui my brother has suffered. It's enough that a week ago, just after you had ostensibly gone to Brussels, something happened to produce an explosion. She found a letter in his pocket—a photograph—a trinket—*que sais-je?* At any rate, the scene was terrible. I didn't listen at the keyhole, and I don't know what was said; but I have reason to believe that my brother was called to account as I fancy none of his ancestors have ever been,—even by injured sweethearts."

Longmore had leaned forward in silent attention with his elbows on his knees, and instinctively he dropped his face into his hands. "Ah, poor woman!" he groaned.

"Voilà!" said Madame Clairin. "You pity her."

"Pity her?" cried Longmore, looking up with ardent eyes and forgetting the spirit of Madame Clairin's narrative in the miserable facts. "Don't you?"

"A little. But I'm not acting sentimentally; I'm acting politically. I wish to arrange things,—to see my brother free to do as he chooses, —to see Euphemia contented. Do you understand me?"

"Very well, I think. You're the most immoral person I've lately had the privilege of conversing with."

Madame Clairin shrugged her shoulders. "Possibly. When was there a great politician who was not immoral?"

"Nay," said Longmore in the same tone. "You're too superficial to be a great politician. You don't begin to know anything about Madame de Mauves."

Madame Clairin inclined her head to one side, eyed Longmore

sharply, mused a moment, and then smiled with an excellent imitation of intelligent compassion. "It's not in my interest to contradict you."

"It would be in your interest to learn, Madame Clairin," the young man went on with unceremonious candor, "what honest men most admire in a woman,—and to recognize it when you see it."

Longmore certainly did injustice to her talents for diplomacy, for she covered her natural annoyance at this sally with a pretty piece of irony. "So you *are* in love!" she quietly exclaimed.

Longmore was silent awhile. "I wonder if you would understand me," he said at last, "if I were to tell you that I have for Madame de Mauves the most devoted friendship?"

"You underrate my intelligence. But in that case you ought to exert your influence to put an end to these painful domestic scenes."

"Do you suppose," cried Longmore, "that she talks to me about her domestic scenes?"

Madame Clairin stared. "Then your friendship isn't returned?" And as Longmore turned away, shaking his head,—"Now, at least," she added, "she will have something to tell you. I happen to know the upshot of my brother's last interview with his wife." Longmore rose to his feet as a sort of protest against the indelicacy of the position into which he was being forced; but all that made him tender made him curious, and she caught in his averted eyes an expression which prompted her to strike her blow. "My brother is monstrously in love with a certain person in Paris; of course he ought not to be; but he wouldn't be a De Mauves if he were not. It was this unsanctified passion that spoke. 'Listen, madam,' he cried at last: 'let us live like people who understand life! It's unpleasant to be forced to say such things outright, but you have a way of bringing one down to the rudiments. I'm faithless, I'm heartless, I'm brutal, I'm everything horrible,—it's understood. Take your revenge, console yourself; you're too pretty a woman to have anything to complain of. Here's a handsome young man sighing himself into a consumption for you. Listen to the poor fellow, and you'll find that virtue is none the less becoming for being good-natured. You'll see that it's not after all such a doleful world, and that there is even an advantage in having the most impudent of husbands.' " Madame Clairin paused; Longmore had turned very pale. "You may believe it," she said; "the speech took place in my presence; things were done in order. And now, Mr. Longmore,"—this with a smile which he was too troubled at the moment to appreciate, but which he remembered later with a kind of awe,—"we count upon you!"

"He said this to her, face to face, as you say it to me now?" Longmore asked slowly, after a silence.

"Word for word, and with the greatest politeness."

"And Madame de Mauves—what did she say?"

Madame Clairin smiled again. "To such a speech as that a woman says—nothing. She had been sitting with a piece of needlework, and I think she had not seen her husband since their quarrel the day before. He came in with the gravity of an ambassador, and I'm sure that when he made his *demande en mariage* his manner was not more respectful. He only wanted white gloves!" said Madame Clairin. "Euphemia sat silent a few moments drawing her stitches, and then without a word, without a glance, she walked out of the room. It was just what she should have done!"

"Yes," Longmore repeated, "it was just what she should have done."

"And I, left alone with my brother, do you know what I said?"

Longmore shook his head. *"Mauvais sujet!"* he suggested.

" 'You've done me the honor,' I said, 'to take this step in my presence. I don't pretend to qualify it. You know what you're about, and it's your own affair. But you may confide in my discretion.' Do you think he has had reason to complain of it?" She received no answer; Longmore was slowly turning away and passing his gloves mechanically round the band of his hat. "I hope," she cried, "you're not going to start for Brussels!"

Plainly, Longmore was deeply disturbed, and Madame Clairin might flatter herself on the success of her plea for old-fashioned manners. And yet there was something that left her more puzzled than satisfied in the reflective tone with which he answered, "No, I shall remain here for the present." The processes of his mind seemed provokingly subterranean, and she would have fancied for a moment that he was linked with her sister in some monstrous conspiracy of asceticism.

"Come this evening," she boldly resumed. "The rest will take care of itself. Meanwhile I shall take the liberty of telling my sister-in-law that I have repeated—in short, that I have put you *au fait*."

Longmore started and colored, and she hardly knew whether he was going to assent or demur. "Tell her what you please. Nothing you can tell her will affect her conduct."

"Voyons! Do you mean to tell me that a woman, young, pretty, sentimental, neglected—insulted, if you will—? I see you don't believe it. Believe simply in your own opportunity! But for heaven's sake, if it's to lead anywhere, don't come back with that *visage de croquemort*. You look as if you were going to bury your heart,—not to offer it to a pretty woman. You're much better when you smile. Come, do yourself justice."

"Yes," he said, "I must do myself justice." And abruptly, with a bow, he took his departure.

VII

He felt, when he found himself unobserved, in the open air, that he must plunge into violent action, walk fast and far, and defer the opportunity for thought. He strode away into the forest, swinging his cane, throwing back his head, gazing away into the verdurous vistas, and following the road without a purpose. He felt immensely excited, but he could hardly have said whether his emotion was a pain or a joy. It was joyous as all increase of freedom is joyous; something seemed to have been knocked down across his path; his destiny appeared to have rounded a cape and brought him into sight of an open sea. But his freedom resolved itself somehow into the need of despising all mankind, with a single exception; and the fact of Madame de Mauves inhabiting a planet contaminated by the presence of this baser multitude kept his elation from seeming a pledge of ideal bliss.

But she was there, and circumstance now forced them to be intimate. She had ceased to have what men call a secret for him, and this fact itself brought with it a sort of rapture. He had no prevision that he should "profit," in the vulgar sense, by the extraordinary position into which they had been thrown; it might be but a cruel trick of destiny to make hope a harsher mockery and renunciation a keener suffering. But above all this rose the conviction that she could do nothing that would not deepen his admiration.

It was this feeling that circumstance—unlovely as it was in itself—was to force the beauty of her character into more perfect relief, that made him stride along as if he were celebrating a kind of spiritual festival. He rambled at random for a couple of hours, and found at last that he had left the forest behind him and had wandered into an unfamiliar region. It was a perfectly rural scene, and the still summer day gave it a charm for which its meagre elements but half accounted.

Longmore thought he had never seen anything so characteristically French; all the French novels seemed to have described it, all the French landscapists to have painted it. The fields and trees were of a cool metallic green; the grass looked as if it might stain your trousers, and the foliage your hands. The clear light had a sort of mild grayness; the sunbeams were of silver rather than gold. A great red-roofed, high-stacked farm-house, with whitewashed walls and a straggling yard, surveyed the high road, on one side, from behind a transparent curtain of poplars. A narrow stream, half choked with emerald rushes and edged with gray aspens, occupied the opposite quarter. The meadows rolled and sloped away gently to the low horizon, which was barely concealed by the continuous line of clipped and marshaled trees. The prospect was not rich, but it had a frank homeliness which touched the young man's fancy. It was full of light atmosphere and diffused sunshine, and if it was prosaic, it was soothing.

Longmore was disposed to walk further, and he advanced along the road beneath the poplars. In twenty minutes he came to a village which straggled away to the right, among orchards and *potagers*. On the left, at a stone's throw from the road, stood a little pink-faced inn, which reminded him that he had not breakfasted, having left home with a prevision of hospitality from Madame de Mauves. In the inn he found a brick-tiled parlor and a hostess in sabots and a white cap, whom, over the omelette she speedily served him,—borrowing license from the bottle of sound red wine which accompanied it,—he assured that she was a true artist. To reward his compliment, she invited him to smoke his cigar in her little garden behind the house.

Here he found a *tonnelle* and a view of ripening crops, stretching down to the stream. The *tonnelle* was rather close, and he preferred to lounge on a bench against the pink wall, in the sun, which was not too hot. Here, as he rested and gazed and mused, he fell into a train of thought which, in an indefinable fashion, was a soft influence from the scene about him. His heart, which had been beating fast for the past three hours, gradually checked its pulses and left him looking at life with a rather more level gaze. The homely tavern sounds coming out through the open windows, the sunny stillness of the fields and crops, which covered so much vigorous natural life, suggested very little that was transcendental, had very little to say about renunciation,—nothing at all about spiritual zeal. They seemed to utter a message from plain ripe nature, to express the unperverted reality of things, to say that the common lot is not brilliantly amusing, and that the part of wisdom is to grasp frankly at experience, lest you miss it altogether. What reason there was for his falling a-wondering after this whether a deeply wounded heart might be soothed and healed by such a scene, it would be difficult to explain; certain it is that, as he sat there, he had a waking dream of an unhappy woman strolling by the slow-flowing stream before him, and pulling down the blossoming boughs in the orchards. He mused and mused, and at last found himself feeling angry that he could not somehow think worse of Madame de Mauves,—or at any rate think otherwise. He could fairly claim that in a sentimental way he asked very little of life,—he made modest demands on passion; why then should his only passion be born to ill-fortune? why should his first—his last—glimpse of positive happiness be so indissolubly linked with renunciation?

It is perhaps because, like many spirits of the same stock, he had in his composition a lurking principle of asceticism to whose authority he had ever paid an unquestioning respect, that he now felt all the vehemence of rebellion. To renounce—to renounce again—to renounce forever—was this all that youth and longing and resolve were meant for? Was experience to be muffled and mutilated, like an indecent picture? Was a man to sit and deliberately condemn his future to be the blank memory of a regret, rather than the long reverberation of a joy? Sacrifice? The word was a trap for minds muddled by fear, an ignoble refuge of weakness. To insist now seemed not to dare, but simply to be, to live on possible terms.

His hostess came out to hang a cloth to dry on the hedge, and, though her guest was sitting quietly enough, she seemed to see in his kindled eyes a flattering testimony to the quality of her wine. As she turned back into the house, she was met by a young man whom Longmore observed in spite of his preoccupation. He was evidently a member of that jovial fraternity of artists whose very shabbiness has an affinity with the element of picturesqueness and unexpectedness in life which provokes a great deal of unformulated envy among people foredoomed to be respectable.

Longmore was struck first with his looking like a very clever man, and then with his looking like a very happy one. The combination, as it was expressed in his face, might have arrested the attention of even a less cynical philosopher. He had a slouched hat and a blond beard, a light easel under one arm, and an unfinished sketch in oils under the other.

He stopped and stood talking for some moments to the landlady with a peculiarly good-humored smile. They were discussing the possibilities of dinner; the hostess enumerated some very savory ones, and he nodded briskly, assenting to everything. It couldn't be, Longmore thought, that he found such soft contentment in the prospect of lamb chops and spinach and a *tarte à la crême*. When the dinner had been ordered, he turned up his sketch, and the good woman fell a-wondering and looking off at the spot by the stream-side where he had made it.

Was it his work, Longmore wondered, that made him so happy? Was a strong talent the best thing in the world? The landlady went back to her kitchen, and the young painter stood as if he were waiting for something, beside the gate which opened upon the path across the fields. Longmore sat brooding and asking himself whether it was better to cultivate an art than to cultivate a passion. Before he had answered the question the painter had grown tired of waiting. He picked up a pebble, tossed it lightly into an upper window, and called, "Claudine!"

Claudine appeared; Longmore heard her at the window, bidding the young man to have patience. "But I'm losing my light," he said; "I must have my shadows in the same place as yesterday."

"Go without me, then," Claudine answered. "I will join you in ten minutes." Her voice was fresh and young; it seemed to say to Longmore that she was as happy as her companion.

"Don't forget the Chénier," cried the young man; and turning away, he passed out of the gate and followed the path across the fields until he disappeared among the trees by the side of the stream. Who was Claudine? Longmore vaguely wondered; and was she as pretty as her voice? Before long he had a chance to satisfy himself; she came out of the house with her hat and parasol, prepared to follow her companion. She had on a pink muslin dress and a little white hat, and she was as pretty as a Frenchwoman needs to be to be pleasing. She had a clear brown skin and a bright dark eye, and a step which seemed to keep time to some slow music, heard only by herself. Her hands were encumbered with various articles which she seemed to intend to carry with her. In one arm she held her parasol and a large roll of needlework, and in the other a shawl and a heavy white umbrella, such as painters use for sketching. Meanwhile she was trying to thrust into her pocket a paper-covered volume which Longmore saw to be the Poems of André Chénier; but in the effort she dropped the large umbrella, and uttered a half-smiling exclamation of disgust. Longmore stepped forward with a bow and picked up the umbrella, and as she, protesting her gratitude, put out her hand to take it, it seemed to him that she was unbecomingly overburdened.

"You have too much to carry," he said; "you must let me help you."

"You're very good, monsieur," she answered. "My husband always forgets something. He can do nothing without his umbrella. He is *d'une étourderie—*"

"You must allow me to carry the umbrella," Longmore said. "It's too heavy for a lady."

She assented, after many compliments to his politeness; and he walked by her side into the meadow. She went lightly and rapidly, picking her steps and glancing forward to catch a glimpse of her husband. She was graceful, she was charming, she had an air of decision and yet of sweetness, and it seemed to Longmore that a young artist would work none the worse for having her seated at his side, reading Chénier's iambics. They were newly married, he supposed, and evidently their path of life had none of the mocking crookedness of some others. They asked little; but what need one ask more than such quiet summer days, with the creature one loves, by a shady stream, with art and books and a wide, unshadowed horizon? To spend such a morning, to stroll back to dinner in the red-tiled parlor of the inn, to ramble away again as the sun got low,—all this was a vision of bliss which floated before him, only to torture him with a sense of the impossible. All Frenchwomen are not coquettes, he remarked, as he kept pace with his companion. She uttered a word now and then, for politeness' sake, but she never looked at him, and seemed not in the least to care that he was a well-favored young man. She cared for nothing but the young artist in the shabby coat and the slouched hat, and for discovering where he had set up his easel.

This was soon done. He was encamped under the trees, close to the stream, and, in the diffused green shade of the little wood, seemed to be in no immediate need of his umbrella. He received a vivacious rebuke, however, for forgetting it, and was informed of what he owed to Longmore's complaisance. He was duly grateful; he thanked our hero warmly, and offered him a seat on the grass. But Longmore felt like a marplot, and lingered only long enough to glance at the young man's sketch, and to see it was a very clever rendering of the silvery stream and the vivid green rushes. The young wife had spread her shawl on the grass at the base of a tree, and meant to seat herself when Longmore had gone, and murmur Chénier's verses to the music of the gurgling river. Longmore looked awhile from one to the other, barely stifled a sigh, bade them good morning, and took his departure.

He knew neither where to go nor what to do; he seemed afloat on the sea of ineffectual longing. He strolled slowly back to the inn, and in the doorway met the landlady coming back from the butcher's with the lamb chops for the dinner of her lodgers.

"Monsieur has made the acquaintance of the *dame* of our young painter," she said with a broad smile,—a smile too broad for malicious meanings. "Monsieur has perhaps seen the young man's picture. It appears that he has a great deal of talent."

"His picture was very pretty," said Longmore, "but his *dame* was prettier still."

"She's a very nice little woman; but I pity her all the more."

"I don't see why she's to be pitied," said Longmore; "they seem a very happy couple."

The landlady gave a knowing nod.

"Don't trust to it, monsieur! Those artists,—*ça n'a pas de principes!* From one day to another he can plant her there! I know them, *allez*. I've had them here very often; one year with one, another year with another."

Longmore was puzzled for a moment. Then, "You mean she's not his wife?" he asked.

She shrugged her shoulders. "What shall I tell you? They are not *des hommes sérieux,* those gentlemen! They don't engage themselves for an eternity. It's none of my business, and I've no wish to speak ill of madame. She's a very nice little woman, and she loves her *jeune homme* to distraction."

"Who is she?" asked Longmore. "What do you know about her?"

"Nothing for certain; but it's my belief that she's better than he. I've even gone so far as to believe that she's a lady,—a true lady,—and that she has given up a great many things for him. I do the best I can for them, but I don't believe she's been obliged all her life to content herself with a dinner of two courses." And she turned over her lamb chops tenderly, as if to say that though a good cook could imagine better things, yet if you could have but one course, lamb chops had much in their favor. "I shall cook them with bread crumbs. *Voilà les femmes, monsieur!*"

Longmore turned away with the feeling that women were indeed a measureless mystery, and that it was hard to say whether there was greater beauty in their strength or in their weakness. He walked back to Saint-Germain, more slowly than he had come, with less philosophic resignation to any event, and more of the urgent egotism of the passion which philosophers call the supremely selfish one. Every now and then the episode of the happy young painter and the charming woman who had given up a great many things for him rose vividly in his mind, and seemed to mock his moral unrest like some obtrusive vision of unattainable bliss.

The landlady's gossip cast no shadow on its brightness; her voice seemed that of the vulgar chorus of the uninitiated, which stands always ready with its gross prose rendering of the inspired passages in human action. Was it possible a man could take *that* from a woman,—take all that lent lightness to that other woman's footstep and intensity to her glance,—and not give her the absolute certainty of a devotion as unalterable as the process of the sun? Was it possible that such a rapturous union had the seeds of trouble,—that the charm of such a perfect accord could be broken by anything but death? Longmore felt an immense desire to cry out a thousand times "No!" for it seemed to him at last that he was somehow spiritually the same as the young painter, and that the latter's companion had the soul of Euphemia de Mauves.

The heat of the sun, as he walked along, became oppressive, and when he re-entered the forest he turned aside into the deepest shade he could find, and stretched himself on the mossy ground at the foot of a great beech. He lay for a while up into the verdurous dusk overhead, and trying to conceive Madame de Mauves hastening toward some quiet stream-side where he waited, as he had seen that trusting creature do an hour before. It would be hard to say how well he succeeded; but the effort soothed him rather than excited him, and as he had had a good deal both of moral and physical fatigue, he sank at last into a quiet sleep.

While he slept he had a strange, vivid dream. He seemed to be in a wood, very much like the one on which his eyes had lately closed; but the wood was divided by the murmuring stream he had left an hour before. He was walking up and down, he thought, restlessly and in intense expectation of some momentous event. Suddenly, at a distance, through the trees, he saw the gleam of a woman's dress, and hurried forward to meet her. As he advanced he recognized her, but he saw at the same time that she was on the opposite bank of the river. She seemed at first not to notice him, but when they were opposite each other she stopped and looked at him very gravely and pityingly. She made him no motion that he should cross the stream, but he wished greatly to stand by her side. He knew the water was deep, and it seemed to him that he knew that he should have to plunge, and that he feared that when he rose to the surface she would have disappeared. Nevertheless, he was going to plunge, when a boat turned into the current from above and came swiftly toward them, guided by an oarsman, who was sitting so that they could not see his face. He brought the boat to the bank where Longmore stood; the latter stepped in, and with a few strokes they touched the opposite shore. Longmore got out, and, though he was sure he had crossed the stream, Madame de Mauves was not there. He turned with a kind of agony and saw that now she was on the other bank,—the one he had left. She gave him a grave, silent glance, and walked away up the stream. The boat and the boatman resumed their course, but after going a short distance they stopped, and the boatman turned back and looked at the still divided couple. Then Longmore recognized him,—just as he had recognized him a few days before at the café in the Bois de Boulogne.

VIII

He must have slept some time after he ceased dreaming, for he had no immediate memory of his dream. It came back to him later, after he had roused himself and had walked nearly home. No great ingenuity was needed to make it seem a rather striking allegory, and it haunted and oppressed him for the rest of the day. He took refuge, however, in his quickened conviction that the only sound policy in life is to grasp unsparingly at happiness; and it seemed no more than one of the vigorous measures dictated by such a policy, to return that evening to Madame de Mauves. And yet when he had decided to do so, and had carefully dressed himself, he felt an irresistible nervous tremor which made it easier to linger at his open window, wondering, with a strange mixture of dread and desire, whether Madame Clairin had told her sister-in-law that she had told him. . . . His presence now might be simply a gratuitous cause of suffering; and yet his absence might seem to imply that it was in the power of circumstances to make them ashamed to meet each other's eyes. He sat a long time with his head in his hands, lost in a painful confusion of hopes and questionings. He felt at moments as if he could throttle Madame Clairin, and yet he could not help asking himself whether it was not possible that she might have done him a service. It was late when he left the hotel, and as he entered the gate of the other house his heart was beating so that he was sure his voice would show it.

The servant ushered him into the drawing-room, which was empty, with the lamp burning low. But the long windows were open, and their light curtains swaying in a soft, warm wind, and Longmore stepped out upon the terrace. There he found Madame de Mauves alone, slowly pacing up and down. She was dressed in white, very simply, and her hair was arranged, not as she usually wore it, but in a single loose coil, like that of a person unprepared for company.

She stopped when she saw Longmore, seemed slightly startled, uttered an exclamation, and stood waiting for him to speak. He looked at her, tried to say something, but found no words. He knew it was awkward, it was offensive, to stand silent, gazing; but he could not say what was suitable, and he dared not say what he wished.

Her face was indistinct in the dim light, but he could see that her eyes were fixed on him, and he wondered what they expressed. Did they warn him, did they plead or did they confess to a sense of provocation? For an instant his head swam; he felt as if it would make all things clear to stride forward and fold her in his arms. But a moment later he was still standing looking at her; he had not moved; he knew that she had spoken, but he had not understood her.

"You were here this morning," she continued, and now, slowly, the meaning of her words came to him. "I had a bad headache and had to shut myself up." She spoke in her usual voice.

Longmore mastered his agitation and answered her without betraying himself: "I hope you are better now."

"Yes, thank you, I'm better—much better."

He was silent a moment, and she moved away to a chair and seated herself. After a pause he followed her and stood before her, leaning against the balustrade of the terrace. "I hoped you might have been able to come out for the morning into the forest. I went alone; it was a lovely day, and I took a long walk."

"It was a lovely day," she said absently, and sat with her eyes lowered, slowly opening and closing her fan. Longmore, as he watched her, felt more and more sure that her sister-in-law had seen her since her interview with him; that her attitude toward him was changed. It was this same something that chilled the ardor with which he had come, or at least converted the dozen passionate speeches which kept rising to his lips into a kind of reverential silence. No, certainly, he could not clasp her to his arms now, any more than some early worshipper could have clasped the marble statue in his temple. But Longmore's statue spoke at last, with a full human voice, and even with a shade of human hesitation. She looked up, and it seemed to him that her eyes shone through the dusk.

"I'm very glad you came this evening," she said. "I have a particular reason for being glad. I half expected you, and yet I thought it possible you might not come."

"As I have been feeling all day," Longmore answered, "it was impossible I should not come. I have spent the day in thinking of you."

She made no immediate reply, but continued to open and close her fan thoughtfully. At last,—"I have something to say to you," she said abruptly. "I want you to know to a certainty that I have a very high opinion of you." Longmore started and shifted his position. To what was she coming? But he said nothing, and she went on.

"I take a great interest in you; there's no reason why I should not say it,—I have a great friendship for you."

He began to laugh; he hardly knew why, unless that this seemed the very mockery of coldness. But she continued without heeding him.

"You know, I suppose, that a great disappointment always implies a great confidence—a great hope?"

"I have hoped," he said, "hoped strongly; but doubtless never rationally enough to have a right to bemoan my disappointment."

"You do yourself injustice. I have such confidence in your reason, that I should be greatly disappointed if I were to find it wanting."

"I really almost believe that you are amusing yourself at my expense," cried Longmore. "My reason? Reason is a mere word! The only reality in the world is *feeling!*"

She rose to her feet and looked at him gravely. His eyes by this time were accustomed to the imperfect light, and he could see that her look was reproachful, and yet that it was beseechingly kind. She shook her head impatiently, and laid her fan upon his arm with a strong pressure.

"If that were so, it would be a weary world. I know your feeling, however, nearly enough. You needn't try to express it. It's enough that it gives me the right to ask a favor of you,—to make an urgent, a solemn request."

"Make it; I listen."

"Don't disappoint me. If you don't understand me now, you will to-morrow, or very soon. When I said just now that I had a very high opinion of you, I meant it very seriously. It was not a vain compliment. I believe that there is no appeal one may make to your generosity which can remain long unanswered. If this were to happen,—if I were to find you selfish where I thought you generous, narrow where I thought you large,"—and she spoke slowly, with her voice lingering with emphasis on each of these words,—"vulgar where I thought you rare,—I should think worse of human nature. I should suffer,—I should suffer keenly. I should say to myself in the dull days of the future, 'There was one man who might have done so and so; and he, too, failed.' But this shall not be. You have made too good an impression on me not to make the very best. If you wish to please me forever, there's a way."

She was standing close to him, with her dress touching him, her eyes fixed on his. As she went on her manner grew strangely intense, and she had the singular appearance of a woman preaching reason with a kind of passion. Longmore was confused, dazzled, almost bewildered. The intention of her words was all remonstrance, refusal, dismissal; but her presence there, so close, so urgent, so personal, seemed a distracting contradiction of it. She had never been so lovely. In her white dress, with her pale face and deeply lighted eyes, she seemed the very spirit of the summer night. When she had ceased speaking, she drew a long breath; Longmore felt it on his cheek, and it stirred in his whole being a sudden, rapturous conjecture. Were her words in their soft severity a mere delusive spell, meant to throw into relief her almost ghostly beauty, and was this the only truth, the only reality, the only law?

He closed his eyes and felt that she was watching him, not without pain and perplexity herself. He looked at her again, met her own eyes, and saw a tear in each of them. Then this last suggestion of his desire seemed to die away with a stifled murmur, and her beauty, more and more radiant in the darkness, rose before him as a symbol of something vague which was yet more beautiful than itself.

"I may understand you to-morrow," he said, "but I don't understand you now."

"And yet I took counsel with myself to-day and asked myself how I had best speak to you. On one side, I might have refused to see you at all." Longmore made a violent movement, and she added: "In that case I should have written to you. I might see you, I thought, and simply say to you that there were excellent reasons why we should part, and that I begged this visit should be your last. This I inclined to do; what made me decide otherwise was—simply friendship! I said to myself that I should be glad to remember in future days, not that I had dismissed you, but that you had gone away out of the fulness of your own wisdom."

"The fulness—the fulness!" cried Longmore.

"I'm prepared, if necessary," Madame de Mauves continued after a pause, "to fall back upon my strict right. But, as I said before, I shall be greatly disappointed, if I am obliged to."

"When I hear you say that," Longmore answered, "I feel so angry, so horribly irritated, that I wonder it is not easy to leave you without more words."

"If you should go away in anger, this idea of mine about our parting would be but half realized. No, I don't want to think of you as angry; I don't want even to think of you as making a serious sacrifice. I want to think of you as—"

"As a creature who never has existed,—who never can exist! A creature who knew you without loving you,—who left you without regretting you!"

She turned impatiently away and walked to the other end of the terrace. When she came back, he saw that her impatience had become a cold sternness. She stood before him again, looking at him from head to foot, in deep reproachfulness, almost in scorn. Beneath her glance he felt a kind of shame. He colored; she observed it and withheld something she was about to say. She turned away again, walked to the other end of the terrace, and stood there looking away into the garden. It seemed to him that she had guessed he understood her, and slowly—slowly—half as the fruit of his vague self-reproach,—he did understand her. She was giving him a chance to do gallantly what it seemed unworthy of both of them he should do meanly.

She liked him, she must have liked him greatly, to wish so to spare him, to go to the trouble of conceiving an ideal of conduct for him. With this sense of her friendship,—her strong friendship she had just called it,—Longmore's soul rose with a new flight, and suddenly felt itself breathing a clearer air. The words ceased to seem a mere bribe to his ardor; they were charged with ardor themselves; they were a present happiness. He moved rapidly toward her with a feeling that this was something he might immediately enjoy.

They were separated by two thirds of the length of the terrace, and he had to pass the drawing-room window. As he did so he started with an exclamation. Madame Clairin stood posted there, watching him. Conscious, apparently, that she might be suspected of eavesdropping, she stepped forward with a smile and looked from Longmore to his hostess.

"Such a tête-à-tête as that," she said, "one owes no apology for interrupting. One ought to come in for good manners."

Madame de Mauves turned round, but she answered nothing. She looked straight at Longmore, and her eyes had extraordinary eloquence. He was not exactly sure, indeed, what she meant them to say; but they seemed to say plainly something of this kind: "Call it what you will, what you have to urge upon me is the thing which this woman can best conceive. What I ask of you is something she can't!" They seemed, somehow, to beg him to suffer her to be herself, and to intimate that that self was as little as possible like Madame Clairin. He felt an immense answering desire not to do anything which would seem natural to this lady. He had laid his hat and cane on the parapet of the terrace. He took them up, offered his hand to Madame de Mauves with a simple good night, bowed silently to Madame Clairin, and departed.

IX

HE WENT home and without lighting his candle flung himself on his bed. But he got no sleep till morning; he lay hour after hour tossing, thinking, wondering; his mind had never been so active. It seemed to him that Euphemia had laid on him in those last moments an inspiring commission, and that she had expressed herself almost as largely as if she had listened assentingly to an assurance of his love. It was neither easy nor delightful thoroughly to understand her; but little by little her perfect meaning sank into his mind and soothed it with a sense of opportunity, which somehow stifled his sense of loss. For, to begin with, she meant that she could love him in no degree nor contingency, in no imaginable future. This was absolute; he felt that he could alter it no more than he could transpose the constellations he lay gazing at through his open window. He wondered what it was, in the background of her life, that she grasped so closely: a sense of duty, unquenchable to the end? a love that no offence could trample out? "Good heavens!" he thought, "is the world so rich in the purest pearls of passion, that such tenderness as that can be wasted forever,—poured away without a sigh into bottomless darkness?" Had she, in spite of the detestable present, some precious memory which contained the germ of a shrinking hope? Was she prepared to submit to everything and yet to believe? Was it strength, was it weakness, was it a vulgar fear, was it conviction, conscience, constancy?

Longmore sank back with a sigh and an oppressive feeling that it was vain to guess at such a woman's motives. He only felt that those of Madame de Mauves were buried deep in her soul, and that they must be of some fine temper, not of a base one. He had a dim, overwhelming sense of a sort of invulnerable constancy being the supreme law of her character,—a constancy which still found a foothold among crumbling ruins. "She has loved once," he said to himself as he rose and wandered to his window; "that's forever. Yes, yes,—if she loved again she would be *common.*" He stood for a long time looking out into the starlit silence of the town and the forest, and thinking of what life would have been if *his* constancy had met hers unpledged. But life was this, now, and he must live. It was living keenly to stand there with a petition from such a woman to revolve. He was not to disappoint her, he was to justify a conception which it had beguiled her weariness to shape. Longmore's imagination swelled; he threw back his head and seemed to be looking for Madame de Mauves's conception among the blinking, mocking stars. But it came to him rather on the mild night-wind, as it wandered in over the house-tops which covered the rest of so many heavy human hearts. What she asked he felt that she was asking, not for her own sake (she feared nothing, she needed nothing), but for that of his own happiness and his own character. He must assent to destiny. Why else was he young and strong, intelligent and resolute? He must not give it to her to reproach him with thinking that she had a moment's attention for his love,—to plead, to argue, to break off in bitterness; he must see everything from above, her indifference and his own ardor; he must prove his strength, he must do the handsome thing; he must decide that the handsome thing was to submit to the inevitable, to be supremely delicate, to spare her all pain, to stifle his passion, to ask no compensation, to depart without delay and try to believe that wisdom is its own reward. All this, neither more nor less, it was a matter of friendship with Madame de Mauves to expect of him. And what should he gain by it? He should have pleased her! . . . He flung himself on his bed again, fell asleep at last, and slept till morning.

Before noon the next day he had made up his mind that he would leave Saint-Germain at once. It seemed easier to leave without seeing her, and yet if he might ask a grain of "compensation," it would be five minutes face to face with her. He passed a restless day. Wherever he went he seemed to see he standing before him in the dusky halo of evening, and looking at him with an air of still negation more intoxicating than the most passionate self-surrender. He must certainly go, and yet it was hideously hard. He compromised and went to Paris to spend the rest of the day. He strolled along the boulevards and looked at the shops, sat awhile in the Tuileries gardens and looked at the shabby unfortunates for whom this only was nature and summer; but simply felt, as a result of it all, that it was a very dusty, dreary, lonely world into which Madame de Mauves was turning him away.

In a sombre mood he made his way back to the boulevards and sat down at a table on the great plain of hot asphalt, before a café. Night came on, the lamps were lighted, the tables near him found occupants, and Paris began to wear that peculiar evening look of hers which seems to say, in the flare of windows and theatre doors, and the muffled rumble of swift-rolling carriages, that this is no world for you unless you have your pockets lined and your scruples drugged. Longmore, however, had neither scruples nor desires; he looked at the swarming city for the first time with an easy sense of repaying its indifference. Before long a carriage drove up to the pavement directly in front of him, and remained standing for several minutes without its occupant getting out. It was one of those neat, plain coupés, drawn by a single powerful horse, in which one is apt to imagine a pale, handsome woman, buried among silk cushions, and yawning as she sees the gas-lamps glittering in the gutters. At last the door opened and out stepped M. de Mauves. He stopped and leaned on the window for some time, talking in an excited manner to a person within. At last he gave a nod and the carriage rolled away. He stood swinging his cane and looking up and down the boulevard, with the air of a man fumbling, as one may say, with the loose change of time. He turned toward the café and was apparently, for want of anything better worth his attention, about to seat himself at one of the tables, when he perceived Longmore. He wavered an instant, and then, without a change in his nonchalant gait, strolled toward him with a bow and a vague smile.

It was the first time they had met since their encounter in the forest after Longmore's false start for Brussels. Madame Clairin's revelations, as we may call them, had not made the Baron especially present to his mind; he had another office for his emotions than disgust. But as M. de Mauves came toward him he felt deep in his heart that he abhorred him. He noticed, however, for the first time, a shadow upon the Baron's cool placidity, and his delight at finding that somewhere at last the shoe pinched *him*, mingled with his impulse to be as exasperatingly impenetrable as possible, enabled him to return the other's greeting with all his own self-possession.

M. de Mauves sat down, and the two men looked at each other across the table, exchanging formal greetings which did little to make their mutual scrutiny seem gracious. Longmore had no reason to suppose that the Baron knew of his sister's revelations. He was sure that M. de Mauves cared very little about his opinions, and yet he had a sense that there was that in his eyes which would have made the Baron change color if keener suspicion had helped him to read it. M. de Mauves did not change color, but he looked at Longmore with a half-defiant intentness, which betrayed at once an irritating memory of the episode in the Bois de Boulogne, and such vigilant curiosity as was natural to a gentleman who had intrusted his "honor" to another gentleman's magnanimity,—or to his artlessness. It would appear that Longmore seemed to the Baron to possess these virtues in rather scantier measure than a few days before; for the cloud deepened on his face, and he turned away and frowned as he lighted a cigar.

The person in the coupé, Longmore thought, whether or not the same person as the heroine of the episode of the Bois de Boulogne, was not a source of unalloyed delight. Longmore had dark blue eyes, of admirable lucidity,—truth-telling eyes which had in his childhood always made his harshest taskmasters smile at his nursery fibs. An observer watching the two men, and knowing something of their relations, would certainly have said that what he saw in those eyes must not a little have puzzled and tormented M. de Mauves. They judged him, they mocked him, they eluded him, they threatened him, they triumphed over him, they treated him as no pair of eyes had ever treated him. The Baron's scheme had been to make no one happy but himself, and here was Longmore already, if looks were to be trusted, primed for an enterprise more inspiring than the finest of his own achievements. Was this candid young barbarian but a *faux bonhomme* after all? He had puzzled the Baron before, and this was once too often.

M. de Mauves hated to seem preoccupied, and he took up the evening paper to help himself to look indifferent. As he glanced over it he uttered some cold commonplace on the political situation, which gave Longmore an easy opportunity of replying by an ironical sally which made him seem for the moment aggressively at his ease. And yet our hero was far from being master of the situation. The Baron's ill-humor did him good, so far as it pointed to a want of harmony with the lady in the coupé; but it disturbed him sorely as he began to suspect that it possibly meant jealousy of himself. It passed through his mind that jealousy is a passion with a double face, and that in some of its moods it bears a plausible likeness to affection. It recurred to him painfully that the Baron might grow ashamed of his political compact with his wife, and he felt that it would be far more tolerable in the future to think of his continued turpitude than of his repentance. The two men sat for half an hour exchanging stinted small-talk, the Baron feeling a nervous need of playing the spy, and Longmore indulging a ferocious relish of his discomfort. These rigid courtesies were interrupted however by the arrival of a friend of M. de Mauves;—a tall, pale, consumptive-looking dandy, who filled the air with the odor of heliotrope. He looked up and down the boulevard wearily, examined the Baron's toilet from head to foot, then surveyed his own in the same fashion, and at last announced languidly that the Duchess was in town! M. de Mauves must come with him to call; she had abused him dreadfully a couple of evenings before,—a sure sign she wanted to see him.

"I depend upon you," said M. de Mauves's friend with an infantine drawl, "to put her *entrain*."

M. de Mauves resisted, and protested that he was *d'une humeur massacrante*; but at last he allowed himself to be drawn to his feet. and stood looking awkwardly—awkwardly for M. de Mauves—at Longmore. "You'll excuse me," he said dryly; "you, too, probably, have occupation for the evening?"

"None but to catch my train," Longmore answered, looking at his watch.

"Ah, you go back to Saint-Germain?"

"In half an hour."

M. de Mauves seemed on the point of disengaging himself from his companion's arm, which was locked in his own; but on the latter uttering some persuasive murmur, he lifted his hat stiffly and turned away.

Longmore packed his trunk the next day with dogged heroism and wandered off to the terrace, to try and beguile the restlessness with which he waited for evening; for he wished to see Madame de Mauves for the last time at the hour of long shadows and pale pink-reflected lights, as he had almost always seen her. Destiny, however, took no account of this humble plea for poetic justice; it was his fortune to meet her on the terrace sitting under a tree, alone. It was an hour when the place was almost empty; the day was warm, but as he took his place beside her a light breeze stirred the leafy edges on the broad circle of shadow in which she sat. She looked at him with candid anxiety, and he immediately told her that he should leave Saint-Germain that evening,—that he must bid her farewell. Her eye expanded and brightened for a moment as he spoke; but she said nothing and turned her glance away toward distant Paris, as it lay twinkling and flashing through its hot exhalations. "I have a request to make of you!" he added. "That you think of me as a man who has felt much and claimed little."

She drew a long breath, which almost suggested pain. "I can't think of you as unhappy. It's impossible. You have a life to lead, you have duties, talents, and interests. I shall hear of your career. And then," she continued after a pause and with the deepest seriousness, "one can't be unhappy through having a better opinion of a friend, instead of a worse."

For a moment he failed to understand her. "Do you mean that there can be varying degrees in my opinion of you?"

She rose and pushed away her chair. "I mean," she said quickly, "that it's better to have done nothing in bitterness,—nothing in passion." And she began to walk.

Longmore followed her, without answering. But he took off his hat and with his pocket-handkerchief wiped his forehead. "Where shall you go? what shall you do?" he asked at last, abruptly.

"Do? I shall do as I've always done,—except perhaps that I shall go for a while to Auvergne."

"I shall go to America. I have done with Europe for the present."

She glanced at him as he walked beside her after he had spoken these words, and then bent her eyes for a long time on the ground. At last, seeing that she was going far, she stopped and put out her hand. "Good by," she said; "may you have all the happiness you deserve!"

He took her hand and looked at her, but something was passing in him that made it impossible to return her hand's light pressure. Something of infinite value was floating past him, and he had taken an oath not to raise a finger to stop it. It was borne by the strong current of the world's great life and not of his own small one. Madame de Mauves disengaged her hand, gathered her shawl, and smiled at him almost as you would do at a child you should wish to encourage. Several moments later he was still standing watching her receding figure. When it had disappeared, he shook himself, walked rapidly back to his hotel, and without waiting for the evening train paid his bill and departed.

Later in the day M. de Mauves came into his wife's drawing-room, where she sat waiting to be summoned to dinner. He was dressed with a scrupulous freshness which seemed to indicate an intention of dining out. He walked up and down for some moments in silence, then rang the bell for a servant, and went out into the hall to meet him. He ordered the carriage to take him to the station, paused a moment with his hand on the knob of the door, dismissed the servant angrily as the latter lingered observing him, re-entered the drawing-room, resumed his restless walk, and at last stepped abruptly before his wife, who had taken up a book. "May I ask the favor," he said with evident effort, in spite of a forced smile of easy courtesy, "of having a question answered?"

"It's a favor I never refused," Madame de Mauves replied.

"Very true. Do you expect this evening a visit from Mr. Longmore?"

"Mr. Longmore," said his wife, "has left Saint-Germain." M. de Mauves started and his smile expired. "Mr. Longmore," his wife continued, "has gone to America."

M. de Mauves stared a moment, flushed deeply, and turned away.

Then recovering himself,—"Had anything happened?" he asked. "Had he a sudden call?"

But his question received no answer. At the same moment the servant threw open the door and announced dinner; Madame Clairin rustled in, rubbing her white hands, Madame de Mauves passed silently into the dining-room, and he stood frowning and wondering. Before long he went out upon the terrace and continued his uneasy walk. At the end of a quarter of an hour the servant came to inform him that the carriage was at the door. "Send it away," he said curtly. "I shall not use it." When the ladies had half finished dinner he went in and joined them, with a formal apology to his wife for his tardiness.

The dishes were brought back, but he hardly tasted them; on the other hand, he drank a great deal of wine. There was little talk; what there was, was supplied by Madame Clairin. Twice she saw her brother's eyes fixed on her own, over his wineglass, with a piercing, questioning glance. She replied by an elevation of the eyebrows, which did the office of a shrug of the shoulders. M. de Mauves was left alone to finish his wine; he sat over it for more than an hour, and let the darkness gather about him. At last the servant came in with a letter and lighted a candle. The letter was a telegram, which M. de Mauves, when he had read it, burnt at the candle. After five minutes' meditation, he wrote a message on the back of a visiting-card and gave it to the servant to carry to the office. The man knew quite as much as his master suspected about the lady to whom the telegram was addressed; but its contents puzzled him; they consisted of the single word, "*Impossible*." As the evening passed without her brother reappearing in the drawing-room, Madame Clairin came to him where he sat, by his solitary candle. He took no notice of her presence for some time; but he was the one person to whom she allowed this license. At last, speaking in a peremptory tone, "The American has gone home at an hour's notice," he said. "What does it mean?"

Madame Clairin now gave free play to the shrug she had been obliged to suppress at the table. "It means that I have a sister-in-law whom I haven't the honor to understand."

He said nothing more, and silently allowed her to depart, as if it had been her duty to provide him with an explanation and he was disgusted with her levity. When she had gone, he went into the garden and walked up and down, smoking. He saw his wife sitting alone on the terrace, but remained below strolling along the narrow paths. He remained a long time. It became late and Madame de Mauves disappeared. Toward midnight he dropped upon a bench, tired, with a kind of angry sigh. It was sinking into his mind that he, too, did not understand Madame Clairin's sister-in-law.

Longmore was obliged to wait a week in London for a ship. It was very hot, and he went out for a day to Richmond. In the garden of the hotel at which he dined he met his friend Mrs. Draper, who was staying there. She made eager inquiry about Madame de Mauves, but Longmore at first, as they sat looking out at the famous view of the Thames, parried her questions and confined himself to small-talk. At last she said she was afraid he had something to conceal; whereupon, after a pause, he asked her if she remembered recommending him, in the letter she sent to him at Saint-Germain, to draw the sadness from her friend's smile. "The last I saw of her was her smile," said he,—"when I bade her good by."

"I remember urging you to 'console' her," Mrs. Draper answered, "and I wondered afterwards whether—a model of discretion as you are—I hadn't given you rather foolish advice."

"She has her consolation in herself," he said; "she needs none that any one else can offer her. That's for troubles for which—be it more, be it less—our own folly has to answer. Madame de Mauves has not a grain of folly left."

"Ah, don't say that!" murmured Mrs. Draper. "Just a little folly is very graceful."

Longmore rose to go, with a quick nervous movement. "Don't talk of grace," he said, "till you have measured her reason."

For two years after his return to America he heard nothing of Madame de Mauves. That he thought of her intently, constantly, I need hardly say: most people wondered why such a clever young man should not "devote" himself to something; but to himself he seemed absorbingly occupied. He never wrote to her; he believed that she preferred it. At last he heard that Mrs. Draper had come home, and he immediately called on her. "Of course," she said after the first greetings, "you are dying for news of Madame de Mauves. Prepare yourself for something strange. I heard from her two or three times during the year after your return. She left Saint-Germain and went to live in the country, on some old property of her husband's. She wrote me very kind little notes, but I felt somehow that—in spite of what you said about 'consolation' —they were the notes of a very sad woman. The only advice I could have given her was to leave her wretch of a husband and come back to her own land and her own people. But this I didn't feel free to do, and yet it made me so miserable not to be able to help her that I preferred to let our correspondence die a natural death. I had no news of her for a year. Last summer, however, I met at Vichy a clever young Frenchman whom I accidentally learned to be a friend of Euphemia's lovely sister-in-law, Madame Clairin. I lost no time in asking him what he knew about Madame de Mauves, —a countrywoman of mine and an old friend. 'I congratulate you on possessing her friendship,' he answered. 'That's the charming little woman who killed her husband.' You may imagine that I promptly asked for an explanation, and he proceeded to relate to me what he called the whole story. M. de Mauves had *fait quelques folies*, which his wife had taken absurdly to heart. He had repented and asked her forgiveness, which she had inexorably refused. She was very pretty, and severity, apparently, suited her style; for whether or no her husband had been in love with her before, he fell madly in love with her now. He was the proudest man in France, but he had begged her on his knees to be readmitted to favor. All in vain! She was stone, she was ice, she was outraged virtue. People noticed a great change in him: he gave up society, ceased to care for anything, looked shockingly. One fine day they learned that he had blown out his brains. My friend had the story of course from Madame Clairin."

Longmore was strongly moved, and his first impulse after he had recovered his composure was to return immediately to Europe. But several years have passed, and he still lingers at home. The truth is, that in the midst of all the ardent tenderness of his memory of Madame de Mauves, he has become conscious of a singular feeling,—a feeling for which awe would be hardly too strong a name.

Daisy Miller

Daisy Miller

DAISY MILLER, the pretty girl from Schenectady who defies European conventions and dies of the Roman fever and a broken heart, is the only one of Henry James's characters to have achieved national renown. For that there is reason enough. Daisy embodies the spirit of her country in a more direct and simple manner than any of her sisters in the Jamesian gallery of native types. And no one has ever offered a better explanation of her great popularity than Edmund Wilson when he said that it is due to the impression somehow conveyed by her creator that "her spirit went marching on."

It should be recalled that originally the story of Daisy Miller was considered by a good many patriots to be a disloyal criticism of American manners and an outrage on American girlhood. Rejected on some such grounds by an editor in Philadelphia, it was first published in England, in *The Cornhill Magazine* (1878). But before long America reclaimed its own, for Daisy was destined to be enshrined in the national pantheon. Not long after her author's death, William Dean Howells wrote in a preface to a new edition of the story that "never was any civilization offered a more precious tribute than that which a great artist paid ours in the character of Daisy Miller." Thus through her phenomenal rise in public favor she finally received what amounted to almost official recognition.

The principal quality of this famous heroine is her spontaneity—a quality retained by her successors in James's novels and stories and invariably rendered as beautifully illustrative of the vigor and innocence of life in the western world. In picturing Daisy, James was mostly concerned with exhibiting her "inscrutable combination of audacity and innocence," for that was the essential characteristic making possible her entry into literature as an altogether new type. Before James no such light had ever been thrown on the character of the American young lady; in Hawthorne, for instance, boldness in the feminine nature is simply the equivalent of badness, and his "good" young ladies (e.g. Priscilla in *The Blithedale Romance* and Hilda in *The Marble Faun*) have literally nothing but their innocence to recommend them. In the observation of his compatriots at home and abroad, James, however, was able to bring to bear the new method of realism absorbed in his study of writers like Balzac, Thackeray, Turgenev and Flaubert. As character creation Daisy is a triumph of the novelist's faculty at work on materials drawn directly from experience. It is interesting, too, to trace the lines of force that radiate from this early Jamesian heroine to later heroines of American fiction. One example that may be cited is Scott Fitzgerald's Daisy in *The Great Gatsby*, who has quite a few features in common with her namesake. And the continuity is primarily of the national experience rather than of literary influence.

One cannot say, however, that in the main it is the quantity of "real life" in Daisy Miller which accounts for her vitality. The mere imitation of life has seldom produced great results in a work of art. The truth is that Daisy—as her author once observed—is at one and the same time a typical little figure and a piece of pure poetry. That is the real secret of her lasting charm—the charm of "a child of nature and of freedom."

PART I

AT THE little town of Vevey, in Switzerland, there is a particularly comfortable hotel. There are, indeed, many hotels; for the entertainment of tourists is the business of the place, which, as many travellers will remember, is seated upon the edge of a remarkably blue lake—a lake that it behooves every tourist to visit. The shore of the lake presents an unbroken array of establishments of this order, of every category, from the "grand hotel" of the newest fashion, with a chalk-white front, a hundred balconies, and a dozen flags flying from its roof, to the little Swiss *pension* of an elder day, with its name inscribed in German-looking lettering upon a pink or yellow wall, and an awkward summer-house in the angle of the garden. One of the hotels at Vevey, however, is famous, even classical, being distinguished from many of its upstart neighbors by an air both of luxury and of maturity. In this region, in the month of June, American travellers are extremely numerous; it may be said, indeed, that Vevey assumes at this period some of the characteristics of an American watering-place. There are sights and sounds which evoke a vision, an echo, of Newport and Saratoga.

There is a flitting hither and thither of "stylish" young girls, a rustling of muslin flounces, a rattle of dance-music in the morning hours, a sound of high-pitched voices at all times. You receive an impression of these things at the excellent inn of the Trois Couronnes, and are transported in fancy to the Ocean House or to Congress Hall. But at the Trois Couronnes, it must be added, there are other features that are much at variance with these suggestions: neat German waiters, who look like secretaries of legation; Russian princesses sitting in the garden; little Polish boys walking about, held by the hand, with their governors; a view of the sunny crest of the Dent du Midi and the picturesque towers of the Castle of Chillon.

I hardly know whether it was the analogies or the differences that were uppermost in the mind of a young American, who, two or three years ago, sat in the garden of the Trois Couronnes, looking about him, rather idly, at some of the graceful objects I have mentioned. It was a beautiful summer morning, and in whatever fashion the young American looked at things they must have seemed to him charming. He had come from Geneva the day before by the little steamer to see his aunt, who was staying at the hotel—Geneva having been for a long time his place of residence. But his aunt had a headache—his aunt had almost always a headache—and now she was shut up in her room, smelling camphor, so that he was at liberty to wander about. He was some seven-and-twenty years of age. When his friends spoke of him, they usually said that he was at Geneva "studying"; when his enemies spoke of him, they said—but, after all, he had no enemies; he was an extremely amiable fellow, and universally liked. What I should say is, simply, that when certain persons spoke of him they affirmed that the reason of his spending so much time at Geneva was that he was extremely devoted to a lady who lived there—a foreign lady—a person older than himself. Very few Americans—indeed I think none—had ever seen this lady, about whom there were some singular stories. But Winterbourne had an old attachment for the little metropolis of Calvinism; he had been put to school there as a boy, and he had afterwards gone to college there—circumstances which had led to his forming a great many youthful friendships. Many of these he had kept, and they were a source of great satisfaction to him.

After knocking at his aunt's door, and learning that she was indisposed, he had taken a walk about the town, and then he had come in to his breakfast. He had now finished his breakfast; but he was drinking a small cup of coffee, which had been served to him on a little table in the garden by one of the waiters who looked like an attaché. At last he finished his coffee and lit a cigarette. Presently a small boy came walking along the path—an urchin of nine or ten. The child, who was diminutive for his years, had an aged expression of countenance: a pale complexion, and sharp little features. He was dressed in knickerbockers, with red stockings, which displayed his poor litle spindle-shanks; he also wore a brilliant red cravat. He carried in his hand a long alpenstock, the sharp point of which he thrust into everything that he approached—the flower-beds, the garden-benches, the trains of the ladies' dresses. In front of Winterbourne he paused, looking at him with a pair of bright, penetrating little eyes.

"Will you give me a lump of sugar?" he asked, in a sharp, hard little voice—a voice immature, and yet, somehow, not young.

Winterbourne glanced at the small table near him, on which his coffee-service rested, and saw that several morsels of sugar remained. "Yes, you may take one," he answered; "but I don't think sugar is good for little boys."

This little boy stepped forward and carefully selected three of the coveted fragments, two of which he buried in the pocket of his knickerbockers, depositing the other as promptly in another place. He poked his alpenstock, lance-fashion, into Winterbourne's bench, and tried to crack the lump of sugar with his teeth.

"Oh, blazes; it's har-r-d!" he exclaimed, pronouncing the adjective in a peculiar manner.

Winterbourne had immediately perceived that he might have the honor of claiming him as a fellow-countryman. "Take care you don't hurt your teeth," he said, paternally.

"I haven't got any teeth to hurt. They have all come out. I have only got seven teeth. My mother counted them last night, and one came out right afterwards. She said she'd slap me if any more came out. I can't help it. It's this old Europe. It's the climate that makes them come out. In America they didn't come out. It's these hotels."

Winterbourne was much amused. "If you eat three lumps of sugar, your mother will certainly slap you," he said.

"She's got to give me some candy, then," rejoined his young

interlocutor. "I can't get any candy here—any American candy. American candy's the best candy."

"And are American little boys the best little boys?" asked Winterbourne.

"I don't know. I'm an American boy," said the child.

"I see you are one of the best!" laughed Winterbourne.

"Are you an American man?" pursued this vivacious infant. And then, on Winterbourne's affirmative reply—"American men are the best!" he declared.

His companion thanked him for the compliment; and the child, who had now got astride of his alpenstock, stood looking about him, while he attacked a second lump of sugar. Winterbourne wondered if he himself had been like this in his infancy, for he had been brought to Europe at about this age.

"Here comes my sister!" cried the child, in a moment. "She's an American girl."

Winterbourne looked along the path and saw a beautiful young lady advancing. "American girls are the best girls!" he said, cheerfully, to his young companion.

"My sister ain't the best!" the child declared. "She's always blowing at me."

"I imagine that is your fault, not hers," said Winterbourne. The young lady meanwhile had drawn near. She was dressed in white muslin, with a hundred frills and flounces, and knots of pale-colored ribbon. She was bareheaded; but she balanced in her hand a large parasol, with a deep border of embroidery; and she was strikingly, admirably pretty. "How pretty they are!" thought Winterbourne, straightening himself in his seat, as if he were prepared to rise.

The young lady paused in front of his bench, near the parapet of the garden, which overlooked the lake. The little boy had now converted his alpenstock into a vaulting-pole, by the aid of which he was springing about in the gravel, and kicking it up a little.

"Randolph," said the young lady, "what *are* you doing?"

"I'm going up the Alps," replied Randolph. "This is the way!" And he gave another little jump, scattering the pebbles about Winterbourne's ears.

"That's the way they come down," said Winterbourne.

"He's an American man!" cried Randolph, in his little hard voice.

The young lady gave no heed to his announcement, but looked straight at her brother. "Well, I guess you had better be quiet," she simply observed.

It seemed to Winterbourne that he had been in a manner presented. He got up and stepped slowly towards the young girl, throwing away his cigarette. "This little boy and I have made acquaintance," he said, with great civility. In Geneva, as he had been perfectly aware, a young man was not at liberty to speak to a young unmarried lady except under certain rarely occurring conditions; but here at Vevey, what conditions could be better than these?—a pretty American girl coming and standing in front of you in a garden. This pretty American girl, however, on hearing Winterbourne's observation, simply glanced at him; she then turned her head and looked over the parapet, at the lake and the opposite mountains. He wondered whether he had gone too far; but he decided that he must advance farther, rather than retreat. While he was thinking of something else to say, the young lady turned to the little boy again.

"I should like to know where you got that pole?" she said.

"I bought it," responded Randolph.

"You don't mean to say you're going to take it to Italy?"

"Yes, I am going to take it to Italy," the child declared.

The young girl glanced over the front of her dress, and smoothed out a knot or two of ribbon. Then she rested her eyes upon the prospect again. "Well, I guess you had better leave it somewhere," she said, after a moment.

"Are you going to Italy?" Winterbourne inquired, in a tone of great respect.

The young lady glanced at him again. "Yes, sir," she replied. And she said nothing more.

"Are you—a—going over the Simplon?" Winterbourne pursued, a little embarrassed.

"I don't know," she said. "I suppose it's some mountain. Randolph, what mountain are we going over?"

"Going where?" the child demanded.

"To Italy," Winterbourne explained.

"I don't know," said Randolph. "I don't want to go to Italy. I want to go to America."

"Oh, Italy is a beautiful place!" rejoined the young man.

"Can you get candy there?" Randolph loudly inquired.

"I hope not," said his sister. "I guess you have had enough candy, and mother thinks so, too."

"I haven't had any for ever so long—for a hundred weeks!" cried the boy, still jumping about.

The young lady inspected her flounces and smoothed her ribbons again, and Winterbourne presently risked an observation upon the beauty of the view. He was ceasing to be embarrassed, for he had begun to perceive that she was not in the least embarrassed herself. There had not been the slightest alteration in her charming complexion; she was evidently neither offended nor fluttered. If she looked another way when he spoke to her, and seemed not particularly to hear him, this was simply her habit, her manner. Yet, as he talked a little more, and pointed out some of the objects of interest in the view, with which she appeared quite unacquainted, she gradually gave him more of the benefit of her glance; and then he saw that this glance was perfectly direct and unshrinking. It was not, however, what would have been called an immodest glance, for the young girl's eyes were singularly honest and fresh. They were wonderfully pretty eyes; and, indeed, Winterbourne had not seen for a long time anything prettier than his fair countrywoman's various features—her complexion, her nose, her ears, her teeth. He had a great relish for feminine beauty; he was addicted to observing and analyzing it; and as regards this young lady's face he made several observations. It was not at all insipid, but it was not exactly expressive; and though it was eminently delicate, Winterbourne mentally accused it—very forgivingly—of a want of finish. He thought it very possible that Master Randolph's sister was a coquette; he was sure she had a spirit of her own; but in her bright, sweet, superficial little visage there was no mockery, no irony. Before long it became obvious that she was much disposed towards conversation. She told him that they were going to Rome for the winter—she and her mother and Randolph. She asked him if he was a "real American"; she shouldn't have taken him for one; he seemed more like a German—this was said after a little hesitation—especially when he spoke. Winterbourne, laughing, answered that he had met Germans who spoke like Americans; but that he had not, so far as he remembered, met an American who spoke like a German. Then he asked her if she should not be more comfortable in sitting upon the bench which he had just quitted. She answered that she liked standing up and walking about; but she presently sat down. She told him she was from New York State—"if you know where that is." Winterbourne learned more about her by catching hold of her small, slippery brother, and making him stand a few minutes by his side.

"Tell me your name, my boy," he said.

"Randolph C. Miller," said the boy, sharply. "And I'll tell you her name;" and he levelled his alpenstock at his sister.

"You had better wait till you are asked!" said this young lady, calmly.

"I should like very much to know your name," said Winterbourne.

"Her name is Daisy Miller!" cried the child. "But that isn't her real name; that isn't her name on her cards."

"It's a pity you haven't got one of my cards!" said Miss Miller.

"Her real name is Annie P. Miller," the boy went on.

"Ask him his name," said his sister, indicating Winterbourne.

But on this point Randolph seemed perfectly indifferent; he continued to supply information in regard to his own family. "My father's name is Ezra B. Miller," he announced. "My father ain't in Europe; my father's in a better place than Europe."

Winterbourne imagined for a moment that this was the manner in which the child had been taught to intimate that Mr. Miller had been removed to the sphere of celestial rewards. But Randolph immediately added, "My father's in Schenectady. He's got a big business. My father's rich, you bet!"

"Well!" ejaculated Miss Miller, lowering her parasol and looking at the embroidered border. Winterbourne presently released the child, who departed, dragging his alpenstock along the path. "He doesn't like Europe," said the young girl. "He wants to go back."

"To Schenectady, you mean?"

"Yes; he wants to go right home. He hasn't got any boys here. There is one boy here, but he always goes round with a teacher; they won't let him play."

"And your brother hasn't any teacher?" Winterbourne inquired.

"Mother thought of getting him one to travel round with us. There was a lady told her of a very good teacher; an American lady —perhaps you know her—Mrs. Sanders. I think she came from Boston. She told her of this teacher, and we thought of getting him to travel round with us. But Randolph said he didn't want a teacher travelling round with us. He said he wouldn't have lessons when he was in the cars. And we *are* in the cars about half the time. There was an English lady we met in the cars—I think her name was Miss Featherstone; perhaps you know her. She wanted to know why I didn't give Randolph lessons—give him 'instructions,' she called it. I guess he could give me more instruction than I could give him. He's very smart."

"Yes," said Winterbourne; "he seems very smart."

"Mother's going to get a teacher for him as soon as we get to Italy. Can you get good teachers in Italy?"

"Very good, I should think," said Winterbourne.

"Or else she's going to find some school. He ought to learn some more. He's only nine. He's going to college." And in this way Miss Miller continued to converse upon the affairs of her family, and upon other topics. She sat there with her extremely pretty hands, ornamented with very brilliant rings, folded in her lap, and with her pretty eyes now resting upon those of Winterbourne, now wandering over the garden, the people who passed by, and the beautiful view. She talked to Winterbourne as if she had known him a long time. He found it very pleasant. It was many years since he had heard a young girl talk so much. It might have been said of this unknown young lady, who had come and sat down beside him upon a bench, that she chattered. She was very quiet; she sat in a charming, tranquil attitude, but her lips and her eyes were constantly moving. She had a soft, slender, agreeable voice, and her tone was decidedly sociable. She gave Winterbourne a history of her movements and intentions, and those of her mother and brother, in Europe, and enumerated, in particular, the various hotels at which they had stopped. "That English lady in the cars," she said—"Miss Featherstone—asked me if we didn't all live in hotels in America. I told her I had never been in so many hotels in my life as since I came to Europe. I have never seen so many— it's nothing but hotels." But Miss Miller did not make this remark with a querulous accent; she appeared to be in the best humor with everything. She declared that the hotels were very good, when once you got used to their ways, and that Europe was perfectly sweet. She was not disappointed—not a bit. Perhaps it was because she had heard so much about it before. She had ever so many intimate friends that had been there ever so many times. And then she had had ever so many dresses and things from Paris. Whenever she put on a Paris dress she felt as if she were in Europe.

"It was a kind of a wishing-cap," said Winterbourne.

"Yes," said Miss Miller, without examining this analogy; "it always made me wish I was here. But I needn't have done that for dresses. I am sure they send all the pretty ones to America; you see the most frightful things here. The only thing I don't like," she proceeded, "is the society. There isn't any society; or, if there is, I don't know where it keeps itself. Do you? I suppose there is some society somewhere, but I haven't seen anything of it. I'm very fond of society, and I have always had a great deal of it. I don't mean only in Schenectady, but in New York. I used to go to New York every winter. In New York I had lots of society. Last winter I had seventeen dinners given me; and three of them were by gentlemen," added Daisy Miller. "I have more friends in New York than in Schenectady—more gentlemen friends; and more young lady friends, too," she resumed in a moment. She paused again for an instant; she was looking at Winterbourne with all her prettiness in her lively eyes, and in her light, slightly monotonous smile. "I have always had," she said, "a great deal of gentlemen's society."

Poor Winterbourne was amused, perplexed, and decidedly charmed. He had never yet heard a young girl express herself in just this fashion—never, at least, save in cases where to say such things seemed a kind of demonstrative evidence of a certain laxity of deportment. And yet was he to accuse Miss Daisy Miller of actual or potential *inconduite*, as they said at Geneva? He felt that he had lived at Geneva so long that he had lost a good deal; he had become dishabituated to the American tone. Never, indeed, since he had grown old enough to appreciate things had he encountered a young American girl of so pronounced a type as this. Certainly she was very charming, but how deucedly sociable! Was she simply a pretty girl from New York State? were they all like that, the pretty girls who had a good deal of gentlemen's society? Or was she also a designing, an audacious, an unscrupulous young person? Winterbourne had lost his instinct in this matter, and his reason could not help him. Miss Daisy Miller looked extremely innocent. Some people had told him that, after all, American girls were exceedingly innocent; and others had told him that, after all, they were not. He was inclined to think Miss Daisy Miller was a flirt—a pretty American flirt. He had never, as yet, had any relations with young ladies of this category. He had known, here in Europe, two or three women—persons older than Miss Daisy Miller, and provided, for respectability's sake, with husbands—who were great coquettes—dangerous, terrible women, with whom one's relations were liable to take a serious turn. But this young girl was not a coquette in that sense; she was very unsophisticated; she was only a pretty American flirt. Winterbourne was almost grateful for having found the formula that applied to Miss Daisy Miller. He leaned back in his seat; he remarked to himself that she had the most charming nose he had ever seen; he wondered what were the regular conditions and limitations of one's intercourse with a pretty American flirt. It presently became apparent that he was on the way to learn.

"Have you been to that old castle?" asked the young girl, pointing with her parasol to the far-gleaming walls of the Château de Chillon.

"Yes, formerly, more than once," said Winterbourne. "You too, I suppose, have seen it?"

"No; we haven't been there. I want to go there dreadfully. Of course I mean to go there. I wouldn't go away from here without having seen that old castle."

"It's a very pretty excursion," said Winterbourne, "and very easy to make. You can drive or go by the little steamer."

"You can go in the cars," said Miss Miller.

"Yes; you can go in the cars," Winterbourne assented.

"Our courier says they take you right up to the castle," the young girl continued. "We were going last week; but my mother gave out. She suffers dreadfully from dyspepsia. She said she couldn't go. Randolph wouldn't go, either; he says he doesn't think much of old castles. But I guess we'll go this week, if we can get Randolph."

"Your brother is not interested in ancient monuments?" Winterbourne inquired, smiling.

"He says he don't care much about old castles. He's only nine. He wants to stay at the hotel. Mother's afraid to leave him alone, and the courier won't stay with him; so we haven't been to many places. But it will be too bad if we don't go up there." And Miss Miller pointed again at the Château de Chillon.

"I should think it might be arranged," said Winterbourne. "Couldn't you get some one to stay for the afternoon with Randolph?"

Miss Miller looked at him a moment, and then very placidly, "I wish *you* would stay with him!" she said.

Winterbourne hesitated a moment. "I should much rather go to Chillon with you."

"With me?" asked the young girl, with the same placidity.

She didn't rise, blushing, as a young girl at Geneva would have done; and yet Winterbourne, conscious that he had been very bold, thought it possible that she was offended. "With your mother," he answered, very respectfully.

But it seemed that both his audacity and his respect were lost upon Miss Daisy Miller. "I guess my mother won't go, after all," she said. "She don't like to ride round in the afternoon. But did you really mean what you said just now, that you would like to go up there?"

"Most earnestly," Winterbourne declared.

"Then we may arrange it. If mother will stay with Randolph, I guess Eugenio will."

"Eugenio?" the young man inquired.

"Eugenio's our courier. He doesn't like to stay with Randolph; he's the most fastidious man I ever saw. But he's a splendid courier. I guess he'll stay at home with Randolph if mother does, and then we can go to the castle."

Winterbourne reflected for an instant as lucidly as possible—"we" could only mean Miss Daisy Miller and himself. This programme seemed almost too agreeable for credence; he felt as if he ought to kiss the young lady's hand. Possibly he would have done so, and quite spoiled the project; but at this moment another person, presumably Eugenio, appeared. A tall, handsome man, with superb whiskers, wearing a velvet morning-coat and a brilliant watch-chain, approached Miss Miller, looking sharply at her companion. "Oh, Eugenio!" said Miss Miller, with the friendliest accent.

Eugenio had looked at Winterbourne from head to foot; he now bowed gravely to the young lady. "I have the honor to inform mademoiselle that luncheon is upon the table."

Miss Miller slowly rose. "See here, Eugenio!" she said; "I'm going to that old castle, anyway."

"To the Château de Chillon, mademoiselle?" the courier inquired. "Mademoiselle has made arangements?" he added, in a tone which struck Winterbourne as very impertinent.

Eugenio's tone apparently threw, even to Miss Miller's own apprehension, a slightly ironical light upon the young girl's situation. She turned to Winterbourne, blushing a little—a very little. "You won't back out?" she said.

"I shall not be happy till we go!" he protested.

"And you are staying in this hotel?" she went on. "And you are really an American?"

The courier stood looking at Winterbourne offensively. The young man, at least, thought his manner of looking an offence to Miss Miller; it conveyed an imputation that she "picked up" acquaintances. "I shall have the honor of presenting to you a person who will tell you all about me," he said, smiling, and referring to his aunt.

"Oh, well, we'll go some day," said Miss Miller. And she gave him a smile and turned away. She put up her parasol and walked back to the inn beside Eugenio. Winterbourne stood looking after her; and as she moved away, drawing her muslin furbelows over the gravel, said to himself that she had the *tournure* of a princess.

He had, however, engaged to do more than proved feasible, in promising to present his aunt, Mrs. Costello, to Miss Daisy Miller. As soon as the former lady had got better of her headache he waited upon her in her apartment; and, after the proper inquiries in regard to her health, he asked her if she had observed in the hotel an American family—a mamma, a daughter, and a little boy.

"And a courier?" said Mrs. Costello. "Oh yes, I have observed them. Seen them—heard them—and kept out of their way." Mrs. Costello was a widow with a fortune; a person of much distinction, who frequently intimated that, if she were not so dreadfully liable to sick-headaches, she would probably have left a deeper impress upon her time. She had a long, pale face, a high nose, and a great deal of very striking white hair, which she wore in large puffs and *rouleaux* over the top of her head. She had two sons married in New York, and another who was now in Europe. This young man was amusing himself at Hombourg; and, though he was on his travels, was rarely perceived to visit any particular city at the moment selected by his mother for her own appearance there. Her nephew, who had come up to Vevey expressly to see her, was therefore more attentive than those who, as she said, were nearer to her. He had imbibed at Geneva the idea that one must always be attentive to one's aunt. Mrs. Costello had not see him for many years, and she was greatly pleased with him, manifesting her approbation by initiating him into many of the secrets of that social sway which, as she gave him to understand, she exerted in the American capital. She admitted that she was very exclusive; but, if he were acquainted with New York, he would see that one had to be. And her picture of the minutely hierarchical constitution of the society of that city, which she presented to him in many different lights, was, to Winterbourne's imagination, almost oppressively striking.

He immediately perceived, from her tone, that Miss Daisy Miller's place in the social scale was low. "I am afraid you don't approve of them," he said.

"They are very common," Mrs. Costello declared. "They are the sort of Americans that one does one's duty by not—not accepting."

"Ah, you don't accept them?" said the young man.

"I can't, my dear Frederick. I would if I could, but I can't."

"The young girl is very pretty," said Winterbourne, in a moment.

"Of course she's pretty. But she is very common."

"I see what you mean, of course," said Winterbourne, after another pause.

"She has that charming look that they all have," his aunt resumed. "I can't think where they pick it up; and she dresses in perfection—no, you don't know how well she dresses. I can't think where they get their taste."

"But, my dear aunt, she is not, after all, a Comanche savage."

"She is a young lady," said Mrs. Costello, "who has an intimacy with her mamma's courier."

"An intimacy with the courier?" the young man demanded.

"Oh, the mother is just as bad! They treat the courier like a familiar friend—like a gentleman. I shouldn't wonder if he dines with them. Very likely they have never seen a man with such good manners, such fine clothes, so like a gentleman. He probably corresponds to the young lady's idea of a count. He sits with them in the garden in the evening. I think he smokes."

Winterbourne listened with interest to these disclosures; they helped him to make up his mind about Miss Daisy. Evidently she was rather wild.

"Well," he said, "I am not a courier, and yet she was very charming to me."

"You had better have said at first," said Mrs. Costello, with dignity, "that you had made her acquaintance."

"We simply met in the garden, and we talked a bit."

"*Tout bonnement*! And pray what did you say?"

"I said I should take the liberty of introducing her to my admirable aunt."

"I am much obliged to you."

"It was to guarantee my respectability," said Winterbourne.

"And pray who is to guarantee hers?"

"Ah, you are cruel," said the young man. "She's a very nice young girl."

"You don't say that as if you believed it," Mrs. Costello observed.

"She is completely uncultivated," Winterbourne went on. "But she is wonderfully pretty, and, in short, she is very nice. To prove that I believe it, I am going to take her to the Château de Chillon."

"You two are going off there together? I should say it proved just the contrary. How long had you known her, may I ask, when this interesting project was formed? You haven't been twenty-four hours in the house."

"I had known her half an hour!" said Winterbourne, smiling.

"Dear me!" cried Mrs. Costello. "What a dreadful girl!"

Her nephew was silent for some moments. "You really think, then," he began, earnestly, and with a desire for trustworthy information—"you really think that——" But he paused again.

"Think what, sir?" said his aunt.

"That she is the sort of young lady who expects a man, sooner or later, to carry her off?"

"I haven't the least idea what such young ladies expect a man to do. But I really think that you had better not meddle with little American girls that are uncultivated, as you call them. You have lived too long out of the country. You will be sure to make some great mistake. You are too innocent."

"My dear aunt, I am not so innocent," said Winterbourne, smiling and curling his mustache.

"You are too guilty, then!"

Winterbourne continued to curl his mustache, meditatively. "You won't let the poor girl know you, then?" he asked at last.

"Is it literally true that she is going to the Château de Chillon with you?"

"I think that she fully intends it."

"Then, my dear Frederick," said Mrs. Costello, "I must decline the honor of her acquaintance. I am an old woman, but I am not too old, thank Heaven, to be shocked!"

"But don't they all do these things—the young girls in America?" Winterbourne inquired.

Mrs. Costello stared a moment. "I should like to see my granddaughters do them!" she declared, grimly.

This seemed to throw some light upon the matter, for Winterbourne remembered to have heard that his pretty cousins in New York were "tremendous flirts." If, therefore, Miss Daisy Miller exceeded the liberal margin allowed to these young ladies, it was probable that anything might be expected of her. Winterbourne was impatient to see her again, and he was vexed with himself that, by instinct, he should not appreciate her justly.

Though he was impatient to see her, he hardly knew what he should say to her about his aunt's refusal to become acquainted with her; but he discovered, promptly enough, that with Miss Daisy Miller there was no great need of walking on tiptoe. He found her that evening in the garden, wandering about in the warm starlight like an indolent sylph, and swinging to and fro the largest fan he had ever beheld. It was ten o'clock. He had dined with his aunt, had been sitting with her since dinner, and had just taken leave of her till the morrow. Miss Daisy Miller seemed very glad to see him; she declared it was the longest evening she had ever passed.

"Have you been all alone?" he asked.

"I have been walking round with mother. But mother gets tired walking round," she answered.

"Has she gone to bed?"

"No; she doesn't like to go to bed," said the young girl. "She doesn't sleep—not three hours. She says she doesn't know how she lives. She's dreadfully nervous. I guess she sleeps more than she thinks. She's gone somewhere after Randolph; she wants to try to get him to go to bed. He doesn't like to go to bed."

"Let us hope she will persuade him," observed Winterbourne.

"She will talk to him all she can; but he doesn't like her to talk to him," said Miss Daisy, opening her fan. "She's going to try to get Eugenio to talk to him. But he isn't afraid of Eugenio. Eugenio's a splendid courier, but he can't make much impression on Randolph! I don't believe he'll go to bed before eleven." It appeared that Randolph's vigil was in fact triumphantly prolonged, for Winterbourne strolled about with the young girl for some time without meeting her mother. "I have been looking round for that lady you want to introduce me to," his companion resumed. "She's your aunt." Then, on Winterbourne's admitting the fact, and expressing some curiosity as to how she had learned it, she said she had heard all about Mrs. Costello from the chambermaid. She was very quiet, and very *comme il faut*; she wore white puffs; she spoke to no one, and she never dined at the *table d'hôte*. Every two days she had a headache. "I think that's a lovely description, headache and all!" said Miss Daisy, chattering along in her thin, gay voice. "I want to know her ever so much. I know just what *your* aunt would be; I know I should like her. She would be very exclusive. I like a lady to be exclusive; I'm dying to be exclusive myself. Well, we *are* exclusive, mother and I. We don't speak to every one—or they don't speak to us. I suppose it's about the same thing. Anyway, I shall be ever so glad to know your aunt."

Winterbourne was embarrassed. "She would be most happy," he said; "but I am afraid those headaches will interfere."

The young girl looked at him through the dusk. "But I suppose she doesn't have a headache every day," she said, sympathetically.

Winterbourne was silent a moment. "She tells me she does," he answered at last, not knowing what to say.

Miss Daisy Miller stopped, and stood looking at him. Her prettiness was still visible in the darkness; she was opening and closing her enormous fan. "She doesn't want to know me!" she said, suddenly. "Why don't you say so? You needn't be afraid. I'm not afraid!" And she gave a little laugh.

Winterbourne fancied there was a tremor in her voice; he was touched, shocked, mortified by it. "My dear young lady," he protested, "she knows no one. It's her wretched health."

The young girl walked on a few steps, laughing still. "You needn't be afraid," she repeated. "Why should she want to know me?" Then she paused again; she was close to the parapet of the garden, and in front of her was the starlit lake. There was a vague sheen upon its surface, and in the distance were dimly-seen mountain forms. Daisy Miller looked out upon the mysterious prospect, and then she gave another little laugh. "Gracious! she *is* exclusive!" she said. Winterbourne wondered whether she was seriously wounded, and for a moment almost wished that her sense of injury might be such as to make it becoming in him to attempt to reassure and comfort her. He had a pleasant sense that she would be very approachable for consolatory purposes. He felt then, for the instant, quite ready to sacrifice his aunt, conversationally; to admit that she was a proud, rude woman, and to declare that they needn't mind her. But before he had time to commit himself to this perilous mixture of gallantry and impiety, the young lady, resuming her walk, gave an exclamation in quite another tone. "Well, here's mother! I guess she hasn't got Randolph to go to bed." The figure of a lady appeared, at a distance, very indistinct in the darkness, and advancing with a slow and wavering movement. Suddenly it seemed to pause.

"Are you sure it is your mother? Can you distinguish her in this thick dusk?" Winterbourne asked.

"Well!" cried Miss Daisy Miller, with a laugh; "I guess I know my own mother. And when she has got on my shawl, too! She is always wearing my things."

The lady in question, ceasing to advance, hovered vaguely about the spot at which she had checked her steps.

"I am afraid your mother doesn't see you," said Winterbourne. "Or perhaps," he added, thinking, with Miss Miller, the joke permissible—"perhaps she feels guilty about your shawl."

"Oh, it's a fearful old thing!" the young girl replied, serenely. "I told her she could wear it. She won't come here, because she sees you."

"Ah, then," said Winterbourne, "I had better leave you."

"Oh no; come on!" urged Miss Daisy Miller.

"I'm afraid your mother doesn't approve of my walking with you."

Miss Miller gave him a serious glance. "It isn't for me; it's for you—that is, it's for *her*. Well, I don't know who it's for! But mother doesn't like any of my gentlemen friends. She's right down timid. She always makes a fuss if I introduce a gentleman. But I *do* introduce them—almost always. If I didn't introduce my gentlemen friends to mother," the young girl added, in her little soft, flat monotone, "I shouldn't think it was natural."

"To introduce me," said Winterbourne, "you must know my name." And he proceeded to pronounce it to her.

"Oh dear, I can't say all that!" said his companion, with a laugh. But by this time they had come up to Mrs. Miller, who, as they drew near, walked to the parapet of the garden and leaned upon it, looking intently at the lake, and turning her back to them. "Mother!" said the young girl, in a tone of decision. Upon this the elder lady turned round. "Mr. Winterbourne," said Miss Daisy Miller, introducing the young man very frankly and prettily. "Common," she was, as Mrs. Costello had pronounced her; yet it was a wonder to Winterbourne that, with her commonness, she had a singularly delicate grace.

Her mother was a small, spare, light person, with a wandering eye, a very exiguous nose, and a large forehead, decorated with a certain amount of thin, much-frizzled hair. Like her daughter, Mrs. Miller was dressed with extreme elegance; she had enormous diamonds in her ears. So far as Winterbourne could observe, she gave him no greeting—she certainly was not looking at him. Daisy was near her, pulling her shawl straight. "What are you doing, poking round here?" this young lady inquired, but by no means with that harshness of accent which her choice of words may imply.

"I don't know," said her mother, turning towards the lake again.

"I shouldn't think you'd want that shawl!" Daisy exclaimed.

"Well, I do!" her mother answered, with a little laugh.

"Did you get Randolph to go to bed?" asked the young girl.

"No; I couldn't induce him," said Mrs. Miller, very gently. "He wants to talk to the waiter. He likes to talk to that waiter."

"I was telling Mr. Winterbourne," the young girl went on; and to the young man's ear her tone might have indicated that she had been uttering his name all her life.

"Oh yes!" said Winterbourne; "I have the pleasure of knowing your son."

Randolph's mamma was silent; she turned her attention to the lake. But at last she spoke. "Well, I don't see how he lives!"

"Anyhow, it isn't so bad as it was at Dover," said Daisy Miller.

"And what occurred at Dover?" Winterbourne asked.

"He wouldn't go to bed at all. I guess he sat up all night in the public parlor. He wasn't in bed at twelve o'clock; I know that."

"It was half-past twelve," declared Mrs. Miller, with mild emphasis.

"Does he sleep much during the day?" Winterbourne demanded.

"I guess he doesn't sleep much," Daisy rejoined.

"I wish he would!" said her mother. "It seems as if he couldn't."

"I think he's real tiresome," Daisy pursued.

Then for some moments there was silence. "Well, Daisy Miller," said the elder lady, presently, "I shouldn't think you'd want to talk against your own brother!"

"Well, he *is* tiresome, mother," said Daisy, quite without the asperity of a retort.

"He's only nine," urged Mrs. Miller.

"Well, he wouldn't go to that castle," said the young girl. "I'm going there with Mr. Winterbourne."

To this announcement, very placidly made, Daisy's mamma offered no response. Winterbourne took for granted that she deeply disapproved of the projected excursion; but he said to himself that she was a simple, easily-managed person, and that a few deferential protestations would take the edge from her displeasure. "Yes," he began; "your daughter has kindly allowed me the honor of being her guide."

Mrs. Miller's wandering eyes attached themselves, with a sort of appealing air, to Daisy, who, however, strolled a few steps farther, gently humming to herself. "I presume you will go in the cars," said her mother.

"Yes, or in the boat," said Winterbourne.

"Well, of course, I don't know," Mrs. Miller rejoined. "I have never been to that castle."

"It is a pity you shouldn't go," said Winterbourne, beginning to feel reassured as to her opposition. And yet he was quite prepared to find that, as a matter of course, she meant to accompany her daughter.

"We've been thinking ever so much about going," she pursued;

"but it seems as if we couldn't. Of course Daisy, she wants to go round. But there's a lady here—I don't know her name—she says she shouldn't think we'd want to go to see castles *here;* she should think we'd want to wait till we got to Italy. It seems as if there would be so many there," continued Mrs. Miller, with an air of increasing confidence. "Of course we only want to see the principal ones. We visited several in England," she presently added.

"Ah, yes! in England there are beautiful castles," said Winterbourne. "But Chillon, here, is very well worth seeing."

"Well, if Daisy feels up to it——" said Mrs. Miller, in a tone impregnated with a sense of the magnitude of the enterprise. "It seems as if there was nothing she wouldn't undertake."

"Oh, I think she'll enjoy it!" Winterbourne declared. And he desired more and more to make it a certainty that he was to have the privilege of a tête-à-tête with the young lady, who was still strolling along in front of them, softly vocalizing. "You are not disposed, madam," he inquired, "to undertake it yourself?"

Daisy's mother looked at him an instant askance, and then walked forward in silence. Then—"I guess she had better go alone," she said, simply. Winterbourne observed to himself that this was a very different type of maternity from that of the vigilant matrons who massed themselves in the forefront of social intercourse in the dark old city at the other end of the lake. But his meditations were interrupted by hearing his name very distinctly pronounced by Mrs. Miller's unprotected daughter.

"Mr. Winterbourne!" murmured Daisy.

"Mademoiselle!" said the young man.

"Don't you want to take me out in a boat?"

"At present!" he asked.

"Of course!" said Daisy.

"Well, Annie Miller!" exclaimed her mother.

"I beg you, madam, to let her go," said Winterbourne, ardently; for he had never yet enjoyed the sensation of guiding through the summer starlight a skiff freighted with a fresh and beautiful young girl.

"I shouldn't think she'd want to go," said her mother. "I should think she'd rather go indoors."

"I'm sure Mr. Winterbourne wants to take me," Daisy declared. "He's so awfully devoted!"

"I will row you over to Chillon in the starlight."

"I don't believe it!" said Daisy.

"Well!" ejaculated the elder lady again.

"You haven't spoken to me for half an hour," her daughter went on.

"I have been having some very pleasant conversation with your mother," said Winterbourne.

"Well, I want you to take me out in a boat!" Daisy repeated. They had all stopped, and she had turned round and was looking at Winterbourne. Her face wore a charming smile, her pretty eyes were gleaming, she was swinging her great fan about. "No; it's impossible to be prettier than that," thought Winterbourne.

"There are half a dozen boats moored at that landing-place," he said, pointing to certain steps which descended from the garden to the lake. "If you will do me the honor to accept my arm, we will go and select one of them."

Daisy stood there smiling; she threw back her head and gave a little light laugh. "I like a gentleman to be formal!" she declared.

"I assure you it's a formal offer."

"I was bound I would make you say something," Daisy went on.

"You see, it's not very difficult," said Winterbourne. "But I am afraid you are chaffing me."

"I think not, sir," remarked Mrs. Miller, very gently.

"Do, then, let me give you a row," he said to the young girl.

"It's quite lovely, the way you say that!" cried Daisy.

"It will be still more lovely to do it."

"Yes, it would be lovely!" said Daisy. But she made no movement to accompany him; she only stood there laughing.

"I should think you had better find out what time it is," interposed her mother.

"It is eleven o'clock, madam," said a voice, with a foreign accent, out of the neighboring darkness; and Winterbourne, turning, perceived the florid personage who was in attendance upon the two ladies. He had apparently just approached.

"Oh, Eugenio," said Daisy, "I am going out in a boat!"

Eugenio bowed. "At eleven o'clock, mademoiselle?"

"I am going with Mr. Winterbourne—this very minute."

"Do tell her she can't," said Mrs. Miller to the courier.

"I think you had better not go out in a boat, mademoiselle," Eugenio declared.

Winterbourne wished to Heaven this pretty girl were not so familiar with her courier; but he said nothing.

"I suppose you don't think it's proper!" Daisy exclaimed. "Eugenio doesn't think anything's proper."

"I am at your service," said Winterbourne.

"Does mademoiselle propose to go alone?" asked Eugenio of Mrs. Miller.

"Oh, no; with this gentleman!" answered Daisy's mamma.

The courier looked for a moment at Winterbourne—the latter thought he was smiling—and then, solemnly, with a bow, "As mademoiselle pleases!" he said.

"Oh, I hoped you would make a fuss!" said Daisy. "I don't care to go now."

"I myself shall make a fuss if you don't go," said Winterbourne.

"That's all I want—a little fuss!" And the young girl began to laugh again.

"Mr. Randolph has gone to bed!" the courier announced, frigidly.

"Oh, Daisy; now we can go!" said Mrs. Miller.

Daisy turned away from Winterbourne, looking at him, smiling, and fanning herself. "Good-night," she said; "I hope you are disappointed, or disgusted, or something!"

He looked at her, taking the hand she offered him. "I am puzzled," he answered.

"Well, I hope it won't keep you awake!" she said, very smartly; and, under the escort of the privileged Eugenio, the two ladies passed towards the house.

Winterbourne stood looking after them; he was indeed puzzled. He lingered beside the lake for a quarter of an hour, turning over the mystery of the young girl's sudden familiarities and caprices. But the only very definite conclusion he came to was that he should enjoy deucedly "going off" with her somewhere.

Two days afterwards he went off with her to the Castle of Chillon. He waited for her in the large hall of the hotel, where the couriers, the servants, the foreign tourists, were lounging about and staring. It was not the place he should have chosen, but she had appointed it. She came tripping downstairs, buttoning her long gloves, squeezing her folded parasol against her pretty figure, dressed in the perfection of a soberly elegant travelling costume. Winterbourne was a man of imagination and, as our ancestors used to say, sensibility; as he looked at her dress and—on the great staircase—her little rapid, confiding step, he felt as if there were something romantic going forward. He could have believed he was going to elope with her. He passed out with her among all the idle people that were assembled there; they were all looking at her very hard; she had begun to chatter as soon as she joined him. Winterbourne's preference had been that they should be conveyed to Chillon in a carriage; but she expressed a lively wish to go in the little steamer; she declared that she had a passion for steamboats. There was always such a lovely breeze upon the water, and you saw such lots of people. The sail was not long, but Winterbourne's companion found time to say a great many things. To the young man himself their little excursion was so much of an escapade—an adventure—that, even allowing for her habitual sense of freedom, he had some expectation of seeing her regard it in the same way. But it must be confessed that, in this particular, he was disappointed. Daisy Miller was extremely animated, she was in charming spirits; but she was apparently not at all excited; she was not fluttered; she avoided neither his eyes nor those of any one else; she blushed neither when she looked at him nor when she felt that people were looking at her. People continued to look at her a great deal, and Winterbourne took much satisfaction in his pretty companion's distinguished air. He had been a little afraid that she would talk loud, laugh overmuch, and even, perhaps, desire to move about the boat a good deal. But he quite forgot his fears; he sat smiling, with his eyes upon her face, while, without moving from her place, she delivered herself of a great number of original reflections. It was the most charming garrulity he had ever heard. He had assented to the idea that she was "common"; but was she so, after all, or was he simply getting used to her commonness? Her conversation was chiefly of what metaphysicians term the objective cast; but every now and then it took a subjective turn.

"What on *earth* are you so grave about?" she suddenly demanded, fixing her agreeable eyes upon Winterbourne's.

"Am I grave?" he asked. "I had an idea I was grinning from ear to ear."

"You look as if you were taking me to a funeral. If that's a grin, your ears are very near together."

"Should you like me to dance a hornpipe on the deck?"

"Pray do, and I'll carry round your hat. It will pay the expenses of our journey."

"I never was better pleased in my life," murmured Winterbourne.

She looked at him a moment, and then burst into a little laugh. "I like to make you say those things! You're a queer mixture!"

In the castle, after they had landed, the subjective element decidedly prevailed. Daisy tripped about the vaulted chambers, rustled her skirts in the corkscrew staircases, flirted back with a pretty little cry and a shudder from the edge of the *oubliettes,* and turned a singularly well-shaped ear to everything that Winterbourne told her about the place. But he saw that she cared very little for feudal antiquities, and that the dusky traditions of Chillon made but a slight impression upon her. They had the good-fortune to have been able to walk without other companionship than that of the custodian; and Winterbourne arranged with this functionary that they should not be hurried—that they should linger and pause wherever they chose. The custodian interpreted the bargain generously—Winterbourne, on his side, had been generous—and ended by leaving them quite to themselves. Miss Miller's observations were not remarkable for logical consistency; for anything she wanted to say she was sure to find a pretext. She found a great many pretexts in the rugged embrasures of Chillon for asking Winterbourne sudden questions about himself—his family, his previous history, his tastes, his habits, his intentions—and for supplying information upon corresponding points in her own personality. Of her own tastes, habits, and intentions Miss Miller was prepared to give the most definite, and, indeed, the most favorable account.

"Well, I hope you know enough!" she said to her companion, after he had told her the history of the unhappy Bonnivard. "I never saw a man who knew so much!" The history of Bonnivard had evidently, as they say, gone into one ear and out of the other. But Daisy went on to say that she wished Winterbourne would travel with them, and "go round" with them; they might know something, in that case. "Don't you want to come and teach Randolph?" she asked. Winterbourne said that nothing could possibly please him so much, but that he had unfortunately other occupations. "Other occupations? I don't believe it!" said Miss Daisy. "What do you mean? You are not in business." The young man admitted that he was not in business; but he had engagements which, even within a day or two, would force him to go back to Geneva. "Oh, bother!" she said; "I don't believe it!" and she began to talk about something else. But a few moments later, when he was pointing out to her the pretty design of an antique fireplace, she broke out irrelevantly, "You don't mean to say you are going back to Geneva?"

"It is a melancholy fact that I shall have to return to-morrow."

"Well, Mr. Winterbourne," said Daisy, "I think you're horrid!"

"Oh, don't say such dreadful things!" said Winterbourne—"just at the last!"

"The last!" cried the young girl; "I call it the first. I have half a mind to leave you here and go straight back to the hotel alone." And for the next ten minutes she did nothing but call him horrid. Poor Winterbourne was fairly bewildered; no young lady had as yet done him the honor to be so agitated by the announcement of his movements. His companion, after this, ceased to pay any attention to the curiosities of Chillon or the beauties of the lake; she opened fire upon the mysterious charmer of Geneva, whom she appeared to have instantly taken for granted that he was hurrying back to see. How did Miss Daisy Miller know that there was a charmer in Geneva? Winterbourne, who denied the existence of such a person, was quite unable to discover; and he was divided between amazement at the rapidity of her induction and amusement at the frankness of her *persiflage*. She seemed to him, in all this, an extraordinary mixture of innocence and crudity. "Does she never allow you more than three days at a time?" asked Daisy, ironically. "Doesn't she give you a vacation in summer? There is no one so hard worked but they can get leave to go off somewhere at this season. I suppose, if you stay another day, she'll come after you in the boat. Do wait over till Friday. and I will go down to the landing to see her arrive!" Winterbourne began to think he had been wrong to feel disappointed in the temper in which the young lady had embarked. If he had missed the personal accent, the personal accent was now making its appearance. It sounded very distinctly, at last, in her telling him she would stop "teasing" him if he would promise her solemnly to come down to Rome in the winter.

"That's not a difficult promise to make," said Winterbourne. "My aunt has taken an apartment in Rome for the winter, and has already asked me to come and see her."

"I don't want you to come for your aunt," said Daisy; "I want you to come for me." And this was the only allusion that the young man was ever to hear her make to his invidious kinswoman. He declared that, at any rate, he would certainly come. After this Daisy stopped teasing. Winterbourne took a carriage, and they drove back to Vevey in the dusk. The young girl was very quiet.

In the evening Winterbourne mentioned to Mrs. Costello that he had spent the afternoon at Chillon with Miss Daisy Miller.

"The Americans—of the courier?" asked this lady.

"Ah, happily," said Winterbourne, "the courier stayed at home."

"She went with you all alone?"

"All alone."

Mrs. Costello sniffed a little at her smelling-bottle. "And that," she exclaimed, "is the young person whom you wanted me to know!"

PART II

ROME

WINTERBOURNE, who had returned to Geneva the day after his excursion to Chillon, went to Rome towards the end of January. His aunt had been established there for several weeks, and he had received a couple of letters from her. "Those people you were so devoted to last summer at Vevey have turned up here, courier and all," she wrote. "They seem to have made several acquaintances, but the courier continues to be the most *intime*. The young lady, however, is also very intimate with some third-rate Italians, with whom she rackets about in a way that makes much talk. Bring me that pretty novel of Cherbuliez's—*Paule Méré*—and don't come later than the 23d."

In the natural course of events, Winterbourne, on arriving in Rome, would presently have ascertained Mrs. Miller's address at the American banker's, and have gone to pay his compliments to Miss Daisy. "After what happened at Vevey, I think I may certainly call upon them," he said to Mrs. Costello.

"If, after what happens—at Vevey and everywhere—you desire to keep up the acquaintance, you are very welcome. Of course a man may know every one. Men are welcome to the privilege!"

"Pray what is it that happens—here, for instance?" Winterbourne demanded.

"The girl goes about alone with her foreigners. As to what happens further, you must apply elsewhere for information. She has picked up half a dozen of the regular Roman fortune-hunters, and she takes them about to people's houses. When she comes to a party she brings with her a gentleman with a good deal of manner and a wonderful mustache."

"And where is the mother?"

"I haven't the least idea. They are very dreadful people."

Winterbourne meditated a moment. "They are very ignorant—very innocent only. Depend upon it they are not bad."

"They are hopelessly vulgar," said Mrs. Costello. "Whether or no being hopelessly vulgar is being 'bad' is a question for the metaphysicians. They are bad enough to dislike, at any rate; and for this short life that is quite enough."

The news that Daisy Miller was surrounded by half a dozen wonderful mustaches checked Winterbourne's impulse to go straightway to see her. He had, perhaps, not definitely flattered himself that he had made an ineffaceable impression upon her heart, but he was annoyed at hearing of a state of affairs so little in harmony with an image that had lately fitted in and out of his own meditations; the image of a very pretty girl looking out of an old Roman window and asking herself urgently when Mr. Winterbourne would arrive. If, however, he determined to wait a little before reminding Miss Miller of his claims to her consideration, he went very soon to call upon two or three other friends. One of these friends was an American lady who had spent several winters at Geneva, where she had placed her children at school. She was a very accomplished woman, and she lived in the Via Gregoriana. Winterbourne found her in a little crimson drawing-room on a third floor; the room was filled with southern sunshine. He had not been there ten minutes when the servant came in, announcing "Madame Mila!" This announcement was presently followed by the entrance of little Randolph Miller, who stopped in the middle of the room and stood staring at Winterbourne. An instant later his pretty sister crossed the threshold; and then, after a considerable interval, Mrs. Miller slowly advanced.

"I know you!" said Randolph.

"I'm sure you know a great many things," exclaimed Winterbourne, taking him by the hand. "How is your education coming on?"

Daisy was exchanging greetings very prettily with her hostess; but when she heard Winterbourne's voice she quickly turned her head. "Well, I declare!" she said.

"I told you I should come, you know," Winterbourne rejoined, smiling.

"Well, I didn't believe it," said Miss Daisy.

"I am much obliged to you," laughed the young man.

"You might have come to see me!" said Daisy.

"I arrived only yesterday."

"I don't believe that!" the young girl declared.

Winterbourne turned with a protesting smile to her mother; but this lady evaded his glance, and, seating herself, fixed her eyes upon her son. "We've got a bigger place than this," said Randolph. "It's all gold on the walls."

Mrs. Miller turned uneasily in her chair. "I told you if I were going to bring you, you would say something!" she murmured.

"I told *you!*" Randolph exclaimed. "I tell *you,* sir!" he added, jocosely, giving Winterbourne a thump on the knee. "It *is* bigger, too!"

Daisy had entered upon a lively conversation with her hostess, and Winterbourne judged it becoming to address a few words to her mother. "I hope you have been well since we parted at Vevey," he said.

Mrs. Miller now certainly looked at him—at his chin. "Not very well, sir," she answered.

"She's got the dyspepsia," said Randolph. "I've got it, too. Father's got it. I've got it most!"

This announcement, instead of embarrassing Mrs. Miller, seemed to relieve her. "I suffer from the liver," she said. "I think it's this climate; it's less bracing than Schenectady, especially in the winter season. I don't know whether you know we reside at Schenectady. I was saying to Daisy that I certainly hadn't found any one like Dr. Davis, and I didn't believe I should. Oh, at Schenectady he stands first; they think everything of him. He has so much to do, and yet there was nothing he wouldn't do for me. He said he never saw anything like my dyspepsia, but he was bound to cure it. I'm sure there was nothing he wouldn't try. He was just going to try something new when we came off. Mr. Miller wanted Daisy to see Europe for herself. But I wrote to Mr. Miller that it seems as if I couldn't get on without Dr. Davis. At Schenectady he stands at the very top; and there's a great deal of sickness there, too. It affects my sleep."

Winterbourne had a good deal of pathological gossip with Dr. Davis's patient, during which Daisy chattered unremittingly to her own companion. The young man asked Mrs. Miller how she was pleased with Rome. "Well, I must say I am disappointed," she answered. "We had heard so much about it; I suppose we had heard too much. But we couldn't help that. We had been led to expect something different."

"Ah, wait a little, and you will become very fond of it," said Winterbourne.

"I hate it worse and worse every day!" cried Randolph.

"You are like the infant Hannibal," said Winterbourne.

"No, I ain't!" Randolph declared, at a venture.

"You are not much like an infant," said his mother. "But we have seen places," she resumed, "that I should put a long way before Rome." And in reply to Winterbourne's interrogation, "There's Zürich," she concluded, "I think Zürich is lovely; and we hadn't heard half so much about it."

"The best place we've seen is the City of Richmond!" said Randolph.

"He means the ship," his mother explained. "We crossed in that ship. Randolph had a good time on the *City of Richmond.*"

"It's the best place I've seen," the child repeated. "Only it was turned the wrong way."

"Well, we've got to turn the right way some time," said Mrs. Miller, with a little laugh. Winterbourne expressed the hope that her daughter at least found some gratification in Rome, and she declared that Daisy was quite carried away. "It's on account of the society—the society's splendid. She goes round everywhere; she has made a great number of acquaintances. Of course she goes round more than I do. I must say they have been very sociable; they have taken her right in. And then she knows a great many gentlemen. Oh, she thinks there's nothing like Rome. Of course, it's a great deal pleasanter for a young lady if she knows plenty of gentlemen."

By this time Daisy had turned her attention again to Winterbourne. "I've been telling Mrs. Walker how mean you were!" the young girl announced.

"And what is the evidence you have offered?" asked Winterbourne, rather annoyed at Miss Miller's want of appreciation of the zeal of an admirer who on his way down to Rome had stopped neither at Bologna nor at Florence, simply because of a certain sentimental impatience. He remembered that a cynical compatriot had once told him that American women—the pretty ones, and this gave a largeness to the axiom—were at once the most exacting in the world and the least endowed with a sense of indebtedness.

"Why, you were awfully mean at Vevey," said Daisy. "You wouldn't do anything. You wouldn't stay there when I asked you."

"My dearest young lady," cried Winterbourne, with eloquence, "have I come all the way to Rome to encounter your reproaches?"

"Just hear him say that!" said Daisy to her hostess, giving a twist to a bow on this lady's dress. "Did you ever hear anything so quaint?"

"So quaint, my dear?" murmured Mrs. Walker, in a tone of a partisan of Winterbourne.

"Well, I don't know," said Daisy, fingering Mrs. Walker's ribbons. "Mrs. Walker, I want to tell you something."

"Mother-r," interposed Randolph, with his rough ends to his words, "I tell you you've got to go. Eugenio'll raise—something!"

"I'm not afraid of Eugenio," said Daisy, with a toss of her head. "Look here, Mrs. Walker," she went on, "you know I'm coming to your party."

"I am delighted to hear it."

"I've got a lovely dress!"

"I am very sure of that."

"But I want to ask a favor—permission to bring a friend."

"I shall be happy to see any of your friends," said Mrs. Walker, turning with a smile to Mrs. Miller.

"Oh, they are not my friends," answered Daisy's mamma, smiling shyly, in her own fashion. "I never spoke to them."

"It's an intimate friend of mine—Mr. Giovanelli," said Daisy, without a tremor in her clear little voice, or a shadow on her brilliant little face.

Mrs. Walker was silent a moment; she gave a rapid glance at Winterbourne. "I shall be glad to see Mr. Giovanelli," she then said.

"He's an Italian," Daisy pursued, with the prettiest serenity. "He's a great friend of mine; he's the handsomest man in the world—except Mr. Winterbourne! He knows plenty of Italians, but he wants to know some Americans. He thinks ever so much of Americans. He's tremendously clever. He's perfectly lovely!"

It was settled that this brilliant personage should be brought to Mrs. Walker's party, and then Mrs. Miller prepared to take her leave. "I guess we'll go back to the hotel," she said.

"You may go back to the hotel, mother, but I'm going to take a walk," said Daisy.

"She's going to walk with Mr. Giovanelli," Randolph proclaimed.

"I am going to the Pincio," said Daisy, smiling.

"Alone, my dear—at this hour?" Mrs. Walker asked. The afternoon was drawing to a close—it was the hour for the throng of carriages and of contemplative pedestrians. "I don't think it's safe, my dear," said Mrs. Walker.

"Neither do I," subjoined Mrs. Miller. "You'll get the fever, as sure as you live. Remember what Dr. Davis told you!"

"Give her some medicine before she goes," said Randolph.

The company had risen to its feet; Daisy, still showing her pretty teeth, bent over and kissed her hostess. "Mrs. Walker, you are too perfect," she said. "I'm not going alone; I am going to meet a friend."

"Your friend won't keep you from getting the fever," Mrs. Miller observed.

"Is it Mr. Giovanelli?" asked the hostess.

Winterbourne was watching the young girl; at this question his attention quickened. She stood there smiling and smoothing her bonnet ribbons; she glanced at Winterbourne. Then, while she glanced and smiled, she answered, without a shade of hesitation, "Mr. Giovanelli—the beautiful Giovanelli."

"My dear young friend," said Mrs. Walker, taking her hand, pleadingly, "don't walk off to the Pincio at this unhealthy hour to meet a beautiful Italian."

"Well, he speaks English," said Mrs. Miller.

"Gracious me!" Daisy exclaimed, "I don't want to do anything improper. There's an easy way to settle it." She continued to glance at Winterbourne. "The Pincio is only a hundred yards distant; and if Mr. Winterbourne were as polite as he pretends, he would offer to walk with me!"

Winterbourne's politeness hastened to affirm itself, and the young girl gave him gracious leave to accompany her. They passed downstairs before her mother, and at the door Winterbourne perceived Mrs. Miller's carriage drawn up, with the ornamental courier, whose acquaintance he had made at Vevey, seated within. "Good-bye, Eugenio!" cried Daisy; "I'm going to take a walk." The distance from the Via Gregoriana to the beautiful garden at the other end of the Pincian Hill is, in fact, rapidly traversed. As the day was splendid, however, and the concourse of vehicles, walkers, and loungers numerous, the young Americans found their progress much delayed. This fact was highly agreeable to Winterbourne, in spite of his consciousness of his singular situation. The slow-moving, idly-gazing Roman crowd bestowed much attention upon the extremely pretty young foreign lady who was passing through it upon his arm; and he wondered what on earth had been in Daisy's mind when she proposed to expose herself, unattended, to its appreciation. His own mission, to her sense, apparently, was to consign her to the hands of Mr. Giovanelli; but Winterbourne, at once annoyed and gratified, resolved that he would do no such thing.

"Why haven't you been to see me?" asked Daisy. "You can't get out of that."

"I have had the honor of telling you that I have only just stepped out of the train."

"You must have stayed in the train a good while after it stopped!" cried the young girl, with her little laugh. "I suppose you were asleep. You have had time to go to see Mrs. Walker."

"I knew Mrs. Walker——" Winterbourne began to explain.

"I know where you knew her. You knew her at Geneva. She told me so. Well, you knew me at Vevey. That's just as good. So you ought to have come." She asked him no other question than this; she began to prattle about her own affairs. "We've got splendid rooms at the hotel; Eugenio says they're the best rooms in Rome. We are going to stay all winter, if we don't die of the fever; and I guess we'll stay then. It's a great deal nicer than I thought; I thought it would be fearfully quiet; I was sure it would be awfully poky. I was sure we should be going round all the time with one of those dreadful old men that explain about the pictures and things. But we only had about a week of that, and now I'm enjoying myself. I know ever so many people, and they are all so charming. The society's extremely select. There are all kinds—English and Germans and Italians. I think I like the English best. I like their style of conversation. But there are some lovely Americans. I never saw anything so hospitable. There's something or other every day. There's not much dancing; but I must say I never thought dancing was everything. I was always fond of conversation. I guess I shall have plenty at Mrs. Walker's, her rooms are so small." When they has passed the gate of the Pincian Gardens, Miss Miller began to wonder where Mr. Giovanelli might be. "We had better go straight to that place in front," she said, "where you look at the view."

"I certainly shall not help you to find him," Winterbourne declared.

"Then I shall find him without you," said Miss Daisy.

"You certainly won't leave me!" cried Winterbourne.

She burst into her little laugh. "Are you afraid you'll get lost—or run over? But there's Giovanelli, leaning against that tree. He's staring at the women in the carriages; did you ever see anything so cool?"

Winterbourne perceived at some distance a little man standing with folded arms nursing his cane. He had a handsome face, an artfully poised hat, a glass in one eye, and a nosegay in his buttonhole. Winterbourne looked at him a moment, and then said, "Do you mean to speak to that man?"

"Do I mean to speak to him? Why, you don't suppose I mean to communicate by signs?"

"Pray understand, then," said Winterbourne, "that I intend to remain with you."

Daisy stopped and looked at him, without a sign of troubled consciousness in her face; with nothing but the presence of her charming eyes, and her happy dimples. "Well, she's a cool one!" thought the young man.

"I don't like the way you say that," said Daisy. "It's too imperious."

"I beg your pardon if I say it wrong. The main point is to give you an idea of my meaning."

The young girl looked at him more gravely, but with eyes that were prettier than ever. "I have never allowed a gentleman to dictate to me, or to interfere with anything I do."

"I think you have made a mistake," said Winterbourne. "You should sometimes listen to a gentleman—the right one."

Daisy began to laugh again. "I do nothing but listen to gentlemen!" she exclaimed. "Tell me if Mr. Giovanelli is the right one."

The gentleman with the nosegay in his bosom had now perceived our two friends, and was approaching the young girl with obsequious rapidity. He bowed to Winterbourne as well as to the latter's companion; he had a brilliant smile, an intelligent eye; Winterbourne thought him not a bad-looking fellow. But he nevertheless said to Daisy, "No, he's not the right one."

Daisy evidently had a natural talent for performing introductions; she mentioned the name of each of her companions to the other. She strolled along with one of them on each side of her; Mr. Giovanelli, who spoke English very cleverly—Winterbourne afterwards learned that he had practised the idiom upon a great many American heiresses—addressed to her a great deal of very polite nonsense; he was extremely urbane, and the young American, who said nothing, reflected upon that profundity of Italian cleverness which enables people to appear more gracious in proportion as they are more acutely disappointed. Giovanelli, of course, had counted upon something more intimate; he had not bargained for a party of three. But he kept his temper in a manner which suggested far-stretching intentions. Winterbourne flattered himself that he had taken his measure. "He is not a gentleman," said the young American; "he is only a clever imitation of one. He is a music-master, or a penny-a-liner, or a third-rate artist. D—n his good looks!" Mr. Giovanelli had certainly a very pretty face; but Winterbourne felt a superior indignation at his own lovely fellow-country woman's not knowing the difference between a spurious gentleman and a real one. Giovanelli chattered and jested, and made himself wonderfully agreeable. It was true that, if he was an imitation, the imitation was brilliant. "Nevertheless." Winterbourne said to himself, "a nice girl ought to know!" And then he came back to the question whether this was, in fact, a nice girl. Would a nice girl, even allowing for her being a little American flirt, make a rendezvous with a presumably low-lived foreigner? The rendezvous in this case, indeed, had been in broad daylight, and in the most crowded corner of Rome; but was it not impossible to regard the choice of these circumstances as a proof of extreme cynicism? Singular though it may seem, Winterbourne was vexed that the young girl, in joining her *amoroso*, should not appear more impatient of his own company, and he was vexed because of his inclination. It was impossible to regard her as a perfectly well-conducted young lady; she was wanting in a certain indispensable delicacy. It would therefore simplify matters greatly to be able to treat her as the object of one of those sentiments which are called by romancers "lawless passions." That she should seem to wish to get rid of him would help him to think more lightly of her, and to be able to think more lightly of her would make her much less perplexing. But Daisy, on this occasion, continued to present herself as an inscrutable combination of audacity and innocence.

She had been walking some quarter of an hour, attended by her two cavaliers, and responding in a tone of very childish gayety, as it seemed to Winterbourne, to the pretty speeches of Mr. Giovanelli, when a carriage that had detached itself from the revolving train drew up beside the path. At the same moment Winterbourne perceived that his friend Mrs. Walker—the lady whose house he had lately left—was seated in the vehicle, and was beckoning to him. Leaving Miss Miller's side, he hastened to obey her summons. Mrs. Walker was flushed; she wore an excited air. "It is really too dreadful," she said. "That girl must not do this sort of thing. She must not walk here with you two men. Fifty people have noticed her."

Winterbourne raised his eyebrows. "I think it's a pity to make too much fuss about it."

"It's a pity to let the girl ruin herself!"

"She is very innocent," said Winterbourne.

"She's very crazy!" cried Mrs. Walker. "Did you ever see anything so imbecile as her mother? After you had all left me just now I could not sit still for thinking of it. It seemed too pitiful not even to attempt to save her. I ordered the carriage and put on my bonnet, and came here as quickly as possible. Thank Heaven I have found you!"

"What do you propose to do with us?" asked Winterbourne. smiling.

"To ask her to get in, to drive her about here for half an hour, so that the world may see that she is not running absolutely wild, and then to take her safely home."

"I don't think it's a very happy thought," said Winterbourne; "but you can try."

Mrs. Walker tried. The young man went in pursuit of Miss Miller, who had simply nodded and smiled at his interlocutor in the carriage, and had gone her way with her companion. Daisy, on learning that Mrs. Walker wished to speak to her, retraced her steps with a perfect good grace and with Mr. Giovanelli at her side. She declared that she was delighted to have a chance to present this gentleman to Mrs. Walker. She immediately achieved the introduction, and declared that she had never in her life seen anything so lovely as Mrs. Walker's carriage-rug.

"I am glad you admire it," said this lady, smiling sweetly. "Will you get in and let me put it over you?"

"Oh no, thank you," said Daisy. "I shall admire it much more as I see you driving round with it."

"Do get in and drive with me!" said Mrs. Walker.

"That would be charming, but it's so enchanting just as I am!" and Daisy gave a brilliant glance at the gentlemen on either side of her.

"It may be enchanting, dear child, but it is not the custom here," urged Mrs. Walker, leaning forward in her victoria, with her hands devoutly clasped.

"Well, it ought to be, then!" said Daisy. "If I didn't walk I should expire."

"You should walk with your mother, dear," cried the lady from Geneva, losing patience.

"With my mother, dear!" exclaimed the young girl. Winterbourne saw that she scented interference. "My mother never walked ten steps in her life. And then, you know," she added, with a laugh, "I am more than five years old."

"You are old enough to be more reasonable. You are old enough, dear Miss Miller, to be talked about."

Daisy looked at Mrs. Walker, smiling intensely. "Talked about? What do you mean?"

"Come into my carriage, and I will tell you."

Daisy turned her quickened glance again from one of the gentlemen beside her to the other. Mr. Giovanelli was bowing to and fro, rubbing down his gloves and laughing very agreeably; Winterbourne thought it a most unpleasant scene. "I don't think I want to know what you mean," said Daisy, presently. "I don't think I should like it."

Winterbourne wished that Mrs. Walker would tuck in her carriage-rug and drive away; but this lady did not enjoy being defied, as she afterwards told him. "Should you prefer being thought a very reckless girl?" she demanded.

"Gracious!" exclaimed Daisy. She looked again at Mr. Giovanelli, then she turned to Winterbourne. There was a little pink flush in her cheek; she was tremendously pretty. "Does Mr. Winterbourne think," she added slowly, smiling, throwing back her head and glancing at him from head to foot, "that, to save my reputation, I ought to get into the carriage?"

Winterbourne colored; for an instant he hesitated greatly. It seemed so strange to hear her speak that way of her "reputation." But he himself, in fact, must speak in accordance with gallantry. The finest gallantry here was simply to tell her the truth, and the truth for Winterbourne—as the few indications I have been able to give have made him known to the reader—was that Daisy Miller should take Mrs. Walker's advice. He looked at her exquisite prettiness, and then said, very gently, "I think you should get into the carriage."

Daisy gave a violent laugh. "I never heard anything so stiff! If this is improper, Mrs. Walker," she pursued, "then I am all improper, and you must give me up. Good-bye; I hope you'll have a lovely ride!" and, with Mr. Giovanelli, who made a triumphantly obsequious salute, she turned away.

Mrs. Walker sat looking after her, and there were tears in Mrs. Walker's eyes. "Get in here, sir," she said to Winterbourne, indicating the place beside her. The young man answered that he felt bound to accompany Miss Miller; whereupon Mrs. Walker declared that if he refused her this favor she would never speak to him again. She was evidently in earnest. Winterbourne overtook Daisy and her companion, and, offering the young girl his hand, told her that Mrs. Walker had made an imperious claim upon his society. He expected that in answer she would say something rather free, something to commit herself still further to that "recklessness" from which Mrs. Walker had so charitably endeavored to dissuade her.

But she only shook his hand, hardly looking at him; while Mr. Giovanelli bade him farewell with a too emphatic flourish of the hat.

Winterbourne was not in the best possible humor as he took his seat in Mrs. Walker's victoria. "That was not clever of you," he said, candidly, while the vehicle mingled again with the throng of carriages.

"In such a case," his companion answered, "I don't wish to be clever; I wish to be *earnest!*"

"Well, your earnestness has only offended her and put her off."

"It has happened very well," said Mrs. Walker. "If she is so perfectly determined to compromise herself, the sooner one knows it the better; one can act accordingly."

"I suspect she meant no harm," Winterbourne rejoined.

"So I thought a month ago. But she has been going too far."

"What has she been doing?"

"Everything that is not done here. Flirting with any man she could pick up; sitting in corners with mysterious Italians; dancing all the evening with the same partners; receiving visits at eleven o'clock at night. Her mother goes away when visitors come."

"But her brother," said Winterbourne, laughing, "sits up till midnight."

"He must be edified by what he sees. I'm told that at their hotel every one is talking about her, and that a smile goes round among all the servants when a gentleman comes and asks for Miss Miller."

"The servants be hanged!" said Winterbourne, angrily. "The poor girl's only fault," he presently added, "is that she is very uncultivated."

"She is naturally indelicate," Mrs. Walker declared. "Take that example this morning. How long had you known her at Vevey?"

"A couple of days."

"Fancy, then, her making it a personal matter that you should have left the place!"

Winterbourne was silent for some moments; then he said, "I suspect, Mrs. Walker, that you and I have lived too long at Geneva!" And he added a request that she should inform him with what particular design she had made him enter her carriage.

"I wished to beg you to cease your relations with Miss Miller—not to flirt with her—to give her no further opportunity to expose herself—to let her alone, in short."

"I'm afraid I can't do that," said Winterbourne. "I like her extremely."

"All the more reason that you shouldn't help her to make a scandal."

"There shall be nothing scandalous in my attentions to her."

"There certainly will be in the way she takes them. But I have said what I had on my conscience," Mrs. Walker pursued. "If you wish to rejoin the young lady I will put you down. Here, by-the-way, you have a chance."

The carriage was traversing that part of the Pincian Garden that overhangs the wall of Rome and overlooks the beautiful Villa Borghese. It is bordered by a large parapet, near which there are several seats. One of the seats at a distance was occupied by a gentleman and a lady, towards whom Mrs. Walker gave a toss of her head. At the same moment these persons rose and walked towards the parapet. Winterbourne had asked the coachman to stop; he now descended from the carriage. His companion looked at him a moment in silence; then, while he raised his hat, she drove majestically away. Winterbourne stood there; he had turned his eyes towards Daisy and her cavalier. They evidently saw no one; they were too deeply occupied with each other. When they reached the low garden-wall they stood a moment looking off at the great flat-topped pine-clusters of the Villa Borghese; then Giovanelli seated himself familiarly upon the broad ledge of the wall. The western sun in the opposite sky sent out a brilliant shaft through a couple of cloud-bars, whereupon Daisy's companion took her parasol out of her hands and opened it. She came a little nearer, and he held the parasol over her; then, still holding it, he let it rest upon her shoulder, so that both of their heads were hidden from Winterbourne. This young man lingered a moment, then he began to walk. But he walked—not towards the couple with the parasol—towards the residence of his aunt, Mrs. Costello.

He flattered himself on the following day that there was no smiling among the servants when he, at least, asked for Mrs. Miller at her hotel. This lady and her daughter, however, were not at home; and on the next day after, repeating his visit, Winterbourne again had the misfortune not to find them. Mrs. Walker's party took place on the evening of the third day, and, in spite of the frigidity of his last interview with the hostess, Winterbourne was among the guests. Mrs. Walker was one of those American ladies who, while residing abroad, make a point, in their own phrase, of studying European society; and she had on this occasion collected several specimens of her diversely-born fellow-mortals to serve, as it were, as text-books. When Winterbourne arrived, Daisy Miller was not there, but in a few moments he saw her mother come in alone, very shyly and ruefully. Mrs. Miller's hair above her exposed-looking temples was more frizzled than ever. As she approached Mrs. Walker, Winterbourne also drew near.

"You see I've come all alone," said poor Mrs. Miller. "I'm so frightened I don't know what to do. It's the first time I've ever been to a party alone, especially in this country. I wanted to bring Randolph, or Eugenio, or some one, but Daisy just pushed me off by myself. I ain't used to going round alone."

"And does not your daughter intend to favor us with her society?" demanded Mrs. Walker, impressively.

"Well, Daisy's all dressed," said Mrs. Miller, with that accent of the dispassionate, if not of the philosophic, historian with which she always recorded the current incidents of her daughter's career. "She got dressed on purpose before dinner. But she's got a friend of hers there; that gentleman—the Italian—that she wanted to bring. They've got going at the piano; it seems as if they couldn't leave off. Mr. Giovanelli sings splendidly. But I guess they'll come before very long," concluded Mrs. Miller, hopefully.

"I'm sorry she should come in that way," said Mrs. Walker.

"Well, I told her that there was no use in her getting dressed before dinner if she was going to wait three hours," responded Daisy's mamma. "I didn't see the use of her putting on such a dress as that to sit round with Mr. Giovanelli."

"This is most horrible!" said Mrs. Walker, turning away and addressing herself to Winterbourne. "*Elle s'affiche*. It's her revenge for my having ventured to remonstrate with her. When she comes I shall not speak to her."

Daisy came after eleven o'clock; but she was not, on such an occasion, a young lady to wait to be spoken to. She rustled forward in radiant loveliness, smiling and chattering, carrying a large bouquet, and attended by Mr. Giovanelli. Every one stopped talking, and turned and looked at her. She came straight to Mrs. Walker. "I'm afraid you thought I never was coming, so I sent mother off to tell you. I wanted to make Mr. Giovanelli practise some things before he came; you know he sings beautifully, and I want you to ask him to sing. This is Mr. Giovanelli; you know I introduced him to you; he's got the most lovely voice, and he knows the most charming set of songs. I made him go over them this evening on purpose; we had the greatest time at the hotel." Of all this Daisy delivered herself with the sweetest, brightest audibleness, looking now at her hostess and now round the room, while she gave a series of little pats round her shoulders to the edges of her dress. "Is there any one I know?" she asked.

"I think every one knows you!" said Mrs. Walker, pregnantly, and she gave a very cursory greeting to Mr. Giovanelli. This gentleman bore himself gallantly. He smiled and bowed, and showed his white teeth; he curled his mustaches and rolled his eyes, and performed all the proper functions of a handsome Italian at an evening party. He sang very prettily half a dozen songs, though Mrs. Walker afterwards declared that she had been quite unable to find out who asked him. It was apparently not Daisy who had given him his orders. Daisy sat at a distance from the piano; and though she had publicly, as it were, professed a high admiration for his singing, talked, not inaudibly, while it was going on.

"It's a pity these rooms are so small; we can't dance," she said to Winterbourne, as if she had seen him five minutes before.

"I am not sorry we can't dance," Winterbourne answered; "I don't dance."

"Of course you don't dance; you're too stiff," said Miss Daisy. "I hope you enjoyed your drive with Mrs. Walker!"

"No, I didn't enjoy it; I preferred walking with you."

"We paired off; that was much better," said Daisy. "But did you ever hear anything so cool as Mrs. Walker's wanting me to get into her carriage and drop poor Mr. Giovanelli, and under the pretext that it was proper? People have different ideas! It would have been most unkind; he had been talking about that walk for ten days."

"He should not have talked about it at all," said Winterbourne; "he would never have proposed to a young lady of this country to walk about the streets with him."

"About the streets?" cried Daisy, with her pretty stare. "Where, then, would he have proposed to her to walk? The Pincio is not the streets, either; and I, thank goodness, am not a young lady of this country. The young ladies of this country have a dreadfully poky time of it, so far as I can learn; I don't see why I should change my habits for *them*."

"I am afraid your habits are those of a flirt," said Winterbourne, gravely.

"Of course they are," she cried, giving him her little smiling stare again. "I'm a fearful, frightful flirt! Did you ever hear of a nice girl that was not? But I suppose you will tell me now that I am not a nice girl."

"You're a very nice girl; but I wish you would flirt with me, and me only," said Winterbourne.

"Ah! thank you—thank you very much; you are the last man I should think of flirting with. As I have had the pleasure of informing you, you are too stiff."

"You say that too often," said Winterbourne.

Daisy gave a delighted laugh. "If I could have the sweet hope of making you angry, I should say it again."

"Don't do that; when I am angry I'm stiffer than ever. But if you won't flirt with me, do cease, at least, to flirt with your friend at the piano; they don't understand that sort of thing here."

"I thought they understood nothing else!" exclaimed Daisy.

"Not in young unmarried women."

"It seems to me much more proper in young unmarried women than in old married ones," Daisy declared.

"Well," said Winterbourne, "when you deal with natives you must go by the custom of the place. Flirting is a purely American custom; it doesn't exist here. So when you show yourself in public with Mr. Giovanelli, and without your mother——"

"Gracious! poor mother!" interposed Daisy.

"Though you may be flirting, Mr. Giovanelli is not; he means something else."

"He isn't preaching, at any rate," said Daisy, with vivacity. "And if you want very much to know, we are neither of us flirting; we are too good friends for that; we are very intimate friends."

"Ah!" rejoined Winterbourne, "if you are in love with each other, it is another affair."

She had allowed him up to this point to talk so frankly that he had no expectation of shocking her by this ejaculation; but she immediately got up, blushing visibly, and leaving him to exclaim mentally that little American flirts were the queerest creatures in the world. "Mr. Giovanelli, at least," she said, giving her interlocutor a single glance, "never says such very disagreeable things to me."

Winterbourne was bewildered; he stood staring. Mr. Giovanelli had finished singing. He left the piano and came over to Daisy. "Won't you come into the other room and have some tea?" he asked, bending before her with his ornamental smile.

Daisy turned to Winterbourne, beginning to smile again. He was still more perplexed, for this inconsequent smile made nothing clear, though it seemed to prove, indeed, that she had a sweetness and softness that reverted instinctively to the pardon of offences. "It has never occurred to Mr. Winterbourne to offer me any tea," she said, with her little tormenting manner.

"I have offered you advice," Winterbourne rejoined.

"I prefer weak tea!" cried Daisy, and she went off with the brilliant Giovanelli. She sat with him in the adjoining room, in the embrasure of the window, for the rest of the evening. There was an interesting performance at the piano, but neither of these young people gave heed to it. When Daisy came to take leave of Mrs. Walker, this lady conscientiously repaired the weakness of which she had been guilty at the moment of the young girl's arrival. She turned her back straight upon Miss Miller, and left her to depart with what grace she might. Winterbourne was standing near the door; he saw it all. Daisy turned very pale, and looked at her mother; but Mrs. Miller was humbly unconscious of any violation of the usual social forms. She appeared, indeed, to have felt an incongruous impulse to draw attention to her own striking observance of them. "Goodnight, Mrs. Walker," she said; "we've had a beautiful evening. You see, if I let Daisy come to parties without me, I don't want her to go away without me." Daisy turned away, looking with a pale, grave face at the circle near the door; Winterbourne saw that, for the first moment, she was too much shocked and puzzled even for indignation. He on his side was greatly touched.

"That was very cruel," he said to Mrs. Walker.

"She never enters my drawing-room again!" replied his hostess.

Since Winterbourne was not to meet her in Mrs. Walker's drawing-room, he went as often as possible to Mrs. Miller's hotel. The ladies were rarely at home; but when he found them the devoted Giovanelli was always present. Very often the brilliant little Roman was in the drawing-room with Daisy alone, Mrs. Miller being apparently constantly of the opinion that discretion is the better part of surveillance. Winterbourne noted, at first with surprise, that Daisy on these occasions was never embarrassed or annoyed by his own entrance; but he very presently began to feel that she had no more surprises for him; the unexpected in her behavior was the only thing to expect. She showed no displeasure at her tête-à-tête with Giovanelli being interrupted; she could chatter as freshly and fully with two gentlemen as with one; there was always, in her conversation, the same odd mixture of audacity and puerility. Winterbourne remarked to himself that if she was seriously interested in Giovanelli, it was very singular that she should not take more trouble to preserve the sanctity of their interviews; and he liked her the more for her innocent-looking indifference and her apparently inexhaustible good-humor. He could hardly have said why, but she seemed to him a girl who would never be jealous. At the risk of exciting a somewhat derisive smile on the reader's part, I may affirm that with regard to the women who had hitherto interested him, it very often seemed to Winterbourne among the possibilities that, given certain contingencies, he should be afraid—literally afraid—of these ladies; he had a pleasant sense that he should never be afraid of Daisy Miller. It must be added that this sentiment was not altogether flattering to Daisy; it was part of his conviction, or rather of his apprehension, that she would prove a very light young person.

But she was evidently very much interested in Giovanelli. She looked at him whenever he spoke; she was perpetually telling him to do this and to do that; she was constantly "chaffing" and abusing him. She appeared completely to have forgotten that Winterbourne had said anything to displease her at Mrs. Walker's little party. One Sunday afternoon, having gone to St. Peter's with his aunt, Winterbourne perceived Daisy strolling about the great church in company with the inevitable Giovanelli. Presently he pointed out the young girl and her cavalier to Mrs. Costello. This lady looked at them a moment through her eye-glass, and then she said,

"That's what makes you so pensive in these days, eh?"

"I had not the least idea I was pensive," said the young man.

"You are very much preoccupied; you are thinking of something."

"And what is it," he asked, " that you accuse me of thinking of?"

"Of that young lady's—Miss Baker's, Miss Chandler's—what's her name?—Miss Miller's intrigue with that little barber's block."

"Do you call it an intrigue," Winterbourne asked—"an affair that goes on with such peculiar publicity?"

"That's their folly," said Mrs. Costello; "it's not their merit."

"No," rejoined Winterbourne, with something of that pensiveness to which his aunt had alluded. "I don't believe that there is anything to be called an intrigue."

"I have heard a dozen people speak of it; they say she is quite carried away by him."

"They are certainly very intimate," said Winterbourne.

Mrs. Costello inspected the young couple again with her optical instrument. "He is very handsome. One easily sees how it is. She thinks him the most elegant man in the world—the finest gentleman. She has never seen anything like him; he is better, even, than the courier. It was the courier, problably, who introduced him; and if he succeeds in marrying the young lady, the courier will come in for a magnificent commission."

"I don't believe she thinks of marrying him," said Winterbourne, "and I don't believe he hopes to marry her."

"You may be very sure she thinks of nothing. She goes on from day to day, from hour to hour, as they did in the Golden Age. I can imagine nothing more vulgar. And at the same time," added Mrs. Costello, "depend upon it that she may tell you any moment that she is 'engaged.'"

"I think that is more than Giovanelli expects," said Winterbourne.

"Who is Giovanelli?"

"The little Italian. I have asked questions about him, and learned something. He is apparently a perfectly respectable little man. I believe he is, in a small way, a *cavaliere avvocato*. But he doesn't move in what are called the first circles. I think it is really not absolutely impossible that the courier introduced him. He is evidently immensely charmed with Miss Miller. If she thinks him the finest gentleman in the world, he, on his side, has never found himself in personal contact with such splendor, such opulence, such expensiveness, as this young lady's. And then she must seem to him wonderfully pretty and interesting. I rather doubt that he dreams of marrying her. That must appear to him too impossible a piece of luck. He has nothing but his handsome face to offer, and there is a substantial Mr. Miller in that mysterious land of dollars. Giovanelli knows that he hasn't a title to offer. If he were only a count or a *marchese*! He must wonder at his luck, at the way they have taken him up."

"He accounts for it by his handsome face, and thinks Miss Miller a young lady *qui se passe ses fantaisies*!" said Mrs. Costello.

"It is very true," Winterbourne pursued, "that Daisy and her mamma have not yet risen to that stage of—what shall I call it?—of culture, at which the idea of catching a count or a *marchese* begins. I believe that they are intellectually incapable of that conception."

"Ah! but the *avvocato* can't believe it," said Mrs. Costello.

Of the observation excited by Daisy's "intrigue," Winterbourne gathered that day at St. Peter's sufficient evidence. A dozen of the American colonists in Rome came to talk with Mrs. Costello, who sat on a little portable stool at the base of one of the great pilasters. The vesper service was going forward in splendid chants and organ-tones in the adjacent choir, and meanwhile, between Mrs. Costello and her friends, there was a great deal said about poor little Miss Miller's going really "too far." Winterbourne was not pleased with what he heard; but when, coming out upon the great steps of the church, he saw Daisy, who had emerged before him, get into an open cab with her accomplice and roll away through the cynical streets of Rome, he could not deny to himself that she was going very far indeed. He felt very sorry for her—not exactly that he believed that she had completely lost her head, but because it was painful to hear so much that was pretty and undefended and natural assigned to a vulgar place among the categories of disorder. He made an attempt after this to give a hint to Mrs. Miller. He met one day in the Corso a friend, a tourist like himself, who had just come out of the Doria Palace, where he had been walking through the beautiful gallery. His friend talked for a moment about the superb portrait of Innocent X., by Velasquez, which hangs in one of the cabinets of the palace, and then said, "And in the same cabinet, by-the-way, I had the pleasure of contemplating a picture of a different kind—that pretty American girl whom you pointed out to me last week." In answer to Winterbourne's inquiries, his friend narrated that the pretty American girl—prettier than ever—was seated with a companion in the secluded nook in which the great papal portrait was enshrined.

"Who was her companion?" asked Winterbourne.

"A little Italian with a bouquet in his button-hole. The girl is delightfully pretty; but I thought I understood from you the other day that she was a young lady *du meilleur monde*."

"So she is!" answered Winterbourne; and having assured himself that his informant had seen Daisy and her companion but five minutes before, he jumped into a cab and went to call on Mrs. Miller. She was at home; but she apologized to him for receiving him in Daisy's absence.

"She's gone out somewhere with Mr. Giovanelli," said Mrs. Miller. "She's always going round with Mr. Giovanelli."

"I have noticed that they are very intimate," Winterbourne observed.

"Oh, it seems as if they couldn't live without each other!" said Mrs. Miller. "Well, he's a real gentleman, anyhow. I keep telling Daisy she's engaged!"

"And what does Daisy say?"

"Oh, she says she isn't engaged. But she might as well be!" this impartial parent resumed; "she goes on as if she was. But I've made Mr. Giovanelli promise to tell me, if *she* doesn't. I should want to write to Mr. Miller about it—shouldn't you?"

Winterbourne replied that he certainly should; and the state of mind of Daisy's mamma struck him as so unprecedented in the annals of parental vigilance that he gave up as utterly irrelevant the attempt to place her upon her guard.

After this Daisy was never at home, and Winterbourne ceased to meet her at the houses of their common acquaintances, because, as he perceived, these shrewd people had quite made up their minds that she was going too far. They ceased to invite her; and they intimated that they desired to express to observant Europeans the great truth that, though Miss Daisy Miller was a young American lady, her behavior was not representative—was regarded by her compatriots as abnormal. Winterbourne wondered how she felt about all the cold shoulders that were turned towards her, and sometimes it annoyed him to suspect that she did not feel at all. He said to himself that she was too light and childish, too uncultivated and unreasoning, too provincial, to have reflected upon her ostracism, or even to have perceived it. Then at other moments he believed that she carried about in her elegant and irresponsible little organism a defiant, passionate, perfectly observant consciousness of the impression she produced. He asked himself whether Daisy's defiance came from the consciousness of innocence, or from her being, essentially, a young person of the reckless class. It must be admitted that holding one's self to a belief in Daisy's "innocence" came to seem to Winterbourne more and more a matter of finespun gallantry. As I have already had occasion to relate, he was angry at finding himself reduced to chopping logic about this young lady; he was vexed at his want of instinctive certitude as to how far her eccentricities were generic, national, and how far they were personal. From either view of them he had somehow missed her, and now it was too late. She was "carried away" by Mr. Giovanelli.

A few days after his brief interview with her mother, he encountered her in that beautiful abode of flowering desolation known as the Palace of the Caesars. The early Roman spring had filled the air with bloom and perfume, and the rugged surface of the Palatine was muffled with tender verdure. Daisy was strolling along the top of one of those great mounds of ruin that are embanked with mossy marble and paved with monumental inscriptions. It seemed to him that Rome had never been so lovely as just then. He stood looking off at the enchanting harmony of line and color that remotely encircles the city, inhaling the softly humid odors, and feeling the freshness of the year and the antiquity of the place reaffirm themselves in mysterious interfusion. It seemed to him, also, that Daisy had never looked so pretty; but this had been an observation of his whenever he met her. Giovanelli was at her side, and Giovanelli, too, wore an aspect of even unwonted brilliancy.

"Well," said Daisy, "I should think you would be lonesome!"

"Lonesome?" asked Winterbourne.

"You are always going round by yourself. Can't you get any one to walk with you?"

"I am not so fortunate," said Winterbourne, "as your companion."

Giovanelli, from the first, had treated Winterbourne with distinguished politeness. He listened with a deferential air to his remarks; he laughed punctiliously at his pleasantries; he seemed disposed to testify to his belief that Winterbourne was a superior young man. He carried himself in no degree like a jealous wooer; he had obviously a great deal of tact; he had no objection to your expecting a little humility of him. It even seemed to Winterbourne at times that Giovanelli would find a certain mental relief in being able to have a private understanding with him—to say to him, as an intelligent man, that, bless you, *he* knew how extraordinary was this young lady, and didn't flatter himself with delusive—or, at least, *too* delusive—hopes of matrimony and dollars. On this occasion he strolled away from his companion to pluck a sprig of almond-blossom, which he carefully arranged in his button-hole.

"I know why you say that," said Daisy, watching Giovanelli. "Because you think I go round too much with *him*." And she nodded at her attendant.

"Every one thinks so—if you care to know," said Winterbourne.

"Of course I care to know!" Daisy exclaimed, seriously. "But I don't believe it. They are only pretending to be shocked. They don't really care a straw what I do. Besides, I don't go round so much."

"I think you will find they do care. They will show it disagreeably."

Daisy looked at him a moment. "How disagreeably?"

"Haven't you noticed anything?" Winterbourne asked.

"I have noticed you. But I noticed you were as stiff as an umbrella the first time I saw you."

"You will find I am not so stiff as several others," said Winterbourne, smiling.

"How shall I find it?"

"By going to see the others."

"What will they do to me?"

"They will give you the cold shoulder. Do you know what that means?"

Daisy was looking at him intently; she began to color.

"Do you mean as Mrs. Walker did the other night?"

"Exactly!" said Winterbourne.

She looked away at Giovanelli, who was decorating himself with his almond-blossom. Then, looking back at Winterbourne, "I shouldn't think you would let people be so unkind!" she said.

"How can I help it?" he asked.

"I should think you would say something."

"I did say something;" and he paused a moment. "I say that your mother tells me that she believes you are engaged."

"Well, she does," said Daisy, very simply.

Winterbourne began to laugh. "And does Randolph believe it?" he asked.

"I guess Randolph doesn't believe anything," said Daisy. Randolph's scepticism excited Winterbourne to further hilarity, and he observed that Giovanelli was coming back to them. Daisy, observing it too, addressed herself again to her countryman. "Since you have mentioned it," she said, "I *am* engaged." . . . Winterbourne looked at her; he had stopped laughing. "You don't believe it!" she added.

He was silent a moment; and then, "Yes, I believe it," he said.

"Oh, no, you don't!" she answered. "Well, then—I am not!"

The young girl and her cicerone were on their way to the gate of the enclosure, so that Winterbourne, who had but lately entered, presently took leave of them. A week afterwards he went to dine at a beautiful villa on the Cælian Hill, and, on arriving, dismissed his hired vehicle. The evening was charming, and he promised himself the satisfaction of walking home beneath the Arch of Constantine and past the vaguely-lighted monuments of the Forum. There was a waning moon in the sky, and her radiance was not brilliant, but she was veiled in a thin cloud-curtain which seemed to diffuse and equalize it. When, on his return from the villa (it was eleven o'clock), Winterbourne approached the dusky circle of the Colosseum, it occurred to him, as a lover of the picturesque, that the interior, in the pale moonshine, would be well worth a glance. He turned aside and walked to one of the empty arches, near which, as he observed, an open carriage—one of the little Roman street-cabs—was stationed. Then he passed in, among the cavernous shadows of the great structure, and emerged upon the clear and silent arena. The place had never seemed to him more impressive. One-half of the gigantic circus was in deep shade, the other was sleeping in the luminous dusk. As he stood there he began to murmur Byron's famous lines, out of "Manfred"; but before he had finished his quotation he remembered that if nocturnal meditations in the Colosseum are recommended by the poets, they are deprecated by the doctors. The historic atmosphere was there, certainly; but the historic atmosphere, scientifically considered, was no better than a villainous miasma. Winterbourne walked to the middle of the arena, to take a more general glance, intending thereafter to make a hasty retreat. The great cross in the centre was covered with shadow; it was only as he drew near it that he made it out distinctly. Then he saw that two persons were stationed upon the low steps which formed its base. One of these was a woman, seated; her companion was standing in front of her.

Presently the sound of the woman's voice came to him distinctly in the warm night air. "Well, he looks at us as one of the old lions or tigers may have looked at the Christian martyrs!" These were the words he heard, in the familiar accent of Miss Daisy Miller.

"Let us hope he is not very hungry," responded the ingenious Giovanelli. "He will have to take me first; you will serve for dessert!"

Winterbourne stopped, with a sort of horror, and, it must be added, with a sort of relief. It was as if a sudden illumination had been flashed upon the ambiguity of Daisy's behavior, and the riddle had become easy to read. She was a young lady whom a gentleman need no longer be at pains to respect. He stood there looking at her—looking at her companion, and not reflecting that though he saw them vaguely, he himself must have been more brightly visible. He felt angry with himself that he had bothered so much about the right way of regarding Miss Daisy Miller. Then, as he was going to advance again, he checked himself; not from the fear that he was doing her injustice, but from the sense of the danger of appearing unbecomingly exhilarated by this sudden revulsion from cautious criticism. He turned away towards the entrance of the place, but, as he did so, he heard Daisy speak again.

"Why, it was Mr. Winterbourne! He saw me, and he cuts me!"

What a clever little reprobate she was, and how smartly she played at injured innocence! But he wouldn't cut her. Winterbourne came forward again, and went towards the great cross. Daisy had got up; Giovanelli lifted his hat. Winterbourne had now begun to think simply of the craziness, from a sanitary point of view, of a delicate young girl lounging away the evening in this nest of malaria. What if she *were* a clever little reprobate? that was no reason for her dying of the *perniciosa*. "How long have you been here?" he asked, almost brutally.

Daisy, lovely in the flattering moonlight, looked at him a moment. Then—"All the evening," she answered, gently. . . . "I never saw anything so pretty."

"I am afraid," said Winterbourne, "that you will not think Roman fever very pretty. This is the way people catch it. I wonder," he added, turning to Giovanelli, "that you, a native Roman, should countenance such a terrible indiscretion."

"Ah," said the handsome native, "for myself I am not afraid."

"Neither am I—for you! I am speaking for this young lady."

Giovanelli lifted his well-shaped eyebrows and showed his brilliant teeth. But he took Winterbourne's rebuke with docility. "I told the signorina it was a grave indiscretion; but when was the signorina ever prudent?"

"I never was sick, and I don't mean to be!" the signorina declared. "I don't look like much, but I'm healthy! I was bound to see the Colosseum by moonlight; I shouldn't have wanted to go home without that; and we have had the most beautiful time, haven't we, Mr. Giovanelli? If there has been any danger, Eugenio can give me some pills. He has got some splendid pills."

"I should advise you," said Winterbourne, "to drive home as fast as possible and take one!"

"What you say is very wise," Giovanelli rejoined. "I will go and make sure the carriage is at hand." And he went forward rapidly.

Daisy followed with Winterbourne. He kept looking at her; she seemed not in the least embarrassed. Winterbourne said nothing; Daisy chattered about the beauty of the place. "Well, I *have* seen the Colosseum by moonlight!" she exclaimed. "That's one good thing." Then, noticing Winterbourne's silence, she asked him why he didn't speak. He made no answer; he only began to laugh. They passed under one of the dark archways; Giovanelli was in front with the carriage. Here Daisy stopped a moment, looking at the young American. "*Did* you believe I was engaged the other day?" she asked.

"It doesn't matter what I believed the other day," said Winterbourne, still laughing.

"Well, what do you believe now?"

"I believe that it makes very little difference whether you are engaged or not!"

He felt the young girl's pretty eyes fixed upon him through the thick gloom of the archway; she was apparently going to answer. But Giovanelli hurried her forward. "Quick! quick!" he said; "if we get in by midnight we are quite safe."

Daisy took her seat in the carriage, and the fortunate Italian placed himself beside her. "Don't forget Eugenio's pills!" said Winterbourne, as he lifted his hat.

"I don't care," said Daisy, in a little strange tone, "whether I have Roman fever or not!" Upon this the cab-driver cracked his whip, and they rolled away over the desultory patches of the antique pavement.

Winterbourne, to do him justice, as it were, mentioned to no one that he had encountered Miss Miller, at midnight, in the Colosseum with a gentleman, but, nevertheless, a couple of days later, the fact of her having been there under these circumstances was known to every member of the little American circle, and commented accordingly. Winterbourne reflected that they had of course known it at the hotel, and that, after Daisy's return, there had been an exchange of remarks between the porter and the cab-driver. But the young man was conscious, at the same moment, that it had ceased to be a matter of serious regret to him that the little American flirt should be "talked about" by low-minded menials. These people, a day or two later, had serious information to give: the little American flirt was alarmingly ill. Winterbourne, when the rumor came to him, immediately went to the hotel for more news. He found that two or three charitable friends had preceded him, and that they were being entertained in Mrs. Miller's salon by Randolph.

"It's going round at night," said Randolph—"that's what made her sick. She's always going round at night. I shouldn't think she'd want to, it's so plaguy dark. You can't see anything here at night, except when there's a moon! In America there's always a moon!" Mrs. Miller was invisible; she was now, at least, giving her daughter the advantage of her society. It was evident that Daisy was dangerously ill.

Winterbourne went often to ask for news of her, and once he saw Mrs. Miller, who, though deeply alarmed, was, rather to his surprise, perfectly composed, and, as it appeared, a most efficient and judicious nurse. She talked a good deal about Dr. Davis, but Winterbourne paid her the compliment of saying to himself that she was not, after all, such a monstrous goose. "Daisy spoke of you the other day," she said to him. "Half the time she doesn't know what she's saying, but that time I think she did. She gave me a message. She told me to tell you—she told me to tell you that she never was engaged to that handsome Italian. I am sure I am very glad. Mr. Giovanelli hasn't been near us since she was taken ill. I thought he was so much of a gentleman; but I don't call that very polite! A lady told me that he was afraid I was angry with him for taking Daisy round at night. Well, so I am; but I suppose he knows I'm a lady. I would scorn to scold him. Anyway, she says she's not engaged. I don't know why she wanted you to know; but she said to me three times, 'Mind you tell Mr. Winterbourne.' And then she told me to ask if you remembered the time you went to that castle in Switzerland. But I said I wouldn't give any such messages as that. Only, if she is not engaged, I'm sure I'm glad to know it."

But, as Winterbourne had said, it mattered very little. A week after this the poor girl died; it had been a terrible case of the fever. Daisy's grave was in the little Protestant cemetery, in an angle of the wall of imperial Rome, beneath the cypresses and the thick spring-flowers. Winterbourne stood there beside it, with a number of other mourners—a number larger than the scandal excited by the young lady's career would have led you to expect. Near him stood Giovanelli, who came nearer still before Winterbourne turned away. Giovanelli was very pale: on this occasion he had no flower in his button-hole; he seemed to wish to say something. At last he said, "She was the most beautiful young lady I ever saw, and the most amiable;" and then he added in a moment, "and she was the most innocent."

Winterbourne looked at him, and presently repeated his words, "And the most innocent?"

"The most innocent!"

Winterbourne felt sore and angry. "Why the devil," he asked, "did you take her to that fatal place?"

Mr. Giovanelli's urbanity was apparently imperturbable. He looked on the ground a moment, and then he said, "For myself I had no fear; and she wanted to go."

"That was no reason!" Winterbourne declared.

The subtle Roman again dropped his eyes. "If she had lived, I should have got nothing. She would never have married me, I am sure."

"She would never have married you?"

"For a moment I hoped so. But no, I am sure."

Winterbourne listened to him: he stood staring at the raw protuberance among the April daisies. When he turned away again, Mr. Giovanelli with his light, slow step, had retired.

Winterbourne almost immediately left Rome; but the following summer he again met his aunt, Mrs. Costello, at Vevey. Mrs. Costello was fond of Vevey. In the interval Winterbourne had often thought of Daisy Miller and her mystifying manners. One day he spoke of her to his aunt—said it was on his conscience that he had done her injustice.

"I am sure I don't know," said Mrs. Costello. "How did your injustice affect her?"

"She sent me a message before her death which I didn't understand at the time; but I have understood it since. She would have appreciated one's esteem."

"Is that a modest way," asked Mrs. Costello, "of saying that she would have reciprocated one's affection?"

Winterbourne offered no answer to this question; but he presently said, "You were right in that remark that you made last summer. I was booked to make a mistake. I have lived too long in foreign parts."

Nevertheless, he went back to live at Geneva, whence there continue to come the most contradictory accounts of his motives of sojourn: a report that he is "studying" hard—an intimation that he is much interested in a very clever foreign lady.

An International Episode

An International Episode

BESSIE ALDEN, the heroine of *An International Episode* (1878), is noteworthy as the first of the James girls to turn down the proposal of an old-world aristocrat. She is a more cultivated and socially entrenched figure than Daisy Miller, though quite as ingenuous in her way. Daisy is a small-town, altogether average American girl who cannot even conceive of herself as the bride of a count or a *marchesse*, whereas Bessie seizes upon such a conception only to rise above it. In her character the primal sincerity of her forebears is combined with a Jamesian sensitivity to the "momentos and reverberations of greatness" in the life of ancient aristocracies; and there is scarcely anything more typical or touching in her treatment of her noble suitor than the solemn manner in which she lectures him on his alleged failure to live up to his social position. Her refusal of Lord Lambeth has as little of the accidental or gratuitous about it as Isabel Archer's refusal of Lord Warburton in *The Portrait of a Lady* (1880). In both cases the American heroine's capacity to say no to a "great personage" is to be taken as a leading motive in the drama of transatlantic relations.

On the biographical plane *An International Episode* can be said to reveal something of James's social experience in London.

Bessie Alden, for example, wholly rejects the assumptions of superiority which come to light as soon as her suitor's family become aware of her existence. It is her idea that an American young lady of good standing in her own country is in every way the equal of the "best people" in Europe; and it is chiefly because of her insistence on this principle that she gives up Lord Lambeth. And in this connection it is interesting to cite the evidence of E. S. Nadal, a secretary at the American Embassy in London in the seventies, who relates in his memoirs that James often spoke to him about "the rudeness encountered from some of the London social leaders." In his writings of that period Nadal could see signs that "his personal relations with English society were very much in his mind."—"An American woman, Mrs. Westagate in *An International Episode,* says that an English woman had said to her, 'In one's own class,' meaning the middle class and meaning also that the American woman belonged to that class. The American woman didn't see what right the English woman had to talk to her in that manner. This was a transcript of an incident James related to me one night when we were walking about the London streets. Some lady of the English middle class, whom he had lately visited in the country, had said to him, 'That is true of the aristocracy, but in one's own class it is different,' meaning, said James, 'her class and mine.' Rather than this, he said he preferred to be regarded as a foreigner."*

Bessie Alden's behavior was resented, of course, by British readers, just as Daisy Miller's was resented by American readers. James, however, took it all in with gloating satisfaction, delighted by the contrast, with the "dramas upon dramas . . . and innumerable points of view," thus disclosed. He felt that the reaction of the public justified his faith in the theme of the "international situation." But conscious as he was of his expatriate status, he was disturbed to learn that some people professed to see a breach of manners in his story of "a Bostonian nymph who rejects an English duke"—as an irate London reviewer summed up Bessie Alden's case. Hence even while the story was running serially in *The Cornhill Magazine* he wrote to his mother that he hoped she would not, like many of his friends in England, take it as an offence against his hosts. "It seems to me myself that I have been very

* Quoted by Van Wyck Brooks in *The Pilgrimage of Henry James.*

delicate; but I shall keep off dangerous ground in future. It is an entirely new sensation for them (the people here) to be (at all delicately) ironized or satirized, from the American point of view. . . ."

An International Episode should be read as a companion-piece to *Daisy Miller*. Both stories have a clarity of outline and a lightness and wit of phrasing which James sacrificed in later years for effects of a different sort; and both stories have a charm of time and place that is unforgettable. The Rome frequented by American travelers of the seventies has never been quite so *done* as in *Daisy Miller*. And the description of summertime New York and of Newport as seen through the eyes of Lord Lambeth and his friend Mr. Beaumont is nearly as captivating.

PART I

FOUR YEARS ago, in 1874, two young Englishmen had occasion to go to the United States. They crossed the ocean at midsummer, and, arriving in New York on the first day of August, were much struck with the fervid temperature of that city. Disembarking upon the wharf, they climbed into one of those huge high-hung coaches which convey passengers to the hotels, and, with a great deal of bouncing and bumping, took their course through Broadway. The midsummer aspect of New York is not, perhaps, the most favorable one; still, it is not without its picturesque and even brilliant side. Nothing could well resemble less a typical English street than the interminable avenue, rich in incongruities, through which our two travellers advanced—looking out on each side of them at the comfortable animation of the sidewalks, the high-colored, heterogeneous architecture, the huge, white marble façades glittering in the strong, crude light, and bedizened with gilded lettering, the multifarious awnings, banners, and streamers, the extraordinary number of omnibuses, horse-cars, and other democratic vehicles, the venders of cooling fluids, the white trousers and big straw-hats of the policemen, the tripping gait of the modish young persons on the pavement, the general brightness, newness, juvenility, both of people and things. The young men had exchanged few observations; but in crossing Union Square, in front of the monument to Washington—in the very shadow, indeed, projected by the image of the *pater patriæ*—one of them remarked to the other, "It seems a rum-looking place."

"Ah, very odd, very odd," said the other, who was the clever man of the two.

"Pity it's so beastly hot," resumed the first speaker, after a pause.

"You know we are in a low latitude," said his friend.

"I dare say," remarked the other.

"I wonder," said the second speaker, presently, "if they can give one a bath?"

"I dare say not," rejoined the other.

"Oh, I say!" cried his comrade.

This animated discussion was checked by their arrival at the hotel, which had been recommended to them by an American gentleman whose acquaintance they made—with whom, indeed, they became very intimate—on the steamer, and who had proposed to accompany them to the inn and introduce them, in a friendly way, to the proprietor. This plan, however, had been defeated by their friend's finding that his "partner" was awaiting him on the wharf, and that his commercial associate desired him instantly to come and give his attention to certain telegrams received from St. Louis. But the two Englishmen, with nothing but their national prestige and personal graces to recommend them, were very well received at the hotel, which had an air of capacious hospitality. They found that a bath was not unattainable, and were indeed struck with the facilities for prolonged and reiterated immersion with which their apartment was supplied. After bathing a good deal—more, indeed, than they had ever done before on a single occasion—they made their way into the dining-room of the hotel, which was a spacious restaurant, with a fountain in the middle, a great many tall plants in ornamental tubs, and an array of French waiters. The first dinner on land after a sea-voyage is, under any circumstances, a delightful occasion, and there was something particularly agreeable in the circumstances in which our young Englishmen found themselves. They were extremely good-natured young men; they were more observant than they appeared; in a sort of inarticulate, accidentally dissimulative fashion, they were highly appreciative. This was, perhaps, especially the case with the elder, who was also, as I have said, the man of talent. They sat down at a little table, which was a very different affair from the great clattering see-saw in the saloon of the steamer. The wide doors and windows of the restaurants stood open, beneath large awnings, to a wide pavement, where there were other plants in tubs and rows of spreading trees, and beyond which there was a large, shady square, without any palings, and with marble-paved walks. And above the vivid verdure rose other façades of white marble and of pale chocolate-colored stone, squaring themselves against the deep blue sky. Here, outside, in the light and the shade and the heat, there was a great tinkling of the bells of innumerable street-cars, and a constant strolling and shuffling and rustling of many pedestrians, a large proportion of whom were young women in Pompadour-looking dresses. Within, the place was cool and vaguely lighted, with the plash of water, the odor of flowers, and the flitting of French waiters, as I have said, upon soundless carpets.

"It's rather like Paris, you know," said the younger of our two travellers.

"It's like Paris—only more so," his companion rejoined.

"I suppose it's the French waiters," said the first speaker. "Why don't they have French waiters in London?"

"Fancy a French waiter at a club," said his friend.

The young Englishman stared a little, as if he could not fancy it. "In Paris I'm very apt to dine at a place where there's an English waiter. Don't you know what's-his-name's, close to the thingumbob? They always set an English waiter at me. I suppose they think I can't speak French."

"Well, you can't." And the elder of the young Englishmen unfolded his napkin.

His companion took no notice whatever of this declaration. "I say," he resumed, in a moment, "we must learn to speak American. I suppose we must take lessons."

"I can't understand them," said the clever man.

"What the deuce is *he* saying?" asked his comrade, appealing from the French waiter.

"He is recommending some soft-shell crabs," said the clever man.

And so, in desultory observation of the idiosyncrasies of the new society in which they found themselves, the young Englishmen proceeded to dine—going in largely, as the phrase is, for cooling draughts and dishes, of which their attendant offered them a very long list. After dinner they went out and slowly walked about the neighboring streets. The early dusk of waning summer was coming on, but the heat was still very great. The pavements were hot even to the stout boot soles of the British travellers, and the trees along the curbstone emitted strange exotic odors. The young men wandered through the adjoining square—that queer place without palings, and with marble walks arranged in black and white lozenges. There were a great many benches, crowded with shabby-looking people, and the travellers remarked, very justly, that it was not much like Belgrave Square. On one side was an enormous hotel, lifting up into the hot darkness an immense array of open, brightly lighted windows. At the base of this populous structure was an eternal jangle of horse-cars, and all round it, in the upper dusk, was a sinister hum of mosquitoes. The ground-floor of the hotel seemed to be a huge transparent cage, flinging a wide glare of gas-light into the street, of which it formed a sort of public adjunct, absorbing and emitting the passers-by promiscuously. The young Englishmen went in with every one else, from curiosity, and saw a couple of hundred men sitting on divans along a great marble-paved corridor, with their legs stretched out, together with several dozen more standing in a *queue*, as at the ticket-office of a railway station, before a brilliantly illuminated counter of vast extent. These latter persons, who carried portmanteaus in their hand, had a dejected, exhausted look; their garments were not very fresh, and they seemed to be rendering some mysterious tribute to a magnificent young man with a waxed mustache, and a shirt-front adorned with diamond buttons, who every now and then dropped an absent glance over their multitudinous patience. They were American citizens doing homage to a hotel clerk.

"I'm glad he didn't tell us to go there," said one of our Englishmen, alluding to their friend on the steamer, who had told them so many things. They walked up Fifth Avenue, where, for instance, he had told them that all the first families lived. But the first families were out of town, and our young travellers had only the satisfaction of seeing some of the second—or, perhaps, even the third—

taking the evening air upon balconies and high flights of doorsteps, in the streets which radiate from the more ornamental thoroughfare. They went a little way down one of these side streets, and they saw young ladies in white dresses—charming-looking persons—seated in graceful attitudes on the chocolate-colored steps. In one or two places these young ladies were conversing across the street with other young ladies seated in similar postures and costumes in front of the opposite houses, and in the warm night air their colloquial tones sounded strange in the ears of the young Englishmen. One of our friends, nevertheless—the younger one—intimated that he felt a disposition to interrupt a few of these soft familiarities; but his companion observed, pertinently enough, that he had better be careful. "We must not begin with making mistakes," said his companion.

"But he told us, you know—he told us," urged the young man, alluding again to the friend on the steamer.

"Never mind what he told us!" answered his comrade, who, if he had greater talents, was also apparently more of a moralist.

By bedtime—in their impatience to taste of a terrestrial couch again, our seafarers went to bed early—it was still insufferably hot, and the buzz of the mosquitoes at the open windows might have passed for an audible crepitation of the temperature. "We can't stand this, you know," the young Englishmen said to each other; and they tossed about all night more boisterously than they had tossed upon the Atlantic billows. On the morrow their first thought was that they would re-embark that day for England; and then it occurred to them that they might find an asylum nearer at hand. The cave of Æolus became their ideal of comfort, and they wondered where the Americans went when they wished to cool off. They had not the least idea, and they determined to apply for information to Mr. J. L. Westgate. This was the name inscribed in a bold hand on the back of a letter carefully preserved in the pocket-book of our junior traveller. Beneath the address, in the left-hand corner of the envelope, were the words, "Introducing Lord Lambeth and Percy Beaumont, Esq." The letter had been given to the two Englishmen by a good friend of theirs in London, who had been in America two years previously, and had singled out Mr. J. L. Westgate from the many friends he had left there as the consignee, as it were, of his compatriots. "He is a capital fellow," the Englishman in London had said, "and he has got an awfully pretty wife. He's tremendously hospitable—he will do everything in the world for you; and as he knows every one over there, it is quite needless I should give you any other introduction. He will make you see every one; trust to him for putting you into circulation. He has got a tremendously pretty wife." It was natural that in the hour of tribulation Lord Lambeth and Mr. Percy Beaumont should have bethought themselves of a gentleman whose attractions had been thus vividly depicted—all the more so that he lived in Fifth Avenue, and that Fifth Avenue, as they had ascertained the night before, was contiguous to their hotel. "Ten to one he'll be out of town," said Percy Beaumont; "but we can at least find out where he has gone, and we can immediately start in pursuit. He can't possibly have gone to a hotter place, you know."

"Oh, there's only one hotter place," said Lord Lambeth, "and I hope he hasn't gone there."

They strolled along the shady side of the street to the number indicated upon the precious letter. The house presented an imposing chocolate-colored expanse, relieved by facings and window cornices of florid sculpture, and by a couple of dusty rose-trees which clambered over the balconies and the portico. This last-mentioned feature was approached by a monumental flight of steps.

"Rather better than a London house," said Lord Lambeth, looking down from this altitude, after they had rung the bell.

"It depends upon what London house you mean," replied his companion. "You have a tremendous chance to get wet between the house door and your carriage."

"Well," said Lord Lambeth, glancing at the burning heavens, "I 'guess' it doesn't rain so much here!"

The door was opened by a long negro in a white jacket, who grinned familiarly when Lord Lambeth asked for Mr. Westgate.

"He ain't at home, sah; he's down-town at his o'fice."

"Oh, at his office?" said the visitor. "And when will he be at home?"

"Well, sah, when he goes out dis way in the mo'ning, he ain't liable to come home all day."

This was discouraging; but the address of Mr. Westgate's office was freely imparted by the intelligent black, and was taken down by Percy Beaumont in his pocket-book. The two gentlemen then returned, languidly, to their hotel, and sent for a hackney-coach, and in this commodious vehicle they rolled comfortably down-town. They measured the whole length of Broadway again, and found it a path of fire; and then, deflecting to the left, they were deposited by their conductor before a fresh, light, ornamental structure, ten stories high, in a street crowded with keen-faced, light-limbed young men, who were running about very quickly, and stopping each other eagerly at corners and in doorways. Passing into this brilliant building, they were introduced by one of the keen-faced young men—he was a charming fellow, in wonderful cream-colored garments and a hat with a blue ribbon, who had evidently perceived them to be aliens and helpless—to a very snug hydraulic elevator, in which they took their place with many other persons, and which, shooting upward in its vertical socket, presently projected them into the seventh horizontal compartment of the edifice. Here, after brief delay, they found themselves face to face with the friend of their friend in London. His office was composed of several different rooms, and they waited very silently in one of them after they had sent in their letter and their cards. The letter was not one which it would take Mr. Westgate very long to read, but he came out to speak to them more instantly than they could have expected; he had evidently jumped up from his work. He was a tall, lean personage, and was dressed all in fresh white linen; he had a thin, sharp, familiar face, with an expression that was at one and the same time sociable and business-like, a quick, intelligent eye, and a large brown mustache, which concealed his mouth and made his chin beneath it look small. Lord Lambeth thought he looked tremendously clever.

"How do you do, Lord Lambeth—how do you do, sir?" he said, holding the open letter in his hand. "I'm very glad to see you; I hope you're very well. You had better come in here; I think it's cooler," and he led the way into another room, where there were law-books and papers, and windows wide open beneath striped awning. Just opposite one of the windows, on a line with his eyes, Lord Lambeth observed the weather-vane of a church steeple. The uproar of the street sounded infinitely far below, and Lord Lambeth felt very high in the air. "I say it's cooler," pursued their host, "but everything is relative. How do you stand the heat?"

"I can't say we like it," said Lord Lambeth; "but Beaumont likes it better than I."

"Well, it won't last," Mr. Westgate very cheerfully declared; "nothing unpleasant lasts over here. It was very hot when Captain Littledale was here; he did nothing but drink sherry-cobblers. He expresses some doubt in his letter whether I will remember him—as if I didn't remember making six sherry-cobblers for him one day in about twenty minutes. I hope you left him well, two years having elapsed since then."

"Oh yes, he's all right," said Lord Lambeth.

"I am always very glad to see your countrymen," Mr. Westgate pursued. "I thought it would be time some of you should be coming along. A friend of mine was saying to me only a day or two ago, 'It's time for the watermelons and the Englishmen.'"

"The Englishmen and the watermelons just now are about the same thing," Percy Beaumont said, wiping his dripping forehead.

"Ah, well, we'll put you on ice, as we do the melons. You must go down to Newport."

"We'll go anywhere," said Lord Lambeth.

"Yes, you want to go to Newport; that's what you want to do," Mr. Westgate affirmed. "But let's see—when did you get here?"

"Only yesterday," said Percy Beaumont.

"Ah, yes, by the *Russia*. Where are you staying?"

"At the Hanover, I think they call it."

"Pretty comfortable?" inquired Mr. Westgate.

"It seems a capital place, but I can't say we like the gnats," said Lord Lambeth.

Mr. Westgate stared and laughed. "Oh no, of course you don't like the gnats. We shall expect you to like a good many things over here, but we sha'n't insist upon your liking the gnats; though certainly you'll admit that, as gnats, they are fine, eh? But you oughtn't to remain in the city."

"So we think," said Lord Lambeth. "If you would kindly suggest something——"

"Suggest something, my dear sir?" and Mr. Westgate looked at him, narrowing his eyelids. "Open your mouth and shut your eyes! Leave it to me, and I'll put you through. It's a matter of national pride with me that all Englishmen should have a good time; and as I have had considerable practice, I have learned to minister to their wants. I find they generally want the right thing. So just please to consider yourselves my property; and if any one should try to appropriate you, please to say, 'Hands off; too late for the market.' But let's see," continued the American, in his slow, humorous voice, with a distinctness of utterance which appeared to his visitors to be a part of a humorous intention—a strangely leisurely speculative voice for a man evidently so busy and, as they felt, so professional—"let's see; are you going to make something of a stay, Lord Lambeth?"

"Oh dear no," said the young Englishman; "my cousin was coming over on some business, so I just came across, at an hour's notice, for the lark."

"Is it your first visit to the United States?"

"Oh dear yes."

"I was obliged to come on some business," said Percy Beaumont, "and I brought Lambeth along."

"And *you* have been here before, sir?"

"Never—never."

"I thought, from your referring to business——" said Mr. Westgate.

"Oh, you see I'm by way of being a barrister," Percy Beaumont answered. "I know some people that think of bringing a suit against one of your railways, and they asked me to come over and take measures accordingly."

Mr. Westgate gave one of his slow, keen looks again. "What's your railroad?" he asked.

"The Tennessee Central."

The American tilted back his chair a little, and poised it an instant. "Well, I'm sorry you want to attack one of our institutions," he said, smiling. "But I guess you had better enjoy yourself *first*!"

"I'm certainly rather afraid I can't work in this weather," the young barrister confessed.

"Leave that to the natives," said Mr. Westgate. "Leave the Tennessee Central to me, Mr. Beaumont. Some day we'll talk it over, and I guess I can make it square. But I didn't know you Englishmen ever did any work, in the upper classes."

"Oh, we do a lot of work; don't we, Lambeth?" asked Percy Beaumont.

"I must certainly be at home by the 19th of September," said the younger Englishman, irrelevantly but gently.

"For the shooting, eh? or is it the hunting, or the fishing?" inquired his entertainer.

"Oh, I must be in Scotland," said Lord Lambeth, blushing a little.

"Well, then," rejoined Mr. Westgate, "you had better amuse yourself first, also. You must go down and see Mrs. Westgate."

"We should be so happy, if you would kindly tell us the train," said Percy Beaumont.

"It isn't a train—it's a boat."

"Oh, I see. And what is the name of—a—the—a—town?"

"It isn't a town," said Mr. Westgate, laughing. "It's a—well, what shall I call it? It's a watering-place. In short, it's Newport. You'll see what it is. It's cool; that's the principal thing. You will greatly oblige me by going down there and putting yourself into the hands of Mrs. Westgate. It isn't perhaps for me to say it, but you couldn't be in better hands. Also in those of her sister, who is staying with her. She is very fond of Englishmen. She thinks there is nothing like them."

"Mrs. Westgate or—a—her sister?" asked Percy Beaumont, modestly, yet in the tone of an inquiring traveller.

"Oh, I mean my wife," said Mr. Westgate. "I don't suppose my sister-in-law knows much about them. She has always led a very quiet life; she has lived in Boston."

Percy Beaumont listened with interest. "That, I believe," he said, "is the most—a—intellectual town?"

"I believe it is very intellectual. I don't go there much," responded his host.

"I say, we ought to go there," said Lord Lambeth to his companion.

"Oh, Lord Lambeth, wait till the great heat is over," Mr. Westgate interposed. "Boston in this weather would be very trying; it's not the temperature for intellectual exertion. At Boston, you know, you have to pass an examination at the city limits; and when you come away they give you a kind of degree."

Lord Lambeth stared, blushing a little; and Percy Beaumont stared a little also—but only with his fine natural complexion—glancing aside after a moment to see that his companion was not looking too credulous, for he had heard a great deal of American humor. "I dare say it is very jolly," said the younger gentleman.

"I dare say it is," said Mr. Westgate. "Only I must impress upon you that at present—to-morrow morning, at an early hour—you will be expected at Newport. We have a house there; half the people of New York go there for the summer. I am not sure that at this very moment my wife can take you in; she has got a lot of people staying with her; I don't know who they all are; only she may have no room. But you can begin with the hotel, and meanwhile you can live at my house. In that way—simply sleeping at the hotel—you will find it tolerable. For the rest, you must make yourself at home at my place. You mustn't be shy, you know; if you are only here for a month, that will be a great waste of time. Mrs. Westgate won't neglect you, and you had better not try to resist her. I know something about that. I expect you'll find some pretty girls on the premises. I shall write to my wife by this afternoon's mail, and to-morrow morning she and Miss Alden will look out for you. Just walk right in and make yourself comfortable. Your steamer leaves from this part of the city, and I will immediately send out and get you a cabin. Then, at half-past four o'clock, just call for me here, and I will go with you and put you on board. It's a big boat; you might get lost. A few days hence, at the end of the week, I will come down to Newport, and see how you are getting on."

The two young Englishmen inaugurated the policy of not resisting Mrs. Westgate by submitting, with great docility and thankfulness, to her husband. He was evidently a very good fellow, and he made an impression upon his visitors; his hospitality seemed to recommend itself consciously—with a friendly wink, as it were—as if it hinted, judiciously, that you could not possibly make a better bargain. Lord Lambeth and his cousin left their entertainer to his labors and returned to their hotel, where they spent three or four hours in their respective shower-baths. Percy Beaumont had suggested that they ought to see something of the town; but "Oh, d—n the town!" his noble kinsman had rejoined. They returned to Mr. Westgate's office in a carriage, with their luggage, very punctually; but it must be reluctantly recorded that, this time, he kept them waiting so long that they felt themselves missing the steamer, and were deterred only by an amiable modesty from dispensing with his attendance, and starting on a hasty scramble to the wharf. But when at last he appeared, and the carriage plunged into the purlieus of Broadway, they jolted to such good purpose that they reached the huge white vessel while the bell for departure was still ringing, and the absorption of passengers still active. It was indeed, as Mr. Westgate had said, a big boat, and his leadership in the innumerable and interminable corridors and cabins, with which he seemed perfectly acquainted, and of which any one and every one appeared to have the entrée, was very grateful to the slightly bewildered voyagers. He showed them their state-room—a spacious apartment, embellished with gas-lamps, mirrors *en pied,* and sculptured furniture—and then, long after they had been intimately convinced that the steamer was in motion and launched upon the unknown stream that they were about to navigate, he bade them a sociable farewell.

"Well, good-bye, Lord Lambeth," he said; "good-bye, Mr. Percy Beaumont. I hope you'll have a good time. Just let them do what they want with you. I'll come down by-and-by and look after you."

The young Englishmen emerged from their cabin and amused themselves with wondering about the immense labyrinthine steamer, which struck them as an extraordinary mixture of a ship and a hotel. It was densely crowded with passengers, the larger number of whom appeared to be ladies and very young children; and in the big saloons, ornamented in white and gold, which followed each other in surprising succession, beneath the swinging gas-light, and among the small side passages where the negro domestics of both sexes assembled with an air of philosophic leisure, every one was moving to and fro and exchanging loud and familiar observations. Eventually, at the instance of a discriminating black, our young men went and had some "supper" in a wonderful place arranged like a theatre, where, in a gilded gallery, upon which little boxes appeared to open, a large orchestra was playing operatic selections, and, below, people were handing about bills of fare, as if they had been programmes. All this was sufficiently curious; but the agreeable thing, later, was to sit out on one of the great white decks of the steamer, in the warm, breezy darkness, and, in the vague starlight, to make out the line of low, mysterious coast. The young Englishmen tried American cigars—those of Mr. Westgate—and talked together as they usually talked, with many odd silences, lapses of logic, and incongruities of transition, like people who have grown old together, and learned to supply each other's missing phrases; or, more especially, like people thoroughly conscious of a common point of view, so that a style of conversation superficially lacking in finish might suffice for reference to a fund of associations in the light of which everything was all right.

"We really seem to be going out to sea," Percy Beaumont observed. "Upon my word, we are going back to England. He has shipped us off again. I call that 'real mean.' "

"I suppose it's all right," said Lord Lambeth. "I want to see those pretty girls at Newport. You know he told us the place was an island; and aren't all islands in the sea?"

"Well," resumed the elder traveller after a while, "if his house is as good as his cigars, we shall do very well indeed."

"He seems a very good fellow," said Lord Lambeth, as if this idea just occurred to him.

"I say, we had better remain at the inn," rejoined his companion, presently. "I don't think I like the way he spoke of his house. I don't like stopping in the house with such a tremendous lot of women."

"Oh, I don't mind," said Lord Lambeth. And then they smoked a while in silence. "Fancy his thinking we do no work in England!" the young man resumed.

"I dare say he didn't really think so," said Percy Beaumont.

"Well I guess they don't know much about England over here!" declared Lord Lambeth, humorously. And then there was another long pause. "He was devilish civil," observed the young nobleman.

"Nothing, certainly, could have been more civil," rejoined his companion.

"Littledale said his wife was great fun," said Lord Lambeth.

"Whose wife—Littledale's?"

"This American's—Mrs. Westgate. What's his name? J. L."

Beaumont was silent a moment. "What was fun to Littledale," he said at last, rather sententiously, "may be death to us."

"What do you mean by that?" asked his kinsman. "I am as good a man as Littledale."

"My dear boy, I hope you won't begin to flirt," said Percy Beaumont.

"I don't care. I dare say I sha'n't begin."

"With a married woman, if she's bent upon it, it's all very well," Beaumont expounded. "But our friend mentioned a young lady—a sister, a sister-in-law. For God's sake, don't get entangled with her!"

"How do you mean entangled?"

"Depend upon it she will try to hook you."

"Oh, bother!" said Lord Lambeth.

"American girls are very clever," urged his companion.

"So much the better," the young man declared.

"I fancy they are always up to some game of that sort," Beaumont continued.

"They can't be worse than they are in England," said Lord Lambeth, judicially.

"Ah, but in England," replied Beaumont, "you have got your natural protectors. You have got your mother and sisters."

"My mother and sisters——" began the young nobleman, with a certain energy. But he stopped in time, puffing at his cigar.

"Your mother spoke to me about it, with tears in her eyes," said Percy Beaumont. "She said she felt very nervous. I promised to keep you out of mischief."

"You had better take care of yourself," said the object of maternal and ducal solicitude.

"Ah," rejoined the young barrister, "I haven't the expectation of a hundred thousand a year, not to mention other attractions."

"Well," said Lord Lambeth, "don't cry out before you're hurt!"

It was certainly very much cooler at Newport, where our travellers found themselves assigned to a couple of diminutive bedrooms in a far-away angle of an immense hotel. They had gone ashore in the early summer twilight, and had very promptly put themselves to bed; thanks to which circumstance, and to their having, during the previous hours in their commodious cabin slept the sleep of youth and health, they began to feel, towards eleven o'clock, very alert and inquisitive. They looked out of their windows across a row of small green fields, bordered with low stone walls of rude construction, and saw a deep blue ocean lying beneath a deep blue sky, and flecked now and then with scintillating patches of foam. A strong, fresh breeze came in through the curtainless casements, and prompted our young men to observe generally that it didn't seem half a bad climate. They made other observations after they had emerged from their rooms in pursuit of breakfast—a meal of which they partook in a huge bare hall, where a hundred negroes in white jackets were shuffling about upon an uncarpeted floor; where the flies were superabundant, and the tables and dishes covered over with a strange, voluminous integument of coarse blue gauze; and where several little boys and girls, who had risen late, were seated in fastidious solitude at the morning repast. These young persons had not the morning paper before them, but they were engaged in languid perusal of the bill of fare.

The latter document was a great puzzle to our friends, who, on reflecting that its bewildering categories had relation to breakfast alone, had uneasy prevision of an encyclopædic dinner list. They found a great deal of entertainment at the hotel, an enormous wooden structure, for the erection of which it seemed to them that the virgin forests of the West must have been terribly deflowered. It was perforated from end to end with immense bare corridors, through which a strong draught was blowing—bearing along wonderful figures of ladies in white morning-dresses and clouds of valenciennes lace, who seemed to float down the long vistas with expanded furbelows like angels spreading their wings. In front was a gigantic veranda, upon which an army might have encamped—a vast wooden terrace, with a roof as lofty as the nave of a cathedral. Here our young Englishmen enjoyed, as they supposed, a glimpse of American society, which was distributed over the measureless expanse in a variety of sedentary attitudes, and appeared to consist largely of pretty young girls, dressed as if for a *fête champêtre*, swaying to and fro in rocking chairs, fanning themselves with large straw fans, and enjoying an enviable exemption from social cares. Lord Lambeth had a theory, which it might be interesting to trace to its origin, that it would be not only agreeable, but easily possible, to enter into relations with one of these young ladies; and his companion (as he had done a couple of days before) found occasion to check the young nobleman's colloquial impulses.

"You had better take care," said Percy Beaumont, "or you will have an offended father or brother pulling out a bowie-knife."

"I assure you it is all right," Lord Lambeth replied. "You know the Americans come to these big hotels to make acquaintances."

"I know nothing about it, and neither do you," said his kinsman, who, like a clever man, had begun to perceive that the observation of American society demanded a readjustment of one's standard.

"Hang it, then, let's find out!" cried Lord Lambeth, with some impatience. "You know I don't want to miss anything."

"We will find out," said Percy Beaumont, very reasonably. "We will go and see Mrs. Westgate, and make all the proper inquiries."

And so the two inquiring Englishmen, who had this lady's address inscribed in her husband's hand upon a card, descended from the veranda of the big hotel and took their way, according to direction, along a large, straight road, past a series of fresh-looking villas embosomed in shrubs and flowers, and enclosed in an ingenious variety of wooden palings. The morning was brilliant and cool, the villas were smart and snug, and the walk of the young travellers was very entertaining. Everything looked as if it had received a coat of fresh paint the day before—the red roofs, the green shutters, the clean, bright browns and buffs of the house fronts. The flower beds on the little lawns seemed to sparkle in the radiant air, and the gravel in the short carriage sweeps to flash and twinkle. Along the road came a hundred little basket-phaetons, in which, almost always, a couple of ladies were sitting—ladies in white dresses and long white gloves, holding the reins and looking at the two Englishmen—whose nationality was not elusive—through thick blue veils tied tightly about their faces, as if to guard their complexions. At last the young men came within sight of the sea again, and then, having interrogated a gardener over the paling of a villa, they turned into an open gate. Here they found themselves face to face with the ocean and with a very picturesque structure, resembling a magnified chalet, which was perched upon a green embankment just above it. The house had a veranda of extraordinary width all around it, and a great many doors and windows standing open to the veranda. These various apertures had, in common, such an accessible, hospitable air, such a breezy flutter within of light curtains, such expansive thresholds and reassuring interiors, that our friends hardly knew which was the regular entrance, and, after hesitating a moment, presented themselves at one of the windows. The room within was dark, but in a moment a graceful figure vaguely shaped itself in the rich-looking gloom, and a lady came to meet them. Then they saw that she had been seated at a table writing, and that she had heard them and had got up. She stepped out into the light; she wore a frank, charming smile, with which she held out her hand to Percy Beaumont.

"Oh, you must be Lord Lambeth and Mr. Beaumont," she said. "I have heard from my husband that you would come. I am extremely glad to see you." And she shook hands with each of her visitors. Her visitors were a little shy, but they had very good manners; they responded with smiles and exclamations, and they apologized for not knowing the front door. The lady rejoined, with vivacity, that when she wanted to see people very much she did not insist upon these distinctions, and that Mr. Westgate had written to her of his English friends in terms that made her really anxious. "He said you were so terribly prostrated," said Mrs. Westgate.

"Oh, you mean by the heat?" replied Percy Beaumont. "We were rather knocked up, but we feel wonderfully better. We had such a jolly—a—voyage down here. It's so very good of you to mind."

"Yes, it's so very kind of you," murmured Lord Lambeth.

Mrs. Westgate stood smiling; she was extremely pretty. "Well, I did mind," she said; "and I thought of sending for you this morning to the Ocean House. I am very glad you are better, and I am charmed you have arrived. You must come round to the other side of the piazza." And she led the way, with a light, smooth step, looking back at the young men and smiling.

The other side of the piazza was, as Lord Lambeth presently remarked, a very jolly place. It was of the most liberal proportions, and with its awnings, its fanciful chairs, its cushions and rugs, its view of the ocean, close at hand, tumbling along the base of the low cliffs whose level tops intervened in lawn-like smoothness, it formed a charming complement to the drawing-room. As such it was in course of use at the present moment; it was occupied by a social circle. There were several ladies and two or three gentlemen, to whom Mrs. Westgate proceeded to introduce the distinguished strangers. She mentioned a great many names very freely and distinctly; the young Englishmen, shuffling about and bowing, were rather bewildered. But at last they were provided with chairs—low, wicker chairs, gilded, and tied with a great many ribbons—and one of the ladies (a very young person, with a little snub-nose and several dimples) offered Percy Beaumont a fan. The fan was also adorned with pink love-knots; but Percy Beaumont declined it, although he was very hot. Presently, however, it became cooler; the breeze from the sea was delicious, the view was charming, and the people sitting there looked exceedingly fresh and comfortable. Several of the ladies seemed to be young girls, and the gentlemen were slim, fair youths, such as our friends had seen the day before in

New York. The ladies were working upon bands of tapestry, and one of the young men had an open book in his lap. Beaumont afterwards learned from one of the ladies that this young man had been reading aloud;that he was from Boston, and was very fond of reading aloud. Beaumont said it was a great pity that they had interrupted him; he should like so much (from all he had heard) to hear a Bostonian read. Couldn't the young man be induced to go on?

"Oh no," said his informant, very freely; "he wouldn't be able to get the young ladies to attend to him now."

There was something very friendly, Beaumont perceived, in the attitude of the company; they looked at the young Englishmen with an air of animated sympathy and interest; they smiled, brightly and unanimously, at everything either of the visitors said. Lord Lambeth and his companion felt that they were being made very welcome. Mrs. Westgate seated herself between them, and, talking a great deal to each, they had occasion to observe that she was as pretty as their friend Littledale had promised. She was thirty years old, with the eyes and the smile of a girl of seventeen, and she was extremely light and graceful—elegant, exquisite. Mrs. Westgate was extremely spontaneous. She was very frank and demonstrative, and appeared always—while she looked at you delightedly with her beautiful young eyes—to be making sudden confessions and concessions after momentary hesitations.

"We shall expect to see a great deal of you," she said to Lord Lambeth, with a kind of joyous earnestness. "We are very fond of Englishmen here—that is, there are a great many we have been fond of. After a day or two you must come and stay with us; we hope you will stay a long time. Newport's a very nice place when you come really to know it—when you know plenty of people. Of course you and Mr. Beaumont will have no difficulty about that. Englishmen are very well received here; there are almost always two or three of them about. I think they always like it, and I must say I should think they would. They receive ever so much attention. I must say I think they sometimes get spoiled; but I am sure you and Mr. Beaumont are proof against that.

"My husband tells me you are a friend of Captain Littledale. He was such a charming man: he made himself most agreeable here, and I am sure I wonder he didn't stay. It couldn't have been pleasanter for him in his own country, though, I suppose, it is very pleasant in

England—for English people. I don't know myself; I have been there very little. I have been a great deal abroad, but I am always on the Continent. I must say I am extremely fond of Paris; you know we Americans always are; we go there when we die. Did you ever hear that before? That was said by a great wit—I mean the good Americans; but we are all good; you'll see that for yourself.

"All I know of England is London, and all I know of London is that place on that little corner, you know, where you buy jackets—jackets with that coarse braid and those big buttons. They made very good jackets in London; I will do you the justice to say that. And some people like the hats; but about the hats I was always a heretic; I always got my hats in Paris. You can't wear an English hat—at least, I never could—unless you dress your hair *à l'Anglaise;* and I must say that is a talent I never possessed. In Paris they will make things to suit your peculiarities; but in England I think you like much more to have—how shall I say it?—one thing for everybody. I mean as regards dress. I don't know about other things; but I have always supposed that in other things everything was different. I mean according to the people—according to the classes, and all that. I am afraid you will think that I don't take a very favorable view; but you know you can't take a very favorable view in Dover Street in the month of November. That has always been my fate.

"Do you know Jones's Hotel, in Dover Street? That's all I know of England. Of course every one admits that the English hotels are your weak point. There was always the most frightful fog; I couldn't see to try my things on. When I got over to America—into the light—I usually found they were twice too big. The next time I mean to go in the season; I think I shall go next year. I want very much to take my sister; she has never been to England. I don't know whether you know what I mean by saying that the Englishmen who come here sometimes get spoiled. I mean that they take things as a matter of course—things that are done for them. Now, naturally, they are only a matter of course when the Englishmen are very nice. But, of course, they are almost always very nice. Of course this isn't nearly such an interesting country as England; there are not nearly so many things to see, and we haven't your country life. I have never seen anything of your country life; when I am in Europe I am always on the Continent. But I have heard a great deal about it; I know that when you are among yourselves in the country you have the most beautiful time. Of course we have nothing of that sort; we have nothing on that scale.

"I don't apologize, Lord Lambeth; some Americans are always apologizing; you must have noticed that. We have the reputation of always boasting and bragging and waving the American flag; but I must say that what strikes me is that we are perpetually making excuses and trying to smooth things over. The American flag has quite gone out of fashion; it's very carefully folded up like an old table-cloth. Why should we apologize? The English never apologize—do they? No; I must say I never apologize. You must take us as we come—with all our imperfections on our heads. Of course we haven't your country life, and your old ruins, and your great estates, and your leisure class, and all that. But if we haven't, I should think you might find it a pleasant change—I think any country is pleasant where they have pleasant manners.

"Captain Littledale told me he had never seen such pleasant manners as at Newport, and he had been a great deal in European society. Hadn't he been in the diplomatic service? He told me the dream of his life was to get appointed to a diplomatic post at Washington. But he doesn't seem to have succeeded. I suppose that in England promotion—and all that sort of thing—is fearfully slow. With us, you know, it's a great deal too fast. You see, I admit our drawbacks. But I must confess I think Newport is an ideal place. I don't know anything like it anywhere. Captain Littledale told me he didn't know anything like it anywhere. It's entirely different from most watering-places; it's a most charming life. I must say I think that when one goes to a foreign country one ought to enjoy the differences. Of course there are differences, otherwise what did one come abroad for? Look for your pleasure in the differences, Lord Lambeth; that's the way to do it; and then I am sure you will find American society—at least, Newport society—most charming and interesting. I wish very much my husband were here; but he's dreadfully confined to New York. I suppose you think that is very strange—for a gentleman. But you see we haven't any leisure class."

Mrs. Westgate's discourse, delivered in a soft, sweet voice, flowed on like a miniature torrent, and was interrupted by a hundred little smiles, glances, and gestures, which might have figured the irregularities and obstructions of such a stream. Lord Lambeth listened to her with, it must be confessed, a rather ineffectual attention, although he indulged in a good many little murmurs and ejaculations of assent and deprecation. He had no great faculty for apprehending generalizations. There were some three or four indeed which, in the play of his own intelligence, he had originated, and which had seemed convenient at the moment; but at the present time he could hardly have been said to follow Mrs. Westgate as she darted gracefully about in the sea of speculation. Fortunately, she asked for no special rejoinder, for she looked about at the rest of the company as well, and smiled at Percy Beaumont, on the other side of her, as if he, too, must understand her and agree with her. He was rather more successful than his companion; for besides being, as we know, cleverer, his attention was not vaguely distracted by close scrutiny to a remarkably interesting young girl with dark hair and blue eyes. This was the case with Lord Lambeth, to whom it occurred after a while that the young girl with blue eyes and dark hair was the pretty sister of whom Mrs. Westgate had spoken. She presently turned to him with a remark which established her identity.

"It's a great pity you couldn't have brought my brother-in-law with you. It's a great shame he should be in New York in these days."

"Oh yes! it's so very hot," said Lord Lambeth.

"It must be dreadful," said the young girl.

"I dare say he is very busy," Lord Lambeth observed.

"The gentlemen in America work too much," the young girl went on.

"Oh, do they? I dare say they like it," said her interlocutor.

"I don't like it. One never sees them."

"Don't you, really?" asked Lord Lambeth. "I shouldn't have fancied that."

"Have you come to study American manners?" asked the young girl.

"Oh, I don't know. I just came over for a lark. I haven't got long." Here there was a pause, and Lord Lambeth began again. "But Mr. Westgate will come down here, will he not?"

"I certainly hope he will. He must help to entertain you and Mr. Beaumont."

Lord Lambeth looked at her a little with his handsome brown

eyes. "Do you suppose he would have come down with us if we had urged him?"

Mr. Westgate's sister-in-law was silent a moment, and then, "I dare say he would," she answered.

"Really!" said the young Englishman. "He was immensely civil to Beaumont and me," he added.

"He is a dear, good fellow," the young lady rejoined, "and he is a perfect husband. But all Americans are that," she continued, smiling.

"Really!" Lord Lambeth exclaimed again, and wondered whether all American ladies had such a passion for generalizing as these two.

He sat there a good while: there was a great deal of talk; it was all very friendly and lively and jolly. Every one present, sooner or later, said something to him, and seemed to make a particular point of addressing him by name. Two or three other persons came in, and there was a shifting of seats and changing of places; the gentlemen all entered into intimate conversation with the two Englishmen, made them urgent offers of hospitality, and hoped they might frequently be of service to them. They were afraid Lord Lambeth and Mr. Beaumont were not very comfortable at their hotel; that it was not, as one of them said, "so private as those dear little English inns of yours." This last gentleman went on to say that unfortunately, as yet, perhaps, privacy was not quite so easily obtained in America as might be desired; still, he continued, you could generally get it by paying for it; in fact, you could get everything in America nowadays by paying for it. American life was certainly growing a great deal more private; it was growing very much like England. Everything at Newport, for instance, was thoroughly private; Lord Lambeth would probably be struck with that. It was also represented to the strangers that it mattered very little whether their hotel was agreeable, as every one would want them to make visits; they would stay with other people, and, in any case, they would be a great deal at Mrs. Westgate's. They would find that very charming; it was the pleasantest house in Newport. It was a pity Mr. Westgate was always away; he was a man of the highest ability—very acute, very acute. He worked like a horse, and he left his wife—well, to do about as she liked. He liked her to enjoy herself, and she seemed to know how. She was extremely brilliant, and a splendid talker. Some people preferred her sister; but Miss

Alden was very different; she was in a different style altogether. Some people even thought her prettier, and, certainly, she was not so sharp. She was more in the Boston style; she had lived a great deal in Boston, and she was very highly educated. Boston girls, it was propounded, were more like English young ladies.

Lord Lambeth had presently a chance to test the truth of this proposition, for on the company rising in compliance with a suggestion from their hostess that they should walk down to the rocks and look at the sea, the young Englishman again found himself, as they strolled across the grass, in proximity to Mrs. Westgate's sister. Though she was but a girl of twenty, she appeared to feel the obligation to exert an active hospitality; and this was, perhaps, the more to be noticed as she seemed by nature a reserved and retiring person, and had little of her sister's fraternizing quality. She was, perhaps, rather too thin, and she was a little pale; but as she moved slowly over the grass, with her arms hanging at her sides, looking gravely for a moment at the sea and then brightly, for all her gravity, at him, Lord Lambeth thought her at least as pretty as Mrs. Westgate, and reflected that if this was the Boston style the Boston style was very charming. He thought she looked very clever; he could imagine that she was highly educated; but at the same time she seemed gentle and graceful. For all her cleverness, however, he felt that she had to think a little what to say; she didn't say the first thing that came into her head; he had come from a different part of the world and from a different society, and she was trying to adapt her conversation. The others were scattering themselves near the rocks; Mrs. Westgate had charge of Percy Beaumont.

"Very jolly place, isn't it?" said Lord Lambeth. "It's a very jolly place to sit."

"Very charming," said the young girl. "I often sit here; there are all kinds of cosey corners—as if they had been made on purpose."

"Ah, I suppose you have had some of them made," said the young man.

Miss Alden looked at him a moment. "Oh no, we have had nothing made. It's pure nature."

"I should think you would have a few little benches—rustic seats, and that sort of thing. It might be so jolly to sit here, you know," Lord Lambeth went on.

"I am afraid we haven't so many of those things as you," said the young girl, thoughtfully.

"I dare say you go in for pure nature, as you were saying. Nature over here must be so grand, you know." And Lord Lambeth looked about him.

The little coast-line hereabouts was very pretty, but it was not at all grand, and Miss Alden appeared to rise to a perception of this fact. "I am afraid it seems to you very rough," she said. "It's not like the coast scenery in Kingsley's novels."

"Ah, the novels always overdo it, you know," Lord Lambeth rejoined. "You must not go by the novels."

They were wandering about a little on the rocks, and they stopped and looked down into a narrow chasm where the rising tide made a curious bellowing sound. It was loud enough to prevent their hearing each other, and they stood there for some moments in silence. The young girl looked at her companion, observing him attentively, but covertly, as women, even when very young, know how to do. Lord Lambeth repaid observation; tall, straight, and strong, he was handsome as certain young Englishmen, and certain young Englishmen, almost alone, are handsome, with a perfect finish of feature and a look of intellectual repose and gentle good-temper which seemed somehow to be consequent upon his well-cut nose and chin. And to speak of Lord Lambeth's expression of intellectual repose is not simply a civil way of saying that he looked stupid. He was evidently not a young man of an irritable imagination; he was not, as he would himself have said, tremendously clever; but though there was a kind of appealing dulness in his eye, he looked thoroughly reasonable and competent, and his appearance proclaimed that to be a nobleman, an athlete, and an excellent fellow was a sufficiently brilliant combination of qualities. The young girl beside him, it may be attested without further delay, thought him the handsomest young man she had ever seen; and Bessie Alden's imagination, unlike that of her companion, was irritable. He, however, was also making up his mind that she was uncommonly pretty.

"I dare say it's very gay here—that you have lots of balls and parties," he said; for, if he was not tremendously clever, he rather prided himself on having, with women, a sufficiency of conversation.

"Oh yes, there is a great deal going on," Bessie Alden replied. "There are not so many balls, but there are a good many other things. You will see for yourself; we live rather in the midst of it."

"It's very kind of you to say that. But I thought you Americans were always dancing."

"I suppose we dance a good deal; but I have never seen much of it. We don't do it much, at any rate, in summer. And I am sure," said Bessie Alden, "that we don't have so many balls as you have in England."

"Really!" exclaimed Lord Lambeth. "Ah, in England it all depends, you know."

"You will not think much of our gayeties," said the young girl, looking at him with a little mixture of interrogation and decision which was peculiar to her. The interrogation seemed earnest and the decision seemed arch; but the mixture, at any rate, was charming. "Those things, with us, are much less splendid than in England."

"I fancy that you don't mean that," said Lord Lambeth, laughing.

"I assure you I mean everything I say," the young girl declared. "Certainly, from what I have read about English society, it is very different."

"Ah well, you know," said her companion, "those things are often described by fellows who know nothing about them. You mustn't mind what you read."

"Oh, I *shall* mind what I read!" Bessie Alden rejoined. "When I read Thackeray and George Eliot, how can I help minding them?"

"Ah, well, Thackeray and George Eliot," said the young nobleman; "I haven't read much of them."

"Don't you suppose they know about society?" asked Bessie Alden.

"Oh, I dare say they know; they were so clever. But these fashionable novels," said Lord Lambeth, "they are awful rot, you know."

His companion looked at him a moment with her dark blue eyes, and then she looked down in the chasm where the water was tumbling about. "Do you mean Mrs. Gore, for instance?" she said, presently, raising her eyes.

"I am afraid I haven't read that, either," was the young man's rejoinder, laughing a little and blushing. "I am afraid you'll think I am not very intellectual."

"Reading Mrs. Gore is no proof of intellect. But I like reading everything about English life—even poor books. I am so curious about it."

"Aren't ladies always curious?" asked the young man, jestingly.

But Bessie Alden appeared to desire to answer his question seriously. "I don't think so—I don't think we are enough so—that we care about many things. So it's all the more of a compliment," she added, "that I should want to know so much about England."

The logic here seemed a little close; but Lord Lambeth, made conscious of a compliment, found his natural modesty just at hand. "I am sure you know a great deal more than I do."

"I really think I know a great deal—for a person who has never been there."

"Have you really never been there?" cried Lord Lambeth. "Fancy!"

"Never—except in imagination," said the young girl.

"Fancy!" repeated her companion. "But I dare say you'll go soon, won't you?"

"It's the dream of my life!" said Bessie Alden, smiling.

"But your sister seems to know a tremendous lot about London," Lord Lambeth went on.

The young girl was silent a moment. "My sister and I are two very different persons," she presently said. "She has been a great deal in Europe. She has been in England several times. She has known a great many English people."

"But you must have known some, too," said Lord Lambeth.

"I don't think that I have ever spoken to one before. You are the first Englishman that—to my knowledge—I have ever talked with."

Bessie Alden made this statement with a certain gravity—almost, as it seemed to Lord Lambeth, an impressiveness. Attempts at impressiveness always made him feel awkward, and he now began to laugh and swing his stick. "Ah, you would have been sure to know!" he said. And then he added, after an instant, "I'm sorry I am not a better specimen."

The young girl looked away; but she smiled, laying aside her impressiveness. "You must remember that you are only a beginning," she said. Then she retraced her steps, leading the way back to the lawn, where they saw Mrs. Westgate come towards them with

Percy Beaumont still at her side. "Perhaps I shall go to England next year," Miss Alden continued; "I want to, immensely. My sister is going to Europe, and she has asked me to go with her. If we go, I shall make her stay as long as possible in London."

"Ah, you must come in July," said Lord Lambeth. "That's the time when there is most going on."

"I don't think I can wait till July," the young girl rejoined. "By the first of May I shall be very impatient." They had gone farther, and Mrs. Westgate and her companion were near them. "Kitty," said Miss Alden, "I have given out that we are going to London next May. So please to conduct yourself accordingly."

Percy Beaumont wore a somewhat animated—even a slightly irritated—air. He was by no means so handsome a man as his cousin, although in his cousin's absence he might have passed for a striking specimen of the tall, muscular, fair-bearded, clear-eyed Englishman. Just now Beaumont's clear eyes, which were small and of a pale gray color, had a rather troubled light, and, after glancing at Bessie Alden while she spoke, he rested them upon his kinsman. Mrs. Westgate meanwhile, with her superfluously pretty gaze, looked at every one alike.

"You had better wait till the time comes," she said to her sister. "Perhaps next May you won't care so much about London. Mr. Beaumont and I," she went on, smiling at her companion, "have had a tremendous discussion. We don't agree about anything. It's perfectly delightful."

"Oh, I say, Percy!" exclaimed Lord Lambeth.

"I disagree," said Beaumont, stroking down his back hair, "even to the point of not thinking it delightful."

"Oh, I say!" cried Lord Lambeth again.

"I don't see anything delightful in my disagreeing with Mrs. Westgate," said Percy Beaumont.

"Well, I do!" Mrs. Westgate declared; and she turned to her sister. "You know you have to go to town. The phaeton is there. You had better take Lord Lambeth."

At this point Percy Beaumont certainly looked straight at his kinsman; he tried to catch his eye. But Lord Lambeth would not look at him; his own eyes were better occupied. "I shall be very happy," cried Bessie Alden. "I am only going to some shops. But I will drive you about and show you the place."

"An American woman who respects herself," said Mrs. Westgate, turning to Beaumont with her bright expository air, "must buy something every day of her life. If she cannot do it herself, she must send out some member of her family for the purpose. So Bessie goes forth to fulfil my mission."

The young girl had walked away, with Lord Lambeth by her side, to whom she was talking still; and Percy Beaumont watched them as they passed towards the house. "She fulfils her own mission," he presently said; "that of being a very attractive young lady."

"I don't know that I should say very attractive," Mrs. Westgate rejoined. "She is not so much that as she is charming, when you really know her. She is very shy."

"Oh, indeed!" said Percy Beaumont.

"Extremely shy," Mrs. Westgate repeated. "But she is a dear, good girl; she is a charming species of a girl. She is not in the least a flirt; that isn't at all her line; she doesn't know the alphabet of that sort of thing. She is very simple, very serious. She has lived a great deal in Boston, with another sister of mine—the eldest of us—who married a Bostonian. She is very cultivated—not at all like me; I am not in the least cultivated. She has studied immensely and read everything; she is what they call in Boston 'thoughtful.'"

"A rum sort of girl for Lambeth to get hold of!" his lordship's kinsman privately reflected.

"I really believe," Mrs. Westgate continued, "that the most charming girl in the world is a Boston superstructure upon a New York *fonds*; or perhaps a New York superstructure upon a Boston *fonds*. At any rate, it's the mixture," said Mrs. Westgate, who continued to give Percy Beaumont a great deal of information.

Lord Lambeth got into a little basket phaeton with Bessie Alden, and she drove him down the long avenue, whose extent he had measured on foot a couple of hours before, into the ancient town, as it was called in that part of the world, of Newport. The ancient town was a curious affair—a collection of fresh-looking little wooden houses, painted white, scattered over a hill-side and clustered about a long, straight street, paved with enormous cobble-stones. There were plenty of shops, a large proportion of which appeared to be those of fruit venders, with piles of huge water-melons and pumpkins stacked in front of them; and, drawn up before the shops, or bumping about on the cobble-stones, were innumerable other basket-phaetons freighted with ladies of high fashion, who greeted each other from vehicle to vehicle, and conversed on the edge of the pavement in a manner that struck Lord Lambeth as demonstrative, with a great many "Oh, my dears," and little, quick exclamations and caresses. His companion went into seventeen shops—he amused himself with counting them—and accumulated at the bottom of the phaeton a pile of bundles that hardly left the young Englishman a place for his feet. As she had no groom nor footman, he sat in the phaeton to hold the ponies, where, although he was not a particularly acute observer, he saw much to entertain him—especially the ladies just mentioned, who wandered up and down with the appearance of a kind of aimless intentness, as if they were looking for something to buy, and who, tripping in and out of their vehicles, displayed remarkably pretty feet. It all seemed to Lord Lambeth very odd and bright and gay. Of course, before they got back to the villa, he had had a great deal of desultory conversation with Bessie Alden.

The young Englishman spent the whole of that day and the whole of many successive days in what the French call the *intimité* of their new friends. They agreed that it was extremely jolly, that they had never known anything more agreeable. It is not proposed to narrate minutely the incidents of their sojourn on this charming shore; though if it were convenient I might present a record of impressions none the less delectable that they were not exhaustively analyzed. Many of them still linger in the minds of our travellers, attended by a train of harmonious images—images of brilliant mornings on lawns and piazzas that overlooked the sea; of innumerable pretty girls; of infinite lounging and talking and laughing and flirting and lunching and dining; of universal friendliness and frankness; of occasions on which they knew every one and everything, and had an extraordinary sense of ease; of drives and rides in the late afternoon over gleaming beaches, on long sea-roads beneath a sky lighted up by marvellous sunsets; of suppers, on the return, informal, irregular, agreeable; of evenings at open windows or on the perpetual verandas, in the summer starlight, above the warm Atlantic. The young Englishmen were introduced to everybody, entertained by everybody, intimate with everybody. At the end of three days they had removed their luggage from the hotel, and gone to stay with Mrs. Westgate—a step to which Percy Beaumont at first offered some conscientious opposition. I call his opposition conscientious, because it was founded upon some talk that he had had, on the second day, with Bessie Alden. He had indeed had a good deal of talk with her, for she was not literally always in conversation with Lord Lambeth. He had meditated upon Mrs. Westgate's account of her sister, and he discovered for himself that the young lady was clever, and appeared to have read a great deal. She seemed very nice, though he could not make out that, as Mrs. Westgate had said, she was shy. If she was shy, she carried it off very well.

"Mr. Beaumont," she had said, "please tell me something about Lord Lambeth's family. How would you say it in England—his position?"

"His position?" Percy Beaumont repeated.

"His rank, or whatever you call it. Unfortunately, we haven't got a 'peerage,' like the people in Thackeray."

"That's a great pity," said Beaumont. "You would find it all set forth there so much better than I can do it."

"He is a peer, then?"

"Oh yes, he is a peer."

"And has he any other title than Lord Lambeth?"

"His title is the Marquis of Lambeth," said Beaumont; and then he was silent. Bessie Alden appeared to be looking at him with interest. "He is the son of the Duke of Bayswater," he added, presently.

"The eldest son?"

"The only son."

"And are his parents living?"

"Oh yes; if his father were not living he would be a duke."

"So that when his father dies," pursued Bessie Alden, with more simplicity than might have been expected in a clever girl, "he will become Duke of Bayswater?"

"Of course," said Percy Beaumont. "But his father is in excellent health."

"And his mother?"

Beaumont smiled a little. "The duchess is uncommonly robust."

"And has he any sisters?"

"Yes, there are two."

"And what are they called?"

"One of them is married. She is the Countess of Pimlico."

"And the other?"

"The other is unmarried; she is plain Lady Julia."

Bessie Alden looked at him a moment. "Is she very plain?"

Beaumont began to laugh again. "You would not find her so handsome as her brother," he said; and it was after this that he attempted to dissuade the heir of the Duke of Bayswater from accepting Mrs. Westgate's invitation. "Depend upon it," he said, "that girl means to try for you."

"It seems to me you are doing your best to make a fool of me," the modest young nobleman answered.

"She has been asking me," said Beaumont, "all about your people and your possessions."

"I am sure it is very good of her!" Lord Lambeth rejoined.

"Well, then," observed his companion, "if you go, you go with your eyes open."

"D—n my eyes!" exclaimed Lord Lambeth. "If one is to be a dozen times a day at the house, it is a great deal more convenient to sleep there. I am sick of travelling up and down this beastly avenue."

Since he had determined to go, Percy Beaumont would, of course, have been very sorry to allow him to go alone; he was a man of conscience, and he remembered his promise to the duchess. It was obviously the memory of this promise that made him say to his companion a couple of days later that he rather wondered he should be so fond of that girl.

"In the first place, how do you know how fond I am of her?" asked Lord Lambeth. "And, in the second place, why shouldn't I be fond of her?"

"I shouldn't think she would be in your line."

"What do you call my 'line'? You don't set her down as 'fast'?"

"Exactly so. Mrs. Westgate tells me that there is no such thing as the 'fast girl' in America; that it's an English invention, and that the term has no meaning here."

"All the better. It's an animal I detest."

"You prefer a blue-stocking."

"Is that what you call Miss Alden?"

"Her sister tells me," said Percy Beaumont, "that she is tremendously literary."

"I don't know anything about that. She is certainly very clever."

"Well," said Beaumont, "I should have supposed you would have found that sort of thing awfully slow."

"In point of fact," Lord Lambeth rejoined, "I find it uncommonly lively."

After this Percy Beaumont held his tongue; but on August 10th he wrote to the Duchess of Bayswater. He was, as I have said, a man of conscience, and he had a strong, incorruptible sense of the proprieties of life. His kinsman, meanwhile, was having a great deal of talk with Bessie Alden—on the red sea-rocks beyond the lawn; in the course of long island rides, with a slow return in the glowing twilight; on the deep veranda late in the evening. Lord Lambeth, who had stayed at many houses, had never stayed at a house in which it was possible for a young man to converse so frequently with a young lady. This young lady no longer applied to Percy Beaumont for information concerning his lordship. She addressed herself directly to the young nobleman. She asked him a great many questions, some of which bored him a little; for he took no pleasure in talking about himself.

"Lord Lambeth," said Bessie Alden, "are you a hereditary legislator?"

"Oh, I say!" cried Lord Lambeth, "don't make me call myself such names as that."

"But you are a member of Parliament," said the young girl.

"I don't like the sound of that either."

"Don't you sit in the House of Lords?" Bessie Alden went on.

"Very seldom," said Lord Lambeth.

"Is it an important position?" she asked.

"Oh dear no," said Lord Lambeth.

"I should think it would be very grand," said Bessie Alden, "to possess, simply by an accident of birth, the right to make laws for a great nation."

"Ah, but one doesn't make laws. It's a great humbug."

"I don't believe that," the young girl declared. "It must be a great privilege, and I should think that if one thought of it in the right way—from a high point of view—it would be very inspiring."

"The less one thinks of it the better," Lord Lambeth affirmed.

"I think it's tremendous," said Bessie Alden; and on another occasion she asked him if he had any tenantry. Hereupon it was that, as I have said, he was a little bored.

"Do you want to buy up their leases?" he asked.

"Well, have you got any livings?" she demanded.

"Oh, I say!" he cried. "Have you got a clergyman that is looking out?" But she made him tell her that he had a castle; he confessed to but one. It was the place in which he had been born and brought up, and, as he had an old-time liking for it, he was beguiled into describing it a little, and saying it was really very jolly. Bessie Alden listened with great interest, and declared that she would give the world to see such a place. Whereupon—"It would be awfully kind of you to come and stay there," said Lord Lambeth. He took a vague satisfaction in the circumstance that Percy Beaumont had not heard him make the remark I have just recorded.

Mr. Westgate all this time had not, as they said at Newport, "come on." His wife more than once announced that she expected him on the morrow; but on the morrow she wandered about a little, with a telegram in her jewelled fingers, declaring it was very tiresome that his business detained him in New York; that he could only hope the Englishmen were having a good time. "I must say," said Mrs. Westgate, "that it is no thanks to him if you are." And she went on to explain, while she continued that slow-paced promenade which enabled her well-adjusted skirts to display themselves so advantageously, that unfortunately in America there was no leisure class. It was Lord Lambeth's theory, freely propounded when the young men were together, that Percy Beaumont was having a very good time with Mrs. Westgate, and that, under the pretext of meeting for the purpose of animated discussion, they were indulging in practices that imparted a shade of hypocrisy to the lady's regret for her husband's absence.

"I assure you we are always discussing and differing," said Percy Beaumont. "She is awfully argumentative. American ladies certainly don't mind contradicting you. Upon my word, I don't think I was ever treated so by a woman before. She's so devilish positive."

Mrs. Westgate's positive quality, however, evidently had its attractions, for Beaumont was constantly at his hostess's side. He detached himself one day to the extent of going to New York to talk over the Tennessee Central with Mr. Westgate; but he was absent only forty-eight hours, during which, with Mr. Westgate's assistance, he completely settled this piece of business. "They certainly do things quickly in New York," he observed to his cousin; and he added that Mr. Westgate had seemed very uneasy lest his wife should miss her visitor—he had been in such an awful hurry to send him back to her. "I'm afraid you'll never come up to an American husband, if that's what the wives expect," he said to Lord Lambeth.

Mrs. Westgate, however, was not to enjoy much longer the entertainment with which an indulgent husband had desired to keep her provided. On August 21st Lord Lambeth received a telegram from his mother, requesting him to return immediately to England; his father had been taken ill, and it was his filial duty to come to him.

The young Englishman was visibly annoyed. "What the deuce does it mean?" he asked of his kinsman. "What am I to do?"

Percy Beaumont was annoyed as well; he had deemed it his duty, as I have narrated, to write to the duchess, but he had not expected that this distinguished woman would act so promptly upon his hint. "It means," he said, "that your father is laid up. I don't suppose it's anything serious; but you have no option. Take the first steamer; but don't be alarmed."

Lord Lambeth made his farewells; but the few last words that he exchanged with Bessie Alden are the only ones that have a place in our record. "Of course I needn't assure you," he said, "that if you should come to England next year, I expect to be the first person that you inform of it."

Bessie Alden looked at him a little and she smiled. "Oh, if we come to London," she answered, "I should think you would hear of it."

Percy Beaumont returned with his cousin, and his sense of duty compelled him, one windless afternoon, in mid-Atlantic, to say to Lord Lambeth that he suspected that the duchess's telegram was in part the result of something he himself had written to her. "I wrote to her—as I explicitly notified you I had promised to do—that you were extremely interested in a little American girl."

Lord Lambeth was extremely angry, and he indulged for some moments in the simple language of indignation. But I have said that he was a reasonable young man, and I can give no better proof of it than the fact that he remarked to his companion at the end of half an hour, "You were quite right, after all. I am very much interested in her. Only, to be fair," he added, "you should have told my mother also that she is not—seriously—interested in me."

Percy Beaumont gave a little laugh. "There is nothing so charming as modesty in a young man in your position. That speech is a capital proof that you are sweet on her."

"She is not interested—she is not!" Lord Lambeth repeated.

"My dear fellow," said his companion, "you are very far gone."

PART II

In point of fact, as Percy Beaumont would have said, Mrs. Westgate disembarked on May 18th on the British coast. She was accompanied by her sister, but she was not attended by any other member of her family. To the deprivation of her husband's society Mrs. Westgate was, however, habituated; she had made half a dozen journeys to Europe without him, and she now accounted for his absence, to interrogative friends on this side of the Atlantic, by allusion to the regrettable but conspicuous fact that in America there was no leisure class. The two ladies came up to London and alighted at Jones's Hotel, where Mrs. Westgate, who had made on former occasions the most agreeable impression at this establishment, received an obsequious greeting. Bessie Alden had felt much excited about coming to England; she had expected the "associations" would be very charming, that it would be an infinite pleasure to rest her eyes upon the things she had read about in the poets and historians. She was very fond of the poets and historians, of the picturesque, of the past, of retrospect, of mementos and reverberations of greatness; so that on coming into the great English world, where strangeness and familiarity would go hand in hand, she was prepared for a multitude of fresh emotions. They began very promptly—these tender, fluttering sensations; they began with the sight of the beautiful English landscape, whose dark richness was quickened and brightened by the season; with the carpeted fields and flowering hedge-rows, as she looked at them from the window of the train; with the spires of the rural churches peeping above the rook-haunted tree-tops; with the oak-studded parks, the ancient homes, the cloudy light, the speech, the manners, the thousand differences. Mrs. Westgate's impressions had, of course, much less novelty and keenness, and she gave but a wandering attention to her sister's ejaculations and rhapsodies.

"You know my enjoyment of England is not so intellectual as Bessie's," she said to several of her friends in the course of her visit to this country. "And yet if it is not intellectual, I can't say it is physical. I don't think I can quite say what it is—my enjoyment of England." When once it was settled that the two ladies should come abroad and should spend a few weeks in England on their way to the Continent, they of course exchanged a good many illusions to their London acquaintance.

"It will certainly be much nicer having friends there," Bessie Alden had said one day, as she sat on the sunny deck of the steamer at her sister's feet, on a large blue rug.

"Whom do you mean by friends?" Mrs. Westgate asked.

"All those English gentlemen whom you have known and entertained. Captain Littledale, for instance. And Lord Lambeth and Mr. Beaumont," added Bessie Alden.

"Do you expect them to give us a very grand reception?"

Bessie reflected a moment; she was addicted, as we know, to reflection. "Well, yes."

"My poor, sweet child!" murmured her sister.

"What have I said that is so silly?" asked Bessie.

"You are a little too simple; just a little. It is very becoming, but it pleases people at your expense."

"I am certainly too simple to understand you," said Bessie.

"Shall I tell you a story?" asked her sister.

"If you would be so good. That is what they do to amuse simple people."

Mrs. Westgate consulted her memory, while her companion sat

gazing at the shining sea. "Did you ever hear of the Duke of Green-Erin?"

"I think not," said Bessie.

"Well, it's no matter," her sister went on.

"It's a proof of my simplicity."

"My story is meant to illustrate that of some other people," said Mrs. Westgate. "The Duke of Green-Erin is what they call in England a great swell, and some five years ago he came to America. He spent most of his time in New York, and in New York he spent his days and his nights at the Butterworths'. You have heard, at least, of the Butterworths. *Bien.* They did everything in the world for him—they turned themselves inside out. They gave him a dozen dinner-parties and balls, and were the means of his being invited to fifty more. At first he used to come into Mrs. Butterworth's box at the opera in a tweed travelling suit; but some one stopped that. At any rate, he had a beautiful time, and they parted the best of friends in the world. Two years elapse, and the Butterworths come abroad and go to London. The first thing they see in all the papers—in England those things are in the most prominent place—is that the Duke of Green-Erin has arrived in town for the season. They wait a little, and then Mr. Butterworth—as polite as ever—goes and leaves a card. They wait a little more; the visit is not returned; they wait three weeks—*silence de mort*—the duke gives no sign. The Butterworths see a lot of other people, put down the Duke of Green-Erin as a rude, ungrateful man, and forget all about him. One fine day they go to the Ascot races, and there they meet him face to face. He stares a moment, and then comes up to Mr. Butterworth, taking something from his pocket-book—something which proves to be bank-note. 'I'm glad to see you, Mr. Butterworth,' he says, 'so that I can pay you that £10 I lost to you in New York. I saw the other day you remembered our bet; here are the £10, Mr. Butterworth. Good-bye, Mr. Butterworth.' And off he goes, and that's the last they see of the Duke of Green-Erin."

"Is that your story?" asked Bessie Alden.

"Don't you think it's interesting?" her sister replied.

"I don't believe it."

"Ah," cried Mrs. Westgate, "you are not so simple, after all! Believe it or not, as you please; there is no smoke without fire."

"Is that the way," asked Bessie, after a moment, "that you expect your friends to treat you?"

"I defy them to treat me very ill, because I shall not give them the opportunity. With the best will in the world, in that case they can't be very offensive."

Bessie Alden was silent a moment. "I don't see what makes you talk that way," she said. "The English are a great people."

"Exactly; and that is just the way they have grown great—by dropping you when you have ceased to be useful. People say they are not clever; but I think they are very clever."

"You know you have liked them—all the Englishmen you have seen," said Bessie.

"They have liked me," her sister rejoined; "it would be more correct to say that. And, of course, one likes that."

Bessie Alden resumed for some moments her studies in sea-green. "Well," she said, "whether they like me or not, I mean to like them. And, happily," she added, "Lord Lambeth does not owe me £10."

During the first few days after their arrival at Jones's Hotel our charming Americans were much occupied with what they would have called looking about them. They found occasion to make a large number of purchases, and their opportunities for conversation were such only as were offered by the deferential London shopmen. Bessie Alden, even in driving from the station, took an immense fancy to the British metropolis, and at the risk of exhibiting her as a young woman of vulgar tastes, it must be recorded that for a considerable period she desired no higher pleasure than to drive about the crowded streets in a hansom cab. To her attentive eyes they were full of a strange, picturesque life, and it is at least beneath the dignity of our historic muse to enumerate the trivial objects and incidents which this simple young lady from Boston found so entertaining. It may be freely mentioned, however, that whenever, after a round of visits in Bond Street and Regent Street, she was about to return with her sister to Jones's Hotel, she made an earnest request that they should be driven home by way of Westminster Abbey. She had begun by asking whether it would not be possible to take in the Tower on the way to their lodgings; but it happened that at a more primitive stage of her culture Mrs. Westgate had paid a visit to this venerable monument, which she spoke of ever afterwards vaguely as a dreadful disappointment; so that she expressed the liveliest disapproval of any attempt to combine historical researches with the purchase of hair-brushes and note-paper. The most she would consent to do in this line was to spend half an hour at Madame Tussaud's, where she saw several dusty wax effigies of members of the royal family. She told Bessie that if she wished to go to the Tower she must get some one else to take her. Bessie expressed hereupon an earnest disposition to go alone; but upon this proposal as well, Mrs. Westgate sprinkled cold water.

"Remember," she said, "that you are not in your innocent little Boston. It is not a question of walking up and down Beacon Street." Then she went on to explain that there were two classes of American girls in Europe—those that walked about alone and those that did not. "You happen to belong, my dear," she said to her sister, "to the class that does not."

"It is only," answered Bessie, laughing, "because you happen to prevent me." And she devoted much private meditation to this question of effecting a visit to the Tower of London.

Suddenly it seemed as if the problem might be solved; the two ladies at Jones's Hotel received a visit from Willie Woodley. Such was the social appellation of a young American who had sailed from New York a few days after their own departure, and who, having the privilege of intimacy with them in that city, had lost no time, on his arrival in London, in coming to pay them his respects. He had, in fact, gone to see them directly after going to see his tailor, than which there can be no greater exhibition of promptitude on the part of a young American who had just alighted at the Charing Cross Hotel. He was a slim, pale youth, of the most amiable disposition, famous for the skill with which he led the "German" in New York. Indeed, by the young ladies who habitually figured in this Terpsichorean revel he was believed to be "the best dancer in the world"; it was in these terms that he was always spoken of, and that his identity was indicated. He was the gentlest, softest young man it was possible to meet; he was beautifully dressed—"in the English style"—and he knew an immense deal about London. He had been at Newport during the previous summer, at the time of our young Englishmen's visit, and he took extreme pleasure in the society of Bessie Alden, whom he always addressed as "Miss Bessie." She immediately arranged with him, in the presence of her sister, that he should conduct her to the scene of Anne Boleyn's execution.

"You may do as you please," said Mrs. Westgate. "Only—if you desire the information—it is not the custom here for young ladies to knock about London with young men."

"Miss Bessie has waltzed with me so often," observed Willie Woodley; "she can surely go out with me in a hansom!"

"I consider waltzing," said Mrs. Westgate, "the most innocent pleasure of our time."

"It's a compliment to our time!" exclaimed the young man, with a little laugh in spite of himself.

"I don't see why I should regard what is done here," said Bessie Alden. "Why should I suffer the restrictions of a society of which I enjoy none of the privileges?"

"That's very good—very good," murmured Willie Woodley.

"Oh, go to the Tower, and feel the axe, if you like," said Mrs. Westgate. "I consent to your going with Mr. Woodley; but I should not let you go with an Englishman."

"Miss Bessie wouldn't care to go with an Englishman!" Mr. Woodley declared, with a faint asperity that was, perhaps, not unnatural in a young man, who, dressing in the manner that I have indicated, and knowing a great deal, as I have said, about London, saw no reason for drawing these sharp distinctions. He agreed upon a day with Miss Bessie—a day of that same week.

An ingenious mind might, perhaps, trace a connection between the young girl's allusion to her destitution of social privileges and a question she asked on the morrow, as she sat with her sister at lunch.

"Don't you mean to write to—to any one?" said Bessie.

"I wrote this morning to Captain Littledale," Mrs. Westgate replied.

"But Mr. Woodley said that Captain Littledale had gone to India."

"He said he thought he had heard so; he knew nothing about it."

For a moment Bessie Alden said nothing more; then, at last, "And don't you intend to write to—to Mr. Beaumont?" she inquired.

"You mean to Lord Lambeth," said her sister.

"I said Mr. Beaumont, because he was so good a friend of yours."

Mrs. Westgate looked at the young girl with sisterly candor. "I don't care two straws for Mr. Beaumont."

"You were certainly very nice to him."

"I am nice to every one," said Mrs. Westgate, simply.

"To every one but me," rejoined Bessie, smiling.

Her sister continued to look at her; then, at last, "Are you in love with Lord Lambeth?" she asked.

The young girl stared a moment, and the question was apparently too humorous even to make her blush. "Not that I know of," she answered.

"Because, if you are," Mrs. Westgate went on, "I shall certainly not send for him."

"That proves what I said," declared Bessie, smiling—"that you are not nice to me."

"It would be a poor service, my dear child," said her sister.

"In what sense? There is nothing against Lord Lambeth that I know of."

Mrs. Westgate was silent a moment. "You *are* in love with him, then?"

Bessie stared again; but this time she blushed a little. "Ah! if you won't be serious," she answered, "we will not mention him again."

For some moments Lord Lambeth was not mentioned again, and it was Mrs. Westgate who, at the end of this period, reverted to him. "Of course I will let him know we are here, because I think he would be hurt—justly enough—if we should go away without seeing him. It is fair to give him a chance to come and thank me for the kindness we showed him. But I don't want to seem eager."

"Neither do I," said Bessie, with a little laugh.

"Though I confess," added her sister, "that I am curious to see how he will behave."

"He behaved very well at Newport."

"Newport is not London. At Newport he could do as he liked; but here it is another affair. He has to have an eye to consequences."

"If he had more freedom, then, at Newport," argued Bessie, "it is the more to his credit that he behaved well; and if he has to be so careful here, it is possible he will behave even better."

"Better—better," repeated her sister. "My dear child, what is your point of view?"

"How do you mean—my point of view?"

"Don't you care for Lord Lambeth—a little?"

This time Bessie Alden was displeased; she slowly got up from the table, turning her face away from her sister. "You will oblige me by not talking so," she said.

Mrs. Westgate sat watching her for some moments as she moved slowly about the room and went and stood at the window. "I will write to him this afternoon," she said at last.

"Do as you please!" Bessie answered; and presently she turned round. "I am not afraid to say that I like Lord Lambeth. I like him very much."

"He is not clever," Mrs. Westgate declared.

"Well, there have been clever people whom I have disliked," said Bessie Alden; "so that I suppose I may like a stupid one. Besides, Lord Lambeth is not stupid."

"Not so stupid as he looks!" exclaimed her sister, smiling.

"If I were in love with Lord Lambeth, as you said just now, it would be bad policy on your part to abuse him."

"My dear child, don't give me lessons in policy!" cried Mrs. Westgate. "The policy I mean to follow is very deep."

The young girl began to walk about the room again; then she stopped before her sister. "I have never heard in the course of five minutes," she said, "so many hints and innuendoes. I wish you would tell me in plain English what you mean."

"I mean that you may be much annoyed."

"That is still only a hint," said Bessie.

Her sister looked at her, hesitating an instant. "It will be said of you that you have come after Lord Lambeth—that you followed him."

Bessie Alden threw back her pretty head like a startled hind, and a look flashed into her face that made Mrs. Westgate rise from her chair. "Who says such things as that?" she demanded.

"People here."

"I don't believe it," said Bessie.

"You have a very convenient faculty of doubt. But my policy will be, as I say, very deep. I shall leave you to find out this kind of thing for yourself."

Bessie fixed her eyes upon her sister, and Mrs. Westgate thought for a moment there were tears in them. "Do they talk that way here?" she asked.

"You will see. I shall leave you alone."

"Don't leave me alone," said Bessie Alden. "Take me away."

"No; I want to see what you make of it," her sister continued.

"I don't understand."

"You will understand after Lord Lambeth has come," said Mrs. Westgate, with a little laugh.

The two ladies had arranged that on this afternoon Willie Woodley should go with them to Hyde Park, where Bessie Alden expected to derive much entertainment from sitting on a little green chair, under the great trees, beside Rotten Row. The want of a suitable escort had hitherto rendered this pleasure inaccessible; but no escort now, for such an expedition, could have been more suitable than their devoted young countryman, whose mission in life, it might almost be said, was to find chairs for ladies, and who appeared on the stroke of half past five with a white camellia in his button-hole.

"I have written to Lord Lambeth, my dear," said Mrs. Westgate to her sister, on coming into the room where Bessie Alden, drawing on her long gray gloves, was entertaining their visitor.

Bessie said nothing, but Willie Woodley exclaimed that his lordship was in town; he had seen his name in the *Morning Post*.

"Do you read the *Morning Post?*" asked Mrs. Westgate.

"Oh yes; it's great fun," Willie Woodley affirmed.

"I want so to see it," said Bessie; "there is so much about it in Thackeray."

"I will send it to you every morning," said Willie Woodley.

He found them what Bessie Alden thought excellent places, under the great trees, beside the famous avenue whose humors had been made familiar to the young girl's childhood by the pictures in *Punch*. The day was bright and warm, and the crowd of riders and spectators, and the great procession of carriages, were proportionately dense and brilliant. The scene bore the stamp of the London Season at its height, and Bessie Alden found more entertainment in it than she was able to express to her companions. She sat silent, under her parasol, and her imagination, according to its wont, let itself loose into the great changing assemblage of striking and suggestive figures. They stirred up a host of old impressions and preconceptions, and she found herself fitting a history to this person and a theory to that, and making a place for them all in her little private museum of types. But if she said little, her sister on one side and Willie Woodley on the other expressed themselves in lively alternation.

"Look at that green dress with blue flounces," said Mrs. Westgate. "*Quelle toilette!*"

"That's the Marquis of Blackborough," said the young man—"the one in the white coat. I heard him speak the other night in the House of Lords; it was something about ramrods; he called them *wamwods*. He's an awful swell."

"Did you ever see anything like the way they are pinned back?" Mrs. Westgate resumed. "They never know where to stop."

"They do nothing but stop," said Willie Woodley. "It prevents them from walking. Here comes a great celebrity, Lady Beatrice Bellevue. She's awfully fast; see what little steps she takes."

"Well, my dear," Mrs. Westgate pursued, "I hope you are getting some ideas for your *couturière?*"

"I am getting plenty of ideas," said Bessie, "but I don't know that my *couturière* would appreciate them."

Willie Woodley presently perceived a friend on horseback, who drove up beside the barrier of the Row and beckoned to him. He went forward, and the crowd of pedestrians closed about him, so that for some ten minutes he was hidden from sight. At last he reappeared, bringing a gentleman with him—a gentleman whom Bessie at first supposed to be his friend dismounted. But at a second glance she found herself looking at Lord Lambeth, who was shaking hands with her sister.

"I found him over there," said Willie Woodley, "and I told him you were here."

And then Lord Lambeth, touching his hat a little, shook hands with Bessie. "Fancy your being here!" he said. He was blushing and smiling; he looked very handsome, and he had a kind of splendor that he had not had in America. Bessie Alden's imagination, as we know, was just then in exercise; so that the tall young Englishman, as he stood there looking down at her, had the benefit of it. "He is handsomer and more splendid than anything I have ever seen," she said to herself. And then she remembered that he was a marquis, and she thought he looked like a marquis.

"I say, you know," he cried, "you ought to have let a man know you were here!"

"I wrote to you an hour ago," said Mrs. Westgate.

"Doesn't all the world know it?" asked Bessie, smiling.

"I assure you I didn't know it!" cried Lord Lambeth. "Upon my honor, I hadn't heard of it. Ask Woodley, now; had I, Woodley?"

"Well, I think you are rather a humbug," said Willie Woodley.

"You don't believe that—do you, Miss Alden?" asked his lordship. "You don't believe I'm a humbug, eh?"

"No," said Bessie, "I don't."

"You are too tall to stand up, Lord Lambeth," Mrs. Westgate observed. "You are only tolerable when you sit down. Be so good as to get a chair."

He found a chair and placed it sidewise, close to the two ladies. "If I hadn't met Woodley I should never have found you," he went on. "Should I, Woodley?"

"Well, I guess not," said the young American.

"Not even with my letter?" asked Mrs. Westgate.

"Ah, well, I haven't got your letter yet; I suppose I shall get it this evening. It was awfully kind of you to write."

"So I said to Bessie," observed Mrs. Westgate.

"Did she say so, Miss Alden?" Lord Lambeth inquired. "I dare say you have been here a month."

"We have been here three," said Mrs. Westgate.

"Have you been here three months?" the young man asked again of Bessie.

"It seems a long time," Bessie answered.

"I say, after that you had better not call me a humbug!" cried Lord Lambeth. "I have only been in town three weeks; but you must have been hiding away; I haven't seen you anywhere."

"Where should you have seen us—where should we have gone?" asked Mrs. Westgate.

"You should have gone to Hurlingham," said Woodley.

"No; let Lord Lambeth tell us," Mrs. Westgate insisted.

"There are plenty of places to go to," said Lord Lambeth; "each one stupider than the other. I mean people's houses; they send you cards."

"No one has sent us cards," said Bessie.

"We are very quiet," her sister declared. "We are here as travellers."

"We have been to Madame Tussaud's," Bessie pursued.

"Oh, I say!" cried Lord Lambeth.

"We thought we should find your image there," said Mrs. Westgate—"yours and Mr. Beaumont's."

"In the Chamber of Horrors?" laughed the young man.

"It did duty very well for a party," said Mrs. Westgate. "All the women were *décolletées*, and many of the figures looked as if they could speak if they tried."

"Upon my word," Lord Lambeth rejoined, "you see people at London parties that look as if they couldn't speak if they tried."

"Do you think Mr. Woodley could find us Mr. Beaumont?" asked Mrs. Westgate.

Lord Lambeth stared and looked round him. "I dare say he could. Beaumont often comes here. Don't you think you could find him, Woodley? Make a dive into the crowd."

"Thank you; I have had enough diving," said Willie Woodley. "I will wait till Mr. Beaumont comes to the surface."

"I will bring him to see you," said Lord Lambeth; "where are you staying?"

"You will find the address in my letter—Jones's Hotel."

"Oh, one of those places just out of Piccadilly? Beastly hole, isn't it?" Lord Lambeth inquired.

"I believe it's the best hotel in London," said Mrs. Westgate.

"But they give you awful rubbish to eat, don't they?" his lordship went on.

"Yes," said Mrs. Westgate.

"I always feel so sorry for the people that come up to town and go to live in those places," continued the young man. "They eat nothing but filth."

"Oh, I say!" cried Willie Woodley.

"Well, how do you like London, Miss Alden?" Lord Lambeth asked, unperturbed by this ejaculation.

"I think it's grand," said Bessie Alden.

"My sister likes it, in spite of the 'filth!' " Mrs. Westgate exclaimed.

"I hope you are going to stay a long time."

"As long as I can," said Bessie.

"And where is Mr. Westgate?" asked Lord Lambeth of this gentleman's wife.

"He's where he always is—in that tiresome New York."

"He must be tremendously clever," said the young man.

"I suppose he is," said Mrs. Westgate.

Lord Lambeth sat for nearly an hour with his American friends; but it is not our purpose to relate their conversation in full. He addressed a great many remarks to Bessie Alden, and finally turned towards her altogether, while Willie Woodley entertained Mrs. Westgate. Bessie herself said very little; she was on her guard, thinking of what her sister had said to her at lunch. Little by little, however, she interested herself in Lord Lambeth again, as she had done at Newport; only it seemed to her that here he might become more interesting. He would be an unconscious part of the antiquity, the impressiveness, the picturesqueness, of England; and poor Bessie Alden, like many a Yankee maiden, was terribly at the mercy of picturesqueness.

"I have often wished I were at Newport again," said the young man. "Those days I spent at your sister's were awfully jolly."

"We enjoyed them very much; I hope your father is better."

"Oh dear, yes. When I got to England he was out grouse-shooting. It was what you call in America a gigantic fraud. My mother had got nervous. My three weeks at Newport seemed like a happy dream."

"America certainly is very different from England," said Bessie.

"I hope you like England better, eh?" Lord Lambeth rejoined, almost persuasively.

"No Englishman can ask that seriously of a person of another country."

Her companion looked at her for a moment. "You mean it's a matter of course?"

"If I were English," said Bessie, "it would certainly seem to me a matter of course that every one should be a good patriot."

"Oh dear, yes, patriotism is everything," said Lord Lambeth, not quite following, but very contented. "Now, what are you going to do here?"

"On Thursday I am going to the Tower."

"The Tower?"

"The Tower of London. Did you never hear of it?"

"Oh yes, I have been there," said Lord Lambeth. "I was taken there by my governess when I was six years old. It's a rum idea, your going there."

"Do give me a few more rum ideas," said Bessie. "I want to see everything of that sort. I am going to Hampton Court, and to Windsor, and to the Dulwich Gallery."

Lord Lambeth seemed greatly amused. "I wonder you don't go to the Rosherville Gardens."

"Are they interesting?" asked Bessie.

"Oh, wonderful!"

"Are they very old? That's all I care for," said Bessie.

"They are tremendously old; they are falling to ruins."

"I think there is nothing so charming as an old ruinous garden," said the young girl. "We must certainly go there."

Lord Lambeth broke into merriment. "I say, Woodley," he cried, "here's Miss Alden wants to go to the Rosherville Gardens!"

Willie Woodley looked a little blank; he was caught in the fact of ignorance of an apparently conspicuous feature of London life. But in a moment he turned it off. "Very well," he said, "I'll write for a permit."

Lord Lambeth's exhilaration increased. "Gad, I believe you Americans would go anywhere!" he cried.

"We wish to go to Parliament," said Bessie. "That's one of the first things."

"Oh, it would bore you to death!" cried the young man.

"We wish to hear you speak."

"I never speak—except to young ladies," said Lord Lambeth, smiling.

Bessie Alden looked at him a while, smiling, too, in the shadow of her parasol. "You are very strange," she murmured. "I don't think I approve of you."

"Ah, now, don't be severe, Miss Alden," said Lord Lambeth, smiling still more. "Please don't be severe. I want you to like me—awfully."

"To like you awfully? You must not laugh at me, then, when I make mistakes. I consider it my right, as a free-born American, to make as many mistakes as I choose."

"Upon my word I didn't laugh at you," said Lord Lambeth.

"And not only that," Bessie went on; "but I hold that all my mistakes shall be set down to my credit. You must think the better of me for them."

"I can't think better of you than I do," the young man declared.

Bessie Alden looked at him a moment. "You certainly speak very well to young ladies. But why don't you address the House?—isn't that what they call it?"

"Because I have nothing to say," said Lord Lambeth.

"Haven't you a great position?" asked Bessie Alden.

He looked a moment at the back of his glove. "I'll set that down," he said, "as one of your mistakes to your credit." And as if he disliked talking about his position, he changed the subject. "I wish you would let me go with you to the Tower, and to Hampton Court, and to all those other places."

"We shall be most happy," said Bessie.

"And of course I shall be delighted to show you the House of Lords—some day that suits you. There are a lot of things I want to do for you. I want to make you have a good time. And I should like very much to present some of my friends to you, if it wouldn't bore you. Then it would be awfully kind of you to come down to Branches."

"We are much obliged to you, Lord Lambeth," said Bessie. "What is Branches?"

"It's a house in the country. I think you might like it."

Willie Woodley and Mrs. Westgate at this moment were sitting in silence, and the young man's ear caught these last words of Lord Lambeth's. "He's inviting Miss Bessie to one of his castles," he murmured to his companion.

Mrs. Westgate, foreseeing what she mentally called "complications," immediately got up; and the two ladies, taking leave of Lord Lambeth, returned, under Mr. Woodley's conduct, to Jones's Hotel.

Lord Lambeth came to see them on the morrow, bringing Percy Beaumont with him—the latter having instantly declared his intention of neglecting none of the usual offices of civility. This declaration, however, when his kinsman informed him of the advent of their American friends, had been preceded by another remark.

"Here they are, then, and you are in for it."

"What am I in for?" demanded Lord Lambeth.

"I will let your mother give it a name. With all respect to

whom," added Percy Beaumont, "I must decline on this occasion to do any more police duty. Her Grace must look after you herself."

"I will give her a chance," said her Grace's son, a trifle grimly. "I shall make her go and see them."

"She won't do it, my boy."

"We'll see if she doesn't," said Lord Lambeth.

But if Percy Beaumont took a sombre view of the arrival of the two ladies at Jones's Hotel, he was sufficiently a man of the world to offer them a smiling countenance. He fell into animated conversation—conversation, at least, that was animated on her side—with Mrs. Westgate, while his companion made himself agreeable to the young lady. Mrs. Westgate began confessing and protesting, declaring and expounding.

"I must say London is a great deal brighter and prettier just now than when I was here last—in the month of November. There is evidently a great deal going on, and you seem to have a good many flowers. I have no doubt it is very charming for all you people, and that you amuse yourselves immensely. It is very good of you to let Bessie and me come and sit and look at you. I suppose you think I am satirical, but I must confess that that's the feeling I have in London."

"I am afraid I don't quite understand to what feeling you allude," said Percy Beaumont.

"The feeling that it's all very well for you English people. Everything is beautifully arranged for you."

"It seems to me it is very well for some Americans, sometimes," rejoined Beaumont.

"For some of them, yes—if they like to be patronized. But I must say I don't like to be patronized. I may be very eccentric and undisciplined and outrageous, but I confess I never was fond of patronage. I like to associate with people on the same terms as I do in my own country; that's a peculiar taste that I have. But here people seem to expect something else—Heaven knows what! I am afraid you will think I am very ungrateful, for I certainly have received a great deal of attention. The last time I was here, a lady sent me a message that I was at liberty to come and see her."

"Dear me! I hope you didn't go," observed Percy Beaumont.

"You are deliciously naïve, I must say that for you!" Mrs. Westgate exclaimed. "It must be a great advantage to you here in

London. I suppose if I myself had a little more naïveté, I should enjoy it more. I should be content to sit on a chair in the park, and see the people pass, and be told that this is the Duchess of Suffolk, and that is the Lord Chamberlain, and that I must be thankful for the privilege of beholding them. I dare say it is very wicked and critical of me to ask for anything else. But I was always critical, and I freely confess to the sin of being fastidious. I am told there is some remarkably superior second-rate society provided here for strangers. *Merci!* I don't want any superior second-rate society. I want the society that I have been accustomed to."

"I hope you don't call Lambeth and me second-rate," Beaumont interposed.

"Oh, I am accustomed to you," said Mrs. Westgate. "Do you know that you English sometimes make the most wonderful speeches? The first time I came to London I went out to dine—as I told you, I have received a great deal of attention. After dinner, in the drawing-room I had some conversation with an old lady; I assure you I had. I forget what we talked about, but she presently said, in allusion to something we were discussing, 'Oh, you know, the aristocracy do so-and-so; but in one' own class of life it is very different.' In one's own class of life! What is a poor unprotected American woman to do in a country where she is liable to have that sort of thing said to her?"

"You seem to get hold of some very queer old ladies; I compliment you on your acquaintance!" Percy Beaumont exclaimed. "If you are trying to bring me to admit that London is an odious place; you'll not succeed. I'm extremely fond of it, and I think it the jolliest place in the world."

"*Pour vous autres.* I never said the contrary," Mrs. Westgate retorted. I make use of this expression, because both interlocutors had begun to raise their voices. Percy Beaumont naturally did not like to hear his country abused, and Mrs. Westgate, no less naturally, did not like a stubborn debater.

"Hallo!" said Lord Lambeth; "what are they up to now?" And he came away from the window, where he had been standing with Bessie Alden.

"I quite agree with a very clever countrywoman of mine," Mrs. Westgate continued, with charming ardor, though with imperfect relevancy. She smiled at the two gentlemen for a moment with terrible brightness, as if to toss at their feet—upon their native heath—the gauntlet of defiance. "For me there are only two social positions worth speaking of—that of an American lady, and that of the Emperor of Russia."

"And what do you do with the American gentlemen?" asked Lord Lambeth.

"She leaves them in America!" said Percy Beaumont.

On the departure of their visitors, Bessie Alden told her sister that Lord Lambeth would come the next day, to go with them to the Tower, and that he had kindly offered to bring his "trap," and drive them thither.

Mrs. Westgate listened in silence to this communication, and for some time afterwards she said nothing. But at last: "If you had not requested me the other day not to mention it," she began, "there is something I should venture to ask you." Bessie frowned a little; her dark blue eyes were more dark than blue. But her sister went on. "As it is, I will take the risk. You are not in love with Lord Lambeth: I believe it, perfectly. Very good. But is there, by chance, any danger of your becoming so? It's a very simple question; don't take offence. I have a particular reason," said Mrs. Westgate, "for wanting to know."

Bessie Alden for some moments said nothing; she only looked displeased. "No; there is no danger," she answered at last, curtly.

"Then I should like to frighten them," declared Mrs. Westgate, clasping her jewelled hands.

"To frighten whom?"

"All these people; Lord Lambeth's family and friends."

"How should you frighten them?" asked the young girl.

"It wouldn't be I—it would be you. It would frighten them to think that you should absorb his lordship's young affections."

Bessie Alden, with her clear eyes still overshadowed by her dark brows, continued to interrogate. "Why should that frighten them?"

Mrs. Westgate poised her answer with a smile before delivering it. "Because they think you are not good enough. You are a charming girl, beautiful and amiable, intelligent and clever, and as *bien-élevée* as it is possible to be; but you are not a fit match for Lord Lambeth."

Bessie Alden was decidedly disgusted. "Where do you get such extraordinary ideas?" she asked. "You have said some such strange things lately. My dear Kitty, where do you collect them?"

Kitty was evidently enamoured of her idea. "Yes, it would put them on pins and needles, and it wouldn't hurt you. Mr. Beaumont is already most uneasy; I could soon see that."

The young girl meditated a moment. "Do you mean that they spy upon him—that they interfere with him?"

"I don't know what power they have to interfere, but I know that a British mamma may worry her son's life out."

It has been intimated that, as regards certain disagreeable things, Bessie Alden had a fund of scepticism. She abstained on the present occasion from expressing disbelief, for she wished not to irritate her sister. But she said to herself that Kitty had been misinformed—that this was a traveller's tale. Though she was a girl of a lively imagination, there could in the nature of things be, to her sense, no reality in the idea of her belonging to vulgar category. What she said aloud was, "I must say that in that case I am very sorry for Lord Lambeth."

Mrs. Westgate, more and more exhilarated by her scheme, was smiling at her again. "If I could only believe it was safe!" she exclaimed. "When you begin to pity him, I, on my side, am afraid."

"Afraid of what?"

"Of your pitying him too much."

Bessie Alden turned away impatiently; but at the end of a minute she turned back. "What if I should pity him too much?" she asked.

Mrs. Westgate hereupon turned away, but after a moment's reflection she also faced her sister again. "It would come, after all, to the same thing," she said.

Lord Lambeth came the next day with his trap, and the two ladies, attended by Willie Woodley, placed themselves under his guidance, and were conveyed eastward, through some of the dusker portions of the metropolis, to the great turreted donjon which overlooks the London shipping. They all descended from their vehicle and entered the famous enclosure; and they secured the services of a venerable beef-eater, who, though there were many other claimants for legendary information, made a fine exclusive party of them, and marched them through courts and corridors, through armories and prisons. He delivered his usual peripatetic discourse, and they stopped and stared, and peeped and stooped, according to the official admonitions. Bessie Alden asked the old man in the crimson doublet a great many questions; she thought it a most fascinating place. Lord Lambeth was in high good-humor; he was constantly laughing; he enjoyed what he would have called the lark. Willie Woodley kept looking at the ceilings and tapping the walls with the knuckle of a pearl-gray glove; and Mrs. Westgate, asking at frequent intervals to be allowed to sit down and wait till they came back, was as frequently informed that they would never come back. To a great many of Bessie's questions—chiefly on collateral points of English history—the ancient warder was naturally unable to reply; whereupon she always appealed to Lord Lambeth. But his lordship was very ignorant. He declared that he knew nothing about that sort of thing, and he seemed greatly diverted at being treated as an authority.

"You can't expect every one to know as much as you," he said.

"I should expect you to know a great deal more," declared Bessie Alden.

"Women always know more than men about names and dates, and that sort of thing," Lord Lambeth rejoined. "There was Lady Jane Grey we have just been hearing about, who went in for Latin and Greek, and all the learning of her age."

"*You* have no right to be ignorant, at all events," said Bessie.

"Why haven't I as good a right as any one else?"

"Because you have lived in the midst of all these things."

"What things do you mean? Axes, and blocks, and thumbscrews?"

"All these historical things. You belong to a historical family."

"Bessie is really too historical," said Mrs. Westgate, catching a word of this dialogue.

"Yes, you are too historical," said Lord Lambeth, laughing, but thankful for a formula. "Upon my honor, you are too historical!"

He went with the ladies a couple of days later to Hampton Court, Willie Woodley being also of the party. The afternoon was charming, the famous horse-chestnuts were in blossom, and Lord Lambeth, who quite entered into the spirit of the cockney excursionist, declared that it was a jolly old place. Bessie Alden was in ecstasies; she went about murmuring and exclaiming.

"It's too lovely," said the young girl; "it's too enchanting; it's too exactly what it ought to be!"

At Hampton Court the little flocks of visitors are not provided with an official bell-wether, but are left to browse at discretion upon the local antiquities. It happened in this manner that, in default of another informant, Bessie Alden, who on doubtful questions was able to suggest a great many alternatives, found herself again applying for intellectual assistance to Lord Lambeth. But he again assured her that he was utterly helpless in such matters—that his education had been sadly neglected.

"And I am sorry it makes you unhappy," he added, in a moment.

"You are very disappointing, Lord Lambeth," she said.

"Ah, now, don't say that!" he cried. "That's the worst thing you could possibly say."

"No," she rejoined, "it is not so bad as to say that I had expected nothing of you."

"I don't know. Give me a notion of the sort of thing you expected."

"Well," said Bessie Alden, "that you would be more what I should like to be—what I should try to be—in your place."

"Ah, my place!" exclaimed Lord Lambeth. "You are always talking about my place!"

The young girl looked at him; he thought she colored a little; and for a moment she made no rejoinder.

"Does it strike you that I am always talking about your place?" she asked.

"I am sure you do it a great honor," he said, fearing he had been uncivil.

"I have often thought about it," she went on, after a moment. "I have often thought about your being a hereditary legislator. A hereditary legislator ought to know a great many things."

"Not if he doesn't legislate."

"But you do legislate; it's absurd your saying you don't. You are very much looked up to here—I am assured of that."

"I don't know that I ever noticed it."

"It is because you are used to it, then. You ought to fill the place."

"How do you mean to fill it?" asked Lord Lambeth.

"You ought to be very clever and brilliant, and to know almost everything."

Lord Lambeth looked at her a moment. "Shall I tell you something?" he asked. "A young man in my position, as you call it——"

"I didn't invent the term," interposed Bessie Alden. "I have seen it in a great many books."

"Hang it! you are always at your books. A fellow in my position, then, does very well whatever he does. That's about what I mean to say."

"Well, if your own people are content with you," said Bessie Alden, laughing, "it is not for me to complain. But I shall always think that, properly, you should have been a great mind—a great character."

"Ah, that's very theoretic," Lord Lambeth declared. "Depend upon it, that's a Yankee prejudice."

"Happy the country," said Bessie Alden, "where even people's prejudices are so elevated!"

"Well, after all," observed Lord Lambeth, "I don't know that I am such a fool as you are trying to make me out."

"I said nothing so rude as that; but I must repeat that you are disappointing."

"My dear Miss Alden," exclaimed the young man, "I am the best fellow in the world!"

"Ah, if it were not for that!" said Bessie Alden, with a smile.

Mrs. Westgate had a good many more friends in London than she pretended, and before long she had renewed acquaintance with most of them. Their hospitality was extreme, so that, one thing leading to another, she began, as the phrase is, to go out. Bessie Alden, in this way, saw something of what she found it a great satisfaction to call to herself English society. She went to balls and danced, she went to dinners and talked, she went to concerts and listened (at concerts Bessie always listened), she went to exhibitions and wondered. Her enjoyment was keen and her curiosity insatiable, and, grateful in general for all her opportunities, she especially prized the privilege of meeting certain celebrated persons—authors and artists, philosophers and statesmen—of whose renown she had been a humble and distant beholder, and who now, as a part of the habitual furniture of London drawing-rooms, struck her as stars fallen from the firmament and become palpable—revealing also sometimes, on contact, qualities not to have been predicted of sidereal bodies.

Bessie, who knew so many of her contemporaries by reputation, had a good many personal disappointments; but, on the other hand, she had innumerable satisfactions and enthusiasms, and she communicated the emotions of either class to a dear friend of her own sex in Boston, with whom she was in voluminous correspondence. Some of her reflections, indeed, she attempted to impart to Lord Lambeth, who came almost every day to Jones's Hotel, and whom Mrs. Westgate admitted to be really devoted. Captain Littledale, it appeared, had gone to India; and of several others of Mrs. Westgate's ex-pensioners—gentlemen who, as she said, had made, in New York, a clubhouse of her drawing-room—no tidings were to be obtained; but Lord Lambeth was certainly attentive enough to make up for the accidental absences, the short memories, all the other irregularities, of every one else. He drove them in the park, he took them to visit private collections of pictures, and, having a house of his own, invited them to dinner. Mrs. Westgate, following the fashion of many of her compatriots, caused herself and her sister to be presented at the English court by her diplomatic representative —for it was in this manner that she alluded to the American minister to England, inquiring what on earth he was put there for, if not to make the proper arrangement for one's going to a Drawing-room.

Lord Lambeth declared that he hated Drawing-rooms, but he participated in the ceremony on the day on which the two ladies at Jones's Hotel repaired to Buckingham Palace in a remarkable coach which his lordship had sent to fetch them. He had a gorgeous uniform, and Bessie Alden was particularly struck with his appearance, especially when on her asking him—rather foolishly, as she felt—if he were a loyal subject, he replied that he was a loyal subject to *her*. This declaration was emphasized by his dancing with her at a royal ball to which the two ladies afterwards went, and was not impaired by the fact that she thought he danced very ill. He seemed to her wonderfully kind; she asked herself, with growing vivacity, why he should be so kind. It was his disposition—that seemed the natural answer. She had told her sister that she liked him very much, and now that she liked him more she wondered why. She liked him for his disposition; to this question as well that seemed the natural answer. When once the impressions of London life began to crowd thickly upon her she completely forgot her sister's warning about the cynicism of public opinion. It had given her great pain at the moment, but there was no particular reason why she should remember it; it corresponded too little with any sensible reality; and it was disagreeable to Bessie to remember disagreeable things. So she was not haunted with the sense of a vulgar imputation. She was not in love with Lord Lambeth—she assured herself of that.

It will immediately be observed that when such assurances become necessary the state of a young lady's affections is already ambiguous; and, indeed, Bessie Alden made no attempt to dissimulate—to herself, of course—a certain tenderness that she felt for the young nobleman. She said to herself that she liked the type to which he belonged—the simple, candid, manly, healthy English temperament. She spoke to herself of him as women speak of young men they like—alluded to his bravery (which she had never in the least seen tested), to his honesty and gentlemanliness, and was not silent upon the subject of his good looks. She was perfectly conscious, moreover, that she liked to think of his more adventitious merits; that her imagination was excited and gratified by the sight of a handsome young man endowed with such large opportunities—opportunities she hardly knew for what, but, as she supposed, for doing great things—for setting an example, for exerting an influence, for conferring happiness, for encouraging the arts. She had a kind of ideal of conduct for a young man who should find himself in this magnificent position, and she tried to adapt it to Lord Lambeth's deportment, as you might attempt to fit a silhouette in cut paper upon a shadow projected upon a wall.

But Bessie Alden's silhouette refused to coincide with his lordship's image, and this want of harmony sometimes vexed her more than she thought reasonable. When he was absent it was, of course, less striking; then he seemed to her a sufficiently graceful combination of high responsibilities and amiable qualities. But when he sat there within sight, laughing and talking with his customary good-humor and simplicity, she measured it more accurately, and she felt acutely that if Lord Lambeth's position was heroic, there was but little of the hero in the young man himself. Then her imagination wandered away from him—very far away; for it was an incontestable fact that at such moments he seemed distinctly dull. I am afraid that while Bessie's imagination was thus invidiously roaming, she cannot have been herself a very lively companion; but it may well have been that these occasional fits of indifference seemed to Lord Lambeth a part of the young girl's personal charm. It had been a part of this charm from the first that he felt that she judged him and measured him more freely and irresponsibly—more at her ease and her leisure, as it were—than several young ladies with whom he had been, on the whole, about as intimate. To feel this, and yet to feel that she also liked him, was very agreeable to Lord Lambeth. He fancied he had compassed that gratification so desirable to young men of title and fortune—being liked for himself. It is true that a cynical counsellor might have whispered to him, "Liked for yourself? Yes; but not so very much!" He had, at any rate, the constant hope of being liked more.

It may seem, perhaps, a trifle singular—but it is nevertheless true—that Bessie Alden, when he struck her as dull, devoted some time, on grounds of conscience, to trying to like him more. I say on grounds of conscience, because she felt that he had been extremely "nice" to her sister, and because she reflected that it was no more than fair that she should think as well of him as he thought of her. This effort was possibly sometimes not so successful as it might have been, for the result of it was occasionally a vague irritation, which expressed itself in hostile criticism of several British institutions. Bessie Alden went to some entertainments at which she met Lord Lambeth; but she went to others at which his lordship was neither actually nor potentially present; and it was chiefly on these latter occasions that she encountered those literary and artistic celebrities of whom mention has been made. After a while she reduced the matter to a principle. If Lord Lambeth should appear anywhere, it was a symbol that there would be no poets and philosophers; and in consequence—for it was almost a strict consequence—she used to enumerate to the young man these objects of her admiration.

"You seem to be awfully fond of those sort of people," said Lord Lambeth one day, as if the idea had just occurred to him.

"They are the people in England I am most curious to see," Bessie Alden replied.

"I suppose that's because you have read so much," said Lord Lambeth, gallantly.

"I have not read so much. It is because we think so much of them at home."

"Oh, I see," observed the young nobleman. "In Boston."

"Not only in Boston; everywhere," said Bessie. "We hold them in great honor; they go to the best dinner-parties."

"I dare say you are right. I can't say I know many of them."

"It's a pity you don't," Bessie Alden declared. "It would do you good."

"I dare say it would," said Lord Lambeth, very humbly. "But I must say I don't like the looks of some of them."

"Neither do I—of some of them. But there are all kinds, and many of them are charming."

"I have talked with two or three of them," the young man went on, "and I thought they had a kind of fawning manner."

"Why should they fawn?" Bessie Alden demanded.

"I'm sure I don't know. Why, indeed?"

"Perhaps you only thought so," said Bessie.

"Well, of course," rejoined her companion, "that's a kind of thing that can't be proved."

"In America they don't fawn," said Bessie.

"Ah, well, then, they must be better company."

Bessie was silent a moment. "That is one of the things I don't like about England," she said—"your keeping the distinguished people apart."

"How do you mean apart?"

"Why, letting them come only to certain places. You never see them."

Lord Lambeth looked at her a moment. "What people do you mean?"

"The eminent people—the authors and artists—the clever people."

"Oh, there are other eminent people besides those," said Lord Lambeth.

"Well, you certainly keep them apart," repeated the young girl.

"And there are other clever people," added Lord Lambeth, simply.

Bessie Alden looked at him, and she gave a light laugh. "Not many," she said.

On another occasion—just after a dinner-party—she told him that there was something else in England she did not like.

"Oh, I say!" he cried, "haven't you abused us enough?"

"I have never abused you at all," said Bessie; "but I don't like your *precedence*."

"It isn't my precedence!" Lord Lambeth declared, laughing.

"Yes, it is yours—just exactly yours; and I think it's odious," said Bessie.

"I never saw such a young lady for discussing things! Has some one had the impudence to go before you?" asked his lordship.

"It is not the going before me that I object to," said Bessie; "it is their thinking that they have a right to do it—*a right that I recognize.*"

"I never saw such a young lady as you are for not 'recognizing.' I have no doubt the thing is *beastly*, but it saves a lot of trouble."

"It makes a lot of trouble. It's horrid," said Bessie.

"But how would you have the first people go?" asked Lord Lambeth. "They can't go last."

"Whom do you mean by the first people?"

"Ah, if you mean to question first principles!" said Lord Lambeth.

"If those are your first principles, no wonder some of your arrangements are horrid," observed Bessie Alden, with a very pretty ferocity. "I am a young girl, so of course I go last; but imagine what Kitty must feel on being informed that she is not at liberty to budge until certain other ladies have passed out."

"Oh, I say she is not 'informed'!" cried Lord Lambeth. "No one would do such a thing as that."

"She is made to feel it," the young girl insisted—"as if they were afraid she would make a rush for the door. No; you have a lovely country," said Bessie Alden, "but your precedence is horrid."

"I certainly shouldn't think your sister would like it," rejoined Lord Lambeth, with even exaggerated gravity. But Bessie Alden could induce him to enter no formal protest against this repulsive custom, which he seemed to think an extreme convenience.

Percy Beaumont all this time had been a very much less frequent visitor at Jones's Hotel than his noble kinsman; he had, in fact, called but twice upon the two American ladies. Lord Lambeth, who often saw him, reproached him with his neglect, and declared that, although Mrs. Westgate had said nothing about it, he was sure that she was secretly wounded by it. "She suffers too much to speak," said Lord Lambeth.

"That's all gammon," said Percy Beaumont; "there's a limit to what people can suffer!" And, though sending no apologies to Jones's Hotel, he undertook, in a manner, to explain his absence.

"You are always there," he said, "and that's reason enough for my not going."

"I don't see why. There is enough for both of us."

"I don't care to be a witness of your—your reckless passion," said Percy Beaumont.

Lord Lambeth looked at him with a cold eye, and for a moment said nothing. "It's not so obvious as you might suppose," he rejoined, dryly, "considering what a demonstrative beggar I am."

"I don't want to know anything about it—nothing whatever," said Beaumont. "Your mother asks me every time she sees me whether I believe you are really lost—and Lady Pimlico does the same. I prefer to be able to answer that I know nothing about it—that I never go there. I stay away for consistency's sake. As I said the other day, they must look after you themselves."

"You are devilish considerate," said Lord Lambeth. "They never question me."

"They are afraid of you. They are afraid of irritating you and making you worse. So they go to work very cautiously, and, somewhere or other, they get their information. They know a great deal about you. They know that you have been with those ladies to the dome of St. Paul's and—where was the other place?—to the Thames Tunnel."

"If all their knowledge is as accurate as that, it must be very valuable," said Lord Lambeth.

"Well, at any rate, they know that you have been visiting the 'sights of the metropolis.' They think—very naturally, as it seems to me—that when you take to visiting the sights of the metropolis with a little American girl, there is serious cause for alarm." Lord Lambeth responded to this intimation by scornful laughter, and his companion continued, after a pause: "I said just now I didn't want to know anything about the affair; but I will confess that I am curious to learn whether you propose to marry Miss Bessie Alden."

On this point Lord Lambeth gave his interlocutor no immediate satisfaction; he was musing, with a frown. "By Jove," he said, "they go rather too far! They *shall* find me dangerous—I promise them."

Percy Beaumont began to laugh. "You don't redeem your promises. You said the other day you would make your mother call."

Lord Lambeth continued to meditate. "I asked her to call," he said, simply.

"And she declined?"

"Yes; but she shall do it yet."

"Upon my word," said Percy Beaumont, "if she gets much more frightened I believe she will." Lord Lambeth looked at him, and he went on. "She will go to the girl herself."

"How do you mean she will go to her?"

"She will beg her off, or she will bribe her. She will take strong measures."

Lord Lambeth turned away in silence, and his companion watched him take twenty steps and then slowly return. "I have invited Mrs. Westgate and Miss Alden to Branches," he said, "and this evening I shall name a day."

"And shall you invite your mother and your sisters to meet them?"

"Explicitly!"

"That will set the duchess off," said Percy Beaumont. "I suspect she will come."

"She may do as she pleases."

Beaumont looked at Lord Lambeth. "You do really propose to marry the little sister, then?"

"I like the way you talk about it!" cried the young man. "She won't gobble me down; don't be afraid."

"She won't leave you on your knees," said Percy Beaumont. "What *is* the inducement?"

"You talk about proposing: wait till I *have* proposed," Lord Lambeth went on.

"That's right, my dear fellow; think about it," said Percy Beaumont.

"She's a charming girl," pursued his lordship.

"Of course she's a charming girl. I don't know a girl more charming, intrinsically. But there are other charming girls nearer home."

"I like her spirit," observed Lord Lambeth, almost as if he were trying to torment his cousin.

"What's the peculiarity of her spirit?"

"She's not afraid, and she says things out, and she thinks herself as good as any one. She is the only girl I have ever seen that was not dying to marry me."

"How do you know that, if you haven't asked her?"

"I don't know how; but I know it."

"I am sure she asked me questions enough about your property and your titles," said Beaumont.

"She has asked me questions, too; no end of them," Lord Lambeth admitted. "But she asked for information, don't you know."

"Information? Aye, I'll warrant she wanted it. Depend upon it that she is dying to marry you just as much and just as little as all the rest of them."

"I shouldn't like her to refuse me—I shouldn't like that."

"If the thing would be so disagreeable, then, both to you and to her, in Heaven's name leave it alone," said Percy Beaumont.

Mrs. Westgate, on her side, had plenty to say to her sister about the rarity of Mr. Beaumont's visits and the non-appearance of the Duchess of Bayswater. She professed, however, to derive more satisfaction from this latter circumstance than she could have done from the most lavish attentions on the part of this great lady. "It is most marked," she said—"most marked. It is a delicious proof that we have made them miserable. The day we dined with Lord Lambeth I was really sorry for the poor fellow." It will have been gathered that the entertainment offered by Lord Lambeth to his American friends had not been graced by the presence of his anxious mother. He had invited several choice spirits to meet them; but the ladies of his immediate family were to Mrs. Westgate's sense—a sense possibly morbidly acute—conspicuous by their absence.

"I don't want to express myself in a manner that you dislike," said Bessie Alden; "but I don't know why you should have so many theories about Lord Lambeth's poor mother. You know a great many young men in New York without knowing their mothers."

Mrs. Westgate looked at her sister, and then turned away. "My dear Bessie, you are superb!" she said.

"One thing is certain," the young girl continued. "If I believed I were a cause of annoyance—however unwitting—to Lord Lambeth's family, I should insist——"

"Insist upon my leaving England," said Mrs. Westgate.

"No, not that. I want to go to the National Gallery again; I want to see Stratford-on-Avon and Canterbury Cathedral. But I should insist upon his coming to see us no more."

"That would be very modest and very pretty of you; but you wouldn't do it now."

"Why do you say 'now'?" asked Bessie Alden. "Have I ceased to be modest?"

"You care for him too much. A month ago, when you said you didn't, I believe it was quite true. But at present, my dear child," said Mrs. Westgate, "you wouldn't find it quite so simple a matter never to see Lord Lambeth again. I have seen it coming on."

"You are mistaken," said Bessie. "You don't understand."

"My dear child, don't be perverse," rejoined her sister.

"I know him better, certainly, if you mean that," said Bessie. "And I like him very much. But I don't like him enough to make trouble for him with his family. However, I don't believe in that."

"I like the way you say 'however,' " Mrs. Westgate exclaimed. "Come; you would not marry him?"

"Oh no," said the young girl.

Mrs. Westgate for a moment seemed vexed. "Why not, pray?" she demanded.

"Because I don't care to," said Bessie Alden.

The morning after Lord Lambeth had had, with Percy Beaumont, that exchange of ideas which has just been narrated, the ladies at Jones's Hotel received from his lordship a written invitation to pay their projected visit to Branches Castle on the following Tuesday. "I think I have made up a very pleasant party," the young nobleman said. "Several people whom you know, and my mother and sisters, who have so long been regrettably prevented from making your acquaintance." Bessie Alden lost no time in calling her sister's attention to the injustice she had done the Duchess of Bayswater, whose hostility was now proved to be a vain illusion.

"Wait till you see if she comes," said Mrs. Westgate. "And if she is to meet us at her son's house, the obligation was all the greater for her to call upon us."

Bessie had not to wait long, and it appeared that Lord Lambeth's mother now accepted Mrs. Westgate's view of her duties. On the morrow, early in the afternoon, two cards were brought to the apartment of the American ladies—one of them bearing the name of the Duchess of Bayswater, and the other that of the Countess of Pimlico. Mrs. Westgate glanced at the clock. "It is not yet four," she said; "they have come early; they wish to see us. We will receive them." And she gave orders that her visitors should be admitted. A few moments later they were introduced, and there was a solemn exchange of amenities. The duchess was a large lady, with a fine fresh color; the Countess of Pimlico was very pretty and elegant.

The duchess looked about her as she sat down—looked not especially at Mrs. Westgate. "I dare say my son has told you that I have been wanting to come and see you," she observed.

"You are very kind," said Mrs. Westgate, vaguely—her conscience not allowing her to assent to this proposition—and, indeed, not permitting her to enunciate her own with any appreciable emphasis.

"He says you were so kind to him in America," said the duchess.

"We are very glad," Mrs. Westgate replied, "to have been able to make him a little more—a little less—a little more comfortable."

"I think that he stayed at your house," remarked the Duchess of Bayswater, looking at Bessie Alden.

"A very short time," said Mrs. Westgate.

"Oh!" said the duchess; and she continued to look at Bessie, who was engaged in conversation with her daughter.

"Do you like London?" Lady Pimlico had asked of Bessie, after looking at her a good deal—at her face and her hands, her dress and her hair.

"Very much indeed," said Bessie.

"Do you like this hotel?"

"It is very comfortable," said Bessie.

"Do you like stopping at hotels?" inquired Lady Pimlico, after a pause.

"I am very fond of travelling," Bessie answered, "and I suppose hotels are a necessary part of it. But they are not the part I am fondest of."

"Oh, I hate travelling," said the Countess of Pimlico, and transferred her attention to Mrs. Westgate.

"My son tells me you are going to Branches," the duchess said, presently.

"Lord Lambeth has been so good as to ask us," said Mrs. Westgate, who perceived that her visitor had now begun to look at her, and who had her customary happy consciousness of a distinguished appearance. The only mitigation of her felicity on this point was that, having inspected her visitor's own costume, she said to herself, "She won't know how well I am dressed!"

"He has asked me to go, but I am not sure I shall be able," murmured the duchess.

"He had offered us the p— the prospect of meeting you," said Mrs. Westgate.

"I hate the country at this season," responded the duchess.

Mrs. Westgate gave a little shrug. "I think it is pleasanter than London."

But the duchess's eyes were absent again; she was looking fixedly at Bessie. In a moment she slowly rose, walked to a chair that stood empty at the young girl's right hand, and silently seated herself. As she was a majestic, voluminous woman, this little transaction had, inevitably, an air of somewhat impressive attention. It diffused a certain awkwardness, which Lady Pimlico, as a sympathetic daughter, perhaps desired to rectify in turning to Mrs. Westgate. "I dare say you go out a great deal," she observed.

"No, very little. We are strangers, and we didn't come here for society."

"I see," said Lady Pimlico. "It's rather nice in town just now."

"It's charming," said Mrs. Westgate. "But we only go to see a few people—whom we like."

"Of course one can't like every one," said Lady Pimlico.

"It depends upon one's society," Mrs. Westgate rejoined.

The duchess meanwhile had addressed herself to Bessie. "My son tells me the young ladies in America are so clever."

"I am glad they made so good an impression on him," said Bessie, smiling.

The duchess was not smiling; her large, fresh face was very tranquil. "He is very susceptible," she said. "He thinks every one clever, and sometimes they are."

"Sometimes," Bessie assented, smiling still.

The duchess looked at her a little, and then went on: "Lambeth is very susceptible, but he is very volatile, too."

"Volatile?" asked Bessie.

"He is very inconstant. It won't do to depend on him."

"Ah," said Bessie, "I don't recognize that description. We have depended on him greatly—my sister and I—and he has never disappointed us."

"He will disappoint you yet," said the duchess.

Bessie gave a little laugh, as if she were amused at the duchess's persistency. "I suppose it will depend on what we expect of him."

"The less you expect the better," Lord Lambeth's mother declared.

"Well," said Bessie, "we expect nothing unreasonable."

The duchess for a moment was silent, though she appeared to have more to say. "Lambeth says he has seen so much of you," she presently began.

"He has been to see us very often; he has been very kind," said Bessie Alden.

"I dare say you are used to that. I am told there is a great deal of that in America."

"A great deal of kindness?" the young girl inquired, smiling.

"Is that what you call it? I know you have different expressions."

"We certainly don't always understand each other," said Mrs. Westgate, the termination of whose interview with Lady Pimlico allowed her to give attention to their elder visitor.

"I am speaking of the young men calling so much upon the young ladies," the duchess explained.

"But surely in England," said Mrs. Westgate, "the young ladies don't call upon the young men?"

"Some of them do—almost!" Lady Pimlico declared. "When the young men are a great *parti*."

"Bessie, you must make a note of that," said Mrs. Westgate. "My sister," she added, "is a model traveller. She writes down all the curious facts she hears in a little book she keeps for the purpose."

The duchess was a little flushed; she looked all about the room, while her daughter turned to Bessie. "My brother told us you were wonderfully clever," said Lady Pimlico.

"He should have said my sister," Bessie answered—"when she says such things as that."

"Shall you be long at Branches?" the duchess asked, abruptly, of the young girl.

"Lord Lambeth has asked us for three days," said Bessie.

"I shall go," the duchess declared, "and my daughter, too."

"That will be charming!" Bessie rejoined.

"Delightful!" murmured Mrs. Westgate.

"I shall expect to see a great deal of you," the duchess continued. "When I go to Branches I monopolize my son's guests."

"They must be most happy," said Mrs. Westgate, very graciously.

"I want immensely to see it—to see the castle," said Bessie to the duchess. "I have never seen one—in England, at least; and you know we have none in America."

"Ah, you are fond of castles?" inquired her Grace.

"Immensely!" replied the young girl. "It has been the dream of my life to live in one."

The duchess looked at her a moment, as if she hardly knew how to take this assurance, which, from her Grace's point of view, was either very artless or very audacious. "Well," she said, rising, "I will show you Branches myself." And upon this the two great ladies took their departure.

"What did they mean by it?" asked Mrs. Westgate, when they were gone.

"They meant to be polite," said Bessie, "because we are going to meet them."

"It is too late to be polite," Mrs. Westgate replied, almost grimly. "They meant to overawe us by their fine manners and their grandeur, and to make you *lâcher prise*."

"*Lâcher prise?* What strange things you say!" murmured Bessie Alden.

"They meant to snub us, so that we shouldn't dare to go to Branches," Mrs. Westgate continued.

"On the contrary," said Bessie, "the duchess offered to show me the place herself."

"Yes, you may depend upon it she won't let you out of her sight. She will show you the place from morning till night."

"You have a theory for everything," said Bessie.

"And you apparently have none for anything."

"I saw no attempt to 'overawe' us," said the young girl. "Their manners were not fine."

"They were not even good!" Mrs. Westgate declared.

Bessie was silent a while, but in a few moments she observed that she had a very good theory. "They came to look at me," she said, as if this had been a very ingenious hypothesis. Mrs. Westgate did it justice; she greeted it with a smile, and pronounced it most brilliant, while, in reality, she felt that the young girl's scepticism, or her charity, or, as she had sometimes called it appropriately, her idealism, was proof against irony. Bessie, however, remained meditative all the rest of the day and well on into the morrow.

On the morrow, before lunch, Mrs. Westgate had occasion to go out for an hour, and left her sister writing a letter. When she came back she met Lord Lambeth at the door of the hotel, coming away. She thought he looked slightly embarrassed; he was certainly very grave. "I am sorry to have missed you. Won't you come back?" she asked.

"No," said the young man, "I can't. I have seen your sister. I can never come back." Then he looked at her a moment, and took her hand. "Good-bye, Mrs. Westgate," he said. "You have been very kind to me." And with what she thought a strange, sad look in his handsome young face, he turned away.

She went in, and she found Bessie still writing her letter—that is, Mrs. Westgate perceived she was sitting at the table with the pen in her hand and not writing. "Lord Lambeth has been here," said the elder lady at last.

Then Bessie got up and showed her a pale, serious face. She bent this face upon her sister for some time, confessing silently and a little pleading. "I told him," she said at last, "that we could not go to Branches."

Mrs. Westgate displayed just a spark of irritation. "He might have waited," she said, with a smile, "till one had seen the castle." Later, an hour afterwards, she said, "Dear Bessie, I wish you might have accepted him."

"I couldn't," said Bessie, gently.

"He is an excellent fellow," said Mrs. Westgate.

"I couldn't," Bessie repeated.

"If it is only," her sister added, "because those women will think that they succeeded—that they paralyzed us!"

Bessie Alden turned away; but presently she added, "They were interesting; I should have liked to see them again."

"So should I!" cried Mrs. Westgate, significantly.

"And I should have liked to see the castle," said Bessie. "But now we must leave England," she added.

Her sister looked at her. "You will not wait to go to the National Gallery?"

"Not now."

"Nor to Canterbury Cathedral?"

Bessie reflected a moment. "We can stop there on our way to Paris," she said.

Lord Lambeth did not tell Percy Beaumont that the contingency he was not prepared at all to like had occurred; but Percy Beaumont, on hearing that the two ladies had left London, wondered with some intensity what had happened—wondered, that is, until the Duchess of Bayswater came a little to his assistance. The two ladies went to Paris, and Mrs. Westgate beguiled the journey to that city by repeating several times: "That's what I regret; they will think they petrified us." But Bessie Alden seemed to regret nothing.

The Siege of London

The Siege of London

The idea of *The Siege of London* came to James one evening in the autumn of 1877, after witnessing a performance at the Théâtre Francais of *Le Demi-Monde,* a play by the younger Dumas. The problem of the play was whether under certain circumstances a gentleman would be justified in "telling on" a lady whom he had once loved though never respected. Typically enough, James found the moral insensibility of the French playwright to be nothing less than "prodigious," and he was sufficiently provoked to think of attempting to pose the same problem through the medium of characters of his own nationality. But it was not till 1882 that he wrote the novelette, which he sent to his friend Leslie Stephen, then editor of *The Cornhill Magazine,* where it appeared in the early months of 1883.

In the process of composition, however, the original idea somehow lost its hold, and the story turned into a brilliant social comedy on the theme of "getting into society." For this is the species of complication faced by Mrs. Headway, the American divorcée from the far West who is finally accepted by London society on the quite interesting ground of her accomplishments as an American humorist. This woman of "absolutely glaring motives" is a type heretofore not treated by James. In relating her adventures he struck that note of the *social picaresque,* so to speak, to which he returned from time to time in later years—as in the account of the marital difficulties of the racy Berrington couple in *A London Life* and of Maisie's parents in *What Maisie Knew.* Relationships involving an element of the socially scandalous or ambiguous or any sort of amalgam of the low and the snobbish intrigued James. In *The Siege of London* this element is so effectively combined with the "international proposition" that it is hardly possible to tell them apart.

PART I

I

THAT solemn piece of upholstery, the curtain of the Comédie Française, had fallen upon the first act of the piece, and our two Americans had taken advantage of the interval to pass out of the huge, hot theatre, in company with the other occupants of the stalls. But they were among the first to return, and they beguiled the rest of the intermission with looking at the house, which had lately been cleansed of its historic cobwebs and ornamented with frescos illustrative of the classic drama. In the month of September the audience at the Théâtre Français is comparatively thin, and on this occasion the drama—*L'Aventurière* of Emile Augier—had no pretensions to novelty. Many of the boxes were empty, others were occupied by persons of provincial or nomadic appearance. The boxes are far from the stage, near which our spectators were placed; but even at a distance Rupert Waterville was able to appreciate certain details. He was fond of appreciating details, and when he went to the theatre he looked about him a good deal, making use of a dainty but remarkably powerful glass. He knew that such a course was wanting in true distinction, and that it was indelicate to level at a lady an instrument which was often only less injurious in effect than a double-barrelled pistol; but he was always very curious, and he was sure, in any case, that at that moment, at that antiquated play—so he was pleased to qualify the masterpiece of an Academician—he would not be observed by any one he knew. Standing up therefore with his back to the stage, he made the circuit of the boxes, while several other persons, near him, performed the same operation with even greater coolness.

"Not a single pretty woman," he remarked at last to his friend; an observation which Littlemore, sitting in his place and staring with a bored expression at the new-looking curtain, received in perfect silence. He rarely indulged in these optical excursions; he had been a great deal in Paris and had ceased to care about it, or wonder about it, much; he fancied that the French capital could have no more surprises for him, though it had had a good many in former days. Waterville was still in the stage of surprise; he suddenly expressed his emotion. "By Jove!" he exclaimed; "I beg your pardon—I beg *her* pardon—there is, after all, a woman that may be called"—he paused a little, inspecting her—"a kind of beauty!"

"What kind?" Littlemore asked, vaguely.

"An unusual kind—an indescribable kind." Littlemore was not heeding his answer, but he presently heard himself appealed to. "I say, I wish very much you would do me a favor."

"I did you a favor in coming here," said Littlemore. "It's insufferably hot, and the play is like a dinner that has been dressed by the kitchen-maid. The actors are all *doublures*."

"It's simply to answer me this: is *she* respectable, now?" Waterville rejoined, inattentive to his friend's epigram.

Littlemore gave a groan, without turning his head. "You are always wanting to know if they are respectable. What on earth can it matter?"

"I have made such mistakes—I have lost all confidence," said poor Waterville, to whom European civilization had not ceased to be a novelty, and who during the last six months had found himself confronted with problems long unsuspected. Whenever he encountered a very nice-looking woman, he was sure to discover that she belonged to the class represented by the heroine of M. Augier's drama; and whenever his attention rested upon a person of a florid style of attraction, there was the strongest probability that she would turn out to be a countess. The countesses looked so superficial and the others looked so exclusive. Now Littlemore distinguished at a glance; he never made mistakes.

"Simply for looking at them, it doesn't matter, I suppose," said Waterville, ingenuously, answering his companion's rather cynical inquiry.

"You stare at them all alike," Littlemore went on, still without moving; "except indeed when I tell you that they are not respectable—then your attention acquires a fixedness!"

"If your judgment is against this lady, I promise never to look at her again. I mean the one in the third box from the passage, in white, with the red flowers," he added, as Littlemore slowly rose and stood beside him. "The young man is leaning forward. It is the young man that makes me doubt of her. Will you have the glass?"

Littlemore looked about him without concentration. "No, I thank you, my eyes are good enough. The young man's a very good young man," he added in a moment.

"Very indeed; but he's several years younger than she. Wait till she turns her head."

She turned it very soon—she apparently had been speaking to the *ouvreuse*, at the door of the box—and presented her face to the public—a fair, well-drawn face, with smiling eyes, smiling lips, ornamented over the brow with delicate rings of black hair and, in each ear, with the sparkle of a diamond sufficiently large to be seen across the Théâtre Français. Littlemore looked at her; then, abruptly, he gave an exclamation. "Give me the glass!"

"Do you know her?" his companion asked, as he directed the little instrument.

Littlemore made no answer; he only looked in silence; then he handed back the glass. "No, she's not respectable," he said. And he dropped into his seat again. As Waterville remained standing, he added, "Please sit down; I think she saw me."

"Don't you want her to see you?" asked Waterville the interrogator, taking his seat.

Littlemore hesitated. "I don't want to spoil her game." By this time the *entr'acte* was at an end; the curtain rose again.

It had been Waterville's idea that they should go to the theatre. Littlemore, who was always for not doing a thing, had recommended that, the evening being lovely, they should simply sit and smoke at the door of the Grand Café, in a decent part of the Boulevard. Nevertheless Rupert Waterville enjoyed the second act even less than he had done the first, which he thought heavy. He began to wonder whether his companion would wish to stay to the end; a useless line of speculation, for now that he had got to the theatre, Littlemore's objection to doing things would certainly keep him from going. Waterville also wondered what he knew about the lady in the box. Once or twice he glanced at his friend, and then he saw that Littlemore was not following the play. He was thinking of something else; he was thinking of that woman. When the curtain fell again he sat in his place, making way for his neighbors, as usual, to edge past him, grinding his knees—his legs were long—with their own protuberances. When the two men were alone in the stalls, Littlemore said: "I think I should like to see her again, after all." He spoke as if Waterville might have known all about her. Waterville was conscious of not doing so, but as there was evidently a good deal to know, he felt that he should lose nothing by being a little discreet. So, for the moment, he asked no questions; he only said—

"Well, here's the glass."

Littlemore gave him a glance of good-natured compassion. "I don't mean that I want to stare at her with that beastly thing. I mean—to see her—as I used to see her."

"How did you use to see her?" asked Waterville, bidding farewell to discretion.

"On the back piazza, at San Diego." And as his interlocutor, in receipt of this information, only stared, he went on—"Come out where we can breathe, and I'll tell you more."

They made their way to the low and narrow door, more worthy of a rabbit-hutch than of a great theatre, by which you pass from the stalls of the Comédie to the lobby, and as Littlemore went first, his ingenuous friend, behind him, could see that he glanced up at the box in the occupants of which they were interested. The more interesting of these had her back to the house; she was apparently just leaving the box, after her companion; but as she had not put on her mantle it was evident that they were not quitting the theatre. Littlemore's pursuit of fresh air did not lead him into the street; he had passed his arm into Waterville's, and when they reached that fine frigid staircase which ascends to the Foyer, he began silently to mount it. Littlemore was averse to active pleasures, but his friend reflected that now at least he had launched himself —he was going to look for the lady whom, with a monosyllable, he appeared to have classified. The young man resigned himself for the moment to asking no questions, and the two strolled together into the shining saloon where Houdon's admirable statue of Voltaire, reflected in a dozen mirrors, is gaped at by visitors obviously less acute than the genius expressed in those living features. Waterville knew that Voltaire was very witty; he had read *Candide*, and had already had several opportunities of appreciating the statue. The Foyer was not crowded; only a dozen groups were scattered over the polished floor, several others having passed out to the balcony which overhangs the square of the Palais Royal. The windows were open, the brilliant lights of Paris made the dull summer evening look like an anniversary or a revolution; a murmur of voices seemed to come up from the streets, and even in the Foyer one heard the slow click of the horses and the rumble of the crookedly-driven fiacres on the hard, smooth asphalt. A lady and a gentleman, with their backs to our friends, stood before the image of Voltaire; the lady was dressed in white, including a white bonnet. Littlemore felt, as so many persons feel in that spot, that the scene was conspicuously Parisian, and he gave a mysterious laugh.

"It seems comical to see her here! The last time was in New Mexico."

"In New Mexico?"

"At San Diego."

"Oh, on the back piazza," said Waterville, putting things together. He had not been aware of the position of San Diego, for if on the occasion of his lately being appointed to a subordinate diplomatic post in London, he had been paying a good deal of attention to European geography, he had rather neglected that of his own country.

They had not spoken loud, and they were not standing near her; but suddenly, as if she had heard them, the lady in white turned round. Her eye caught Waterville's first, and in that glance he saw that if she had heard them it was not because they were audible but because she had extraordinary quickness of ear. There was no recognition in it—there was none, at first, even when it rested lightly upon George Littlemore. But recognition flashed out a moment later, accompanied with a delicate increase of color and a quick extension of her apparently constant smile. She had turned completely round; she stood there in sudden friendliness, with parted lips, with a hand, gloved to the elbow, almost imperiously offered. She was even prettier than at a distance. "Well, I declare!" she exclaimed; so loud that every one in the room appeared to feel personally addressed. Waterville was surprised; he had not been prepared, even after the mention of the back piazza, to find her an American. Her companion turned round as she spoke; he was a fresh, lean young man, in evening dress; he kept his hands in his pockets; Waterville imagined that he at any rate was not an American. He looked very grave—for such a fair, festive young man—and gave Waterville and Littlemore, though his height was not superior to theirs, a narrow, vertical glance. Then he turned back to the statue of Voltaire, as if it had been, after all, among his premonitions that the lady he was attending would recognize people he didn't know, and didn't even, perhaps, care to know. This possibly confirmed slightly Littlemore's assertion that she was not respectable. The young man was, at least; consummately so. "Where in the world did you drop from?" the lady inquired.

"I have been here some time," Littlemore said, going forward, rather deliberately, to shake hands with her. He smiled a little, but he was more serious than she; he kept his eye on her own as if she had been just a trifle dangerous; it was the manner in which a duly discreet person would have approached some glossy, graceful animal which had an occasional trick of biting.

"Here in Paris, do you mean?"

"No; here and there—in Europe generally."

"Well, it's queer I haven't met you."

"Better late than never!" said Littlemore. His smile was a little fixed.

"Well, you look very natural," the lady went on.

"So do you—or very charming—it's the same thing," Littlemore answered, laughing, and evidently wishing to be easy. It was as if, face to face, and after a considerable lapse of time, he had found her more imposing than he expected when, in the stalls below, he determined to come and meet her. As he spoke, the young man who was with her gave up his inspection of Voltaire and faced about, listlessly, without looking either at Littlemore or at Waterville.

"I want to introduce you to my friend," she went on. "Sir Arthur Demesne—Mr. Littlemore. Mr. Littlemore—Sir Arthur Demesne. Sir Arthur Demesne is an Englishman—Mr. Littlemore is a countryman of mine, an old friend. I haven't seen him for years. For how long? Don't let's count!—I wonder you knew me," she continued, addressing Littlemore. "I'm fearfully changed." All this was said in a clear, gay tone, which was the more audible as she spoke with a kind of caressing slowness. The two men, to do honor to her introduction, silently exchanged a glance; the Englishman, perhaps, colored a little. He was very conscious of his companion. "I haven't introduced you to many people yet," she remarked.

"Oh, I don't mind," said Sir Arthur Demesne.

"Well, it's queer to see you!" she exclaimed, looking still at Littlemore. "You have changed, too—I can see that."

"Not where you are concerned."

"That's what I want to find out. Why don't you introduce your friend? I see he's dying to know me!"

Littlemore proceeded to this ceremony; but he reduced it to its simplest elements, merely glancing at Rupert Waterville, and murmuring his name.

"You didn't tell him *my* name," the lady cried, while Waterville made her a formal salutation. "I hope you haven't forgotten it!"

Littlemore gave her a glance which was intended to be more penetrating than what he had hitherto permitted himself; if it had been put into words it would have said, "Ah, but *which* name?"

She answered the unspoken question, putting out her hand, as she had done to Littlemore, "Happy to make your acquaintance, Mr. Waterville. I'm Mrs. Headway—perhaps you've heard of me. If you've ever been in America, you must have heard of me. Not so much in New York, but in the Western cities. You *are* an American? Well, then, we are all compatriots—except Sir Arthur Demesne. Let me introduce you to Sir Arthur. Sir Arthur Demesne, Mr. Waterville—Mr. Waterville, Sir Arthur Demesne. Sir Arthur Demesne is a member of Parliament; don't he look young?" She waited for no answer to this question, but suddenly asked another, as she moved her bracelets back over her long, loose gloves. "Well, Mr. Littlemore, what are you thinking of?"

He was thinking that he must indeed have forgotten her name, for the one that she had pronounced awakened no association. But he could hardly tell her that.

"I'm thinking of San Diego."

"The back piazza, at my sister's? Oh, don't; it was too horrid. She has left now. I believe every one has left."

Sir Arthur Demesne drew out his watch with the air of a man who could take no part in these domestic reminiscences; he appeared to combine a generic self-possession with a degree of individual shyness. He said something about its being time they should go back to their seats, but Mrs. Headway paid no attention to the remark. Waterville wished her to linger; he felt in looking at her as if he had been looking at a charming picture. Her low-growing hair, with its fine dense undulations, was of a shade of blackness that has now become rare; her complexion had the bloom of a white flower; her profile, when she turned her head, was as pure and fine as the outline of a cameo.

"You know this is the first theatre," she said to Waterville, as if she wished to be sociable. "And this is Voltaire, the celebrated writer."

"I'm devoted to the Comédie Française," Waterville answered, smiling.

"Dreadfully bad house; we didn't hear a word," said Sir Arthur.

"Ah, yes, the boxes!" murmured Waterville.

"I'm rather disappointed," Mrs. Headway went on. "But I want to see what becomes of that woman."

"Doña Clorinde? Oh, I suppose they'll shoot her; they generally shoot the women, in French plays," Littlemore said.

"It will remind me of San Diego!" cried Mrs. Headway.

"Ah, at San Diego the women did the shooting."

"They don't seem to have killed you!" Mrs. Headway rejoined, archly.

"No, but I'm riddled with wounds."

"Well, this is very remarkable," the lady went on, turning to Houdon's statue. "It's beautifully modelled."

"You are perhaps reading M. de Voltaire," Littlemore suggested.

"No; but I've purchased his works."

"They are not proper reading for ladies," said the young Englishman, severely, offering his arm to Mrs. Headway.

"Ah, you might have told me before I had bought them!" she exclaimed, in exaggerated dismay.

"I couldn't imagine you would buy a hundred and fifty volumes."

"A hundred and fifty? I have only bought two."

"Perhaps two won't hurt you?" said Littlemore with a smile.

She darted him a reproachful ray. "I know what you mean,—that I'm too bad already! Well, bad as I am, you must come and see me." And she threw him the name of her hotel, as she walked away with her Englishman. Waterville looked after the latter with a certain interest; he had heard of him in London, and had seen his portrait in "Vanity Fair."

It was not yet time to go down, in spite of this gentleman's saying so, and Littlemore and his friend passed out on the balcony of the Foyer. "Headway—Headway? Where the deuce did she get that name?" Littlemore asked, as they looked down into the animated dusk.

"From her husband, I suppose," Waterville suggested.

"From her husband? From which? The last was named Beck."

"How many has she had?" Waterville inquired, anxious to hear how it was that Mrs. Headway was not respectable.

"I haven't the least idea. But it wouldn't be difficult to find out, as I believe they are all living. She was Mrs. Beck—Nancy Beck—when I knew her."

"Nancy Beck!" cried Waterville, aghast. He was thinking of her delicate profile, like that of a pretty Roman empress. There was a great deal to be explained.

Littlemore explained it in a few words before they returned to their places, admitting indeed that he was not yet able to elucidate her present situation. She was a memory of his Western days; he had seen her last some six years before. He had known her very well and in several places; the circle of her activity was chiefly the Southwest. This activity was of a vague character, except in the sense that it was exclusively social. She was supposed to have a husband, one Philadelphus Beck, the editor of a Democratic newspaper, the *Dakotah Sentinel*; but Littlemore had never seen him—the pair were living apart—and it was the impression at San Diego that matrimony, for Mr. and Mrs. Beck, was about played out. He remembered now to have heard afterwards that she was getting a divorce. She got divorces very easily, she was so taking in court.

She had got one or two before from a man whose name he had forgotten, and there was a legend that even these were not the first. She had been exceedingly divorced! When he first met her in California, she called herself Mrs. Grenville, which he had been given to understand was not an appellation acquired in matrimony, but her parental name, resumed after the dissolution of an unfortunate union. She had had these episodes—her unions were all unfortunate—and had borne half a dozen names. She was a charming woman, especially for New Mexico; but she had been divorced too often—it was a tax on one's credulity; she must have repudiated more husbands than she had married.

At San Diego she was staying with her sister, whose actual spouse (she, too, had been divorced), the principal man of the place, kept a bank (with the aid of a six-shooter), and who had never suffered Nancy to want for a home during her unattached periods. Nancy had begun very young; she must be about thirty-seven to-day. That was all he meant by her not being respectable. The chronology was rather mixed; her sister at least had once told him that there was one winter when she didn't know herself *who* was Nancy's husband. She had gone in mainly for editors—she esteemed the journalistic profession. They must all have been dreadful ruffians, for her own amiability was manifest. It was well known that whatever she had done she had done in self-defense. In fine, she had done things; that was the main point now! She was very pretty, good-natured and clever, and quite the best company in those parts. She was a genuine product of the far West—a flower of the Pacific slope; ignorant, audacious, crude, but full of pluck and spirit, of natural intelligence, and of a certain intermittent, haphazard good taste. She used to say that she only wanted a chance—apparently she had found it now. At one time, without her, he didn't see how he could have put up with the life. He had started a cattle-ranch, to which San Diego was the nearest town, and he used to ride over to see her. Sometimes he stayed there for a week; then he went to see her every evening. It was horribly hot; they used to sit on the back piazza. She was always as attractive, and very nearly as well-dressed, as they had just beheld her. As far as appearance went, she might have been transplanted at an hour's notice from that dusty old settlement to the city by the Seine.

"Some of those Western women are wonderful," Littlemore said. "Like her, they only want a chance."

He had not been in love with her—there never was anything of that sort between them. There might have been of course; but as it happened there was not. Headway apparently was the successor of Beck; perhaps there had been others between. She was in no sort of "society"; she only had a local reputation ("the elegant and accomplished Mrs. Beck," the newspapers called her—the other editors, to whom she wasn't married), though, indeed, in that spacious civilization the locality was large. She knew nothing of the East, and to the best of his belief at that period had never seen New York. Various things might have happened in those six years, however; no doubt she had "come up." The West was sending us everything (Littlemore spoke as a New Yorker); no doubt it would send us at last our brilliant women. This little woman used to look quite over the head of New York; even in those days she thought and talked of Paris, which there was no prospect of her knowing; that was the way she had got on in New Mexico. She had had her ambition, her presentiments; she had known she was meant for better things. Even at San Diego she had prefigured her little Sir Arthur; every now and then a wandering Englishman came within her range. They were not all baronets and M. P.'s, but they were usually a change from the editors. What she was doing with her present acquisition he was curious to see. She was certainly—if he had any capacity for that state of mind, which was not too apparent—making him happy. She looked very splendid; Headway had probably made a "pile," an achievement not to be imputed to any of the others. She didn't accept money—he was sure she didn't accept money.

On their way back to their seats Littlemore, whose tone had been humorous, but with that strain of the pensive which is inseparable from retrospect, suddenly broke into audible laughter.

"The modelling of a statue and the works of Voltaire!" he exclaimed, recurring to two or three things she had said. "It's comical to hear her attempt those flights, for in New Mexico she knew nothing about modelling."

"She didn't strike me as affected," Waterville rejoined, feeling a vague impulse to take a considerate view of her.

"Oh, no; she's only—as she says—fearfully changed."

They were in their places before the play went on again, and they both gave another glance at Mrs. Headway's box. She leaned back, slowly fanning herself, and evidently watching Littlemore, as if she had been waiting to see him come in. Sir Arthur Demesne sat beside her, rather gloomily, resting a round pink chin upon a high stiff collar; neither of them seemed to speak.

"Are you sure she makes him happy?" Waterville asked.

"Yes—that's the way those people show it."

"But does she go about alone with him that way? Where's her husband?"

"I suppose she has divorced him."

"And does she want to marry the baronet?" Waterville asked, as if his companion were omniscient.

It amused Littlemore for the moment to appear so. "He wants to marry her, I guess."

"And be divorced, like the others?"

"Oh, no; this time she has got what she wants," said Littlemore, as the curtain rose.

He suffered three days to elapse before he called at the Hôtel Meurice, which she had designated, and we may occupy this interval in adding a few words to the story we have taken from his lips. George Littlemore's residence in the far West had been of the usual tentative sort—he had gone there to replenish a pocket depleted by youthful extravagance. His first attempts had failed; the days were passing away when a fortune was to be picked up even by a young man who might be supposed to have inherited from an honorable father, lately removed, some of those fine abilities, mainly dedicated to the importation of tea, to which the elder Mr. Littlemore was indebted for the power of leaving his son well off. Littlemore had dissipated his patrimony, and he was not quick to discover his talents, which, consisting chiefly of an unlimited faculty for smoking and horse-breaking, appeared to lie in the direction of none of the professions called liberal. He had been sent to Harvard to have his aptitudes cultivated, but here they took such a form that repression had been found more necessary than stimulus—repression embodied in an occasional sojourn in one of the lovely villages of the Connecticut valley. Rustication saved him, perhaps, in the sense that it detached him; it destroyed his ambitions, which had been foolish. At the age of thirty, Littlemore had mastered none of the useful arts, unless we include in the number the great art of indifference. He was roused from his indifference by a stroke of good luck. To oblige a friend who was even in more pressing need of cash than himself, he had purchased for a moderate sum (the proceeds of a successful game of poker) a share in a silver-mine which the disposer, with unusual candor, admitted to be destitute of metal. Littlemore looked into his mine and recognized the truth of the contention, which, however, was demolished some two years later by a sudden revival of curiosity on the part of one of the other shareholders. This gentleman, convinced that a silver-mine without silver is as rare as an effect without a cause, discovered the sparkle of the precious element deep down in the reasons of things. The discovery was agreeable to Littlemore, and was the beginning of a fortune which, through several dull years and in many rough places, he had repeatedly despaired of, and which a man whose purpose was never very keen did not perhaps altogether deserve. It was before he saw himself successful that he had made the acquaintance of the lady now established at the Hôtel Meurice. To-day he owned the largest share in his mine, which remained perversely productive, and which enabled him to buy, among other things, in Montana, a cattle-ranch of much finer proportions than the dry acres near San Diego. Ranches and mines encourage security, and the consciousness of not having to watch the sources of his income too anxiously (an obligation which for a man of his disposition spoils everything) now added itself to his usual coolness. It was not that this same coolness had not been considerably tried. To take only one—the principal—instance: he had lost his wife after only a twelve-month of marriage, some three years before the date at which we meet him. He was more than forty when he encountered and wooed a young girl of twenty-three, who, like himself, had consulted all the probabilities in expecting a succession of happy years. She left him a small daughter, now intrusted to the care of his only sister, the wife of an English squire and mistress of a dull park in Hampshire. This lady, Mrs. Dolphin by name, had captivated her landowner during a journey in which Mr. Dolphin had promised himself to examine the institutions of the United States. The institution on which he reported most favorably was the pretty girls of the larger towns, and he returned to New York a year or two later to marry Miss Littlemore, who, unlike her brother, had not wasted her patrimony. Her sister-in-law, married many years later, and coming to Europe on this occasion, had died in London—where she flattered herself the doctors were infallible—a week after the birth of her little girl; and poor Littlemore, though relinquishing his child for the moment, remained in these disappointing countries, to be within call of the Hampshire nursery. He was rather a noticeable man, especially since his hair and mustache had turned white. Tall and strong, with a good figure and a bad carriage, he looked capable but indolent, and was usually supposed to have an importance of which he was far from being conscious. His eye was at once keen and quiet, his smile dim and dilatory, but exceedingly genuine. His principal occupation to-day was doing nothing, and he did it with a sort of artistic perfection. This faculty excited real envy on the part of Rupert Waterville, who was ten years younger than he, and who had too many ambitions and anxieties—none of them very important, but making collectively a considerable incubus—to be able to wait for inspiration. He thought it a great accomplishment, he hoped some day to arrive at it; it made a man so independent; he had his resources within his own breast. Littlemore could sit for a whole evening, without utterance or movement, smoking cigars and looking absently at his finger-nails. As every one knew that he was a good fellow and had made his fortune, this dull behavior could not well be attributed to stupidity or to moroseness. It seemed to imply a fund of reminiscence, an experience of life which had left him hundreds of things to think about. Waterville felt that if he could make a good use of these present years, and keep a sharp look-out for experience, he too, at forty-five, might have time to look at his finger-nails. He had an idea that such contemplations—not of course in their literal, but in their symbolic intensity—were a sign of a man of the world. Waterville, reckoning possibly without an ungrateful Department of State, had also an idea that he had embraced the diplomatic career. He was the junior of the two Secretaries who render the *personnel* of the United States Legation in London exceptionally numerous, and was at present enjoying his annual leave of absence. It became a diplomatist to be inscrutable, and though he had by no means, as a whole, taken Littlemore as his model—there were much better ones in the diplomatic body in London—he thought he looked inscrutable when of an evening, in Paris, after he had been asked what he would like to do, he replied that he should like to do nothing, and simply sat for an interminable time in front of the Grand Café, on the Boulevard de la Madeleine (he was very fond of cafés), ordering a succession of *demitasses.* It was very rarely that Littlemore cared even to go to the theatre, and the visit to the Comédie Française, which we have described, had been undertaken at Waterville's instance. He had seen *Le Demi-Monde* a few nights before, and had been told that *L'Aventurière* would show him a particular treatment of the same subject—the justice to be meted out to unscrupulous women who attempt to thrust themselves into honorable families. It seemed to him that in both of these cases the ladies had deserved their fate, but he wished it might have been brought about by a little less lying on the part of the representatives of honor. Littlemore and he, without being intimate, were very good friends, and spent much of their time together. As it turned out, Littlemore was very glad he had gone to the theatre, for he found himself much interested in this new incarnation of Nancy Beck.

II

His delay in going to see her was nevertheless calculated; there were more reasons for it than it is necessary to mention. But when he went, Mrs. Headway was at home, and Littlemore was not surprised to see Sir Arthur Demesne in her sitting-room. There was something in the air which seemed to indicate that this gentleman's visit had already lasted a certain time. Littlemore thought it probable that, given the circumstances, he would now bring it to a close; he must have learned from their hostess that Littlemore was an old and familiar friend. He might of course have definite rights—he had every appearance of it; but the more definite they were the more gracefully he could afford to waive them. Littlemore made these reflections while Sir Arthur Demesne sat there looking at him without giving any sign of departure. Mrs. Headway was very gracious—she had the manner of having known you a hundred years; she scolded Littlemore extravagantly for not having been to see her sooner, but this was only a form of the gracious. By daylight she looked a little faded; but she had an expression which could never fade. She had the best rooms in the hotel, and an air of extreme opulence and prosperity; her courier sat outside in the ante-chamber, and she evidently knew how to live. She attempted to include Sir Arthur in the conversation, but though the young man remained in his place, he declined to be included. He smiled, in silence; but he was evidently uncomfortable. The conversation, therefore, remained superficial—a quality that, of old, had by no means belonged to Mrs. Headway's interviews with her friends. The Englishman looked at Littlemore with a strange, perverse expression which Littlemore, at first, with a good deal of private amusement, simply attributed to jealousy.

"My dear Sir Arthur, I wish very much you would go," Mrs. Headway remarked, at the end of a quarter of an hour.

Sir Arthur got up and took his hat. "I thought I should oblige you by staying."

"To defend me against Mr. Littlemore? I've known him since I was a baby—I know the worst he can do." She fixed her charming smile for a moment on her retreating visitor, and she added, with much unexpectedness, "I want to talk to him about my past!"

"That's just what I want to hear," said Sir Arthur, with his hand on the door.

"We are going to talk American; you wouldn't understand us!—He speaks in the English style," she explained, in her little sufficient way, as the baronet, who announced that at all events he would come back in the evening, let himself out.

"He doesn't know about your past?" Littlemore inquired, trying not to make the question sound impertinent.

"Oh, yes; I've told him everything; but he doesn't understand. The English are so peculiar; I think they are rather stupid. He has never heard of a woman being—" But here Mrs. Headway checked herself, while Littlemore filled out the blank. "What are you laughing at? It doesn't matter," she went on; "there are more things in the world than those people have heard of. However, I like them very much; at least I like him. He's such a gentleman; do you know what I mean? Only, he stays too long, and he isn't amusing. I'm very glad to see you, for a change."

"Do you mean I'm not a gentleman?" Littlemore asked.

"No indeed; you used to be, in New Mexico. I think you were the only one—and I hope you are still. That's why I recognized you the other night; I might have cut you, you know."

"You can still, if you like. It's not too late."

"Oh, no; that's not what I want. I want you to help me."

"To help you?"

Mrs. Headway fixed her eyes for a moment on the door. "Do you suppose that man is there still?"

"That young man—your poor Englishman?"

"No; I mean Max. Max is my courier," said Mrs. Headway, with a certain impressiveness.

"I haven't the least idea. I'll see, if you like."

"No; in that case I should have to give him an order, and I don't know what in the world to ask him to do. He sits there for hours; with my simple habits I afford him no employment. I am afraid I have no imagination."

"The burden of grandeur," said Littlemore.

"Oh yes, I'm very grand. But on the whole I like it. I'm only afraid he'll hear. I talk so very loud; that's another thing I'm trying to get over."

"Why do you want to be different?"

"Well, because everything else is different," Mrs. Headway rejoined, with a little sigh. "Did you hear that I'd lost my husband?" she went on, abruptly.

"Do you mean—a—Mr.——?" and Littlemore paused, with an effect that did not seem to come home to her.

"I mean Mr. Headway," she said, with dignity. "I've been through a good deal since you saw me last: marriage, and death, and trouble, and all sorts of things."

"You had been through a good deal of marriage before that," Littlemore ventured to observe.

She rested her eyes on him with soft brightness, and without a change of color. "Not so much—not so much—"

"Not so much as might have been thought."

"Not so much as was reported. I forget whether I was married when I saw you last."

"It was one of the reports," said Littlemore. "But I never saw Mr. Beck."

"You didn't lose much; he was a simple *wretch*! I have done certain things in my life which I have never understood; no wonder others can't understand them. But that's all over! Are you sure Max doesn't hear?" she asked, quickly.

"Not at all sure. But if you suspect him of listening at the keyhole, I would send him away."

"I don't think he does that. I am always rushing to the door."

"Then he doesn't hear. I had no idea you had so many secrets. When I parted with you, Mr. Headway was in the future."

"Well, now he's in the past. He was a pleasant man—I can understand my doing that. But he only lived a year. He had neuralgia of the heart; he left me very well off." She mentioned these various facts as if they were quite of the same order.

"I'm glad to hear it; you used to have expensive tastes."

"I have plenty of money," said Mrs. Headway. "Mr. Headway had property at Denver, which has increased immensely in value. After his death I tried New York. But I don't like New York." Littlemore's hostess uttered this last sentence in a tone which was the *résumé* of a social episode. "I mean to live in Europe—I like Europe," she announced; and the manner of the announcement had a touch of prophecy, as the other words had had a reverberation of history.

Littlemore was very much struck with all this, and he was greatly entertained with Mrs. Headway. "Are you travelling with that young man?" he inquired, with the coolness of a person who wishes to make his entertainment go as far as possible.

She folded her arms as she leaned back in her chair. "Look here, Mr. Littlemore," she said; "I'm about as good-natured as I used to be in America, but I know a great deal more. Of course I ain't travelling with that young man; he's only a friend."

"He isn't a lover?" asked Littlemore, rather cruelly.

"Do people travel with their lovers? I don't want you to laugh at me—I want you to help me." She fixed her eyes on him with an air of tender remonstrance that might have touched him; she looked so gentle and reasonable. "As I tell you, I have taken a great fancy to this old Europe; I feel as if I should never go back. But I want to see something of the life. I think it would suit me—if I could get started a little. Mr. Littlemore," she added, in a moment—"I may as well be frank, for I ain't at all ashamed. I want to get into society. That's what I'm after!"

Littlemore settled himself in his chair, with the feeling of a man who, knowing that he will have to pull, seeks to obtain a certain leverage. It was in a tone of light jocosity, almost of encouragement, however, that he repeated: "Into society? It seems to me you are in it already, with baronets for your adorers."

"That's just what I want to know!" she said, with a certain eagerness. "Is a baronet much?"

"So they are apt to think. But I know very little about it."

"Ain't you in society yourself?"

"I? Never in the world! Where did you get that idea? I care no more about society than about that copy of the *Figaro*."

Mrs. Headway's countenance assumed for a moment a look of extreme disappointment, and Littlemore could see that, having heard of his silver-mine and his cattle-ranch, and knowing that he was living in Europe, she had hoped to find him immersed in the world of fashion. But she speedily recovered herself. "I don't believe a word of it. You know you're a gentleman—you can't help yourself."

"I may be a gentleman, but I have none of the habits of one." Littlemore hesitated a moment, and then he added—"I lived too long in the great Southwest."

She flushed quickly; she instantly understood—understood even more than he had meant to say. But she wished to make use of him, and it was of more importance that she should appear forgiving—especially as she had the happy consciousness of being so, than that she should punish a cruel speech. She could afford, however, to be lightly ironical. "That makes no difference—a gentleman is always a gentleman."

"Not always," said Littlemore, laughing.

"It's impossible that, through your sister, you shouldn't know something about European society," said Mrs. Headway.

At the mention of his sister, made with a studied lightness of reference which he caught as it passed, Littlemore was unable to repress a start. "What in the world have you got to do with my sister?" he would have liked to say. The introduction of this lady was disagreeable to him; she belonged to quite another order of ideas, and it was out of the question that Mrs. Headway should ever make her acquaintance—if this was what, as that lady would have said—she was "after." But he took advantage of a side-issue. "What do you mean by European society? One can't talk about that. It's a very vague phrase."

"Well, I mean English society—I mean the society your sister lives in—that's what I mean," said Mrs. Headway, who was quite prepared to be definite. "I mean the people I saw in London last May—the people I saw at the opera and in the park, the people who go to the Queen's drawing-rooms. When I was in London I stayed at that hotel on the corner of Piccadilly—that looking straight down St. James's Street—and I spent hours together at the window looking at the people in the carriages. I had a carriage of my own, and when I was not at my window I was driving all round. I was all alone; I saw every one, but I knew no one—I had no one to tell me. I didn't know Sir Arthur then—I only met him a month ago at Homburg. He followed me to Paris—that's how he came to be my guest." Serenely, prosaically, without any of the inflation of vanity, Mrs. Headway made this last assertion; it was as if she were used to being followed, or as if a gentleman one met at Homburg would inevitably follow. In the same tone she went on: "I attracted a good deal of attention in London—I could easily see that."

"You'll do that wherever you go," Littlemore said, insufficiently enough, as he felt.

"I don't want to attract so much; I think it's vulgar," Mrs. Headway rejoined, with a certain soft sweetness which seemed to denote the enjoyment of a new idea. She was evidently open to new ideas.

"Every one was looking at you the other night at the theatre," Littlemore continued. "How can you hope to escape notice?"

"I don't want to escape notice—people have always looked at me, and I suppose they always will. But there are different ways of being looked at, and I know the way I want. I mean to have it, too!" Mrs. Headway exclaimed. Yes, she was very definite.

Littlemore sat there, face to face with her, and for some time he said nothing. He had a mixture of feelings, and the memory of other places, other hours, was stealing over him. There had been of old a very considerable absence of interposing surfaces between these two—he had known her as one knew people only in the great Southwest. He had liked her extremely, in a town where it would have been ridiculous to be difficult to please. But his sense of this fact was somehow connected with Southwestern conditions; his liking for Nancy Beck was an emotion of which the proper setting was a back piazza. She presented herself here on a new basis—she appeared to desire to be classified afresh. Littlemore said to himself that this was too much trouble; he had taken her in that way—he couldn't begin at this time of day to take her in another way. He asked himself whether she were going to be a bore. It was not easy to suppose Mrs. Headway capable of this offence; but she might become tiresome if she were bent upon being different. It made him rather afraid when she began to talk about European society, about his sister, about things being vulgar. Littlemore was a very good fellow, and he had at least the average human love of justice; but there was in his composition an element of the indolent, the sceptical, perhaps even the brutal, which made him desire to preserve the simplicity of their former terms of intercourse. He had no particular desire to see a woman rise again, as the mystic process was called; he didn't believe in women's rising again. He believed in their not going down; thought it perfectly possible and eminently desirable, but held it was much better for society that they should not endeavor, as the French say, to *mêler les genres*. In general, he didn't pretend to say what was good for society—society seemed to him in rather a bad way; but he had a conviction on this particular point. Nancy Beck going in for the great prizes, that spectacle might be entertaining for a simple spectator; but it would be a nuisance, an embarrassment, from the moment anything more than contemplation should be expected of him. He had no wish to be rough, but it might be well to show her that he was not to be humbugged.

"Oh, if there's anything you want you'll have it," he said in answer to her last remark. "You have always had what you want."

"Well, I want something new this time. Does your sister reside in London?"

"My dear lady, what do you know about my sister?" Littlemore asked. "She's not a woman you would care for."

Mrs. Headway was silent a moment. "You don't respect me!" she exclaimed suddenly in a loud, almost gay tone of voice. If Littlemore wished, as I say, to preserve the simplicity of their old terms of intercourse, she was apparently willing to humor him.

"Ah, my dear Mrs. Beck . . .!" he cried, vaguely, protestingly, and using her former name quite by accident. At San Diego he had never thought whether he respected her or not; that never came up.

"That's a proof of it—calling me by that hateful name! Don't you believe I'm married? I haven't been fortunate in my names," she added, pensively.

"You make it very awkward when you say such mad things. My

sister lives most of the year in the country; she is very simple, rather dull, perhaps a trifle narrow-minded. You are very clever, very lively, and as wide as all creation. That's why I think you wouldn't like her."

"You ought to be ashamed to run down your sister!" cried Mrs. Headway. "You told me once—at San Diego—that she was the nicest woman you knew. I made a note of that, you see. And you told me she was just my age. So that makes it rather uncomfortable for you, if you won't introduce me!" And Littlemore's hostess gave a pitiless laugh. "I'm not in the least afraid of her being dull. It's very distinguished to be dull. I'm ever so much too lively."

"You are indeed, ever so much! But nothing is more easy than to know my sister," said Littlemore, who knew perfectly that what he said was untrue. And then, as a diversion from this delicate topic, he suddenly asked, "Are you going to marry Sir Arthur?"

"Don't you think I've been married about enough?"

"Possibly; but this is a new line, it would be different. An Englishman—that's a new sensation."

"If I should marry, it would be a European," said Mrs. Headway calmly.

"Your chance is very good; they are all marrying Americans."

"He would have to be some one fine, the man I should marry now. I have a good deal to make up for! That's what I want to know about Sir Arthur; all this time you haven't told me."

"I have nothing in the world to tell—I have never heard of him. Hasn't he told you himself?"

"Nothing at all; he is very modest. He doesn't brag, nor make himself out anything great. That's what I like him for: I think it's in such good taste. I like good taste!" exclaimed Mrs. Headway. "But all this time," she added, "you haven't told me you would help me."

"How can I help you? I'm no one, I have no power."

"You can help me by not preventing me. I want you to promise not to prevent me." She gave him her fixed, bright gaze again; her eyes seemed to look far into his.

"Good Lord, how could I prevent you?"

"I'm not sure that you could. But you might try."

"I'm too indolent, and too stupid," said Littlemore jocosely.

"Yes," she replied, musing as she still looked at him. "I think you are too stupid. But I think you are also too kind," she added more graciously. She was almost irresistible when she said such a thing as that.

They talked for a quarter of an hour longer, and at last—as if she had had scruples—she spoke to him of his own marriage, of the death of his wife, matters to which she alluded more felicitously (as he thought) than to some other points. "If you have a little girl you ought to be very happy; that's what I should like to have. Lord, I should make her a nice woman! Not like me—in another style!" When he rose to leave her, she told him that he must come and see her very often; she was to be some weeks longer in Paris; he must bring Mr. Waterville.

"Your English friend won't like that—our coming very often," Littlemore said, as he stood with his hand on the door.

"I don't know what he has got to do with it," she answered, staring.

"Neither do I. Only he must be in love with you."

"That doesn't give him any right. Mercy, if I had had to put myself out for all the men that have been in love with me!"

"Of course you would have had a terrible life! Even doing as you please, you have had rather an agitated one. But your young Englishman's sentiments appear to give him the right to sit there, after one comes in, looking blighted and bored. That might become very tiresome."

"The moment he becomes tiresome I send him away. You can trust me for that."

"Oh," said Littlemore, "it doesn't matter, after all." He remembered that it would be very inconvenient to him to have undisturbed possession of Mrs. Headway.

She came out with him into the antechamber. Mr. Max, the courier, was fortunately not there. She lingered a little; she appeared to have more to say.

"On the contrary, he likes you to come," she remarked in a moment; "he wants to study my friends."

"To study them?"

"He wants to find out about me, and he thinks they may tell him something. Some day he will ask you right out, 'What sort of a woman is she, anyway?' "

"Hasn't he found out yet?"

"He doesn't understand me," said Mrs. Headway, surveying the front of her dress. "He has never seen any one like me."

"I should imagine not!"

"So he will ask you, as I say."

"I will tell him you are the most charming woman in Europe."

"That ain't a description! Besides, he knows it. He wants to know if I'm respectable."

"He's very curious!" Littlemore cried, with a laugh.

She grew a little pale; she seemed to be watching his lips. "Mind you tell him," she went on with a smile that brought none of her color back.

"Respectable? I'll tell him you're adorable!"

Mrs. Headway stood a moment longer. "Ah, you're no use!" she murmured. And she suddenly turned away and passed back into her sitting-room, slowly drawing her far-trailing skirts.

III

E*lle ne se doute de rien*!" Littlemore said to himself as he walked away from the hotel; and he repeated the phrase in talking about her to Waterville. "She wants to be right," he added; "but she will never really succeed; she has begun too late, she will never be more than half-right. However, she won't know when she's wrong, so it doesn't signify!" And then he proceeded to assert that in some respects she would remain incurable; she had no delicacy; no discretion, no shading; she was a woman who suddenly said to you, "You don't respect me!" As if that were a thing for a woman to say!

"It depends upon what she meant by it." Waterville liked to see the meanings of things.

"The more she meant by it the less she ought to say it!" Littlemore declared.

But he returned to the Hôtel Meurice, and on the next occasion he took Waterville with him. The Secretary of Legation, who had not often been in close quarters with a lady of this ambiguous quality, was prepared to regard Mrs. Headway as a very curious type.

He was afraid she might be dangerous; but, on the whole, he felt secure. The object of his devotion at present was his country, or at least the Department of State; he had no intention of being diverted from that allegiance. Besides, he had his ideal of the attractive woman—a person pitched in a very much lower key than this shining, smiling, rustling, chattering daughter of the Territories. The woman he should care for would have repose, a certain love of privacy—she would sometimes let one alone. Mrs. Headway was personal, familiar, intimate; she was always appealing or accusing, demanding explanations and pledges, saying things one had to answer. All this was accompanied with a hundred smiles and radiations and other natural graces, but the general effect of it was slightly fatiguing. She had certainly a great deal of charm, an immense desire to please, and a wonderful collection of dresses and trinkets; but she was eager and preoccupied, and it was impossible that other people should share her eagerness. If she wished to get into society, there was no reason why her bachelor visitors should wish to see her there; for it was the absence of the usual social incumbrances which made her drawing-room attractive. There was no doubt whatever that she was several women in one, and she ought to content herself with that sort of numerical triumph. Littlemore said to Waterville that it was stupid of her to wish to scale the heights; she ought to know how much more she was in her place down below. She appeared vaguely to irritate him; even her fluttering attempts at self-culture—she had become a great critic, and handled many of the productions of the age with a bold, free touch—constituted a vague invocation, an appeal for sympathy which was naturally annoying to a man who disliked the trouble of revising old decisions, consecrated by a certain amount of reminiscence that might be called tender. She had, however, one palpable charm; she was full of surprises. Even Waterville was obliged to confess that an element of the unexpected was not to be excluded from his conception of the woman who should have an ideal repose. Of course there were two kinds of surprises, and only one of them was thoroughly pleasant, though Mrs. Headway dealt impartially in both. She had the sudden delights, the odd exclamations, the queer curiosities of a person who has grown up in a country where everything is new and many things ugly, and who, with a natural turn for the arts and amenities of life, makes a tardy acquaintance with some of the finer usages, the higher pleasures. She was provincial—it was easy to see that she was provincial; that took no great cleverness. But what was Parisian enough—if to be Parisian was the measure of success—was the way she picked up ideas and took a hint from every circumstance. "Only give me time, and I shall know all I have need of," she said to Littlemore, who watched her progress with a mixture of admiration and sadness. She delighted to speak of herself as a poor little barbarian who was trying to pick up a few crumbs of knowledge, and this habit took great effect from her delicate face, her perfect dress, and the brilliancy of her manners.

One of her surprises was that after that first visit she said no more to Littlemore about Mrs. Dolphin. He did her perhaps the grossest injustice; but he had quite expected her to bring up this lady whenever they met. "If she will only leave Agnes alone, she may do what she will," he said to Waterville, expressing his relief. "My sister would never look at her, and it would be very awkward to have to tell her so." She expected assistance; she made him feel that simply by the way she looked at him; but for the moment she demanded no definite service. She held her tongue, but she waited, and her patience itself was a kind of admonition. In the way of society, it must be confessed, her privileges were meagre, Sir Arthur Demesne and her two compatriots being, so far as the latter could discover, her only visitors. She might have had other friends, but she held her head very high, and liked better to see no one than not to see the best company. It was evident that she flattered herself that she produced the effect of being, not neglected, but fastidious. There were plenty of Americans in Paris, but in this direction she failed to extend her acquaintance; the nice people wouldn't come and see her, and nothing would have induced her to receive the others. She had the most exact conception of the people she wished to see and to avoid. Littlemore expected every day that she would ask him why he didn't bring some of his friends, and he had his answer ready. It was a very poor one, for it consisted simply of a conventional assurance that he wished to keep her for himself. She would be sure to retort that this was very "thin," as, indeed, it was; but the days went by without her calling him to account. The little American colony in Paris is rich in amiable women, but there were none to whom Littlemore could make up his mind to say that it would be a favor to him to call on Mrs. Headway. He shouldn't like them the better for doing so, and he wished to like those of whom he might ask a favor. Except, therefore, that he occasionally spoke of her as a little Western woman, very pretty and rather queer, who had formerly been a great chum of his, she remained unknown in the *salons* of the Avenue Gabriel and the streets that encircle the Arch of Triumph. To ask the men to go and see her, without asking the ladies, would only accentuate the fact that he didn't ask the ladies; so he asked no one at all. Besides, it was true—just a little—that he wished to keep her to himself, and he was fatuous enough to believe that she cared much more for him than for her Englishman. Of course, however, he would never dream of marrying her, whereas the Englishman apparently was immersed in that vision. She hated her past; she used to announce that very often, talking of it as if it were an appendage of the same order as a dishonest courier, or even an inconvenient protrusion of drapery. Therefore, as Littlemore was part of her past, it might have been supposed that she would hate him too, and wish to banish him, with all the images he recalled, from her sight. But she made an exception in his favor, and if she disliked their old relations as a chapter of her own history, she seemed still to like them as a chapter of his. He felt that she clung to him, that she believed he could help her and in the long run would. It was to the long run that she appeared little by little to have attuned herself.

She succeeded perfectly in maintaining harmony between Sir Arthur Demesne and her American visitors, who spent much less time in her drawing-room. She had easily persuaded him that there were no grounds for jealousy, and that they had no wish, as she said, to crowd him out; for it was ridiculous to be jealous of two persons at once, and Rupert Waterville, after he had learned the way to her hospitable apartment, appeared there as often as his friend Littlemore. The two, indeed, usually came together, and they ended by relieving their competitor of a certain sense of responsibility. This amiable and excellent but somewhat limited and slightly pretentious young man, who had not yet made up his mind, was sometimes rather oppressed with the magnitude of his undertaking, and when he was alone with Mrs. Headway the tension of his thoughts occasionally became quite painful. He was very slim and straight, and looked taller than his height; he had the prettiest, silkiest hair, which waved away from a large white forehead, and he was endowed with a nose of the so-called Roman model. He looked younger than his years (in spite of those last two attributes), partly on account of the delicacy of his complexion and the almost childlike candor of his round blue eye. He was diffident and self-conscious; there were certain letters he could not pronounce. At the same time he had the manners of a young man who had been brought up to fill a considerable place in the world, with whom a certain correctness had become a habit, and who, though he might occasionally be a little awkward about small things, would be sure to acquit himself honorably in great ones. He was very simple, and he believed himself very serious; he had the blood of a score of Warwickshire squires in his veins; mingled in the last instance with the somewhat paler fluid which animated the long-necked daughter of a banker who had expected an earl for his son-in-law, but who had consented to regard Sir Baldwin Demesne as the least insufficient of baronets. The boy, the only one, had come into his title at five years of age; his mother, who disappointed her auriferous sire a second time when poor Sir Baldwin broke his neck in the hunting field, watched over him with a tenderness that burned as steadily as a candle shaded by a transparent hand. She never admitted, even to herself, that he was not the cleverest of men; but it took all her own cleverness, which was much greater than his, to maintain this appearance. Fortunately he was not wild, so that he would never marry an actress or a governess, like two or three of the young men who had been at Eton with him. With this ground of nervousness the less, Lady Demesne awaited with an air of confidence his promotion to some high office. He represented in Parliament the Conservative instincts and vote of a red-roofed market town, and sent regularly to his bookseller for all the new publications on economical subjects, for he was determined that his political attitude should have a firm statistical basis. He was not conceited; he was only misinformed—misinformed, I mean, about himself. He thought himself indispensable in the scheme of things—not as an individual, but as an institution. This conviction, however, was too sacred to betray itself by vulgar assumptions. If he was a little man in a big place, he never strutted nor talked loud; he merely felt it as a kind of luxury that he had a large social circumference. It was like sleeping in a big bed; one didn't toss about the more, but one felt a greater freshness.

He had never seen anything like Mrs. Headway; he hardly knew by what standard to measure her. She was not like an English lady—not like those at least with whom he had been accustomed to converse; and yet it was impossible not to see that she had a standard of her own. He suspected that she was provincial, but as he was very much under the charm he compromised matters by saying to himself that she was only foreign. It was of course provincial to be foreign; but this was, after all, a peculiarity which she shared with a great many nice people. He was not wild, and his mother had flattered herself that in this all-important matter he would not be perverse; but it was all the same most unexpected that he should have taken a fancy to an American widow, five years older than himself, who knew no one and who sometimes didn't appear to understand exactly who he was. Though he disapproved of it, it was precisely her foreignness that pleased him; she seemed to be as little as possible of his own race and creed; there was not a touch of Warwickshire in her composition. She was like an Hungarian or a Pole, with the difference that he could almost understand her language. The unfortunate young man was fascinated, though he had not yet admitted to himself that he was in love. He would be very slow and deliberate in such a position, for he was deeply conscious of its importance. He was a young man who had arranged his life; he had determined to marry at thirty-two. A long line of ancestors was watching him; he hardly knew what they would think of Mrs. Headway. He hardly knew what he thought himself; the only thing he was absolutely sure of was that she made the time pass as it passed in no other pursuit. He was vaguely uneasy; he was by no means sure it was right the time should pass like that. There was nothing to show for it but the fragments of Mrs. Headway's conversation, the peculiarities of her accent, the sallies of her wit, the audacities of her fancy, her mysterious allusions to her past. Of course he knew that she had a past; she was not a young girl, she was a widow—and widows are essentially an expression of an accomplished fact. He was not jealous of her antecedents, but he wished to understand them, and it was here that the difficulty occurred. The subject was illumined with fitful flashes, but it never placed itself before him as a general picture. He asked her a good many questions, but her answers were so startling that, like sudden luminous points, they seemed to intensify the darkness round their edges. She had apparently spent her life in an inferior province of an inferior country;

but it didn't follow from this that she herself had been low. She had been a lily among thistles; and there was something romantic in a man in his position taking an interest in such a woman. It pleased Sir Arthur to believe he was romantic; that had been the case with several of his ancestors, who supplied a precedent without which he would perhaps not have ventured to trust himself. He was the victim of perplexities from which a single spark of direct perception would have saved him. He took everything in the literal sense; he had not a grain of humor. He sat there vaguely waiting for something to happen, and not committing himself by rash declarations. If he was in love, it was in his own way, reflectively, inexpressively, obstinately. He was waiting for the formula which would justify his conduct and Mrs. Headway's peculiarities. He hardly knew where it would come from; you might have thought from his manner that he would discover it in one of the elaborate *entrées* that were served to the pair when Mrs. Headway consented to dine with him at Bignon's or the Café Anglais; or in one of the numerous bandboxes that arrived from the Rue de la Paix, and from which she often lifted the lid in the presence of her admirer. There were moments when he got weary of waiting in vain, and at these moments the arrival of her American friends (he often wondered that she had so few), seemed to lift the mystery from his shoulders and give him a chance to rest. This formula—she herself was not yet able to give it, for she was not aware how much ground it was expected to cover. She talked about her past, because she thought it the best thing to do; she had a shrewd conviction that it was better to make a good use of it than to attempt to efface it. To efface it was impossible, though that was what she would have preferred. She had no objection to telling fibs, but now that she was taking a new departure, she wished to tell only those that were necessary. She would have been delighted if it had been possible to tell none at all. A few, however, were indispensable, and we need not attempt to estimate more closely the ingenious re-arrangements of fact with which she entertained and mystified Sir Arthur. She knew of course that as a product of fashionable circles she was nowhere, but she might have great success as a child of nature.

IV

RUPERT WATERVILLE, in the midst of intercourse in which every one perhaps had a good many mental reservations, never forgot that he was in a representative position, that he was responsible, official; and he asked himself more than once how far it was permitted to him to countenance Mrs. Headway's pretensions to being an American lady typical even of the newer phases. In his own way he was as puzzled as poor Sir Arthur, and indeed he flattered himself that he was as particular as any Englishman could be. Suppose that after all this free association Mrs. Headway should come over to London and ask at the Legation to be presented to the Queen? It would be so awkward to refuse her—of course they would have to refuse her—that he was very careful about making tacit promises. She might construe anything as a tacit promise—he knew how the smallest gestures of diplomatists were studied and interpreted. It was his effort therefore to be really the diplomatist in his relations with this attractive but dangerous woman. The party of four used often to dine together—Sir Arthur pushed his confidence so far—and on these occasions Mrs. Headway, availing herself of one of the privileges of a lady, even at the most expensive restaurant—used to wipe her glasses with her napkin. One evening, when after polishing a goblet she held it up to the light, giving it, with her head on one side, the least glimmer of a wink, he said to himself as he watched her that she looked like a modern bacchante. He noticed at this moment that the baronet was gazing at her too, and he wondered if the same idea had come to him. He often wondered what the baronet thought; he had devoted first and last a good deal of speculation to the baronial class. Littlemore, alone, at this moment, was not observing Mrs. Headway; he never appeared to observe her, though she often observed him. Waterville asked himself among other things why Sir Arthur had not brought his own friends to see her, for Paris during the several weeks that now elapsed was rich in English visitors. He wondered whether she had asked him and he had refused; he would have liked very much to know whether she had asked him. He explained his curiosity to Littlemore, who, however, took very little interest in it. Littlemore said, nevertheless, that he had no doubt she had asked him; she never would be deterred by false delicacy.

"She has been very delicate with you," Waterville replied. "She hasn't been at all pressing of late."

"It is only because she has given me up; she thinks I'm a brute."

"I wonder what she thinks of me," Waterville said, pensively.

"Oh, she counts upon you to introduce her to the Minister. It's lucky for you that our representative here is absent."

"Well," Waterville rejoined, "the Minister has settled two or three difficult questions, and I suppose he can settle this one. I shall do nothing but by the orders of my chief." He was very fond of talking about his chief.

"She does me injustice," Littlemore added in a moment. "I have spoken to several people about her."

"Ah; but what have you told them?"

"That she lives at the Hôtel Meurice; and that she wants to know nice people."

"They are flattered, I suppose, at your thinking them nice, but they don't go," said Waterville.

"I spoke of her to Mrs. Bagshaw, and Mrs. Bagshaw has promised to go."

"Ah," Waterville murmured; "you don't call Mrs. Bagshaw nice? Mrs. Headway won't see her."

"That's exactly what she wants,—to be able to cut some one!"

Waterville had a theory that Sir Arthur was keeping Mrs. Headway as a surprise—he meant perhaps to produce her during the next London season. He presently, however, learned as much about the matter as he could have desired to know. He had once offered to accompany his beautiful compatriot to the Museum of the Luxembourg and tell her a little about the modern French school. She had not examined this collection, in spite of her determination to see everything remarkable (she carried her *Murray* in her lap even when she went to see the great tailor in the Rue de la Paix, to whom, as she said, she had given no end of points); for she usually went to such places with Sir Arthur, and Sir Arthur was indifferent to the modern painters of France. "He says there are much better men in England. I must wait for the Royal Academy, next year. He seems to think one can wait for anything, but I'm not so good at waiting as he. I can't afford to wait—I've waited long enough." So much as this Mrs. Headway said on the occasion of her arranging with Rupert Waterville that they should some day visit the Luxembourg together. She alluded to the Englishman as if he were her husband or her brother, her natural protector and companion.

"I wonder if she knows how that sounds?" Waterville said to himself. "I don't believe she would do it if she knew how it sounds." And he made the further reflection that when one arrived from San Diego there was no end to the things one had to learn: it took so many things to make a well-bred woman. Clever as she was, Mrs. Headway was right in saying that she couldn't afford to wait. She must learn quickly. She wrote to Waterville one day to propose that they should go to the Museum on the morrow; Sir Arthur's mother was in Paris, on her way to Cannes, where she was to spend the winter. She was only passing through, but she would be there three days and he would naturally give himself up to her. She appeared to have the properest ideas as to what a gentleman would propose to do for his mother. She herself, therefore, would be free, and she named the hour at which she should expect him to call for her. He was punctual to the appointment, and they drove across the river in the large high-hung barouche in which she constantly rolled about Paris. With Mr. Max on the box—the courier was ornamented with enormous whiskers—this vehicle had an appearance of great respectability, though Sir Arthur assured her—she repeated this to her other friends—that in London, next year, they would do the thing much better for her. It struck her other friends of course that the baronet was prepared to be very consistent, and this on the whole was what Waterville would have expected of him. Littlemore simply remarked that at San Diego she drove herself about in a rickety buggy, with muddy wheels, and with a mule very often in the shafts. Waterville felt something like excitement as he asked himself whether the baronet's mother would now consent to know her. She must of course be aware that it was a woman who was keeping her son in Paris at a season when English gentlemen were most naturally employed in shooting partridges.

"She is staying at the Hôtel du Rhin, and I have made him feel that he mustn't leave her while she is here," Mrs. Headway said, as they drove up the narrow Rue de Seine. "Her name is Lady Demesne. but her full title is the Honorable Lady Demesne, as she's a Baron's daughter. Her father used to be a banker, but he did something or other for the Government—the Tories, you know, they call them—and so he was raised to the peerage. So you see one *can* be raised! She has a lady with her as a companion." Waterville's neighbor gave him this information with a seriousness that made him smile; he wondered whether she thought he didn't know how a Baron's daughter was addressed. In that she was very provincial; she had a way of exaggerating the value of her intellectual acquisitions and of assuming that others had been as ignorant as she. He noted, too, that she had ended by suppressing poor Sir Arthur's name altogether, and designating him only by a sort of conjugal pronoun. She had been so much, and so easily, married, that she was full of these misleading references to gentlemen.

V

THEY walked through the gallery of the Luxembourg, and except that Mrs. Headway looked at everything at once and at nothing long enough, talked, as usual, rather too loud, and bestowed too much attention on the bad copies that were being made of several indifferent pictures, she was a very agreeable companion and a grateful recipient of knowledge. She was very quick to understand, and Waterville was sure that before she left the gallery she knew something about the French school. She was quite prepared to compare it critically with London exhibitions of the following year. As Littlemore and he had remarked more than once, she was a very odd mixture. Her conversation, her personality, were full of little joints and seams, all of them very visible, where the old and the new had been pieced together. When they had passed through the different rooms of the palace Mrs. Headway proposed that instead of returning directly they should take a stroll in the adjoining gardens, which she wished very much to see and was sure she should like. She had quite seized the difference between the old Paris and the new, and felt the force of the romantic associations of the Latin quarter as perfectly as if she had enjoyed all the benefits of modern culture. The autumn sun was warm in the alleys and terraces of the Luxembourg; the masses of foilage above them, clipped and squared, rusty with ruddy patches, shed a thick lacework over the white sky, which was streaked with the palest blue. The beds of flowers near the palace were of the vividest yellow and red, and the sunlight rested on the smooth gray walls of those parts of its basement that looked south; in front of which, on the long green benches, a row of brown-cheeked nurses, in white caps and white aprons, sat offering nutrition to as many bundles of white drapery. There were other white caps wandering in the broad paths, attended by little brown French children; the small, straw-seated chairs were piled and stacked in some places and disseminated in others. An old lady in black, with white hair fastened over each of her temples by a large black comb, sat on the edge of a stone bench (too high for her delicate length), motionless, staring straight before her and holding a large door-key; under a tree a priest was reading—you could see his lips move at a distance; a young soldier, dwarfish and red-legged, strolled past with his hands in his pockets, which were very much distended. Waterville sat down with Mrs. Headway on the straw-bottomed chairs, and she presently said, "I like this; it's even better than the pictures in the gallery. It's more of a picture."

"Everything in France is a picture—even things that are ugly," Waterville replied. "Everything makes a subject."

"Well, I like France!" Mrs. Headway went on, with a little incongruous sigh. Then, suddenly, from an impulse even more inconsequent than her sigh, she added, "He asked me to go and see her, but I told him I wouldn't. She may come and see me if she likes." This was so abrupt that Waterville was slightly confounded; but he speedily perceived that she had returned by a short cut to Sir Arthur Demesne and his honorable mother. Waterville liked to know about other people's affairs, but he did not like this taste to be imputed to him; and therefore, though he was curious to see how the old lady, as he called her, would treat his companion, he was rather displeased with the latter for being so confidential. He had never imagined he was so intimate with her as that. Mrs. Headway, however, had a manner of taking intimacy for granted; a manner which Sir Arthur's mother at least would be sure not to like. He pretended to wonder a little what she was talking about, but she scarcely explained. She only went on, through untraceable transitions: "The least she can do is to come. I have been very kind to her son. That's not a reason for my going to her—it's a reason for her coming to me. Besides, if she doesn't like what I've done, she can leave me alone. I want to get into European society, but I want to get in in my own way. I don't want to run after people; I want them to run after me. I guess they will, some day!" Waterville listened to this with his eyes on the ground; he felt himself blushing a little. There was something in Mrs. Headway that shocked and mortified him, and Littlemore had been right in saying that she had a deficiency of shading. She was terribly distinct; her motives, her impulses, her desires were absolutely glaring. She needed to see, to hear, her own thoughts. Vehement thought, with Mrs. Headway, was inevitably speech, though speech was not always thought, and now she had suddenly become vehement. "If she does once come—then, ah, then, I shall be too perfect with her; I sha'n't let her go! But she must take the first step. I confess, I hope she'll be nice."

"Perhaps she won't," said Waterville perversely.

"Well, I don't care if she isn't. He has never told me anything about her; never a word about any of his own belongings. If I wished, I might believe he's ashamed of them."

"I don't think it's that."

"I know it isn't. I know what it is. It's just modesty. He doesn't want to brag—he's too much of a gentleman. He doesn't want to dazzle me—he wants me to like him for himself. Well, I do like him," she added in a moment. "But I shall like him still better if he brings his mother. They shall know that in America."

"Do you think it will make an impression in America?" Waterville asked, smiling.

"It will show them that I am visited by the British aristocracy. They won't like that."

"Surely they grudge you no innocent pleasure," Waterville murmured, smiling still.

"They grudged me common politeness—when I was in New York! Did you ever hear how they treated me, when I came on from the West?"

Waterville stared; this episode was quite new to him. His companion had turned towards him; her pretty head was tossed back like a flower in the wind: there was a flush in her cheek, a sharper light in her eye. "Ah! my dear New Yorkers, they're incapable of rudeness!" cried the young man.

"You're one of them, I see. But I don't speak of the men. The men were well enough—though they did allow it."

"Allow what, Mrs. Headway?" Waterville was quite in the dark.

She wouldn't answer at once; her eyes, glittering a little, were fixed upon absent images. "What did you hear about me over there? Don't pretend you heard nothing."

He had heard nothing at all; there had not been a word about Mrs. Headway in New York. He couldn't pretend, and he was obliged to tell her this. "But I have been away," he added, "and in America I didn't go out. There's nothing to go out for in New York—only little boys and girls."

"There are plenty of old women! They decided I was improper. I'm very well known in the West—I'm known from Chicago to San Francisco—if not personally (in all cases), at least by reputation. People can tell you out there. In New York they decided I wasn't good enough. Not good enough for New York! What do you say to that?" And she gave a sweet little laugh. Whether she had struggled with her pride before making this avowal, Waterville never knew. The crudity of the avowal seemed to indicate that she had no pride, and yet there was a spot in her heart which, as he now perceived, was intensely sore and had suddenly begun to throb. "I took a house for the winter—one of the handsomest houses in the place—but I sat there all alone. They didn't think me proper. Such as you see me here, I wasn't a success! I tell you the truth, at whatever cost. Not a decent woman came to see me!"

Waterville was embarrassed; diplomatist as he was, he hardly knew what line to take. He could not see what need there was of her telling him the truth, though the incident appeared to have been most curious, and he was glad to know the facts on the best authority. It was the first he knew of this remarkable woman's having spent a winter in his native city—which was virtually a proof of her having come and gone in complete obscurity. It was vain for him to pretend that he had been a good deal away, for he had been appointed to his post in London only six months before, and Mrs. Headway's social failure preceded that event. In the midst of these reflections he had an inspiration. He attempted neither to explain, to minimize, nor to apologize; he ventured simply to lay his hand for an instant on her own and to exclaim, as tenderly as possible, "I wish *I* had known you were there!"

"I had plenty of men—but men don't count. If they are not a positive help, they're a hinderance, and the more you have, the worse it looks. The women simply turned their backs."

"They were afraid of you—they were jealous," Waterville said.

"It's very good of you to try and explain it away; all I know is, not one of them crossed my threshold. You needn't try and tone it down; I know perfectly how the case stands. In New York, if you please, I was a failure!"

"So much the worse for New York!" cried Waterville, who, as he afterwards said to Littlemore, had got quite worked up.

"And now you know why I want to get into society over here?" She jumped up and stood before him; with a dry, hard smile she looked down at him. Her smile itself was an answer to her question; it expressed an urgent desire for revenge. There was an abruptness in her movements which left Waterville quite behind; but as he still sat there, returning her glance, he felt that he at last, in the light of that smile, the flash of that almost fierce question, understood Mrs. Headway.

She turned away, to walk to the gate of the garden, and he went with her, laughing vaguely, uneasily, at her tragic tone. Of course she expected him to help her to her revenge; but his female relations, his mother and his sisters, his innumerable cousins, had been a party to the slight she suffered, and he reflected as he walked along that after all they had been right. They had been right in not going to see a woman who could chatter that way about her social wrongs; whether Mrs. Headway were respectable or not, they had a correct instinct, for at any rate she was vulgar. European society might let her in, but European society would be wrong. New York, Waterville said to himself with a glow of civic pride, was quite capable of taking a higher stand in such a matter than London. They went some distance without speaking; at last he said, expressing honestly the thought which at that moment was uppermost in his mind, "I hate that phrase, 'getting into society.' I don't think one ought to attribute to one's self that sort of ambition. One ought to assume that one is in society—that one *is* society—and to hold that if one has good manners, one has, from the social point of view, achieved the great thing. The rest regards others."

For a moment she appeared not to understand; then she broke out: "Well, I suppose I haven't good manners; at any rate, I'm not satisfied! Of course, I don't talk right—I know that very well. But let me get where I want to first—then I'll look after my expressions. If I once get there, I shall be perfect!" she cried with a tremor of passion. They reached the gate of the garden and stood a moment outside, opposite to the low arcade of the Odéon, lined with book-stalls at which Waterville cast a slightly wistful glance, waiting for Mrs. Headway's carriage, which had drawn up a short distance. The whiskered Max had seated himself within, and on the tense, elastic cushions had fallen into a doze. The carriage got into motion without his awaking; he came to his senses only as it stopped again. He started up, staring; then, without confusion, he proceeded to descend.

"I have learned it in Italy—they say the *siesta,*" he remarked with an agreeable smile, holding the door open to Mrs. Headway.

"Well, I should think you had!" this lady replied, laughing amicably as she got into the vehicle, whither Waterville followed her. It was not a surprise to him to perceive that she spoiled her courier; she naturally would spoil her courier. But civilization begins at home, said Waterville; and the incident threw an ironical light upon her desire to get into society. It failed, however, to divert her thoughts from the subject she was discussing with Waterville, for as Max ascended the box and the carriage went on its way, she threw out another little note of defiance. "If once I'm all right over here, I can snap my fingers at New York! You'll see the faces those women will make."

Waterville was sure his mother and sisters would make no faces; but he felt afresh, as the carriage rolled back to the Hôtel Meurice, that now he understood Mrs. Headway. As they were about to enter the court of the hotel a closed carriage passed before them, and while a few moments later he helped his companion to alight, he saw that Sir Arthur Demesne had descended from the other vehicle. Sir Arthur perceived Mrs. Headway, and instantly gave his hand to a lady seated in the *coupé*. This lady emerged with a certain slow impressiveness, and as she stood before the door of the hotel—a woman still young and fair, with a good deal of height, gentle, tranquil, plainly dressed, yet distinctly imposing—Waterville saw that the baronet had brought his mother to call upon Nancy Beck.

Mrs. Headway's triumph had begun; the Dowager Lady Demesne had taken the first step. Waterville wondered whether the ladies in New York, notified by some magnetic wave, were distorting their features. Mrs. Headway, quickly conscious of what had happened, was neither too prompt to appropriate the visit, nor too slow to acknowledge it. She just paused, smiling at Sir Arthur.

"I wish to introduce my mother—she wants very much to know you." He approached Mrs. Headway; the lady had taken his arm. She was at once simple and circumspect; she had all the resources of an English matron.

Mrs. Headway, without advancing a step, put out her hands as if to draw her visitor quickly closer. "I declare, you're too sweet!" Waterville heard her say.

He was turning away, as his own business was over; but the young Englishman, who had surrendered his mother to the embrace, as it might now almost be called, of their hostess, just checked him with a friendly gesture. "I daresay I sha'n't see you again—I'm going away."

"Good-by, then," said Waterville. "You return to England?"

"No; I go to Cannes with my mother."

"You remain at Cannes?"

"Till Christmas very likely."

The ladies, escorted by Mr. Max, had passed into the hotel, and Waterville presently quitted his interlocutor. He smiled as he walked away reflecting that this personage had obtained a concession from his mother only at the price of a concession.

The next morning he went to see Littlemore, from whom he had a standing invitation to breakfast, and who, as usual, was smoking a cigar and looking through a dozen newspapers. Littlemore had a large apartment and an accomplished cook; he got up late and wandered about his room all the morning, stopping from time to time to look out of his windows which overhung the Place de la Madeleine. They had not been seated many minutes at breakfast when Waterville announced that Mrs. Headway was about to be abandoned by Sir Arthur, who was going to Cannes.

"That's no news to me," Littlemore said. "He came last night to bid me good-by."

"To bid you good-by? He was very civil all of a sudden."

"He didn't come from civility—he came from curiosity. Having dined here, he had a pretext for calling."

"I hope his curiosity was satisfied," Waterville remarked, in the manner of a person who could enter into such a sentiment.

Littlemore hesitated. "Well, I suspect not. He sat here some time, but we talked about everything but what he wanted to know."

"And what did he want to know?"

"Whether I know anything against Nancy Beck."

Waterville stared. "Did he call her Nancy Beck?"

"We never mentioned her; but I saw what he wanted, and that he wanted me to lead up to her—only I wouldn't do it."

"Ah, poor man!" Waterville murmured.

"I don't see why you pity him," said Littlemore. "Mrs. Beck's admirers were never pitied."

"Well, of course he wants to marry her.'

"Let him do it, then. I have nothing to say to it."

"He believes there's something in her past that's hard to swallow."

"Let him leave it alone, then."

"How can he, if he's in love with her?" Waterville asked, in the tone of a man who could enter into that sentiment too.

"Ah, my dear fellow, he must settle it himself. He has no right, at any rate, to ask me such a question. There was a moment, just as he was going, when he had it on his tongue's end. He stood there in the doorway, he couldn't leave me—he was going to plump out with it. He looked at me straight, and I looked straight at him; we remained that way for almost a minute. Then he decided to hold his tongue, and took himself off."

Waterville listened to this little description with intense interest. "And if he had asked you, what would you have said?"

"What do you think?"

"Well, I suppose you would have said that his question wasn't fair?"

"That would have been tantamount to admitting the worst."

"Yes," said Waterville, thoughtfully, "you couldn't do that. On the other hand, if he had put it to you on your honor whether she were a woman to marry, it would have been very awkward."

"Awkward enough. Fortunately, he has no business to put things to me on my honor. Moreover, nothing has passed between us to give him the right to ask me questions about Mrs. Headway. As she is a great friend of mine, he can't pretend to expect me to give confidential information about her."

"You don't think she's a woman to marry, all the same," Waterville declared. "And if a man were to ask you that, you might knock him down, but it wouldn't be an answer."

"It would have to serve," said Littlemore. He added in a moment, "There are certain cases where it's a man's duty to commit perjury."

Waterville looked grave. "Certain cases?"

"Where a woman's honor is at stake."

"I see what you mean. That's of course if he has been himself concerned—"

"Himself or another. It doesn't matter."

"I think it does matter. I don't like perjury," said Waterville. "It's a delicate question."

They were interrupted by the arrival of the servant with a second course, and Littlemore gave a laugh as he helped himself. "It would be a joke to see her married to that superior being!"

"It would be a great responsibility."

"Responsibility or not, it would be very amusing."

"Do you mean to assist her, then?"

"Heaven forbid! But I mean to bet on her."

Waterville gave his companion a serious glance; he thought him strangely superficial. The situation, however, was difficult, and he laid down his fork with a little sigh.

PART II

VI

THE Easter holidays that year were unusually genial; mild, watery sunshine assisted the progress of the spring. The high, dense hedges, in Warwickshire, were like walls of hawthorn imbedded in banks of primrose, and the finest trees in England, springing out of them with a regularity which suggested conservative principles, began to cover themselves with a kind of green downiness. Rupert Waterville, devoted to his duties and faithful in attendance at the Legation, had had little time to enjoy that rural hospitality which is the great invention of the English people and the most perfect expression of their character. He had been invited now and then—for in London he commended himself to many people as a very sensible young man—but he had been obliged to decline more proposals than he accepted. It was still, therefore, rather a novelty to him to stay at one of those fine old houses, surrounded with hereditary acres, which from the first of his coming to England he had thought of with such curiosity and such envy. He proposed to himself to see as many of them as possible, but he disliked to do things in a hurry, or when his mind was preoccupied, as it was so apt to be, with what he believed to be business of importance. He kept the country-houses in reserve; he would take them up in their order, after he should have got a little more used to London. Without hesitation, however, he had accepted the invitation to Longlands; it had come to him in a simple and familiar note, from Lady Demesne, with whom he had no acquaintance. He knew of her return from Cannes, where she had spent the whole winter, for he had seen it related in a Sunday newspaper; yet it was with a certain surprise that he heard from her in these informal terms. "Dear Mr. Waterville," she wrote, "my son tells me that you will perhaps be able to come down here on the 17th, to spend two or three days. If you can, it will give us much pleasure. We can promise you the society of your charming countrywoman, Mrs. Headway."

He had seen Mrs. Headway; she had written to him a fortnight before from an hotel in Cork Street, to say that she had arrived in London for the season and should be very glad to see him. He had gone to see her, trembling with the fear that she would break ground about her presentation; but he was agreeably surprised to observe that she neglected this topic. She had spent the winter in Rome, travelling directly from that city to England, with just a little stop in Paris, to buy a few clothes. She had taken much satisfaction in Rome, where she made many friends; she assured him that she knew half the Roman nobility. "They are charming people; they have only one fault, they stay too long," she said. And, in answer to his inquiring glance, "I mean when they come to see you," she explained. "They used to come every evening, and they wanted to stay till the next day. They were all princes and counts. I used to give them cigars, &c. I knew as many people as I wanted," she added, in a moment, discovering perhaps in Waterville's eye the traces of that sympathy with which six months before he had listened to her account of her discomfiture in New York. "There were lots of English; I knew all the English, and I mean to visit them here. The Americans waited to see what the English would do, so as to do the opposite. Thanks to that, I was spared some precious specimens. There are, you know, some fearful ones. Besides, in Rome, society doesn't matter, if you have a feeling for the ruins and the Campagna; I had an immense feeling for the Campagna. I was always mooning round in some damp old temple. It reminded me a good deal of the country round San Diego—if it hadn't been for the temples. I liked to think it all over, when I was driving round; I was always brooding over the past." At this moment, however, Mrs. Headway had dismissed the past; she was prepared to give herself up wholly to the actual. She wished Waterville to advise her as to how she should live—what she should do. Should she stay at a hotel or should she take a house? She guessed she had better take a house, if she could find a nice one. Max wanted to look for one, and she didn't know but she'd let him; he got her such a nice one in Rome. She said nothing about Sir Arthur Demesne, who, it seemed to Waterville, would have been her natural guide and sponsor; he wondered whether her relations with the baronet had come to an end. Waterville had met him a couple of times since the opening of Parliament, and they had exchanged twenty words, none of which, however, had reference to Mrs. Headway. Waterville had been recalled to London just after the incident of which he was witness in the court of the Hôtel Meurice; and all he knew of its consequence was what he had learned from Littlemore, who, on his way back to America, where he had suddenly ascertained that there were reasons for his spending the winter, passed through the British capital. Littlemore had reported that Mrs. Headway was enchanted with Lady Demesne, and had no words to speak of her kindness and sweetness. "She told me she liked to know her son's friends, and I told her I liked to know my friends' mothers," Mrs. Headway had related. "I should be willing to be old if I could be like that," she had added, oblivious for the moment that she was at least as near to the age of the mother as to that of the son. The mother and son, at any rate, had retired to Cannes together, and at this moment Littlemore had received letters from home which caused him to start for Arizona. Mrs. Headway had accordingly been left to her own devices, and he was afraid she had bored herself, though Mrs. Bagshaw had called upon her. In November she had travelled to Italy, not by way of Cannes.

"What do you suppose she'll do in Rome?" Waterville had asked; his imagination failing him here, for he had not yet trodden the Seven Hills.

"I haven't the least idea. And I don't care!" Littlemore added in a moment. Before he left London he mentioned to Waterville that Mrs. Headway, on his going to take leave of her in Paris, had made another, and a rather unexpected, attack. "About the society business—she said I must really do something—she couldn't go on in that way. And she appealed to me in the name—I don't think I quite know how to say it."

"I should be very glad if you would try," said Waterville, who was constantly reminding himself that Americans in Europe were, after all, in a manner, to a man in his position, as the sheep to the shepherd.

"Well, in the name of the affection that we had formerly entertained for each other."

"The affection?"

"So she was good enough to call it. But I deny it all. If one had to have an affection for every woman one used to sit up 'evenings' with—!" And Littlemore paused, not defining the result of such an obligation. Waterville tried to imagine what it would be; while his friend embarked for New York, without telling him how, after all, he had resisted Mrs. Headway's attack.

At Christmas, Waterville knew of Sir Arthur's return to England, and believed that he also knew that the baronet had not gone down to Rome. He had a theory that Lady Demesne was a very clever woman—clever enough to make her son do what she preferred and yet also make him think it his own choice. She had been politic, accommodating, about going to see Mrs. Headway; but, having seen her and judged her, she had determined to break the thing off. She had been sweet and kind, as Mrs. Headway said, because for the moment that was easiest; but she had made her last visit on the same occasion as her first. She had been sweet and kind, but she had set her face as a stone, and if poor Mrs. Headway, arriving in London for the season, expected to find any vague promises redeemed, she would taste of the bitterness of shattered hopes. He had made up his mind that, shepherd as he was, and Mrs. Headway one of his sheep, it was none of his present duty to run about after her, especially as she could be trusted not to stray too far. He saw her a second time, and she still said nothing about Sir Arthur. Waterville, who always had a theory, said to himself that she was waiting, that the baronet had not turned up. She was also getting into a house; the courier had found her in Chesterfield Street, Mayfair, a little gem, which was to cost her what jewels cost. After all this, Waterville was greatly surprised at Lady Demesne's note, and he went down to Longlands with much the same impatience with which, in Paris, he would have gone, if he had been able, to the first night of a new comedy. It seemed to him that, through a sudden stroke of good fortune, he had received a *billet d'auteur.*

It was agreeable to him to arrive at an English country-house at the close of the day. He liked the drive from the station in the twilight, the sight of the fields and copses and cottages, vague and lonely in contrast to his definite, lighted goal; the sound of the wheels on the long avenue, which turned and wound repeatedly without bringing him to what he reached however at last—the wide, gray front, with a glow in its scattered windows and a sweep of still firmer gravel up to the door. The front at Longlands, which was of this sober complexion, had a grand, pompous air; it was attributed to the genius of Sir Christopher Wren. There were wings which came forward in a semicircle, with statues placed at intervals on the cornice; so that in the flattering dusk it looked like an Italian palace, erected through some magical evocation in an English park. Waterville had taken a late train, which left him but twenty minutes to dress for dinner. He prided himself considerably on the art of dressing both quickly and well; but this operation left him no time to inquire whether the apartment to which he had been assigned befitted the dignity of a Secretary of Legation. On emerging from his room he found there was an ambassador in the house, and this discovery was a check to uneasy reflections. He tacitly assumed that he would have had a better room if it had not been for the ambassador, who was of course counted first. The large, brilliant house gave an impression of the last century and of foreign taste, of light colors, high, vaulted ceilings, with pale mythological frescos, gilded doors, surmounted by old French panels, faded tapestries and delicate damasks, stores of ancient china, among which great jars of pink roses were conspicuous. The people in the house had assembled for dinner in the principal hall, which was animated by a fire of great logs, and the company was so numerous that Waterville was afraid he was the last. Lady Demesne gave him a smile and a touch of her hand; she was very tranquil, and, saying nothing in particular, treated him as if he had been a constant visitor. Waterville was not sure whether he liked this or hated it; but these alternatives mattered equally little to his hostess, who looked at her guests as if to see whether the number were right.

The master of the house was talking to a lady before the fire; when he caught sight of Waterville across the room, he waved him "how d'ye do," with an air of being delighted to see him. He had never had that air in Paris, and Waterville had a chance to observe, what he had often heard, to how much greater advantage the English appear in their country houses. Lady Demesne turned to him again, with her sweet vague smile, which looked as if it were the same for everything.

"We are waiting for Mrs. Headway," she said.

"Ah, she has arrived?" Waterville had quite forgotten her.

"She came at half-past five. At six she went to dress. She has had two hours."

"Let us hope that the results will be proportionate," said Waterville, smiling.

"Oh, the results; I don't know," Lady Demesne murmured, without looking at him; and in these simple words Waterville saw the confirmation of his theory that she was playing a deep game. He wondered whether he should sit next to Mrs. Headway at dinner, and hoped, with due deference to this lady's charms, that he should have something more novel. The results of a toilet which she had protracted through two hours were presently visible. She appeared on the staircase which descended to the hall, and which, for three minutes, as she came down rather slowly, facing the people beneath, placed her in considerable relief. Waterville, as he looked at her, felt that this was a moment of importance for her: it was virtually her entrance into English society. Mrs. Headway entered English society very well, with her charming smile upon her lips and with the trophies of the Rue de la Paix trailing behind her. She made a portentous rustling as she moved. People turned their eyes toward her; there was soon a perceptible diminution of talk, though talk had not been particularly audible. She looked very much alone, and it was rather pretentious of her to come down last, though it was possible that this was simply because, before her glass, she had been unable to please herself. For she evidently felt the importance of the occasion, and Waterville was sure that her heart was beating. She was very valiant, however; she smiled more intensely, and advanced like a woman who was used to being looked at. She had at any rate the support of knowing that she was pretty; for nothing on this occasion was wanting to her prettiness, and the determination to succeed, which might have made her hard, was veiled in the virtuous consciousness that she had neglected nothing. Lady Demesne went forward to meet her; Sir Arthur took no notice of her; and presently Waterville found himself proceeding to dinner with the wife of an ecclesiastic, to whom Lady Demesne had presented him for this purpose when the hall was almost empty. The rank of this ecclesiastic in the hierarchy he learned early on the morrow; but in the mean time it seemed to him strange, somehow, that in England ecclesiastics should have wives. English life, even at the end of a year, was full of those surprises. The lady, however, was very easily accounted for; she was in no sense a violent exception, and there had been no need of the Reformation to produce her. Her name was Mrs. April; she was wrapped in a large lace shawl; to eat her dinner she removed but one glove, and the other gave Waterville at moments an odd impression that the whole repast, in spite of its great completeness, was something of the picnic order. Mrs. Headway was opposite, at a little distance; she had been taken in, as Waterville learned from his neighbor, by a general, a gentleman with a lean, aquiline face and a cultivated whisker, and she had on the other side a smart young man of an identity less definite. Poor Sir Arthur sat between two ladies much older than himself, whose names, redolent of history, Waterville had often heard, and had associated with figures more romantic. Mrs. Headway gave Waterville no greeting; she evidently had not seen him till they were seated at table, when she simply stared at him with a violence of surprise that for a moment almost effaced her smile. It was a copious and well-ordered banquet, but as Waterville looked up and down the table he wondered whether some of its elements might not be a little dull. As he made this reflection he became conscious that he was judging the affair much more from Mrs. Headway's point of view than from his own. He knew no one but Mrs. April, who, displaying an almost motherly desire to give him information, told him the names of many of their companions; in return for which he explained to her that he was not in that set. Mrs. Headway got on in perfection with her general; Waterville watched her more than he appeared to do, and saw that the general, who evidently was a cool hand, was drawing her out. Waterville hoped she would be careful. He was a man of fancy, in his way, and as he compared her with the rest of the company he said to himself that she was a very plucky little woman, and that her present undertaking had a touch of the heroic. She was alone against many, and her opponents were a very serried phalanx; those who were there represented a thousand others. They looked so different from her that to the eye of the imagination she stood very much on her merits. All those people seemed so completely made up, so unconscious of effort, so surrounded with things to rest upon; the men with their clean complexions, their well-hung chins, their cold, pleasant eyes, their shoulders set back, their absence of gesture; the women, several very handsome, half strangled in strings of pearls, with smooth plain tresses, seeming to look at nothing in particular, supporting silence as if it were as becoming as candlelight, yet talking a little, sometimes, in fresh, rich voices. They were all wrapped in a community of ideas, of traditions; they understood each other's accent, even each other's variations. Mrs. Headway, with all her prettiness, seemed to transcend these variations; she looked foreign, exaggerated; she had too much expression; she might have been engaged for the evening. Waterville remarked, moreover, that English society was always looking out for amusement and that its transactions were conducted on a cash basis. If Mrs. Headway were amusing enough she would probably succeed, and her fortune—if fortune there was—would not be a hindrance.

In the drawing-room, after dinner, he went up to her, but she gave him no greeting. She only looked at him with an expression he had never seen before—a strange, bold expression of displeasure.

"Why have you come down here?" she asked. "Have you come to watch me?"

Waterville colored to the roots of his hair. He knew it was terribly little like a diplomatist; but he was unable to control his blushes. Besides, he was shocked, he was angry, and in addition he was mystified. "I came because I was asked," he said.

"Who asked you?"

"The same person that asked you, I suppose—Lady Demesne."

"She's an old cat!" Mrs. Headway exclaimed, turning away from him.

He turned away from her as well. He didn't know what he had done to deserve such treatment. It was a complete surprise; he had never seen her like that before. She was a very vulgar woman; that was the way people talked, he supposed, at San Diego. He threw himself almost passionately into the conversation of the others, who all seemed to him, possibly a little by contrast, extraordinarily genial and friendly. He had not, however, the consolation of seeing Mrs. Headway punished for her rudeness, for she was not in the least neglected. On the contrary, in the part of the room where she sat the group was denser, and every now and then it was agitated with unanimous laughter. If she should amuse them, he said to himself, she would succeed, and evidently she was amusing them.

VII

If she was strange, he had not come to the end of her strangeness. The next day was a Sunday and uncommonly fine; he was down before breakfast, and took a walk in the park, stopping to gaze at the thin-legged deer, scattered like pins on a velvet cushion over some of the remoter slopes, and wandering along the edge of a large sheet of ornamental water, which had a temple, in imitation of that of Vesta, on an island in the middle. He thought at this time no more about Mrs. Headway; he only reflected that these stately objects had for more than a hundred years furnished a background to a great deal of family history. A little more reflection would perhaps have suggested to him that Mrs. Headway was possibly an incident of some importance in the history of a family. Two or three ladies failed to appear at breakfast; Mrs. Headway was one of them.

"She tells me she never leaves her room till noon," he heard Lady Demesne say to the general, her companion of the previous evening, who had asked about her. "She takes three hours to dress."

"She's a monstrous clever woman!" the general exclaimed.

"To do it in three hours?"

"No, I mean the way she keeps her wits about her."

"Yes; I think she's very clever," said Lady Demesne, in a tone in which Waterville flattered himself that he saw more meaning than the general could see. There was something in this tall, straight, deliberate woman, who seemed at once benevolent and distant, that Waterville admired. With her delicate surface, her conventional mildness, he could see that she was very strong; she had set her patience upon a height, and she carried it like a diadem. She had very little to say to Waterville, but every now and then she made some inquiry of him that showed she had not forgotten him. Demesne himself was apparently in excellent spirits, though there was nothing bustling in his deportment, and he only went about looking very fresh and fair, as if he took a bath every hour or two, and very secure against the unexpected. Waterville had less conversation with him than with his mother; but the young man had found occasion to say to him the night before, in the smoking-room, that he was delighted Waterville had been able to come, and that if he was fond of real English scenery there were several things about there he should like very much to show him.

"You must give me an hour or two before you go, you know; I really think there are some things you'll like."

Sir Arthur spoke as if Waterville would be very fastidious; he seemed to wish to attach a vague importance to him. On the Sunday morning after breakfast he asked Waterville if he should care to go to church; most of the ladies and several of the men were going.

"It's just as you please, you know; but it's rather a pretty walk across the fields, and a curious little church of King Stephen's time."

Waterville knew what this meant; it was already a picture. Besides, he liked going to church, especially when he sat in the Squire's pew, which was sometimes as big as a boudoir. So he replied that he should be delighted. Then he added, without explaining his reason—

"Is Mrs. Headway going?"

"I really don't know," said his host, with an abrupt change of tone—as if Waterville had asked him whether the housekeeper were going.

"The English are awfully queer!" Waterville indulged mentally in this exclamation, to which since his arrival in England he had had recourse whenever he encountered a gap in the consistency of things. The church was even a better picture than Sir Arthur's description of it, and Waterville said to himself that Mrs. Headway had been a great fool not to come. He knew what she was after; she wished to study English life, so that she might take possession of it, and to pass in among a hedge of bobbing rustics, and sit among the monuments of the old Demesnes, would have told her a great deal about English life. If she wished to fortify herself for the struggle she had better come to that old church. When he returned to Longlands—he had walked back across the meadows with the canon's wife, who was a vigorous pedestrian—it wanted half an hour of luncheon, and he was unwilling to go indoors. He remembered that he had not yet seen the gardens, and he wandered away in search of them. They were on a scale which enabled him to find them without difficulty, and they looked as if they had been kept up unremittingly for a century or two. He had not advanced very far between their blooming borders when he heard a voice that he recognized, and a moment after, at the turn of an alley, he came upon Mrs. Headway, who was attended by the master of Longlands. She was bareheaded beneath her parasol, which she flung back, stopping short, as she beheld her compatriot.

"Oh, it's Mr. Waterville come to spy me out as usual!" It was with this remark that she greeted the slightly embarrassed young man.

"Hallo! you've come home from church," Sir Arthur said, pulling out his watch.

Waterville was struck with his coolness. He admired it; for, after all, he said to himself, it must have been disagreeable to him to be interrupted. He felt a little like a fool, and wished he had kept Mrs. April with him, to give him the air of having come for her sake.

Mrs. Headway looked adorably fresh, in a toilet which Waterville, who had his ideas of such matters, was sure would not be regarded as the proper thing for a Sunday morning in an English country house: a *négligé* of white flounces and frills, interspersed with yellow ribbons—a garment which Madame de Pompadour might have worn when she received a visit from Louis XV., but would probably not have worn when she went into the world. The sight of this costume gave the finishing touch to Waterville's impression that Mrs. Headway knew, on the whole, what she was about. She would take a line of her own; she would not be too accommodating. She would not come down to breakfast; she would not go to church; she would wear on Sunday mornings little elaborately informal dresses, and look dreadfully un-British and un-Protestant. Perhaps, after all, this was better. She began to talk with a certain volubility.

"Isn't this too lovely? I walked all the way from the house. I'm not much at walking, but the grass in this place is like a parlor. The whole thing is beyond everything. Sir Arthur, you ought to go and look after the Ambassador; it's shameful the way I've kept you. You didn't care about the Ambassador? You said just now you had scarcely spoken to him, and you must make it up. I never saw such a way of neglecting your guests. Is that the usual style over here? Go and take him out for a ride, or make him play a game of billiards. Mr. Waterville will take me home; besides, I want to scold him for spying on me."

Waterville sharply resented this accusation. "I had no idea you were here," he declared.

"We weren't hiding," said Sir Arthur quietly. "Perhaps you'll see Mrs. Headway back to the house. I think I ought to look after old Davidoff. I believe lunch is at two."

He left them, and Waterville wandered through the gardens with Mrs. Headway. She immediately wished to know if he had come there to look after her; but this inquiry was accompanied, to his surprise, with the acrimony she had displayed the night before. He was determined not to let that pass, however; when people had treated him in that way they should not be allowed to forget it.

"Do you suppose I am always thinking of you?" he asked. "You're out of my mind sometimes. I came here to look at the gardens, and if you hadn't spoken to me I should have passed on."

Mrs. Headway was perfectly good-natured; she appeared not even to hear his defense. "He has got two other places," she simply rejoined. "That's just what I wanted to know."

But Waterville would not be turned away from his grievance. That mode of reparation to a person whom you had insulted which consisted in forgetting that you had done so, was doubtless largely in use in New Mexico; but a person of honor demanded something more. "What did you mean last night by accusing me of having come down here to watch you? You must excuse me if I tell you that I think you were rather rude." The sting of this accusation lay in the fact that there was a certain amount of truth in it; yet for a moment Mrs. Headway, looking very blank, failed to recognize the allusion. "She's a barbarian, after all," thought Waterville. "She thinks a woman may slap a man's face and run away!"

"Oh!" cried Mrs. Headway, suddenly, "I remember, I was angry with you; I didn't expect to see you. But I didn't really care about it at all. Every now and then I am angry, like that, and I work it off on any one that's handy. But it's over in three minutes, and I never think of it again. I was angry last night; I was furious with the old woman."

"With the old woman?"

"With Sir Arthur's mother. She has no business here, anyway. In this country, when the husband dies, they're expected to clear out. She has a house of her own, ten miles from here, and she has another in Portman Square; so she's got plenty of places to live. But she sticks—she sticks to him like a plaster. All of a sudden it came over me that she didn't invite me here because she liked me, but because she suspects me. She's afraid we'll make a match, and she thinks I ain't good enough for her son. She must think I'm in a great hurry to get hold of him. I never went after him, he came after me. I should never have thought of anything if it hadn't been for him. He began it last summer at Homburg; he wanted to know why I didn't come to England; he told me I should have great success. He doesn't know much about it, any way; he hasn't got much gumption. But he's a very nice man, all the same; it's very pleasant to see him surrounded by his—" And Mrs. Headway paused a moment, looking admiringly about her—"Surrounded by all his old heirlooms. I like the old place," she went on; "it's beautifully mounted; I'm quite satisfied with what I've seen. I thought Lady Demesne was very friendly; she left a card on me in London, and very soon after, she wrote to me to ask me here. But I'm very quick; I sometimes see things in a flash. I saw something yesterday, when she came to speak to me at dinner-time. She saw I looked pretty, and it made her blue with rage; she hoped I would be ugly. I should like very much to oblige her; but what can one do? Then I saw that she had asked me here only because he insisted. He didn't come to see me when I first arrived—he never came near me for ten days. She managed to prevent him; she got him to make some promise. But he changed his mind after a little, and then he had to do something really polite. He called three days in succession, and he made her come. She's one of those women that resists as long as she can, and then seems to give in, while she's really resisting more than ever. She hates me like poison; I don't know what she thinks I've done. She's very underhand; she's a regular old cat. When I saw you last night at dinner, I thought she had got you here to help her."

"To help her?" Waterville asked.

"To tell her about me. To give her information, that she can make use of against me. You may tell her what you like!"

Waterville was almost breathless with the attention he had given this extraordinary burst of confidence, and now he really felt faint. He stopped short; Mrs. Headway went on a few steps, and then, stopping too, turned and looked at him. "You're the most unspeakable woman!" he exclaimed. She seemed to him indeed a barbarian.

She laughed at him—he felt she was laughing at his expression of face—and her laugh rang through the stately gardens. "What sort of a woman is that?"

"You've got no delicacy," said Waterville, resolutely.

She colored quickly, though, strange to say, she appeared not to be angry. "No delicacy?" she repeated.

"You ought to keep those things to yourself."

"Oh, I know what you mean; I talk about everything. When I'm excited I've got to talk. But I must do things in my own way. I've got plenty of delicacy, when people are nice to me. Ask Arthur Demesne if I ain't delicate—ask George Littlemore if I ain't. Don't stand there all day; come in to lunch!" And Mrs. Headway resumed her walk, while Rupert Waterville, raising his eyes for a moment, slowly overtook her. "Wait till I get settled; then I'll be delicate," she pursued. "You can't be delicate when you're trying to save your life. It's very well for *you* to talk, with the whole American Legation to back you. Of course I'm excited. I've got hold of this thing, and I don't mean to let go!" Before they reached the house she told him why he had been invited to Longlands at the same time as herself. Waterville would have liked to believe that his personal attractions sufficiently explained the fact; but she took no account of this supposition. Mrs. Headway preferred to think that she lived in an element of ingenious machination, and that most things that happened had reference to herself. Waterville had been asked because he represented, however modestly, the American Legation, and their host had a friendly desire to make it appear that this pretty American visitor, of whom no one knew anything, was under the protection of that establishment. "It would start me better," said Mrs. Headway, serenely. "You can't help yourself—you've helped to start me. If he had known the Minister he would have asked him—or the first secretary. But he don't know them."

They reached the house by the time Mrs. Headway had developed this idea, which gave Waterville a pretext more than sufficient for detaining her in the portico. "Do you mean to say Sir Arthur told you this?" he inquired, almost sternly.

"Told me? Of course not! Do you suppose I would let him take the tone with me that I need any favors? I should like to hear him tell me that I'm in want of assistance!"

"I don't see why he shouldn't—at the pace you go yourself. You say it to every one."

"To every one? I say it to you, and to George Littlemore—when I'm nervous. I say it to you because I like you, and to him because I'm afraid of him. I'm not in the least afraid of you, by the way. I'm all alone—I haven't got any one. I must have some comfort, mustn't I? Sir Arthur scolded me for putting you off last night—he noticed it; and that was what made me guess his idea."

"I'm much obliged to him," said Waterville, rather bewildered.

"So mind you answer for me. Don't you want to give me your arm, to go in?"

"You're a most extraordinary combination," he murmured, as she stood smiling at him.

"Oh, come, don't *you* fall in love with me!" she cried, with a laugh; and, without taking his arm, passed in before him.

That evening, before he went to dress for dinner, Waterville wandered into the library, where he felt sure that he should find some superior bindings. There was no one in the room, and he spent a happy half-hour among the treasures of literature and the triumphs of old morocco. He had a great esteem for good literature; he held that it should have handsome covers. The daylight had begun to wane, but whenever, in the rich-looking dimness, he made out the glimmer of a well-gilded back, he took down the volume and carried it to one of the deep-set windows. He had just finished the inspection of a delightfully fragrant folio, and was about to carry it back to its niche, when he found himself standing face to face with Lady Demesne. He was startled for a moment, for her tall, slim figure, her fair visage, which looked white in the high, brown room, and the air of serious intention with which she presented herself, gave something spectral to her presence. He saw her smile, however, and heard her say, in that tone of hers which was sweet almost to sadness, "Are you looking at our books? I'm afraid they are rather dull."

"Dull? Why, they are as bright as the day they were bound." And he turned the glittering panels of his folio towards her.

"I'm afraid I haven't looked at them for a long time," she murmured, going nearer to the window, where she stood looking out. Beyond the clear pane the park stretched away, with the grayness of evening beginning to hang itself on the great limbs of the oaks. The place appeared cold and empty, and the trees had an air of conscious importance, as if nature herself had been bribed somehow to take the side of county families. Lady Demesne was not an easy person to talk with; she was neither spontaneous nor abundant; she was conscious of herself, conscious of many things. Her very simplicity was conventional, though it was rather a noble convention. You might have pitied her, if you had seen that she lived in constant unrelaxed communion with certain rigid ideals. This made her at times seem tired, like a person who has undertaken too much. She gave an impression of still brightness, which was not at all brilliancy, but a carefully preserved purity. She said nothing for a moment, and there was an appearance of design in her silence, as if she wished to let him know that she had a certain business with him, without taking the trouble to announce it. She had been accustomed to expect that people would suppose things, and to be saved the trouble of explanations. Waterville made some haphazard remark about the beauty of the evening (in point of fact, the weather had changed for the worse), to which she vouchsafed no reply. Then, presently, she said, with her usual gentleness, "I hoped I should find you here—I wish to ask you something."

"Anything I can tell you—I shall be delighted!" Waterville exclaimed.

She gave him a look, not imperious, almost appealing, which

seemed to say—"Please be very simple—very simple indeed." Then she glanced about her, as if there had been other people in the room; she didn't wish to appear closeted with him, or to have come on purpose. There she was, at any rate, and she went on. "When my son told me he should ask you to come down, I was very glad. I mean, of course, that we were delighted—" And she paused a moment. Then she added, simply, "I want to ask you about Mrs. Headway."

"Ah, here it is!" cried Waterville within himself. More superficially, he smiled, as agreeably as possible, and said, "Ah yes, I see!"

"Do you mind my asking you? I hope you don't mind. I haven't any one else to ask."

"Your son knows her much better than I do." Waterville said this without an intention of malice, simply to escape from the difficulties of his situation; but after he had said it, he was almost frightened by its mocking sound.

"I don't think he knows her. She knows him, which is very different. When I ask him about her, he merely tells me she is fascinating. She *is* fascinating," said her ladyship, with inimitable dryness.

"So I think, myself. I like her very much," Waterville rejoined, cheerfully.

"You are in all the better position to speak of her, then."

"To speak well of her," said Waterville, smiling.

"Of course, if you can. I should be delighted to hear you do that. That's what I wish—to hear some good of her."

It might have seemed, after this, that nothing would have remained but for Waterville to launch himself in a panegyric of his mysterious countrywoman; but he was no more to be tempted into that danger than into another. "I can only say I like her," he repeated. "She has been very kind to me."

"Every one seems to like her," said Lady Demesne, with an unstudied effect of pathos. "She is certainly very amusing."

"She is very good-natured; she has lots of good intentions."

"What do you call good intentions?" asked Lady Demesne, very sweetly.

"Well, I mean that she wants to be friendly and pleasant."

"Of course you have to defend her. She's your countrywoman."

"To defend her—I must wait till she's attacked," said Waterville, laughing.

"That's very true. I needn't call your attention to the fact that I am not attacking her. I should never attack a person staying in this house. I only want to know something about her, and if you can't tell me, perhaps at least you can mention some one who will."

"She'll tell you herself. Tell you by the hour!"

"What she has told my son? I shouldn't understand it. My son doesn't understand it. It's very strange. I rather hoped you might explain it."

Waterville was silent a moment. "I'm afraid I can't explain Mrs. Headway," he remarked at last.

"I see you admit she is very peculiar."

Waterville hesitated again. "It's too great a responsibility to answer you." He felt that he was very disobliging; he knew exactly what Lady Demesne wished him to say. He was unprepared to blight the reputation of Mrs. Headway to accommodate Lady Demesne; and yet, with his active little imagination, he could enter perfectly into the feelings of this tender, formal, serious woman, who—it was easy to see—had looked for her own happiness in the cultivation of duty and in extreme constancy to two or three objects of devotion chosen once for all. She must, indeed, have had a vision of things which would represent Mrs. Headway as both displeasing and dangerous. But he presently became aware that she had taken his last words as a concession in which she might find help.

"You know why I ask you these things, then?"

"I think I have an idea," said Waterville, persisting in irrelevant laughter. His laugh sounded foolish in his own ears.

"If you know that, I think you ought to assist me." Her tone changed as she spoke these words; there was a quick tremor in it; he could see it was a confession of distress. Her distress was deep; he immediately felt that it must have been, before she made up her mind to speak to him. He was sorry for her, and determined to be very serious.

"If I could help you I would. But my position is very difficult."

"It's not so difficult as mine!" She was going all lengths; she was really appealing to him. "I don't imagine that you are under any obligation to Mrs. Headway—you seem to me very different," she added.

Waterville was not insensible to any discrimination that told in his favor; but these words gave him a slight shock, as if they had been an attempt at bribery. "I am surprised that you don't like her," he ventured to observe.

Lady Demesne looked out of the window a little. "I don't think you are really surprised, though possibly you try to be. I don't like her, at any rate, and I can't fancy why my son should. She's very pretty, and she appears to be very clever; but I don't trust her. I don't know what has taken possession of him; it is not usual in his family to marry people like that. I don't think she's a lady. The person I should wish for him would be so very different—perhaps you can see what I mean. There's something in her history that we don't understand. My son understands it no better than I. If you could only explain to us, that might be a help. I treat you with great confidence the first time I see you; it's because I don't know where to turn. I am exceedingly anxious."

It was very plain that she was anxious; her manner had become more vehement; her eyes seemed to shine in the thickening dusk. "Are you very sure there is danger?" Waterville asked. "Has he asked her to marry him, and has she consented?"

"If I wait till they settle it all, it will be too late. I have reason to believe that my son is not engaged, but he is terribly entangled. At the same time he is very uneasy, and that may save him yet. He has a great sense of honor. He is not satisfied about her past life; he doesn't know what to think of what we have been told. Even what she admits is so strange. She has been married four of five times—she has been divorced again and again—it seems so extraordinary. She tells him that in America it is different, and I daresay you have not our ideas; but really there is a limit to everything. There must have been some great irregularities—I am afraid some great scandals. It's dreadful to have to accept such things. He has not told me all this; but it's not necessary he should tell me; I know him well enough to guess."

"Does he know that you have spoken to me?" Waterville said.

"Not in the least. But I must tell you that I shall repeat to him anything that you may say against her."

"I had better say nothing, then. It's very delicate. Mrs. Headway is quite undefended. One may like her or not, of course. I have seen nothing of her that is not perfectly correct."

"And you have heard nothing?"

Waterville remembered Littlemore's assertion that there were cases in which a man was bound in honor to tell an untruth, and he wondered whether this were such a case. Lady Demesne imposed herself, she made him believe in the reality of her grievance, and he saw the gulf that divided her from a pushing little woman who had lived with Western editors. She was right to wish not to be connected with Mrs. Headway. After all, there had been nothing in his relations with that lady to make it incumbent on him to lie for her. He had not sought her acquaintance, she had sought his; she had sent for him to come and see her. And yet he couldn't give her away, as they said in New York; that stuck in his throat. "I am afraid I really can't say anything. And it wouldn't matter. Your son won't give her up because I happen not to like her."

"If he were to believe she has done wrong, he would give her up."

"Well, I have no right to say so," said Waterville.

Lady Demesne turned away; she was much disappointed in him. He was afraid she was going to break out—"Why, then, do you suppose I asked you here?" She quitted her place near the window and was apparently about to leave the room. But she stopped short. "You know something against her, but you won't say it."

Waterville hugged his folio and looked awkward. "You attribute things to me. I shall never say anything."

"Of course you are perfectly free. There is some one else who knows, I think—another American—a gentleman who was in Paris when my son was there. I have forgotten his name."

"A friend of Mrs. Headway's? I suppose you mean George Littlemore."

"Yes—Mr. Littlemore. He has a sister, whom I have met; I didn't know she was his sister till to-day. Mrs. Headway spoke of her, but I find she doesn't know her. That itself is a proof, I think. Do you think *he* would help me?" Lady Demesne asked, very simply.

"I doubt it, but you can try."

"I wish he had come with you. Do you think he would come?"

"He is in America at this moment, but I believe he soon comes back."

"I shall go to his sister; I will ask her to bring him to see me.

She is extremely nice; I think she will understand. Unfortunately there is very little time."

"Don't count too much on Littlemore," said Waterville, gravely.

"You men have no pity."

"Why should we pity you? How can Mrs. Headway hurt such a person as you?"

Lady Demesne hesitated a moment. "It hurts me to hear her voice."

"Her voice is very sweet."

"Possibly. But she's horrible!"

This was too much, it seemed to Waterville; poor Mrs. Headway was extremely open to criticism, and he himself had declared she was a barbarian. Yet she was not horrible. "It's for your son to pity you. If he doesn't, how can you expect it of others?"

"Oh, but he does!" And with a majesty that was more striking even than her logic, Lady Demesne moved towards the door.

Waterville advanced to open it for her, and as she passed out he said, "There's one thing you can do—try to like her!"

She shot him a terrible glance. "That would be worst of all!"

VIII

George Littlemore arrived in London on the twentieth of May, and one of the first things he did was to go and see Waterville at the Legation, where he made known to him that he had taken for the rest of the season a house at Queen Anne's Gate, so that his sister and her husband, who, under the pressure of diminished rents, had let their own town-residence, might come up and spend a couple of months with him.

"One of the consequences of your having a house will be that you will have to entertain Mrs. Headway," Waterville said.

Littlemore sat there with his hands crossed upon his stick; he looked at Waterville with an eye that failed to kindle at the mention of this lady's name. "Has she got into European society?" he asked, rather languidly.

"Very much, I should say. She has a house, and a carriage, and diamonds, and everything handsome. She seems already to know a lot of people; they put her name in the *Morning Post*. She has come up very quickly; she's almost famous. Every one is asking about her—you'll be plied with questions."

Littlemore listened gravely. "How did she get in?"

"She met a large party at Longlands, and made them all think her great fun. They must have taken her up; she only wanted a start."

Littlemore seemed suddenly to be struck with the grotesqueness of this news, to which his first response was a burst of quick laughter. "To think of Nancy Beck! The people here are queer people. There's no one they won't go after. They wouldn't touch her in New York."

"Oh, New York's old-fashioned," said Waterville; and he announced to his friend that Lady Demesne was very eager for his arrival, and wanted to make him help her prevent her son's bringing such a person into the family. Littlemore apparently was not alarmed at her ladyship's projects, and intimated, in the manner of a man who thought them rather impertinent, that he could trust himself to keep out of her way. "It isn't a proper marriage, at any rate," Waterville declared.

"Why not, if he loves her?"

"Oh, if that's all you want!" cried Waterville, with a degree of cynicism that rather surprised his companion. "Would you marry her yourself?"

"Certainly, if I were in love with her."

"You took care not to be that."

"Yes, I did—and so Demesne had better have done. But since he's bitten—!" and Littlemore terminated his sentence in a suppressed yawn.

Waterville presently asked him how he would manage, in view of his sister's advent, about asking Mrs. Headway to his house; and he replied that he would manage by simply not asking her. Upon this, Waterville declared that he was very inconsistent; to which Littlemore rejoined that it was very possible. But he asked whether they couldn't talk about something else than Mrs. Headway. He couldn't enter into the young man's interest in her, and was sure to have enough of her later.

Waterville would have been sorry to give a false idea of his interest in Mrs. Headway; for he flattered himself the feeling had definite limits. He had been two or three times to see her; but it was a relief to think that she was now quite independent of him. There had been no revival of that intimate intercourse which occurred during the visit to Longlands. She could dispense with assistance now; she knew herself that she was in the current of success. She pretended to be surprised at her good fortune, especially at its rapidity; but she was really surprised at nothing. She took things as they came, and, being essentially a woman of action, wasted almost as little time in elation as she would have done in despondence. She talked a great deal about Lord Edward and Lady Margaret, and about such other members of the nobility as had shown a desire to cultivate her acquaintance; professing to understand perfectly the sources of a popularity which apparently was destined to increase. "They come to laugh at me," she said; "they come simply to get things to repeat. I can't open my mouth but they burst into fits. It's a settled thing that I'm an American humorist; if I say the simplest things, they begin to roar. I must express myself somehow; and indeed when I hold my tongue they think me funnier than ever. They repeat what I say to a great person, and a great person told some of them the other night that he wanted to hear me for himself. I'll do for him what I do for the others; no better and no worse. I don't know how I do it; I talk the only way I can. They tell me it isn't so much the things I say as the way I say them. Well, they're very easy to please. They don't care for me; it's only to be able to repeat Mrs. Headway's 'last.' Every one wants to have it first; it's a regular race." When she found what was expected of her, she undertook to supply the article in abundance; and the poor little woman really worked hard at her Americanisms. If the taste of London lay that way, she would do her best to gratify it; it was only a pity she hadn't known it before; she would have made more extensive preparations. She thought it a disadvantage, of old, to live in Arizona, in Dakota, in the newly admitted States; but now she perceived that, as she phrased it to herself, this was the best thing that ever had happened to her. She tried to remember all the queer stories she had heard out there, and keenly regretted that she had not taken them down in writing; she drummed up the echoes of the Rocky Mountains and practised the intonations of the Pacific slope. When she saw her audience in convulsions, she said to herself that this was success, and believed that, if she had only come to London five years sooner, she might have married a duke. That would have been even a more absorbing spectacle for the London world than the actual proceedings of Sir

Arthur Demesne, who, however, lived sufficiently in the eye of society to justify the rumor that there were bets about town as to the issue of his already protracted courtship. It was food for curiosity to see a young man of his pattern—one of the few "earnest" young men of the Tory side, with an income sufficient for tastes more marked than those by which he was known—make up to a lady several years older than himself, whose fund of California slang was even larger than her stock of dollars. Mrs. Headway had got a good many new ideas since her arrival in London, but she also retained several old ones. The chief of these—it was now a year old—was that Sir Arthur Demesne was the most irreproachable young man in the world. There were, of course, a good many things that he was not. He was not amusing; he was not insinuating; he was not of an absolutely irrepressible ardor. She believed he was constant; but he was certainly not eager. With these things, however, Mrs. Headway could perfectly dispense; she had, in particular, quite outlived the need of being amused. She had had a very exciting life, and her vision of happiness at present was to be magnificently bored. The idea of complete and uncriticised respectability filled her soul with satisfaction; her imagination prostrated itself in the presence of this virtue. She was aware that she had achieved it but ill in her own person; but she could now, at least, connect herself with it by sacred ties. She could prove in that way what was her deepest feeling. This was a religious appreciation of Sir Arthur's great quality—his smooth and rounded, his blooming, lily-like exemption from social flaws.

She was at home when Littlemore went to see her and surrounded by several visitors, to whom she was giving a late cup of tea and to whom she introduced her compatriot. He stayed till they dispersed, in spite of the manoeuvres of a gentleman who evidently desired to outstay him, but who, whatever might have been his happy fortune on former visits, received on this occasion no encouragement from Mrs. Headway. He looked at Littlemore slowly, beginning with his boots and travelling upwards, as if to discover the reason of so unexpected a preference, and then, without a salutation, left him face to face with their hostess.

"I'm curious to see what you'll do for me, now that you've got your sister with you," Mrs. Headway presently remarked, having heard of this circumstance from Rupert Waterville. "I suppose you'll have to do something, you know. I'm sorry for you; but I don't see how you can get off. You might ask me to dine some day when she's dining out. I would come even then, I think, because I want to keep on the right side of you."

"I call that the wrong side," said Littlemore.

"Yes, I see. It's your sister that's on the right side. You're in rather an embarrassing position, ain't you? However, you take those things very quietly. There's something in you that exasperates me. What does your sister think of me? Does she hate me?"

"She knows nothing about you."

"Have you told her nothing?"

"Never a word."

"Hasn't she asked you? That shows that she hates me. She thinks I ain't creditable to America. I know all that. She wants to show people over here that, however they may be taken in by me, she knows much better. But she'll have to ask you about me; she can't go on for ever. Then what'll you say?"

"That you're the most successful woman in Europe."

"Oh, bother!" cried Mrs. Headway, with irritation.

"Haven't you got into European society?"

"Maybe I have, maybe I haven't. It's too soon to see. I can't tell this season. Every one says I've got to wait till next, to see if it's the same. Sometimes they take you up for a few weeks, and then never know you again. You've got to fasten the thing somehow—to drive in a nail."

"You speak as if it were your coffin," said Littlemore.

"Well, it is a kind of coffin. I'm burying my past!"

Littlemore winced at this. He was tired to death of her past. He changed the subject, and made her talk about London, a topic which she treated with a great deal of humor. She entertained him for half an hour, at the expense of most of her new acquaintances and of some of the most venerable features of the great city. He himself looked at England from the outside, as much as it was possible to do; but in the midst of her familiar allusions to people and things known to her only since yesterday, he was struck with the fact that she would never really be initiated. She buzzed over the surface of things like a fly on a window-pane. She liked it immensely; she was flattered, encouraged, excited; she dropped her confident judgments as if she were scattering flowers, and talked about her intentions, her prospects, her wishes. But she knew no more about English life than about the molecular theory. The words in which he had described her of old to Waterville came back to him: "*Elle ne se doute de rien*!" Suddenly she jumped up; she was going out to dine, and it was time to dress. "Before you leave I want you to promise me something," she said off-hand, but with a look which he had seen before and which meant that the point was important. "You'll be sure to be questioned about me." And then she paused.

"How do people know I know you?"

"You haven't bragged about it? Is that what you mean? You can be a brute when you try. They do know it, at any rate. Possibly I may have told them. They'll come to you, to ask about me. I mean from Lady Demesne. She's in an awful state—she's so afraid her son'll marry me."

Littlemore was unable to control a laugh. "I'm not, if he hasn't done it yet."

"He can't make up his mind. He likes me so much, yet he thinks I'm not a woman to marry." It was positively grotesque, the detachment with which she spoke of herself.

"He must be a poor creature if won't marry you as you are," Littlemore said.

This was not a very gallant form of speech; but Mrs. Headway let it pass. She only replied, "Well, he wants to be very careful, and so he ought to be!"

"If he asks too many questions, he's not worth marrying."

"I beg your pardon—he's worth marrying whatever he does—he's worth marrying for me. And I want to marry him—that's what I want to do."

"Is he waiting for me, to settle it?"

"He's waiting for I don't know what—for some one to come and tell him that I'm the sweetest of the sweet. Then he'll believe it. Some one who has been out there and knows all about me. Of course you're the man, you're created on purpose. Don't you remember how I told you in Paris that he wanted to ask you? He was ashamed, and he gave it up; he tried to forget me. But now it's all on again; only, meanwhile, his mother has been at him. She works at him night and day, like a weasel in a hole, to persuade him that I'm far beneath him. He's very fond of her, and he's very open to influence—I mean from his mother, not from any one else. Except me, of course. Oh, I've influenced him, I've explained everything fifty times over. But some things are rather complicated, don't you know; and he keeps coming back to them. He wants every little speck explained. He won't come to you himself, but his mother will, or she'll send some of her people. I guess she'll send the lawyer—the family solicitor, they call him. She wanted to send him out to America to make inquiries, only she didn't know where to send. Of course I couldn't be expected to give the places, they've got to find them out for themselves. She knows all about you, and she has made the acquaintance of your sister. So you see how much I know. She's waiting for you; she means to catch you. She has an idea she can fix you—make you say what'll meet her views. Then she'll lay it before Sir Arthur. So you'll be so good as to deny everything."

Littlemore listened to this little address attentively, but the conclusion left him staring. "You don't mean that anything I can say will make a difference?"

"Don't be affected! You know it will as well as I."

"You make him out a precious idiot."

"Never mind what I make him out. I want to marry him, that's all. And I appeal to you solemnly. You can save me, as you can lose me. If you lose me, you'll be a coward. And if you say a word against me, I shall be lost."

"Go and dress for dinner, that's your salvation," Littlemore answered, separating from her at the head of the stairs.

IX

It was very well for him to take that tone; but he felt as he walked home that he should scarcely know what to say to people who were determined, as Mrs. Headway put it, to catch him. She had worked a certain spell; she had succeeded in making him feel responsible. The sight of her success, however, rather hardened his heart; he was irritated by her ascending movement. He dined alone that evening, while his sister and her husband, who had engagements every day for a month, partook of their repast at the expense of some friends. Mrs. Dolphin, however, came home rather early, and immediately sought admittance to the small apartment at the foot of the staircase, which was already spoken of as Littlemore's den. Reginald had gone to a "squash" somewhere, and she had returned without delay, having something particular to say to her brother. She was too impatient even to wait till the next morning. She looked impatient; she was very unlike George Littlemore. "I want you to tell me about Mrs. Headway," she said, while he started slightly at the coincidence of this remark with his own thoughts. He was just making up his mind at last to speak to her. She unfastened her cloak and tossed it over a chair, then pulled off her long tight black gloves, which were not so fine as those Mrs. Headway wore; all this as if she were preparing herself for an important interview. She was a small, neat woman, who had once been pretty, with a small, thin voice, a sweet, quiet manner, and a perfect knowledge of what it was proper to do on every occasion in life. She always did it, and her conception of it was so definite that failure would have left her without excuse. She was usually not taken for an American, but she made a point of being one, because she flattered herself that she was of a type which, in that nationality, borrowed distinction from its rarity. She was by nature a great conservative, and had ended by being a better Tory than her husband. She was thought by some of her old friends to have changed immensely since her marriage. She knew as much about English society as if she had invented it; had a way, usually, of looking as if she were dressed for a ride; had also thin lips and pretty teeth; and was as positive as she was amiable. She told her brother that Mrs. Headway had given out that he was her most intimate friend, and she thought it rather odd he had never spoken of her. He admitted that he had known her a long time, referred to the circumstances in which the acquaintance had sprung up, and added that he had seen her that afternoon. He sat there smoking his cigar and looking at the ceiling, while Mrs. Dolphin delivered herself of a series of questions. Was it true that he liked her so much, was it true he thought her a possible woman to marry, was it not true that her antecedents had been most peculiar?

"I may as well tell you that I have a letter from Lady Demesne," Mrs. Dolphin said. "It came to me just before I went out, and I have it in my pocket."

She drew forth the missive, which she evidently wished to read to him; but he gave her no invitation to do so. He knew that she had come to him to extract a declaration adverse to Mrs. Headway's projects, and however little satisfaction he might take in this lady's upward flight, he hated to be urged and pushed. He had a great esteem for Mrs. Dolphin, who, among other Hampshire notions, had picked up that of the preponderance of the male members of a family, so that she treated him with a consideration which made his having an English sister rather a luxury. Nevertheless he was not very encouraging about Mrs. Headway. He admitted once for all that she had not behaved properly—it wasn't worth while to split hairs about that—but he couldn't see that she was much worse than many other women, and he couldn't get up much feeling about her marrying or not marrying. Moreover, it was none of his business, and he intimated that it was none of Mrs. Dolphin's.

"One surely can't resist the claims of common humanity!" his sister replied; and she added that he was very inconsistent. He didn't respect Mrs. Headway, he knew the most dreadful things about her, he didn't think her fit company for his own flesh and blood. And yet he was willing to let poor Arthur Demesne be taken in by her!

"Perfectly willing!" Littlemore exclaimed. "All I've got to do is not to marry her myself."

"Don't you think we have any responsibilities, any duties?"

"I don't know what you mean. If she can succeed she's welcome. It's a splendid sight in its way."

"How do you mean splendid?"

"Why, she has run up the tree as if she were a squirrel!"

"It's very true that she has an audacity *à toute épreuve*. But English society has become scandalously easy. I never saw anything like the people that are taken up. Mrs. Headway has had only to appear to succeed. If they think there's something bad about you they'll be sure to run after you. It's like the decadence of the Roman Empire. You can see to look at Mrs. Headway that she's not a lady. She's pretty, very pretty, but she looks like a dissipated dressmaker. She failed absolutely in New York. I have seen her three times—she apparently goes everywhere. I didn't speak of her —I was wanting to see what you would do. I saw that you meant to do nothing, then this letter decided me. It's written on purpose to be shown to you; it's what she wants you to do. She wrote to me before I came to town, and I went to see her as soon as I arrived. I think it very important. I told her that if she would draw up a little statement I would put it before you as soon as we got settled. She's in real distress. I think you ought to feel for her. You ought to communicate the facts exactly as they stand. A woman has no right to do such things and come and ask to be accepted. She may make it up with her conscience, but she can't make it up with society. Last night at Lady Dovedale's I was afraid she would know who I was and come and speak to me. I was so frightened that I went away. If Sir Arthur wishes to marry her for what she is, of course he's welcome. But at least he ought to know."

Mrs. Dolphin was not excited nor voluble; she moved from point to point with a calmness which had all the air of being used to have reason on its side. She deeply desired, however, that Mrs. Headway's triumphant career should be checked; she had sufficiently abused the facilities of things. Herself a party to an international marriage, Mrs. Dolphin naturally wished that the class to which she belonged should close its ranks and carry its standard high.

"It seems to me that she's quite as good as the little baronet," said Littlemore, lighting another cigar.

"As good? What do you mean? No one has ever breathed a word against him."

"Very likely. But he's a nonentity, and she at least is somebody. She's a person, and a very clever one. Besides, she's quite as good as the women that lots of them have married. I never heard that the British gentry were so unspotted."

"I know nothing about other cases," Mrs. Dolphin said, "I only know about this one. It so happens that I have been brought near to it, and that an appeal has been made to me. The English are very romantic—the most romantic people in the world, if that's what you mean. They do the strangest things, from the force of passion—even those from whom you would least expect it. They marry their cooks—they marry their coachmen—and their romances always have the most miserable end. I'm sure this one would be most wretched. How can you pretend that such a woman as that is to be trusted? What I see is a fine old race—one of the oldest and most honorable in England, people with every tradition of good conduct and high principle—and a dreadful, disreputable, vulgar little woman, who hasn't an idea of what such things are, trying to force her way into it. I hate to see such things—I want to go to the rescue!"

"I don't—I don't care anything about the fine old race."

"Not from interested motives, of course, any more than I. But surely, on artistic grounds, on grounds of decency?"

"Mrs. Headway isn't indecent—you go too far. You must remember that she's an old friend of mine." Littlemore had become rather stern; Mrs. Dolphin was forgetting the consideration due, from an English point of view, to brothers.

She forgot it even a little more. "Oh, if you are in love with her, too!" she murmured, turning away.

He made no answer to this, and the words had no sting for him. But at last, to finish the affair, he asked what in the world the old lady wanted him to do. Did she want him to go out into Piccadilly and announce to the passers-by that there was one winter when even Mrs. Headway's sister didn't know who was her husband?

Mrs. Dolphin answered this inquiry by reading out Lady Demesne's letter, which her brother, as she folded it up again, pronounced one of the most extraordinary letters he had ever heard.

"It's very sad—it's a cry of distress," said Mrs. Dolphin. "The whole meaning of it is that she wishes you would come and see her. She doesn't say so in so many words, but I can read between the lines. Besides, she told me she would give anything to see you. Let me assure you it's your duty to go."

"To go and abuse Nancy Beck?"

"Go and praise her, if you like!" This was very clever of Mrs. Dolphin, but her brother was not so easily caught. He didn't take that view of his duty, and he declined to cross her ladyship's threshold. "Then she'll come and see you," said Mrs. Dolphin, with decision.

"If she does, I'll tell her Nancy's an angel."

"If you can say so conscientiously, she'll be delighted to hear it," Mrs. Dolphin replied, as she gathered up her cloak and gloves.

Meeting Rupert Waterville the next day, as he often did, at the St. George's Club, which offers a much-appreciated hospitality to secretaries of legation and to the natives of the countries they assist in representing, Littlemore let him know that his prophecy had been fulfilled and that Lady Desmesne had been making proposals for an interview. "My sister read me a most remarkable letter from her," he said.

"What sort of a letter?"

"The letter of a woman so scared that she will do anything. I may be a great brute, but her fright amuses me."

"You're in the position of Olivier de Jalin, in the *Demi-Monde,*" Waterville remarked.

"In the *Demi-Monde*?" Littlemore was not quick at catching literary allusions.

"Don't you remember the play we saw in Paris? Or like Don

Fabrice in *L'Aventurière*. A bad woman tries to marry an honorable man, who doesn't know how bad she is, and they who do know step in and push her back."

"Yes, I remember. There was a good deal of lying, all round."

"They prevented the marriage, however, which is the great thing."

"The great thing, if you care about it. One of them was the intimate friend of the fellow, the other was his son. Demesne's nothing to me."

"He's a very good fellow," said Waterville.

"Go and tell him then."

"Play the part of Olivier de Jalin? Oh, I can't; I'm not Olivier. But I wish he would come along. Mrs. Headway oughtn't really to be allowed to pass."

"I wish to heaven they'd let me alone," Littlemore murmured, ruefully, staring for a while out of the window.

"Do you still hold to that theory you propounded in Paris? Are you willing to commit perjury?" Waterville asked.

"Of course I can refuse to answer questions—even that one."

"As I told you before, that will amount to a condemnation."

"It may amount to what it pleases. I think I will go to Paris."

"That will be the same as not answering. But it's quite the best thing you can do. I have been thinking a great deal about it, and it seems to me, from the social point of view, that, as I say, she really oughtn't to pass." Waterville had the air of looking at the thing from a great elevation; his tone, the expression of his face, indicated this lofty flight; the effect of which, as he glanced down at his didactic young friend, Littlemore found peculiarly irritating.

"No, after all, hanged if they shall drive me away!" he exclaimed abruptly; and walked off, while his companion looked after him.

X

THE morning after this Littlemore received a note from Mrs. Headway—a short and simple note, consisting merely of the words, "I shall be at home this afternoon; will you come and see me at five? I have something particular to say to you." He sent no answer to this inquiry, but he went to the little house in Chesterfield Street at the hour that its mistress had designated.

"I don't believe you know what sort of woman I am!" she exclaimed, as soon as he stood before her.

"Oh, Lord!" Littlemore groaned, dropping into a chair. Then he added, "Don't begin on that sort of thing!"

"I shall begin—that's what I wanted to say. It's very important. You don't know me—you don't understand me. You think you do—but you don't."

"It isn't for the want of your having told me—many, many times!" And Littlemore smiled, though he was bored at the prospect that opened before him. The last word of all was, decidedly, that Mrs. Headway was a nuisance. She didn't deserve to be spared!

She glared at him a little, at this; her face was no longer the face that smiled. She looked sharp and violent, almost old; the change was complete. But she gave a little angry laugh. "Yes, I know; men are so stupid. They know nothing about women but what women tell them. And women tell them things on purpose, to see how stupid they can be. I've told you things like that, just for amusement, when it was dull. If you believed them, it was your own fault. But now I am serious, I want you really to know."

"I don't want to know. I know enough."

"How do you mean, you know enough?" she cried, with a flushed face. "What business have you to know anything?" The poor little woman, in her passionate purpose, was not obliged to be consistent, and the loud laugh with which Littlemore greeted this interrogation must have seemed to her unduly harsh. "You shall know what I want you to know, however. You think me a bad woman—you don't respect me; I told you that in Paris. I have done things I don't understand, myself, to-day; that I admit, as fully as you please. But I've completely changed, and I want to change everything. You ought to enter into that; you ought to see what I want. I hate everything that has happened to me before this; I loathe it, I despise it. I went on that way trying—one thing and another. But now I've got what I want. Do you expect me to go down on my knees to you? I believe I will, I'm so anxious. You can help me—no one else can do a thing—no one can do anything—they are only waiting to see if he'll do it. I told you in Paris you could help me, and it's just as true now. Say a good word for me, for God's sake! You haven't lifted your little finger, or I should know it by this time. It will just make the difference. Or if your sister would come and see me, I should be all right. Women are pitiless, pitiless, and you are pitiless too. It isn't that she's anything so great, most of my friends are better than that!—but she's the one woman who *knows*, and people know that she knows. *He* knows that she knows, and he knows she doesn't come. So she kills me—she kills me! I understand perfectly what he wants—I shall do everything, be anything, I shall be the most perfect wife. The old woman will adore me when she knows me—it's too stupid of her not to see. Everything in the past is over; it has all fallen away from me; it's the life of another woman. This was what I wanted; I knew I should find it some day. What could I do in those horrible places? I had to take what I could. But now I've got a nice country. I want you to do me justice; you have never done me justice; that's what I sent for you for."

Littlemore suddenly ceased to be bored; but a variety of feelings had taken the place of a single one. It was impossible not to be touched; she really meant what she said. People don't change their nature; but they change their desires, their ideal, their effort. This incoherent and passionate protestation was an assurance that she was literally panting to be respectable. But the poor woman, whatever she did, was condemned, as Littlemore had said of old, in Paris, to Waterville, to be only half-right. The color rose to her visitor's face as he listened to this outpouring of anxiety and egotism; she had not managed her early life very well, but there was no need of her going down on her knees. "It's very painful to me to hear all this," he said. "You are under no obligation to say such things to me. You entirely misconceive my attitude—my influence."

"Oh yes, you shirk it—you only wish to shirk it!" she cried, flinging away fiercely the sofa-cushion on which she had been resting.

"Marry whom you please!" Littlemore almost shouted, springing to his feet.

He had hardly spoken when the door was thrown open, and the servant announced Sir Arthur Demesne. The baronet entered with a certain briskness, but he stopped short on seeing that Mrs. Headway had another visitor. Recognizing Littlemore, however, he gave a slight exclamation, which might have passed for a greeting. Mrs. Headway, who had risen as he came in, looked with extraordinary earnestness from one of the men to the other; then, like a person who had a sudden inspiration, she clasped her hands together and cried out, "I'm so glad you've met; if I had arranged it, it couldn't be better!"

"If you had arranged it?" said Sir Arthur, crinkling a little his high, white forehead, while the conviction rose before Littlemore that she had indeed arranged it.

"I'm going to do something very strange," she went on, and her eye glittered with a light that confirmed her words.

"You're excited, I'm afraid you're ill." Sir Arthur stood there with his hat and his stick; he was evidently much annoyed.

"It's an excellent opportunity; you must forgive me if I take advantage." And she flashed a tender, touching ray at the baronet. "I have wanted this a long time—perhaps you have seen I wanted it. Mr. Littlemore has known me a long, long time; he's an old, old friend. I told you that in Paris, don't you remember? Well, he's my only one, and I want him to speak for me." Her eyes had turned now to Littlemore; they rested upon him with a sweetness that only made the whole proceeding more audacious. She had begun to smile again, though she was visibly trembling. "He's my only one," she continued; "it's a great pity, you ought to have known others. But I'm very much alone, I must make the best of what I have. I want so much that some one else than myself should speak for me. Women usually can ask that service of a relative, or of another woman. I can't; it's a great pity, but it's not my fault, it's my misfortune. None of my people are here; and I'm terribly alone in the world. But Mr. Littlemore will tell you; he will say he has known me for years. He will tell you whether he knows any reason—whether he knows anything against me. He's been wanting the chance; but he thought he couldn't begin himself. You see I treat you as an old friend, dear Mr. Littlemore. I will leave you with Sir Arthur. You will both excuse me." The expression of her face, turned towards Littlemore, as she delivered herself of this singular proposal had the intentness of a magician who wishes to work a spell. She gave Sir Arthur another smile, and then she swept out of the room.

The two men remained in the extraordinary position that she had created for them; neither of them moved even to open the door for her. She closed it behind her, and for a moment there was a deep, portentous silence. Sir Arthur Demesne, who was very pale, stared hard at the carpet.

"I am placed in an impossible situation," Littlemore said at last, "and I don't imagine that you accept it any more than I do."

The baronet kept the same attitude; he neither looked up nor answered. Littlemore felt a sudden gush of pity for him. Of course he couldn't accept the situation; but all the same, he was half sick with anxiety to see how this nondescript American, who was both so valuable and so superfluous, so familiar and so inscrutable, would consider Mrs. Headway's challenge.

"Have you any questions to ask me?" Littlemore went on.

At this Sir Arthur looked up. Littlemore had seen the look before; he had described it to Waterville after the baronet came to call on him in Paris. There were other things mingled with it now—shame, annoyance, pride; but the great thing, the intense desire to *know,* was paramount.

"Good God, how can I tell him?" Littlemore exclaimed to himself.

Sir Arthur's hesitation was probably extremely brief; but Littlemore heard the ticking of the clock while it lasted. "Certainly, I have no question to ask," the young man said in a voice of cool, almost insolent surprise.

"Good-day, then."

"Good-day."

And Littlemore left Sir Arthur in possession. He expected to find Mrs. Headway at the foot of the staircase; but he quitted the house without interruption.

On the morrow, after lunch, as he was leaving the little mansion at Queen Anne's Gate, the postman handed him a letter. Littlemore opened and read it on the steps of his house, an operation which took but a moment. It ran as follows:—

"Dear Mr. Littlemore,—It will interest you to know that I am engaged to be married to Sir Arthur Demesne, and that our marriage is to take place as soon as their stupid old Parliament rises. But it's not to come out for some days, and I am sure that I can trust meanwhile to your complete discretion.

"Yours very sincerely,

"Nancy H.

"P.S.—He made me a terrible scene for what I did yesterday, but he came back in the evening and made it up. That's how the thing comes to be settled. He won't tell me what passed between you—he requested me never to allude to the subject. I don't care; I was bound you should speak!"

Littlemore thrust this epistle into his pocket and marched away with it. He had come out to do various things, but he forgot his business for the time, and before he knew it had walked into Hyde Park. He left the carriages and riders to one side of him and followed the Serpentine into Kensington Gardens, of which he made the complete circuit. He felt annoyed, and more disappointed than he understood—than he would have understood if he had tried. Now that Nancy Beck had succeeded, her success seemed offensive, and he was almost sorry he had not said to Sir Arthur—"Oh, well, she was pretty bad, you know." However, now the thing was settled, at least they would leave him alone. He walked off his irritation, and before he went about the business he had come out for, had ceased to think about Mrs. Headway. He went home at six o'clock, and the servant who admitted him informed him in doing so that Mrs. Dolphin had requested he should be told on his return that she wished to see him in the drawing-room. "It's another trap!" he said to himself, instinctively; but, in spite of this reflection, he went upstairs. On entering the apartment in which Mrs. Dolphin was accustomed to sit, he found that she had a visitor. This visitor, who was apparently on the point of departing, was a tall, elderly woman, and the two ladies stood together in the middle of the room.

"I'm so glad you've come back," said Mrs. Dolphin, without meeting her brother's eye. "I want so much to introduce you to Lady Demesne, and I hoped you would come in. Must you really go—won't you stay a little?" she added, turning to her companion; and without waiting for an answer, went on hastily—"I must leave you a moment—excuse me. I will come back!" Before he knew it, Littlemore found himself alone with Lady Demesne, and he understood that, since he had not been willing to go and see her, she had taken upon herself to make an advance. It had the queerest effect, all the same, to see his sister playing the same tricks as Nancy Beck!

"Ah, she must be in a fidget!" he said to himself as he stood before Lady Demesne. She looked delicate and modest, even timid, as far as a tall, serene woman who carried her head very well could look so; and she was such a different type from Mrs. Headway that his present vision of Nancy's triumph gave her by contrast something of the dignity of the vanquished. It made him feel sorry for her. She lost no time; she went straight to the point. She evidently felt that in the situation in which she had placed herself, her only advantage could consist in being simple and business-like.

"I'm so glad to see you for a moment. I wish so much to ask you if you can give me any information about a person you know and about whom I have been in correspondence with Mrs. Dolphin. I mean Mrs. Headway."

"Won't you sit down?" asked Littlemore.

"No, I thank you. I have only a moment."

"May I ask you why you make this inquiry?"

"Of course I must give you my reason. I am afraid my son will marry her."

Littlemore was puzzled for a moment; then he felt sure that she was not aware of the fact imparted to him in Mrs. Headway's note. "You don't like her?" he said, exaggerating in spite of himself the interrogative inflexion.

"Not at all," said Lady Demesne, smiling and looking at him. Her smile was gentle, without rancor; Littlemore thought it almost beautiful.

"What would you like me to say?" he asked.

"Whether you think her respectable."

"What good will that do you? How can it possibly affect the event?"

"It will do me no good, of course, if your opinion is favorable. But if you tell me it is not, I shall be able to say to my son that the one person in London who has known her more than six months thinks her a bad woman."

This epithet, on Lady Demesne's clear lips, evoked no protest from Littlemore. He had suddenly become conscious of the need to utter the simple truth with which he had answered Rupert Waterville's first question at the Théâtre Français. "I don't think Mrs. Headway respectable," he said.

"I was sure you would say that." Lady Demesne seemed to pant a little.

"I can say nothing more—not a word. That's my opinion. I don't think it will help you."

"I think it will. I wished to have it from your own lips. That makes all the difference," said Lady Demesne. "I am exceedingly obliged to you." And she offered him her hand; after which he acccompanied her in silence to the door.

He felt no discomfort, no remorse, at what he had said; he only felt relief. Perhaps it was because he believed it would make no difference. It made a difference only in what was at the bottom of all things—his own sense of fitness. He only wished he had remarked to Lady Demesne that Mrs. Headway would probably make her son a capital wife. But that, at least, would make no difference. He requested his sister, who had wondered greatly at the brevity of his interview with Lady Demesne, to spare him all questions on this subject; and Mrs. Dolphin went about for some days in the happy faith that there were to be no dreadful Americans in English society compromising her native land.

Her faith, however, was short-lived. Nothing had made any difference; it was, perhaps, too late. The London world heard in the first days of July, not that Sir Arthur Demesne was to marry Mrs. Headway, but that the pair had been privately, and it was to be hoped, as regards Mrs. Headway, on this occasion indissolubly, united. Lady Demesne gave neither sign nor sound; she only retired to the country.

"I think you might have done differently," said Mrs. Dolphin, very pale, to her brother. "But of course everything will come out now."

"Yes, and make her more the fashion than ever!" Littlemore answered, with cynical laughter. After his little interview with the elder Lady Demesne, he did not feel himself at liberty to call again upon the younger; and he never learned—he never even wished to know—whether in the pride of her success she forgave him.

Waterville—it was very strange—was positively scandalized at this success. He held that Mrs. Headway ought never to have been allowed to marry a confiding gentleman; and he used, in speaking to Littlemore, the same words as Mrs. Dolphin. He thought Littlemore might have done differently.

He spoke with such vehemence that Littlemore looked at him hard—hard enough to make him blush.

"Did you want to marry her yourself?" his friend inquired. "My dear fellow, you're in love with her! That's what's the matter with you."

This, however, blushing still more, Waterville indignantly denied. A little later he heard from New York that people were beginning to ask who in the world was Mrs. Headway.

Lady Barberina

Lady Barberina

IN THE "international" novels and tales the basic Jamesian relation between Europe and America is a relation of marriage—a marriage symbolizing the reconciliation of competing cultures, the union of innocence and experience, faith and civilization. If you are disposed to take a less idealistic view of the matter you might see it simply as the inevitable conjunction of wealth and aristocracy. In some cases the marriage fails to come off because no way is found to bridge the conflict of manners or morals; yet regardless of the specific turn of the plot, the American side of the equation is nearly always represented by a young woman and the European by a young man. *Lady Barberina* (1884) is among the very few exceptions, for its story deals with the marriage of an English noblewoman and an American doctor. This reversal of the social law is in the nature of an experiment on the author's part, and considering the historical circumstances, the experiment could hardly have been expected to yield positive results. Dr. Jackson Lemon may regard himself as the "heir of all the ages," yet even he must confess his blunder in attempting to adapt "a flower of the British aristocracy" to American soil.

In the preface to *Lady Barberina* (New York Edition, 1907-17)

James noted his deviation in this instance from the norm of transatlantic marriages, explaining at some length that though the "bridal migrations were eastward without exception—as rigidly as if settled by custom," it was precisely the "observed rarity of the case" which prompted him to select it for an imaginative test. "There was nothing . . . to 'go by'; we had seen the American girl 'of position' absorbed again and again into the European social system, but we had only seen young foreign candidates for places as cooks and housemaids absorbed into the American. The more one viewed the possible instance, accordingly, the more it appealed to speculative study; so that, failing all valid testimony, one had studiously, as it were, to forge the very documents."

At this point the observant reader might well ask whether James doesn't go too far in his preoccupation with national differences. The Europe-America contrast can scarcely be made to pay endless dividends; it is, after all, but a limited subject. This objection is one of which James was aware and in the above-mentioned preface he tried to meet it. He points out that in quite a few of his fictions his concern is with matters altogether apart from the "international" relation, and that in others it is reduced to a subordinate level of interest. But he goes on to defend his "unnatural mixture" by remarking that no artist is really free to choose his general range of vision and "the experience from which ideas and themes and suggestions spring: this proves ever what it has *had* to be, this is one with the very turn one's life has taken; so that whatever it 'gives,' whatever it makes us feel and think of, we regard very much as imposed and inevitable. The subject thus pressed upon the artist is the necessity of his case and the fruit of his consciousness; which truth has ever made of any quarrel with his subject, any stupid attempt to go behind *that,* the true stultification of criticism." As for himself, he has "never pretended to *go behind*" his own experience, for the profitable thing is "to have your experience, to recognize and understand it. . . ."

James's argument is more than plausible; its truth is guaranteed by his great and intimate knowledge of the creative process. Nothing more needs to be said, except to note the complex uses to which James put his "international" subject. There is its documentary or social and historical use; but beyond that it is employed aesthetically as a kind of individual theatre or personal convention, a framework enclosing a representation of life at once pictorial and dramatic. Thus in *Lady Barberina* the American hero and the English heroine move toward and away from each other like figures in a ballet, and the beauty of their movement lies in its stylization, in its intricate and delicate choreography. The Americanism of the one figure and the Anglicism of the other serve only as the principle of animation by which the dancers are released for their ritual dance of fate.

PART I

I

It is well known that there are few sights in the world more brilliant than the main avenues of Hyde Park of a fine afternoon in June. This was quite the opinion of two persons, who on a beautiful day at the beginning of that month, four years ago, had established themselves under the great trees in a couple of iron chairs (the big ones with arms, for which, if I mistake not, you pay twopence), and sat there with the slow procession of the Drive behind them, while their faces were turned to the more vivid agitation of the Row. They were lost in the multitude of observers, and they belonged, superficially, at least, to that class of persons who, wherever they may be, rank rather with the spectators than with the spectacle. They were quiet, simple, elderly, of aspect somewhat neutral; you would have liked them extremely, but you would scarcely have noticed them. Nevertheless, in all that shining host, it is to them, obscure, that we must give our attention. The reader is begged to have confidence; he is not asked to make vain concessions. There was that in the faces of our friends which indicated that they were growing old together, and that they were fond enough of each other's company not to object (if it was a condition), even to that. The reader will have guessed that they were husband and wife; and perhaps while he is about it, he will have guessed that they were of that nationality for which Hyde Park at the height of the season is most completely illustrative. They were familiar strangers, as it were; and people at once so initiated and so detached could only be Americans. This reflection, indeed, you would have made only after some delay; for it must be admitted that they carried few patriotic signs on the surface. They had the American turn of mind, but that was very subtle; and to your eye—if your eye had cared about it—they might have been of English, or even of Continental, parentage. It was as if it suited them to be colorless; their color was all in their talk. They were not in the least verdant; they were gray, rather, of monotonous hue. If they were interested in the riders, the horses, the walkers, the great exhibition of English wealth and health, beauty, luxury, and leisure, it was because all this referred itself to other impressions, because they had the key to almost everything that needed an answer,—because, in a word, they were able to compare. They had not arrived, they had only returned; and recognition much more than surprise was expressed in their quiet gaze. It may as well be said outright that Dexter Freer and his wife belonged to that class of Americans who are constantly "passing through" London. Possessors of a fortune of which, from any standpoint, the limits were plainly visible, they were unable to command that highest of luxuries,—a habitation in their own country. They found it much more possible to economize at Dresden or Florence than at Buffalo or Minneapolis. The economy was as great, and the inspiration was greater. From Dresden, from Florence, moreover, they constantly made excursions which would not have been possible in those other cities; and it is even to be feared that they had some rather expressive methods of saving. They came to London to buy their portmanteaus, their toothbrushes, their writing-paper; they occasionally even crossed the Atlantic to assure themselves that prices over there were still the same. They were eminently a social pair; their interests were mainly personal. Their point of view, always, was so distinctly human, that they passed for being fond of gossip; and they certainly knew a good deal about the affairs of other people. They had friends in every country, in every town; and it was not their fault if people told them their secrets. Dexter Freer was a tall, lean man, with an interested eye, and a nose that rather drooped than aspired, yet was salient withal. He brushed his hair, which was streaked with white, forward over his ears, in those locks which are represented in the portraits of clean-shaven gentlemen who flourished fifty years ago, and wore an old-fashioned neckcloth and gaiters. His wife, a small, plump person, of superficial freshness, with a white face, and hair that was still perfectly black, smiled perpetually, but had never laughed since the death of a son whom she had lost ten years after her marriage. Her husband, on the other hand, who was usually quite grave, indulged on great occasions in resounding mirth. People confided in her less than in him; but that mattered little, as she confided sufficiently in herself. Her dress, which was always black or dark gray, was so harmoniously simple, that you could see she was fond of it; it was never smart by accident. She was full of intentions of the most judicious sort; and though she was perpetually moving about the world, she had the air of being perfectly stationary. She was celebrated for the promptitude with which she made her sitting-room at an inn, where she might be spending a night or two, look like an apartment long inhabited. With books, flowers, photographs, draperies, rapidly distributed,—she had even a way, for the most part, of having a piano,—the place seemed almost hereditary. The pair were just back from America, where they had spent three months, and now were able to face the world with something of the elation which people feel who have been justified in a prevision. They had found their native land quite ruinous.

"There he is again!" said Mr. Freer, following with his eyes a young man who passed along the Row, riding slowly. "That's a beautiful thorough-bred!"

Mrs. Freer asked idle questions only when she wished for time to think. At present she had simply to look and see who it was her husband meant. "The horse is too big," she remarked, in a moment.

"You mean that the rider is too small," her husband rejoined; "he is mounted on his millions."

"Is it really millions?"

"Seven or eight, they tell me."

"How disgusting!" It was in this manner that Mrs. Freer usually spoke of the large fortunes of the day. "I wish he would see us," she added.

"He does see us, but he doesn't like to look at us. He is too conscious; he isn't easy."

"Too conscious of his big horse?"

"Yes, and of his big fortune; he is rather ashamed of it."

"This is an odd place to come, then," said Mrs. Freer.

"I am not sure of that. He will find people here richer than himself, and other big horses in plenty, and that will cheer him up. Perhaps, too, he is looking for that girl."

"The one we heard about? He can't be such a fool."

"He isn't a fool," said Dexter Freer. "If he is thinking of her, he has some good reason."

"I wonder what Mary Lemon would say."

"She would say it was right, if he should do it. She thinks he can do no wrong. He is exceedingly fond of her."

"I sha'n't be sure of that if he takes home a wife that will despise her."

"Why should the girl despise her? She is a delightful woman."

"The girl will never know it,—and if she should, it would make no difference; she will despise everything."

"I don't believe it, my dear; she will like some things very much. Every one will be very nice to her."

"She will despise them all the more. But we are speaking as if it were all arranged; I don't believe in it at all," said Mrs. Freer.

"Well, something of the sort—in this case or in some other—is sure to happen sooner or later," her husband replied, turning round a little toward the part of the delta which is formed, near the entrance to the Park, by the divergence of the two great vistas of the Drive and the Row.

Our friends had turned their backs, as I have said, to the solemn revolution of wheels and the densely-packed mass of spectators who had chosen that part of the show. These spectators were now agitated by a unanimous impulse: the pushing back of chairs, the shuffle of feet, the rustle of garments, and the deepening murmur of voices sufficiently expressed it. Royalty was approaching—royalty was passing—royalty had passed. Freer turned his head and his ear a little; but he failed to alter his position further, and his wife took no notice of the flurry. They had seen royalty pass, all over Europe, and they knew that it passed very quickly. Sometimes it came back; sometimes it didn't; for more than once they had seen it pass for the last time. They were veteran tourists, and they knew perfectly when to get up and when to remain seated. Mr. Freer went on with his proposition: "Some young fellow is certain to do it, and one of these girls is certain to take the risk. They must take risks, over here, more and more."

"The girls, I have no doubt, will be glad enough; they have had very little chance as yet. But I don't want Jackson to begin."

"Do you know I rather think I do," said Dexter Freer; "it will be very amusing."

"For us, perhaps, but not for him; he will repent of it, and be wretched. He is too good for that."

"Wretched, never! He has no capacity for wretchedness; and that's why he can afford to risk it."

"He will have to make great concessions," Mrs. Freer remarked.

"He won't make one."

"I should like to see."

"You admit, then, that it will be amusing, which is all I contend for. But, as you say, we are talking as if it were settled, whereas there is probably nothing in it after all. The best stories always turn out false. I shall be sorry in this case."

They relapsed into silence, while people passed and repassed them—continuous, successive, mechanical, with strange sequences of faces. They looked at the people, but no one looked at them, though every one was there so admittedly to see what was to be seen. It was all striking, all pictorial, and it made a great composition. The wide, long area of the Row, its red-brown surface dotted with bounding figures, stretched away into the distance and became suffused and misty in the bright, thick air. The deep, dark English verdure that bordered and overhung it, looked rich and old, revived and refreshed though it was by the breath of June. The mild blue of the sky was spotted with great silvery clouds, and the light drizzled down in heavenly shafts over the quieter spaces of the Park, as one saw them beyond the Row. All this, however, was only a background, for the scene was before everything personal; superbly so, and full of the gloss and lustre, the contrasted tones, of a thousand polished surfaces. Certain things were salient, pervasive,—the shining flanks of the perfect horses, the twinkle of bits and spurs, the smoothness of fine cloth adjusted to shoulders and limbs, the sheen of hats and boots, the freshness of complexions, the expression of smiling, talking faces, the flash and flutter of rapid gallops. Faces were everywhere, and they were the great effect,—above all, the fair faces of women on tall horses, flushed a little under their stiff black hats, with figures stiffened, in spite of much definition of curve, by their tight-fitting habits. Their hard little helmets, their neat, compact heads, their straight necks, their firm, tailor-made armor, their blooming, competent physique, made them look doubly like amazons about to ride a charge. The men, with their eyes before them, with hats of undulating brim, good profiles, high collars, white flowers on their chests, long legs and long feet, had an air more elaboratively decorative, as they jolted beside the ladies, always out of step. These were youthful types; but it was not all youth, for many a saddle was surmounted by a richer rotundity, and ruddy faces, with short white whiskers or with matronly chins, looked down comfortably from an equilibrium which was moral as well as physical. The walkers differed from the riders only in being on foot, and in looking at the riders more than these looked at them; for they would have done as well in the saddle and ridden as the others ride. The women had tight little bonnets and still tighter little knots of hair; their round chins rested on a close swathing of lace, or, in some cases, of silver chains and circlets. They had flat backs and small waists, they walked slowly, with their elbows out, carrying vast parasols, and turning their heads very little to the right or the left. They were amazons unmounted, quite ready to spring into the saddle. There was a great deal of beauty and a suffused look of successful development, which came from clear, quiet eyes and from well-cut lips, on which syllables were liquid and sentences brief. Some of the young men, as well as the women, had the happiest proportions and oval faces, in which line and color were pure and fresh, and the idea of the moment was not very intense.

"They are very good-looking," said Mr. Freer, at the end of ten minutes; "they are the finest whites."

"So long as they remain white they do very well; but when they venture upon color!" his wife replied. She sat with her eyes on a level with the skirts of the ladies who passed her; and she had been following the progress of a green velvet robe, enriched with ornaments of steel and much gathered up in the hands of its wearer, who, herself apparently in her teens, was accompanied by a young lady draped in scanty pink muslin, embroidered, aesthetically, with flowers that simulated the iris.

"All the same, in a crowd, they are wonderfully well turned out," Dexter Freer went on; "take the men, and women, and horses together. Look at that big fellow on the light chestnut: what could be more perfect? By the way, it's Lord Canterville," he added in a moment, as if the fact were of some importance.

Mrs. Freer recognized its importance to the degree of raising her glass to look at Lord Canterville. "How do you know it's he?" she asked, with her glass still up.

"I heard him say something the night I went to the House of Lords. It was very few words, but I remember him. A man who was near me told me who he was."

"He is not so handsome as you," said Mrs. Freer, dropping her glass.

"Ah, you're too difficult!" her husband murmured. "What a pity the girl isn't with him," he went on; "we might see something."

It appeared in a moment that the girl was with him. The nobleman designated had ridden slowly forward from the start, but just opposite our friends he pulled up to look behind him, as if he had been waiting for some one. At the same moment a gentleman in the Walk engaged his attention, so that he advanced to the barrier which protects the pedestrians, and halted there, bending a little from his saddle and talking with his friend, who leaned against the rail. Lord Canterville was indeed perfect, as his American admirer had said. Upwards of sixty, and of great stature and great presence, he was really a splendid apparition. In exquisite preservation, he had the freshness of middle life, and would have been young to the eye if the lapse of years were not needed to account for his considerable girth. He was clad from head to foot in garments of a radiant gray, and his fine florid countenance was surmounted with a white hat, of which the majestic curves were a triumph of good form. Over his mighty chest was spread a beard of the richest growth, and of a color, in spite of a few streaks, vaguely grizzled, to which the coat of his admirable horse appeared to be a perfect match. It left no opportunity, in his uppermost button-hole, for the customary gardenia; but this was of comparatively little consequence, as the vegetation of the beard itself was tropical. Astride his great steed, with his big fist, gloved in pearl-gray, on his swelling thigh, his face lighted up with good-humored indifference, and all his magnificent surface reflecting the mild sunshine, he was a very imposing man indeed, and visibly, incontestably, a personage. People almost lingered to look at him as they passed. His halt was brief, however, for he was almost immediately joined by two handsome girls, who were as well turned-out, in Dexter Freer's phrase, as himself. They had been detained a moment at the entrance to the Row, and now advanced side by side, their groom close behind them. One was taller and older than the other, and it was apparent at a glance that they were sisters. Between them, with their charming shoulders, contracted waists, and skirts that hung without a wrinkle, like a plate of zinc, they represented in a singularly complete form the pretty English girl in the position in which she is prettiest.

"Of course they are his daughters," said Dexter Freer, as they rode away with Lord Canterville; "and in that case one of them must be Jackson Lemon's sweetheart. Probably the bigger; they said it was the eldest. She is evidently a fine creature."

"She would hate it over there," Mrs. Freer remarked, for all answer to this cluster of inductions.

"You know I don't admit that. But granting she should, it would do her good to have to accommodate herself."

"She wouldn't accommodate herself."

"She looks so confoundedly fortunate, perched up on that saddle," Dexter Freer pursued, without heeding his wife's rejoinder.

"Aren't they supposed to be very poor?"

"Yes, they look it!" And his eyes followed the distinguished trio, as, with the groom, as distinguished in his way as any of them, they started on a canter.

The air was full of sound, but it was low and diffused; and when, near our friends, it became articulate, the words were simple and few.

"It's as good as the circus, isn't it, Mrs. Freer?" These words correspond to that description, but they pierced the air more effectually than any our friends had lately heard. They were uttered by a young man who had stopped short in the path, absorbed by the sight of his compatriots. He was short and stout, he had a round, kind face, and short, stiff-looking hair, which was reproduced in a small bristling beard. He wore a double-breasted walking-coat, which was not, however, buttoned, and on the summit of his round head was perched a hat of exceeding smallness, and of the so-called "pot" category. It evidently fitted him, but a hatter himself would not have known why. His hands were encased in new gloves, of a dark-brown color, and they hung with an air of unaccustomed inaction at his sides. He sported neither umbrella nor stick. He extended one of his hands, almost with eagerness, to Mrs. Freer, blushing a little as he became aware that he had been eager.

"Oh, Dr. Feeder!" she said, smiling at him. Then she repeated to her husband, "Dr. Feeder, my dear!" and her husband said, "Oh, Doctor, how d'ye do?" I have spoken of the composition of his appearance; but the items were not perceived by these two. They saw only one thing, his delightful face, which was both simple and clever, and unreservedly good. They had lately made the voyage from New York in his company, and it was plain that he would be very genial at sea. After he had stood in front of them a moment, a chair beside Mrs. Freer became vacant, on which he took possession of it, and sat there telling her what he thought of the Park, and how he liked London. As she knew every one, she had known many of his people at home; and while she listened to him she remembered how large their contribution had been to the virtue and culture of Cincinnati. Mrs. Freer's social horizon included even that city; she had been on terms almost familiar with several families from Ohio, and was acquainted with the position of the Feeders there. This family, very numerous, was interwoven into an enormous cousinship. She herself was quite out of such a system, but she could have told you whom Dr. Feeder's great-grandfather had married. Every one, indeed, had heard of the good deeds of the descendants of this worthy, who were generally physicians, excellent ones, and whose name expressed not inaptly their numerous acts of charity. Sidney Feeder, who had several cousins of this name established in the same line at Cincinnati, had transferred himself and his ambition to New York, where his practice, at the end of three years, had begun to grow. He had studied his profession at Vienna, and was impregnated with German science; indeed, if he had only worn spectacles, he might perfectly, as he sat there watching the riders in Rotten Row as if their proceedings were a successful demonstration, have passed for a young German of distinction. He had come over to London to attend a medical congress which met this year in the British capital; for his interest in the healing art was by no means limited to the cure of his patients, it embraced every form of experiment; and the expression of his honest eyes would almost have reconciled you to vivisection. It was the first time he had come to the Park; for social experiments he had little leisure. Being aware, however, that it was a very typical, and as it were symptomatic, sight, he had conscientiously reserved an afternoon, and had dressed himself carefully for the occasion. "It's quite a brilliant show," he said to Mrs. Freer; "it makes me wish I had a mount." Little as he resembled Lord Canterville, he rode very well.

"Wait till Jackson Lemon passes again, and you can stop him and make him let you take a turn." This was the jocular suggestion of Dexter Freer.

"Why, is he here? I have been looking out for him; I should like to see him."

"Doesn't he go to your medical congress?" asked Mrs. Freer.

"Well yes, he attends; but he isn't very regular. I guess he goes out a good deal."

"I guess he does," said Mr. Freer; "and if he isn't very regular, I guess he has a good reason. A beautiful reason, a charming reason," he went on, bending forward to look down toward the beginning of the Row. "Dear me, what a lovely reason!"

Dr. Feeder followed the direction of his eyes, and after a moment understood his allusion. Little Jackson Lemon, on his big horse, passed along the avenue again, riding beside one of the young girls who had come that way shortly before in the company of Lord Canterville. His lordship followed, in conversation with the other, his younger daughter. As they advanced, Jackson Lemon turned his eyes toward the multitude under the trees, and it so happened that they rested upon the Dexter Freers. He smiled, and raised his hat with all possible friendliness; and his three companions turned to see to whom he was bowing with so much cordiality. As he settled his hat on his head, he espied the young man from Cincinnati, whom he had at first overlooked; whereupon he smiled still more brightly, and waved Sidney Feeder an airy salutation with his hand, reining in a little at the same time just for an instant, as if he half expected the Doctor to come and speak to him. Seeing him with strangers, however, Sidney Feeder hung back, staring a little as he rode away.

It is open to us to know that at this moment the young lady by whose side he was riding said to him familiarly enough: "Who are those people you bowed to?"

"Some old friends of mine,—Americans," Jackson Lemon answered.

"Of course they are Americans; there is nothing but Americans nowadays."

"Oh, yes, our turn's coming round!" laughed the young man.

"But that doesn't say who they are," his companion continued. "It's so difficult to say who Americans are," she added, before he had time to answer her.

"Dexter Freer and his wife,—there is nothing difficult about that; every one knows them."

"I never heard of them," said the English girl.

"Ah, that's your fault. I assure you everybody knows them."

"And does everybody know the little man with the fat face whom you kissed your hand to?"

"I didn't kiss my hand; but I would if I had thought of it. He is a great chum of mine,—a fellow student at Vienna."

"And what's *his* name?"

"Dr. Feeder."

Jackson Lemon's companion was silent a moment. "Are *all* your friends doctors?" she presently inquired.

"No; some of them are in other businesses."

"Are they all in some business?"

"Most of them; save two or three, like Dexter Freer."

"Dexter Freer? I thought you said Dr. Freer."

The young man gave a laugh. "You heard me wrong. You have got doctors on the brain, Lady Barb."

"I am rather glad," said Lady Barb, giving the rein to her horse, who bounded away.

"Well yes, she's very handsome, the reason," Dr. Feeder remarked, as he sat under the trees.

"Is he going to marry her?" Mrs. Freer inquired.

"Marry her? I hope not."

"Why do you hope not?"

"Because I know nothing about her. I want to know something about the woman that man marries."

"I suppose you would like him to marry in Cincinnati," Mrs. Freer rejoined, lightly.

"Well, I am not particular where it is; but I want to know her first." Dr. Feeder was very sturdy.

"We were in hopes you would know all about it," said Mr. Freer.

"No; I haven't kept up with him there."

"We have heard from a dozen people that he has been always with her for the last month; and that kind of thing, in England, is supposed to mean something. Hasn't he spoken of her when you have seen him?"

"No, he has only talked about the new treatment of spinal meningitis. He is very much interested in spinal meningitis."

"I wonder if he talks about it to Lady Barb," said Mrs. Freer.

"Who is she, anyway?" the young man inquired.

"Lady Barberina Clement."

"And who is Lady Barberina Clement?"

"The daughter of Lord Canterville."

"And who is Lord Canterville?"

"Dexter must tell you that," said Mrs. Freer.

And Dexter accordingly told him that the Marquis of Canterville had been in his day a great sporting nobleman and an ornament to English society, and had held more than once a high post in her Majesty's household. Dexter Freer knew all these things,—how his lordship had married a daughter of Lord Treherne, a very serious, intelligent, and beautiful woman, who had redeemed him from the extravagance of his youth and presented him in rapid succession with a dozen little tenants for the nurseries at Pasterns,—this being, as Mr. Freer also knew, the name of the principal seat of the Cantervilles. The Marquis was a Tory, but very liberal for a Tory, and very popular in society at large; good-natured, good-looking, knowing how to be genial, and yet to remain a *grand seigneur,* clever enough to make an occasional speech, and much associated with the fine old English pursuits, as well as with many of the new improvements,—the purification of the Turf, the opening of the museums on Sunday, the propagation of coffee-taverns, the latest ideas on sanitary reform. He disapproved of the extension of the suffrage, but he positively had drainage on the brain. It had been said of him at least once (and I think in print) that he was just the man to convey to the popular mind the impression that the British aristocracy is still a living force. He was not very rich, unfortunately (for a man who had to exemplify such truths), and of his twelve children, no less than seven were daughters. Lady Barberina, Jackson Lemon's friend, was the second; the eldest had married Lord Beauchemin. Mr. Freer had caught quite the right pronunciation of this name: he called it Bitumen. Lady Lucretia had done very well, for her husband was rich, and she had brought him nothing to speak of; but it was hardly to be expected that the others would do as well. Happily the younger girls were still in the schoolroom; and before they had come up, Lady Canterville, who was a woman of resources, would have worked off the two that were out. It was Lady Agatha's first season; she was not so pretty as her sister, but she was thought to be cleverer. Half-a-dozen people had spoken to him of Jackson Lemon's being a great deal at the Cantervilles. He was supposed to be enormously rich.

"Well, so he is," said Sidney Feeder, who had listened to Mr. Freer's little recital with attention, with eagerness even, but with an air of imperfect apprehension.

"Yes, but not so rich as they probably think."

"Do they want his money? Is that what they're after?"

"You go straight to the point," Mrs. Freer murmured.

"I haven't the least idea," said her husband. "He is a very nice fellow in himself."

"Yes, but he's a doctor," Mrs. Freer remarked.

"What have they got against that?" asked Sidney Feeder.

"Why, over here, you know, they only call them in to prescribe," said Dexter Freer; "the profession isn't—a—what you'd call aristocratic."

"Well, I don't know it, and I don't know that I want to know it. How do you mean, aristocratic? What profession is? It would be rather a curious one. Many of the gentlemen at the congress there are quite charming."

"I like doctors very much," said Mrs. Freer; "my father was a doctor. But they don't marry the daughters of marquises."

"I don't believe Jackson wants to marry that one."

"Very possibly not—people are such asses," said Dexter Freer. "But he will have to decide. I wish you would find out, by the way; you can if you will."

"I will ask him—up at the congress; I can do that. I suppose he has got to marry some one." Sidney Feeder added, in a moment, "And she may be a nice girl."

"She is said to be charming."

"Very well, then; it won't hurt him. I must say, however, I am not sure I like all that about her family."

"What I told you? It's all to their honor and glory."

"Are they quite on the square? It's like those people in Thackeray."

"Oh, if Thackeray could have done this!" Mrs. Freer exclaimed, with a good deal of expression.

"You mean all this scene?" asked the young man.

"No; the marriage of a British noblewoman and an American doctor. It would have been a subject for Thackeray."

"You see you do want it, my dear," said Dexter Freer, quietly.

"I want it as a story, but I don't want it for Dr. Lemon."

"Does he call himself 'Doctor' still?" Mr. Freer asked of young Feeder.

"I suppose he does; I call him so. Of course he doesn't practice. But once a doctor, always a doctor."

"That's doctrine for Lady Barb!"

Sidney Feeder stared. "Hasn't she got a title too? What would she expect him to be? President of the United States? He's a man of real ability; he might have stood at the head of his profession. When I think of that, I want to swear. What did his father want to go and make all that money for!"

"It must certainly be odd to them to see a 'medical man' with six or eight millions," Mr. Freer observed.

"They use the same term as the Choctaws," said his wife.

"Why, some of their own physicians made immense fortunes," Sidney Feeder declared.

"Couldn't he be made a baronet by the Queen?" This suggestion came from Mrs. Freer.

"Yes, then he would be aristocratic," said the young man. "But I don't see why he should want to marry over here; it seems to me to be going out of his way. However, if he is happy, I don't care. I like him very much; he has got lots of ability. If it hadn't been for his father he would have made a splendid doctor. But, as I say, he takes a great interest in medical science, and I guess he means to promote it all he can—with his fortune. He will always be doing something in the way of research. He thinks we *do* know something, and he is bound we shall know more. I hope she won't prevent him, the young marchioness—is that her rank? And I hope they are really good people. He ought to be very useful. I should want to know a good deal about the family I was going to marry into."

"He looked to me, as he rode there, as if he knew a good deal about the Clements," Dexter Freer said, rising, as his wife suggested that they ought to be going; "and he looked to me pleased with the knowledge. There they come, down on the other side. Will you walk away with us, or will you stay?"

"Stop him and ask him, and then come and tell us—in Jermyn Street." This was Mrs. Freer's parting injunction to Sidney Feeder.

"He ought to come himself—tell him that," her husband added.

"Well, I guess I'll stay," said the young man, as his companions merged themselves in the crowd that now was tending toward the gates. He went and stood by the barrier, and saw Dr. Lemon and his friends pull up at the entrance to the Row, where they apparently prepared to separate. The separation took some time, and Sidney Feeder became interested. Lord Canterville and his younger daughter lingered to talk with two gentlemen, also mounted, who looked a good deal at the legs of Lady Agatha's horse. Jackson Lemon and Lady Barberina were face to face, very near each other; and she, leaning forward a little, stroked the overlapping neck of his glossy bay. At a distance he appeared to be talking, and she to be listening and saying nothing. "Oh, yes, he's making love to her," thought Sidney Feeder. Suddenly her father turned away to leave the Park, and she joined him and disappeared, while Dr. Lemon came up on the left again, as if for a final gallop. He had not gone far before he perceived his *confrère*, who awaited him at the rail; and he repeated the gesture which Lady Barberina had spoken of as a kissing of his hand, though it must be added that, to his friend's eyes, it had not quite that significance. When he reached the point where Feeder stood, he pulled up.

"If I had known you were coming here, I would have given you a moment," he said. There was not in his person that irradiation of wealth and distinction which made Lord Canterville glow like a picture; but as he sat there with his little legs stuck out, he looked very bright, and sharp, and happy, wearing in his degree the aspect of one of Fortune's favorites. He had a thin, keen, delicate face, a nose very carefully finished, a rapid eye, a trifle hard in expression, and a small mustache, a good deal cultivated. He was not striking, but he was very positive, and it was easy to see that he was full of purpose.

"How many horses have you got—about forty?" his compatriot inquired, in response to his greeting.

"About five hundred," said Jackson Lemon.

"Did you mount your friends—the three you were riding with?"

"Mount them? They have got the best horses in England?"

"Did they sell you this one?" Sidney Feeder continued, in the same humorous strain.

"What do you think of him?" said his friend, not deigning to answer this question.

"He's an awful old screw; I wonder he can carry you."

"Where did you get your hat?" asked Dr. Lemon, in return.

"I got it in New York. What's the matter with it?"

"It's very beautiful; I wish I had bought one like it."

"The head's the thing—not the hat. I don't mean yours, but mine. There is something very deep in your question; I must think it over."

"Don't—don't," said Jackson Lemon; "you will never get to the bottom of it. Are you having a good time?"

"A glorious time. Have you been up to-day?"

"Up among the doctors? No; I have had a lot of things to do."

"We had a very interesting discussion. I made a few remarks."

"You ought to have told me. What were they about?"

"About the intermarriage of races, from the point of view——." And Sidney Feeder paused a moment, occupied with the attempt to scratch the nose of his friend's horse.

"From the point of view of the progeny, I suppose?"

"Not at all; from the point of view of the old friends."

"Damn the old friends!" Dr. Lemon exclaimed, with jocular crudity.

"Is it true that you are going to marry a young marchioness?"

The face of the young man in the saddle became just a trifle rigid, and his firm eyes fixed themselves on Dr. Feeder.

"Who has told you that?"

"Mr. and Mrs. Freer, whom I met just now."

"Mr. and Mrs. Freer be hanged! And who told them?"

"Ever so many people; I don't know who."

"Gad, how things are tattled!" cried Jackson Lemon, with some asperity.

"I can see it's true, by the way you say that."

"Do Freer and his wife believe it?" Jackson Lemon went on, impatiently.

"They want you to go and see them: you can judge for yourself."

"I will go and see them, and tell them to mind their business."

"In Jermyn Street; but I forget the number. I am sorry the marchioness isn't American," Sidney Feeder continued.

"If I should marry her, she would be," said his friend. "But I don't see what difference it can make to you."

"Why, she'll look down on the profession; and I don't like that from your wife."

"That will touch me more than you."

"Then it *is* true?" cried Feeder, more seriously, looking up at his friend.

"She won't look down; I will answer for that."

"You won't care, you are out of it all now."

"No, I am not; I mean to do a great deal of work."

"I will believe that when I see it," said Sidney Feeder, who was by no means perfectly incredulous, but who thought it salutary to take that tone. "I am not sure that you have any right to work, —you oughtn't to have everything; you ought to leave the field to us. You must pay the penalty of being so rich. You would have been celebrated if you had continued to practice,—more celebrated than any one. But you won't be now,—you can't be. Some one else will be, in your place."

Jackson Lemon listened to this, but without meeting the eyes of the speaker; not, however, as if he were avoiding them, but as if the long stretch of the Ride, now less and less obstructed, invited him, and made his companion's talk a little retarding. Nevertheless, he answered, deliberately and kindly enough: "I hope it will be you"; and he bowed to a lady who rode past.

"Very likely it will. I hope I make you feel badly,—that's what I'm trying to do."

"Oh, awfully!" cried Jackson Lemon; "all the more that I am not in the least engaged."

"Well, that's good. Won't you come up to-morrow?" Dr. Feeder went on.

"I'll try, my dear fellow; I can't be sure. By by!"

"Oh, you're lost anyway!" cried Sidney Feeder, as the other started away.

II

IT WAS Lady Marmaduke, the wife of Sir Henry Marmaduke, who had introduced Jackson Lemon to Lady Beauchemin; after which Lady Beauchemin had made him acquainted with her mother and sisters. Lady Marmaduke was also transatlantic; she had been for her conjugal baronet the most permanent consequence of a tour in the United States. At present, at the end of ten years, she knew her London as she had never known her New York, so that it had been easy for her to be, as she called herself, Jackson Lemon's social godmother. She had views with regard to his career, and these views fitted into a social scheme which, if our space permitted, I should be glad to lay before the reader in its magnitude. She wished to add an arch or two to the bridge on which she had effected her transit from America; and it was her belief that Jackson Lemon might furnish the materials. This bridge, as yet a somewhat sketchy and rickety structure, she saw (in the future) boldly stretching from one solid pillar to another. It would have to go both ways, for reciprocity was the keynote of Lady Marmaduke's plan. It was her belief that an ultimate fusion was inevitable, and that those who were the first to understand the situation would gain the most. The first time Jackson Lemon had dined with her, he met Lady Beauchemin, who was her intimate friend. Lady Beauchemin was remarkably gracious; she asked him to come and see her as if she really meant it. He presented himself, and in her drawing-room met her mother, who happened to be calling at the same moment. Lady Canterville, not less friendly than her daughter, invited him down to Pasterns for Easter Week; and before a month had passed it seemed to him that, though he was not what he would have called intimate at any house in London, the door of the house of Clement opened to him pretty often. This was a considerable good fortune, for it always opened upon a charming picture. The inmates were a blooming and beautiful race, and their interior had an aspect of the ripest comfort. It was not the splendor of New York (as New York had lately begun to appear to the young man), but a splendor in which there was an unpurchasable ingredient of age. He himself had a great deal of money, and money was good, even when it was new; but old money was the best. Even after he learned that Lord Canterville's fortune was more ancient than abundant, it was still the mellowness of the golden element that struck him. It was Lady Beauchemin who had told him that her father was not rich; having told him, besides this, many surprising things,—things that were surprising in themselves, or surprising on her lips. This struck him afresh later that evening—the day he met Sidney Feeder in the Park. He dined out, in the company of Lady Beauchemin, and afterward, as she was alone,—her husband had gone down to listen to a debate,—she offered to "take him on." She was going to several places, and he must be going to some of them. They compared notes; and it was settled that they should proceed together to the Trumpington's whither, also, it appeared at eleven o'clock that all the world was going, the approach to the house being choked for half a mile with carriages. It was a close, muggy night; Lady Beauchemin's chariot, in its place in the rank, stood still for long periods. In his corner beside her, through the open window, Jackson Lemon, rather hot, rather oppressed, looked out on the moist, greasy pavement, over which was flung, a considerable distance up and down, the flare of a public-house. Lady Beauchemin, however, was not impatient, for she had a purpose in her mind, and now she could say what she wished.

"Do you really love her?" That was the first thing she said.

"Well, I guess so," Jackson Lemon answered, as if he did not recognize the obligation to be serious.

Lady Beauchemin looked at him a moment in silence; he felt her gaze, and turning his eyes, saw her face, partly shadowed, with the aid of a street-lamp. She was not so pretty as Lady Barberina; her countenance had a certain sharpness; her hair, very light in color and wonderfully frizzled, almost covered her eyes, the expression of which, however, together with that of her pointed nose, and the glitter of several diamonds, emerged from the gloom. "You don't seem to know. I never saw a man in such an odd state," she presently remarked.

"You push me a little too much; I must have time to think of it," the young man went on. "You know in my country they allow us plenty of time." He had several little oddities of expression, of which he was perfectly conscious, and which he found convenient, for they protected him in a society in which a lonely American was rather exposed; they gave him the advantage which corresponded with certain drawbacks. He had very few natural Americanisms, but the occasional use of one, discreetly chosen, made him appear simpler than he really was, and he had his reasons for wishing this result. He was not simple; he was subtle, circumspect, shrewd, and perfectly aware that he might make mistakes. There was a danger of his making a mistake at present,—a mistake which would be immensely grave. He was determined only to succeed. It is true that for a great success he would take a certain risk; but the risk was to be considered, and he gained time while he multiplied his guesses and talked about his country.

"You may take ten years if you like," said Lady Beauchemin. "I am in no hurry whatever to make you my brother-in-law. Only you must remember that you spoke to me first."

"What did I say?"

"You told me that Barberina was the finest girl you had seen in England."

"Oh, I am willing to stand by that; I like her type."

"I should think you might!"

"I like her very much,—with all her peculiarities."

"What do you mean by her peculiarities?"

"Well, she has some peculiar ideas," said Jackson Lemon, in a tone of the sweetest reasonableness, "and she has a peculiar way of speaking."

"Ah, you can't expect us to speak as well as you!" cried Lady Beauchemin.

"I don't know why not; you do some things much better."

"We have our own ways, at any rate, and we think them the best in the world. One of them is not to let a gentleman devote himself to a girl for three or four months without some sense of responsibility. If you don't wish to marry my sister, you ought to go away."

"I ought never to have come," said Jackson Lemon.

"I can scarcely agree to that; for I should have lost the pleasure of knowing you."

"It would have spared you this duty, which you dislike very much."

"Asking you about you intentions? I don't dislike it at all; it amuses me extremely."

"Should you like your sister to marry me?" asked Jackson Lemon, with great simplicity.

If he expected to take Lady Beauchemin by surprise he was disappointed; for she was perfectly prepared to commit herself. "I should like it very much. I think English and American society ought to be but one—I mean the best of each—a great whole."

"Will you allow me to ask whether Lady Marmaduke suggested that to you?"

"We have often talked of it."

"Oh yes, that's her aim."

"Well, it's my aim too. I think there's a great deal to be done."

"And you would like me to do it?"

"To begin it, precisely. Don't you think we ought to see more of each other?—I mean the best in each country."

Jackson Lemon was silent a moment. "I am afraid I haven't any general ideas. If I should marry an English girl, it wouldn't be for the good of the species."

"Well, we want to be mixed a little; that I am sure of," Lady Beauchemin said.

"You certainly got that from Lady Marmaduke."

"It's too tiresome, your not consenting to be serious! But my father will make you so," Lady Beauchemin went on. "I may as well let you know that he intends in a day or two to ask you your intentions. That's all I wished to say to you. I think you ought to be prepared."

"I am much obliged to you; Lord Canterville will do quite right."

There was, to Lady Beauchemin, something really unfathomable in this little American doctor, whom she had taken up on grounds of large policy, and who, though he was assumed to have sunk the medical character, was neither handsome nor distinguished, but only immensely rich and quite original, for he was not insignificant. It was unfathomable, to begin with, that a medical man should be so rich, or that so rich a man should be a doctor; it was even, to an eye which was always gratified by suitability, rather irritating. Jackson Lemon himself could have explained it better than any one else, but this was an explanation that one could scarcely ask for. There were other things: his cool acceptance of certain situations; his general indisposition to explain; his way of taking refuge in jokes, which at times had not even the merit of being American; his way, too, of appearing to be a suitor without being an aspirant. Lady Beauchemin, however, was, like Jackson Lemon, prepared to run a certain risk. His reserves made him slippery; but that was only when one pressed. She flattered herself that she could handle people lightly. "My father will be sure to act with perfect tact," she said; "of course, if you shoudn't care to be questioned, you can go out of town." She had the air of really wishing to make everything easy for him.

"I don't want to go out of town; I am enjoying it far too much here," her companion answered. "And wouldn't your father have a right to ask me what I meant by that?"

Lady Beauchemin hesitated; she was slightly perplexed. But in a moment she exclaimed: "He is incapable of saying anything vulgar!"

She had not really answered his inquiry, and he was conscious of that; but he was quite ready to say to her, a little later, as he guided her steps from the brougham to the strip of carpet which, between a somewhat rickety border of striped cloth and a double row of waiting footmen, policemen, and dingy amateurs of both sexes, stretched from the curbstone to the portal of the Trumpingtons, "Of course I shall not wait for Lord Canterville to speak to me."

He had been expecting some such announcement as this from

Lady Beauchemin, and he judged that her father would do no more than his duty. He knew that he ought to be prepared with an answer to Lord Canterville, and he wondered at himself for not yet having come to the point. Sidney Feeder's question in the Park had made him feel rather pointless; it was the first allusion that had been made to his possible marriage, except on the part of Lady Beauchemin. None of his own people were in London; he was perfectly independent, and even if his mother had been within reach he could not have consulted her on the subject. He loved her dearly, better than any one; but she was not a woman to consult, for she approved of whatever he did: it was her standard. He was careful not to be too serious when he talked with Lady Beauchemin; but he was very serious indeed as he thought over the matter within himself, which he did even among the diversions of the next half hour, while he squeezed obliquely and slowly through the crush in Mrs. Trumpington's drawing-room. At the end of the half-hour he came away, and at the door he found Lady Beauchemin, from whom he had separated on entering the house, and who, this time with a companion of her own sex, was awaiting her carriage and still "going on." He gave her his arm into the street, and as she stepped into the vehicle she repeated that she wished he would go out of town for a few days.

"Who, then, would tell me what to do?" he asked, for answer, looking at her through the window.

She might tell him what to do, but he felt free, all the same; and he was determined this should continue. To prove it to himself he jumped into a hansom and drove back to Brook Street to his hotel, instead of proceeding to a bright-windowed house in Portland Place, where he knew that after midnight he should find Lady Canterville and her daughters. There had been a reference to the subject between Lady Barberina and himself during their ride, and she would probably expect him; but it made him taste his liberty not to go, and he liked to taste his liberty. He was aware that to taste it in perfection he ought to go to bed; but he did not go to bed, he did not even take off his hat. He walked up and down his sitting-room, with his head surmounted by this ornament, a good deal tipped back, and his hands in his pockets. There were a good many cards stuck into the frame of the mirror over his chimney-piece, and every time he passed the place he seemed to see what was written on one of them,—the name of the mistress of the house in Portland Place, his own name, and, in the lower left-hand corner, the words: "A small Dance." Of course, now, he must make up his mind; he would make it up to the next day: that was what he said to himself as he walked up and down; and according to his decision he would speak to Lord Canterville, or he would take the night-express to Paris. It was better meanwhile that he should not see Lady Barberina. It was vivid to him, as he paused occasionally, looking vaguely at that card in the chimney-glass, that he had come pretty far; and he had come so far because he was under the charm, —yes, he was in love with Lady Barb. There was no doubt whatever of that; he had a faculty for diagnosis, and he knew perfectly well what was the matter with him. He wasted no time in musing upon the mystery of this passion, in wondering whether he might not have escaped it by a little vigilance at first, or whether it would die out if he should go away. He accepted it frankly, for the sake of the pleasure it gave him,—the girl was the delight of his eyes,—and confined himself to considering whether such a marriage would square with his general situation. This would not at all necessarily follow from the fact that he was in love; too many other things would come in between. The most important of these was the change, not only of the geographical, but of the social, standpoint for his wife, and a certain readjustment that it would involve in his own relation to things. He was not inclined to readjustments, and there was no reason why he should be; his own position was in most respects so advantageous. But the girl tempted him almost irresistibly, satisfying his imagination both as a lover and as a student of the human organism; she was so blooming, so complete, of a type so rarely encountered in that degree of perfection. Jackson Lemon was not an Anglo-maniac, but he admired the physical conditions of the English,—their complexion, their temperament, their tissue; and Lady Barberina struck him in flexible, virginal form, as a wonderful compendium of these elements. There was something simple and robust in her beauty; it had the quietness of an old Greek statue, without the vulgarity of the modern simper or of contemporary prettiness. Her head was antique; and though her conversation was quite of the present period, Jackson Lemon had said to himself that there was sure to be in her soul a certain primitive sincerity which would match with the outline of her brow. He saw her as she might be in the future, the beautiful mother of beautiful children, in whom the look of race should be conspicuous. He should like his children to have the look of race, and he was not unaware that he must take his precautions accordingly. A great many people had it in England; and it was a pleasure to him to see it, especially as no one had it so unmistakably as the second daughter of Lord Canterville. It would be a great luxury to call such a woman one's own; nothing could be more evident than that, because it made no difference that she was not strikingly clever. Striking cleverness was not a part of harmonious form and the English complexion; it was associated with the modern simper, which was a result of modern nerves. If Jackson Lemon had wanted a nervous wife, of course he could have found her at home; but this tall, fair girl, whose character, like her figure, appeared mainly to have been formed by riding across country, was differently put together. All the same, would it suit his book, as they said in London, to marry her and transport her to New York? He came back to this question; came back to it with a persistency which, had she been admitted to a view of it, would have tried the patience of Lady Beauchemin. She had been irritated, more than once, at his appearing to attach himself so exclusively to this horn of the dilemma,—as if it could possibly fail to be a good thing for a little American doctor to marry the daughter of an English peer. It would have been more becoming, in her ladyship's eyes, that he should take that for granted a little more, and the consent of her ladyship's—of their ladyships'—family a little less. They looked at the matter so differently! Jackson Lemon was conscious that if he should marry Lady Barberina Clement, it would be because it suited him, and not because it suited his possible sisters-in-law. He believed that he acted in all things by his own will,—an organ for which he had the highest respect.

It would have seemed, however, that on this occasion it was not working very regularly, for though he had come home to go to bed, the stroke of half-past twelve saw him jump, not into his couch, but into a hansom which the whistle of the porter had summoned to the door of his hotel, and in which he rattled off to Portland Place. Here he found—in a very large house—an assembly of three hundred people, and a band of music concealed in a bower of azaleas. Lady Canterville had not arrived; he wandered through the rooms and assured himself of that. He also discovered a very good conservatory, where there were banks and pyramids of azaleas. He watched the top of the staircase, but it was a long time before he saw what he was looking for, and his impatience at last was extreme. The reward, however, when it came, was all that he could have desired. It was a little smile from Lady Barberina, who stood behind her mother while the latter extended her finger-tips to the hostess. The entrance of this charming woman, with her beautiful daughters—always a noticeable incident—was effected with a certain brilliancy, and just now it was agreeable to Jackson Lemon to think that it concerned him more than any one else in the house. Tall, dazzling, indifferent, looking about her as if she saw very little, Lady Barberina was certainly a figure round which a young man's fancy might revolve. She was very quiet and simple, had little manner and little movement; but her detachment was not a vulgar art. She appeared to efface herself, to wait till, in the natural course, she should be attended to; and in this there was evidently no exaggeration, for she was too proud not to have perfect confidence. Her sister, smaller, slighter, with a little surprised smile, which seemed to say that in her extreme innocence she was yet prepared for anything, having heard, indirectly, such extraordinary things about society, was much more impatient and more expressive, and projected across a threshold the pretty radiance of her eyes and teeth before her mother's name was announced. Lady Canterville was thought by many persons to be very superior to her daughters; she had kept even more beauty than she had given them; and it was a beauty which had been called intellectual. She had extraordinary sweetness, without any definite professions; her manner was mild almost to tenderness; there was even a kind of pity in it. Moreover, her features were perfect, and nothing could be more gently gracious than a way she had of speaking, or rather, of listening, to people, with her head inclined a little to one side. Jackson Lemon liked her very much, and she had certainly been most kind to him. He approached Lady Barberina as soon as he could do so without an appearance of precipitation, and said to her that he hoped very much she would not dance. He was a master of the art which flourishes in New York above every other, and he had guided her through a dozen waltzes with a skill which, as she felt, left absolutely nothing to be desired. But dancing was not his business to-night. She smiled a little at the expression of his hope.

"That is what mamma has brought us here for," she said; "she doesn't like it if we don't dance."

"How does she know whether she likes it or not? You have always danced."

"Once I didn't," said Lady Barberina.

He told her that, at any rate, he would settle it with her mother, and persuaded her to wander with him into the conservatory, where there were colored lights suspended among the plants, and a vault of verdure overhead. In comparison with the other rooms the conservatory was dusky and remote. But they were not alone; half a dozen other couples were in possession. The gloom was rosy with the slopes of azalea, and suffused with mitigated music, which made it possible to talk without consideration of one's neighbors. Nevertheless, though it was only in looking back on the scene later that Lady Barberina perceived this, these dispersed couples were talking very softly. She did not look at them; it seemed to her that, virtually, she was alone with Jackson Lemon. She said something about the flowers, about the fragrance of the air; for all answer to which he asked her, as he stood there before her, a question by which she might have been exceedingly startled.

"How do people who marry in England ever know each other before marriage? They have no chance."

"I am sure I don't know," said Lady Barberina; "I never was married."

"It's very different in my country. There a man may see much of a girl; he may come and see her, he may be constantly alone with her. I wish you allowed that over here."

Lady Barberina suddenly examined the less ornamental side of her fan, as if it had never occurred to her before to look at it. "It must be so very odd, America," she murmured at last.

"Well, I guess in that matter we are right; over here it's a leap in the dark."

"I'm sure I don't know," said the girl. She had folded her fan; she stretched out her arm mechanically, and plucked a sprig of azalea.

"I guess it doesn't signify, after all," Jackson Lemon remarked. "They say that love is blind at the best." His keen young face was bent upon hers; his thumbs were in the pockets of his trousers; he smiled a little, showing his fine teeth. She said nothing, but only pulled her azalea to pieces. She was usually so quiet, that this small movement looked restless.

"This is the first time I have seen you in the least without a lot of people," he went on.

"Yes, it's very tiresome," she said.

"I have been sick of it; I didn't want to come here to-night."

She had not met his eyes, though she knew they were seeking her own. But now she looked at him a moment. She had never objected to his appearance, and in this respect she had no repugnance to overcome. She liked a man to be tall and handsome, and Jackson Lemon was neither; but when she was sixteen, and as tall herself as she was to be at twenty, she had been in love (for three weeks) with one of her cousins, a little fellow in the Hussars, who was shorter even than the American, shorter, consequently, than herself. This proved that distinction might be independent of stature—not that she ever reasoned it out. Jackson Lemon's facial spareness, his bright little eye, which seemed always to be measuring things, struck her as original, and she thought them very cutting, which would do very well for a husband of hers. As she made this reflection, of course it never occurred to her that she herself might be cut; she was not a sacrificial lamb. She perceived that his features expressed a mind—a mind that would be rather superior. She would never have taken him for a doctor; though, indeed, when all was said, that was very negative, and didn't account for the way he imposed himself.

"Why, then, did you come?" she asked, in answer to his last speech.

"Because it seems to me after all better to see you in this way than not to see you at all; I want to know you better."

"I don't think I ought to stay here," said Lady Barberina, looking round her.

"Don't go till I have told you I love you," murmured the young man.

She made no exclamation, indulged in no start; he could not see even that she changed color. She took his request with a noble simplicity, with her head erect and her eyes lowered.

"I don't think you have a right to tell me that."

"Why not?" Jackson Lemon demanded. "I wish to claim the right; I wish you to give it to me."

"I can't—I don't know you. You have said it yourself."

"Can't you have a little faith? That will help us to know each other better. It's disgusting, the want of opportunity; even at Pasterns I could scarcely get a walk with you. But I have the greatest faith in you. I feel that I love you, and I couldn't do more than that at the end of six months. I love your beauty—I love you from head to foot. Don't move, please don't move." He lowered his tone; but it went straight to her ear, and it must be believed that it had a certain eloquence. For himself, after he had heard himself say these words, all his being was in a glow. It was a luxury to speak to her of her beauty; it brought him nearer to her than he had ever been. But the color had come into her face, and it seemed to remind him that her beauty was not all. "Everything about you is sweet and noble," he went on; "everything is dear to me. I am sure you are good. I don't know what you think of me; I asked Lady Beauchemin to tell me, and she told me to judge for myself. Well, then, I judge you like me. Haven't I a right to assume that till the contrary is proved? May I speak to your father? That's what I want to know. I have been waiting; but now what should I wait for longer? I want to be able to tell him that you have given me some hope. I suppose I ought to speak to him first. I meant to, to-morrow, but meanwhile, to-night, I thought I would just put this in. In my country it wouldn't matter particularly. You must see all that over there for yourself. If you should tell me not to speak to your father, I wouldn't; I would wait. But I like better to ask your leave to speak to him than to ask his to speak to you."

His voice had sunk almost to a whisper; but, though it trembled, his emotion gave it peculiar intensity. He had the same attitude, his thumbs in his trousers, his attentive head, his smile, which was a matter of course; no one would have imagined what he was saying. She had listened without moving, and at the end she raised her eyes. They rested on his a moment, and he remembered, a good while later, the look which passed her lids.

"You may say anything that you please to my father, but I don't wish to hear any more. You have said too much, considering how little idea you have given me before."

"I was watching you," said Jackson Lemon.

Lady Barberina held her head higher, looking straight at him. Then, quite seriously, "I don't like to be watched," she remarked.

"You shouldn't be so beautiful, then. Won't you give me a word of hope?" he added.

"I have never supposed I should marry a foreigner," said Lady Barberina.

"Do you call me a foreigner?"

"I think your ideas are very different, and your country is different; you have told me so yourself."

"I should like to show it to you; I would make you like it."

"I am not sure what you would make me do," said Lady Barberina, very honestly.

"Nothing that you don't want."

"I am sure you would try," she declared, with a smile.

"Well," said Jackson Lemon, "after all, I am trying now."

To this she simply replied she must go to her mother, and he was obliged to lead her out of the conservatory. Lady Canterville was not immediately found, so that he had time to murmur as they went, "Now that I have spoken, I am very happy."

"Perhaps you are happy too soon," said the girl.

"Ah, don't say that, Lady Barb."

"Of course I must think of it."

"Of course you must!" said Jackson Lemon; "I will speak to your father to-morrow."

"I can't fancy what he will say."

"How can he dislike me?" the young man asked, in a tone which Lady Beauchemin, if she had heard him, would have been forced to attribute to his general affectation of the jocose. What Lady Beauchemin's sister thought of it is not recorded; but there is perhaps a clue to her opinion in the answer she made him after a moment's silence: "Really, you know, you *are* a foreigner!" With this she turned her back upon him, for she was already in her mother's hands. Jackson Lemon said a few words to Lady Canterville; they were chiefly about its being very hot. She gave him her vague, sweet attention, as if he were saying something ingenious, of which she missed the point. He could see that she was thinking of the doings of her daughter Agatha, whose attitude toward the contemporary young man was wanting in the perception of differences,— a madness without method; she was evidently not occupied with Lady

Barberina, who was more to be trusted. This young woman never met her suitor's eyes again; she let her own rest, rather ostentatiously, upon other objects. At last he was going away without a glance from her. Lady Canterville had asked him to come to lunch on the morrow, and he had said he would do so if she would promise him he should see his lordship. "I can't pay you another visit until I have had some talk with him," he said.

"I don't see why not; but if I speak to him, I dare say he will be at home," she answered.

"It will be worth his while!"

Jackson Lemon left the house reflecting that as he had never proposed to a girl before, he could not be expected to know how women demean themselves in this emergency. He had heard, indeed, that Lady Barb had had no end of offers; and though he thought it probable that the number was exaggerated, as it always is, it was to be supposed that her way of appearing suddenly to have dropped him was but the usual behavior for the occasion.

III

At her mother's the next day she was absent from luncheon, and Lady Canterville mentioned to him (he didn't ask) that she had gone to see a dear old great-aunt, who was also her godmother, and who lived at Roehampton. Lord Canterville was not present, but our young man was informed by his hostess that he had promised her he would come in exactly at three o'clock. Jackson Lemon lunched with Lady Canterville and the children, who appeared in force at this repast, all the younger girls being present, and two little boys, the juniors of the two sons who were in their teens. Jackson, who was very fond of children, and thought these absolutely the finest in the world,—magnificent specimens of a magnificent brood, such as it would be so satisfactory in future days to see about his own knee,—Jackson felt that he was being treated as one of the family, but was not frightened by what he supposed the privilege to imply. Lady Canterville betrayed no consciousness whatever of his having mooted the question of becoming her son-in-law, and he believed that her eldest daughter had not told her of their talk the night before. This idea gave him pleasure; he liked to think that Lady Barb was judging him for herself. Perhaps, indeed, she was taking counsel of the old lady at Roehampton: he believed that he was the sort of lover of whom a godmother would approve. Godmothers in his mind were mainly associated with fairy-tales (he had had no baptismal sponsors of his own); and that point of view would be favorable to a young man with a great deal of gold who had suddenly arrived from a foreign country,—an apparition, surely, sufficiently elfish. He made up his mind that he should like Lady Canterville as a mother-in-law; she would be too well-bred to meddle. Her husband came in at three o'clock, just after they had left the table, and said to Jackson Lemon that it was very good in him to have waited.

"I haven't waited," Jackson replied, with his watch in his hand; "you are punctual to the minute."

I know not how Lord Canterville may have judged his young friend, but Jackson Lemon had been told more than once in his life that he was a very good fellow, but rather too literal. After he had lighted a cigarette in his lordship's "den," a large brown apartment on the ground-floor, which partook at once of the nature of an office and of that of a harness-room (it could not have been called in any degree a library), he went straight to the point in these terms: "Well now, Lord Canterville, I feel as if I ought to let you know without more delay that I am in love with Lady Barb, and that I should like to marry her." So he spoke, puffing his cigarette, with his conscious but unextenuating eye fixed on his host.

No man, as I have intimated, bore better being looked at than this noble personage; he seemed to bloom in the envious warmth of human contemplation, and never appeared so faultless as when he was most exposed. "My dear fellow, my dear fellow," he murmured, almost in disparagement, stroking his ambrosial beard from before the empty fireplace. He lifted his eyebrows, but he looked perfectly good-natured.

"Are you surprised, sir?" Jackson Lemon asked.

"Why, I suppose any one is surprised at a man wanting one of his children. He sometimes feels the weight of that sort of thing so much, you know. He wonders what the devil another man wants of them." And Lord Canterville laughed pleasantly out of the copious fringe of his lips.

"I only want one of them," said Jackson Lemon, laughing too, but with a lighter organ.

"Polygamy would be rather good for the parents. However, Lucy told me the other night that she thought you were looking the way you speak of."

"Yes, I told Lady Beauchemin that I love Lady Barb, and she seemed to think it was natural."

"Oh, yes, I suppose there's no want of nature in it! But, my dear fellow, I really don't know what to say."

"Of course you'll have to think of it." Jackson Lemon, in saying this, felt that he was making the most liberal concession to the point of view of his interlocutor; being perfectly aware that in his own country it was not left much to the parents to think of.

"I shall have to talk it over with my wife."

"Lady Canterville has been very kind to me; I hope she will continue."

"My dear fellow, we are excellent friends. No one could appreciate you more than Lady Canterville. Of course we can only consider such a question on the—a—the highest grounds. You would never want to marry without knowing, as it were, exactly what you are doing. I, on my side, naturally, you know, am bound to do the best I can for my own child. At the same time, of course, we don't want to spend our time in—a—walking round the horse. We want to keep to the main lines." It was settled between them after a little that the main lines were that Jackson Lemon knew to a certainty the state of his affections, and was in a position to pretend to the hand of a young lady who Lord Canterville might say—of course, you know, without swaggering about it—had a right to expect to do well, as the women call it.

"I should think she had," Jackson Lemon said; "she's a beautiful type."

Lord Canterville stared a moment. "She is a clever, well-grown girl, and she takes her fences like a grasshopper. Does she know all this, by the way?" he added.

"Oh yes, I told her last night."

Again Lord Canterville had the air, unusual with him, of returning his companion's regard. "I am not sure that you ought to have done that, you know."

"I couldn't have spoken to you first—I couldn't," said Jackson Lemon. "I meant to; but it stuck in my crop."

"They don't in your country, I guess," his lordship returned, smiling.

"Well, not as a general thing; however, I find it very pleasant to discuss with you now." And in truth it was very pleasant. Nothing could be easier, friendlier, more informal, than Lord Canterville's manner, which implied all sorts of equality, especially that of age and fortune, and made Jackson Lemon feel at the end of three minutes almost as if he too were a beautifully preserved and somewhat straitened nobleman of sixty, with the views of a man of the world about his own marriage. The young American perceived that Lord Canterville waived the point of his having spoken first to the girl herself, and saw in this indulgence a just concession to the ardor of young affection. For Lord Canterville seemed perfectly to appreciate the sentimental side,—at least so far as it was embodied in his visitor,—when he said without deprecation: "Did she give you any encouragement?"

"Well, she didn't box my ears. She told me that she would think of it, but that I must speak to you. But naturally I shouldn't have said what I did to her if I hadn't made up my mind during the last fortnight that I am not disagreeable to her."

"Ah, my dear young man, women are odd cattle!" Lord Canterville exclaimed, rather unexpectedly. "But of course you know all that," he added in an instant; "you take the general risk."

"I am perfectly willing to take the general risk; the particular risk is small."

"Well, upon my honor I don't really know my girls. You see a man's time, in England, is tremendously taken up; but I dare say it's the same in your country. Their mother knows them—I think I had better send for their mother. If you don't mind I'll just suggest that she join us here."

"I'm rather afraid of you both together, but if it will settle it any quicker—" said Jackson Lemon. Lord Canterville rang the bell, and, when a servant appeared, despatched him with a message to her ladyship. While they were waiting, the young man remembered that it was in his power to give a more definite account of his pecuniary basis. He had simply said before that he was abundantly able to marry; he shrank from putting himself forward as a billionnaire. He had a fine taste, and he wished to appeal to Lord Canterville primarily as a gentleman. But now that he had to make a double impression, he bethought himself of his millions, for millions were always impressive. "I think it only fair to let you know that my fortune is really very considerable," he remarked.

"Yes, I dare say you are beastly rich," said Lord Canterville.

"I have about seven millions."

"Seven millions?"

"I count in dollars; upwards of a million and a half sterling."

Lord Canterville looked at him from head to foot, with an air of cheerful resignation to a form of grossness which threatened to become common. Then he said, with a touch of that inconsequence of which he had already given a glimpse: "What the deuce, then, possessed you to turn doctor?"

Jackson Lemon colored a little, hesitated, and then said quickly: "Because I had the talent for it."

"Of course, I don't for a moment doubt of your ability; but don't you find it rather a bore?"

"I don't practise much. I am rather ashamed to say that."

"Ah, well, of course, in your country it's different. I dare say you've got a door-plate, eh?"

"Oh yes, and a tin sign tied to the balcony!" said Jackson Lemon, smiling.

"What did your father say to it?"

"To my going into medicine? He said he would be hanged if he'd take any of my doses. He didn't think I should succeed; he wanted me to go into the house."

"Into the House—a—" said Lord Canterville, hesitating a little. "Into your Congress—yes, exactly."

"Ah, no, not so bad as that. Into the store," Jackson Lemon replied, in the candid tone in which he expressed himself when, for reasons of his own, he wished to be perfectly national.

Lord Canterville stared, not venturing, even for the moment, to hazard an interpretation; and before a solution had presented itself, Lady Canterville came into the room.

"My dear, I thought we had better see you. Do you know he wants to marry our second girl?" It was in these simple terms that her husband acquainted her with the question.

Lady Canterville expressed neither surprise nor elation; she simply stood there, smiling, with her head a little inclined to the side, with all her customary graciousness. Her charming eyes rested on those of Jackson Lemon; and though they seemed to show that she had to think a little of so serious a proposition, his own discovered in them none of the coldness of calculation. "Are you talking about Barberina?" she asked in a moment, as if her thoughts had been far away.

Of course they were talking about Barberina, and Jackson Lemon repeated to her ladyship what he had said to the girl's father. He had thought it all over, and his mind was quite made up. Moreover, he had spoken to Lady Barb.

"Did she tell you that, my dear?" asked Lord Canterville, while he lighted another cigar.

She gave no heed to this inquiry, which had been vague and accidental on his lordship's part, but simply said to Jackson Lemon that the thing was very serious, and that they had better sit down for a moment. In an instant he was near her on the sofa on which she had placed herself, still smiling and looking up at her husband with an air of general meditation, in which a sweet compassion for every one concerned was apparent.

"Barberina has told me nothing," she said after a little.

"That proves she cares for me!" Jackson Lemon exclaimed, eagerly.

Lady Canterville looked as if she thought this almost too ingenious, almost professional; but her husband said cheerfully, jovially: "Ah well, if she cares for you, I don't object."

This was a little ambiguous; but before Jackson Lemon had time to look into it, Lady Canterville asked, gently: "Should you expect her to live in America?"

"Oh, yes; that's my home, you know."

"Shouldn't you be living sometimes in England?"

"Oh, yes, we'll come over and see you." The young man was in love, he wanted to marry, he wanted to be genial, and to commend himself to the parents of Lady Barb; at the same time it was in his nature not to accept conditions, save in so far as they exactly suited him, to tie himself, or, as they said in New York, to give himself away. In any transaction he preferred his own terms to those of any one else. Therefore, the moment Lady Canterville gave signs of wishing to extract a promise, he was on his guard.

"She'll find it very different; perhaps she won't like it," her ladyship suggested.

"If she likes me, she'll like my country," said Jackson Lemon, with decision.

"He tells me he has got a plate on his door," Lord Canterville remarked, humorously.

"We must talk to her, of course; we must understand how she feels," said his wife, looking more serious than she had done as yet.

"Please don't discourage her, Lady Canterville," the young man begged; "and give me a chance to talk to her a little more myself. You haven't given me much chance, you know."

"We don't offer our daughters to people, Mr. Lemon." Lady Canterville was always gentle, but now she was a little majestic.

"She isn't like some women in London, you know," said Jackson Lemon's host, who seemed to remember that to a discussion of such importance he ought from time to time to contribute a word of wisdom. And Jackson Lemon, certainly, if the idea had been presented to him, would have said that, No, decidedly, Lady Barberina had not been thrown at him.

"Of course not," he declared, in answer to her mother's remark. "But, you know, you mustn't refuse them too much, either; you mustn't make a poor fellow wait too long. I admire her, I love her, more than I can say; I give you my word of honor for that."

"He seems to think that settles it," said Lord Canterville, smiling down at the young American, very pleasantly, from his place before the cold chimney-piece.

"Of course that's what we desire, Phillip," her ladyship returned, very nobly.

"Lady Barb believes it; I am sure she does!" Jackson Lemon exclaimed. "Why should I pretend to be in love with her if I am not?"

Lady Canterville received this inquiry in silence, and her husband, with just the least air in the world of repressed impatience, began to walk up and down the room. He was a man of many engagements, and he had been closeted for more than a quarter of an hour with the young American doctor. "Do you imagine you should come often to England?" Lady Canterville demanded, with a certain abruptness, returning to that important point.

"I'm afraid I can't tell you that; of course we shall do whatever seems best." He was prepared to suppose they should cross the Atlantic every summer: that prospect was by no means displeasing to him; but he was not prepared to give any such pledge to Lady Canterville, especially as he did not believe it would really be necessary. It was in his mind, not as an overt pretension, but as a tacit implication that he should treat with Barberina's parents on a footing of perfect equality; and there would somehow be nothing equal if he should begin to enter into engagements which didn't belong to the essence of the matter. They were to give their daughter, and he was to take her: in this arrangement there would be as much on one side as on the other. But beyond this he had nothing to ask of them; there was nothing he wished them to promise, and his own pledges, therefore, would have no equivalent. Whenever his wife should wish it, she should come over and see her people. Her home was to be in New York; but he was tacitly conscious that on the question of absences he should be very liberal. Nevertheless, there was something in the very grain of his character which forbade that he should commit himself at present in respect to times and dates.

Lady Canterville looked at her husband, but her husband was not attentive; he was taking a peep at his watch. In a moment, however, he threw out a remark to the effect that he thought it a capital thing that the two countries should become more united, and there was nothing that would bring it about better than a few of the best people on both sides pairing off together. The English, indeed, had begun it; a lot of fellows had brought over a lot of pretty girls, and it was quite fair play that the Americans should take their pick. They were all one race, after all; and why shouldn't they make one society,—the best on both sides, of course? Jackson Lemon smiled as he recognized Lady Marmaduke's philosophy, and he was pleased to think that Lady Beauchemin had some influence with her father; for he was sure the old gentleman (as he mentally designated his host) had got all this from her, though he expressed himself less happily than the cleverest of his daughters. Our hero had no objection to make to it, especially if there was anything in it that would really help his case. But it was not in the least on these high grounds that he had sought the hand of Lady Barb. He wanted her not in order that her people and his (the best on both sides!) should make one society; he wanted her simply because he wanted her. Lady Canterville smiled; but she seemed to have another thought.

"I quite appreciate what my husband says; but I don't see why poor Barb should be the one to begin."

"I dare say she'll like it," said Lord Canterville, as if he were attempting a short cut. "They say you spoil your women awfully."

"She's not one of their women yet," her ladyship remarked, in the sweetest tone in the world; and then she added, without Jackson Lemon's knowing exactly what she meant, "It seems so strange."

He was a little irritated; and perhaps these simple words added to the feeling. There had been no positive opposition to his suit, and Lord and Lady Canterville were most kind; but he felt that they held back a little; and though he had not expected them to throw themselves on his neck, he was rather disappointed; his pride was touched. Why should they hesitate? He considered himself such a good *parti*. It was not so much the old gentleman, it was Lady Canterville. As he saw the old gentleman look, covertly, a second time at his watch, he could have believed he would have been glad to settle the matter on the spot. Lady Canterville seemed to wish her daughter's lover to come forward more, to give certain assurances and guaranties. He felt that he was ready to say or do anything that was a matter of proper form; but he couldn't take the tone of trying to purchase her ladyship's consent, penetrated as he was with the conviction that such a man as he could be trusted to care for his wife rather more than an impecunious British peer and *his* wife could be supposed (with the lights he had acquired in English society) to care even for the handsomest of a dozen children. It was a mistake on Lady Canterville's part not to recognize that. He humored her mistake to the extent of saying, just a little dryly, "My wife shall certainly have everything she wants."

"He tells me he is disgustingly rich," Lord Canterville added, pausing before their companion with his hands in his pockets.

"I am glad to hear it; but it isn't so much that," she answered, sinking back a little on her sofa. If it was not that, she did not say what it was, though she had looked for a moment as if she were going to. She only raised her eyes to her husband's face, as if to ask for inspiration. I know not whether she found it, but in a moment she said to Jackson Lemon, seeming to imply that it was quite another point: "Do you expect to continue your profession?"

He had no such intention, so far as his profession meant getting up at three o'clock in the morning to assuage the ills of humanity; but here, as before, the touch of such a question instantly stiffened him. "Oh, my profession! I am rather ashamed of that matter. I have neglected my work so much, I don't know what I shall be able to do, once I am really settled at home."

Lady Canterville received these remarks in silence; fixing her eyes again upon her husband's face. But this nobleman was really not helpful; still with his hands in his pockets, save when he needed to remove his cigar from his lips, he went and looked out of the window. "Of course we know you don't practice, and when you're a married man you will have less time even than now. But I should really like to know if they call you Doctor over there."

"Oh, yes, universally. We are nearly as fond of titles as your people."

"I don't call that a title."

"It's not so good as duke or marquis, I admit; but we have to take what we have got."

"Oh, bother, what does it signify?" Lord Canterville demanded, from his place at the window. "I used to have a horse named Doctor, and a devilish good one too."

"You may call me bishop, if you like," said Jackson Lemon, laughing.

Lady Canterville looked grave, as if she did not enjoy this pleasantry. "I don't care for any titles," she observed; "I don't see why a gentleman shouldn't be called Mr."

It suddenly appeared to Jackson Lemon that there was something helpless, confused, and even slightly comical, in the position of this noble and amiable lady. The impression made him feel kindly; he too, like Lord Canterville, had begun to long for a short cut. He relaxed a moment, and leaning toward his hostess, with a smile and his hands on his little knees, he said, softly, "It seems to me a question of no importance; all I desire is that you should call me your son-in-law."

Lady Canterville gave him her hand, and he pressed it almost affectionately. Then she got up, remarking that before anything was decided she must see her daughter, she must learn from her own lips the state of her feelings. "I don't like at all her not having spoken to me already," she added.

"Where has she gone—to Roehampton? I dare say she has told it all to her godmother," said Lord Canterville.

"She won't have much to tell, poor girl!" Jackson Lemon exclaimed. "I must really insist upon seeing with more freedom the person I wish to marry."

"You shall have all the freedom you want, in two or three days," said Lady Canterville. She smiled with all her sweetness; she appeared to have accepted him, and yet still to be making tacit assumptions. "Are there not certain things to be talked of first?"

"Certain things, dear lady?"

Lady Canterville looked at her husband, and though he was still at his window, this time he felt it in her silence, and had to come away and speak. "Oh, she means settlements, and that kind of thing." This was an allusion which came with a much better grace from him.

Jackson Lemon looked from one of his companions to the other; he colored a little, and gave a smile that was perhaps a trifle fixed. "Settlements? We don't make them in the United States. You may be sure I shall make a proper provision for my wife."

"My dear fellow, over here—in our class, you know, it's the custom," said Lord Canterville, with a richer brightness in his face at the thought that the discussion was over.

"I have my own ideas," Jackson answered, smiling.

"It seems to me it's a question for the solicitors to discuss," Lady Canterville suggested.

"They may discuss it as much as they please," said Jackson Lemon, with a laugh. He thought he saw his solicitors discussing it! He had indeed his own ideas. He opened the door for Lady Canterville, and the three passed out of the room together, walking into the hall in a silence in which there was just a tinge of awkwardness. A note had been struck which grated and scratched a little. A pair of brilliant footmen, at their approach, rose from a bench to a great altitude, and stood there like sentinels presenting arms. Jackson Lemon stopped, looking for a moment into the interior of his hat, which he had in his hand. Then, raising his keen eyes, he fixed them a moment on those of Lady Canterville, addressing her, instinctively, rather than her husband. "I guess you and Lord Canterville had better leave it to me!"

"We have our traditions, Mr. Lemon," said her ladyship, with nobleness. "I imagine you don't know—" she murmured.

Lord Canterville laid his hand on the young man's shoulder. "My dear boy, those fellows will settle it in three minutes."

"Very likely they will!" said Jackson Lemon. Then he asked of Lady Canterville when he might see Lady Barb.

She hesitated a moment, in her gracious way. "I will write you a note."

One of the tall footmen, at the end of the impressive vista, had opened wide the portals, as if even he were aware of the dignity to which the little visitor had virtually been raised. But Jackson lingered a moment; he was visibly unsatisfied, though apparently so little unconscious that he was unsatisfying. "I don't think you understand me."

"Your ideas are certainly different," said Lady Canterville.

"If the girl understands you, that's enough!" Lord Canterville exclaimed in a jovial, detached, irrelevant way.

"May not *she* write to me?" Jackson asked of her mother. "I certainly must write to her, you know, if you won't let me see her."

"Oh, yes, you may write to her, Mr. Lemon."

There was a point for a moment in the look that he gave Lady Canterville, while he said to himself that if it were necessary he would transmit his notes through the old lady at Roehampton. "All right, good by; you know what I want, at any rate." Then, as he was going, he turned and added: "You needn't be afraid that I won't bring her over in the hot weather!"

"In the hot weather?" Lady Canterville murmured, with vague visions of the torrid zone, while the young American quitted the house with the sense that he had made great concessions.

His host and hostess passed into a small morning-room, and (Lord Canterville having taken up his hat and stick to go out again) stood there a moment, face to face.

"It's clear enough he wants her," said his lordship, in a summary manner.

"There's something so odd about him," Lady Canterville answered. "Fancy his speaking so about settlements."

"You had better give him his head; he'll go much quieter."

"He's so obstinate—very obstinate; it's easy to see that. And he seems to think a girl in your daughter's position can be married from one day to the other—with a ring and a new frock—like a housemaid."

"Well, of course, over there, that's the kind of thing. But he seems really to have a most extraordinary fortune; and every one does say their women have *carte blanche*."

"*Carte blanche* is not what Barb wishes; she wishes a settlement. She wants a definite income; she wants to be safe."

Lord Canterville stared a moment. "Has she told you so? I thought you said—." And then he stopped. "I beg your pardon," he added.

Lady Canterville gave no explanation of her inconsistency. She went on to remark that American fortunes were notoriously insecure; one heard of nothing else; they melted away like smoke. It was their duty to their child to demand that something should be fixed.

"He has a million and a half sterling," said Lord Canterville. "I can't make out what he does with it."

"She ought to have something very handsome," his wife remarked.

"Well, my dear, you must settle it: you must consider it; you must send for Hilary. Only take care you don't put him off; it may be a very good opening you know. There is a great deal to be done out there; I believe in all that," Lord Canterville went on, in the tone of a conscientious parent.

"There is no doubt that he *is* a doctor—in those places," said Lady Canterville, musingly.

"He may be a pedlar for all I care."

"If they should go out, I think Agatha might go with them," her ladyship continued, in the same tone, a little disconnectedly.

"You may send them all out if you like. Good by!" And Lord Canterville kissed his wife.

But she detained him a moment, with her hand on his arm. "Don't you think he is very much in love?"

"Oh, yes, he's very bad; but he's a clever little beggar."

"She likes him very much," Lady Canterville announced, rather formally, as they separated.

PART II

IV

JACKSON LEMON had said to Sidney Feeder in the Park that he would call on Mr. and Mrs. Freer; but three weeks elapsed before he knocked at their door in Jermyn Street. In the meantime he had met them at dinner, and Mrs. Freer had told him that she hoped very much he would find time to come and see her. She had not reproached him, nor shaken her finger at him; and her clemency, which was calculated, and very characteristic of her, touched him so much (for he was in fault; she was one of his mother's oldest and best friends), that he very soon presented himself. It was on a fine Sunday afternoon, rather late, and the region of Jermyn Street looked forsaken and inanimate; the native dulness of the landscape appeared in all its purity. Mrs. Freer, however, was at home, resting on a lodging-house sofa—an angular couch, draped in faded chintz—before she went to dress for dinner. She made the young man very welcome; she told him she had been thinking of him a great deal; she had wished to have a chance to talk with him. He immediately perceived what she had in mind, and then he remembered that Sidney Feeder had told him what it was that Mr. and Mrs. Freer took upon themselves to say. This had provoked him at the time, but he had forgotten it afterward; partly because he became aware, that same evening, that he did wish to marry the "young marchioness," and partly because since then he had had much greater annoyances. Yes, the poor young man, so conscious of liberal intentions, of a large way of looking at the future, had had much to irritate and disgust him. He had seen the mistress of his affections but three or four times, and he had received letters from Mr. Hilary, Lord Canterville's solicitor, asking him, in terms the most obsequious, it is true, to designate some gentleman of the law with whom the preliminaries of his marriage to Lady Barberina Clement might be arranged. He had given Mr. Hilary the name of such a functionary, but he had written by the same post to his own solicitor (for whose services in other matters he had had much occasion, Jackson Lemon being distinctly contentious), instructing him that he was at liberty to meet Mr. Hilary, but not at liberty to entertain any proposals as to this odious English idea of a settlement. If marrying Jackson Lemon were not settlement enough, then Lord and Lady Canterville had better alter their point of view. It was quite out of the question that he should alter his. It would perhaps be difficult to explain the strong aversion that he entertained to the introduction into his prospective union of this harsh diplomatic element; it was as if they mistrusted him, suspected him; as if his hands were to be tied, so that he could not handle his own fortune as he thought best. It was not the idea of parting with his money that displeased him, for he flattered himself that he had plans of expenditure for his wife beyond even the imagination of her distinguished parents. It struck him even that they were fools not to have perceived that they should make a much better thing of it by leaving him perfectly free. This intervention of the solicitor was a nasty little English tradition—totally at variance with the large spirit of American habits—to which he would not submit. It was not his way to submit when he disapproved: why should he change his way on this occasion, when the matter lay so near him? These reflections, and a hundred more, had flowed freely through his mind for several days before he called in Jermyn Street, and they had engendered a lively indignation and a really bitter sense of wrong. As may be imagined, they had infused a certain awkwardness into his relations with the house of Canterville, and it may be said of these relations that they were for the moment virtually suspended. His first interview with Lady Barb, after his conference with the old couple, as he called her august elders, had been as tender as he could have desired. Lady Canterville, at the end of three days, had sent him an invitation—five words on a card—asking him to dine with them to-morrow, quite *en famille*. This had been the only formal intimation that his engagement to Lady Barb was recognized; for even at the family banquet, which included half a dozen outsiders, there had been no allusion on the part either of his host or his hostess to the subject of their conversation in Lord Canterville's den. The only allusion was a wandering ray, once or twice, in Lady Barberina's eyes. When, however, after dinner, she strolled away with him into the music-room, which was lighted and empty, to play for him something out of *Carmen,* of which he had spoken at table, and when the young couple were allowed to enjoy for upwards of an hour, unmolested, the comparative privacy of this rich apartment, he felt that Lady Canterville definitely counted upon him. She didn't believe in any serious difficulties. Neither did he, then; and that was why it was a nuisance there should be a vain appearance of them. The arrangements, he supposed Lady Canterville would have said, were pending, and indeed they were; for he had already given orders in Bond Street for the setting of an extraordinary number of diamonds. Lady Barb, at any rate, during that hour he spent with her, had had nothing to say about arrangements; and it had been an hour of pure satisfaction. She had seated herself at the piano and had played perpetually, in a soft, incoherent manner, while he leaned over the instrument, very close to her, and said everything that came into his head. She was very bright and serene, and she looked at him as if she liked him very much.

This was all he expected of her, for it did not belong to the cast of her beauty to betray a vulgar infatuation. That beauty was more delightful to him than ever; and there was a softness about her which seemed to say to him that from this moment she was quite his own. He felt more than ever the value of such a possession; it came over him more than ever that it had taken a great social outlay to produce such a mixture. Simple and girlish as she was, and not particularly quick in the give and take of conversation, she seemed to him to have a part of the history of England in her blood; she was a *résumé* of generations of privileged people, and of centuries of rich country-life. Between these two, of course, there was no allusion to the question which had been put into the hands of Mr. Hilary, and the last thing that occurred to Jackson Lemon was that Lady Barb had views as to his settling a fortune upon her before their marriage. It may appear singular, but he had not asked himself whether his money operated upon her in any degree as a bribe; and this was because, instinctively, he felt that such a speculation was idle,—the point was not to be ascertained,—and because he was willing to assume that it was agreeable to her that she should continue to live in luxury. It was eminently agreeable to him that he might enable her to do so. He was acquainted with the mingled character of human motives, and he was glad that he was rich enough to pretend to the hand of a young woman who, for the best of reasons, would be very expensive. After that happy hour in the music-room he had ridden with her twice; but he had not found her otherwise accessible. She had let him know, the second time they rode, that Lady Canterville had directed her to make, for the moment, no further appointment with him; and on his presenting himself, more than once at the house, he had been told that neither the mother nor the daughter was at home; it had been added that Lady Barberina was staying at Roehampton. On giving him that information in the Park, Lady Barb had looked at him with a mute reproach,—there was always a certain superior dumbness in her eyes,—as if he were exposing her to an annoyance that she ought to be spared; as if he were taking an eccentric line on a question that all well-bred people treated in the conventional way. His induction from this was not that she wished to be secure about his money, but that, like a dutiful English daughter, she received her opinions (on points that were indifferent to her) ready-made from a mamma whose fallibility had never been exposed. He knew by this that his solicitor had answered Mr. Hilary's letter, and that Lady Canterville's coolness was the fruit of this correspondence. The effect of it was not in the least to make him come round, as he phrased it; he had not the smallest intention of doing that. Lady Canterville had spoken of the traditions of her family; but he had no need to go to his family for his own. They resided within himself; anything that he had definitely made up his mind to, acquired in an hour the force of a tradition. Meanwhile, he was in the detestable position of not knowing whether or no he were engaged. He wrote to Lady Barb to inquire,—it being so strange that she should not receive him; and she answered, in a very pretty little letter, which had to his mind a sort of bygone quality, an old-fashioned freshness, as if it might have been written in the last century by Clarissa or Amelia: she answered that she did not in the least understand the situation; that, of course, she would never give him up; that her mother had said that there were the best reasons for their not going too fast; that, thank God, she was yet young, and could wait as long as he would; but that she begged he wouldn't write her anything about money-matters, as she could never comprehend them. Jackson felt that he was in no danger whatever of making this last mistake; he only noted how Lady Barb thought it natural that there should be a discussion; and this made it vivid to him afresh that he had got hold of a daughter of the Crusaders. His ingenious mind could appreciate this hereditary assumption perfectly, at the same time that, to light his own footsteps, it remained entirely modern. He believed—or he thought he believed—that in the end he should marry Barberina Clement on his own terms; but in the interval there was a sensible indignity in being challenged and checked. One effect of it, indeed, was to make him desire the girl more keenly. When she was not before his eyes in the flesh, she hovered before him as an image; and this image had reasons of its own for being a radiant picture. There were moments, however, when he wearied of looking at it; it was so impalpable and thankless, and then Jackson Lemon, for the first time in his life, was melancholy. He felt alone in London, and very much out of it, in spite of all the acquaintances he had made, and the bills he had paid; he felt the need of a greater intimacy than any he had formed (save, of course, in the case of Lady Barb). He wanted to vent his disgust, to relieve himself, from the American point of view. He felt that in engaging in a contest with the great house of Canterville, he was, after all, rather single. That singleness was, of course, in a great measure an inspiration; but it pinched him a little at moments. Then he wished his mother had been in London, for he used to talk of his affairs a great deal with this delightful parent, who had a soothing way of advising him in the sense he liked best. He had even gone so far as to wish he had never laid eyes on Lady Barb, and had fallen in love with some transatlantic maiden of a similar composition. He presently came back, of course, to the knowledge that in the United States there was—and there could be

—nothing similar to Lady Barb; for was it not precisely as a product of the English climate and the British constitution that he valued her? He had relieved himself, from his American point of view, by speaking his mind to Lady Beauchemin, who confessed that she was very much vexed with her parents. She agreed with him that they had made a great mistake; they ought to have left him free; and she expressed her confidence that that freedom would be for her family, as it were, like the silence of the sage, golden. He must excuse them; he must remember that what was asked of him had been their custom for centuries. She did not mention her authority as to the origin of customs, but she assured him that she would say three words to her father and mother, which would make it all right. Jackson answered that customs were all very well, but that intelligent people recognized, when they saw it, the right occasion for departing from them; and with this he awaited the result of Lady Beauchemin's remonstrance. It had not as yet been perceptible, and it must be said that this charming woman was herself much bothered. When, on her venturing to say to her mother that she thought a wrong line had been taken with regard to her sister's *prétendant,* Lady Canterville had replied that Mr. Lemon's unwillingness to settle anything was in itself a proof of what they had feared, the unstable nature of his fortune (for it was useless to talk—this gracious lady could be very decided—there could be no serious reason but that one)—on meeting this argument, as I say, Jackson's protectress felt considerably baffled. It was perhaps true, as her mother said, that if they didn't insist upon proper guaranties, Barberina might be left in a few years with nothing but the stars and stripes (this odd phrase was a quotation from Mr. Lemon) to cover her. Lady Beauchemin tried to reason it out with Lady Marmaduke; but these were complications unforseen by Lady Marmaduke in her project of an Anglo-American society. She was obliged to confess that Mr. Lemon's fortune could not have the solidity of long-established things; it was a very new fortune indeed. His father had made the greater part of it all in a lump, a few years before his death, in the extraordinary way in which people made money in America; that, of course, was why the son had those singular professional attributes. He had begun to study to be a doctor very young, before his expectations were so great. Then he had found he was very clever, and very fond of it; and he had kept on, because, after all, in America, where there were no country gentlemen, a young man had to have something to do, don't you know? And Lady Marmaduke, like an enlightened woman, intimated that in such a case she thought it in much better taste not to try to sink anything. "Because, in America, don't you see," she reasoned, "you can't sink it—nothing *will* sink. Everything is floating about—in the newspapers." And she tried to console her friend by remarking that if Mr. Lemon's fortune was precarious, it was at all events so big. That was just the trouble for Lady Beauchemin; it was so big, and yet they were going to lose it. He was as obstinate as a mule; she was sure he would never come round. Lady Marmaduke declared that he would come round; she even offered to bet a dozen pair of *gants de Suède* on it; and she added that this consummation lay quite in the hands of Barberina. Lady Beauchemin promised herself to converse with her sister; for it was not for nothing that she herself had felt the international contagion.

Jackson Lemon, to dissipate his chagrin, had returned to the sessions of the medical congress, where, inevitably, he had fallen into the hands of Sidney Feeder, who enjoyed in this disinterested assembly a high popularity. It was Dr. Feeder's earnest desire that his old friend should share it, which was all the more easy as the medical congress was really, as the young physician observed, a perpetual symposium. Jackson Lemon entertained the whole body—entertained it profusely, and in a manner befitting one of the patrons of science rather than its humbler votaries; but these dissipations only made him forget for a moment that his relations with the house of Canterville were anomalous. His great difficulty punctually came back to him, and Sidney Feeder saw it stamped upon his brow. Jackson Lemon, with his acute inclination to open himself, was on the point, more than once, of taking the sympathetic Sidney into his confidence. His friend gave him easy opportunity; he asked him what it was he was thinking of all the time, and whether the young marchioness had concluded she couldn't swallow a doctor. These forms of speech were displeasing to Jackson Lemon, whose fastidiousness was nothing new; but it was for even deeper reasons that he said to himself that, for such complicated cases as his, there was no assistance in Sidney Feeder. To understand his situation one must know the world; and the child of Cincinnati didn't know the world,—at least the world with which his friend was now concerned.

"Is there a hitch in your marriage? Just tell me that," Sidney Feeder had said, taking everything for granted, in a manner which was in itself a proof of great innocence. It is true he had added that he supposed he had no business to ask; but he had been anxious about it ever since hearing from Mr. and Mrs. Freer that the British aristocracy was down on the medical profession. "Do they want you to give it up? Is that what the hitch is about? Don't desert your colors, Jackson. The repression of pain, the mitigation of misery, constitute surely the noblest profession in the world."

"My dear fellow, you don't know what you are talking about," Jackson observed, for answer to this. "I haven't told any one I was going to be married; still less have I told any one that any one objected to my profession. I should like to see them do it. I have got out of the swim to-day, but I don't regard myself as the sort of person that people object to. And I do expect to do something, yet."

"Come home, then, and do it. And excuse me if I say that the facilities for getting married are much greater over there."

"You don't seem to have found them very great."

"I have never had time. Wait till my next vacation, and you will see."

"The facilities over there are too great. Nothing is good but what is difficult," said Jackson Lemon, in a tone of artificial sententiousness that quite tormented his interlocutor.

"Well, they have got their backs up, I can see that. I'm glad you like it. Only if they despise your profession, what will they say to that of your friends? If they think you are queer, what would they think of me?" asked Sidney Feeder, the turn of whose mind was not, as a general thing, in the least sarcastic, but who was pushed to this sharpness by a conviction that (in spite of declarations which seemed half an admission and half a denial) his friend was suffering himself to be bothered for the sake of a good which might be obtained elsewhere without bother. It had come over him that the bother was of an unworthy kind.

"My dear fellow, all that is idiotic." That had been Jackson Lemon's reply; but it expressed but a portion of his thoughts. The rest was inexpressible, or almost; being connected with a sentiment of rage at its having struck even so genial a mind as Sidney Feeder's, that in proposing to marry a daughter of the highest civilization he was going out of his way—departing from his natural line. Was he then so ignoble, so pledged to inferior things, that when he saw a girl who (putting aside the fact that she had not genius, which was rare, and which, though he prized rarity, he didn't want) seemed to him the most complete feminine nature he had known, he was to think himself too different, too incongruous, to mate with her? He would mate with whom he chose; that was the upshot of Jackson Lemon's reflections. Several days elapsed, during which everybody—even the pure-minded, like Sidney Feeder—seemed to him very abject.

I relate all this to show why it was that in going to see Mrs. Freer he was prepared much less to be angry with people who, like the Dexter Freers, a month before, had given it out that he was engaged to a peer's daughter, than to resent the insinuation that there were obstacles to such a prospect. He sat with Mrs. Freer alone for half an hour, in the sabbatical stillness of Jermyn Street. Her husband had gone for a walk in the Park; he always walked in the Park on Sunday. All the world might have been there, and Jackson and Mrs. Freer in sole possession of the district of St. James's. This perhaps had something to do with making him at last rather confidential; the influences were conciliatory, persuasive. Mrs. Freer was extremely sympathetic; she treated him like a person she had known from the age of ten; asked his leave to continue recumbent; talked a great deal about his mother; and seemed almost, for a while, to perform the kindly functions of that lady. It had been wise of her from the first not to allude, even indirectly, to his having neglected so long to call; her silence on this point was in the best taste. Jackson Lemon had forgotten that it was a habit with her, and indeed a high accomplishment, never to reproach people with these omissions. You might have left her alone for two years, her greeting was always the same; she was never either too delighted to see you, or not delighted enough. After a while, however, he perceived that her silence had been to a certain extent a reference; she appeared to take for granted that he devoted all his hours to a certain young lady. It came over him, for a moment, that his country people took a great deal for granted; but when Mrs. Freer, rather abruptly, sitting up on her sofa, said to him, half simply, half solemnly, "And now, my dear Jackson, I want you to tell m thing!"—he perceived that, after all, she didn't pretend to know more about the impending matter than he himself did. In the course of a quarter of an hour—so appreciatively she listened—he had told her a good deal about it. It was the first time he had said so much to any one, and the process relieved him even more than he would have supposed. It made certain things clear to him, by bringing them to a point—above all, the fact that he had been wronged. He made no allusion whatever to its being out of the usual way that, as an American doctor, he should sue for the hand of a marquis's daughter; and this reserve was not voluntary, it was quite unconscious. His mind was too full of the offensive conduct of the Cantervilles, and the sordid side of their want of confidence. He could not imagine that while he talked to Mrs. Freer—and it amazed him afterward that he should have chattered so; he could account for it only by the state of his nerves—she should be thinking only of the strangeness of the situation he sketched for her. She thought Americans as good as other people, but she didn't see where, in American life, the daughter of a marquis would, as she phrased it, work in. To take a simple instance,—they coursed through Mrs. Freer's mind with extraordinary speed,—would she not always expect to go in to dinner first? As a novelty, over there, they might like to see her do it, at first; there might be even a pressure for places for the spectacle. But with the increase of every kind of sophistication that was taking place in America, the humorous view to which she would owe her safety might not continue to be taken; and then where would Lady Barberina be? This was but a small instance; but Mrs. Freer's vivid imagination—much as she had lived in Europe, she knew her native land so well—saw a host of others massing themselves behind it. The consequence of all of which was that after listening to him in the most engaging silence, she raised her clasped hands, pressed them against her breast, lowered her voice to a tone of entreaty, and, with her perpetual little smile, uttered three words: "My dear Jackson, don't—don't—don't."

"Don't what?" he asked, staring.

"Don't neglect the chance you have of getting out of it; it would never do."

He knew what she meant by his chance of getting out of it; in his many meditations he had, of course, not overlooked that. The ground the old couple had taken about settlements (and the fact that

Lady Beauchemin had not come back to him to tell him, as she promised, that she had moved them, proved how firmly they were rooted) would have offered an all-sufficient pretext to a man who should have repented of his advances. Jackson Lemon knew that; but he knew at the same time that he had not repented. The old couple's want of imagination did not in the least alter the fact that Barberina was, as he had told her father, a beautiful type. Therefore, he simply said to Mrs. Freer that he didn't in the least wish to get out of it; he was as much in it as ever, and he intended to remain there. But what did she mean, he inquired in a moment, by her statement that it would never do? Why wouldn't it do? Mrs. Freer replied by another inquiry,—Should he really like her to tell him? It wouldn't do, because Lady Barb would not be satisfied with her place at dinner. She would not be content—in a society of commoners—with any but the best; and the best she could not expect (and it was to be supposed that he did not expect her) always to have.

"What do you mean by commoners?" Jackson Lemon demanded, looking very serious.

"I mean you, and me, and my poor husband, and Dr. Feeder," said Mrs. Freer.

"I don't see how there can be commoners where there are not lords. It is the lord that makes the commoner; and *vice versa*."

"Won't a lady do as well? Lady Barberina—a single English girl—can make a million inferiors."

"She will be, before anything else, my wife; and she will not talk about inferiors any more than I do. I never do; it's very vulgar."

"I don't know what she'll talk about, my dear Jackson, but she will think; and her thoughts won't be pleasant,—I mean for others. Do you expect to sink her to your own rank?"

Jackson Lemon's bright little eyes were fixed more brightly than ever upon his hostess. "I don't understand you; and I don't think you understand yourself." This was not absolutely candid, for he did understand Mrs. Freer to a certain extent; it has been related that before he asked Lady Barb's hand of her parents there had been moments when he himself was not very sure that the flower of the British aristocracy would flourish in American soil. But an intimation from another person that it was beyond his power to pass off his wife—whether she were the daughter of a peer or of a shoemaker—set all his blood on fire. It quenched on the instant his own perception of difficulties of detail, and made him feel only that he was dishonored—he, the heir of all the ages,—by such insinuations. It was his belief—though he had never before had occasion to put it forward—that his position, one of the best in the world, was one of those positions that make everything possible. He had had the best education the age could offer, for if he had rather wasted his time at Harvard, where he entered very young, he had, as he believed, been tremendously serious at Heidelberg and at Vienna. He had devoted himself to one of the noblest of professions,—a profession recognized as such everywhere but in England,—and he had inherited a fortune far beyond the expectation of his earlier years, the years when he cultivated habits of work, which alone—or rather in combination with talents that he neither exaggerated nor minimized—would have conduced to distinction. He was one of the most fortunate inhabitants of an immense, fresh, rich country, a country whose future was admitted to be incalculable, and he moved with perfect ease in a society in which he was not overshadowed by others. It seemed to him, therefore, beneath his dignity to wonder whether he could afford, socially speaking, to marry according to his taste. Jackson Lemon pretended to be strong; and what was the use of being strong if you were not prepared to undertake things that timid people might find difficult? It was his plan to marry the woman he liked, and not to be afraid of her afterward. The effect of Mrs. Freer's doubt of his success was to represent to him that his own character would not cover his wife's; she couldn't have made him feel otherwise if she had told him that he was marrying beneath him, and would have to ask for indulgence. "I don't believe you know how much I think that any woman who marries me will be doing very well," he added, directly.

"I am very sure of that; but it isn't so simple—one's being an American," Mrs. Freer rejoined, with a little philosophic sigh.

"It's whatever one chooses to make it."

"Well, you'll make it what no one has done yet, if you take that young lady to America and make her happy there."

"Do you think it's such a very dreadful place?"

"No, indeed; but she will."

Jackson Lemon got up from his chair, and took up his hat and stick. He had actually turned a little pale, with the force of his emotion; it had made him really quiver that his marriage to Lady Barberina should be looked at as too high a flight. He stood a moment leaning against the mantelpiece, and very much tempted to say to Mrs. Freer that she was a vulgar-minded old woman. But he said something that was really more to the point: "You forgot that she will have her consolations."

"Don't go away, or I shall think I have offended you. You can't console a wounded marchioness."

"How will she be wounded? People will be charming to her."

"They will be charming to her—charming to her!" These words fell from the lips of Dexter Freer, who had opened the door of the room and stood with the knob in his hand, putting himself into relation to his wife's talk with their visitor. This was accomplished in an instant. "Of course I know whom you mean," he said, while he exchanged greetings with Jackson Lemon. "My wife and I—of course you know we are great busybodies—have talked of your affair, and we differ about it completely: she sees only the dangers, and I see the advantages."

"By the advantages he means the fun for us," Mrs. Freer remarked, settling her sofa-cushions.

Jackson looked with a certain sharp blankness from one of these disinterested judges to the other; and even yet they did not perceive how their misdirected familiarities wrought upon him. It was hardly more agreeable to him to know that the husband wished to see Lady Barb in America, than to know that the wife had a dread of such a vision; for there was that in Dexter Freer's face which seemed to say that the thing would take place somehow for the benefit of the spectators. "I think you both see too much—a great deal too much," he answered, rather coldly.

"My dear young man, at my age I can take certain liberties," said Dexter Freer. "Do it—I beseech you to do it; it has never been done before." And then, as if Jackson's glance had challenged this last assertion, he went on: "Never, I assure you, this particular thing. Young female members of the British aristocracy have married coachmen and fish-mongers, and all that sort of thing; but they have never married you and me."

"They certainly haven't married you," said Mrs. Freer.

"I am much obliged to you for your advice." It may be thought that Jackson Lemon took himself rather seriously; and indeed I am afraid that if he had not done so there would have been no occasion for my writing this little history. But it made him almost sick to hear his engagement spoken of as a curious and ambiguous phenomenon. He might have his own ideas about it—one always had about one's engagement; but the ideas that appeared to have peopled the imagination of his friends ended by kindling a little hot spot in each of his cheeks. "I would rather not talk any more about my little plans," he added to Dexter Freer. "I have been saying all sorts of absurd things to Mrs. Freer."

"They have been most interesting," that lady declared. "You have been very stupidly treated."

"May she tell me when you go?" her husband asked of the young man.

"I am going now; she may tell you whatever she likes."

"I am afraid we have displeased you," said Mrs. Freer; "I have said too much what I think. You must excuse me, it's all for your mother."

"It's she whom I want Lady Barberina to see!" Jackson Lemon exclaimed, with the inconsequence of filial affection.

"Deary me!" murmured Mrs. Freer.

"We shall go back to America to see how you get on," her husband said; "and if you succeed, it will be a great precedent."

"Oh, I shall succeed!" and with this he took his departure. He walked away with the quick step of a man laboring under a certain excitement; walked up to Piccadilly and down past Hyde Park Corner. It relieved him to traverse these distances, for he was thinking hard, under the influence of irritation; and locomotion helped him to think. Certain suggestions that had been made him in the last half-hour rankled in his mind, all the more that they seemed to have a kind of representative value, to be an echo of the common voice. If his prospects wore that face to Mrs. Freer, they would probably wear it to others; and he felt a sudden need of showing such others that they took a pitiful measure of his position. Jackson Lemon walked and walked till he found himself on the highway of Hammersmith. I have represented him as a young man of much strength of purpose, and I may appear to undermine this plea when I relate that he wrote that evening to his solicitor that Mr. Hilary was to be informed that he would agree to any proposals for settlements that Mr. Hilary should make. Jackson's strength of purpose was shown in his deciding to marry Lady Barberina on any terms. It seemed to him, under the influence of his desire to prove that he was not afraid—so odious was the imputation—that terms of any kind were very superficial things. What was fundamental, and of the essence of the matter, would be to marry Lady Barb and carry everything out.

V

ON SUNDAYS, now, you might be at home," Jackson Lemon said to his wife in the following month of March, more than six months after his marriage.

"Are the people any nicer on Sundays than they are on other days?" Lady Barberina replied, from the depths of her chair, without looking up from a stiff little book.

He hesitated a single instant before answering: "I don't know whether they are, but I think you might be."

"I'm as nice as I know how to be. You must take me as I am. You knew when you married me that I was not an American."

Jackson Lemon stood before the fire, towards which his wife's face was turned and her feet were extended; stood there some time, with his hands behind him and his eyes dropped a little obliquely upon the bent head and richly-draped figure of Lady Barberina. It may be said without delay that he was irritated, and it may be added that he had a double cause. He felt himself to be on the verge of the first crisis that had occurred between himself and his wife,—the reader will perceive that it had occurred rather promptly,

—and he was annoyed at his annoyance. A glimpse of his state of mind before his marriage has been given to the reader, who will remember that at that period Jackson Lemon somehow regarded himself as lifted above possibilities of irritation. When one was strong, one was not irritable; and a union with a kind of goddess would of course be an element of strength. Lady Barb was a goddess still, and Jackson Lemon admired his wife as much as the day he led her to the altar; but I am not sure that he felt as strong.

"How do you know what people are?" he said in a moment. "You have seen so few; you are perpetually denying yourself. If you should leave New York to-morrow, you would know wonderfully little about it."

"It's all the same," said Lady Barb; "the people are all exactly alike."

"How can you tell? You never see them."

"Didn't I go out every night for the first two months we were here?"

"It was only to about a dozen houses,—always the same; people, moreover, you had already met in London. You have got no general impressions."

"That's just what I have got; I had them before I came. Every one is just the same; they have just the same names—just the same manners."

Again, for an instant, Jackson Lemon hesitated; then he said, in that apparently artless tone of which mention has already been made, and which he sometimes used in London during his wooing: "Don't you like it over here?"

Lady Barb raised her eyes from her book. "Did you expect me to like it?"

"I hoped you would, of course. I think I told you so."

"I don't remember. You said very little about it; you seemed to make a kind of mystery. I knew, of course, you expected me to live here, but I didn't know you expected me to like it."

"You thought I asked of you the sacrifice, as it were."

"I am sure I don't know," said Lady Barb. She got up from her chair and tossed the volume she had been reading into the empty seat. "I recommend you read that book," she added.

"Is it interesting?"

"It's an American novel."

"I never read novels."

"You had better look at that one; it will show you the kind of people you want me to know."

"I have no doubt it's very vulgar," said Jackson Lemon; "I don't see why you read it."

"What else can I do? I can't always be riding in the Park; I hate the Park," Lady Barb remarked.

"It's quite as good as your own," said her husband.

She glanced at him with a certain quickness, her eyebrows slightly lifted. "Do you mean the park at Pasterns?"

"No; I mean the park in London."

"I don't care about London. One was only in London a few weeks."

"I suppose you miss the country," said Jackson Lemon. It was his idea of life that he should not be afraid of anything, not be afraid, in any situation, of knowing the worst that was to be known about it; and the demon of a courage with which discretion was not properly commingled prompted him to take soundings which were perhaps not absolutely necessary for safety, and yet which revealed unmistakable rocks. It was useless to know about rocks if he couldn't avoid them; the only thing was to trust to the wind.

"I don't know what I miss. I think I miss everything!" This was his wife's answer to his too-curious inquiry. It was not peevish, for that is not the tone of a goddess; but it expressed a good deal—a good deal more than Lady Barb, who was rarely eloquent, had expressed before. Nevertheless, though his question had been precipitate, Jackson Lemon said to himself that he might take his time to think over what his wife's little speech contained; he could not help seeing that the future would give him abundant opportunity for that. He was in no hurry to ask himself whether poor Mrs. Freer, in Jermyn Street, might not, after all, have been right in saying that, in regard to marrying the product of an English caste, it was not so simple to be an American doctor—might avail little even, in such a case, to be the heir of all the ages. The transition was complicated, but in his bright mind it was rapid, from the brush of a momentary contact with such ideas to certain considerations which led him to say, after an instant, to his wife, "Should you like to go down into Connecticut?"

"Into Connecticut?"

"That's one of our States; it's about as large as Ireland. I'll take you there if you like."

"What does one do there?"

"We can try and get some hunting."

"You and I alone?"

"Perhaps we can get a party to join us."

"The people in the State?"

"Yes; we might propose it to them."

"The tradespeople in the towns?"

"Very true; they will have to mind their shops," said Jackson Lemon. "But we might hunt alone."

"Are there any foxes?"

"No; but there are a few old cows."

Lady Barb had already perceived that her husband took it into his head once in a while to laugh at her, and she was aware that the present occasion was neither worse nor better than some others. She didn't mind it particularly now, though in England it would have disgusted her; she had the consciousness of virtue,—an immense comfort,—and flattered herself that she had learned the lesson of an altered standard of fitness; there were, moreover, so many more disagreeable things in America than being laughed at by one's husband. But she pretended to mind it, because it made him stop, and above all it stopped discussion, which with Jackson was so often jocular, and none the less tiresome for that. "I only want to be left alone," she said, in answer—though, indeed, it had not the manner of an answer—to his speech about the cows. With this she wandered away to one of the windows which looked out in the Fifth Avenue. She was very fond of these windows, and she had taken a great fancy to the Fifth Avenue, which, in the high-pitched winter weather, when everything sparkled, was a spectacle full of novelty. It will be seen that she was not wholly unjust to her adoptive country; she found it delightful to look out of the window. This was a pleasure she had enjoyed in London only in the most furtive manner; it was not the kind of thing that girls did in England. Besides, in London, in Hill Street, there was nothing particular to see; but in the Fifth Avenue everything and every one went by, and observation was made consistent with dignity by the quantities of brocade and lace in which the windows were draped, which, somehow, would not have been tidy in England, and which made an ambush, without concealing the brilliant day. Hundreds of women —the curious women of New York, who were unlike any that Lady Barb had hitherto seen—passed the house every hour; and her ladyship was infinitely entertained and mystified by the sight of their clothes. She spent a good deal more time than she was aware of in this amusement; and if she had been addicted to returning upon herself, or asking herself for an account of her conduct—an inquiry which she did not, indeed, completely neglect, but treated very cursorily,—it would have made her smile sadly to think what she appeared mainly to have come to America for, conscious though she was that her tastes were very simple, and that so long as she didn't hunt, it didn't much matter what she did.

Her husband turned about to the fire, giving a push with his foot to a log that had fallen out of its place. Then he said,—and the connection with the words she had just uttered was apparent enough,—"You really must be at home on Sundays, you know. I used to like that so much in London. All the best women here do it. You had better begin to-day. I am going to see my mother; if I meet any one I will tell them to come."

"Tell them not to talk so much," said Lady Barb, among her lace curtains.

"Ah, my dear," her husband replied, "it isn't every one that has your concision." And he went and stood behind her in the window, putting his arm around her waist. It was as much of a satisfaction to him as it had been six months before, at the time the solicitors were settling the matter, that this flower of an ancient stem should be worn upon his own breast; he still thought its fragrance a thing quite apart, and it was as clear as day to him that his wife was the handsomest woman in New York. He had begun, after their arrival, by telling her this very often; but the assurance brought no color to her cheek, no light to her eyes; to be the handsomest woman in New York evidently did not seem to her a position in life. Moreover, the reader may be informed that, oddly enough, Lady Barb did not particularly believe this assertion. There were some very pretty women in New York, and without in the least wishing to be like them—she had seen no woman in America whom she desired to resemble—she envied some of their looks. It is probable that her own finest points were those of which she was most unconscious.

But her husband was aware of all of them; nothing could exceed the minuteness of his appreciation of his wife. It was a sign of this that after he had stood behind her a moment he kissed her very tenderly. "Have you any message for my mother?" he asked.

"Please give her my love. And you might take her that book."

"What book?"

"That nasty one I have been reading."

"Oh, bother your books," said Jackson Lemon, with a certain irritation, as he went out of the room.

There had been a good many things in her life in New York that cost Lady Barb an effort; but sending her love to her mother-in-law was not one of these. She liked Mrs. Lemon better than any one she had seen in America; she was the only person who seemed to Lady Barb really simple, as she understood that quality. Many people had struck her as homely and rustic, and many others as pretentious and vulgar; but in Jackson's mother she had found the golden mean of a simplicity which, as she would have said, was really nice. Her sister, Lady Agatha, was even fonder of Mrs. Lemon; but then Lady Agatha had taken the most extraordinary fancy to every one and everything, and talked as if America were the most delightful country in the world. She was having a lovely time (she already spoke the most beautiful American), and had been, during the winter that was just drawing to a close, the most prominent girl in New York. She had gone out at first with her sister; but for some weeks past Lady Barb had let so many occasions pass, that Agatha threw herself into the arms of Mrs. Lemon, who found her extraordinarly quaint and amusing, and was delighted to take her into society. Mrs. Lemon, as an old woman, had given up such vanities; but she only wanted a motive, and in her good nature she ordered a dozen new caps, and sat smiling against the wall while her little English maid, on polished floors, to the sound of music, cultivated the American step as well as the American tone. There was no trouble, in New York, about going out, and the winter was not half over before the little English maid found herself an accomplished diner, rolling about, without any chaperon at all, to banquets where she could count upon a bouquet at her plate. She had had a great deal of correspondence with her mother on this point, and Lady Canterville at last withdrew her protest, which in the meantime had been perfectly useless. It was ultimately Lady

Canterville's feeling that if she had married the handsomest of her daughters to an American doctor, she might let another become a professional *raconteuse* (Agatha had written to her that she was expected to talk so much), strange as such a destiny seemed for a girl of nineteen. Mrs. Lemon was even a much simpler woman than Lady Barberina thought her; for she had not noticed that Lady Agatha danced much oftener with Herman Longstraw than with any one else. Jackson Lemon, though he went little to balls, had discovered this truth, and he looked slightly preoccupied when, after he had sat five minutes with his mother on the Sunday afternoon through which I have invited the reader to trace so much more than (I am afraid) is easily apparent of the progress of this simple story, he learned that his sister-in-law was entertaining Mr. Longstraw in the library. He had called half an hour before, and she had taken him into the other room to show him the seal of the Cantervilles, which she had fastened to one of her numerous trinkets (she was adorned with a hundred bangles and chains), and the proper exhibition of which required a taper and a stick of wax. Apparently he was examining it very carefully, for they had been absent a good while. Mrs. Lemon's simplicity was further shown by the fact that she had not measured their absence; it was only when Jackson questioned her that she remembered.

Herman Longstraw was a young Californian who had turned up in New York the winter before, and who travelled on his mustache, as they were understood to say in his native State. This mustache, and some of the accompanying features, were very ornamental; several ladies in New York had been known to declare that they were as beautiful as a dream. Taken in connection with his tall stature, his familiar good-nature, and his remarkable Western vocabulary, they constituted his only social capital; for of the two great divisions, the rich Californians and the poor Californians, it was well known to which he belonged. Jackson Lemon looked at him as a slightly mitigated cowboy, and was somewhat vexed at his dear mother, though he was aware that she could scarcely figure to herself what an effect such an account as that would produce in the halls of Canterville. He had no desire whatever to play a trick on the house to which he was allied, and knew perfectly that Lady Agatha had not been sent to America to become entangled with a Californian of the wrong denomination. He had been perfectly willing to bring her; he thought, a little vindictively, that this would operate as a hint to her parents as to what he might have been inclined to do if they had not sent Mr. Hilary after him. Herman Longstraw, according to the legend, had been a trapper, a squatter, a miner, a pioneer,—had been everything that one could be in the romantic parts of America, and had accumulated masses of experience before the age of thirty. He had shot bears in the Rockies and buffaloes on the plains; and it was even believed that he had brought down animals of a still more dangerous kind, among the haunts of men. There had been a story that he owned a cattle-ranch in Arizona; but a later and apparently more authentic version of it, though it represented him as looking after the cattle, did not depict him as their proprietor. Many of the stories told about him were false; but there is no doubt that his mustache, his good-nature, and his accent were genuine. He danced very badly; but Lady Agatha had frankly told several persons that that was nothing new to her; and she liked (this, however, she did not tell) Mr. Herman Longstraw. What she enjoyed in America was the revelation of freedom; and there was no such proof of freedom as conversation with a gentleman who dressed in skins when he was not in New York, and who, in his usual pursuits, carried his life (as well as that of other people) in his hand. A gentleman whom she had sat next to at dinner in the early part of her stay in New York, remarked to her that the United States were the paradise of women and mechanics; and this had seemed to her at the time very abstract, for she was not conscious, as yet, of belonging to either class. In England she had been only a girl; and the principal idea connected with that was simply that, for one's misfortune, one was not a boy. But presently she perceived that New York was a paradise; and this helped her to know that she must be one of the people mentioned in the axiom of her neighbor—people who could do whatever they wanted, had a voice in everything, and made their taste and their ideas felt. She saw that it was great fun to be a woman in America, and that that was the best way to enjoy the New York winter,—the wonderful, brilliant New York winter, the queer, long-shaped, glittering city, the heterogeneous hours, among which you couldn't tell the morning from the afternoon, or the night from either of them, the perpetual liberties and walks, the rushings-out and the droppings-in, the intimacies, the endearments, the comicalities, the sleigh-bells, the cutters, the sunsets on the snow, the ice-parties in the frosty clearness, the bright, hot, velvety houses, the bouquets, the bonbons, the little cakes, the big cakes, the irrepressible inspirations of shopping, the innumerable luncheons and dinners that were offered to youth and innocence, the quantities of chatter of quantities of girls, the perpetual motion of the german, the suppers at restaurants after the play, the way in which life was pervaded by Delmonico and Delmonico by the sense that though one's hunting was lost, and this so different, it was almost as good —and in all, through all, a kind of suffusion of bright, loud, friendly sound, which was very local, but very human.

Lady Agatha at present was staying, for a little change, with Mrs. Lemon, and such adventures as that were part of the pleasure of her American season. The house was too close; but, physically, the girl could bear anything, and it was all she had to complain of; for Mrs. Lemon, as we know, thought her a quaint little damsel, and had none of those old-world scruples in regard to spoiling young people to which Lady Agatha now perceived that she herself, in the past, had been unduly sacrificed. In her own way —it was not at all her sister's way—she liked to be of importance; and this was assuredly the case when she saw that Mrs. Lemon had apparently nothing in the world to do (after spending a part of the morning with her servants) but invent little distractions (many of them of the edible sort) for her guest. She appeared to have certain friends, but she had no society to speak of, and the people who came into her house came principally to see Lady Agatha. This, as we have seen, was strikingly the case with Herman Longstraw. The whole situation gave Lady Agatha a great feeling of success,—success of a new and unexpected kind. Of course, in England, she had been born successful, in a manner, in coming into the world in one of the most beautiful rooms at Pasterns; but her present triumph was achieved more by her own effort (not that she had tried very hard) and by her merit. It was not so much what she said (for she could never say half as much as the girls in New York), as the spirit of enjoyment that played in her fresh young face, with its pointless curves, and shone in her gray English eyes. She enjoyed everything, even the street-cars, of which she made liberal use; and more than everything she enjoyed Mr. Longstraw and his talk about buffaloes and bears. Mrs. Lemon promised to be very careful, as soon as her son had begun to warn her; and this time she had a certain understanding of what she promised. She thought people ought to make the matches they liked; she had given proof of this in her late behavior to Jackson, whose own union was, in her opinion, marked with all the arbitrariness of pure love. Nevertheless, she could see that Herman Longstraw would probably be thought rough in England; and it was not simply that he was so inferior to Jackson, for, after all, certain things were not to be expected. Jackson Lemon was not oppressed with his mother-in-law, having taken his precautions against such a danger; but he was aware that he should give Lady Canterville a permanent advantage over him if while she was in America, her daughter Agatha should attach herself to a mere mustache.

It was not always, as I have hinted, that Mrs. Lemon entered completely into the views of her son, though in form she never failed to subscribe to them devoutly. She had never yet, for instance, apprehended his reason for marrying Lady Barberina Clement. This was a great secret, and Mrs. Lemon was determined that no one should ever know it. For herself, she was sure that, to the end of time, she should not discover Jackson's reason. She could never ask about it, for that, of course, would betray her. From the first she had told him she was delighted; there being no need of asking for explanations then, as the young lady herself, when she should come to know her, would explain. But the young lady had not yet explained; and after this, evidently, she never would. She was very tall, very handsome, she answered exactly to Mrs. Lemon's prefigurement of the daughter of a lord, and she wore her clothes, which were peculiar, but, to her, remarkably becoming, very well. But she did not elucidate; we know ourselves that there was very little that was explanatory about Lady Barb. So Mrs. Lemon continued to wonder, to ask herself, "Why that one, more than so many others, who would have been more natural?" The choice appeared to her, as I have said, very arbitrary. She found Lady Barb very different from other girls she had known, and this led her almost immediately to feel sorry for her daughter-in-law. She said to herself that Barb was to be pitied if she found her husband's people as peculiar as his mother found *her*; for the result of that would be to make her very lonesome. Lady Agatha was different, because she seemed to keep nothing back; you saw all there was of her, and she was evidently not homesick. Mrs. Lemon could see that Barberina was ravaged by this last passion, and that she was too proud to show it. She even had a glimpse of the ultimate truth; namely, that Jackson's wife had not the comfort of crying, because that would have amounted to a confession that she had been idiotic enough to believe in advance that, in an American town, in the society of doctors, she should escape such pangs. Mrs. Lemon treated her with the greatest gentleness,—all the gentleness that was due to a young woman who was in the unfortunate position of having been married one couldn't tell why. The world, to Mrs. Lemon's view, contained two great departments,—that of people, and that of things; and she believed that you must take an interest either in one or the other. The incomprehensible thing in Lady Barb was that she cared for neither side of the show. Her house apparently inspired her with no curiosity and no enthusiasm, though it had been thought magnificent enough to be described in successive columns of the American newspapers; and she never spoke of her furniture or her domestics, though she had a prodigious quantity of such possessions. She was the same with regard to her acquaintance, which was immense, inasmuch as every one in the place had called on her. Mrs. Lemon was the least critical woman in the world; but it had sometimes exasperated her just a little that her daughter-in-law should receive every one in New York in exactly the same way. There were differences, Mrs. Lemon knew, and some of them were of the highest importance; but poor Lady Barb appeared never to suspect them. She accepted every one and everything, and asked no questions. She had no curiosity about her fellow citizens, and as she never assumed it for a moment, she gave Mrs. Lemon no opportunity to enlighten her. Lady Barb was a person with whom you could do nothing unless she gave you an opening; and nothing would have been more difficult than to enlighten her against her will. Of course she picked up a little knowledge; but she confounded and transposed American attributes in the most extraordinary way. She had a way of calling every one Doctor; and Mrs. Lemon could scarcely convince her that this distinction was too precious to be so freely bestowed. She had once said to her mother-in-law that in New York there was nothing to know people by, their names were so very monotonous; and Mrs. Lemon had entered into this enough to see that there was something that stood out a good deal in Barberina's own prefix. It is probable that during her short stay in New York complete justice was not done Lady Barb; she never got credit, for instance, for repressing her annoyance at the aridity of the social nomenclature, which seemed to her hideous. That little speech to her mother was the most reckless sign she gave of it; and there were few things that contributed more to the good conscience she habitually enjoyed, than her self-control on this particular point.

Jackson Lemon was making some researches, just now, which took up a great deal of his time; and, for the rest, he passed his hours abundantly with his wife. For the last three months, therefore, he had seen his mother scarcely more than once a week. In spite of researches, in spite of medical societies, where Jackson, to her knowledge, read papers, Lady Barb had more of her husband's company than she had counted upon at the time she married. She had never known a married pair to be so much together as she and Jackson; he appeared to expect her to sit with him in the library in the morning. He had none of the occupations of gentlemen and noblemen in England, for the element of politics appeared to be as absent as the hunting. There were politics in Washington, she had been told, and even at Albany, and Jackson had proposed to introduce her to these cities; but the proposal, made to her once at dinner before several people, had excited such cries of horror that it fell dead on the spot. "We don't want you to see anything of that kind," one of the ladies had said, and Jackson had appeared to be discouraged,—that is if, in regard to Jackson, she could really tell.

"Pray, what is it you want me to see?" Lady Barb had asked on this occasion.

"Well, New York; and Boston, if you want to very much—but not otherwise; and Niagara; and, more than anything, Newport."

Lady Barb was tired of their eternal Newport; she had heard of it a thousand times, and felt already as if she had lived there half her life; she was sure, moreover, that she should hate it. This is perhaps as near as she came to having a lively conviction on any American subject. She asked herself whether she was then to spend her life in the Fifth Avenue, with alternations of a city of villas (she detested villas), and wondered whether that was all the great American country had to offer her. There were times when she thought that she should like the backwoods, and that the Far West might be a resource; for she had analyzed her feelings just deep enough to discover that when she had—hesitating a good deal—turned over the question of marrying Jackson Lemon, it was not in the least of American barbarism that she was afraid; her dread was of American civilization. She believed the little lady I have just quoted was a goose; but that did not make New York any more interesting. It would be reckless to say that she suffered from an overdose of Jackson's company, because she had a view of the fact that he was much her most important social resource. She could talk to him about England; about her own England, and he understood more or less what she wished to say, when she wished to say anything, which was not frequent. There were plenty of other people who talked about England; but with them the range of allusion was always the hotels, of which she knew nothing, and the shops, and the opera, and the photographs: they had a mania for photographs. There were other people who were always wanting her to tell them about Pasterns, and the manner of life there, and the parties; but if there was one thing Lady Barb disliked more than another, it was describing Pasterns. She had always lived with people who knew, of themselves, what such a place would be, without demanding these pictorial efforts, proper only, as she vaguely felt, to persons belonging to the classes whose trade was the arts of expression. Lady Barb, of course, had never gone into it; but she knew that in her own class the business was not to express, but to enjoy; not to represent, but to be represented,—though, indeed, this latter liability might convey offense; for it may be noted that even for an aristocrat Jackson Lemon's wife was aristocratic.

Lady Agatha and her visitor came back from the library in course of time, and Jackson Lemon felt it his duty to be rather cold to Herman Longstraw. It was not clear to him what sort of a husband his sister-in-law would do well to look for in America,—if there were to be any question of husbands; but as to this he was not bound to be definite, provided he should rule out Mr. Longstraw. This gentleman, however, was not given to perceive shades of manner; he had little observation, but very great confidence.

"I think you had better come home with me," Jackson said to Lady Agatha; "I guess you have stayed here long enough."

"Don't let him say that, Mrs. Lemon!" the girl cried. "I like being with you so very much."

"I try to make it pleasant," said Mrs. Lemon. "I should really miss you now; but perhaps it's your mother's wish." If it was a question of defending her guest from ineligible suitors, Mrs. Lemon felt, of course, that her son was more competent than she; though she had a lurking kindness for Herman Longstraw, and a vague idea that he was a gallant, genial specimen of young America.

"Oh, mamma wouldn't see any difference!" Lady Agatha exclaimed, looking at Jackson with pleading blue eyes. "Mamma wants me to see every one; you know she does. That's what she sent me to America for; she knew it was not like England. She wouldn't like it if I didn't sometimes stay with people; she always wanted us to stay at other houses. And she knows all about you, Mrs. Lemon, and she likes you immensely. She sent you a message the other day, and I am afraid I forgot to give it to you,—to thank you for being so kind to me and taking such a lot of trouble. Really she did, but I forgot it. If she wants me to see as much as possible of America, it's much better I should be here than always with Barb,—it's much less like one's own country. I mean it's much nicer—for a girl," said Lady Agatha, affectionately, to Mrs. Lemon, who began also to look at Jackson with a kind of tender argumentativeness.

"If you want the genuine thing, you ought to come out on the plains," Mr. Longstraw interposed, with smiling sincerity. "I guess that was your mother's idea. Why don't you all come out?" He had been looking intently at Lady Agatha while the remarks I have just repeated succeeded each other on her lips,—looking at her with a kind of fascinated approbation, for all the world as if he had been a slightly slow-witted English gentleman, and the girl had been a flower of the West,—a flower that knew how to talk. He made no secret of the fact that Lady Agatha's voice was music to him, his ear being much more susceptible than his own inflections would have indicated. To Lady Agatha those inflections were not displeasing, partly because, like Mr. Herman himself, in general, she had not a perception of shades; and partly because it never occurred to her to compare them with any other tones. He seemed to her to speak a foreign language altogether,—a romantic dialect, through which the most comical meanings gleamed here and there.

"I should like it above all things," she said, in answer to his last observation.

"The scenery's superior to anything round here," Mr. Longstraw went on.

Mrs. Lemon, as we know, was the softest of women; but, as an old New Yorker, she had no patience with some of the new fashions. Chief among these was the perpetual reference, which had become common only within a few years, to the outlying parts of the country, the States and Territories of which children, in her time, used to learn the names, in their order, at school, but which no one ever thought of going to or talking about. Such places, in Mrs. Lemon's opinion, belonged to the geography-books, or at most to the literature of newspapers, but not to society nor to conversation; and the change—which, so far as it lay in people's talk, she thought at bottom a mere affectation—threatened to make her native land appear vulgar and vague. For this amiable daughter of Manhattan, the normal existence of man, and, still more, of woman, had been "located," as she would have said, between Trinity Church and the beautiful Reservoir at the top of the Fifth Avenue,—monuments of which she was personally proud; and if we could look into the deeper parts of her mind, I am afraid we should discover there an impression that both the countries of Europe and the remainder of her own continent were equally far from the centre and the light.

"Well, scenery isn't everything," she remarked, mildly, to Mr. Longstraw; "and if Lady Agatha should wish to see anything of that kind, all she has got to do is to take the boat up the Hudson."

Mrs. Lemon's recognition of this river, I should say, was all that it need have been; she thought that it existed for the purpose of supplying New Yorkers with poetical feelings, helping them to face comfortably occasions like the present, and, in general, meet foreigners with confidence,—part of the oddity of foreigners being their conceit about their own places.

"That's a good idea, Lady Agatha; let's take the boat," said Mr. Longstraw. "I've had great times on the boats."

Lady Agatha looked at her cavalier a little with those singular, charming eyes of hers,—eyes of which it was impossible to say, at any moment, whether they were the shyest or the frankest in the world; and she was not aware, while this contemplation lasted, that her brother-in-law was observing her. He was thinking of certain things while he did so, of things he had heard about the English; who still, in spite of his having married into a family of that nation, appeared to him very much through the medium of hearsay. They were more passionate than the Americans, and they did things that would never have been expected; though they seemed steadier and less excitable, there was much social evidence to show that they were more impulsive.

"It's so very kind of you to propose that," Lady Agatha said in a moment to Mrs. Lemon. "I think I have never been in a ship,—except, of course, coming from England. I am sure mamma would wish me to see the Hudson. We used to go in immensely for boating in England."

"Did you boat in a ship?" Herman Longstraw asked, showing his teeth hilariously, and pulling his mustaches.

"Lots of my mother's people have been in the navy." Lady Agatha perceived vaguely and good-naturedly that she had said something which the odd Americans thought odd, and that she must justify herself. Her standard of oddity was getting dreadfully dislocated.

"I really think you had better come back to us," said Jackson; "your sister is very lonely without you."

"She is much more lonely with me. We are perpetually having differences. Barb is dreadfully vexed because I like America, instead of—instead of—" And Lady Agatha paused a moment; for it just occurred to her that this might be a betrayal.

"Instead of what?" Jackson Lemon inquired.

"Instead of perpetually wanting to go to England, as she does," she went on, only giving her phrase a little softer turn; for she felt the next moment that her sister could have nothing to hide, and must, of course, have the courage of her opinions. "Of course England's best, but I dare say I like to be bad," said Lady Agatha, artlessly.

"Oh, there's no doubt you are awfully bad," Mr. Longstraw exclaimed, with joyous eagerness. Of course he could not know that what she had principally in mind was an exchange of opinions that had taken place between her sister and herself just before she came to stay with Mrs. Lemon. This incident, of which Longstraw was the occasion, might indeed have been called a discussion, for it had carried them quite into the realms of the abstract. Lady Barb had said she didn't see how Agatha could look at such a creature as that, —an odious, familiar, vulgar being, who had not about him the rudiments of a gentleman. Lady Agatha had replied that Mr. Longstraw was familiar and rough, and that he had a twang, and thought it amusing to talk of her as "the Princess"; but that he was a gentleman for all that, and that at any rate he was tremendous fun. Her sister to this had rejoined that if he was rough and familiar he couldn't be a gentleman, inasmuch as that was just what a gentleman meant,—a man who was civil, and well-bred, and well-born. Lady Agatha had argued that this was just where she differed; that a man might perfectly be a gentleman, and yet be rough, and even ignorant, so long as he was really nice. The only thing was that he should be really nice, which was the case with Mr. Longstraw, who, moreover, was quite extraordinary civil—as civil as a man could be. And then Lady Agatha made the strongest point she had ever made in her life, she had never been so inspired, in saying that Mr. Longstraw was rough, perhaps, but not rude,—a distinction altogether wasted on her sister, who declared that she had not come to America, of all places, to learn what a gentleman was. The discussion, in short, had been lively. I know not whether it was the tonic effect on them, too, of the fine winter weather, or, on the other hand, that of Lady Barb's being bored and having nothing else to do; but Lord Canterville's daughters went into the question with the moral earnestness of a pair of Bostonians. It was part of Lady Agatha's view of her admirer that he, after all, much resembled other tall people, with smiling eyes and mustaches, who had ridden a good deal in rough countries, and whom she had seen in other places. If he was more familiar, he was also more alert; still, the difference was not in himself, but in the way she saw him,—the way she saw everybody in America. If she should see the others in the same way, no doubt they would be quite the same; and Lady Agatha sighed a little over the possibilities of life; for this peculiar way, especially regarded in connection with gentlemen, had become very pleasant to her.

She had betrayed her sister more than she thought, even though Jackson Lemon did not particularly show it in the tone in which he said: "Of course she knows that she is going to see your mother in the summer." His tone, rather, was that of irritation at the repetition of a familiar idea.

"Oh, it isn't only mamma," replied Lady Agatha.

"I know she likes a cool house," said Mrs. Lemon, suggestively.

"When she goes, you had better bid her good-by," the girl went on.

"Of course I shall bid her good-by," said Mrs. Lemon, to whom, apparently, this remark was addressed.

"I shall never bid you good-by, Princess," Herman Longstraw interposed. "I can tell you that you never will see the last of me."

"Oh, it doesn't matter about me, for I shall come back; but if Barb once gets to England, she will never come back."

"Oh, my dear child," murmured Mrs. Lemon, addressing Lady Agatha, but looking at her son.

Jackson looked at the ceiling, at the floor; above all, he looked very conscious.

"I hope you don't mind my saying that, Jackson dear," Lady Agatha said to him, for she was very fond of her brother-in-law.

"Ah, well, then, she shan't go, then," he remarked, after a moment, with a dry little laugh.

"But you promised mamma, you know," said the girl, with the confidence of her affection.

Jackson looked at her with an eye which expressed none even of his very moderate hilarity. "Your mother, then, must bring her back."

"Get some of your navy people to supply an ironclad!" cried Mr. Longstraw.

"It would be very pleasant if the Marchioness could come over," said Mrs. Lemon.

"Oh, she would hate it more than poor Barb," Lady Agatha quickly replied. It did not suit her mood at all to see a marchioness inserted into the field of her vision.

"Doesn't she feel interested, from what you have told her?" Herman Longstraw asked of Lady Agatha. But Jackson Lemon did not heed his sister-in-law's answer; he was thinking of something else. He said nothing more, however, about the subject of his thought, and before ten minutes were over, he took his departure, having, meanwhile, neglected also to revert to the question of Lady Agatha's bringing her visit to his mother to a close. It was not to speak to him of this (for, as we know, she wished to keep the girl, and, somehow, could not bring herself to be afraid of Herman Longstraw) that when Jackson took leave she went with him to the door of the house detaining him a little, while she stood on the steps, as people had always done in New York in her time, though it was another of the new fashions she did not like, not to come out of the parlor. She placed her hand on his arm to keep him on the "stoop," and looked up and down into the brilliant afternoon and the beautiful city,—its chocolate-colored houses, so extraordinarly smooth,—in which it seemed to her that even the most fastidious people ought to be glad to live. It was useless to attempt to conceal it; her son's marriage had made a difference, had put up a kind of barrier. It had brought with it a problem much more difficult than his old problem of how to make his mother feel that she was still, as she had been in his childhood, the dispenser of his rewards. The old problem had been easily solved; the new one was a visible preoccupation. Mrs. Lemon felt that her daughter-in-law did not take her seriously; and that was a part of the barrier. Even if Barberina liked her better than any one else, this was mostly because she liked every one else so little. Mrs. Lemon had not a grain of resentment in her nature; and it was not to feed a sense of wrong that she permitted herself to criticise her son's wife. She could not help feeling that his marriage was not altogether fortunate if his wife didn't take his mother seriously. She knew she was not otherwise remarkable than as being his mother; but that position, which was no merit of hers (the merit was all Jackson's, in being her son), seemed to her one which, familiar as Lady Barb appeared to have been in England with positions of various kinds, would naturally strike the girl as a very high one, to be accepted as freely as a fine morning. If she didn't think of his mother as an indivisible part of him, perhaps she didn't think of other things either; and Mrs. Lemon vaguely felt that, remarkable as Jackson was, he was made up of parts, and that it would never do that these parts should be rated lower one by one, for there was no knowing what that might end in. She feared that things were rather cold for him at home when he had to explain so much to his wife,—explain to her, for instance, all the sources of happiness that were to be found in New York. This struck her as a new kind of problem altogether for a husband. She had never thought of matrimony without a community of feeling in regard to religion and country; one took those great conditions for granted, just as one assumed that one's food was to be cooked; and if Jackson should have to discuss them with his wife, he might, in spite of his great abilities, be carried into regions where he would get entangled and embroiled,—from which, even, possibly, he would not come back at all. Mrs. Lemon had a horror of losing him in some way; and this fear was in her eyes as she stood on the steps of her house, and, after she had glanced up and down the street, looked at him a moment in silence. He simply kissed her again, and said she would take cold.

"I am not afraid of that, I have a shawl!" Mrs. Lemon, who was very small and very fair, with pointed features and an elaborate cap, passed her life in a shawl, and owed to this habit her reputation for being an invalid,—an idea which she scorned, naturally enough, inasmuch as it was precisely her shawl that (as she believed) kept her from being one. "Is it true Barberina won't come back?" she asked of her son.

"I don't know that we shall ever find out; I don't know that I shall take her to England."

"Didn't you promise, dear?"

"I don't know that I promised; not absolutely."

"But you wouldn't keep her here against her will?" said Mrs. Lemon, inconsequently.

"I guess she'll get used to it," Jackson answered, with a lightness he did not altogether feel.

Mrs. Lemon looked up and down the street again, and gave a little sigh. "What a pity she isn't American!" She did not mean this as a reproach, a hint of what might have been; it was simply embarrassment resolved into speech.

"She couldn't have been American," said Jackson, with decision.

"Couldn't she, dear?" Mrs. Lemon spoke with a kind of respect; she felt that there were imperceptible reasons in this.

"It was just as she is that I wanted her," Jackson added.

"Even if she won't come back?" his mother asked, with a certain wonder.

"Oh, she has got to come back!" Jackson said, going down the steps.

VI

Lady barb, after this, did not decline to see her New York acquaintances on Sunday afternoons, though she refused for the present to enter into a project of her husband's, who thought it would be a pleasant thing that she should entertain his friends on the evening of that day. Like all good Americans, Jackson Lemon devoted much consideration to the great question how, in his native land, society should be brought into being. It seemed to him that it would help the good cause, for which so many Americans are ready to lay down their lives, if his wife should, as he jocularly called it, open a saloon. He believed, or he tried to believe, the *salon* now possible in New York, on condition of its being reserved entirely for adults; and in having taken a wife out of a country in which social traditions were rich and ancient, he had done something towards qualifying his own house—so splendidly qualified in all strictly material respects—to be the scene of such an effort. A charming woman, accustomed only to the best in each country, as Lady Beauchemin said, what might she not achieve by being at home (to the elder generation) in an easy, early, inspiring, comprehensive way, on the evening in the week on which worldly engagements were least numerous? He laid this philosophy before Lady Barb, in pursuance of a theory that if she disliked New York on a short acquaintance, she could not fail to like it on a long one. Jackson Lemon believed in the New York mind,—not so much, indeed, in its literary, artistic, or political achievements, as in its general quickness and nascent adaptability. He clung to this belief, for it was a very important piece of material in the structure that he was attempting to rear. The New York mind would throw its glamour over Lady Barb if she would only give it a chance; for it was exceedingly bright, entertaining, and sympathetic. If she would only have a *salon,* where this charming organ might expand, and where she might inhale its fragrance in the most convenient and luxurious way, without, as it were, getting up from her chair; if she would only just try this graceful, good-natured experiment (which would make every one like *her* so much, too),—he was sure that all the wrinkles in the gilded scroll of his fate would be smoothed out. But Lady Barb did not rise at all to his conception, and had not the least curiosity about the New York mind. She thought it would be extremely disagreeable to have a lot of people tumbling in on Sunday evening without being invited; and altogether her husband's sketch of the Anglo-American saloon seemed to her to suggest familiarity, high-pitched talk (she had already made a remark to him about "screeching women"), and exaggerated laughter. She did not tell him—for this, somehow, it was not in her power to express, and, strangely enough, he never completely guessed it,—that she was singularly deficient in any natural, or indeed acquired, understanding of what a saloon might be. She had never seen one, and for the most part she never thought of things she had not seen. She had seen great dinners, and balls, and meets, and runs, and races; she had seen garden-parties, and a lot of people, mainly women (who, however, didn't screech), at dull, stuffy teas, and distinguished companies collected in splendid castles; but all this gave her no idea of a tradition of conversation, of a social agreement that its continuity, its accumulations from season to season, should not be lost. Conversation, in Lady Barb's experience, had never been continuous; in such a case it would surely have been a bore. It had been occasional and fragmentary, a trifle jerky, with allusions that were never explained; it had a dread of detail; it seldom pursued anything very far, or kept hold of it very long.

There was something else that she did not say to her husband in reference to his visions of hospitality, which was, that if she should open a saloon (she had taken up the joke as well, for Lady Barb was eminently good-natured), Mrs. Vanderdecken would straightway open another, and Mrs. Vanderdecken's would be the more successful of the two. This lady, for reasons that Lady Barb had not yet explored, was supposed to be the great personage in New York; there were legends of her husband's family having behind them a fabulous antiquity. When this was alluded to, it was spoken of as something incalculable, and lost in the dimness of time. Mrs. Vanderdecken was young, pretty, clever, incredibly pretentious (Lady Barb thought), and had a wonderfully artistic house. Ambition, also, was expressed in every rustle of her garments; and if she was the first person in America (this had an immense sound), it was plain that she intended to remain so. It was not till after she had been several months in New York that it came over Lady Barb that this brilliant native had flung down the glove; and when the idea presented itself, lighted up by an incident which I have no space to relate, she simply blushed a little (for Mrs. Vanderdecken), and held her tongue. She had not come to America to bandy words about precedence with such a woman as that. She had ceased to think about it much (of course one thought about it in England); but an instinct of self-preservation led her not to expose herself to occasions on which her claim might be tested. This, at bottom, had much to do with her having, very soon after the first flush of the honors paid her on her arrival, and which seemed to her rather grossly overdone, taken the line of scarcely going out. "They can't keep *that* up!" she had said to herself; and, in short, she would stay at home. She had a feeling that whenever she should go forth she would meet Mrs. Vanderdecken, who would withhold, or deny, or contest something,—poor Lady Barb could never imagine what. She did not try to, and gave little thought to all this; for she was not prone to confess to herself fears, especially fears from which terror was absent. But, as I have said, it abode within her as a presentiment, that if she should set up a drawing-room in the foreign style (it was curious, in New York, how they tried to be foreign), Mrs. Vanderdecken would be beforehand with her. The continuity of conversation, oh! that idea she would certainly have; there was no one so continuous as Mrs. Vanderdecken. Lady Barb, as I have related, did not give her husband the surprise of telling him of these thoughts, though she had given him some other surprises. He would have been very much astonished, and perhaps, after a bit, a little encouraged, at finding that she was liable to this particular form of irritation.

On the Sunday afternoon she was visible; and on one of these occasions, going into her drawing-room late, he found her entertaining two ladies and a gentleman. The gentleman was Sidney Feeder, and one of the ladies was Mrs. Vanderdecken, whose ostensible relations with Lady Barb were of the most cordial nature. If she intended to crush her (as two or three persons, not conspicuous for a narrow accuracy, gave out that she privately declared), Mrs. Vanderdecken wished at least to study the weak points of the invader, to penetrate herself with the character of the English girl. Lady Barb, indeed, appeared to have a mysterious fascination for the representative of the American patriciate. Mrs. Vanderdecken could not take her eyes off her victim; and whatever might be her estimate of her importance, she at least could not let her alone. "Why does she come to see me?" poor Lady Barb asked herself. "I am sure I don't want to see her; she has done enough for civility long ago." Mrs. Vanderdecken had her own reasons; and one of them was simply the pleasure of looking at the Doctor's wife, as she habitually called the daughter of the Cantervilles. She was not guilty of the folly of depreciating this lady's appearance, and professed an unbounded admiration for it, defending it on many occasions against superficial people, who said there were fifty women in New York that were handsomer. Whatever might have been Lady Barb's weak points, they were not the curve of her cheek and chin, the setting of her head on her throat, or the quietness of her deep eyes, which were as beautiful as if they had been blank, like those of antique busts. "The head is enchanting—perfectly enchanting," Mrs. Vanderdecken used to say irrelevantly, as if there were only one head in the place. She always used to ask about the Doctor; and that was another reason why she came. She brought up the Doctor at every turn; asked if he were often called up at night; found it the greatest of luxuries, in a word, to address Lady Barb as the wife of a medical man, more or less *au courant* of her husband's patients. The other lady, on this Sunday afternoon, was a certain little Mrs. Chew, who had the appearance of a small, but very expensive doll, and was always asking Lady Barb about England, which Mrs. Vanderdecken never did. The latter visitor conversed with Lady Barb on a purely American basis, with that continuity (on her own side) of which mention has already been made, while Mrs. Chew engaged Sidney Feeder on topics equally local. Lady Barb liked Sidney Feeder; she only hated his name, which was constantly in her ears during the half-hour the ladies sat with her, Mrs. Chew having the habit, which annoyed Lady Barb, of repeating perpetually the appellation of her interlocutor.

Lady Barb's relations with Mrs. Vanderdecken consisted mainly in wondering, while she talked, what she wanted of her, and in looking, with her sculptured eyes, at her visitor's clothes, in which there was always much to examine. "Oh, Dr. Feeder!" "Now, Dr. Feeder!" "Well, Dr. Feeder,"—these exclamations, on the lips of Mrs. Chew, were an undertone in Lady Barb's consciousness. When I say that she liked her husband's *confrère*, as he used to call himself, I mean that she smiled at him when he came, and gave him her hand, and asked him if he would have some tea. There was nothing nasty (as they said in London) in Lady Barb and she would have been incapable of inflicting a deliberate snub upon a man who had the air of standing up so squarely to any work that he might have in hand. But she had nothing to say to Sidney Feeder. He apparently had the art of making her shy, more shy than usual; for she was always a little so; she discouraged him, discouraged him completely. He was not a man who wanted drawing out, there was nothing of that in him, he was remarkably copious; but Lady Barb appeared unable to follow him, and half the time, evidently, did not know what he was saying. He tried to adapt his conversation to her needs; but when he spoke of the world, of what was going on in society, she was more at sea even than when he spoke of hospitals and laboratories, and the health of the city, and the progress of science. She appeared, indeed, after her first smile, when he came in, which was always charming, scarcely to see him, looking past him, and above him, and below him, and everywhere but at him, until he got up to go again, when she gave him another smile, as expressive of pleasure and of casual acquaintance as that with which she had greeted his entry; it seemed to imply that they had been having delightful talk for an hour. He wondered what the deuce Jackson Lemon could find interesting in such a woman, and he believed that his perverse, though gifted, colleague was not destined to feel that she illuminated his life. He pitied Jackson, he saw that Lady Barb, in New York, would neither assimilate nor be assimilated; and yet he was afraid to betray his incredulity, thinking it might be depressing to poor Lemon to show him how his marriage—now so dreadfully irrevocable—struck others. Sidney Feeder was a man of a strenuous conscience, and he did his duty overmuch by his old friend and his wife, from the simple fear that he should not do it enough. In order not to appear to neglect them, he called upon Lady Barb heroically, in spite of pressing engagements, week after week, enjoying his virtue himself as little as he made it fruitful for his hostess, who wondered at last what she had done to deserve these visitations. She spoke of them to her husband, who wondered also what poor Sidney had in his head, and yet was unable, of course, to hint to him that he need not think it necessary to come so often. Between Dr. Feeder's wish not to let Jackson see that his marriage had made a difference, and Jackson's hesitation to reveal to Sidney that his standard of friendship was too high, Lady Barb passed a good many of those numerous hours during which she asked herself if she had come to America for that. Very little had ever passed between her and her husband on the subject of Sidney Feeder; for an instinct told her that if they were ever to have scenes, she must choose the occasion well; and this odd person was not an occasion. Jackson had tacitly admitted that his friend Feeder was anything he chose to think him; he was not a man to be guilty, in a discussion, of the disloyalty of damning him with praise that was faint. If Lady Agatha had usually been with her sister, Dr. Feeder would have been better entertained; for the younger of the English visitors prided herself, after several months of New York, on understanding everything that was said, and catching every allusion, it mattered not from what lips it fell. But Lady Agatha was never at home; she had learned how to describe herself perfectly by the time she wrote to her mother that she was always "on the go." None of the innumerable victims of old-world tyranny who have fled to the United States as to a land of freedom, have ever offered more lavish incense to that goddess than this emancipated London *débutante*. She had enrolled herself in an amiable band which was known by the humorous name of "the Tearers," —a dozen young ladies of agreeable appearance, high spirits, and good wind, whose most general characteristic was that, when wanted, they were to be sought anywhere in the world but under the roof that was supposed to shelter them. They were never at home; and when Sidney Feeder, as sometimes happened, met Lady Agatha at other houses, she was in the hands of the irrepressible Longstraw. She had come back to her sister, but Mr. Longstraw had followed her to the door. As to passing it, he had received direct discouragement from her brother-in-law; but he could at least hang about and wait for her. It may be confided to the reader, at the risk of diminishing the effect of the only incident which in the course of this very level narrative may startle him, that he never had to wait very long.

When Jackson Lemon came in, his wife's visitors were on the point of leaving her; and he did not ask even Sidney Feeder to remain, for he had something particular to say to Lady Barb.

"I haven't asked you half what I wanted—I have been talking so much to Dr. Feeder," the dressy Mrs. Chew said, holding the hand of her hostess in one of her own, and toying with one of Lady Barb's ribbons with the other.

"I don't think I have anything to tell you; I think I have told people everything," Lady Barb answered, rather wearily.

"You haven't told *me* much!" Mrs. Vanderdecken said, smiling brightly.

"What could one tell you?—you know everything," Jackson Lemon interposed.

"Ah, no; there are some things that are great mysteries for me," the lady returned. "I hope you are coming to me on the 17th," she added, to Lady Barb.

"On the 17th? I think we are going somewhere."

"Do go to Mrs. Vanderdecken's," said Mrs. Chew; "you'll see the cream of the cream."

"Oh, gracious!" Mrs. Vanderdecken exclaimed.

"Well, I don't care; she will, won't she, Dr. Feeder?—the very pick of American society." Mrs. Chew stuck to her point.

"Well, I have no doubt Lady Barb will have a good time," said Sidney Feeder. "I'm afraid you miss the bran," he went on, with irrelevant jocosity, to Lady Barb. He always tried to be jocose, when other elements had failed.

"The bran?" asked Lady Barb, staring.

"Where you used to ride in the Park."

"My dear fellow, you speak as if it were the circus," Jackson Lemon said, smiling; "I haven't married a mountebank!"

"Well, they put some stuff on the road," Sidney Feeder explained, not holding much to his joke.

"You must miss a great many things," said Mrs. Chew, tenderly.

"I don't see what," Mrs. Vanderdecken remarked, "except the fogs and the Queen. New York is getting more and more like London. It's a pity; you ought to have known us thirty years ago."

"You are the queen, here," said Jackson Lemon; "but I don't know what you know about thirty years ago."

"Do you think she doesn't go back?—she goes back to the last century!" cried Mrs. Chew.

"I dare say I should have liked that," said Lady Barb; "but I can't imagine." And she looked at her husband—a look she often had—as if she vaguely wished him to do something.

He was not called upon, however, to take any violent steps, for Mrs. Chew presently said: "Well, Lady Barberina, good-by"; and Mrs. Vanderdecken smiled in silence at her hostess, and addressed a farewell, accompanied very audibly with his title, to her host; and Sidney Feeder made a joke about stepping on the trains of the ladies' dresses as he accompanied them to the door. Mrs. Chew had always a great deal to say at the last; she talked till she was in the street, and then she did not cease. But at the end of five minutes Jackson Lemon was alone with his wife; and then he told her a piece of news. He prefaced it, however, by an inquiry as he came back from the hall.

"Where is Agatha, my dear?"

"I haven't the least idea. In the streets somewhere, I suppose."

"I think you ought to know a little more."

"How can I know about things here? I have given her up; I can do nothing with her. I don't care what she does."

"She ought to go back to England," Jackson Lemon said, after a pause.

"She ought never to have come."

"It was not my proposal, God knows!" Jackson answered, rather sharply.

"Mamma could never know what it really is," said his wife.

"No, it has not been as yet what your mother supposed! Herman Longstraw wants to marry her. He has made me a formal proposal. I met him half an hour ago in Madison Avenue, and he asked me to come with him into the Columbia Club. There, in the billiard-room, which to-day is empty, he opened himself—thinking evidently that in laying the matter before me he was behaving with extraordinary propriety. He tells me he is dying of love, and that she is perfectly willing to go and live in Arizona."

"So she is," said Lady Barb. "And what did you tell him?"

"I told him that I was sure it would never do, and that at any rate I could have nothing to say to it. I told him explicitly, in short, what I had told him virtually before. I said that we should send Agatha straight back to England, and that if they had the courage they must themselves broach the question over there."

"When shall you send her back?" asked Lady Barb.

"Immediately; by the very first steamer."

"Alone, like an American girl?"

"Don't be rough, Barb," said Jackson Lemon. "I shall easily find some people; lots of people are sailing now."

"I must take her myself," Lady Barb declared in a moment. "I brought her out, and I must restore her to my mother's hands."

Jackson Lemon had expected this, and he believed he was prepared for it. But when it came he found his preparation was not complete; for he had no answer to make—none, at least, that seemed to him to go to the point. During these last weeks it had come over him, with a quiet, irresistible, unmerciful force, that Mrs. Dexter Freer had been right when she said to him, that Sunday afternoon in Jermyn Street, the summer before, that he would find it was not so simple to be an American. Such an identity was complicated, in just the measure that she had foretold, by the difficulty of domesticating one's wife. The difficulty was not dissipated by his having taken a high tone about it; it pinched him from morning till night, like a misfitting shoe. His high tone had given him courage when he took the great step; but he began to perceive that the highest tone in the world cannot change the nature of things. His ears tingled when he reflected that if the Dexter Freers, whom he had thought alike abject in their hopes and their fears, had been by ill-luck spending the winter in New York, they would have found his predicament as entertaining as they could desire. Drop by drop the conviction had entered his mind—the first drop had come in the form of a word from Lady Agatha—that if his wife should return to England she would never again cross the Atlantic to the west. That word from Lady Agatha had been the touch from the outside, at which, often, one's fears crystallize. What she would do, how she would resist,—this he was not yet prepared to tell himself; but he felt, every time he looked at her, that this beautiful woman whom he had adored was filled with a dumb, insuperable, ineradicable purpose. He knew that if she should plant herself, no power on earth would move her; and her blooming, antique beauty, and the general loftiness of her breeding, came to seem to him—rapidly—but the magnificent expression of a dense, patient, imperturbable obstinacy. She was not light, she was not supple, and after six months of marriage he had made up his mind that she was not clever; but nevertheless she would elude him. She had married him, she had come into his fortune and his consideration—for who was she, after all? Jackson Lemon was once so angry as to ask himself, reminding himself that in England Lady Claras and Lady Florences were as thick as blackberries—but she would have nothing to do, if she could help it, with his country. She had gone in to dinner first in every house in the place, but this had not satisfied her. It *had* been simple to be an American, in this sense, that no one else in New York had made any difficulties; the difficulties had sprung from her peculiar feelings, which were after all what he had married her for, thinking they would be a fine temperamental heritage for his brood. So they would, doubtless, in the coming years, after the brood should have appeared; but meanwhile they interfered with the best heritage of all—the nationality of his possible children. Lady Barb would do nothing violent; he was tolerably certain of that. She would not return to England without his consent; only, when she should return, it would be once for all. His only possible line, then, was not to take her back, —a position replete with difficulties, because, of course, he had, in a manner, given his word, while she had given no word at all, beyond the general promise she murmured at the altar. She had been general, but he had been specific; the settlements he had made were a part of that. His difficulties were such as he could not directly face. He must tack in approaching so uncertain a coast. He said to Lady Barb presently that it would be very inconvenient for him to leave New York at that moment: she must remember that their plans had been laid for a later departure. He could not think of letting her make the voyage without him, and, on the other hand, they must pack her sister off without delay. He would therefore make instant inquiry for a chaperon, and he relieved his irritation by expressing considerable disgust at Herman Longstraw.

Lady Barb did not trouble herself to denounce this gentleman; her manner was that of having for a long time expected the worst. She simply remarked dryly, after having listened to her husband for some minutes in silence: "I would as lief she should marry Dr. Feeder!"

The day after this, Jackson Lemon closeted himself for an hour with Lady Agatha, taking great pains to set forth to her the reasons why she should not marry her Californian. Jackson was kind, he was affectionate; he kissed her and put his arm round her waist, he reminded her that he and she were the best of friends, and that she had always been awfully nice to him; therefore he counted upon her. She would break her mother's heart, she would deserve her father's curse, and she would get him, Jackson, into a pickle from which no human power could ever disembroil him. Lady Agatha listened and cried, and returned his kiss very affectionately, and admitted that her father and mother would never consent to such a marriage; and when he told her that he had made arrangements for her to sail for Liverpool (with some charming people) the next day but one, she embraced him again and assured him that she could never thank him enough for all the trouble he had taken about her. He flattered himself that he had convinced, and in some degree comforted her, and reflected with complacency that even should his wife take it into her head, Barberina would never get ready to embark for her native land between a Monday and a Wednesday. The next morning Lady Agatha did not appear at breakfast; but as she usually rose very late, her absence excited no alarm. She had not rung her bell, and she was supposed still to be sleeping. But she had never yet slept later than mid-day; and as this hour approached her sister went to her room. Lady Barb then discovered that she had left the house at seven o'clock in the morning, and had gone to meet Herman Longstraw at a neighboring corner. A little note on the table explained it very succinctly, and put beyond the power of Jackson Lemon and his wife to doubt that by the time this news reached them their wayward sister had been united to the man of her preference as closely as the laws of the State of New York could bind her. Her little note set forth that as she knew she should never be permitted to marry him, she had determined to marry him without permission, and that directly after the ceremony, which would be of the simplest kind, they were to take a train for the Far West. Our history is concerned only with the remote consequences of this incident, which made, of course, a great deal of trouble for Jackson Lemon. He went to the Far West in pursuit of the fugitives, and overtook them in California; but he had not the audacity to propose to them to separate, as it was easy for him to see that Herman Longstraw was at least as well married as himself. Lady Agatha was already popular in the new States, where the history of her elopement, emblazoned in enormous capitals, was circulated in a thousand newspapers. This question of the newspapers had been for Jackson Lemon one of the most definite results of his sister-in-law's *coup de tête*. His first thought had been of the public prints, and his first exclamation a prayer that they should not get hold of the story. But they did get hold of it, and they treated the affair with their customary energy and eloquence. Lady Barb never saw them; but an affectionate friend of the family, travelling at that time in the United States, made a parcel of some of the leading journals, and sent them to Lord Canterville. This missive elicited from her ladyship a letter addressed to Jackson Lemon which shook the young man's position to the base. The phials of an unnamable vulgarity had been opened upon the house of Canterville, and his mother-in-law demanded that in compensation for the affronts and injuries that were being heaped upon her family, and bereaved and dishonored as she was, she should at least be allowed to look on the face of her other daughter. "I suppose you will not, for very pity, be deaf to such a prayer as that," said Lady Barb; and though shrinking from recording a second act of weakness on the part of a man who had such pretensions to be strong, I must relate that poor Jackson, who blushed dreadfully over the newspapers, and felt afresh, as he read them, the force of Mrs. Freer's terrible axiom,—poor Jackson paid a visit to the office of the Cunarders. He said to himself afterward that it was the newspapers that had done it; he could not bear to appear to be on their side; they made it so hard to deny that the country was vulgar, at a time when one was in such need of all one's arguments. Lady Barb, before sailing, definitely refused to mention any week or month as the date of their pre-arranged return to New York. Very many weeks and months have elapsed since then, and she gives no sign of coming back. She will never fix a date. She is much missed by Mrs. Vanderdecken, who still alludes to her—still says the line of the shoulders was superb; putting the statement, pensively, in the past tense. Lady Beauchemin and Lady Marmaduke are much disconcerted; the international project has not, in their view, received an impetus.

Jackson Lemon has a house in London, and he rides in the Park with his wife, who is as beautiful as the day, and a year ago presented him with a little girl, with features that Jackson already scans for the look of race,—whether in hope or fear, to-day, is more than my muse has revealed. He has occasional scenes with Lady Barb, during which the look of race is very visible in her own countenance; but they never terminate in a visit to the Cunarders. He is exceedingly restless, and is constantly crossing to the Continent; but he returns with a certain abruptness, for he cannot bear to meet the Dexter Freers, and they seem to pervade the more comfortable parts of Europe. He dodges them in every town. Sidney Feeder feels very badly about him; it is months since Jackson has sent him any "results." The excellent fellow goes very often, in a consolatory spirit, to see Mrs. Lemon; but he has not yet been able to answer her standing question: "Why that girl more than another?" Lady Agatha Longstraw and her husband arrived a year ago in England, and Mr. Longstraw's personality had immense success during the last London season. It is not exactly known what they live on, though it is perfectly known that he is looking for something to do. Meanwhile it is as good as known that Jackson Lemon supports them.

The Author of Beltraffio

The Author of Beltraffio

IN THE eighties and nineties James wrote a number of short stories and short novels about the life of artists and writers. *The Author of Beltraffio* (1884) is one of the earliest and finest narratives in this series, which includes *The Figure in the Carpet, The Lesson of the Master, The Death of the Lion, The Coxon Fund, The Middle Years, The Next Time, Greville Fane, The Real Thing* and *Broken Wings.* It is his own artistic idealism, the lessons he drew from his experience as a professional writer, and his complex and ironic sense of the artist's position in society that James dramatized in these stories. And their importance is not limited to their Jamesian reference; for complete understanding, it is necessary to grasp their significant relation to that entire section of modern literature in which the creative process and the creative personality are at once analyzed and celebrated.

The hero of some of these stories is a novelist who, in his literary if not personal traits, bears a distinct resemblance to Henry James himself. Such types as Hugh Vereker in *The Figure in the Carpet* and Dencombe in *The Middle Years* appear in no other role than that of the literary artist; their sole function is to exhibit the triumphs and passions, embarrassments and humiliations of the artist *qua* artist. Other stories, of a more mixed intention, recall the English literary world of the late nineteenth century, though none so concretely as *The Author of Beltraffio*—its hero, Mark Ambient, being a character said to be modelled on John Addington Symonds. For a long time, because of certain statements made by Edmund Gosse, it was thought that the original of Mark Ambient was Robert Louis Stevenson; but Professor F. O. Matthiessen, who had had access to James's unpublished notebooks, has recently established the identity of Symonds as the subject of the anecdote that James was told one day about the situation of an eminent author whose wife found his work objectionable—"immoral, pagan, hyperaesthetic." Such was the "air-blown grain" which produced the story of Mark Ambient—a figure interesting not so much for his personal qualities as for qualities richly evocative of the aesthetic movement in England at the time of Pater and Swinburne. This is what makes Mark Ambient perhaps the very best portrait in fiction of the English gentleman-aesthete of the late Victorian age.

The plot of the story is a piece of wonderful invention from beginning to end. The deathly struggle between the author of *Beltraffio* and his wife—the guardian-spirit of British respectability—for the possession of their beautiful child has that element of psychological horror which James knew so well how to manipulate. One of the typical motives of his fiction is the use of the innocence of children as the precipitant of the corrupt and the sinister. Mark Ambient's child is the little brother of Pansy in *The Portrait of a Lady*, and of Maisie in *What Maisie Knew*, and of Morgan Moreen in *The Pupil*, and of course of those two strange children in *The Turn of the Screw* who are really beyond everything.

PART I

Much as I wished to see him, I had kept my letter of introduction for three weeks in my pocket-book. I was nervous and timid about meeting him,—conscious of youth and ignorance, convinced that he was tormented by strangers, and especially by my country-people, and not exempt from the suspicion that he had the irritability as well as the brilliancy of genius. Moreover, the pleasure if it should occur (for I could scarcely believe it was near at hand), would be so great that I wished to think of it in advance, to feel that it was in my pocket, not to mix it with satisfactions more superficial and usual. In the little game of new sensations that I was playing with my ingenious mind, I wished to keep my visit to the author of *Beltraffio* as a trump card. It was three years after the publication of that fascinating work, which I had read over five times, and which now, with my riper judgment, I admire on the whole as much as ever. This will give you about the date of my first visit (of any duration) to England; for you will not have forgotten the commotion—I may even say the scandal—produced by Mark Ambient's masterpiece. It was the most complete presentation that had yet been made of the gospel of art; it was a kind of æsthetic war-cry. People had endeavored to sail nearer to "truth" in the cut of their sleeves and the shape of their sideboards; but there had not as yet been, among English novels, such an example of beauty of execution and genuineness of substance. Nothing had been done in that line from the point of view of art for art. This was my own point of view, I may mention, when I was twenty-five; whether it is altered now I won't take upon myself to say—especially as the discerning reader will be able to judge for himself. I had been in England, briefly, a twelvemonth before the time to which I began by alluding, and had learned then that Mr. Ambient was in distant lands—was making a considerable tour in the East: so there was nothing to do but to keep my letter till I should be in London again. It was of little use to me to hear that his wife had not left England, and, with her little boy, their only child, was spending the period of her husband's absence—a good many months—at a small place they had down in Surrey. They had a house in London which was let. All this I learned, and also that Mrs. Ambient was charming (my friend the American poet, from whom I had my introduction, had never seen her, his relations with the great man being only epistolary); but she was not, after all, though she had lived so near the rose, the author of *Beltraffio,* and I did not go down into Surrey to call on her. I went to the Continent, spent the following winter in Italy, and returned to London in May. My visit to Italy opened my eyes to a good many things, but to nothing more than the beauty of certain pages in the works of Mark Ambient. I had every one of his productions in my portmanteau,—they are not, as you know, very numerous, but he had preluded to *Beltraffio* by some exquisite things,—and I used to read them over in the evening at the inn. I used to say to myself that the man who drew those characters and wrote that style understood what he saw and knew what he was doing. This is my only reason for mentioning my winter in Italy. He had been there much in former years, and he was saturated with what painters call the "feeling" of that classic land. He expressed the charm of the old hill-cities of Tuscany, the look of certain lonely grassgrown places which, in the past, had echoed with life; he understood the great artists, he understood the spirit of the Renaissance, he understood everything. The scene of one of his earlier novels was laid in Rome, the scene of another in Florence, and I moved through these cities in company with the figures whom Mark Ambient had set so vividly upon their feet. This is why I was now so much happier even than before in the prospect of making his acquaintance.

At last, when I had dallied with this privilege long enough, I despatched to him the missive of the American poet. He had already gone out of town; he shrank from the rigor of the London "season," and it was his habit to migrate on the first of June. Moreover, I had heard that this year he was hard at work on a new book, into which some of his impressions of the East were to be wrought, so that he desired nothing so much as quiet days. This knowledge, however, did not prevent me—*cet âge est sans pitié*—from sending with my friend's letter a note of my own, in which I asked Mr. Ambient's leave to come down and see him for an hour or two, on a day to be designated by himself. My proposal was accompanied with a very frank expression of my sentiments, and the effect of the whole projectile was to elicit from the great man the kindest possible invitation. He would be delighted to see me, especially if I should turn up on the following Saturday and would remain till the Monday morning. We would take a walk over the Surrey commons, and I could tell him all about the other great man, the one in America. He indicated to me the best train, and it may be imagined whether on the Saturday afternoon I was punctual at Waterloo. He carried his benevolence to the point of coming to meet me at the little station at which I was to alight, and my heart beat very fast as I saw his handsome face, surmounted with a soft wide-awake, and which I knew by a photograph long since enshrined upon my mantel-shelf, scanning the carriage windows as the train rolled up. He recognized me as infallibly as I had recognized him; he appeared to know by instinct how a young American of an æsthetic turn would look when much divided between eagerness and modesty. He took me by the hand, and smiled at me, and said: "You must be—a—*you*, I think!" and asked if I should mind going on foot to his house, which would take but a few minutes. I remember thinking it a piece of extraordinary affability that he should give directions about the conveyance of my bag, and feeling altogether very happy and rosy, in fact quite transported, when he laid his hand on my shoulder as we came out of the station.

I surveyed him, askance, as we walked together; I had already—

I had indeed instantly—seen that he was a delightful creature. His face is so well known that I needn't describe it; he looked to me at once an English gentleman and a man of genius, and I thought that a happy combination. There was just a little of the Bohemian in his appearance; you would easily have guessed that he belonged to the guild of artists and men of letters. He was addicted to velvet jackets, to cigarettes, to loose shirt-collars, to looking a little dishevelled. His features, which were fine, but not perfectly regular, are fairly enough represented in his portraits; but no portrait that I have seen gives any idea of his expression. There were so many things in it, and they chased each other in and out of his face. I have seen people who were grave and gay in quick alternation; but Mark Ambient was grave and gay at one and the same moment. There were other strange oppositions and contradictions in his slightly faded and fatigued countenance. He seemed both young and old, both anxious and indifferent. He had evidently had an active past, which inspired one with curiosity, and yet it was impossible not to be more curious still about his future. He was just enough above middle height to be spoken of as tall, and rather lean and long in the flank. He had the friendliest, frankest manner possible, and yet I could see that he was shy. He was thirty-eight years old at the time *Beltraffio* was published. He asked me about his friend in America, about the length of my stay in England, about the last news in London and the people I had seen there; and I remember looking for the signs of genius in the very form of his questions, and thinking I found it. I liked his voice.

There was genius in his house, too, I thought, when we got there; there was imagination in the carpets and curtains, in the pictures and books, in the garden behind it, where certain old brown walls were muffled in creepers that appeared to me to have been copied from a masterpiece of one of the pre-Raphaelites. That was the way many things struck me at that time, in England; as if they were reproductions of something that existed primarily in art or literature. It was not the picture, the poem, the fictive page, that seemed to me a copy; these things were the originals, and the life of happy and distinguished people was fashioned in their image. Mark Ambient called his house a cottage, and I perceived afterwards that he was right; for if it had not been a cottage it must have been a villa, and a villa, in England at least, was not a place in which one could fancy him at home. But it was, to my vision, a cottage glorified and translated; it was a palace of art, on a slightly reduced scale,—it was an old English demesne. It nestled under a cluster of magnificent beeches, it had little creaking lattices that opened out of, or into, pendent mats of ivy, and gables, and old red tiles, as well as a general aspect of being painted in water-colors and inhabited by people whose lives would go on in chapters and volumes. The lawn seemed to me of extraordinary extent, the garden-walls of incalculable height, the whole air of the place delightfully still, private, proper to itself. "My wife must be somewhere about," Mark Ambient said, as we went in. "We shall find her perhaps; we have got about an hour before dinner. She may be in the garden. I will show you my little place."

We passed through the house, and into the grounds, as I should have called them, which extended into the rear. They covered but three or four acres, but, like the house, they were very old and crooked, and full of traces of long habitation, with inequalities of level and little steps—mossy and cracked were these—which connected the different parts with each other. The limits of the place, cleverly dissimulated, were muffled in the deepest verdure. They made, as I remember, a kind of curtain at the further end, in one of the folds of which, as it were, we presently perceived, from afar, a little group. "Ah, there she is!" said Mark Ambient; "and she has got the boy." He made this last remark in a slightly different tone from any in which he yet had spoken. I was not fully aware of it at the time, but it lingered in my ear and I afterwards understood it.

"Is it your son?" I inquired, feeling the question not to be brilliant.

"Yes, my only child. He's always in his mother's pocket. She coddles him too much." It came back to me afterwards, too—the manner in which he spoke these words. They were not petulant; they expressed rather a sudden coldness, a kind of mechanical submission. We went a few steps further, and then he stopped short and called the boy, beckoning to him repeatedly.

"Dolcino, come and see your daddy!" There was something in the way he stood still and waited that made me think he did it for a purpose. Mrs. Ambient had her arm around the child's waist, and he was leaning against her knee; but though he looked up at the sound of his father's voice, she gave no sign of releasing him. A lady, apparently a neighbor, was seated near her, and before them was a garden-table, on which a tea-service had been placed.

Mark Ambient called again, and Dolcino struggled in the maternal embrace, but he was too tightly held, and after two or three fruitless efforts he suddenly turned round and buried his head deep in his mother's lap. There was a certain awkwardness in the scene; I thought it rather odd that Mrs. Ambient should pay so little attention to her husband. But I would not for the world have betrayed my thought, and, to conceal it, I observed that it must be such a pleasant thing to have tea in the garden. "Ah, she won't let him come!" said Mark Ambient, with a sigh; and we went our way till we reached the two ladies. He mentioned my name to his wife, and I noticed that he addressed her as "My dear," very genially, without any trace of resentment at her detention of the child. The quickness of the transition made me vaguely ask myself whether he were henpecked,—a shocking conjecture, which I instantly dismissed. Mrs. Ambient was quite such a wife as I should have expected him to have; slim and fair, with a long neck and pretty eyes and an air of great refinement. She was a little cold, and a little shy; but she was very sweet, and she had a certain look of race, justified by my afterwards learning that she was "connected" with two or three great families. I have seen poets married to women of whom it was difficult to conceive that they should gratify the poetic fancy,—women with dull faces and glutinous minds, who were none the less, however, excellent wives. But there was no obvious incongruity in Mark Ambient's union. Mrs. Ambient, delicate and quiet, in a white dress, with her beautiful child at her side, was worthy of the author of a work so distinguished as *Beltraffio*. Round her neck she wore a black velvet ribbon, of which the long ends, tied behind, hung down her back, and to which, in front, was attached a miniature portrait of her little boy. Her smooth, shining hair was confined in a net. She gave me a very pleasant greeting, and Dolcino—I thought this little name of endearment delightful—took advantage of her getting up to slip away from her and go to his father, who said nothing to him, but simply seized him and held him high in his arms for a moment, kissing him several times.

I had lost no time in observing that the child, who was not more than seven years old, was extraordinarily beautiful. He had the face of an angel,—the eyes, the hair, the more than mortal bloom, the smile of innocence. There was something touching, almost alarming, in his beauty, which seemed to be composed of elements too fine and pure for the breath of this world. When I spoke to him, and he came and held out his hand and smiled at me, I felt a sudden pity for him, as if he had been an orphan, or a changeling, or stamped with some social stigma. It was impossible to be, in fact, more exempt from these misfortunes, and yet, as one kissed him, it was hard to keep from murmuring "Poor little devil!" though why one should have applied this epithet to a living cherub is more than I can say. Afterwards, indeed, I knew a little better; I simply discovered that he was too charming to live, wondering at the same time that his parents should not have perceived it, and should not be in proportionate grief and despair. For myself, I had no doubt of his evanescence, having already noticed that there is a kind of charm which is like a death-warrant.

The lady who had been sitting with Mrs. Ambient was a jolly, ruddy personage, dressed in velveteen and rather limp feathers, whom I guessed to be the vicar's wife,—our hostess did not introduce me,—and who immediately began to talk to Ambient about chrysanthemums. This was a safe subject, and yet there was a certain surprise for me in seeing the author of *Beltraffio* even in such superficial communion with the Church of England. His writings implied so much detachment from that institution, expressed a view of life so profane, as it were, so independent, and so little likely, in general, to be thought edifying, that I should have expected to find him an object of horror to vicars and their ladies—of horror repaid on his own part by good-natured but brilliant mockery. This proves how little I knew as yet of the English people and their extraordinary talent for keeping up their forms, as well as of some of the mysteries of Mark Ambient's hearth and home. I found afterwards that he had, in his study, between smiles and cigar-smoke, some wonderful comparisons for his clerical neighbors; but meanwhile the chrysanthemums were a source of harmony, for he and the vicaress were equally fond of them, and I was surprised at the knowledge they exhibited of this interesting plant. The lady's visit, however, had presumably already been long, and she presently got up, saying she must go, and kissed Mrs. Ambient. Mark started to walk with her to the gate of the grounds, holding Dolcino by the hand.

"Stay with me, my darling," Mrs. Ambient said to the boy, who was wandering away with his father.

Mark Ambient paid no attention to the summons, but Dolcino turned round and looked with eyes of shy entreaty at his mother. "Can't I go with papa?"

"Not when I ask you to stay with me."

"But please don't ask me, mamma," said the child, in his little clear, new voice.

"I must ask you when I want you. Come to me, my darling." And Mrs. Ambient, who had seated herself again, held out her long, slender hands.

Her husband stopped, with his back turned to her, but without releasing the child. He was still talking to the vicaress, but this good lady, I think, had lost the thread of her attention. She looked at Mrs. Ambient and at Dolcino, and then she looked at me, smiling very hard, in an extremely fixed, cheerful manner.

"Papa," said the child, "mamma wants me not to go with you."

"He's very tired—he has run about all day. He ought to be quiet till he goes to bed. Otherwise he won't sleep." These declarations fell successively and gravely from Mrs. Ambient's lips.

Her husband, still without turning round, bent over the boy and looked at him in silence. The vicaress gave a genial, irrelevant laugh, and observed that he was a precious little pet. "Let him choose," said Mark Ambient. "My dear little boy, will you go with me or will you stay with your mother?"

"Oh, it's a shame!" cried the vicar's lady, with increased hilarity.

"Papa, I don't think I can choose," the child answered, making his voice very low and confidential. "But I have been a great deal with mamma to-day," he added in a moment.

"And very little with papa! My dear fellow, I think you have chosen!" And Mark Ambient walked off with his son, accompanied by re-echoing but inarticulate comments from my fellow-visitor.

His wife had seated herself again, and her fixed eyes, bent upon the ground, expressed for a few moments so much mute agitation that I felt as if almost any remark from my own lips would be a false note. But Mrs. Ambient quickly recovered herself, and said to me civilly enough that she hoped I didn't mind having had to walk from the station. I reassured her on this point, and she went on, "We have got a thing that might have gone for you, but my husband wouldn't order it."

"That gave me the pleasure of a walk with him," I rejoined.

She was silent a minute, and then she said, "I believe the Americans walk very little."

"Yes, we always run," I answered laughingly.

She looked at me seriously, and I began to perceive a certain coldness in her pretty eyes. "I suppose your distances are so great."

"Yes; but we break our marches! I can't tell you what a pleasure it is for me to find myself here," I added. "I have the greatest admiration for Mr. Ambient."

"He will like that. He likes being admired."

"He must have a very happy life, then. He has many worshippers."

"Oh, yes, I have seen some of them," said Mrs. Ambient, looking away, very far from me, rather as if such a vision were before her at the moment. Something in her tone seemed to indicate that the vision was scarcely edifying, and I guessed very quickly that she was not in sympathy with the author of *Beltraffio*. I thought the fact strange, but, somehow, in the glow of my own enthusiasm, I didn't think it important; it only made me wish to be rather explicit about that enthusiasm.

"For me, you know," I remarked, "he is quite the greatest of living writers."

"Of course I can't judge. Of course he's very clever," said Mrs. Ambient, smiling a little.

"He's magnificent, Mrs. Ambient! There are pages in each of his books that have a perfection that classes them with the greatest things. Therefore, for me to see him in this familiar way,—in his habit as he lives,—and to find, apparently, the man as delightful as the artist, I can't tell you how much too good to be true it seems, and how great a privilege I think it." I knew that I was gushing, but I couldn't help it, and what I said was a good deal less than what I felt. I was by no means sure that I should dare to say even so much as this to Ambient himself, and there was a kind of rapture in speaking it out to his wife which was not affected by the fact that, as a wife, she appeared peculiar. She listened to me with her face grave again, and with her lips a little compressed, as if there were no doubt, of course, that her husband was remarkable, but at the same time she had heard all this before and couldn't be expected to be particularly interested in it. There was even in her manner an intimation that I was rather young, and that people usually got over that sort of thing. "I assure you that for me this is a red-letter day," I added.

She made no response, until after a pause, looking round her, she said abruptly, though gently, "We are very much afraid about the fruit this year."

My eyes wandered to the mossy, mottled, garden walls, where plum-trees and pear-trees, flattened and fastened upon the rusty bricks, looked like crucified figures with many arms. "Doesn't it promise well?" I inquired.

"No, the trees look very dull. We had such late frosts."

Then there was another pause. Mrs. Ambient kept her eyes fixed on the opposite end of the grounds, as if she were watching for her husband's return with the child. "Is Mr. Ambient fond of gardening?" it occurred to me to inquire, irresistibly impelled as I felt myself, moreover, to bring the conversation constantly back to him.

"He's very fond of plums," said his wife.

"Ah, well then, I hope your crop will be better than you fear. It's a lovely old place," I continued. "The whole character of it is that of certain places that he describes. Your house is like one of his pictures."

"It's a pleasant little place. There are hundreds like it."

"Oh, it has got his tone," I said, laughing, and insisting on my point the more that Mrs. Ambient appeared to see in my appreciation of her simple establishment a sign of limited experience.

It was evident that I insisted too much. "His tone?" she repeated, with a quick look at me, and a slightly heightened color.

"Surely he has a tone, Mrs. Ambient."

"Oh, yes, he has indeed! But I don't in the least consider that I am living in one of his books; I shouldn't care for that, at all," she went on, with a smile which had in some degree the effect of converting her slightly sharp protest into a joke deficient in point. "I am afraid I am not very literary," said Mrs. Ambient. "And I am not artistic."

"I am very sure you are not ignorant, not stupid," I ventured to reply, with the accompaniment of feeling immediately afterwards that I had been both familiar and patronizing. My only consolation was in the reflection that it was she, and not I who had begun it. She had brought her idiosyncrasies into the discussion.

"Well, whatever I am, I am very different from my husband. If you like him, you won't like me. You needn't say anything. Your liking me isn't in the least necessary!"

"Don't defy me!" I exclaimed.

She looked as if she had not heard me, which was the best thing she could do; and we sat some time without further speech. Mrs. Ambient had evidently the enviable English quality of being able to be silent without being restless. But at last she spoke; she asked me if there seemed to be many people in town. I gave her what satisfaction I could on this point, and we talked a little about London and of some pictures it presented at that time of the year. At the end of this I came back, irrepressibly, to Mark Ambient.

"Doesn't he like to be there now? I suppose he doesn't find the proper quiet for his work. I should think his things had been written, for the most part, in a very still place. They suggest a great stillness, following on a kind of tumult. Don't you think so? I suppose London is a tremendous place to collect impressions, but a refuge like this, in the country, must be much better for working them up. Does he get many of his impressions in London, do you think?" I proceeded from point to point in this malign inquiry, simply because my hostess, who probably thought me a very pushing and talkative young man, gave me time; for when I paused—I have not represented my pauses—she simply continued to let her eyes wander, and, with her long fair fingers, played with the medallion on her neck. When I stopped altogether, however, she was obliged to say something, and what she said was that she had not the least idea where her husband got his impressions. This made me think her, for a moment, positively disagreeable; delicate and proper and rather aristocratically dry as she sat there. But I must either have lost the impression a moment later, or been goaded by it to further aggression, for I remember asking her whether Mr. Ambient were in a good vein of work, and when we might look for the appearance of the book on which he was engaged. I have every reason now to know that she thought me an odious person.

She gave a strange, small laugh as she said, "I am afraid you think I know a great deal more about my husband's work than I do. I haven't the least idea what he is doing," she added presently, in a slightly different, that is a more explanatory, tone, as if she recognized in some degree the enormity of her confession. "I don't read what he writes!"

She did not succeed (and would not, even had she tried much harder) in making it seem to me anything less than monstrous. I stared at her, and I think I blushed. "Don't you admire his genius? Don't you admire *Beltraffio*?"

She hesitated a moment, and I wondered what she could possibly say. She did not speak—I could see—the first words that rose to her lips; she repeated what she had said a few minutes before. "Oh, of course he's very clever!" And with this she got up; her husband and little boy had reappeared. Mrs. Ambient left me and went to meet them; she stopped and had a few words with her husband, which I did not hear, and which ended in her taking the child by the hand and returning to the house with him. Her husband joined me in a moment, looking, I thought, the least bit conscious and constrained, and said that if I would come in with him he would show me my room. In looking back upon these first moments of my visit to him, I find it important to avoid the error of appearing to have understood his situation from the first, and to have seen in him the signs of things which I learnt only afterwards. This later knowledge throws a backward light, and makes me forget that at least on the occasion of which I am speaking now (I mean that first afternoon), Mark Ambient struck me as a fortunate man. Allowing for this, I think he was rather silent and irresponsive as we walked back to the house, though I remember well the answer he made to a remark of mine in relation to his child.

"That's an extraordinary little boy of yours," I said. "I have never seen such a child."

"Why do you call him extraordinary?"

"He's so beautiful, so fascinating. He's like a little work of art."

He turned quickly, grasping my arm an instant. "Oh, don't call him that, or you'll—you'll—!" And in his hesitation he broke off suddenly, laughing at my surprise. But immediately afterwards he added, "You will make his little future very difficult."

I declared that I wouldn't for the world take any liberties with his little future—it seemed to me to hang by threads of such delicacy. I should only be highly interested in watching it.

"You Americans are very sharp," said Ambient. "You notice more things than we do."

"Ah, if you want visitors who are not struck with you, you shouldn't ask me down here!"

He showed me my room, a little bower of chintz, with open windows where the light was green, and before he left me he said irrelevantly, "As for my little boy, you know, we shall probably kill him between us, before we have done with him!" And he made this assertion as if he really believed it, without any appearance of jest, with his fine, near-sighted, expressive eyes looking straight into mine.

"Do you mean by spoiling him?"

"No; by fighting for him!"

"You had better give him to me to keep for you," I said. "Let me remove the apple of discord."

I laughed, of course, but he had the air of being perfectly serious. "It would be quite the best thing we could do. I should be quite ready to do it."

"I am greatly obliged to you for your confidence."

Mark Ambient lingered there, with his hands in his pockets. I felt, within a few moments, as if I had, morally speaking, taken several steps nearer to him. He looked weary, just as he faced me then, looked preoccupied, and as if there were something one might do for him. I was terribly conscious of the limits of my own ability, but I wondered what such a service might be, feeling at bottom, however, that the only thing I could do for him was to like him. I suppose he guessed this, and was grateful for what was in my mind; for he went on presently, "I haven't the advantage of being an American. But I also notice a little, and I have an idea that—a—" here he smiled and laid his hand on my shoulder, "that even apart from your nationality, you are not destitute of intelligence! I have only known you half an hour, but—a—" And here he hesitated again. "You are very young, after all."

"But you may treat me as if I could understand you!" I said; and before he left me to dress for dinner he had virtually given me a promise that he would.

When I went down into the drawing-room—I was very punctual

—I found that neither my hostess nor my host had appeared. A lady rose from a sofa, however, and inclined her head as I rather surprisedly gazed at her. "I dare say you don't know me," she said, with the modern laugh. "I am Mark Ambient's sister." Whereupon I shook hands with her, saluting her very low. Her laugh was modern—by which I mean that it consisted of the vocal agitation which, between people who meet in drawing-rooms, serves as the solvent of social mysteries, the medium of transitions; but her appearance was —what shall I call it?—mediæval. She was pale and angular, with a long, thin face, inhabited by sad, dark eyes, and black hair intertwined with golden fillets and curious chains. She wore a faded velvet robe, which clung to her when she moved, fashioned, as to the neck and sleeves, like the garments of old Venetians and Florentines. She looked pictorial and melancholy, and was so perfect an image of a type which I, in my ignorance, supposed to be extinct, that while she rose before me I was almost as much startled as if I had seen a ghost. I afterwards perceived that Miss Ambient was not incapable of deriving pleasure from the effect she produced, and I think this sentiment had something to do with her sinking again into her seat, with her long, lean, but not ungraceful arms locked together in an archaic manner on her knees, and her mournful eyes addressing themselves to me with an intentness which was a menace of what they were destined subsequently to inflict upon me. She was a singular, self-conscious, artificial creature, and I never, subsequently, more than half penetrated her motives and mysteries. Of one thing I am sure, however: that they were considerably less extraordinary than her appearance announced. Miss Ambient was a restless, disappointed, imaginative spinster, consumed with the love of Michael-Angelesque attitudes and mystical robes; but I am pretty sure she had not in her nature those depths of unutterable thought which, when you first knew her, seemed to look out from her eyes and to prompt her complicated gestures. Those features, in especial, had a misleading eloquence; they rested upon you with a far-off dimness, an air of obstructed sympathy, which was certainly not always a key to the spirit of their owner; and I suspect that a young lady could not really have been so dejected and disillusioned as Miss Ambient looked, without having committed a crime for which she was consumed with remorse, or parted with a hope which she could not sanely have entertained.

She had, I believe, the usual allowance of vulgar impulses: she wished to be looked at, she wished to be married, she wished to be thought original.

It costs me something to speak in this irreverent manner of Mark Ambient's sister, but I shall have still more disagreeable things to say before I have finished my little anecdote, and moreover,—I confess it,—I owe the young lady a sort of grudge. Putting aside the curious cast of her face, she had no natural aptitude for an artistic development,—she had little real intelligence. But her affectations rubbed off on her brother's renown, and as there were plenty of people who disapproved of him totally, they could easily point to his sister as a person formed by his influence. It was quite possible to regard her as a warning, and she had done him but little good with the world at large. He was the original, and she was the inevitable imitation. I think he was scarcely aware of the impression she produced, beyond having a general idea that she made up very well as a Rossetti; he was used to her, and he was sorry for her,—wishing she would marry and observing that she didn't. Doubtless I take her too seriously, for she did me no harm, though I am bound to add that I feel I can only half account for her. She was not so mystical as she looked, but she was a strange, indirect, uncomfortable, embarrassing woman. My story will give the reader at best so very small a knot to untie that I need not hope to excite his curiosity by delaying to remark that Mrs. Ambient hated her sister-in-law. This I only found out afterwards, when I found out some other things. But I mention it at once, for I shall perhaps not seem to count too much on having enlisted the imagination of the reader if I say that he will already have guessed it. Mrs. Ambient was a person of conscience, and she endeavored to behave properly to her kinswoman, who spent a month with her twice a year; but it required no great insight to discover that the two ladies were made of a very different paste, and that the usual feminine hypocrisies must have cost them, on either side, much more than the usual effort. Mrs. Ambient, smooth-haired, thin-lipped, perpetually fresh, must have regarded her crumpled and dishevelled visitor as a very stale joke; she herself was not a Rossetti, but a Gainsborough or a Lawrence, and she had in her appearance no elements more romantic than a cold, ladylike candor, and a well-starched muslin dress.

It was in a garment, and with an expression of this kind, that she made her entrance, after I had exchanged a few words with Miss Ambient. Her husband presently followed her, and there being no other company we went to dinner. The impression I received from that repast is present to me still. There were elements of oddity in my companions, but they were vague and latent, and didn't interfere with my delight. It came mainly, of course, from Ambient's talk, which was the most brilliant and interesting I had ever heard. I know not whether he laid himself out to dazzle a rather juvenile pilgrim from over the sea; but it matters little, for it was very easy for him to shine. He was almost better as a talker than as a writer; that is, if the extraordinary finish of his written prose be really, as some people have maintained, a fault. There was such a kindness in him, however, that I have no doubt it gave him ideas to see me sit open-mouthed, as I suppose I did. Not so the two ladies, who not only were very nearly dumb from beginning to the end of the meal, but who had not the air of being struck with such an exhibition of wit and knowledge. Mrs. Ambient, placid and detached, met neither my eye nor her husband's; she attended to her dinner, watched the servants, arranged the puckers in her dress, exchanged at wide intervals a remark with her sister-in-law, and while she slowly rubbed her white hands between the courses, looked out of the window at the first signs of twilight—the long June day allowing us to dine without candles. Miss Ambient appeared to give little direct heed to her brother's discourse; but on the other hand she was much engaged in watching its effect upon me. Her lustreless pupils continued to attach themselves to my countenance, and it was only her air of belonging to another century that kept them from being importunate. She seemed to look at me across the ages, and the interval of time diminished the vividness of the performance. It was as if she knew in a general way that her brother must be talking very well, but she herself was so rich in ideas that she had no need to pick them up, and was at liberty to see what would become of a young American when subjected to a high aesthetic temperature.

The temperature was aesthetic, certainly, but it was less so than I could have desired, for I was unsuccessful in certain little attempts to make Mark Ambient talk about himself. I tried to put him on the ground of his own writings, but he slipped through my fingers every time and shifted the saddle to one of his contemporaries. He talked about Balzac and Browning, and what was being done in foreign countries, and about his recent tour in the East, and the extraordinary forms of life that one saw in that part of the world. I perceived that he had reasons for not wishing to descant upon literature, and suffered him without protest to deliver himself on certain social topics, which he treated with extraordinary humor and with constant revelations of that power of ironical portraiture of which his books are full. He had a great deal to say about London, as London appears to the observer who doesn't fear the accusation of cynicism, during the high-pressure time—from April to July—of its peculiarities. He flashed his faculty of making the fanciful real and the real fanciful over the perfunctory pleasures and desperate exertions of so many of his compatriots, among whom there were evidently not a few types for which he had little love. London bored him, and he made capital sport of it; his only allusion, that I can remember, to his own work was his saying that he meant some day to write an immense grotesque epic of London society. Miss Ambient's perpetual gaze seemed to say to me: "Do you perceive how artistic we are? Frankly now, is it possible to be more artistic than this? You surely won't deny that we are remarkable." I was irritated by her use of the plural pronoun, for she had no right to pair herself with her brother; and moreover, of course, I could not see my way to include Mrs. Ambient. But there was no doubt that, for that matter, they were all remarkable, and, with all allowances, I had never heard anything so artistic. Mark Ambient's conversation seemed to play over the whole field of knowledge and taste, and to flood it with light and color.

After the ladies had left us he took me into his study to smoke, and here I led him on to talk freely enough about himself. I was bent upon proving to him that I was worthy to listen to him, upon repaying him for what he had said to me before dinner, by showing him how perfectly I understood. He liked to talk; he liked to defend his ideas (not that I attacked them); he liked a little perhaps—it was a pardonable weakness—to astonish the youthful mind and to feel its admiration and sympathy. I confess that my own youthful mind was considerably astonished at some of his speeches; he startled me and he made me wince. He could not help forgetting, or rather he couldn't know, how little personal contact I had had with the school in which he was master; and he promoted me at a jump, as it were, to the study of its innermost mysteries. My trepidations, however, were delightful; they were just what I had hoped for, and their only fault was that they passed away too quickly; for I found that, as regards most things, I very soon seized Mark Ambient's point of view. It was the point of view of the artist to whom every manifestation of human energy was a thrilling spectacle, and who felt forever the desire to resolve his experience of life into a literary form. On this matter of the passion for form,—the attempt at perfection, the quest for which was to his mind the real search for the holy grail,—he said the most interesting, the most inspiring things. He mixed with them a thousand illustrations from his own life, from other lives that he had known, from history and fiction, and above all from the annals of the time that was dear to him beyond all periods,—the Italian *cinque-cento*. I saw that in his books he had only said half of his thought, and what he had kept back—from motives that I deplored when I learnt them later—was the richer part. It was his fortune to shock a great many people, but there was not a grain of bravado in his pages (I have always maintained it, though often contradicted), and at bottom the poor fellow, an artist to his finger-tips, and regarding a failure of completeness as a crime, had an extreme dread of scandal. There are people who regret that having gone so far he did not go further; but I regret nothing (putting aside two or three of the motives I just mentioned), for he arrived at perfection, and I don't see how you can go beyond that. The hours I spent in his study—this first one and the few that followed it; they were not, after all, so numerous—seem to glow, as I look back on them, with a tone which is partly that of the brown old room, rich, under the shaded candlelight where we sat and smoked, with the dusky, delicate bindings of valuable books; partly that of his voice, of which I still catch the echo, charged with the images that came at his command. When we went back to the drawing-room we found Miss Ambient alone in possession of it; and she informed us that her sister-in-law had a quarter of an hour before been called by the nurse to see Dolcino, who appeared to be a little feverish.

"Feverish! how in the world does he come to be feverish?" Ambient asked. "He was perfectly well this afternoon."

"Beatrice says you walked him about too much—you almost killed him."

"Beatrice must be very happy—she has an opportunity to triumph!" Mark Ambient said, with a laugh of which the bitterness was just perceptible.

"Surely not if the child is ill," I ventured to remark, by way of pleading for Mrs. Ambient.

"My dear fellow, you are not married—you don't know the nature of wives!" my host exclaimed.

"Possibly not; but I know the nature of mothers."

"Beatrice is perfect as a mother," said Miss Ambient, with a tremendous sigh and her fingers interlaced on her embroidered knees.

"I shall go up and see the child," her brother went on. "Do you suppose he's asleep?"

"Beatrice won't let you see him, Mark," said the young lady, looking at me, though she addressed our companion.

"Do you call that being perfect as a mother?" Ambient inquired.

"Yes, from her point of view."

"Damn her point of view!" cried the author of *Beltraffio.* And he left the room; after which we heard him ascend the stairs.

I sat there for some ten minutes with Miss Ambient, and we naturally had some conversation, which was begun, I think, by my asking her what the point of view of her sister-in-law could be.

"Oh, it's so very odd," she said. "But we are so very odd, altogether. Don't you find us so? We have lived so much abroad. Have you people like us in America?"

"You are not all alike, surely; so that I don't think I understand your question. We have no one like your brother—I may go so far as that."

"You have probably more persons like his wife," said Miss Ambient, smiling.

"I can tell you that better when you have told me about her point of view."

"Oh, yes—oh, yes. Well, she doesn't like his ideas. She doesn't like them for the child. She thinks them undesirable."

Being quite fresh from the contemplation of some of Mark Ambient's *arcana,* I was particularly in a position to appreciate this announcement. But the effect of it was to make me, after staring a moment, burst into laughter, which I instantly checked when I remembered that there was a sick child above.

"What has that infant to do with ideas?" I asked. "Surely, he can't tell one from another. Has he read his father's novels?"

"He's very precocious and very sensitive, and his mother thinks she can't begin to guard him too early." Miss Ambient's head drooped a little to one side, and her eyes fixed themselves on futurity. Then suddenly there was a strange alteration in her face; she gave a smile that was more joyless than her gravity—a conscious, insincere smile, and added, "When one has children, it's a great responsibility—what one writes."

"Children are terrible critics," I answered. "I am rather glad I haven't got any."

"Do you also write then? And in the same style as my brother? And do you like that style? And do people appreciate it in America? I don't write, but I think I feel." To these and various other inquiries and remarks the young lady treated me, till we heard her brother's step in the hall again, and Mark Ambient reappeared. He looked flushed and serious, and I supposed that he had seen something to alarm him in the condition of his child. His sister apparently had another idea; she gazed at him a moment as if he were a burning ship on the horizon, and simply murmured, "Poor old Mark!"

"I hope you are not anxious," I said.

"No, but I'm disappointed. She won't let me in. She has locked the door, and I'm afraid to make a noise." I suppose there might have been something ridiculous in a confession of this kind, but I liked my new friend so much that for me it didn't detract from his dignity. "She tells me—from behind the door—that she will let me know if he is worse."

"It's very good of her," said Miss Ambient.

I had exchanged a glance with Mark in which it is possible that he read that my pity for him was untinged with contempt, though I know not why he should have cared; and as, presently, his sister got up and took her bedroom candlestick, he proposed that we should go back to his study. We sat there till after midnight; he put himself into his slippers, into an old velvet jacket, lighted an ancient pipe, and talked considerably less than he had done before. There were longish pauses in our communion, but they only made me feel that we had advanced in intimacy. They helped me, too, to understand my friend's personal situation, and to perceive that it was by no means the happiest possible. When his face was quiet, it was vaguely troubled; it seemed to me to show that for him, too, life was a struggle, as it has been for many another man of genius. At last I prepared to leave him, and then, to my ineffable joy, he gave me some of the sheets of his forthcoming book,—it was not finished, but he had indulged in the luxury, so dear to writers of deliberation, of having it "set up," from chapter to chapter, as he advanced,—he gave me, I say, the early pages, the *prémices,* as the French have it, of this new fruit of his imagination, to take to my room and look over at my leisure. I was just quitting him when the door of his study was noiselessly pushed open, and Mrs. Ambient stood before us. She looked at us a moment, with her candle in her hand, and then she said to her husband that as she supposed he had not gone to bed, she had come down to tell him that Dolcino was more quiet and would probably be better in the morning. Mark Ambient made no reply; he simply slipped past her in the doorway, as if he were afraid she would seize him in his passage, and bounded upstairs, to judge for himself of his child's condition. Mrs. Ambient looked slightly discomfited, and for a moment I thought she was going to give chase to her husband. But she resigned herself, with a sigh, while her eyes wandered over the lamp-lit room, where various books, at which I had been looking, were pulled out of their places on the shelves, and the fumes of tobacco seemed to hang in mid-air. I bade her good-night, and then, without intention, by a kind of fatality, the perversity which had already made me insist unduly on talking with her about her husband's achievements, I alluded to the precious proof-sheets with which Ambient had intrusted me and which I was nursing there under my arm. "It is the opening chapters of his new book," I said. "Fancy my satisfaction at being allowed to carry them to my room!"

She turned away, leaving me to take my candlestick from the table in the hall; but before we separated, thinking it apparently a good occasion to let me know once for all—since I was beginning, it would seem, to be quite "thick" with my host—that there was no fitness in my appealing to her for sympathy in such a case; before we separated, I say, she remarked to me with her quick, round, well-bred utterance, "I dare say you attribute to me ideas that I haven't got. I don't take that sort of interest in my husband's proof-sheets. I consider his writings most objectionable!"

PART II

I HAD some curious conversation the next morning with Miss Ambient, whom I found strolling in the garden before breakfast. The whole place looked as fresh and trim, amid the twitter of the birds, as if, an hour before, the housemaids had been turned into it with their dustpans and feather-brushes. I almost hesitated to light a cigarette, and was doubly startled when, in the act of doing so, I suddenly perceived the sister of my host, who had, in any case, something of the oddity of an apparition, standing before me. She might have been posing for her photograph. Her sad-colored robe arranged itself in serpentine folds at her feet; her hands locked themselves listlessly together in front; and her chin rested upon a cinquecento ruff. The first thing I did, after bidding her good-morning, was to ask her for news of her little nephew,—to express the hope that she had heard he was better. She was able to gratify this hope, and spoke as if we might expect to see him during the day. We walked through the shrubberies together, and she gave me a great deal of information about her brother's ménage, which offered me an opportunity to mention to her that his wife had told me, the night before, that she thought his productions objectionable.

"She doesn't usually come out with that so soon!" Miss Ambient exclaimed, in answer to this piece of gossip.

"Poor lady, she saw that I am a fanatic."

"Yes, she won't like you for that. But you mustn't mind, if the rest of us like you! Beatrice thinks a work of art ought to have a 'purpose.' But she's a charming woman—don't you think her charming? —she's such a type of the lady."

"She's very beautiful," I answered; while I reflected that though it was true, apparently, that Mark Ambient was mis-mated, it was also perceptible that his sister was perfidious. She told me that her brother and his wife had no other difference but this one, that she thought his writings immoral and his influence pernicious. It was a fixed idea; she was afraid of these things for the child. I answered that it was not a trifle—a woman's regarding her husband's mind as a well of corruption and she looked quite struck with the novelty of my remark. "But there hasn't been any of the sort of trouble that there so often is among married people," she said. "I suppose you can judge for yourself that Beatrice isn't at all—well, whatever they call it when a woman misbehaves herself. And Mark doesn't make love to other people, either. I assure you he doesn't! All the same, of course, from her point of view, you know, she has a dread of my brother's influence on the child—on the formation of his character, of his principles. It is as if it were a subtle poison, or a contagion, or something that would rub off on Dolcino when his father kisses him or holds him on his knee. If she could, she would prevent Mark from ever touching him. Every one knows it; visitors see it for themselves; so there is no harm in my telling you. Isn't it excessively odd? It comes from Beatrice's being so religious, and so tremendously moral, and all that. And then, of course, we mustn't forget," my companion added, unexpectedly, "that some of Mark's ideas are—well, really—rather queer!"

I reflected, as we went into the house, where we found Ambient unfolding the *Observer* at the breakfast-table, that none of them were probably quite so queer as his sister. Mrs. Ambient did not appear at breakfast, being rather tired with her ministrations, during the night, to Dolcino. Her husband mentioned, however, that she was hoping to go to church. I afterwards learned that she did go, but I may as well announce without delay that he and I did not accompany her. It was while the church-bell was murmuring in the distance that the author of *Beltraffio* led me forth for the ramble he had spoken of in his note. I will not attempt to say where we went, or to describe what we saw. We kept to the fields and copses and commons, and breathed the same sweet air as the nibbling donkeys and the browsing sheep, whose woolliness seemed to me, in those early days of my acquaintance with English objects, but a part of the general texture of the small, dense landscape, which looked as if the harvest were gathered by the shears. Everything was full of expression for Mark Ambient's visitor,—from the big, bandy-legged geese, whose whiteness was a "note," amid all the tones of green, as they wandered beside a neat little oval pool, the foreground of a thatched and whitewashed inn, with a grassy approach and a pictorial sign,—from these humble wayside animals to the crests of high woods which let a gable or a pinnacle peep here and there, and looked, even at a distance, like trees of good company, conscious of an individual profile. I admired the hedgerows. I plucked the faint-hued heather, and I was forever stopping to say how charming I thought the thread-like footpaths across the fields, which wandered, in a diagonal of finer grain, from one smooth stile to another. Mark Ambient was abundantly good-natured, and was as much entertained with my observations as I was with the literary allusions of the landscape. We sat and smoked upon stiles, broaching paradoxes in the decent English air; we took short cuts across a park or two, where the bracken was deep and my companion nodded to the old woman at the gate; we skirted rank covers, which rustled here and there as we passed, and we stretched ourselves at last on a heathery hillside, where, if the sun was not too hot, neither was the earth too cold, and where the country lay beneath us in a rich blue mist. Of course I had already told Ambient what I thought of his new novel, having the previous night read every word of the opening chapters before I went to bed.

"I am not without hope of being able to make it my best," he said, as I went back to the subject, while we turned up our heels to the sky. "At least the people who dislike my prose—and there are a great many of them, I believe—will dislike this work most." This was the first time I had heard him allude to the people who couldn't read him,—a class which is supposed always to sit heavy upon the consciousness of the man of letters. A man organized for literature, as Mark Ambient was, must certainly have had the normal proportion of sensitiveness, of irritability; the artistic *ego,* capable in some cases of such monstrous development, must have been, in his composition, sufficiently erect and definite. I will not therefore go so far as to say that he never thought of his detractors, or that he had any illusions with regard to the number of his admirers (he could never so far have deceived himself as to believe he was popular); but I may at least affirm that adverse criticism, as I had occasion to perceive later, ruffled him visibly but little, that he had an air of thinking it quite natural he should be offensive to many minds, and that he very seldom talked about the newspapers, which, by the way, were always very stupid in regard to the author of *Beltraffio.* Of course he may have thought about them—the newspapers—night and day; the only point I wish to make is that he didn't show it; while, at the same time, he didn't strike one as a man who was on his guard. I may add that, as regards his hope of making the work on which he was then engaged the best of his books, it was only partly carried out. That place belongs, incontestably, to *Beltraffio,* in spite of the beauty of certain parts of its successor. I am pretty sure, however, that he had, at the moment of which I speak, no sense of failure; he was in love with his idea, which was indeed magnificent, and though for him, as, I suppose, for every artist, the act of execution had in it as much torment as joy, he saw his work growing a little every day and filling out the largest plan he had yet conceived. "I want to be truer than I have ever been," he said, settling himself on his back, with his hands clasped behind his head; "I want to give an impression of life itself. No, you may say what you will, I have always arranged things too much, always smoothed them down and rounded them off and tucked them in,—done everything to them that life doesn't do. I have been a slave to the old superstitions."

"You a slave, my dear Mark Ambient? You have the freest imagination of our day!"

"All the more shame to me to have done some of the things I have! The reconciliation of the two women in *Ginistrella,* for instance, which could never really have taken place. That sort of thing is ignoble; I blush when I think of it! This new affair must be a golden vessel, filled with the purest distillation of the actual; and oh, how it bothers me, the shaping of the vase—the hammering of the metal! I have to hammer it so fine, so smooth; I don't do more than an inch or two a day. And all the while I have to be so careful not to let a drop of the liquor escape! When I see the kind of things that Life does, I despair of ever catching her peculiar trick. She has an impudence, Life! If one risked a fiftieth part of the effects she risks! It takes ever so long to believe it. You don't know yet, my dear fellow. It isn't till one has been watching Life for forty years that one finds out half of what she's up to! Therefore one's earlier things must inevitably contain a mass of rot. And with what one sees, on one side, with its tongue in its cheek, defying one to be real enough, and on the other the *bonnes gens* rolling up their eyes at one's cynicism, the situation has elements of the ludicrous which the artist himself is doubtless in a position to appreciate better than any one else. Of course one mustn't bother about the *bonnes gens*," Mark Ambient went on, while my thoughts reverted to his ladylike wife, as interpreted by his remarkable sister.

"To sink your shaft deep, and polish the plate through which people look into it—that's what your work consists of," I remember remarking.

"Ah, polishing one's plate—that is the torment of execution!" he exclaimed, jerking himself up and sitting forward. "The effort to arrive at a surface—if you think a surface necessary—some people don't, happily for them! My dear fellow, if you could see the surface I dream of, as compared with the one with which I have to content myself. Life is really too short for art—one hasn't time to make one's shell ideally hard. Firm and bright—firm and bright!—the devilish thing has a way, sometimes, of being bright without being firm. When I rap it with my knuckles it doesn't give the right sound. There are horrible little flabby spots where I have taken the second-best word, because I couldn't for the life of me think of the best. If you knew how stupid I am sometimes! They look to me now like pimples and ulcers on the brow of beauty!"

"That's very bad—very bad," I said, as gravely as I could.

"Very bad? It's the highest social offence I know; it ought—it absolutely ought—I'm quite serious—to be capital. If I knew I should be hanged else, I should manage to find the best word. The people who couldn't—some of them don't know it when they see it—would shut their inkstands, and we shouldn't be deluged by this flood of rubbish!"

I will not attempt to repeat everything that passed between us, or to explain just how it was that, every moment I spent in his company, Mark Ambient revealed to me more and more that he looked at all things from the standpoint of the artist, felt all life as literary material. There are people who will tell me that this is a poor way of feeling it, and I am not concerned to defend my statement, having space merely to remark that there is something to be said for any interest which makes a man feel so much. If Mark Ambient did really, as I suggested above, have imaginative contact with "all life," I, for my part envy him his *arrière-pensée*. At any rate it was through the receipt of this impression of him that by the time we returned I had acquired the feeling of intimacy I have noted. Before we got up for the homeward stretch, he alluded to his wife's having once—or perhaps more than once—asked him whether he should like Dolcino to read *Beltraffio*. I think he was unconscious at the moment of all that this conveyed to me—as well, doubtless, of my extreme curiosity to hear what he had replied. He had said that he hoped very much Dolcino would read all his works—when he was twenty; he should like him to know what his father had done. Before twenty it would be useless; he wouldn't understand them.

"And meanwhile do you propose to hide them,—to lock them up in a drawer?" Mrs. Ambient had inquired.

"Oh, no; we must simply tell him that they are not intended for small boys. If you bring him up properly, after that he won't touch them."

To this Mrs. Ambient had made answer that it would be very awkward when he was about fifteen; and I asked her husband if it was his opinion in general, then, that young people should not read novels.

"Good ones—certainly not!" said my companion. I suppose I had had other views, for I remember saying that, for myself, I was not sure it was bad for them, if the novels were "good" enough. "Bad for *them,* I don't say so much!" Ambient exclaimed. "But very bad, I am afraid, for the novel!" That oblique, accidental allusion to his wife's attitude was followed by a franker style of reference as we walked home. "The difference between us is simply the opposition between two distinct ways of looking at the world, which have never succeeded in getting on together, or making any kind of common ménage, since the beginning of time. They have borne all sorts of names, and my wife would tell you it's the difference between Christian and Pagan. I may be a pagan, but I don't like the name; it sounds sectarian. She thinks me, at any rate, no better than an ancient Greek. It's the difference between making the most of life and making the least, so that you'll get another better one in some other time and place. Will it be a sin to make the most of that one too, I wonder; and shall we have to be bribed off in future state, as well as in the present? Perhaps I care too much for beauty—I don't know; I delight in it, I adore it, I think of it continually, I try to produce it, to reproduce it. My wife holds that we shouldn't think too much about it. She's always afraid of that, always on her guard. I don't know what she has got on her back! And she's so pretty, too, herself! Don't you thing she's lovely? She was, at any rate, when I married her. At that time I wasn't aware of that difference I speak of—I thought it all came to the same thing: in the end, as they say. Well, perhaps it will, in the end. I don't know what the end will be. Moreover, I care for seeing things as they are; that's the way I try to show them in my novels. But you mustn't talk to Mrs. Ambient about things as they are. She has a mortal dread of things as they are."

"She's afraid of them for Dolcino," I said: surprised a moment afterwards at being in a position—thanks to Miss Ambient—to be so explanatory; and surprised even now that Mark shouldn't have shown visibly that he wondered what the deuce I knew about it. But he didn't; he simply exclaimed, with a tenderness that touched me,—

"Ah, nothing shall ever hurt *him*!" He told me more about his wife before we arrived at the gate of his house, and if it be thought that he was querulous, I am afraid I must admit that he had some of the foibles as well as the gifts of the artistic temperament; adding, however, instantly, that hitherto, to the best of my belief, he had very rarely complained. "She thinks me immoral—that's the long and short of it," he said, as we paused outside a moment, and his hand rested on one of the bars of his gate; while his conscious, demonstrative, expressive, perceptive eyes,—the eyes of a foreigner, I had begun to account them, much more than of the usual Englishman,—viewing me now evidently as quite a familiar friend, took part in the declaration. "It's very strange, when one thinks it all over, and there's a grand comicality in it which I should like to bring out. She is a very nice woman, extraordinarily well behaved, upright and clever, and with a tremendous lot of good sense about a good many matters. Yet her conception of a novel—she has explained it to me once or twice, and she doesn't do it badly, as exposition—is a thing so false that it makes me blush. It is a thing so hollow, so dishonest, so lying, in which life is so blinked and blinded, so dodged and disfigured, that it makes my ears burn. It's two different ways of looking at the whole affair," he repeated, pushing open the gate. "And they are irreconcilable!" he added, with a sigh. We went forward to the house, but on the walk, half way to the door, he stopped, and said to me, "If you are going into this kind of thing, there's a fact you should know beforehand; it may save you some disappointment. There's a hatred of art, there's a hatred of literature!" I looked up at the charming house, with its genial color and crookedness, and I answered, with a smile, that those evil passions might exist, but that I should never have expected to find them there. "Oh, it doesn't matter, after all," he said, laughing; which I was glad to hear, for I was reproaching myself with having excited him.

If I had, his excitement soon passed off, for at lunch he was delightful; strangely delightful, considering that the difference between himself and his wife was, as he had said, irreconcilable. He had the art, by his manner, by his smile, by his natural kindliness, of reducing the importance of it in the common concerns of life; and Mrs. Ambient, I must add, lent herself to this transaction with a very good grace. I watched her, at table, for further illustrations of that fixed idea of which Miss Ambient had spoken to me; for, in the light of the united revelations of her sister-in-law and her husband, she had come to seem to me a very singular personage. I am obliged to say that the signs of a fanatical temperament were not more striking in my hostess than before; it was only after a while that her air of incorruptible conformity, her tapering, monosyllabic correctness, began to appear to be themselves a cold, thin flame. Certainly, at first, she looked like a woman with as few passions as possible; but if she had a passion at all, it would be that of Philistinism. She might have been—for there are guardian-spirits, I suppose, of all great principles—the angel of propriety. Mark Ambient, apparently, ten years before, had simply perceived that she was an angel, without asking himself of what. He had been quite right in calling my attention to her beauty. In looking for the reason why he should have married her, I saw, more than before, that she was, physically speaking, a wonderfully cultivated human plant—that she must have given him many ideas and images. It was impossible to be more pencilled, more garden-like, more delicately tinted and petalled.

If I had had it in my heart to think Ambient a little of a hypocrite for appearing to forget at table everything he had said to me during our walk, I should instantly have cancelled such a judgment, on reflecting that the good news his wife was able to give him about their little boy was reason enough for his sudden air of happiness. It may have come partly, too, from a certain remorse at having complained to me of the fair lady who sat there,—a desire to show me that he was after all not so miserable. Dolcino continued to be much better, and he had been promised he should come downstairs after he had had his dinner. As soon as we had risen from our own meal Ambient slipped away, evidently for the purpose of going to his child; and no sooner had I observed this than I became aware that his wife had simultaneously vanished. It happened that Miss Ambient and I, both at the same moment, saw the tail of her dress whisk out of a doorway, which led the young lady to smile at me, as if I now knew all the secrets of the Ambients. I passed with her into the garden, and we sat down on a dear old bench which rested against the west wall of the house. It was a perfect spot for the middle period of a Sunday in June, and its felicity seemed to come partly from an antique sun-dial which, rising in front of us and forming the centre of a small, intricate parterre, measured the moments ever so slowly, and made them safe for leisure and talk. The garden bloomed in the suffused afternoon, the tall beeches stood still for an example, and, behind and above us, a rose-tree of many seasons, clinging to the faded grain of the brick, expressed the whole character of the place in a familiar, exquisite smell. It seemed to me a place for genius to have every sanction, and not to encounter challenges and checks. Miss Ambient asked me if I had enjoyed my walk with her brother, and whether we had talked of many things.

"Well, of most things," I said, smiling, though I remembered that we had not talked of Miss Ambient.

"And don't you think some of his theories are very peculiar?"

"Oh, I guess I agree with them all." I was very particular, for Miss Ambient's entertainment, to guess.

"Do you think art is everything?" she inquired in a moment.

"In art, of course I do!"

"And do you think beauty is everything?"

"I don't know about its being everything. But it's very delightful."

"Of course it is difficult for a woman to know how far to go," said my companion. "I adore everything that gives a charm to life. I am intensely sensitive to form. But sometimes I draw back—don't you see what I mean?—I don't quite see where I shall be landed. I only want to be quiet, after all," Miss Ambient continued, in a tone of stifled yearning which seemed to indicate that she had not yet arrived at her desire. "And one must be good, at any rate, must not one?" she inquired, with a cadence apparently intended for an assurance that my answer would settle this recondite question for her. It was difficult for me to make it very original, and I am afraid I repaid her confidence with an unblushing platitude. I remember, moreover, appending to it an inquiry equally destitute of freshness, and still more wanting perhaps in tact, as to whether she did not mean to go to church, as that was an obvious way of being good. She replied that she had performed this duty in the morning, and that for her, on Sunday afternoon, supreme virtue consisted in answering the week's letters. Then suddenly, without transition, she said to me, "It's quite a mistake about Dolcino being better. I have seen him, and he's not at all right."

"Surely his mother would know, wouldn't she?" I suggested.

She appeared for a moment to be counting the leaves on one of the great beeches. "As regards most matters, one can easily say what, in a given situation, my sister-in-law would do. But as regards this one, there are strange elements at work."

"Strange elements? Do you mean in the constitution of the child?"

"No, I mean in my sister-in-law's feelings."

"Elements of affection, of course; elements of anxiety. Why do you call them strange?"

She repeated my words. "Elements of affection, elements of anxiety. She is very anxious."

Miss Ambient made me vaguely uneasy; she almost frightened

me, and I wished she would go and write her letters. "His father will have seen him now," I said, "and if he is not satisfied he will send for the doctor."

"The doctor ought to have been here this morning. He lives only two miles away."

I reflected that all this was very possibly only a part of the general tragedy of Miss Ambient's view of things; but I asked her why she hadn't urged such a necessity upon her sister-in-law. She answered me with a smile of extraordinary significance, and told me that I must have very little idea of what her relations with Beatrice were; but I must do her the justice to add that she went on to make herself a little more comprehensible by saying that it was quite reason enough for her sister not to be alarmed that Mark would be sure to be. He was always nervous about the child, and as they were predestined by nature to take opposite views, the only thing for Beatrice was to cultivate a false optimism. If Mark were not there, she would not be at all easy. I remembered what he had said to me about their dealings with Dolcino,—that between them they would put an end to him; but I did not repeat this to Miss Ambient: the less so that just then her brother emerged from the house, carrying his child in his arms. Close behind him moved his wife, grave and pale; the boy's face was turned over Ambient's shoulder, towards his mother. We got up to receive the group, and as they came near us Dolcino turned round. I caught, on his enchanting little countenance, a smile of recognition, and for the moment would have been quite content with it. Miss Ambient, however, received another impression, and I make haste to say that her quick sensibility, in which there was something maternal, argues that, in spite of her affectations, there was a strain of kindness in her. "It won't do at all—it won't do at all," she said to me under her breath. "I shall speak to Mark about the doctor."

The child was rather white, but the main difference I saw in him was that he was even more beautiful than the day before. He had been dressed in his festal garments,—a velvet suit and a crimson sash,—and he looked like a little invalid prince, too young to know condescension, and smiling familiarly on his subjects.

"Put him down, Mark, he's not comfortable," Mrs. Ambient said.

"Should you like to stand on your feet, my boy?" his father asked.

"Oh, yes; I'm remarkably well," said the child.

Mark placed him on the ground; he had shining, pointed slippers, with enormous bows. "Are you happy now, Mr. Ambient?"

"Oh, yes, I am particularly happy," Dolcino replied. The words were scarcely out of his mouth when his mother caught him up, and in a moment, holding him on her knees, she took her place on the bench where Miss Ambient and I had been sitting. This young lady said something to her brother, in consequence of which the two wandered away into the garden together. I remained with Mrs. Ambient; but as a servant had brought out a couple of chairs I was not obliged to seat myself beside her. Our conversation was not animated, and I, for my part, felt there would be a kind of hypocrisy in my trying to make myself agreeable to Mrs. Ambient. I didn't dislike her—I rather admired her; but I was aware that I differed from her inexpressibly. Then I suspected, what I afterwards definitely knew and have already intimated, that the poor lady had taken a dislike to me; and this of course was not encouraging. She thought me an obtrusive and even depraved young man, whom a perverse Providence had dropped upon their quiet lawn to flatter her husband's worst tendencies. She did me the honor to say to Miss Ambient, who repeated the speech, that she didn't know when she had seen her husband take such a fancy to a visitor; and she measured, apparently, my evil influence by Mark's appreciation of my society. I had a consciousness, not yet acute, but quite sufficient, of all this; but I must say that if it chilled my flow of small-talk, it didn't prevent me from thinking that the beautiful mother and beautiful child, interlaced there against their background of roses, made a picture such as I perhaps should not soon see again. I was free, I supposed, to go into the house and write letters, to sit in the drawing-room, to repair to my own apartment and take a nap; but the only use I made of my freedom was to linger still in my chair and say to myself that the light hand of Sir Joshua might have painted Mark Ambient's wife and son. I found myself looking perpetually at Dolcino, and Dolcino looked back at me, and that was enough to detain me. When he looked at me he smiled, and I felt it was an absolute impossibility to abandon a child who was smiling at one like that. His eyes never wandered; they attached themselves to mine, as if among all the small incipient things of his nature there was a desire to say something to me. If I could have taken him upon my own knee, he perhaps would have managed to say it; but it would have been far too delicate a matter to ask his mother to give him up, and it has remained a constant regret for me that on that Sunday afternoon I did not, even for a moment, hold Dolcino in my arms. He had said that he felt remarkably well, and that he was especially happy; but though he may have been happy, with his charming head pillowed on his mother's breast, and his little crimson silk legs depending from her lap, I did not think he looked well. He made no attempt to walk about; he was content to swing his legs softly and strike one as languid and angelic.

Mark came back to us with his sister; and Miss Ambient, making some remark about having to attend to her correspondence, passed into the house. Mark came and stood in front of his wife, looking down at the child, who immediately took hold of his hand, keeping it while he remained. "I think Allingham ought to see him," Ambient said: "I think I will walk over and fetch him."

"That's Gwendolen's idea, I suppose," Mrs. Ambient replied, very sweetly.

"It's not such an out-of-the-way idea, when one's child is ill."

"I'm not ill, papa; I'm much better now," Dolcino remarked.

"Is that the truth, or are you only saying it to be agreeable? You have a great idea of being agreeable, you know."

The boy seemed to meditate on this distinction, this imputation, for a moment; then his exaggerated eyes, which had wandered, caught my own as I watched him. "Do *you* think me agreeable?" he inquired, with the candor of his age, and with a smile that made his father turn round to me, laughing, and ask, mutely, with a glance, "Isn't he adorable?"

"Then why don't you hop about, if you feel so lusty?" Ambient went on, while the boy swung his hand.

"Because mamma is holding me close!"

"Oh, yes; I know how mamma holds you when I come near!" Ambient exclaimed, looking at his wife.

She turned her charming eyes up to him, without deprecation or concession, and after a moment she said, "You can go for Allingham if you like. I think myself it would be better. You ought to drive."

"She says that to get me away," Ambient remarked to me, laughing; after which he started for the doctor's.

I remained there with Mrs. Ambient, though our conversation had more pauses than speeches. The boy's little fixed white face seemed, as before, to plead with me to stay, and after a while it produced still another effect, a very curious one, which I shall find it difficult to express. Of course I expose myself to the charge of attempting to give fantastic reasons for an act which may have been simply the fruit of a native want of discretion; and indeed the traceable consequences of that perversity were too lamentable to leave me any desire to trifle with the question. All I can say is that I acted in perfect good faith, and that Dolcino's friendly little gaze gradually kindled the spark of my inspiration. What helped it to glow were the other influences,—the silent, suggestive garden-nook, the perfect opportunity (if it was not an opportunity for that, it was an opportunity for nothing) and the plea that I speak of, which issued from the child's eyes, and seemed to make him say, "The mother that bore me and that presses me here to her bosom —sympathetic little organism that I am—has really the kind of sensibility which she has been represented to you as lacking; if you only look for it patiently and respectfully. How is it possible that she shouldn't have it? How is it possible that *I* should have so much of it (for I am quite full of it, dear, strange gentleman), if it were not also in some degree in her? I am my father's child, but I am also my mother's, and I am sorry for the difference between them!" So it shaped itself before me, the vision of reconciling Mrs. Ambient with her husband, of putting an end to their great disagreement. The project was absurd, of course, for had I not had his word for it—spoken with all the bitterness of experience —that the gulf that divided them was wellnigh bottomless? Nevertheless, a quarter of an hour after Mark had left us, I said to his wife that I couldn't get over what she told me the night before about her thinking her husband's writings "objectionable." I had been so very sorry to hear it, had thought of it constantly, and wondered whether it were not possible to make her change her mind. Mrs. Ambient gave me rather a cold stare; she seemed to be recommending me to mind my own business. I wish I had taken this mute counsel, but I did not. I went on to remark that it seemed an immense pity so much that was beautiful should be lost upon her.

"Nothing is lost upon me," said Mrs. Ambient. "I know they are very beautiful."

"Don't you like papa's books?" Dolcino asked, addressing his mother, but still looking at me. Then he added to me, "Won't you read them to me, American gentleman?"

"I would rather tell you some stories of my own," I said. "I know some that are very interesting."

"When will you tell them? To-morrow?"

"To-morrow, with pleasure, if that suits you."

Mrs. Ambient was silent at this. Her husband, during our walk, had asked me to remain another day; my promise to her son was an implication that I had consented, and it is not probable that the prospect was agreeable to her. This ought, doubtless, to have made me more careful as to what I said next; but all I can say is that it didn't. I presently observed that just after leaving her the evening before, and after hearing her apply to her husband's writings the epithet I had already quoted, I had, on going up to my room, sat down to the perusal of those sheets of his new book which he had been so good as to lend me. I had sat entranced till nearly three in the morning. I had read them twice over. "You say you haven't looked at them. I think it's such a pity you shouldn't. Do let me beg you to take them up. They are so very remarkable. I'm sure they will convert you. They place him in—really—such a dazzling light. All that is best in him is there. I have no doubt it's a great liberty, my saying all this; but excuse me, and *do* read them!"

"Do read them, mamma!" Dolcino repeated; "do read them!"

She bent her head and closed his lips with a kiss. "Of course I know he has worked immensely over them," she said; and after this she made no remark, but sat there looking thoughtful, with her eyes on the ground. The tone of these last words was such as to leave me no spirit for further pressure, and after expressing a fear that her husband had not found the doctor at home, I got up and took a turn about the grounds. When I came back, ten minutes later, she was still in her place watching her boy, who had fallen asleep in her lap. As I drew near she put her finger on her lips, and a moment afterwards she rose, holding the child, and murmured something about its being better that he should go upstairs. I offered to carry him, and held out my hands to take him; but she thanked me and turned away with the child seated on her arm, his head on her shoulder. "I am very strong," she said, as she passed into the house, and her slim, flexible figure bent backwards with the filial weight. So I never touched Dolcino.

I betook myself to Ambient's study, delighted to have a quiet hour to look over his books by myself. The windows were open into the garden; the sunny stillness, the mild light of the English summer, filled the room, without quite chasing away the rich dusky tone which was a part of its charm, and which abode in the serried shelves where old morocco exhaled the fragrance of curious learning, and in the brighter intervals, where medals and prints and miniatures were suspended upon a surface of faded stuff. The place had both color and quiet; I thought it a perfect room for work, and went so far as to say to myself that, if it were mine to sit and scribble in, there was no knowing but that I might learn to write as well as the author of *Beltraffio*. This distinguished man did not turn up, and I rummaged freely among his treasures. At last I took down a book that detained me awhile, and seated myself in a fine old leather chair by the window to turn it over. I had been occupied in this way for half an hour,—a good part of the afternoon had waned,—when I became conscious of another presence in the room, and, looking up from my quarto, saw that Mrs. Ambient, having pushed open the door in the same noiseless way that marked, or disguised, her entrance the night before, had advanced across the threshold. On seeing me she stopped; she had not, I think, expected to find me. But her hesitation was only of a moment; she came straight to her husband's writing-table as if she were looking for something. I got up and asked her if I could help her. She glanced about an instant, and then put her hand upon a roll of papers which I recognized, as I had placed it in that spot in the morning on coming down from my room.

"Is this the new book?" she asked, holding it up.

"The very sheets, with precious annotations."

"I mean to take your advice"; and she tucked the little bundle under her arm. I congratulated her cordially, and ventured to make of my triumph, as I presumed to call it, a subject of pleasantry. But she was perfectly grave, and turned away from me, as she had presented herself, without a smile; after which I settled down to my quarto again, with the reflection that Mrs. Ambient was a queer woman. My triumph, too, suddenly seemed to me rather vain. A woman who couldn't smile in the right place would never understand Mark Ambient. He came in at last in person, having brought the doctor back with him. "He was away from home," Mark said, "and I went after him, to where he was supposed to be. He had left the place, and I followed him to two or three others, which accounts for my delay." He was now with Mrs. Ambient looking at the child, and was to see Mark again before leaving the house. My host noticed, at the end of ten minutes, that the proof-sheets of his new book had been removed from the table; and when I told him, in reply to his question as to what I knew about them, that Mrs. Ambient had carried them off to read, he turned almost pale for an instant with surprise. "What has suddenly made her so curious?" he exlaimed; and I was obliged to tell him that I was at the bottom of the mystery. I had had it on my conscience to assure her that she really ought to know of what her husband was capable. "Of what I am capable? *Elle ne s'en doute que trop!*" said Ambient, with a laugh; but he took my meddling very good-naturedly, and contented himself with adding that he was very much afraid she would burn up the sheets, with his emendations, of which he had no duplicate. The doctor paid a long visit in the nursery, and before he came down I retired to my own quarters, where I remained till dinner-time. On entering the drawing-room at this hour, I found Miss Ambient in possession, as she had been the evening before.

"I was right about Dolcino," she said, as soon as she saw me, with a strange little air of triumph. "He is really very ill."

"Very ill! Why, when I last saw him, at four o'clock, he was in fairly good form."

"There has been a change for the worse, very sudden and rapid, and when the doctor got here he found diphtheritic symptoms. He ought to have been called, as I knew, in the morning, and the child oughtn't to have been brought into the garden."

"My dear lady, he was very happy there," I answered, much appalled.

"He would be happy anywhere. I have no doubt he is happy now, with his poor little throat in a state—" she dropped her voice as her brother came in, and Mark let us know that, as a matter of course, Mrs. Ambient would not appear. It was true that Dolcino had developed diphtheritic symptoms, but he was quiet for the present, and his mother was earnestly watching him. She was a perfect nurse, Mark said, and the doctor was coming back at ten o'clock. Our dinner was not very gay; Ambient was anxious and alarmed, and his sister irritated me by her constant tacit assumption, conveyed in the very way she nibbled her bread and sipped her wine, of having "told me so." I had had no disposition to deny anything she told me, and I could not see that her satisfaction in being justified by the event made poor Dolcino's throat any better. The truth is that, as the sequel proved, Miss Ambient had some of the qualities of the sibyl, and had therefore, perhaps, a right to the sibylline contortions. Her brother was so preoccupied that I felt my presence to be an indiscretion, and was sorry I had promised to remain over the morrow. I said to Mark that, evidently, I had better leave them in the morning; to which he replied that, on the contrary, if he was to pass the next days in the fidgets, my company would be an extreme relief to him. The fidgets had already begun for him, poor fellow; and as we sat in his study with our cigars after dinner, he wandered to the door whenever he heard the sound of the doctor's wheels. Miss Ambient, who shared this apartment with us, gave me at such moments significant glances; she had gone upstairs before rejoining us to ask after the child. His mother and his nurse gave a tolerable account of him; but Miss Ambient found his fever high and his symptoms very grave. The doctor came at ten o'clock, and I went to bed after hearing from Mark that he saw no present cause for alarm. He had made every provision for the night, and was to return early in the morning.

I quitted my room at eight o'clock the next day, and, as I came downstairs, saw, through the open door of the house, Mrs. Ambient standing at the front gate of the grounds, in colloquy with the physician. She wore a white dressing-gown, but her shining hair was carefully tucked away in its net, and in the freshness of the morning, after a night of watching, she looked as much "the type of the lady" as her sister-in-law had described her. Her appearance, I suppose, ought to have reassured me; but I was still nervous and uneasy, so that I shrank from meeting her with the necessary question about Dolcino. None the less, however, was I impatient to learn how the morning found him; and, as Mrs. Ambient had not seen me, I passed into the grounds by a roundabout way, and, stopping at a further gate, hailed the doctor just as he was driving away. Mrs. Ambient had returned to the house before he got into his gig.

"Excuse me, but as a friend of the family, I should like very much to hear about the little boy."

The doctor, who was a stout, sharp man, looked at me from head to foot, and then he said, "I'm sorry to say I haven't seen him."

"Haven't seen him?"

"Mrs. Ambient came down to meet me as I alighted, and told me that he was sleeping so soundly, after a restless night, that she didn't wish him disturbed. I assured her I wouldn't disturb him, but she said he was quite safe now and she could look after him herself."

"Thank you very much. Are you coming back?"

"No, sir; I'll be hanged if I come back!" exclaimed Dr. Allingham, who was evidently very angry. And he started his horse again with the whip.

I wandered back into the garden, and five minutes later Miss Ambient came forth from the house to greet me. She explained that breakfast would not be served for some time, and that she wished to catch the doctor before he went away. I informed her that this functionary had come and departed, and I repeated to her what he had told me about his dismissal. This made Miss Ambient very serious, very serious indeed, and she sank into a bench, with dilated eyes, hugging her elbows with crossed arms. She indulged in many ejaculations, she confessed that she was infinitely perplexed, and she finally told me what her own last news of her nephew had been. She had sat up very late,—after me, after Mark,—and before going to bed had knocked at the door of the child's room, which was opened to her by the nurse. This good woman had admitted her, and she had found Dolcino quiet, but flushed and "unnatural," with his mother sitting beside his bed. "She held his hand in one of hers," said Miss Ambient, "and in the other—what do you think?—the proof-sheets of Mark's new book! She was reading them there, intently: did you ever hear of anything so extraordinary? Such a very odd time to be reading an author whom she never could abide!" In her agitation Miss Ambient was guilty of this vulgarism of speech, and I was so impressed by her narrative that it was only in recalling her words later that I noticed the lapse. Mrs. Ambient had looked up from her reading with her finger on her lips—I recognized the gesture she had addressed to me in the afternoon—and, though the nurse was about to go to rest, had not encouraged her sister-in-law to relieve her of any part of her vigil. But certainly, then, Dolcino's condition was far from reassuring, —his poor little breathing was most painful; and what change could have taken place in him in those few hours that would justify Beatrice in denying the physician access to him? This was the moral of Miss Ambient's anecdote, the moral for herself at least. The moral for me, rather, was that it *was* a very singular time for Mrs. Ambient to be going into a novelist she had never appreciated, and who had simply happened to be recommended to her by a young American she disliked. I thought of her sitting there in the sick-chamber in the still hours of the night, after the nurse had left her, turning over those pages of genius and wrestling with their magical influence.

I must relate very briefly the circumstances of the rest of my visit to Mark Ambient,—it lasted but a few hours longer,—and devote but three words to my later acquaintance with him. That lasted five years,—till his death,—and was full of interest, of satisfaction, and, I may add, of sadness. The main thing to be said with regard to it, is that I had a secret from him. I believe he never suspected it, though of this I am not absolutely sure. If he did, the line he had taken, the line of absolute negation of the matter to himself, shows an immense effort of the will. I may tell my secret now, giving it for what it is worth, now that Mark Ambient has gone, that he has begun to be alluded to as one of the famous early dead, and that his wife does not survive him; now, too, that Miss Ambient, whom I also saw at intervals during the years that followed, has, with her embroideries and her attitudes, her necromantic glances and strange intuitions, retired to a Sisterhood, where, as I am told, she is deeply immured and quite lost to the world.

Mark came in to breakfast after his sister and I had for some time been seated there. He shook hands with me in silence, kissed his sister, opened his letters and newspapers, and pretended to drink his coffee. But I could see that these movements were mechanical, and I was little surprised when, suddenly, he pushed away everything that was before him, and, with his head in his hands and his elbows on the table, sat staring strangely at the cloth.

"What is the matter, *fratello mio*?" Miss Ambient inquired, peeping from behind the urn.

He answered nothing, but got up with a certain violence and strode to the window. We rose to our feet, his sister and I, by a common impulse, exchanging a glance of some alarm, while he stared for a moment into the garden. "In Heaven's name what has got possession of Beatrice?" he cried at last, turning round with an almost haggard face. And he looked from one of us to the other; the appeal was addressed to me as well as to his sister.

Miss Ambient gave a shrug. "My poor Mark, Beatrice is always —Beatrice!"

"She has locked herself up with the boy—bolted and barred the door; she refuses to let me come near him!" Ambient went on.

"She refused to let the doctor see him an hour ago!" Miss Ambient remarked, with intention, as they say on the stage.

"Refused to let the doctor see him? By heaven, I'll smash in the door!" And Mark brought his fist down upon the table, so that all the breakfast-service rang.

I begged Miss Ambient to go up and try to have speech of her sister-in-law, and I drew Mark out into the garden. "You're exceedingly nervous, and Mrs. Ambient is probably right," I said to him. "Women know; women should be supreme in such a situation. Trust a mother—a devoted mother, my dear friend!" With such words as these I tried to soothe and comfort him, and, marvellous to relate, I succeeded, with the help of many cigarettes, in making him walk about the garden and talk, or listen at least to my own ingenious chatter, for nearly an hour. At the end of this time Miss Ambient returned to us, with a very rapid step, holding her hand to her heart.

"Go for the doctor, Mark, go for the doctor this moment!"

"Is he dying? Has she killed him?" poor Ambient cried, flinging away his cigarette.

"I don't know what she has done! But she's frightened, and now she wants the doctor."

"He told me he would be hanged if he came back!" I felt myself obliged to announce.

"Precisely—therefore Mark himself must go for him, and not a messenger. You must see him, and tell him it's to save your child. The trap has been ordered—it's ready."

"To save him? I'll save him, please God!" Ambient cried, bounding with his great strides across the lawn.

As soon as he had gone I felt that I ought to have volunteered in his place, and I said as much to Miss Ambient; but she checked me by grasping my arm quickly, while we heard the wheels of the dog-cart rattle away from the gate. "He's off—he's off—and now I can think! To get him away—while I think—while I think!"

"While you think of what, Miss Ambient?"

"Of the unspeakable thing that has happened under this roof!"

Her manner was habitually that of such a prophetess of ill that my first impulse was to believe I must allow here for a great exaggeration. But in a moment I saw that her emotion was real. "Dolcino *is* dying then,—he is dead?"

"It's too late to save him. His mother has let him die! I tell you that because you are sympathetic, because you have imagination," Miss Ambient was good enough to add, interrupting my expression of horror. "That's why you had the idea of making her read Mark's new book!"

"What has that to do with it? I don't understand you; your accusation is monstrous."

"I see it all; I'm not stupid," Miss Ambient went on, heedless of the harshness of my tone. "It was the book that finished her; it was that decided her!"

"Decided her? Do you mean she has murdered her child?" I demanded, trembling at my own words.

"She sacrificed him; she determined to do nothing to make him live. Why else did she lock herself up, why else did she turn away the doctor? The book gave her a horror; she determined to rescue him,—to prevent him from ever being touched. He had a crisis at two o'clock in the morning. I know that from the nurse, who had left her then, but whom, for a short time, she called back. Dolcino got much worse, but she insisted on the nurse's going back to bed, and after that she was alone with him for hours."

"Do you pretend that she has no pity, that she's insane?"

"She held him in her arms, she pressed him to her breast, not to see him; but she gave him no remedies; she did nothing the doctor ordered. Everything is there, untouched. She has had the honesty not even to throw the drugs away!"

I dropped upon the nearest bench, overcome with wonder and

agitation, quite as much at Miss Ambient's terrible lucidity as at the charge she made against her sister-in-law. There was an amazing coherency in her story, and it was dreadful to me to see myself figuring in it as so proximate a cause.

"You are a very strange woman, and you say strange things."

"You think it necessary to protest, but you are quite ready to believe me. You have received an impression of my sister-in-law, you have guessed of what she is capable."

I do not feel bound to say what concession, on this point, I made to Miss Ambient, who went on to relate to me that within the last half-hour Beatrice had had a revulsion; that she was tremendously frightened at what she had done; that her fright itself betrayed her; and that she would now give heaven and earth to save the child. "Let us hope she will!" I said, looking at my watch and trying to time poor Ambient; whereupon my companion repeated, in a singular tone, "Let us hope so!" When I asked her if she herself could do nothing, and whether she ought not to be with her sister-in-law, she replied, "You had better go and judge; she is like a wounded tigress!"

I never saw Mrs. Ambient till six months after this, and therefore cannot pretend to have verified the comparison. At the latter period she was again the type of the lady. "She'll treat him better after this," I remember Miss Ambient saying, in response to some quick outburst (on my part) of compassion for her brother. Although I had been in the house but thirty-six hours, this young lady had treated me with extraordinary confidence, and there was therefore a certain demand which, as an intimate, I might make of her. I extracted from her a pledge that she would never say to her brother what she had just said to me; she would leave him to form his own theory of his wife's conduct. She agreed with me that there was misery enough in the house, without her contributing a new anguish, and that Mrs. Ambient's proceedings might be explained, to her husband's mind, by the extravagance of a jealous devotion. Poor Mark came back with the doctor much sooner than we could have hoped, but we knew, five minutes afterwards, that they arrived too late. Poor little Dolcino was more exquisitely beautiful in death than he had been in life. Mrs. Ambient's grief was frantic; she lost her head and said strange things. As for Mark's—but I will not speak of that. *Basta,* as he used to say. Miss Ambient kept her secret,—I have already had occasion to say that she had her good points,—but it rankled in her conscience like a guilty participation, and, I imagine, had something to do with her retiring ultimately to a Sisterhood. And, *à propos* of consciences, the reader is now in a position to judge of my compunction for my effort to convert Mrs. Ambient. I ought to mention that the death of her child in some degree converted her. When the new book came out—it was long delayed—she read it over as a whole, and her husband told me that a few months before her death,—she failed rapidly after losing her son, sank into a consumption, and faded away at Mentone,—during those few supreme weeks she even dipped into *Beltraffio*.

The Aspern Papers

The Aspern Papers

THE ASPERN PAPERS (1888) is undoubtedly one of the finest of James's short novels. The short novel, or *nouvelle,* as he preferred to call it, is of a dimension that suited him perfectly, and there is no greater master of the genre in English. His work in it compares favorably in some instances with the great novels of his later manner. As Stephen Spender has said, it is precisely in such *nouvelles* as *The Aspern Papers* and *The Turn of the Screw* that we find a "rare, inaccessible and pure poetry"—a poetry that resembles nothing so much as the musical art of a composer like Gluck.

In his prefaces to the New York Edition, James distinguished again and again between the short story and the "beautiful and blest *nouvelle.*" To the former he ascribed a function chiefly anecdotal, whereas in the latter he saw the possibility of the complete integration of pattern and plot, picture and drama—an integration making for the happiest development of the writer's idea. He pointed out that though in other languages the very best results had been obtained "under the star of the *nouvelle,*" this form was still neglected and excluded from editorial favor in England and America because of the "blank misery of our Anglo-Saxon sense in such matters." It is clear, too, that James found the *nouvelle* so adaptable to his gifts because within its range he could satisfy his need for psychological elaboration even while practicing that "exquisite economy in composition" which he valued above all else.

Most of James's narratives owe their first impulse to some small fact or circumstance of real life. The particle of fact in *The Aspern Papers* was identified by James in Florence, where he was told one day of the presence in that city of the still-surviving Jane Clairmont, the half-sister of Shelley's second wife and the mother of Byron's daughter Allegra. To the legend was added the rich detail of an American traveler—"an ardent Shelleyite"—who contrived to enter the forgotten Clairmont household in the guise of a lodger in order to get hold of "literary remains." This was quite enough to provide James with the "germ" he wanted; and since he believed that the "minimum of valid suggestion serves the man of imagination better than the maximum," he literally shrank from any further investigation of the facts. Years later, when it came to writing the preface to *The Aspern Papers*, he recalled that he had at once perceived a romantic image in the legend, sensing an opportunity to mount the "final scene of the dim Shelley drama . . . in the very theatre of our modernity." He felt that it was still possible to catch the fragrance of the Byronic age, an age not so irrevocably of the past as to elude altogether the venturesome storyteller.

It is partly with the intention of covering his tracks that James transposed the scene from Florence to Venice. He invented, moreover, an American Byron—Jeffrey Aspern—to make ghostly love to an American Miss Clairmont. Venice furnished a background of mouldy rococo for his little drama, and the addition of an experimental American element promised to heighten the charm. James asked but scarcely answered the question of what the Byronic age had come to on the banks of the Hudson, for in the text the American reference remained on the level of a mere conceit. It turned out that for interest and actuality nothing more was needed than to make the scheming lodger come up against the senile mask of the "beautiful Juliana" flanked by the face of her niece, a face expressive of the quality of fatal honesty in Miss Tina's nature. The release of the unspeakable irony of the situation sufficed to create the story.

There is a considerable modern literature dealing with the ambiguity of the artist in his social and moral character, and in a sense this theme is also implicit in *The Aspern Papers.* Such a reading of the story is suggested by the position of Juliana's lodger —the "publishing scoundrel" as she calls him—a position only at one remove from that of the artist-type. The lodger has all of the artist's presumption and ruthless curiosity; and again like the latter he cannot conceivably justify his behavior except on the somewhat ambiguous ground of the artist's "right" to make public that which is intrinsically private. Thus the intrigue of *The Aspern Papers* might be seen as symbolic of the perpetual danger and intrigue of art, whose practitioners have always risked moral annihilation in searching out and "publishing" those secrets which because of fear, pride, delicacy or shame all "decent people" are resolved to keep to themselves.

I

I HAD taken Mrs. Prest into my confidence; without her in truth I should have made but little advance, for the fruitful idea in the whole business dropped from her friendly lips. It was she who found the short cut and loosed the Gordian knot. It is not supposed easy for women to rise to the large free view of anything, anything to be done; but they sometimes throw off a bold conception—such as a man wouldn't have risen to—with singular serenity. "Simply make them take you in on the footing of a lodger"—I don't think that unaided I should have risen to that. I was beating about the bush, trying to be ingenious, wondering by what combination of arts I might become an acquaintance, when she offered this happy suggestion that the way to become an acquaintance was first to become an intimate. Her actual knowledge of the Misses Bordereau was scarcely larger than mine, and indeed I had brought with me from England some definite facts that were new to her. Their name had been mixed up ages before with one of the greatest names of the century, and they now lived obscurely in Venice, lived on very small means, unvisited, unapproachable, in a sequestered and dilapidated old palace: this was the substance of my friend's impression of them. She herself had been established in Venice some fifteen years and had done a great deal of good there; but the circle of her benevolence had never embraced the two shy, mysterious and, as was somehow supposed, scarcely respectable Americans—they were believed to have lost in their long exile all national quality, besides being as their name implied of some remoter French affiliation—who asked no favours and desired no attention. In the early years of her residence she had made an attempt to see them, but this had been successful only as regards the little one, as Mrs. Prest called the niece; though in fact I afterwards found her the bigger of the two in inches. She had heard Miss Bordereau was ill and had a suspicion she was in want, and had gone to the house to offer aid, so that if there were suffering, American suffering in particular, she shouldn't have it on her conscience. The "little one" had received her in the great cold tarnished Venetian *sala,* the central hall of the house, paved with marble and roofed with dim cross-beams, and hadn't even asked her to sit down. This was not encouraging for me, who wished to sit so fast, and I remarked as much to Mrs. Prest. She replied, however, with profundity "Ah, but there's all the difference: I went to confer a favour and you'll go to ask one. If they're proud you'll be on the right side." And she offered to show me their house to begin with—to row me thither in her gondola. I let her know I had already been to look at it half a dozen times; but I accepted her invitation, for it charmed me to hover about the place. I had made my way to it the day after my arrival in Venice—it had been described to me in advance by the friend in England to whom I owed definite information as to their possession of the papers—laying siege to it with my eyes while I considered my plan of campaign. Jeffrey Aspern had never been in it that I knew of, but some note of his voice seemed to abide there by a roundabout implication and in a "dying fall."

Mrs. Prest knew nothing about the papers, but was interested in my curiosity, as always in the joys and sorrows of her friends. As we went, however, in her gondola, gliding there under the sociable hood with the bright Venetian picture framed on either side by the moveable window, I saw how my eagerness amused her and that she found my interest in my possible spoil a fine case of monomania. "One would think you expected from it the answer to the riddle of the universe," she said; and I denied the impeachment only by replying that if I had to choose between that precious solution and a bundle of Jeffrey Aspern's letters I knew indeed which would appear to me the greater boon. She pretended to make light of his genius and I took no pains to defend him. One doesn't defend one's god: one's god is in himself a defence. Besides, to-day, after his long comparative obscuration, he hangs high in the heaven of our literature for all the world to see; he's a part of the light by which we walk. The most I said was that he was no doubt not a woman's poet: to which she rejoined aptly enough that he had been at least Miss Bordereau's. The strange thing had been for me to discover in England that she was still alive: it was as if I had been told Mrs. Siddons was, or Queen Caroline, or the famous Lady Hamilton, for it seemed to me that she belonged to a generation as extinct. "Why she must be tremendously old—at least a hundred," I had said; but on coming to consider dates I saw it not strictly involved that she should have far exceeded the common span. None the less she was of venerable age and her relations with Jeffrey Aspern had occurred in her early womanhood. "That's her excuse," said Mrs. Prest half sententiously and yet also somewhat as if she were ashamed of making a speech so little in the real tone of Venice. As if a woman needed an excuse for having loved the divine poet! He had been not only one of the most brilliant minds of his day—and in those years, when the century was young, there were, as every one knows, many—but one of the most genial men and one of the handsomest.

The niece, according to Mrs. Prest, was of minor antiquity, and the conjecture was risked that she was only a grand-niece. This was possible; I had nothing but my share in the very limited knowledge of my English fellow-worshipper John Cumnor, who had never seen the couple. The world, as I say, had recognised Jeffrey Aspern, but Cumnor and I had recognised him most. The multitude to-day flocked to his temple, but of that temple he and I regarded ourselves as the appointed ministers. We held, justly, as I think, that we had done more for his memory than any one else, and had done it simply by opening lights into his life. He had nothing to fear from us because he had nothing to fear from the truth, which alone at such a distance of time we could be interested in establishing. His early death had been the only dark spot, as it were, on his fame, unless the papers in Miss Bordereau's hands should perversely bring out others. There had been an impression about 1825 that he had "treated her badly," just as there had been an impression that he had "served," as the London populace says, several other ladies in the same masterful way. Each of these cases Cumnor and I had been able to investigate, and we had never failed to acquit him conscientiously of any grossness. I judged him perhaps more indulgently than my friend; certainly, at any rate, it appeared to me that no man could have walked straighter in the given circumstances. These had been almost always difficult and dangerous. Half the women of his time, to speak liberally, had flung themselves at his head, and while the fury raged—the more that it was very catching—accidents, some of them grave, had not failed to occur. He was not a woman's poet, as I had said to Mrs. Prest, in the modern phase of his reputation; but the situation had been different when the man's own voice was mingled with his song. That voice, by every testimony, was one of the most charming ever heard. "Orpheus and the Mænads!" had been of course my foreseen judgement when first I turned over his correspondence. Almost all the Mænads were unreasonable and many of them unbearable; it struck me that he had been kinder and more considerate than in his place—if I could imagine myself in any such box—I should have found the trick of.

It was certainly strange beyond all strangeness, and I shall not take up space with attempting to explain it, that whereas among all these other relations and in these other directions of research we had to deal with phantoms and dust, the mere echoes of echoes, the one living source of information that had lingered on into our time had been unheeded by us. Every one of Aspern's contemporaries had, according to our belief, passed away; we had not been able to look into a single pair of eyes into which his had looked or to feel a transmitted contact in any aged hand that his had touched. Most dead of all did poor Miss Bordereau appear, and yet she alone had survived. We exhausted in the course of months our wonder that we had not found her out sooner, and the substance of our explanation was that she had kept so quiet. The poor lady on the whole had had reason for doing so. But it was a revelation to us that self-effacement on such a scale had been possible in the latter half of the nineteenth century—the age of newspapers and telegrams and photographs and interviewers. She had taken no great trouble for it either—hadn't hidden herself away in an undiscoverable hole, had boldly settled down in a city of exhibition. The one apparent secret of her safety had been that Venice contained so many much greater curiosities. And then accident had somehow favoured her, as was shown for example in the fact that Mrs. Prest had never happened to name her to me, though I had spent three weeks in Venice—under her nose, as it were—five years before. My friend indeed had not named her much to any one; she appeared almost to have forgotten the fact of her continuance. Of course Mrs. Prest hadn't the nerves of an editor. It was meanwhile no explanation of the old woman's having eluded us to say that she lived abroad, for our researches had again and again taken us—not only by correspondence but by personal enquiry—to France, to Germany, to Italy, in which countries, not counting his important stay in England, so many of the too few years of Aspern's career had been spent. We were glad to think at least that in all our promulgations—some people now consider I believe that we have overdone them—we had only touched in passing and in the most discreet manner on Miss Bordereau's connexion. Oddly enough, even if we had had the material—and we had often wondered what could have become of it—this would have been the most difficult episode to handle.

The gondola stopped, the old palace was there; it was a house of the class which in Venice carries even in extreme dilapidation the dignified name. "How charming! It's gray and pink!" my companion exclaimed; and that is the most comprehensive description of it. It was not particularly old, only two or three centuries; and it had an air not so much of decay as of quiet discouragement, as if it had rather missed its career. But its wide front, with a stone balcony from end to end of the *piano nobile* or most important floor, was architectural enough, with the aid of various pilasters and arches; and the stucco with which in the intervals it had long ago been endued was rosy in the April afternoon. It overlooked a clean melancholy rather lonely canal, which had a narrow *riva* or convenient footway on either side. "I don't know why—there are no brick gables," said Mrs. Prest, "but this corner has seemed to me before more Dutch than Italian, more like Amsterdam than like Venice. It's eccentrically neat, for reasons of its own; and though you may pass on foot scarcely any one ever thinks of doing so. It's as negative—considering *where* it is—as a Protestant Sunday. Perhaps the people are afraid of the Misses Bordereau. I dare say they have the reputation of witches."

I forget what answer I made to this—I was given up to two other reflexions. The first of these was that if the old lady lived in such a big and imposing house she couldn't be in any sort of misery and therefore wouldn't be tempted by a chance to let a couple of rooms. I expressed this fear to Mrs. Prest, who gave me a very straight answer. "If she didn't live in a big house how could it be a question of her having rooms to spare? If she were not amply lodged you'd lack ground to approach her. Besides, a big house here, and especially in this *quartier perdu*, proves nothing at all: it's perfectly consistent with a state of penury. Dilapidated old palazzi, if you'll go out of the way for them, are to be had for five shillings a year. And as for the people who live in them—no, until you've explored Venice socially as much as I have, you can form no idea of their domestic desolation. They live on nothing, for they've nothing to live on." The other idea that had come into my head was connected with a high blank wall which appeared to confine an expanse of ground on one side of the house. Blank I call it, but it was figured over with the patches that please a painter, repaired breaches, crumblings of plaster, extrusions of brick that had turned pink with time; while a few thin trees, with the poles of certain rickety trellises, were visible over the top. The place was a garden and apparently attached to the house. I suddenly felt that so attached it gave me my pretext.

I sat looking out on all this with Mrs. Prest (it was covered with the golden glow of Venice) from the shade of our *felze*, and she asked me if I would go in then, while she waited for me, or come back another time. At first I couldn't decide—it was doubtless very weak of me. I wanted still to think I *might* get a footing, and was afraid to meet failure, for it would leave me, as I remarked to my companion, without another arrow for my bow. "Why not another?" she enquired as I sat there hesitating and thinking it over; and she wished to know why even now and before taking the trouble of becoming an inmate—which might be wretchedly uncomfortable after all, even if it succeeded—I hadn't the resource of simply offering them a sum of money down. In that way I might get what I wanted without bad nights.

"Dearest lady," I exclaimed, "excuse the impatience of my tone when I suggest that you must have forgotten the very fact—surely I communicated it to you—which threw me on your ingenuity. The old woman won't have her relics and tokens so much as spoken of; they're personal, delicate, intimate, and she hasn't the feelings of the day, God bless her! If I should sound that note first I should certainly spoil the game. I can arrive at my spoils only by putting her off her guard, and I can put her off her guard only by ingratiating diplomatic arts. Hypocrisy, duplicity are my only chance. I'm sorry for it, but there's no baseness I wouldn't commit for Jeffrey Aspern's sake. First I must take tea with her—then tackle the main job." And I told over what had happened to John Cumnor on his respectfully writing to her. No notice whatever had been taken of his first letter, and the second had been answered very sharply, in six lines, by the niece. "Miss Bordereau requested her to say that she couldn't imagine what he meant by troubling them. They had none of Mr. Aspern's 'literary remains,' and if they *had* had wouldn't have dreamed of showing them to any one on any account whatever. She couldn't imagine what he was talking about and begged he would let her alone." I certainly didn't want to be met that way.

"Well," said Mrs. Prest after a moment and all provokingly, "perhaps they really haven't anything. If they deny it flat how are you sure?"

"John Cumnor's sure, and it would take me long to tell you how his conviction, or his very strong presumption—strong enough to stand against the old lady's not unnatural fib—has built itself up. Besides, he makes much of the internal evidence of the niece's letter."

"The internal evidence?"

"Her calling him 'Mr. Aspern.' "

"I don't see what that proves."

"It proves familiarity, and familiarity implies the possession of mementoes, of tangible objects I can't tell you how that 'Mr.' affects me—how it bridges over the gulf of time and brings our hero near to me—nor what an edge it gives to my desire to see Juliana. You don't say 'Mr.' Shakespeare."

"Would I, any more, if I had a box full of his letters?"

"Yes, if he had been your lover and some one wanted them!" And I added that John Cumnor was so convinced, and so all the more convinced by Miss Bordereau's tone, that he would have come himself to Venice on the undertaking were it not for the obstacle of his having, for any confidence, to disprove his identity with the person who had written to them, which the old ladies would be sure to suspect in spite of dissimulation and a change of name. If they were to ask him point-blank if he were not their snubbed correspondent it would be too awkward for him to lie; whereas I was fortunately not tied in that way. I was a fresh hand—I could protest without lying.

"But you'll have to take a false name," said Mrs. Prest. "Juliana lives out of the world as much as it is possible to live, but she has none the less probably heard of Mr. Aspern's editors. She perhaps possesses what you've published."

"I've thought of that," I returned; and I drew out of my pocket-book a visiting card neatly engraved with a well-chosen *nom de guerre.*

"You're very extravagant—it adds to your immorality. You might have done it in pencil or ink," said my companion.

"This looks more genuine."

"Certainly you've the courage of your curiosity. But it will be awkward about your letters; they won't come to you in that mask."

"My banker will take them in and I shall go every day to get them. It will give me a little walk."

"Shall you depend all on that?" asked Mrs. Prest. "Aren't you coming to see me?"

"Oh you'll have left Venice for the hot months long before there are any results. I'm prepared to roast all summer—as well as through the long hereafter perhaps you'll say! Meanwhile John Cumnor will bombard me with letters addressed, in my feigned name, to the care of the padrona."

"She'll recognise his hand," my companion suggested.

"On the envelope he can disguise it."

"Well, you're a precious pair! Doesn't it occur to you that even if you're able to say you're not Mr. Cumnor in person they may still suspect you of being his emissary?"

"Certainly, and I see only one way to parry that."

"And what may that be?"

I hesitated a moment. "To make love to the niece."

"Ah," cried my friend, "wait till you see her!"

II

I MUST work the garden—I must work the garden," I said to myself five minutes later and while I waited, upstairs, in the long, dusky sala, where the bare scagliola floor gleamed vaguely in a chink of the closed shutters. The place was impressive, yet looked somehow cold and cautious. Mrs. Prest had floated away, giving me a rendezvous at the end of half an hour by some neighbouring water-steps; and I had been let into the house, after pulling the rusty bell-wire, by a small red-headed and white-faced maid-servant, who was very young and not ugly and wore clicking pattens and a shawl in the fashion of a hood. She had not contented herself with opening the door from above by the usual arrangement of a creaking pulley, though she had looked down at me first from an upper window, dropping the cautious challenge which in Italy precedes the act of admission. I was irritated as a general thing by this survival of mediæval manners, though as so fond, if yet so special, an antiquarian I suppose I ought to have liked it; but, with my resolve to be genial from the threshold at any price, I took my false card out of my pocket and held it up to her, smiling as if it were a magic token. It had the effect of one indeed, for it brought her, as I say, all the way down. I begged her to hand it to her mistress, having first written on it in Italian the words: "Could you very kindly see a gentleman, a travelling American, for a moment?" The little maid wasn't hostile—even that was perhaps something gained. She coloured, she smiled and looked both frightened and pleased. I could see that my arrival was a great affair, that visits in such a house were rare and that she was a person who would have liked a bustling place. When she pushed forward the heavy door behind me I felt my foot in the citadel and promised myself ever so firmly to keep it there. She pattered across the damp stony lower hall and I followed her up the high staircase—stonier still, as it seemed—without an invitation. I think she had meant I should wait for her below, but such was not my idea, and I took up my station in the sala. She flitted, at the far end of it, into impenetrable regions, and I looked at the place with my heart beating as I had known it to do in dentists' parlours. It had a gloomy grandeur, but owed its character almost all to its noble shape and to the fine architectural doors, as high as those of grand frontages, which, leading into the various rooms, repeated themselves on either side at intervals. They were surmounted with old faded painted escutcheons, and here and there in the spaces between them hung brown pictures, which I noted as speciously bad, in battered and tarnished frames that were yet more desirable than the canvases themselves. With the exception of several straw-bottomed chairs that kept their backs to the wall the grand obscure vista contained little else to minister to effect. It was evidently never used save as a passage, and scantly even as that. I may add that by the time the door through which the maid-servant had escaped opened again my eyes had grown used to the want of light.

I hadn't meanwhile meant by my private ejaculation that I must myself cultivate the soil of the tangled enclosure which lay beneath the windows, but the lady who came toward me from the distance over the hard shining floor might have supposed as much from the way in which, as I went rapidly to meet her, I exclaimed, taking care to speak Italian: "The garden, the garden—do me the pleasure to tell me if it's yours!"

She stopped short, looking at me with wonder; and then, "Nothing here is mine," she answered in English, coldly and sadly.

"Oh you're English; how delightful!" I ingenuously cried. "But surely the garden belongs to the house?"

"Yes, but the house doesn't belong to me." She was a long lean pale person, habited apparently in a dull-coloured dressing-gown, and she spoke very simply and mildly. She didn't ask me to sit down, any more than years before—if she were the niece—she had asked Mrs. Prest, and we stood face to face in the empty pompous hall.

"Well then, would you kindly tell me to whom I must address myself? I'm afraid you will think me horribly intrusive, but you know I *must* have a garden—upon my honour I must!"

Her face was not young, but it was candid; it was not fresh, but it was clear. She had large eyes which were not bright, and a great deal of hair which was not "dressed," and long fine hands which were—possibly—not clean. She clasped these members almost convulsively as, with a confused alarmed look, she broke out: "Oh, don't take it away from us; we like it ourselves!"

"You have the use of it then?"

"Oh yes. If it wasn't for that—!" And she gave a wan vague smile.

"Isn't it a luxury, precisely? That's why intending to be in Venice some weeks, possibly all summer, and having some literary work, some reading and writing to do, so that I must be quiet and yet if possible a great deal in the open air—that's why I've felt a garden to be really indispensable. I appeal to your own experience," I went on with as sociable a smile as I could risk. "Now can't I look at yours?"

"I don't know, I don't understand," the poor woman murmured, planted there and letting her weak wonder deal—helplessly enough, as I felt—with my strangeness.

"I mean only from one of those windows—such grand ones as you have here—if you'll let me open the shutters." And I walked toward the back of the house. When I had advanced halfway I stopped and waited as in the belief she would accompany me. I had been of necessity quite abrupt, but I strove at the same time to give her the impression of extreme courtesy. "I've looked at furnished rooms all over the place, and it seems impossible to find any with a garden attached. Naturally in a place like Venice gardens are rare. It's absurd if you like, for a man, but I can't live without flowers."

"There are none to speak of down there." She came nearer, as if, though she mistrusted me, I had drawn her by an invisible thread. I went on again, and she continued as she followed me: "We've a few, but they're very common. It costs too much to cultivate them; one has to have a man."

"Why shouldn't I be the man?" I asked. "I'll work without wages; or rather I'll put in a gardener. You shall have the sweetest flowers in Venice."

She protested against this with a small quaver of sound that might have been at the same time a gush of rapture for my free sketch. Then she gasped: "We don't know you—we don't know you."

"You know me as much as I know you, or rather much more, because you know my name. And if you're English I'm almost a countryman."

"We're not English," said my companion, watching me in practical submission while I threw open the shutters of one of the divisions of the wide high window.

"You speak the language so beautifully: might I ask what you are?" Seen from above the garden was in truth shabby, yet I felt at a glance that it had great capabilities. She made no rejoinder, she was so lost in her blankness and gentleness, and I exclaimed, "You don't mean to say you're also by chance American?"

"I don't know. We used to be."

"Used to be? Surely you haven't changed?"

"It's so many years ago. We don't seem to be anything now."

"So many years that you've been living here? Well, I don't wonder at that; it's a grand old house. I suppose you all use the garden," I went on, "but I assure you I shouldn't be in your way. I'd be very quiet and stay quite in one corner."

"We all use it?" she repeated after me vaguely, not coming close to the window but looking at my shoes. She appeared to think me capable of throwing her out.

"I mean all your family—as many as you are."

"There's only one other than me. She's very old. She never goes down."

I feel again my thrill at this close identification of Juliana; in spite of which, however, I kept my head. "Only one other in all this great house!" I feigned to be not only amazed but almost scandalized. "Dear lady, you must have space then to spare!"

"To spare?" she repeated—almost as for the rich unwonted joy to her of spoken words.

"Why you surely don't live (two quiet women—I see *you* are quiet, at any rate) in fifty rooms!" Then with a burst of hope and cheer I put the question straight: "Couldn't you for a good rent *let* me two or three? That would set me up!"

I had now struck the note that translated my purpose, and I needn't reproduce the whole of the tune I played. I ended by making my entertainer believe me an undesigning person, though of course I didn't even attempt to persuade her I was not an eccentric one. I repeated that I had studies to pursue; that I wanted quiet; that I delighted in a garden and had vainly sought one up and down the city; that I would undertake that before another month was over the dear old house should be smothered in flowers. I think it was the flowers that won my suit, for I afterwards found that Miss Tina—for such the name of this high tremulous spinster proved somewhat incongruously to be—had an insatiable appetite for them. When I speak of my suit as won I mean that before I left her she had promised me she would refer the question to her aunt. I invited information as to who her aunt might be and she answered "Why Miss Bordereau!" with an air of surprise, as if I might have been expected to know. There were contradictions like this in Miss Tina which, as I observed later, contributed to make her rather pleasingly incalculable and interesting. It was the study of the two ladies to live so that the world shouldn't talk of them or touch them, and yet they had never altogether accepted the idea that it didn't hear of them. In Miss Tina at any rate a grateful susceptibility to human contact had not died out, and contact of a limited order there would be if I should come to live in the house.

"We've never done anything of the sort; we've never had a lodger or any kind of inmate." So much as this she made a point of saying to me. "We're very poor, we live very badly—almost on nothing. The rooms are very bare—those you might take; they've nothing at all in them. I don't know how you'd sleep, how you'd eat."

"With your permission I could easily put in a bed and a few tables and chairs. *C'est la moindre des choses* and the affair of an hour or two. I know a little man from whom I can hire for a trifle what I should so briefly want, what I should use; my gondolier can bring the things round in his boat. Of course in this great house you must have a second kitchen, and my servant who's a wonderfully handy fellow"—this personage was an evocation of the moment—"can easily cook me a chop there. My tastes and habits are of the simplest; I live on flowers!" And then I ventured to add that if they were very poor it was all the more reason they should let their rooms. They were bad economists—I had never heard of such a waste of material.

I saw in a moment my good lady had never before been spoken to in any such fashion—with a humorous firmness that didn't exclude sympathy, that was quite founded on it. She might easily have told me that my sympathy was impertinent, but this by good fortune didn't occur to her. I left her with the understanding that she would submit the question to her aunt and that I might come back the next day for their decision.

"The aunt will refuse; she'll think the whole proceeding very *louche*!" Mrs. Prest declared shortly after this, when I had resumed my place in her gondola. She had put the idea into my head and now—so little are women to be counted on—she appeared to take a despondent view of it. Her pessimism provoked me and I pretended to have the best hopes; I went so far as to boast of a distinct prevision of success. Upon this Mrs. Prest broke out, "Oh I see what's in your head! You fancy you've made such an impression in five minutes that she's dying for you to come and can be depended on to bring the old one round. If you do get in you'll count it as a triumph."

I did count it as a triumph, but only for the commentator—in the last analysis—not for the man, who had not the tradition of personal conquest. When I went back on the morrow the little maid-servant conducted me straight through the long sala—it opened there as before in large perspective and was lighter now, which I thought a good omen—into the apartment from which the recipient of my former visit had emerged on that occasion. It was a spacious shabby parlour with a fine old painted ceiling under which a strange figure sat alone at one of the windows. They come back to me now almost with the palpitation they caused, the successive states marking my consciousness that as the door of the room closed behind me I was really face to face with the Juliana of some of Aspern's most exquisite and most renowned lyrics. I grew used to her afterwards, though never completely; but as she sat there before me my heart beat as fast as if the miracle of resurrection had taken place for my benefit. Her presence seemed somehow to contain and express his own, and I felt nearer to him at that first moment of seeing her than I ever had been before or ever have been since. Yes, I remember my emotions in their order, even including a curious little tremor that took me when I saw the niece not to be there. With her, the day before, I had become sufficiently familiar, but it almost exceeded my courage—much as I had longed for the event—to be left alone with so terrible a relic as the aunt. She was too strange, too literally resurgent. Then came a check from the perception that we weren't really face to face, inasmuch as she had over her eyes a horrible green shade which served for her almost as a mask. I believed for the instant that she had put it on expressly, so that from underneath it she might take me all in without my getting at herself. At the same time it created a presumption of some ghastly death's head lurking behind it. The divine Juliana as a grinning skull—the vision hung there until it passed. Then it came to me that she *was* tremendously old—so old that death might take her at any moment, before I should have time to compass my end. The next thought was a correction to that; it lighted up the situation. She would die next week, she would die to-morrow—then I could pounce on her possessions and ransack her drawers. Meanwhile she sat there neither moving nor speaking. She was very small and shrunken, bent forward with her hands in her lap. She was dressed in black and her head was wrapped in a piece of old black lace which showed no hair.

My emotion keeping me silent she spoke first, and the remark she made was exactly the most unexpected.

III

"Our house is very far from the centre, but the little canal is very *comme il faut.*"

"It's the sweetest corner of Venice and I can imagine nothing more charming," I hastened to reply. The old lady's voice was very thin and weak, but it had an agreeable, cultivated murmur and there was wonder in the thought that that individual note had been in Jeffrey Aspern's ear.

"Please to sit down there. I hear very well," she said quietly, as if perhaps I had been shouting; and the chair she pointed to was at a certain distance. I took possession of it, assuring her I was perfectly aware of my intrusion and of my not having been properly introduced, and that I could but throw myself on her indulgence. Perhaps the other lady, the one I had had the honour of seeing the day before, would have explained to her about the garden. That was literally what had given me courage to take a step so unconventional. I had fallen in love at sight with the whole place—she herself was probably so used to it that she didn't know the impression it was capable of making on a stranger—and I had felt it really a case to risk something. Was her own kindness in receiving me a sign that I was not wholly out in my calculation? It would make me extremely happy to think so. I could give her my word of honour that I was a most respectable inoffensive person and that as a co-tenant of the palace, so to speak, they would be barely conscious of my existence. I would conform to any regulations, any restrictions, if they would only let me enjoy the garden. Moreover I should be delighted to give her references, guarantees; they would be of the very best, both in Venice and in England, as well as in America.

She listened to me in perfect stillness and I felt her look at me with great penetration, though I could see only the lower part of her bleached and shrivelled face. Independently of the refining process of old age it had a delicacy which once must have been great. She had been very fair, she had had a wonderful complexion. She was silent a little after I had ceased speaking; then she began: "If you're so fond of a garden why don't you go to *terra firma*, where there are so many far better than this?"

"Oh it's the combination!" I answered, smiling; and then with rather a flight of fancy; "It's the idea of a garden in the middle of the sea."

"This isn't the middle of the sea; you can't so much as see the water."

I stared a moment, wondering if she wished to convict me of fraud. "Can't see the water? Why, dear madam, I can come up to the very gate in my boat."

She appeared inconsequent, for she said vaguely in reply to this: "Yes, if you've got a boat. I haven't any; it's many years since I have been in one of the *gondole*." She uttered these words as if they designed a curious far-away craft known to her only by hearsay.

"Let me assure you of the pleasure with which I would put mine at your service!" I returned. I had scarcely said this however before I became aware that the speech was in questionable taste and might also do me the injury of making me appear too eager, too possessed of a hidden motive. But the old woman remained impenetrable and her attitude worried me by suggesting that she had a fuller vision of me than I had of her. She gave me no thanks for my somewhat extravagant offer, but remarked that the lady I had seen the day before was her niece; she would presently come in. She had asked her to stay away a little on purpose—had had her reasons for seeing me first alone. She relapsed into silence and I turned over the fact of these unmentioned reasons and the question of what might come yet; also that of whether I might venture on some judicious remark in praise of her companion. I went so far as to say I should be delighted to see our absent friend again: she had been so very patient with me, considering how odd she must have thought me—a declaration which drew from Miss Bordereau another of her whimsical speeches.

"She has very good manners; I bred her up myself!" I was on the point of saying that that accounted for the easy grace of the niece, but I arrested myself in time, and the next moment the old woman went on: "I don't care who you may be—I don't want to know; it signifies very little to-day." This had all the air of being a formula of dismissal, as if her next words would be that I might take myself off now that she had had the amusement of looking on the face of such a monster of indiscretion. Therefore I was all the more surprised when she added in her soft venerable quaver: "You may have as many rooms as you like—if you'll pay me a good deal of money."

I hesitated but an instant, long enough to measure what she meant in particular by this condition. First it struck me that she must have really a large sum in her mind; then I reasoned quickly that her idea of a large sum would probably not correspond to my own. My deliberation, I think, was not so visible as to diminish the promptitude with which I replied: "I will pay with pleasure and of course in advance whatever you may think it proper to ask me."

"Well then, a thousand francs a month," she said instantly, while her baffling green shade continued to cover her attitude.

The figure, as they say, was startling and my logic had been at fault. The sum she had mentioned was, by the Venetian measure of such matters, exceedingly large; there was many an old palace in an out-of-the-way corner that I might on such terms have enjoyed the whole of by the year. But so far as my resources allowed I was prepared to spend money, and my decision was quickly taken. I would pay her with a smiling face what she asked, but in that case I would make it up by getting hold of my "spoils" for nothing. Moreover if she had asked five times as much I should have risen to the occasion, so odious would it have seemed to me to stand chaffering with Aspern's Juliana. It was queer enough to have a question of money with her at all. I assured her that her views perfectly met my own and that on the morrow I should have the pleasure of putting three months' rent into her hand. She received this announcement with apparent complacency and with no discoverable sense that after all it would become her to say that I ought to see the rooms first. This didn't occur to her, and indeed her serenity was mainly what I wanted. Our little agreement was just concluded when the door opened and the younger lady appeared on the threshold. As soon as Miss Bordereau saw her niece she cried out almost gaily: "He'll give three thousand—three thousand to-morrow!"

Miss Tina stood still, her patient eyes turning from one of us to the other; then she brought out, scarcely above her breath: "Do you mean francs?"

"Did you mean francs or dollars?" the old woman asked of me at this.

"I think francs were what you said," I sturdily smiled.

"That's very good," said Miss Tina, as if she had felt how overreaching her own question might have looked.

"What do *you* know? You're ignorant," Miss Bordereau remarked; not with acerbity but with a strange soft coldness.

"Yes, of money—certainly of money!" Miss Tina hastened to concede.

"I'm sure you've your own fine branches of knowledge," I took the liberty of saying genially. There was something painful to me, somehow, in the turn the conversation had taken, in the discussion of dollars and francs.

"She had a very good education when she was young. I looked into that myself," said Miss Bordereau. Then she added: "But she has learned nothing since."

"I have always been with *you,*" Miss Tina rejoined very mildly, and of a certainty with no intention of an epigram.

"Yes, but for that—!" her aunt declared with more satirical force. She evidently meant that but for this her niece would never have got on at all; the point of the observation however being lost on Miss Tina, though she blushed at hearing her history revealed to a stranger. Miss Bordereau went on, addressing herself to me: "And what time will you come to-morrow with the money?"

"The sooner the better. If it suits you I'll come at noon."

"I am always here, but I have my hours," said the old woman as if her convenience were not to be taken for granted.

"You mean the times when you receive?"

"I never receive. But I'll see you at noon when you come with the money."

"Very good, I shall be punctual." To which I added: "May I shake hands with you on our contract?" I thought there ought to be some little form; it would make me really feel easier, for I was sure there would be no other. Besides, though Miss Bordereau couldn't to-day be called personally attractive and there was something even in her wasted antiquity that bade one stand at one's distance, I felt an irresistible desire to hold in my own for a moment the hand Jeffrey Aspern had pressed.

For a minute she made no answer, and I saw that my proposal failed to meet with her approbation. She indulged in no movement of withdrawal, which I half expected; she only said coldly: "I belong to a time when that was not the custom."

I felt rather snubbed but I exclaimed good-humouredly to Miss Tina, "Oh you'll do as well!" I shook hands with her while she assented with a small flutter. "Yes, yes, to show it's all arranged!"

"Shall you bring the money in gold?" Miss Bordereau demanded as I was turning to the door.

I looked at her a moment. "Aren't you a little afraid, after all, of keeping such a sum as that in the house?" It was not that I was annoyed at her avidity, but was truly struck with the disparity between such a treasure and such scanty means of guarding it.

"Whom should I be afraid of if I'm not afraid of you?" she asked with her shrunken grimness.

"Ah well," I laughed, "I shall be in point of fact a protector and I'll bring gold if you prefer."

"Thank you," the old woman returned with dignity and with an inclination of her head which evidently signified my dismissal. I passed out of the room, thinking how hard it would be to circumvent her. As I stood in the sala again I saw that Miss Tina had followed me, and I supposed that as her aunt had neglected to suggest I should take a look at my quarters it was her purpose to repair the omission. But she made no such overture; she only stood there with a dim, though not a languid smile, and with an effect of irresponsible incompetent youth almost comically at variance with the faded facts of her person. She was not infirm, like her aunt, but she struck me as more deeply futile, because her inefficiency was inward, which was not the case with Miss Bordereau's. I waited to see if she would offer to show me the rest of the house but I didn't precipitate the question, inasmuch as my plan was from this moment to spend as much of my time as possible in her society. A minute indeed elapsed before I committed myself.

"I've had better fortune than I hoped. It was very kind of her to see me. Perhaps you said a good word for me."

"It was the idea of the money," said Miss Tina.

"And did you suggest that?"

"I told her you'd perhaps pay largely."

"What made you think that?"

"I told her I thought you were rich."

"And what put that into your head?"

"I don't know; the way you talked."

"Dear me, I must talk differently now," I returned. "I'm sorry to say it's not the case."

"Well," said Miss Tina, "I think that in Venice the *forestieri* in general often give a great deal for something that after all isn't much." She appeared to make this remark with a comforting intention, to wish to remind me that if I had been extravagant I wasn't foolishly singular. We walked together along the sala, and as I took its magnificent measure I said that I was afraid it wouldn't form a part of my *quartiere*. Were my rooms by chance to be among those that opened into it? "Not if you go above—to the second floor," she answered as if she had rather taken for granted I would know my proper place.

"And I infer that that's where your aunt would like me to be."

"She said your apartments ought to be very distinct."

"That certainly would be best." And I listened with respect while she told me that above I should be free to take whatever I might like; that there was another staircase, but only from the floor on which we stood, and that to pass from it to the garden-level or to come up to my lodging I should have in effect to cross the great hall. This was an immense point gained; I foresaw that it would constitute my whole leverage in my relations with the two ladies. When I asked Miss Tina how I was to manage at present to find my way up she replied with an access of that sociable shyness which constantly marked her manner:

"Perhaps you can't. I don't see—unless I should go with you." She evidently hadn't thought of this before.

We ascended to the upper floor and visited a long succession of empty rooms. The best of them looked over the garden; some of the others had above the opposite rough-tiled house-tops a view of the blue lagoon. They were all dusty and even a little disfigured with long neglect, but I saw that by spending a few hundred francs I should be able to make three or four of them habitable enough. My experiment was turning out costly, yet now that I had all but taken possession I ceased to allow this to trouble me. I mentioned to my companion a few of the things I should put in, but she replied rather more precipitately than usual that I might do exactly what I liked: she seemed to wish to notify me that the Misses Bordereau would take none but the most veiled interest in my proceedings. I guessed that her aunt had instructed her to adopt this tone, and I may as well say now that I came afterwards to distinguish perfectly (as I believed) between the speeches she made on her own responsibility and those the old woman imposed upon her. She took no notice of the unswept condition of the rooms and indulged neither in explanations nor in apologies. I said to myself that this was a sign Juliana and her niece—disenchanting idea!—were untidy persons with a low Italian standard; but I afterwards recognised that a lodger who had forced an entrance had no *locus standi* as a critic. We looked out of a good many windows, for there was nothing within the rooms to look at, and still I wanted to linger. I asked her what several different objects in the prospect might be, but in no case did she appear to know. She was evidently not familiar with the view—it was as if she had not looked at it for years—and I presently saw that she was too preoccupied with something else to pretend to care for it. Suddenly she said—the remark was not suggested:

"I don't know whether it will make any difference to you, but the money is for me."

"The money—?"

"The money you're going to bring."

"Why you'll make me wish to stay here two or three years!" I spoke as benevolently as possible, though it had begun to act on my nerves that these women so associated with Aspern should so constantly bring the pecuniary question back.

"That would be very good for me," she answered almost gaily.

"You put me on my honour!"

She looked as if she failed to understand this, but went on: "She wants me to have more. She thinks she's going to die."

"Ah not soon I hope!" I cried with genuine feeling. I had perfectly considered the possibility of her destroying her documents on the day she should feel her end at hand. I believed that she would cling to them till then, and I was as convinced of her reading Aspern's letters over every night or at least pressing them to her withered lips. I would have given a good deal for some view of those solemnities. I asked Miss Tina if her venerable relative were seriously ill, and she replied that she was only very tired—she had lived so extraordinarily long. That was what she said herself—she wanted to die for a change. Besides, all her friends had been dead for ages; either they ought to have remained or she ought to have gone. That was another thing her aunt often said: she was not at all resigned—resigned, that is, to life.

"But people don't die when they like, do they?" Miss Tina inquired. I took the liberty of asking why, if there was actually enough money to maintain both of them, there would not be more than enough in case of her being left alone. She considered this difficult problem a moment and then said: "Oh well, you know, she takes care of me. She thinks that when I'm alone I shall be a great fool and shan't know how to manage."

"I should have supposed rather that you took care of *her*. I'm afraid she's very proud."

"Why, have you discovered that already?" Miss Tina cried with a dimness of glad surprise.

"I was shut up with her there for a considerable time and she struck me, she interested me extremely. It didn't take me long to make my discovery. She won't have much to say to me while I'm here."

"No, I don't think she will," my companion averred.

"Do you suppose she has some suspicion of me?"

Miss Tina's honest eyes gave me no sign I had touched a mark. "I shouldn't think so—letting you in after all so easily."

"You call it easily? She has covered her risk," I said. "But where is it one could take an advantage of her?"

"I oughtn't to tell you if I knew, ought I?" And Miss Tina added, before I had time to reply to this, smiling dolefully: "Do you think we've any weak points?"

"That's exactly what I'm asking. You'd only have to mention them for me to respect them religiously."

She looked at me hereupon with that air of timid but candid and even gratified curiosity with which she had confronted me from the first; after which she said: "There's nothing to tell. We're terribly quiet. I don't know how the days pass. We've no life."

"I wish I might think I should bring you a little."

"Oh we know what we want," she went on. "It's all right."

There were twenty things I desired to ask her: how in the world they did live; whether they had any friends or visitors, any relations in America or in other countries. But I judged such probings premature; I must leave it to a later chance. "Well, don't *you* be proud," I contented myself with saying. "Don't hide from me altogether."

"Oh I must stay with my aunt," she returned without looking at me. And at the same moment, abruptly, without any ceremony of parting, she quitted me and disappeared, leaving me to make my own way downstairs. I stayed a while longer, wandering about the bright desert—the sun was pouring in—of the old house, thinking the situation over on the spot. Not even the pattering little *serva* came to look after me, and I reflected that after all this treatment showed confidence.

IV

Perhaps it did, but all the same, six weeks later, towards the middle of June, the moment when Mrs. Prest undertook her annual migration, I had made no measurable advance. I was obliged to confess to her that I had no results to speak of. My first step had been unexpectedly rapid, but there was no appearance it would be followed by a second. I was a thousand miles from taking tea with my hostesses—that privilege of which, as I reminded my good friend, we both had had a vision. She reproached me with lacking boldness and I answered that even to be bold you must have an opportunity: you may push on through a breach, but you can't batter down a dead wall. She returned that the breach I had already made was big enough to admit an army and accused me of wasting precious hours in whimpering in her salon when I ought to have been carrying on the struggle in the field. It is true that I went to see her very often—all on the theory that it would console me (I freely expressed my discouragement) for my want of success on my own premises. But I began to feel that it didn't console me to be perpetually chaffed for my scruples, especially since I was really so vigilant; and I was rather glad when my ironic friend closed her house for the summer. She had expected to gather amusement from the drama of my intercourse with the Misses Bordereau, and was disappointed that the intercourse, and consequently the drama, had not come off. "They'll lead you on to your ruin," she said before she left Venice. "They'll get all your money without showing you a scrap." I think I settled down to my business with more concentration after her departure.

It was a fact that up to that time I had not, save on a single brief occasion, had even a moment's contact with my queer hostesses. The exception had occurred when I carried them according to my promise the terrible three thousand francs. Then I found Miss Tina awaiting me in the hall, and she took the money from my hand with a promptitude that prevented my seeing her aunt. The old lady had promised to receive me, yet apparently thought nothing of breaking that vow. The money was contained in a bag of chamois leather, of respectable dimensions, which my banker had given me, and Miss Tina had to make a big fist to receive it. This she did with extreme solemnity though I tried to treat the affair a little as a joke. It was in no jocular strain, yet it was with a clearness akin to a brightness that she enquired, weighing the money in her two palms: "Don't you think it's too much?" To which I replied that this would depend on the amount of pleasure I should get for it. Hereupon she turned away from me quickly, as she had done the day before, murmuring in a tone different from any she had used hitherto: "Oh pleasure, pleasure—there's no pleasure in this house!"

After that, for a long time, I never saw her, and I wondered the common chances of the day shouldn't have helped us to meet. It could only be evident that she was immensely on her guard against them; and in addition to this the house was so big that for each other we were lost in it. I used to look out for her hopefully as I crossed the sala in my comings and goings, but I was not rewarded with a glimpse of the tail of her dress. It was as if she never peeped out of her aunt's apartment. I used to wonder what she did there week after week and year after year. I had never met so stiff a policy of seclusion; it was more than keeping quiet—it was like hunted creatures feigning death. The two ladies appeared to have no visitors whatever and no sort of contact with the world. I judged at least that people couldn't have come to the house and that Miss Tina couldn't have gone out without my catching some view of it. I did what I disliked myself for doing—considering it but as once in a way: I questioned my servant about their habits and let him infer that I should be interested in any information he might glean. But he gleaned amazingly little for a knowing Venetian: it must be added that where there is a perpetual fast there are very few crumbs on the floor. His ability in other ways was sufficient, if not quite all I had attributed to him on the occasion of my first interview with Miss Tina. He had helped my gondolier to bring me round a boat-load of furniture; and when these articles had been carried to the top of the palace and distributed according to our associated wisdom he organized my household with such dignity as answered to its being composed exclusively of himself. He made me in short as comfortable as I could be with my indifferent prospects. I should have been glad if he had fallen in love with Miss Bordereau's maid or, failing this, had taken her in aversion; either event might have brought about some catastrophe, and a catastrophe might have led to some parley. It was my idea that she would have been sociable, and I myself on various occasions saw her flit to and fro on domestic errands, so that I was sure she was accessible. But I tasted of no gossip from that fountain, and I afterwards learned that Pasquale's affections were fixed upon an object that made him heedless of other women. This was a young lady with a powdered face, a yellow cotton gown and much leisure, who used often to come to see him. She practised, at her convenience, the art of a stringer of beads—these ornaments are made in Venice to profusion; she had her pocket full of them and I used to find them on the floor of my apartment—and kept an eye on the possible rival in the house. It was not for me of course to make the domestics tattle, and I never said a word to Miss Bordereau's cook.

It struck me as a proof of the old woman's resolve to have nothing to do with me that she should never have sent me a receipt for my three months' rent. For some days I looked out for it and then, when I had given it up, wasted a good deal of time in wondering what her reason had been for neglecting so indispensable and familiar a form. At first I was tempted to send her a reminder; after which I put by the idea—against my judgement as to what was right in the particular case—on the general ground of wishing to keep quiet. If Miss Bordereau suspected me of ulterior aims she would suspect me less if I should be businesslike, and yet I consented not to be. It was possible she intended her omission as an impertinence, a visible irony, to show how she could overreach people who attempted to overreach her. On that hypothesis it was well to let her see that one didn't notice her little tricks. The real reading of the matter, I afterwards gathered, was simply the poor lady's desire to emphasise the fact that I was in the enjoyment of a favour as rigidly limited as it had been liberally bestowed. She had given me part of her house, but she wouldn't add to that so much as a morsel of paper with her name on it. Let me say that even at first this didn't make me too miserable, for the whole situation had the charm of its oddity. I foresaw that I should have a summer after my own literary heart, and the sense of playing with my opportunity was much greater after all than any sense of being played with. There could be no Venetian business without patience, and since I adored the place I was much more in the spirit of it for having laid in a large provision. That spirit kept me perpetual company and seemed to look out at me from the revived immortal face—in which all his genius shone—of the great poet who was my prompter. I had invoked him and he had come; he hovered before me half the time; it was as if his bright ghost had returned to earth to assure me he regarded the affair as his own no less than as mine and that we should see it fraternally and fondly to a conclusion. It was as if he had said: "Poor dear, be easy with her; she has some natural prejudices; only give her time. Strange as it may appear to you she was very attractive in 1820. Meanwhile aren't we in Venice together, and what better place is there for the meeting of dear friends? See how it glows with the advancing summer; how the sky and the sea and the rosy air and the marble of the palaces all shimmer and melt together." My eccentric private errand became a part of the general romance and the general glory—I felt even a mystic companionship, a moral fraternity with all those who in the past had been in the service of art. They had worked for beauty, for a devotion; and what else was I doing? That element was in everything that Jeffrey Aspern had written, and I was only bringing it to light.

I lingered in the sala when I went to and fro; I used to watch —as long as I thought decent—the door that led to Miss Bordereau's part of the house. A person observing me might have supposed I was trying to cast a spell on it or attempting some odd experiment in hypnotism. But I was only praying it might open or thinking what treasure probably lurked behind it. I hold it singular, as I look back, that I should never have doubted for a moment that the sacred relics were there; never have failed to know the joy of being beneath the same roof with them. After all they were under my hand—they had not escaped me yet; and they made my life continuous, in a fashion, with the illustrious life they had touched at the other end. I lost myself in this satisfaction to the point of assuming—in my quiet extravagance—that poor Miss Tina also went back, and still went back, as I used to phrase it. She did indeed, the gentle spinster, but not quite so far as Jeffrey Aspern, who was simple hearsay to her quite as he was to me. Only she had lived for years with Juliana, she had seen and handled all mementoes and—even though she was stupid—some esoteric knowledge had rubbed off on her. That was what the old woman represented—esoteric knowledge; and this was the idea with which my critical heart used to thrill. It literally beat faster often, of an evening when I had been out, as I stopped with my candle in the re-echoing hall on my way up to bed. It was as if at such a moment as that, in the stillness and after the long contradiction of the day, Miss Bordereau's secrets were in the air, the wonder of her survival more vivid. These were the acute impressions. I had them in another form, with more of a certain shade of reciprocity, during the hours I sat in the garden looking up over the top of my book at the closed windows of my hostess. In these windows no sign of life ever appeared; it was as if, for fear of my catching a glimpse of them, the two ladies passed their days in the dark. But this only emphasised their having matters to conceal; which was what I had wished to prove. Their motionless shutters became as expressive as eyes consciously closed, and I took comfort in the probability that, though invisible themselves, they kept me in view between the lashes.

I made a point of spending as much time as possible in the garden, to justify the picture I had originally given of my horticultural passion. And I not only spent time, but (hang it! as I said) spent precious money. As soon as I had got my rooms arranged and could give the question proper thought I surveyed the place with a clever expert and made terms for having it put in order. I was sorry to do this, for personally I liked it better as it was, with its weeds and its wild rich tangle, its sweet characteristic Venetian shabbiness. I had to be consistent, to keep my promise that I would smother the house in flowers. Moreover I clung to the fond fancy that by flowers I should make my way—I should succeed by big nosegays. I would batter the old women with lilies—I would bombard their citadel with roses. Their door would have to yield to the pressure when a mound of fragrance should be heaped against it. The place in truth had been brutally neglected. The Venetian capacity for dawdling is of the largest, and for a good many days unlimited litter was all my gardener had to show for his ministrations. There was a great digging of holes and carting about of earth, and after a while I grew so impatient that I had thoughts of sending for my "results" to the nearest stand. But I felt sure my friends would see through the chinks of their shutters where such tribute *couldn't* have been gathered, and might so make up their minds against my veracity. I possessed my soul and finally, though the delay was long, perceived some appearances of bloom. This encouraged me and I waited serenely enough till they multiplied. Meanwhile the real summer days arrived and began to pass, and as I look back upon them they seem to me almost the happiest of my life. I took more and more care to be in the garden whenever it was not too hot. I had an arbour arranged and a low table and an armchair put into it; and I carried out books and portfolios—I had always some business of writing in hand—and worked and waited and mused and hoped, while the golden hours elapsed and the plants drank in the light and the inscrutable old palace turned pale and then, as the day waned, began to recover and flush and my papers rustled in the wandering breeze of the Adriatic.

Considering how little satisfaction I got from it at first it is wonderful I shouldn't have grown more tired of trying to guess what mystic rites of ennui the Misses Bordereau celebrated in their darkened rooms; whether this had always been the tenor of their life and how in previous years they had escaped elbowing their neighbours. It was supposable they had then had other habits, forms and resources; that they must once have been young or at least middle-aged. There was no end to the questions it was possible to ask about them and no end to the answers it was not possible to frame. I had known many of my country-people in Europe and was familiar with the strange ways they were liable to take up there; but the Misses Bordereau formed altogether a new type of the American absentee. Indeed it was clear the American name had ceased to have any application to them—I had seen this in the ten minutes I spent in the old woman's room. You could never have said whence they came from the appearance of either of them; wherever it was they had long ago shed and unlearned all native marks and notes. There was nothing in them one recognised or fitted, and, putting the question of speech aside, they might have been Norwegians or Spaniards. Miss Bordereau, after all, had been in Europe nearly three-quarters of a century; it appeared by some verses addressed to her by Aspern on the occasion of his own second absence from America—verses of which Cumnor and I had after infinite conjecture established solidly enough the date—that she was even then, as a girl of twenty, on the foreign side of the sea. There was a profession in the poem—I hope not just for the phrase—that he had come back for her sake. We had no real light on her circumstances at that moment, any more than we had upon her origin, which we believed to be of the sort usually spoken of as modest. Cumnor had a theory that she had been a governess in some family in which the poet visited and that, in consequence of her position, there was from the first something unavowed, or rather something quite clandestine, in their relations. I on the other hand had hatched a little romance according to which she was the daughter of an artist, a painter or a sculptor, who had left the Western world, when the century was fresh, to study in the ancient schools. It was essential to my hypothesis that this amiable man should have lost his wife, should have been poor and unsuccessful and should have had a second daughter of a disposition quite different from Juliana's. It was also indispensable that he should have been accompanied to Europe by these young ladies and should have established himself there for the remainder of a struggling saddened life. There was a further implication that Miss Bordereau had had in her youth a perverse and reckless, albeit a generous and fascinating character, and that she had braved some wondrous chances. By what passions had she been ravaged, by what adventures and sufferings had she been blanched, what store of memories had she laid away for the monotonous future?

I asked myself these things as I sat spinning theories about her in my arbour and the bees droned in the flowers. It was incontestable that, whether for right or for wrong, most readers of certain of Aspern's poems (poems not as ambiguous as the sonnets—scarcely more divine, I think—of Shakespeare) had taken for granted that Juliana had not always adhered to the steep footway of renunciation. There hovered about her name a perfume of impenitent passion, an intimation that she had not been exactly as the respectable young person in general. Was this a sign that her singer had betrayed her, had given her away, as we say nowadays, to posterity? Certain it is that it would have been difficult to put one's finger on the passage in which her fair fame suffered injury. Moreover was not any fame fair enough that was so sure of duration and was associated with works immortal through their beauty? It was a part of my idea that the young lady had had a foreign lover—and say an unedifying tragical rupture—before her meeting with Jeffrey Aspern. She had lived with her father and sister in a queer old-fashioned expatriated artistic Bohemia of the days when the æsthetic was only the academic and the painters who knew the best models for *contadina* and *pifferaro* wore peaked hats and long hair. It was a society less awake than the coteries of to-day—in its ignorance of the wonderful chances, the opportunities of the early bird, with which its path was strewn—to tatters of old stuff and fragments of old crockery; so that Miss Bordereau appeared not to have picked up or have inherited many objects of importance. There was no enviable *bric-â-brac,* with its provoking legend of cheapness, in the room in which I had seen her. Such a fact as that suggested bareness, but none the less it worked happily into the sentimental interest I had always taken in the early movements of my countrymen as visitors to Europe. When Americans went abroad in 1820 there was something romantic, almost heroic in it, as compared with the perpetual ferryings of the present hour, the hour at which photography and other conveniences have annihilated surprise. Miss Bordereau had sailed with her family on a tossing brig in the days of long voyages and sharp differences; she had had her emotions on the top of yellow diligences, passed the night at inns where she dreamed of travellers' tales, and was most struck, on reaching the Eternal City, with the elegance of Roman pearls and scarfs and mosaic brooches. There was something touching to me in all that, and my imagination frequently went back to the period. If Miss Bordereau carried it there of course Jeffrey Aspern had at other times done so with greater force. It was a much more important fact, if one was looking at his genius critically, that he had lived in the days before the general transfusion. It had happened to me to regret that he had known Europe at all; I should have liked to see what he would have written without that experience, by which he had incontestably been enriched. But as his fate had ruled otherwise I went with him—I tried to judge how the general old order would have struck him. It was not only there, however, I watched him; the relations he had entertained with the special new had even a livelier interest. His own country after all had had most of his life, and his muse, as they said at that time, was essentially American. That was originally what I had prized him for: that at a period when our native land was nude and crude and provincial, when the famous "atmosphere" it is supposed to lack was not even missed, when literature was lonely there and art and form almost impossible, he had found means to live and write like one of the first; to be free and general and not at all afraid; to feel, understand and express everything.

V

I WAS seldom at home in the evening, for when I attempted to occupy myself in my apartments the lamplight brought in a swarm of noxious insects, and it was too hot for closed windows. Accordingly I spent the late hours either on the water—the moonlights of Venice are famous—or in the splendid square which serves as a vast forecourt to the strange old church of Saint Mark. I sat in front of Florian's café eating ices, listening to music, talking with acquaintances: the traveller will remember how the immense cluster of tables and little chairs stretches like a promontory into the smooth lake of the Piazza. The whole place, of a summer's evening, under the stars and with all the lamps, all the voices and light footsteps on marble—the only sounds of the immense arcade that encloses it—is an open-air saloon dedicated to cooling drinks and to a still finer degustation, that of the splendid impressions received during the day. When I didn't prefer to keep mine to myself there was always a stray tourist, disencumbered of his Bädeker, to discuss them with, or some domesticated painter rejoicing in the return of the season of strong effects. The great basilica, with its low domes and bristling embroideries, the mystery of its mosaic and sculpture, looked ghostly in the tempered gloom, and the sea-breeze passed between the twin columns of the Piazzetta, the lintels of a door no longer guarded, as gently as if a rich curtain swayed there. I used sometimes on these occasions to think of the Misses Bordereau and of the pity of their being shut up in apartments which in the Venetian July even Venetian vastness couldn't relieve of some stuffiness. Their life seemed miles away from the life of the Piazza, and no doubt it was really too late to make the austere Juliana change her habits. But poor Miss Tina would have enjoyed one of Florian's ices, I was sure; sometimes I even had thoughts of carrying one home to her. Fortunately my patience bore fruit and I was not obliged to do anything so ridiculous.

One evening about the middle of July I came in earlier than usual—I forgot what chance had led to this—and instead of going up to my quarters made my way into the garden. The temperature was very high; it was such a night as one would gladly have spent in the open air, and I was in no hurry to go to bed. I had floated home in my gondola, listening to the slow splash of the oar in the dark narrow canals, and now the only thought that occupied me was that it would be good to recline at one's length in the fragrant darkness on a garden bench. The odour of the canal was doubtless at the bottom of that aspiration, and the breath of the garden, as I entered it, gave consistency to my purpose. It was delicious—just such an air as must have trembled with Romeo's vows when he stood among the thick flowers and raised his arms to his mistress's balcony. I looked at the windows of the palace to see if by chance the example of Verona—Verona being not far off—had been followed; but everything was dim, as usual, and everything was still. Juliana might on the summer nights of her youth have murmured down from open windows at Jeffrey Aspern, but Miss Tina was not a poet's mistress any more than I was a poet. This however didn't prevent my gratification from being great as I became aware on reaching the end of the garden that my younger padrona was seated in one of the bowers. At first I made out but an indistinct figure, not in the least counting on such an overture from one of my hostesses; it even occurred to me that some enamoured maidservant had stolen in to keep a tryst with her sweetheart. I was going to turn away, not to frighten her, when the figure rose to its height and I recognised Miss Bordereau's niece. I must do myself the justice that I didn't wish to frighten her either, and much as I had longed for some such accident I should have been capable of retreating. It was as if I had laid a trap for her by coming home earlier than usual and by adding to that oddity my invasion of the garden. As she rose she spoke to me, and then I guessed that perhaps, secure in my almost inveterate absence, it was her nightly practice to take a lonely airing. There was no trap in truth, because I had had no suspicion. At first I took the words she uttered for an impatience of my arrival; but as she repeated them—I hadn't caught them clearly—I had the surprise of hearing her say: "Oh dear, I'm so glad you've come!" She and her aunt had in common the property of unexpected speeches. She came out of the arbour almost as if to throw herself in my arms.

I hasten to add that I escaped this ordeal and that she didn't even then shake hands with me. It was an ease to her to see me and presently she told me why—because she was nervous when out-of-doors at night alone. The plants and shrubs looked so strange in the dark, and there were all sorts of queer sounds—she couldn't tell what they were—like the noises of animals. She stood close to me, looking about her with an air of greater security but without any demonstration of interest in me as an individual. Then I felt how little nocturnal prowlings could have been her habit, and I was also reminded—I had been afflicted by the same in talking with her before I took possession—that it was impossible to allow too much for her simplicity.

"You speak as if you were lost in the backwoods," I cheeringly laughed. "How you manage to keep out of this charming place when you've only three steps to take to get into it is more than I've yet been able to discover. You hide away amazingly so long as I'm on the premises, I know; but I had a hope you peeped out a little at other times. You and your poor aunt are worse off than Carmelite nuns in their cells. Should you mind telling me how you exist without air, without exercise, without any sort of human contact? I don't see how you carry on the common business of life."

She looked at me as if I had spoken a strange tongue, and her answer was so little of one that I felt it make for irritation. "We go to bed very early—earlier than you'd believe." I was on the point of saying that this only deepened the mystery, but she gave me some relief by adding: "Before you came we weren't so private. But I've never been out at night."

"Never in these fragrant alleys, blooming here under your nose?"

"Ah," said Miss Tina, "they were never nice till now!" There was a finer sense in this and a flattering comparison, so that it seemed to me I had gained some advantage. As I might follow that further by establishing a good grievance I asked her why, since she thought my garden nice, she had never thanked me in any way for the flowers I had been sending up in such quantities for the previous three weeks. I had not been discouraged—there had been, as she would have observed, a daily armful; but I had been brought up in the common forms and a word of recognition now and then would have touched me in the right place.

"Why I didn't know they were for me!"

"They were for both of you. Why should I make a difference?"

Miss Tina reflected as if she might be thinking of a reason for that, but she failed to produce one. Instead of this she asked abruptly: "Why in the world do you want so much to know us?"

"I ought after all to make a difference," I replied. "That question's your aunt's; it isn't yours. You wouldn't ask it if you hadn't been put up to it."

"She didn't tell me to ask you," Miss Tina replied without confusion. She was indeed the oddest mixture of shyness and straightness.

"Well, she has often wondered about it herself and expressed her wonder to you. She has insisted on it, so that she has put the idea into your head that I'm insufferably pushing. Upon my word I think I've been very discreet. And how completely your aunt must have lost every tradition of sociability, to see anything out of the way in the idea that respectable intelligent people, living as we do under the same roof, should occasionally exchange a remark! What could be more natural? We are of the same country and have at least some of the same tastes, since, like you, I'm intensely fond of Venice."

My friend seemed incapable of grasping more than one clause in any proposition, and she now spoke quickly, eagerly, as if she were answering my whole speech: "I'm not in the least fond of Venice. I should like to go far away!"

"Has she always kept you back so?" I went on, to show her I could be as irrelevant as herself.

"She told me to come out to-night; she has told me very often," said Miss Tina. "It is I who wouldn't come. I don't like to leave her."

"Is she too weak, is she really failing?" I demanded, with more emotion, I think, than I meant to betray. I measured this by the way her eyes rested on me in the darkness. It embarrassed me a little, and to turn the matter off I continued genially: "Do let us sit down together comfortably somewhere—while you tell me all about her."

Miss Tina made no resistance to this. We found a bench less secluded, less confidential, as it were, than the one in the arbour; and we were still sitting there when I heard midnight ring out from those clear bells of Venice which vibrate with a solemnity of their own over the lagoon and hold the air so much more than the chimes of other places. We were together more than an hour and our interview gave, as it struck me, a great lift to my undertaking. Miss Tina accepted the situation without a protest; she had avoided me for three months, yet now she treated me almost as if these three months had made me an old friend. If I had chosen I might have gathered from this that though she had avoided me she had given a good deal of consideration to doing so. She paid no attention to the flight of time—never worried at my keeping her so long away from her aunt. She talked freely, answering questions and asking them and not even taking advantage of certain longish pauses by which they were naturally broken to say she thought she had better go in. It was almost as if she were waiting for something—something I might say to her—and intended to give me my opportunity. I was the more struck by this as she told me how much less well her aunt had been for a good many days, and in a way that was rather new. She was markedly weaker; at moments she showed no strength at all; yet more than ever before she wished to be left alone. That was why she had told her to come out—not even to remain in her own room, which was alongside; she pronounced poor Miss Tina "a worry, a bore and a source of aggravation." She sat still for hours together, as if for long sleep; she had always done that, musing and dozing; but at such times formerly she gave, in breaks, some small sign of life, of interest, liking her companion to be near her with her work. This sad personage confided to me that at present her aunt was so motionless as to create the fear she was dead; moreover she scarce ate or drank—one couldn't see what she lived on. The great thing was that she still on most days got up; the serious job was to dress her, to wheel her out of her bedroom. She clung to as many of her old habits as possible and had always, little company as they had received for years, made a point of sitting in the great parlour.

I scarce knew what to think of all this—of Miss Tina's sudden conversion to sociability and of the strange fact that the more the old woman appeared to decline to her end the less she should desire to be looked after. The story hung indifferently together, and I even asked myself if it mightn't be a trap laid for me, the result of a design to make me show my hand. I couldn't have told why my companions (as they could only by courtesy be called) should have this purpose—why they should try to trip up so lucrative a lodger. But at any hazard I kept on my guard, so that Miss Tina shouldn't have occasion again to ask me what I might really be "up to." Poor woman, before we parted for the night my mind was at rest as to what *she* might be. She was up to nothing at all.

She told me more about their affairs than I had hoped; there was no need to be prying, for it evidently drew her out simply to feel me listen and care. She ceased wondering why I *should,* and at last while describing the brilliant life they had led years before, she almost chattered. It was Miss Tina who judged it brilliant; she said that when they first came to live in Venice, years and years back—I found her essentially vague about dates and the order in which events had occurred—there was never a week they hadn't some visitor or didn't make some pleasant *passeggio* in the town. They had seen all the curiosities; they had even been to the Lido in a boat—she spoke as if I might think there was a way on foot; they had had a collation there, brought in three baskets and spread out on the grass. I asked her what people they had known and she said Oh very nice ones—the Cavaliere Bombicci and the Contessa Altemura, with whom they had had a great friendship! Also English people—the Churtons and the Goldies and Mrs. Stock-Stock, whom they had loved dearly; she was dead and gone, poor dear. That was the case with most of their kind circle—this expression was Miss Tina's own; though a few were left, which was a wonder considering how they had neglected them. She mentioned the names of two or three Venetian old women; of a certain doctor, very clever, who was so attentive—he came as a friend, he had really given up practice; of the *avvocato* Pochintesta, who wrote beautiful poems and had addressed one to her aunt. These people came to see them without fail every year, usually at the *capo d'anno,* and of old her aunt used to make them some little present—her aunt and she together: small things that she, Miss Tina, turned out with her own hand, paper lamp-shades, or mats for the decanters of wine at dinner, or those woollen things that in cold weather are worn on the wrists. The last few years there hadn't been many presents; she couldn't think what to make and her aunt had lost interest and never suggested. But the people came all the same; if the good Venetians liked you once they liked you for ever.

There was affecting matter enough in the good faith of this sketch of former social glories; the picnic at the Lido had remained vivid through the ages and poor Miss Tina evidently was of the impression that she had had a dashing youth. She had in fact had a glimpse of the Venetian world in its gossiping home-keeping parsimonious professional walks; for I noted for the first time how nearly she had acquired by contact the trick of the familiar soft-sounding almost infantile prattle of the place. I judged her to have imbibed this invertebrate dialect from the natural way the names of things and people—mostly purely local—rose to her lips. If she knew little of what they represented she knew still less of anything else. Her aunt had drawn in—the failure of interest in the table-mats and lamp-shades was a sign of that—and she hadn't been able to mingle in society or to entertain it alone; so that her range of reminiscence struck one as an old world altogether. Her tone, hadn't it been so decent, would have seemed to carry one back to the queer rococo Venice of Goldoni and Casanova. I found myself mistakenly think of her too as one of Jeffrey Aspern's contemporaries; this came from her having so little in common with my own. It was possible, I indeed reasoned, that she hadn't even heard of him; it might very well be that Juliana had forborne to lift for innocent eyes the veil that covered the temple of her glory. In this case she perhaps wouldn't know of the existence of the papers, and I welcomed that presumption—it made me feel more safe with her—till I remembered we had believed the letter of disavowal received by Cumnor to be in the handwriting of the niece. If it had been dictated to her she had of course to know what it was about; though the effect of it withal was to repudiate the idea of any connexion with the poet. I held it probable at all events that Miss

Tina hadn't read a word of his poetry. Moreover if, with her companion, she had always escaped invasion and research, there was little occasion for her having got it into her head that people were "after" the letters. People had not been after them, for people hadn't heard of them. Cumnor's fruitless feeler would have been a solitary accident.

When midnight sounded Miss Tina got up; but she stopped at the door of the house only after she had wandered two or three times with me round the garden. "When shall I see you again?" I asked before she went in; to which she replied with promptness that she should like to come out the next night. She added, however, that she shouldn't come—she was so far from doing everything she liked.

"You might do a few things *I* like," I quite sincerely sighed.

"Oh you—I don't believe you!" she murmured at this, facing me with her simple solemnity.

"Why don't you believe me?"

"Because I don't understand you."

"That's just the sort of occasion to have faith." I couldn't say more, though I should have liked to, as I saw I only mystified her; for I had no wish to have it on my conscience that I might pass for having made love to her. Nothing less should I have seemed to do had I continued to beg a lady to "believe in me" in an Italian garden on a midsummer night. There was some merit in my scruples, for Miss Tina lingered and lingered: I made out in her conviction that she shouldn't really soon come down again and the wish therefore to protract the present. She insisted too on making the talk between us personal to ourselves; and altogether her behaviour was such as would have been possible only to a perfectly artless and a considerably witless woman.

"I shall like the flowers better now that I know them also meant for me."

"How could you have doubted it? If you'll tell me the kind you like best I'll send a double lot."

"Oh I like them all best!" Then she went on familiarly: "Shall you study—shall you read and write—when you go up to your rooms?"

"I don't do that at night—at this season. The lamplight brings in the animals."

"You might have known that when you came."

"I did know it!"

"And in winter do you work at night?"

"I read a good deal, but I don't often write." She listened as if these details had a rare interest, and suddenly a temptation quite at odds with all the prudence I had been teaching myself glimmered at me in her plain mild face. Ah yes, she was safe and I could make her safer! It seemed to me from one moment to another that I couldn't wait longer—that I really must take a sounding. So I went on: "In general before I go to sleep (very often in bed; it's a bad habit, but I confess to it) I read some great poet. In nine cases out of ten it's a volume of Jeffrey Aspern."

I watched her well as I pronounced that name, but I saw nothing wonderful. Why should I indeed? Wasn't Jeffrey Aspern the property of the human race?

"Oh *we* read him—we *have* read him," she quietly replied.

"He's my poet of poets—I know him almost by heart."

For an instant Miss Tina hesitated; then her sociability was too much for her. "Oh by heart—that's nothing;" and, though dimly, she quite lighted. "My aunt used to know him—to know him"—she paused an instant and I wondered what she was going to say—"to know him as a visitor."

"As a visitor?" I guarded my tone.

"He used to call on her and take her out."

I continued to stare. "My dear lady, he died a hundred years ago!"

"Well," she said amusingly, "my aunt's a hundred and fifty."

"Mercy on us!" I cried; "why didn't you tell me before? I should like so to ask her about him."

"She wouldn't care for that—she wouldn't tell you," Miss Tina returned.

"I don't care what she cares for! She *must* tell me—it's not a chance to be lost."

"Oh you should have come twenty years ago. Then she still talked about him."

"And what did she say?" I eagerly asked.

"I don't know—that he liked her immensely."

"And she—didn't she like *him*?"

"She said he was a god." Miss Tina gave me this information flatly, without expression; her tone might have made it a piece of trivial gossip. But it stirred me deeply as she dropped the words into the summer night; their sound might have been the light rustle of an old unfolded love-letter.

"Fancy, fancy!" I murmured. And then, "Tell me this, please—has she got a portrait of him? They're distressingly rare."

"A portrait? I don't know," said Miss Tina; and now there was discomfiture in her face. "Well, good-night!" she added; and she turned into the house.

I accompanied her into the wide dusky stone-paved passage that corresponded on the ground floor with our grand sala. It opened at one end into the garden, at the other upon the canal, and was lighted now only by the small lamp always left for me to take up as I went to bed. An extinguished candle which Miss Tina apparently had brought down with her stood on the same table with it. "Good-night, good-night!" I replied, keeping beside her as she went to get her light. "Surely you'd know, shouldn't you, if she had one?"

"If she had what?" the poor lady asked, looking at me queerly over the flame of her candle.

"A portrait of the god. I don't know what I wouldn't give to see it."

"I don't know what she has got. She keeps her things locked up." And Miss Tina went away toward the staircase with the sense evidently of having said too much.

I let her go—I wished not to frighten her—and I contented myself with remarking that Miss Bordereau wouldn't have locked up such a glorious possession as that: a thing a person would be proud of and hang up in a prominent place on the parlour-wall. Therefore of course she hadn't any portrait. Miss Tina made no direct answer to this and, candle in hand, with her back to me, mounted two or three degrees. Then she stopped short and turned round, looking at me across the dusky space.

"Do you write—do you write?" There was a shake in her voice—she could scarcely bring it out.

"Do I write? Oh don't speak of my writing on the same day with Aspern's!"

"Do you write about *him*—do you pry into his life?"

"Ah that's your aunt's question; it can't be yours!" I said in a tone of slightly wounded sensibility.

"All the more reason then that you should answer it. Do you, please?"

I thought I had allowed for the falsehoods I should have to tell, but I found that in fact when it came to the point I hadn't. Besides, now that I had an opening there was a kind of relief in being frank. Lastly—it was perhaps fanciful, even fatuous—I guessed that Miss Tina personally wouldn't in the last resort be less my friend. So after a moment's hesitation I answered: "Yes, I've written about him and I'm looking for more material. In heaven's name have you got any?"

"Santo Dio!" she exclaimed without heeding my question; and she hurried upstairs and out of sight. I might count upon her in the last resort, but for the present she was visibly alarmed. The proof of it was that she began to hide again, so that for a fortnight I kept missing her. I found my patience ebbing and after four or five days of this I told the gardener to stop the "floral tributes."

VI

ONE afternoon, at last, however, as I came down from my quarters to go out, I found her in the sala: it was our first encounter on that ground since I had come to the house. She put on no air of being there by accident; there was an ignorance of such arts in her honest angular diffidence. That I might be quite sure she was waiting for me she mentioned it at once, but telling me with it that Miss Bordereau wished to see me: she would take me into the room at that moment if I had time. If I had been late for a love-tryst I would have stayed for this, and I quickly signified that I should be delighted to wait on my benefactress. "She wants to talk with you—to know you," Miss Tina said, smiling as if she herself appreciated that idea; and she led me to the door of her aunt's apartment. I stopped her a moment before she had opened it, looking at her with some curiosity. I told her that this was a great satisfaction to me and a great honour; but all the same I should like to ask what had made Miss Bordereau so markedly and suddenly change. It had been only the other day that she wouldn't suffer me near her. Miss Tina was not embarrassed by my question; she had as many little unexpected serenities, plausibilities almost, as if she told fibs, but the odd part of them was that they had on the contrary their source in her truthfulness. "Oh my aunt varies," she answered; "it's so terribly dull—I suppose she's tired."

"But you told me she wanted more and more to be alone."

Poor Miss Tina coloured as if she found me too pushing. "Well, if you don't believe she wants to see you, I haven't invented it! I think people often are capricious when they're very old."

"That's perfectly true. I only wanted to be clear as to whether you've repeated to her what I told you the other night."

"What you told me?"

"About Jeffrey Aspern—that I'm looking for materials."

"If I had told her do you think she'd have sent for you?"

"That's exactly what I want to know. If she wants to keep him to herself she might have sent for me to tell me so."

"She won't speak of him," said Miss Tina. Then as she opened the door she added in a lower tone: "I told her nothing."

The old woman was sitting in the same place in which I had seen her last, in the same position, with the same mystifying bandage over her eyes. Her welcome was to turn her almost invisible face to me and show me that while she sat silent she saw me clearly. I made no motion to shake hands with her; I now felt too well that this was out of place for ever. It had been sufficiently enjoined on me that she was too sacred for trivial modernisms—too venerable to touch. There was something so grim in her aspect—it was partly the accident of her green shade—as I stood there to be measured, that I ceased on the spot to doubt her suspecting me, though I didn't in the least myself suspect that Miss Tina hadn't just spoken the truth. She hadn't betrayed me, but the old woman's brooding instinct had served her; she had turned me over and over in the long still hours and had guessed. The worst of it was that she looked terribly like an old woman who at a pinch would, even like Sardanapalus, burn her treasure. Miss Tina pushed a chair forward, saying to me: "This will be a good place for you to sit." As I took possession of it I asked after Miss Bordereau's health; expressed the hope that in spite of the very hot weather it was satisfactory. She answered that it was good enough—good enough; that it was a great thing to be alive.

"Oh as to that, it depends upon what you compare it with!" I returned with a laugh.

"I don't compare—I don't compare. If I did that I should have given everything up long ago."

I liked to take this for a subtle allusion to the rapture she had known in the society of Jeffrey Aspern—though it was true that such an allusion would have accorded ill with the wish I imputed to her to keep him buried in her soul. What it accorded with was my constant conviction that no human being had ever had a happier social gift than his, and what it seemed to convey was that nothing in the world was worth speaking of if one pretended to speak of that. But one didn't pretend! Miss Tina sat down beside her aunt, looking as if she had reason to believe some wonderful talk would come off between us.

"It's about the beautiful flowers," said the old lady; "you sent us so many—I ought to have thanked you for them before. But I don't write letters and I receive company but at long intervals."

She hadn't thanked me while the flowers continued to come, but she departed from her custom so far as to send for me as soon as she began to fear they wouldn't come any more. I noted this; I remembered what an acquisitive propensity she had shown when it was a question of extracting gold from me, and I privately rejoiced at the happy thought I had had in suspending my tribute. She had missed it and was willing to make a concession to bring it back. At the first sign of this concession I could only go to meet her. "I'm afraid you haven't had many, of late, but they shall begin again immediately—to-morrow, to-night."

"Oh do send us some to-night!" Miss Tina cried as if it were a great affair.

"What else should you do with them? It isn't a manly taste to make a bower of your room," the old woman remarked.

"I don't make a bower of my room, but I'm exceedingly fond of growing flowers, of watching their ways. There's nothing unmanly in that: it has been the amusement of philosophers, of statesmen in retirement; even I think of great captains."

"I suppose you know you can sell them—those you don't use," Miss Bordereau went on. "I dare say they wouldn't give you much for them; still, you could make a bargain."

"Oh I've never in my life made a bargain, as you ought pretty well to have gathered. My gardener disposes of them and I ask no questions."

"I'd ask a few, I can promise you!" said Miss Bordereau; and it was so I first heard the strange sound of her laugh, which was as if the faint "walking" ghost of her old-time tone had suddenly cut a caper. I couldn't get used to the idea that this vision of pecuniary profit was most what drew out the divine Juliana.

"Come into the garden yourself and pick them; come as often as you like; come every day. The flowers are all for you," I pursued, addressing Miss Tina and carrying off this veracious statement by treating it as an innocent joke. "I can't imagine why she doesn't come down," I added for Miss Bordereau's benefit.

"You must make her come; you must come up and fetch her," the old woman said to my stupefaction. "That odd thing you've made in the corner will do very well for her to sit in."

The allusion to the most elaborate of my shady coverts, a sketchy "summer-house," was irreverent; it confirmed the impression I had already received that there was a flicker of impertinence in Miss Bordereau's talk, a vague echo of the boldness or the archness of her adventurous youth and which had somehow automatically outlived passions and faculties. None the less I asked: "Wouldn't it be possible for you to come down there yourself? Wouldn't it do you good to sit there in the shade and the sweet air?"

"Oh, sir, when I move out of this it won't be to sit in the air, and I'm afraid that any that may be stirring around me won't be particularly sweet! It will be a very dark shade indeed. But that won't be just yet," Miss Bordereau continued cannily, as if to correct any hopes this free glance at the last receptacle of her mortality might lead me to entertain. "I've sat here many a day and have had enough of arbours in my time. But I'm not afraid to wait till I'm called."

Miss Tina had expected, as I felt, rare conversation, but perhaps she found it less gracious on her aunt's side—considering I had been sent for with a civil intention—than she had hoped. As to give the position a turn that would put our companion in a light more favourable she said to me: "Didn't I tell you the other night that she had sent me out? You see I can do what I like!"

"Do you pity her—do you teach her to pity herself?" Miss

Bordereau demanded, before I had time to answer this appeal. "She has a much easier life than I had at her age."

"You must remember it has been quite open to me," I said, "to think you rather inhuman."

"Inhuman? That's what the poets used to call the women a hundred years ago. Don't try that; you won't do as well as they!" Juliana went on. "There's no more poetry in the world—that *I* know of at least. But I won't bandy words with you," she said, and I well remember the old-fashioned artificial sound she gave the speech. "You make me talk, talk, talk! It isn't good for me at all." I got up at this and told her I would take no more of her time; but she detained me to put a question, "Do you remember, the day I saw you about the rooms, that you offered us the use of your gondola?" And when I assented promptly, struck again with her disposition to make a "good thing" of my being there and wondering what she now had in her eye, she produced: "Why don't you take that girl out in it and show her the place?"

"Oh dear aunt, what do you want to do with me?" cried the "girl" with a piteous quaver. "I know all about the place!"

"Well then go with him and explain!" said Miss Bordereau, who gave an effect of cruelty to her implacable power of retort. This showed her as a sarcastic profane cynical old woman. "Haven't we heard that there have been all sorts of changes in all these years? You ought to see them, and at your age—I don't mean because you're so young—you ought to take the chances that come. You're old enough, my dear, and this gentleman won't hurt you. He'll show you the famous sunsets, if they still go on—*do* they go on? The sun set for me so long ago. But that's not a reason. Besides, I shall never miss you; you think you're too important. Take her to the Piazza; it used to be very pretty," Miss Bordereau continued, addressing herself to me. "What have they done with the funny old church? I hope it hasn't tumbled down. Let her look at the shops; she may take some money, she may buy what she likes."

Poor Miss Tina had got up, discountenanced and helpless, and as we stood there before her aunt it would certainly have struck a spectator of the scene that our venerable friend was making rare sport of us. Miss Tina protested in a confusion of exclamations and murmurs; but I lost no time in saying that if she would do me the honour to accept the hospitality of my boat I would engage she really shouldn't be bored. Or if she didn't want so much of my company, the boat itself, with the gondolier, was at her service; he was a capital oar and she might have every confidence. Miss Tina, without definitely answering this speech, looked away from me and out of the window, quite as if about to weep, and I remarked that once we had Miss Bordereau's approval we could easily come to an understanding. We would take an hour, whichever she liked, one of the very next days. As I made my obeisance to the old lady I asked her if she would kindly permit me to see her again.

For a moment she kept me; then she said: "Is it very necessary to your happiness?"

"It diverts me more than I can say."

"You're wonderfully civil. Don't you know it almost kills *me*?"

"How can I believe that when I see you more animated, more brilliant than when I came in?"

"That's very true, aunt," said Miss Tina. "I think it does you good."

"Isn't it touching, the solicitude we each have that the other shall enjoy herself?" sneered Miss Bordereau. "If you think me brilliant to-day you don't know what you are talking about; you've never seen an agreeable woman. What do you people know about good society?" she cried; but before I could tell her, "Don't try to pay me a compliment; I've been spoiled," she went on. "My door's shut, but you may sometimes knock."

With this she dismissed me and I left the room. The latch closed behind me, but Miss Tina, contrary to my hope, had remained within. I passed slowly across the hall and before taking my way downstairs waited a little. My hope was answered; after a minute my conductress followed me. "That's a delightful idea about the Piazza," I said. "When will you go—to-night, to-morrow?"

She had been disconcerted, as I have mentioned, but I had already perceived, and I was to observe again, that when Miss Tina was embarrassed she didn't—as most women would have in like case—turn away, floundering and hedging, but came closer, as it were, with a deprecating, a clinging appeal to be spared, to be protected. Her attitude was a constant prayer for aid and explanation, and yet no woman in the world could have been less of a comedian. From the moment you were kind to her she depended on you absolutely; her self-consciousness dropped and she took the greatest intimacy, the innocent intimacy that was all she could conceive, for granted. She didn't know, she now declared, what possessed her aunt, who had changed so quickly, who had got some idea. I replied that she must catch the idea and let me have it: we would go and take an ice together at Florian's and she should report while we listened to the band.

"Oh, it will take me a long time to be able to 'report'!" she said rather ruefully; and she could promise me this satisfaction neither for that night nor for the next. I was patient now, however, for I felt I had only to wait; and in fact at the end of the week, one lovely evening after dinner, she stepped into my gondola, to which in honour of the occasion I had attached a second oar.

We swept in the course of five minutes into the Grand Canal; whereupon she uttered a murmur of ecstasy as fresh as if she had been a tourist just arrived. She had forgotten the splendour of the great water-way on a clear summer evening, and how the sense of floating between marble palaces and reflected lights disposed the mind to freedom and ease. We floated long and far, and though my friend gave no high-pitched voice to her glee I was sure of her full surrender. She was more than pleased, she was transported; the whole thing was an immense liberation. The gondola moved with slow strokes, to give her time to enjoy it, and she listened to the plash of the oars, which grew louder and more musically liquid as we passed into narrow canals, as if it were a revelation of Venice. When I asked her how long it was since she had thus floated, she answered: "Oh I don't know; a long time—not since my aunt began to be ill." This was not the only show of her extreme vagueness about the previous years and the line marking off the period of Miss Bordereau's eminence. I was not at liberty to keep her out long, but we took a considerable *giro* before going to the Piazza. I asked her no questions, holding off by design from her life at home and the things I wanted to know; I poured, rather, treasures of information about the objects before and around us into her ears, describing also Florence and Rome, discoursing on the charms and advantages of travel. She reclined, receptive, on the deep leather cushions, turned her eyes conscientiously to everything I noted and never mentioned to me till some time afterwards that she might be supposed to know Florence better than I, as she had lived there for years with her kinswoman. At last she said with the shy impatience of a child: "Are we not really going to the Piazza? That's what I want to see!" I immediately gave the order that we should go straight, after which we sat silent with the expectation of arrival. As some time still passed, however, she broke out of her own movement: "I've found out what's the matter with my aunt: she's afraid you'll go!"

I quite gasped. "What has put that into her head?"

"She has had an idea you've not been happy. That's why she is different now."

"You mean she wants to make me happier?"

"Well, she wants you not to go. She wants you to stay."

"I suppose you mean on account of the rent," I remarked candidly.

Miss Tina's candour but profited. "Yes, you know; so that I shall have more."

"How much does she want you to have?" I asked with all the gaiety I now felt. "She ought to fix the sum, so that I may stay till it's made up."

"Oh that wouldn't please me," said Miss Tina. "It would be unheard of, your taking that trouble."

"But suppose I should have my own reasons for staying in Venice?"

"Then it would be better for you to stay in some other house."

"And what would your aunt say to that?"

"She wouldn't like it at all. But I should think you'd do well to give up your reasons and go away altogether."

"Dear Miss Tina," I said, "it's not so easy to give up my reasons!"

She made no immediate answer to this, but after a moment broke out afresh: "I think I know what your reasons are!"

"I dare say, because the other night I almost told you how I wished you'd help me to make them good."

"I can't do that without being false to my aunt."

"What do you mean by being false to her?"

"Why she would never consent to what you want. She has been asked, she has been written to. It makes her fearfully angry."

"Then she *has* papers of value" I precipitately cried.

"Oh she has everything!" sighed Miss Tina, with a curious weariness, a sudden lapse into gloom.

These words caused all my pulses to throb, for I regarded them as precious evidence. I felt them too deeply to speak, and in the interval the gondola approached the Piazzetta. After we had disembarked I asked my companion if she would rather walk round the square or go and sit before the great café; to which she replied that she would do whichever I liked best—I must only remember again how little time she had. I assured her there was plenty to do both, and we made the circuit of the long arcades. Her spirits revived at the sight of the bright shop-windows, and she lingered and stopped, admiring or disapproving of their contents, asking me what I thought of things, theorizing about prices. My attention wandered from her; her words of a while before "Oh she has everything!" echoed so in my consciousness. We sat down at last in the crowded circle at Florian's, finding an unoccupied table among those that were ranged in the square. It was a splendid night and all the world out-of-doors; Miss Tina couldn't have wished the elements more auspicious for her return to society. I saw she felt it all even more than she told, but her impressions were well-nigh too many for her. She had forgotten the attraction of the world and was learning that she had for the best years of her life been rather mercilessly cheated of it. This didn't make her angry; but as she took in the charming scene her face had, in spite of its smile of appreciation, the flush of a wounded surprise. She didn't speak, sunk in the sense of opportunities, for ever lost, that ought to have been easy; and this gave me a chance to say to her: "Did you mean a while ago that your aunt has a plan of keeping me on by admitting me occasionally to her presence?"

"She thinks it will make a difference with you if you sometimes see her. She wants you so much to stay that she's willing to make that concession."

"And what good does she consider I think it will do me to see her?"

"I don't know; it must be interesting," said Miss Tina simply. "You told her you found it so."

"So I did; but every one doesn't think that."

"No, of course not, or more people would try."

"Well, if she's capable of making that reflexion she's capable also of making this further one," I went on: "that I must have a particular reason for not doing as others do, in spite of the interest she offers—for not leaving her alone." Miss Tina looked as if she failed to grasp this rather complicated proposition; so I continued: "If you've not told her what I said to you the other night may she not at least have guessed it?"

"I don't know—she's very suspicious."

"But she hasn't been made so by indiscreet curiosity, by persecution?"

"No, no; it isn't that," said Miss Tina, turning on me a troubled face. "I don't know how to say it; it's on account of something—ages ago, before I was born—in her life."

"Something? What sort of thing?"—and I asked it as if I could have no idea.

"Oh she has never told me." And I was sure my friend spoke the truth.

Her extreme limpidity was almost provoking, and I felt for the moment that she would have been more satisfactory if she had been less ingenuous. "Do you suppose it's something to which Jeffrey Aspern's letters and papers—I mean the things in her possession—have reference?"

"I dare say it is!" my companion exclaimed as if this were a very happy suggestion. "I've never looked at any of those things."

"None of them? Then how do you know what they are?"

"I don't," said Miss Tina placidly. "I've never had them in my hands. But I've seen them when she has had them out."

"Does she have them out often?"

"Not now, but she used to. She's very fond of them."

"In spite of their being compromising?"

"Compromising?" Miss Tina repeated as if vague as to what that meant. I felt almost as one who corrupts the innocence of youth.

"I allude to their containing painful memories."

"Oh I don't think anything's painful."

"You mean there's nothing to affect her reputation?"

An odder look even than usual came at this into the face of Miss Bordereau's niece—a confession, it seemed, of helplessness, an appeal to me to deal fairly, generously with her. I had brought her to the Piazza, placed her among charming influences, paid her an attention she appreciated, and now I appeared to show it all as a bribe—a bribe to make her turn in some way against her aunt. She was of a yielding nature and capable of doing almost anything to please a person markedly kind to her; but the greatest kindness of all would be not to presume too much on this. It was strange enough, as I afterwards thought, that she had not the least air of resenting my want of consideration for her aunt's character, which would have been in the worst possible taste if anything less vital—from my point of view—had been at stake. I don't think she really measured it. "Do you mean she ever did something bad?" she asked in a moment.

"Heaven forbid I should say so, and it's none of my business. Besides, if she did," I agreeably put it, "that was in other ages, in another world. But why shouldn't she destroy her papers?"

"Oh she loves them too much."

"Even now, when she may be near her end?"

"Perhaps when she's sure of that she will."

"Well, Miss Tina," I said, "that's just what I should like you to prevent."

"How can I prevent it?"

"Couldn't you get them away from her?"

"And give them to you?"

This put the case, superficially, with sharp irony, but I was sure of her not intending that. "Oh I mean that you might let me see them and look them over. It isn't for myself, or that I should want them at any cost to any one else. It's simply that they would be of such immense interest to the public, such immeasurable importance as a contribution to Jeffrey Aspern's history."

She listened to me in her usual way, as if I abounded in matters she had never heard of, and I felt almost as base as the reporter of a newspaper who forces his way into a house of mourning. This was marked when she presently said: "There was a gentleman who some time ago wrote to her in very much those words. He also wanted her papers."

"And did she answer him?" I asked, rather ashamed of not having my friend's rectitude.

"Only when he had written two or three times. He made her very angry."

"And what did she say?"

"She said he was a devil," Miss Tina replied categorically.

"She used that expression in her letter?"

"Oh no; she said it to me. She made me write to him."

"And what did you say?"

"I told him there were no papers at all."

"Ah poor gentleman!" I groaned.

"I knew there were, but I wrote what she bade me."

"Of course you had to do that. But I hope I shan't pass for a devil."

"It will depend upon what you ask me to do for you," my companion smiled.

"Oh if there's a chance of *your* thinking so my affair's in a bad way! I shan't ask you to steal for me, nor even to fib—for you *can't* fib, unless on paper. But the principal thing is this—to prevent her destroying the papers."

"Why I've no control of her," said Miss Tina. "It's she who controls me."

"But she doesn't control her own arms and legs, does she? The way she would naturally destroy her letters would be to burn them. Now she can't burn them without fire, and she can't get fire unless you give it to her."

"I've always done everything she has asked," my poor friend pleaded. "Besides, there's Olimpia."

I was on the point of saying that Olimpia was probably corruptible, but I thought it best not to sound that note. So I simply put it that this frail creature might perhaps be managed.

"Every one can be managed by my aunt," said Miss Tina. And then she remembered that her holiday was over; she must go home.

I laid my hand on her arm, across the table, to stay her a moment. "What I want of you is a general promise to help me."

"Oh how *can* I, how *can* I?" she asked, wondering and troubled. She was half-surprised, half-frightened at my attaching that importance to her, at my calling on her for action.

"This is the main thing: to watch our friend carefully and warn me in time, before she commits that dreadful sacrilege."

"I can't watch her when she makes me go out."

"That's very true."

"And when you do too."

"Mercy on us—do you think she'll have done anything to-night?"

"I don't know. She's very cunning."

"Are you trying to frighten me?" I asked.

I felt this question sufficiently answered when my companion murmured in a musing, almost envious way: "Oh but she loves them—she loves them!"

This reflexion, repeated with such emphasis, gave me great comfort; but to obtain more of that balm I said: "If she shouldn't intend to destroy the objects we speak of before her death she'll probably have made some disposition by will."

"By will?"

"Hasn't she made a will for your benefit?"

"Ah she has so little to leave. That's why she likes money," said Miss Tina.

"Might I ask, since we're really talking things over, what you and she live on?"

"On some money that comes from America, from a gentleman—I think a lawyer—in New York. He sends it every quarter. It isn't much!"

"And won't she have disposed of that?"

My companion hesitated—I saw she was blushing. "I believe it's mine," she said; and the look and tone which accompanied these words betrayed so the absence of the habit of thinking of herself that I almost thought her charming. The next instant she added: "But she had in an *avvocato* here once, ever so long ago. And some people came and signed something."

"They were probably witnesses. And you weren't asked to sign? Well then," I argued, rapidly and hopefully, "it's because you're the legatee. She must have left all her documents to you!"

"If she has it's with very strict conditions," Miss Tina responded, rising quickly, while the movement gave the words a small character of decision. They seemed to imply that the bequest would be accompanied with a proviso that the articles bequeathed should remain concealed from every inquisitive eye, and that I was very much mistaken if I thought her the person to depart from an injunction so absolute.

"Oh of course you'll have to abide by the terms," I said; and she uttered nothing to mitigate the rigour of this conclusion. None the less, later on, just before we disembarked at her own door after a return which had taken place almost in silence, she said to me abruptly: "I'll do what I can to help you." I was grateful for this—it was very well so far as it went; but it didn't keep me from remembering that night in a worried waking hour that I now had her word for it to re-enforce my own impression that the old woman was full of craft.

VII

THE fear of what this side of her character might have led her to do made me nervous for days afterwards. I waited for an intimation from Miss Tina; I almost read it as her duty to keep me informed, to let me know definitely whether or no Miss Bordereau had sacrificed her treasures. But as she gave no sign I lost patience and determined to put the case to the very touch of my own senses. I sent late one afternoon to ask if I might pay the ladies a visit, and my servant came back with surprising news. Miss Bordereau could be approached without the least difficulty; she had been moved out into the sala and was sitting by the window that overlooked the garden. I descended and found this picture correct; the old lady had been wheeled forth into the world and had a certain air, which came mainly perhaps from some brighter element in her dress, of being prepared again to have converse with it. It had not yet, however, begun to flock about her; she was perfectly alone and, though the door leading to her own quarters stood open, I had at first no glimpse of Miss Tina. The window at which she sat had the afternoon shade and, one of the shutters having been pushed back, she could see the pleasant garden, where the summer sun had by this time dried up too many of the plants—she could see the yellow light and the long shadows.

"Have you come to tell me you'll take the rooms for six months more?" she asked as I approached her, startling me by something coarse in her cupidity almost as much as if she hadn't already given me a specimen of it. Juliana's desire to make our acquaintance lucrative had been, as I have sufficiently indicated, a false note in my image of the woman who had inspired a great poet with immortal lines; but I may say here definitely that I after all recognised large allowance to be made for her. It was I who had kindled the unholy flame; it was I who had put into her head that she had the means of making money. She appeared never to have thought of that; she had been living wastefully for years, in a house five times too big for her, on a footing that I could explain only by the presumption that, excessive as it was, the space she enjoyed cost her next to nothing and that, small as were her revenues, they left her, for Venice, an appreciable margin. I had descended on her one day and taught her to calculate, and my almost extravagant comedy on the subject of the garden had presented me irresistibly in the light of a victim. Like all persons who achieve the miracle of changing their point of view late in life, she had been intensely converted; she had seized my hint with a desperate tremulous clutch.

I invited myself to go and get one of the chairs that stood, at a distance, against the wall—she had given herself no concern as to whether I should sit or stand; and while I placed it near her I began gaily: "Oh dear madam, what an imagination you have, what an intellectual sweep! I'm a poor devil of a man of letters who lives from day to day. How can I take palaces by the year? My existence is precarious. I don't know whether six months hence I shall have bread to put in my mouth. I've treated myself for once; it has been an immense luxury. But when it comes to going on——!"

"Are your rooms too dear? If they are you can have more for the same money," Juliana responded. "We can arrange, we can *combinare*, as they say here."

"Well yes, since you ask me, they're too dear, much too dear," I said. "Evidently you suppose me richer than I am."

She looked at me as from the mouth of her cave. "If you write books don't you sell them?"

"Do you mean don't people buy them? A little, a very little—not so much as I could wish. Writing books, unless one be a great genius—and even then!—is the last road to fortune. I think there's no more money to be made by good letters."

"Perhaps you don't choose nice subjects. What do you write about?" Miss Bordereau implacably pursued.

"About the books of other people. I'm a critic, a commentator, an historian, in a small way." I wondered what she was coming to.

"And what other people now?"

"Oh better ones than myself: the great writers mainly—the great philosophers and poets of the past; those who are dead and gone and can't, poor darlings, speak for themselves."

"And what do you say about them?"

"I say they sometimes attached themselves to very clever women!" I replied as for pleasantness. I had measured, as I thought, my risk, but as my words fell upon the air they were to strike me as imprudent. However, I had launched them and I wasn't sorry, for perhaps after all the old woman would be willing to treat. It seemed tolerably obvious that she knew my secret; why therefore drag the process out? But she didn't take what I had said as a confession; she only asked:

"Do you think it's right to rake up the past?"

"I don't feel that I know what you mean by raking it up. How can we get at it unless we dig a little? The present has such a rough way of treading it down."

"Oh I like the past, but I don't like critics," my hostess declared with her hard complacency.

"Neither do I, but I like their discoveries."

"Aren't they mostly lies?"

"The lies are what they sometimes discover," I said, smiling at the quiet impertinence of this. "They often lay bare the truth."

"The truth is God's, it isn't man's; we had better leave it alone. Who can judge of it?—who can say?"

"We're terribly in the dark, I know," I admitted; "but if we give up trying what becomes of all the fine things? What becomes of the work I just mentioned, that of the great philosophers and poets? It's all vain words if there's nothing to measure it by."

"You talk as if you were a tailor," said Miss Bordereau whimsically; and then she added quickly and in a different manner: "This house is very fine; the proportions are magnificent. To-day I wanted to look at this part again. I made them bring me out here. When your man came just now to learn if I would see you I was on the point of sending for you to ask if you didn't mean to go on. I wanted to judge what I'm letting you have. This sala is very grand," she pursued like an auctioneer, moving a little, as I guessed, her invisible eyes. "I don't believe you often have lived in such a house, eh?"

"I can't often afford to!" I said.

"Well then how much will you give me for six months?"

I was on the point of exclaiming—and the air of excruciation in my face would have denoted a moral fact—"Don't, Juliana; for *his* sake, don't!" But I controlled myself and asked less passionately: "Why should I remain so long as that?"

"I thought you liked it," said Miss Bordereau with her shrivelled dignity.

"So I thought I should."

For a moment she said nothing more, and I left my own words to suggest to her what they might. I half-expected her to say, coldly enough, that if I had been disappointed we needn't continue the discussion, and this in spite of the fact that I believed her now to have in her mind—however it had come there—what would have told her that my disappointment was natural. But to my extreme surprise she ended by observing: "If you don't think we've treated you well enough perhaps we can discover some way of treating you better." This speech was somehow so incongruous that it made me laugh again, and I excused myself by saying that she talked as if I were a sulky boy pouting in the corner and having to be "brought round." I hadn't a grain of complaint to make; and could anything have exceeded Miss Tina's graciousness in accompanying me a few nights before to the Piazza? At this the old woman went on: "Well, you brought it on yourself!" And then in a different tone: "She's a very fine girl." I assented cordially to this proposition, and she expressed the hope that I did so not merely to be obliging, but that I really liked her. Meanwhile I wondered still more what Miss Bordereau was coming to. "Except for me, to-day," she said, "she hasn't a relation in the world." Did she by describing her niece as amiable and unencumbered wish to represent her as a *parti?*

It was perfectly true that I couldn't afford to go on with my rooms at a fancy price and that I had already devoted to my undertaking almost all the hard cash I had set apart for it. My patience and my time were by no means exhausted, but I should be able to draw upon them only on a more usual Venetian basis. I was willing to pay the precious personage with whom my pecuniary dealings were such a discord twice as much as any other *padrona di casa* would have asked, but I wasn't willing to pay her twenty times as much. I told her so plainly, and my plainness appeared to have some success, for she exclaimed: "Very good; you've done what I asked—you've made an offer!"

"Yes, but not for half a year. Only by the month."

"Oh I must think of that then." She seemed disappointed that I wouldn't tie myself to a period, and I guessed that she wished both to secure me and to discourage me; to say severely: "Do you dream that you can get off with less than six months? Do you dream that even by the end of that time you'll be appreciably nearer your victory?" What was most in my mind was that she had a fancy to play me the trick of making me engage myself when in fact she had sacrificed her treasure. There was a moment when my suspense on this point was so acute that I all but broke out with the question, and what kept it back was but an instinctive recoil—lest it should be a mistake—from the last violence of self-exposure. She was such a subtle old witch that one could never tell where one stood with her. You may imagine whether it cleared up the puzzle when, just after she had said she would think of my proposal and without any formal transition, she drew out of her pocket with an embarrassed hand a small object wrapped in crumpled white paper. She held it there a moment and then resumed: "Do you know much about curiosities?"

"About curiosities?"

"About antiquities, the old gimcracks that people pay so much for to-day. Do you know the kind of price they bring?"

I thought I saw what was coming, but I said ingenuously: "Do you want to buy something?"

"No, I want to sell. What would an amateur give me for that?" She unfolded the white paper and made a motion for me to take from her a small oval portrait. I possessed myself of it with fingers of which I could only hope that they didn't betray the intensity of their clutch, and she added: "I would part with it only for a good price."

At the first glance I recognized Jeffrey Aspern, and was well aware that I flushed with the act. As she was watching me however I had the consistency to exclaim: "What a striking face! Do tell me who it is."

"He's an old friend of mine, a very distinguished man in his day. He gave it me himself, but I'm afraid to mention his name, lest you never should have heard of him, critic and historian as you are. I know the world goes fast and one generation forgets another. He was all the fashion when I was young."

She was perhaps amazed at my assurance, but I was surprised at hers; at her having the energy, in her state of health and at her time of life, to wish to sport with me to that tune simply for her private entertainment—the humour to test me and practise on me and befool me. This at least was the interpretation that I put upon her production of the relic, for I couldn't believe she really desired to sell it or cared for any information I might give her. What she wished was to dangle it before my eyes and put a prohibitive price on it. "The face comes back to me, it torments me," I said, turning the object this way and that and looking at it very critically. It was a careful but not a supreme work of art, larger than the ordinary miniature and representing a young man with a remarkably handsome face, in a high-collared green coat and a buff waistcoat. I felt in the little work a virtue of likeness and judged it to have been painted when the model was about twenty-five. There are, as all the world knows, three other portraits of the poet in existence, but none of so early a date as this elegant image. "I've never seen the original, clearly a man of a past age, but I've seen other reproductions of this face," I went on. "You expressed doubt of this generation's having heard of the gentleman, but he strikes me for all the world as a celebrity. Now who is he? I can't put my finger on him—I can't give him a label. Wasn't he a writer? Surely he's a poet." I was determined that it should be she, not I, who should first pronounce Jeffrey Aspern's name.

My resolution was taken in ignorance of Miss Bordereau's extremely resolute character, and her lips never formed in my hearing the syllables that meant so much for her. She neglected to answer my question, but raised her hand to take back the picture, using a gesture which though impotent was in a high degree peremptory. "It's only a person who should know for himself that would give me my price," she said with a certain dryness.

"Oh then you have a price?" I didn't restore the charming thing; not from any vindictive purpose, but because I instinctively clung to it. We looked at each other hard while I retained it.

"I know the least I would take. What it occurred to me to ask you about is the most I shall be able to get."

She made a movement, drawing herself together as if, in a spasm of dread at having lost her prize she had been impelled to the immense effort of rising to snatch it from me. I instantly placed it in her hand again, saying as I did so: "I should like to have it myself, but with your ideas it would be quite beyond my mark."

She turned the small oval plate over in her lap, with its face down, and I heard her catch her breath as after a strain or an escape. This however did not prevent her saying in a moment: "You'd buy a likeness of a person you don't know by an artist who has no reputation?"

"The artist may have no reputation, but that thing's wonderfully well painted," I replied, to give myself a reason.

"It's lucky you thought of saying that, because the painter was my father."

"That makes the picture indeed precious!" I returned with gaiety; and I may add that a part of my cheer came from this proof I had been right in my theory of Miss Bordereau's origin. Aspern had of course met the young lady on his going to her father's studio as a sitter. I observed to Miss Bordereau that if she would entrust me with her property for twenty-four hours I should be happy to take advice on it; but she made no other reply than to slip it in silence into her pocket. This convinced me still more that she had no sincere intention of selling it during her lifetime, though she may have desired to satisfy herself as to the sum her niece, should she leave it to her, might expect eventually to obtain for it. "Well, at any rate, I hope you won't offer it without giving me notice," I said as she remained irresponsive. "Remember me as a possible purchaser."

"I should want your money first!" she returned with unexpected rudeness; and then, as if she bethought herself that I might well complain of such a tone and wished to turn the matter off, asked abruptly what I talked about with her niece when I went out with her that way of an evening.

"You speak as if we had set up the habit," I replied. "Certainly I should be very glad if it were to become our pleasant custom. But in that case I should feel a still greater scruple at betraying a lady's confidence."

"Her confidence? Has my niece confidence?"

"Here she is—she can tell you herself," I said; for Miss Tina now appeared on the threshold of the old woman's parlour. "Have you confidence, Miss Tina? Your aunt wants very much to know."

"Not in her, not in her!" the younger lady declared, shaking her head with a dolefulness that was neither jocular nor affected. "I don't know what to do with her; she has fits of horrid imprudence. She's so easily tired—and yet she has begun to roam, to drag herself about the house." And she looked down at her yoke-fellow of long years with a vacancy of wonder, as if all their contact and custom hadn't made her perversities, on occasion, any more easy to follow.

"I know what I'm about. I'm not losing my mind. I dare say you'd like to think so," said Miss Bordereau with a crudity of cynicism.

"I don't suppose you came out here yourself. Miss Tina must have had to lend you a hand," I interposed for conciliation.

"Oh she insisted we should push her; and when she insists!" said Miss Tina, in the same tone of apprehension; as if there were no knowing what service she disapproved of her aunt might force her next to render.

"I've always got most things done I wanted, thank God! The people I've lived with have humoured me," the old woman continued, speaking out of the white ashes of her vanity.

I took it pleasantly up. "I suppose you mean they've obeyed you."

"Well, whatever it is—when they like one."

"It's just because I like you that I want to resist," said Miss Tina with a nervous laugh.

"Oh I suspect you'll bring Miss Bordereau upstairs next to pay me a visit," I went on; to which the old lady replied:

"Oh no; I can keep an eye on you from here!"

"You're very tired; you'll certainly be ill to-night!" cried Miss Tina.

"Nonsense, dear; I feel better at this moment than I've done for a month. To-morrow I shall come out again. I want to be where I can see this clever gentleman."

"Shouldn't you perhaps see me better in your sitting-room?" I asked.

"Don't you mean shouldn't you have a better chance at *me?*" she returned, fixing me a moment with her green shade.

"Ah I haven't that anywhere! I look at you but don't see you."

"You agitate her dreadfully—and that's not good," said Miss Tina, giving me a reproachful deterrent headshake.

"I want to watch you—I want to watch you!" Miss Bordereau went on.

"Well then let us spend as much of our time together as possible —I don't care where. That will give you every facility."

"Oh I've seen you enough for to-day. I'm satisfied. Now I'll go home," Juliana said. Miss Tina laid her hands on the back of the wheeled chair and began to push, but I begged her to let me take her place. "Oh yes, you may move me this way—you shan't in any other!" the old woman cried as she felt herself propelled firmly and easily over the smooth hard floor. Before we reached the door of her own apartment she bade me stop, and she took a long last look up and down the noble sala. "Oh it's a prodigious house!" she murmured; after which I pushed her forward. When we had entered the parlour Miss Tina let me know she should now be able to manage, and at the same moment the little red-haired *donna* came to meet her mistress. Miss Tina's idea was evidently to get her aunt immediately back to bed. I confess that in spite of this urgency I was guilty of the indiscretion of lingering; it held me there to feel myself so close to the objects I coveted—which would be probably put away somewhere in the faded unsociable room. The place had indeed a bareness that suggested no hidden values; there were neither dusky nooks nor curtained corners, neither massive cabinets nor chests with iron bands. Moreover it was possible, it was perhaps even likely, that the old lady had consigned her relics to her bedroom, to some battered box that was shoved under the bed, to the drawer of some lame dressing-table, where they would be in the range of vision by the dim night-lamp. None the less I turned an eye on every article of furniture, on every conceivable cover for a hoard, and noticed that there were half a dozen things with drawers, and in particular a tall old secretary with brass ornaments of the style of the Empire—a receptacle somewhat infirm but still capable of keeping rare secrets. I don't know why this article so engaged me, small purpose as I had of breaking into it; but I stared at it so hard that Miss Tina noticed me and changed colour. Her doing this made me think I was right and that, wherever they might have been before, the Aspern papers at that moment languished behind the peevish little lock of the secretary. It was hard to turn my attention from the dull mahogany front when I reflected that a plain panel divided me from the goal of my hopes; but I gathered up my slightly scattered prudence and with an effort took leave of my hostess. To make the effort graceful I said to her that I should certainly bring her an opinion about the little picture.

"The little picture?" Miss Tina asked in surprise.

"What do *you* know about it, my dear?" the old woman demanded. "You needn't mind. I've fixed my price."

"And what may that be?"

"A thousand pounds."

"Oh Lord!" cried poor Miss Tina irrepressibly.

"Is that what she talks to you about?" said Miss Bordereau.

"Imagine your aunt's wanting to know!" I had to separate from my younger friend with only those words, though I should have liked immensely to add: "For heaven's sake meet me to-night in the garden!"

VIII

As it turned out the precaution had not been needed, for three hours later, just as I had finished my dinner, Miss Tina appeared, unannounced, in the open doorway of the room in which my simple repasts were served. I remember well that I felt no surprise at seeing her; which is not a proof of my not believing in her timidity. It was immense, but in a case in which there was a particular reason for boldness it never would have prevented her from running up to my floor. I saw that she was now quite full of a particular reason; it threw her forward—made her seize me, as I rose to meet her, by the arm.

"My aunt's very ill; I think she's dying!"

"Never in the world," I answered bitterly. "Don't you be afraid!"

"Do go for a doctor—do, do! Olimpia's gone for the one we always have, but she doesn't come back; I don't know what has happened to her. I told her that if he wasn't at home she was to follow him where he had gone; but apparently she's following him all over Venice. I don't know what to do—she looks so as if she were sinking."

"May I see her, may I judge?" I asked. "Of course I shall be delighted to bring some one; but hadn't we better send my man instead, so that I may stay with you?"

Miss Tina assented to this and I dispatched my servant for the best doctor in the neighbourhood. I hurried downstairs with her, and on the way she told me that an hour after I quitted them in the afternoon Miss Bordereau had had an attack of "oppression," a terrible difficulty in breathing. This had subsided, but had left her so exhausted that she didn't come up: she seemed all spent and gone. I repeated that she wasn't gone, that she wouldn't go yet; whereupon Miss Tina gave me a sharper sidelong glance than she had ever favoured me withal and said: "Really, what do you mean? I suppose you don't accuse her of making-believe!" I forget what reply I made to this, but I fear that in my heart I thought the old woman capable of any weird manœuvre. Miss Tina wanted to know what I had done to her; her aunt had told her I had made her so angry. I declared I had done nothing whatever—I had been exceedingly careful; to which my companion rejoined that our friend had assured her she had had a scene with me—a scene that had upset her. I answered with some resentment that the scene had been of *her* making—that I couldn't think what she was angry with me for unless for not seeing my way to give a thousand pounds for the portrait of Jeffrey Aspern. "And did she show you that? Oh gracious—oh deary me!" groaned Miss Tina, who seemed to feel the situation pass out of her control and the elements of her fate thicken round her. I answered her I'd give anything to possess it, yet that I had no thousand pounds; but I stopped when we came to the door of Miss Bordereau's room. I had an immense curiosity to pass it, but I thought it my duty to represent to Miss Tina that if I made the invalid angry she ought perhaps to be spared the sight of me. "The sight of you? Do you think she can *see?*" my companion demanded, almost with indignation. I did think so but forbore to say it, and I softly followed my conductress.

I remember that what I said to her as I stood for a moment beside the old woman's bed was: "Does she never show you her eyes then? Have you never seen them?" Miss Bordereau had been divested of her green shade, but—it was not my fortune to behold Juliana in her nightcap—the upper half of her face was covered by the fall of a piece of dingy lacelike muslin, a sort of extemporised hood which, wound round her head, descended to the end of her nose, leaving nothing visible but her white withered cheeks and puckered mouth, closed tightly and, as it were, consciously. Miss Tina gave me a glance of surprise, evidently not seeing a reason for my impatience. "You mean she always wears something? She does it to preserve them."

"Because they're so fine?"

"Oh to-day, to-day!" And Miss Tina shook her head speaking very low. "But they used to be magnificent!"

"Yes indeed—we've Aspern's word for that." And as I looked again at the old woman's wrappings I could imagine her not having wished to allow any supposition that the great poet had overdone it. But I didn't waste my time in considering Juliana, in whom the appearance of respiration was so slight as to suggest that no human attention could ever help her more. I turned my eyes once more all over the room, rummaging with them the closets, the chests of drawers, the tables. Miss Tina at once noted their direction and read, I think, what was in them; but she didn't answer it, turning away restlessly, anxiously, so that I felt rebuked, with reason, for an appetite well-nigh indecent in the presence of our dying companion. All the same I took another view, endeavouring to pick out mentally the receptacle to try first, for a person who should wish to put his hand on Miss Bordereau's papers directly after her death. The place was a dire confusion; it looked like the dressing-room of an old actress. There were clothes hanging over chairs, odd-looking shabby bundles here and there, and various pasteboard boxes piled together, battered, bulging and discoloured, which might have been fifty years old. Miss Tina after a moment noticed the direction of my eyes again, and, as if she guessed how I judged such appearances—forgetting I had no business to judge them at all—said, perhaps to defend herself from the imputation of complicity in the disorder:

"She likes it this way; we can't move things. There are old band-boxes she has had most of her life." Then she added, half-taking pity on my real thought: "Those things were *there*." And she pointed to a small low trunk which stood under a sofa that just allowed room for it. It struck me as a queer superannuated coffer, of painted wood, with elaborate handles and shrivelled straps and with the colour—it had last been endued with a coat of light green

—much rubbed off. It evidently had travelled with Juliana in the olden time—in the days of her adventures, which it had shared. It would have made a strange figure arriving at a modern hotel.

"*Were* there—they aren't now?" I asked, startled by Miss Tina's implication.

She was going to answer, but at that moment the doctor came in—the doctor whom the little maid had been sent to fetch and whom she had at last overtaken. My servant, going on his own errand, had met her with her companion in tow, and in the sociable Venetian spirit, retracing his steps with them, had also come up to the threshold of the padrona's room, where I saw him peep over the doctor's shoulder. I motioned him away the more instantly that the sight of his prying face reminded me how little I myself had to do there—an admonition confirmed by the sharp way the little doctor eyed me, his air of taking me for a rival who had the field before him. He was a short fat brisk gentleman who wore the tall hat of his profession and seemed to look at everything but his patient. He kept me still in range, as if it struck him I too should be better for a dose, so that I bowed to him and left him with the women, going down to smoke a cigar in the garden. I was nervous; I couldn't go further; I couldn't leave the place. I don't know exactly what I thought might happen, but I felt it important to be there. I wandered about the alleys—the warm night had come on—smoking cigar after cigar and studying the light in Miss Bordereau's windows. They were open now, I could see; the situation was different. Sometimes the light moved, but not quickly; it didn't suggest the hurry of a crisis. Was the old woman dying or was she already dead? Had the doctor said that there was nothing to be done at her tremendous age but to let her quietly pass away? or had he simply announced with a look a little more conventional that the end of the end had come? Were the other two women just going and coming over the offices that follow in such a case? It made me uneasy not to be nearer, as if I thought the doctor himself might carry away the papers with him. I bit my cigar hard while it assailed me again that perhaps there were now no papers to carry!

I wandered about an hour and more. I looked out for Miss Tina at one of the windows, having a vague idea that she might come there to give me some sign. Wouldn't she see the red tip of my cigar in the dark and feel sure I was hanging on to know what the doctor had said? I'm afraid it's a proof of the grossness of my anxieties that I should have taken in some degree for granted at such an hour, in the midst of the greatest change that could fall on her, poor Miss Tina's having also a free mind for them. My servant came down and spoke to me; he knew nothing save that the doctor had gone after a visit of half an hour. If he had stayed half an hour then Miss Bordereau was still alive: it couldn't have taken so long to attest her decease. I sent the man out of the house; there were moments when the sense of his curiosity annoyed me, and this was one of them. *He* had been watching my cigar-tip from an upper window, if Miss Tina hadn't; he couldn't know what I was after and I couldn't tell him, though I suspected in him fantastic private theories about me which he thought fine and which, had I more exactly known them, I should have thought offensive.

I went upstairs at last, but I mounted no higher than the sala. The door of Miss Bordereau's apartment was open, showing from the parlour the dimness of a poor candle. I went toward it with a light tread, and at the same moment Miss Tina apppeared and stood looking at me as I approached. "She's better, she's better," she said even before I had asked. "The doctor has given her something; she woke up, came back to life while he was there. He says there's no immediate danger."

"No immediate danger? Surely he thinks her condition serious!"

"Yes, because she had been excited. That affects her dreadfully."

"It will do so again then, because she works herself up. She did so this afternoon."

"Yes, she mustn't come out any more," said Miss Tina with one of her lapses into a deeper detachment.

"What's the use of making such a remark as that," I permitted myself to ask, "if you begin to rattle her about again the first time she bids you?"

"I won't—I won't do it any more."

"You must learn to resist her," I went on.

"Oh yes, I shall; I shall do so better if you tell me it's right."

"You mustn't do it for me—you must do it for yourself. It all comes back to you, if you're scared and upset."

"Well, I'm not upset now," said Miss Tina placidly enough. "She's very quiet."

"Is she conscious again—does she speak?"

"No, she doesn't speak, but she takes my hand. She holds it fast."

"Yes," I returned, "I can see what force she still has by the way she grabbed that picture this afternoon. But if she holds you fast how comes it that you're here?"

Miss Tina waited a little; though her face was in deep shadow—she had her back to the light in the parlour and I had put down my own candle far off, near the door of the sala—I thought I saw her smile ingenuously. "I came on purpose—I had heard your step."

"Why I came on tiptoe, as soundlessly as possible."

"Well, I had heard you," said Miss Tina.

"And is your aunt alone now?"

"Oh no—Olimpia sits there."

On my side I debated. "Shall we then pass in there?" And I nodded at the parlour; I wanted more and more to be on the spot.

"We can't talk there—she'll hear us."

I was on the point of replying that in that case we'd sit silent, but I felt too much this wouldn't do, there was something I desired so immensely to ask her. Thus I hinted we might walk a little in the sala, keeping more at the other end, where we shouldn't disturb our friend. Miss Tina assented unconditionally; the doctor was coming again, she said, and she would be there to meet him at the door. We strolled through the fine superfluous hall, where on the marble floor—particularly as at first we said nothing—our footsteps were more audible than I had expected. When we reached the other end—the wide window, inveterately closed, connecting with the balcony that overhung the canal—I submitted that we had best remain there, as she would see the doctor arrive the sooner. I opened the window and we passed out on the balcony. The air of the canal seemed even heavier, hotter than that of the sala. The place was hushed and void; the quiet neighborhood had gone to sleep. A lamp, here and there, over the narrow black water, glimmered in double; the voice of a man going homeward singing, his jacket on his shoulder and his hat on his ear, came to us from a distance. This didn't prevent the scene from being very *comme il faut*, as Miss Bordereau had called it the first time I saw her. Presently a gondola passed along the canal with its slow rhythmical plash, and as we listened we watched it in silence. It didn't stop, it didn't carry the doctor; and after it had gone on I said to Miss Tina:

"And where are they now—the things that were in the trunk?"

"In the trunk?"

"That green box you pointed out to me in her room. You said her papers had been there; you seemed to mean she had transferred them."

"Oh yes; they're not in the trunk," said Miss Tina.

"May I ask if you've looked?"

"Yes, I've looked—for you."

"How for me, dear Miss Tina? Do you mean you'd have given them to me if you had found them?"—and I fairly trembled with the question.

She delayed to reply and I waited. Suddenly she broke out: "I don't know what I'd do—what I wouldn't!"

"Would you look again—somewhere else?"

She had spoken with a strange unexpected emotion, and she went on in the same tone: "I can't—I can't—while she lies there. It isn't decent."

"No, it isn't decent," I replied gravely. "Let the poor lady rest in peace." And the words, on my lips, were not hypocritical, for I felt reprimanded and shamed.

Miss Tina added in a moment, as if she had guessed this and were sorry for me, but at the same time wished to explain that I did push her, or at least harp on the chord, too much: "I can't deceive her that way. I can't deceive her—perhaps on her death-bed."

"Heaven forbid I should ask you, though I've been guilty myself!"

"You've been guilty?"

"I've sailed under false colours." I felt now I must make a clean breast of it, must tell her I had given her an invented name on account of my fear her aunt would have heard of me and so refuse to take me in. I explained this as well as that I had really been a party to the letter addressed them by John Cumnor months before.

She listened with great attention, almost in fact gaping for wonder, and when I had made my confession she said: "Then your real name—what is it?" She repeated it over twice when I had told her, accompanying it with the exclamation "Gracious, gracious!" Then she added: "I like your own best."

"So do I,"—and I felt my laugh rueful. "Ouf! it's a relief to get rid of the other."

"So it was a regular plot—a kind of conspiracy?"

"Oh a conspiracy—we were only two," I replied, leaving out of course Mrs. Prest.

She considered; I thought she was perhaps going to pronounce us very base. But this was not her way, and she remarked after a moment, as in candid impartial contemplation: "How much you must want them!"

"Oh I do, passionately!" I grinned, I fear to admit. And this chance made me go on, forgetting my compunction of a moment before. "How can she possibly have changed their place herself? How can she walk? How can she arrive at that sort of muscular exertion? How can she lift and carry things?"

"Oh when one wants and when one has so much will!" said Miss Tina as if she had thought over my question already herself and had simply had no choice but that answer—the idea that in the dead of night, or at some moment when the coast was clear, the old woman had been capable of a miraculous effort.

"Have you questioned Olimpia? Hasn't she helped her—hasn't she done it for her?" I asked; to which my friend replied promptly and positively that their servant had had nothing to do with the matter, though without admitting definitely that she had spoken to her. It was as if she were a little shy, a little ashamed now, of letting me see how much she had entered into my uneasiness and had me on her mind. Suddenly she said to me without any immediate relevance:

"I rather feel you a new person, you know, now that you've a new name."

"It isn't a new one; it's a very good old one, thank fortune!"

She looked at me a moment. "Well, I do like it better."

"Oh if you didn't I would almost go on with the other!"

"Would you really?"

I laughed again, but I returned for all answer: "Of course if she can rummage about that way she can perfectly have burnt them."

"You must wait—you must wait," Miss Tina mournfully moralised; and her tone ministered little to my patience, for it seemed after all to accept that wretched possibility. I would teach myself to wait, I declared nevertheless; because in the first place I couldn't do otherwise and in the second I had her promise, given me the other night, that she would help me.

"Of course if the papers are gone that's no use," she said; not as if she wished to recede, but only to be conscientious.

"Naturally. But if you could only find out!" I groaned, quivering again.

"I thought you promised you'd wait."

"Oh you mean wait even for that?"

"For what then?"

"Ah, nothing," I answered rather foolishly, being ashamed to tell her what had been implied in my acceptance of delay—the idea that she would perhaps do more for me than merely find out.

I know not if she guessed this; at all events she seemed to bethink herself of some propriety of showing me more rigour. "I didn't promise to deceive, did I? I don't think I did."

"It doesn't much matter whether you did or not, for you couldn't!"

Nothing is more possible than that she wouldn't have contested this even hadn't she been diverted by our seeing the doctor's gondola shoot into the little canal and approach the house. I noted that he came as fast as if he believed our proprietress still in danger. We looked down at him while he disembarked and then went back into the sala to meet him. When he came up, however, I naturally left Miss Tina to go off with him alone, only asking her leave to come back later for news.

I went out of the house and walked far, as far as the Piazza, where my restlessness declined to quit me. I was unable to sit down; it was very late now though there were people still at the little tables in front of the cafés: I could but uneasily revolve, and I did so half a dozen times. The only comfort, none the less, was in my having told Miss Tina who I really was. At last I took my way home again, getting gradually and all but inextricably lost, as I did whenever I went out in Venice: so that it was considerably past midnight when I reached my door. The sala, upstairs, was as dark as usual and my lamp as I crossed it found nothing satisfactory to show me. I was disappointed, for I had notified Miss Tina that I would come back for a report, and I thought she might have left a light there as a sign. The door of the ladies' apartment was closed; which seemed a hint that my faltering friend had gone to bed in impatience of waiting for me. I stood in the middle of the place, considering, hoping she would hear me and perhaps peep out, saying to myself too that she would never go to bed with her aunt in a state so critical; she would sit up and watch—she would be in a chair, in her dressing-gown. I went nearer the door; I stopped there and listened. I heard nothing at all and at last I tapped gently. No answer came and after another minute I turned the handle. There was no light in the room; this ought to have prevented my entrance, but it had no such effect. If I have frankly stated the importunities, the indelicacies, of which my desire to possess myself of Jeffrey Aspern's papers had made me capable I needn't shrink, it seems to me, from confessing this last indiscretion. I regard it as the worst thing I did, yet there were extenuating circumstances. I was deeply though doubtless not disinterestedly anxious for more news of Juliana, and Miss Tina had accepted from me, as it were, a rendezvous which it might have been a point of honour with me to keep. It may be objected that her leaving the place dark was a positive sign that she released me, and to this I can only reply that I wished not to be released.

The door to Miss Bordereau's room was open and I could see beyond it the faintness of a taper. There was no sound—my footstep caused no one to stir. I came further into the room; I lingered there lamp in hand. I wanted to give Miss Tina a chance to come to me if, as I couldn't doubt, she were still with her aunt. I made no noise to call her; I only waited to see if she wouldn't notice my light. She didn't, and I explained this—I found afterwards I was right—by the idea that she had fallen asleep. If she had fallen asleep her aunt was not on her mind, and my explanation ought to have led me to go out as I had come. I must repeat again that it didn't, for I found myself at the same moment given up to something else. I had no definite purpose, no bad intention, but felt myself held to the spot by an acute, though absurd, sense of opportunity. Opportunity for what I couldn't have said, inasmuch as it wasn't in my mind that I might proceed to thievery. Even had this tempted me I was confronted with the evident fact that Miss Bordereau didn't leave her secretary, her cupboard and the drawers of her tables gaping. I had no keys, no tools and no ambition to smash her furniture. None the less it came to me that I was now, perhaps alone, unmolested, at the hour of freedom and safety, nearer to the source of my hopes than I had ever been. I held up my lamp, let the light play on the different objects as if it could tell me something. Still there came no movement from the other room. If Miss Tina was sleeping she was sleeping sound. Was she doing so—generous creature—on purpose to leave me the field? Did she know I was there and was she just keeping quiet to see what I would do—what I *could* do? Yet might I, when it came to that? She herself knew even better than I how little.

I stopped in front of the secretary, gaping at it vainly and no doubt grotesquely; for what had it to say to me after all? In the first place it was locked, and in the second it almost surely contained nothing in which I was interested. Ten to one the papers had been destroyed, and even if they hadn't the keen old woman wouldn't have put them in such a place as that after removing them from the green trunk—wouldn't have transferred them, with the idea of their safety on her brain, from the better hiding-place to the worse. The secretary was more conspicuous, more exposed in a room in which she could no longer mount guard. It opened with a key, but there was a small brass handle, like a button as well; I saw this as I played my lamp over it. I did something more, for the climax of my crisis; I caught a glimpse of the possibility that Miss Tina wished me really to understand. If she didn't so wish me, if she wished me to keep away, why hadn't she locked the door of communication between the sitting-room and the sala? That would have been a definite sign that I was to leave them alone. If I didn't leave them alone she meant me to come for a purpose—a purpose now represented by the super-subtle inference that to oblige me she had unlocked the secretary. She hadn't left the key, but the lid would probably move if I touched the button. This possibility pressed me hard and I bent very close to judge. I didn't propose to do anything, not even—not in the least—to let down the lid; I only wanted to test my theory, to see if the cover *would* move. I touched the button with my hand—a mere touch would tell me; and as I did so—it is embarrassing for me to relate it—I looked over my shoulder. It was a chance, an instinct, for I had really heard nothing. I almost let my luminary drop and certainly I stepped back, straightening myself up at what I saw. Juliana stood there in her nightdress, by the doorway of her room, watching me; her hands were raised, she had lifted the everlasting curtain that covered half her face, and for the first, the last, the only time I beheld her extraordinary eyes. They glared at me; they were like the sudden drench, for a caught burglar, of a flood of gaslight; they made me horribly ashamed. I never shall forget her strange little bent white tottering figure, with its lifted head, her attitude, her expression; neither shall I forget the tone in which as I turned, looking at her, she hissed out passionately, furiously:

"Ah you publishing scoundrel!"

I can't now say what I stammered to excuse myself, to explain; but I went toward her to tell her I meant no harm. She waved me off with her old hands, retreating before me in horror; and the next thing I knew she had fallen back with a quick spasm, as if death had descended on her, into Miss Tina's arms.

IX

I LEFT Venice the next morning, directly on learning that my hostess had not succumbed, as I feared at the moment, to the shock I had given her—the shock I may also say she had given me. How in the world could I have supposed her capable of getting out of bed by herself? I failed to see Miss Tina before going; I only saw the *donna,* whom I entrusted with a note for her younger mistress. In this note I mentioned that I should be absent but a few days. I went to Treviso, to Bassano, to Castelfranco; I took walks and drives and looked at musty old churches with ill-lighted pictures; I spent hours seated smoking at the doors of cafés, where there were flies and yellow curtains, on the shady side of sleepy little squares. In spite of these pasttimes, which were mechanical and perfunctory, I scantly enjoyed my travels: I had had to gulp down a bitter draught and couldn't get rid of the taste. It had been devilish awkward, as the young men say, to be found by Juliana in the dead of night examining the attachment of her bureau; and it had not been less so to have to believe for a good many hours after that it was highly probable I had killed her. My humiliation galled me, but I had to make the best of it, had, in writing to Miss Tina to minimise it, as well as account for the posture in which I had been discovered. As she gave me no word of answer I couldn't know what impression I made on her. It rankled for me that I had been called a publishing scoundrel, since certainly I did publish and no less certainly hadn't been very delicate. There was a moment when I stood convinced that the only way to purge my dishonour was to take myself straight away on the instant; to sacrifice my hopes and relieve the two poor women for ever of the oppression of my intercourse. Then I reflected that I had better try a short absence first, for I must already have had a sense (unexpressed and dim) that in disappearing completely it wouldn't be merely my own hopes I should condemn to extinction. It would perhaps answer if I kept dark long enough to give the elder lady time to believe herself rid of me. That she would wish to be rid of me after this—if I wasn't rid of her—was now not to be doubted: that midnight monstrosity would have cured her of the disposition to put up with my company for the sake of my dollars. I said to myself that after all I couldn't abandon Miss Tina, and I continued to say this even while I noted that she quite ignored my earnest request—I had given her two or three addresses, at little towns, *poste restante*—for some sign of her actual state. I would have made my servant write me news but that he was unable to manage a pen. Couldn't I measure the scorn of Miss Tina's silence—little disdainful as she had ever been? Really the soreness pressed; yet if I had scruples about going back I had others about not doing so, and I wanted to put myself on a better footing. The end of it was that I did return to Venice on the twelfth day; and as my gondola gently bumped against our palace steps a fine palpitation of suspense showed me the violence my absence had done me.

I had faced about so abruptly that I hadn't even telegraphed to my servant. He was therefore not at the station to meet me, but he poked out his head from an upper window when I reached the house. "They have put her into earth, *quella vecchia,*" he said to me in the lower hall while he shouldered my valise; and he grinned and almost winked as if he knew I should be pleased with his news.

"She's dead!" I cried, giving him a very different look.

"So it appears, since they've buried her."

"It's all over then? When was the funeral?"

"The other yesterday. But a funeral you could scarcely call it, signore: *roba da niente—un piccolo passeggio brutto* of two gondolas. Poveretta!" the man continued, referring apparently to Miss Tina. His conception of funerals was that they were mainly to amuse the living.

I wanted to know about Miss Tina, how she might be and generally where; but I asked him no more questions till we had got upstairs. Now that the fact had met me I took a bad view of it, especially of the idea that poor Miss Tina had had to manage by herself after the end. What did she know about arrangements, about the steps to take in such a case? Poveretta indeed! I could only hope the doctor had given her support and that she hadn't been neglected by the old friends of whom she had told me, the little band of the faithful whose fidelity consisted in coming to the house once a year. I elicited from my servant that two old ladies and an old gentleman had in fact rallied round Miss Tina and had supported her—they had come for her in a gondola of their own—during the journey to the cemetery, the little red-walled island of tombs which lies to the north of the town and on the way to Murano. It appeared from these signs that the Misses Bordereau were Catholics, a discovery I had never made, as the old woman couldn't go to church and her niece, so far as I perceived, either didn't, or went only to early mass in the parish before I was stirring. Certainly even the priests respected their seclusion; I had never caught the whisk of the curato's skirt. That evening, an hour later, I sent my servant down with five words on a card to ask if Miss Tina would see me for a few moments. She was not in the house, where he had sought her, he told me when he came back, but in the garden walking about to refresh herself and picking the flowers quite as if they belonged to her. He had found her there and she would be happy to see me.

I went down and passed half an hour with poor Miss Tina. She had always had a look of musty mourning, as if she were wearing out old robes of sorrow that wouldn't come to an end; and in this particular she made no different show. But she clearly had been crying, crying a great deal—simply, satisfyingly, refreshingly, with a primitive retarded sense of solitude and violence. But she had none of the airs or graces of grief, and I was almost surprised to see her stand there in the first dusk with her hands full of admirable roses and smile at me with reddened eyes. Her white face, in the frame of her mantilla, looked longer, leaner than usual. I hadn't doubted her being irreconcilably disgusted with me, her considering I ought to have been on the spot to advise her, to help her; and, though I believed there was no rancour in her composition and no great conviction of the importance of her affairs, I had prepared myself for a change in her manner, for some air of injury and estrangement, which should say to my conscience: "Well, you're a nice person to have professed things!" But historic truth compels me to declare that this poor lady's dull face ceased to be dull, almost ceased to be plain, as she turned it gladly to her late aunt's lodger. That touched him extremely and he thought it simplified his situation until he found it didn't. I was as kind to her that evening as I knew how to be, and I walked about the garden with her as long as seemed good. There was no explanation of any sort between us; I didn't ask her why she hadn't answered my letter. Still less did I repeat what I had said to her in that communication; if she chose to let me suppose she had forgotten the position in which Miss Bordereau had surprised me and the effect of the discovery on the old woman, I was quite willing to take it that way: I was grateful to her for not treating me as if I had killed her aunt.

We strolled and strolled, though really not much passed between us save the recognition of her bereavement, conveyed in my manner and in the expression she had of depending on me now, since I let her see I still took an interest in her. Miss Tina's was no breast for the pride or the pretense of independence; she didn't in the least suggest that she knew at present what would become of her. I forbore to press on that question, however, for I certainly was not prepared to say that I would take charge of her. I was cautious; not ignobly, I think, for I felt her knowledge of life to be so small that in her unsophisticated vision there would be no reason why—since I seemed to pity her—I shouldn't somehow look after her. She told me how her aunt had died, very peacefully at the last, and how everything had been done afterwards by the care of her good friends—fortunately, thanks to me, she said, smiling, there was money in the house. She repeated that when once the "nice" Italians like you they are your friends for life, and when we had gone into this she asked me about my *giro,* my impressions, my adventures, the places I had seen. I told her what I could, making it up partly,

I'm afraid, as in my disconcerted state I had taken little in; and after she had heard me she exclaimed, quite as if she had forgotten her aunt and her sorrow, "Dear, dear, how much I should like to do such things—to take an amusing little journey!" It came over me for the moment that I ought to propose some enterprise, say I would accompany her anywhere she liked; and I remarked at any rate that a pleasant excursion—to give her a change—might be managed; we would think of it, talk it over. I spoke never a word of the Aspern documents, asked no question as to what she had ascertained or what had otherwise happened with regard to them before Juliana's death. It wasn't that I wasn't on pins and needles to know, but that I thought it more decent not to show greed again so soon after the catastrophe. I hoped she herself would say something, but she never glanced that way, and I thought this natural at the time. Later on, however, that night, it occurred to me that her silence was matter for suspicion; since if she had talked of my movements, of anything so detached as the Giorgione at Castelfranco, she might have alluded to what she could easily remember was in my mind. It was not to be supposed that the emotion produced by her aunt's death had blotted out the recollection that I was interested in that lady's relics, and I fidgeted afterwards as it came to me that her reticence might very possibly just mean that no relics survived. We separated in the garden—it was she who said she must go in; now that she was alone on the *piano nobile* I felt that (judged at any rate by Venetian ideas) I was on rather a different footing in regard to the invasion of it. As I shook hands with her for good-night I asked her if she had some general plan, had thought over what she had best do. "Oh yes, oh yes, but I haven't settled anything yet," she replied quite cheerfully. Was her cheerfulness explained by the impression that I would settle for her?

I was glad the next morning that we had neglected practical questions, as this gave me a pretext for seeing her again immediately. There was a practical enough question now to be touched on. I owed it to her to let her know formally that of course I didn't expect her to keep me on as a lodger, as also to show some interest in her own tenure, what she might have on her hands in the way of a lease. But I was not destined, as befell, to converse with her for more than an instant on either of these points. I sent her no message; I simply went down to the sala and walked to and fro there.

I knew she would come out; she would promptly see me accessible. Somehow I preferred not to be shut up with her; gardens and big halls seemed better places to talk. It was a splendid morning, with something in the air that told of the waning of the long Venetian summer; a freshness from the sea that stirred the flowers in the garden and made a pleasant draught in the house, less shuttered and darkened now than when the old woman was alive. It was the beginning of autumn, of the end of the golden months. With this it was the end of my experiment—or would be in the course of half an hour, when I should really have learned that my dream had been reduced to ashes. After that there would be nothing left for me but to go to the station; for seriously—and as it struck me in the morning light—I couldn't linger there to act as guardian to a piece of middle-aged female helplessness. If she hadn't saved the papers wherein should I be indebted to her? I think I winced a little as I asked myself how much, if she *had* saved them, I should have to recognise and, as it were, reward such a courtesy. Mightn't that service after all saddle me with a guardianship? If this idea didn't make me more uncomfortable as I walked up and down it was because I was convinced I had nothing to look to. If the old woman hadn't destroyed everything before she pounced on me in the parlour she had done so the next day.

It took Miss Tina rather longer than I had expected to act on my calculation; but when at last she came out she looked at me without surprise. I mentioned I had been waiting for her and she asked why I hadn't let her know. I was glad a few hours later on that I had checked myself before remarking that a friendly intuition might have told her: it turned to comfort for me that I hadn't played even to that mild extent on her sensibility. What I did say was virtually the truth—that I was too nervous, since I expected her now to settle my fate.

"Your fate?" said Miss Tina, giving me a queer look; and as she spoke I noticed a rare change in her. Yes, she was other than she had been the evening before—less natural and less easy. She had been crying the day before and was not crying now, yet she struck me as less confident. It was as if something had happened to her during the night, or at least as if she had thought of something that troubled her—something in particular that affected her relations with me, made them more embarrassing and more complicated.

Had she simply begun to feel that her aunt's not being there now altered my position?

"I mean about our papers. *Are* there any? You must know now."

"Yes, there are a great many; more than I supposed." I was struck with the way her voice trembled as she told me this.

"Do you mean you've got them in there—and that I may see them?"

"I don't think you can see them," said Miss Tina, with an extraordinary expression of entreaty in her eyes, as if the dearest hope she had in the world now was that I wouldn't take them from her. But how could she expect me to make such a sacrifice as that after all that had passed between us? What had I come back to Venice for but to see them, to take them? My joy at learning they were still in existence was such that if the poor woman had gone down on her knees to beseech me never to mention them again I would have treated the proceeding as a bad joke. "I've got them but I can't show them," she lamentably added.

"Not even to me? Ah Miss Tina!" I broke into a tone of infinite remonstrance and reproach.

She colored and the tears came back to her eyes; I measured the anguish it cost her to take such a stand which a dreadful sense of duty had imposed on her. It made me quite sick to find myself confronted with that particular obstacle; all the more that it seemed to me I had been distinctly encouraged to leave it out of account. I quite held Miss Tina to have assured me that if she had no greater hindrance than that——! "You don't mean to say you made her a death-bed promise? It was precisely against your doing anything of that sort that I thought I was safe. Oh I would rather she had burnt the papers outright than have to reckon with such a treachery as that."

"No, it isn't a promise," said Miss Tina.

"Pray what is it then?"

She hung fire, but finally said: "She tried to burn them, but I prevented it. She had hid them in her bed."

"In her bed—?"

"Between the mattresses. That's where she put them when she took them out of the trunk. I can't understand how she did it, because Olimpia didn't help her. She tells me so and I believe her. My aunt only told her afterwards, so that she shouldn't undo the bed—anything but the sheets. So it was very badly made," added Miss Tina simply.

"I should think so! And how did she try to burn them?"

"She didn't try much; she was too weak those last days. But she told me—she charged me. Oh it was terrible! She couldn't speak after that night. She could only make signs."

"And what did you do?"

"I took them away. I locked them up."

"In the secretary?"

"Yes, in the secretary," said Miss Tina, reddening again.

"Did you tell her you'd burn them?"

"No, I didn't—on purpose."

"On purpose to gratify me?"

"Yes, only for that."

"And what good will you have done me if after all you won't show them?"

"Oh none. I know that—I know that," she dismally sounded.

"And did she believe you had destroyed them?"

"I don't know what she believed at the last. I couldn't tell—she was too far gone."

"Then if there was no promise and no assurance I can't see what ties you."

"Oh she hated it so—she hated it so! She was so jealous. But here's the portrait—you may have that," the poor woman announced, taking the little picture, wrapped up in the same manner in which her aunt had wrapped it, out of her pocket.

"I may have it—do you mean you give it to me?" I gasped as it passed into my hand.

"Oh yes."

"But it's worth money—a large sum."

"Well!" said Miss Tina, still with her strange look.

I didn't know what to make of it, for it could scarcely mean that she wanted to bargain like her aunt. She spoke as for making me a present. "I can't take it from you as a gift," I said, "and yet I can't afford to pay you for it according to the idea Miss Bordereau had of its value. She rated it at a thousand pounds."

"Couldn't we sell it?" my friend threw off.

"God forbid! I prefer the picture to the money."

"Well then keep it."

"You're very generous."

"So are you."

"I don't know why you should think so," I returned; and this was true enough, for the good creature appeared to have in her mind some rich reference that I didn't in the least seize.

"Well, you've made a great difference for me," she said.

I looked at Jeffrey Aspern's face in the little picture, partly in order not to look at that of my companion, which had begun to trouble me, even to frighten me a little—it had taken so very odd, so strained and unnatural a cast. I made no answer to this last declaration; I but privately consulted Jeffrey Aspern's delightful eyes with my own—they were so young and brilliant yet so wise and so deep; I asked him what on earth was the matter with Miss Tina. He seemed to smile at me with mild mockery; he might have been amused at my case. I had got into a pickle for him—as if he needed it! He was unsatisfactory for the only moment since I had known him. Nevertheless, now that I held the little picture in my hand I felt it would be a precious possession. "Is this a bribe to make me give up the papers?" I presently and all perversely asked. "Much as I value this, you know, if I were to be obliged to choose the papers are what I should prefer. Ah but ever so much!"

"How can you choose—how can you choose?" Miss Tina returned slowly and woefully.

"I see! Of course there's nothing to be said if you regard the interdiction that rules on you as quite insurmountable. In this case it must seem to you that to part with them would be an impiety of the worst kind, a simple sacrilege!"

She shook her head, only lost in the queerness of her case. "You'd understand if you had known her. I'm afraid," she quavered suddenly—"I'm afraid! She was terrible when she was angry."

"Yes, I saw something of that, that night. She was terrible. Then I saw her eyes. Lord, they were fine!"

"I see them—they stare at me in the dark!" said Miss Tina.

"You've grown nervous with all you've been through."

"Oh yes, very—very!"

"You mustn't mind; that will pass away," I said kindly. Then I added resignedly, for it really seemed to me that I must accept the situation: "Well, so it is, and it can't be helped. I must renounce." My friend, at this, with her eyes on me, gave a low soft moan, and I went on: "I only wish to goodness she had destroyed them; then there would be nothing more to say. And I can't understand why, with her ideas, she didn't."

"Oh she lived on them!" said Miss Tina.

"You can imagine whether that makes me want less to see them," I returned not quite so desperately. "But don't let me stand here as if I had it in my soul to tempt you to anything base. Naturally, you understand, I give up my rooms. I leave Venice immediately." And I took up my hat, which I had placed on a chair. We were still rather awkwardly on our feet in the middle of the sala. She had left the door of the apartments open behind her, but had not led me that way.

A strange spasm came into her face as she saw me take my hat. "Immediately—do you mean to-day?" The tone of the words was tragic—they were a cry of desolation.

"Oh no; not so long as I can be of the least service to you."

"Well, just a day or two more—just two or three days," she panted. Then controlling herself she added in another manner: "She wanted to say something to me—the last day—something very particular. But she couldn't."

"Something very particular?"

"Something more about the papers."

"And did you guess—have you any idea?"

"No, I've tried to think—but I don't know. I've thought all kinds of things."

"As for instance?"

"Well, that if you were a relation it would be different."

I wondered. "If I were a relation—?"

"If you weren't a stranger. Then it would be the same for you as for me. Anything that's mine would be yours, and you could do what you like. I shouldn't be able to prevent you—and you'd have no responsibility."

She brought out this droll explanation with a nervous rush and as if speaking words got by heart. They gave me an impression of a subtlety which at first I failed to follow. But after a moment her face helped me to see further, and then the queerest of light came to me. It was embarrassing, and I bent my head over Jeffrey Aspern's portrait. What an odd expression was in his face! "Get out of it as you can, my dear fellow!" I put the picture into the pocket of my coat and said to Miss Tina: "Yes, I'll sell it for you. I shan't get a thousand pounds by any means, but I shall get something good."

She looked at me through pitiful tears, but seemed to try to smile as she returned: "We can divide the money."

"No, no, it shall be all yours." Then I went on: "I think I know what your poor aunt wanted to say. She wanted to give directions that the papers should be buried with her."

Miss Tina appeared to weigh this suggestion; after which she answered with striking decision, "Oh no, she wouldn't have thought that safe!"

"It seems to me nothing could be safer."

"She had an idea that when people want to publish they're capable—!" And she paused, very red.

"Of violating a tomb? Mercy on us, what must she have thought of me!"

"She wasn't just, she wasn't generous!" my companion cried with sudden passion.

The light that had come into my mind a moment before spread further. "Ah don't say that, for we *are* a dreadful race." Then I pursued: "If she left a will that may give you some idea."

"I've found nothing of the sort—she destroyed it. She was very fond of me," Miss Tina added with an effect of extreme inconsequence. "She wanted me to be happy. And if any person should be kind to me—she wanted to speak of that."

I was almost awestricken by the astuteness with which the good lady found herself inspired, transparent astuteness as it was and stitching, as the phrase is, with white thread. "Depend upon it she didn't want to make any provision that would be agreeable to *me*."

"No, not to you, but quite to me. She knew I should like it if you could carry out your idea. Not because she cared for you, but because she did think of me," Miss Tina went on with her unexpected persuasive volubility. "You could see the things—you could use them." She stopped, seeing I grasped the sense of her conditional—stopped long enough for me to give some sign that I didn't give. She must have been conscious, however, that though my face showed the greatest embarrassment ever painted on a human countenance it was not set as a stone, it was also full of compassion. It was a comfort to me a long time afterwards to consider that she couldn't have seen in me the smallest symptom of disrespect. "I don't know what to do; I'm too tormented, I'm too ashamed!" she continued with vehemence. Then turning away from me and burying her face in her hands she burst into a flood of tears. If she didn't know what to do it may be imagined whether I knew better. I stood there dumb, matching her while her sobs resounded in the great empty hall. In a moment she was up at me again with her streaming eyes. "I'd give you everything, and she'd understand, where she is—she'd forgive me!"

"Ah Miss Tina—ah Miss Tina," I stammered for all reply. I didn't know what to do, as I say, but at a venture I made a wild vague movement in consequence of which I found myself at the door. I remember standing there and saying, "It wouldn't do, it wouldn't do!"—saying it pensively, awkwardly, grotesquely, while I looked away to the opposite end of the sala as at something very interesting. The next thing I remembered is that I was downstairs and out of the house. My gondola was there and my gondolier, reclining on the cushions, sprang up as soon as he saw me. I jumped in and to his usual "*Dove commanda?*" replied, in a tone that made him stare: "Anywhere, anywhere; out into the lagoon!"

He rowed me away and I sat there prostrate, groaning softly to myself, my hat pulled over my brow. What in the name of the preposterous did she mean if she didn't mean to offer me her hand? That was the price—that was the price! And did she think I wanted it, poor deluded infatuated extravagant lady? My gondolier, behind me, must have seen my ears red as I wondered, motionless there under the fluttering *tenda* with my hidden face, noticing nothing as we passed—wondered whether her delusion, her infatuation had been my own reckless work. Did she think I had made love to her even to get the papers? I hadn't, I hadn't; I repeated that over to myself for an hour, for two hours, till I was wearied if not convinced. I don't know where, on the lagoon, my gondolier took me; we floated aimlessly and with slow rare strokes. At last I became conscious that we were near the Lido, far up, on the right hand, as you turn your back to Venice, and I made him put me ashore. I wanted to walk, to move, to shed some of my bewilderment. I crossed the narrow strip and got to the sea-beach—I took my way toward Malamocco. But presently I flung myself down again on the warm sand, in the breeze, on the coarse dry grass. It took it out of me to think I had been so much at fault, that I had unwittingly but none the less deplorably trifled. But I hadn't given her cause—distinctly I hadn't. I had said to Mrs. Prest that I would make love to her; but it had been a joke without consequences and I had never said it to my victim. I had been as kind as possible because I really liked her; but since when had that become a crime where a woman of such an age and such an appearance was concerned? I am far from remembering clearly the succession of events and feelings during this long day of confusion, which I spent entirely in wandering about, without going home, until late at night; it only comes back to me that there were moments when I pacified my conscience and others when I lashed it into pain. I didn't laugh all day—that I do recollect; the case, however it might have struck others, seemed to me so little amusing. I should have been better employed perhaps in taking in the comic side of it. At any rate, whether I had given cause or not, there was no doubt whatever that I couldn't pay the price. I couldn't accept the proposal. I couldn't, for a bundle of tattered papers, marry a ridiculous pathetic provincial old woman. It was a proof of how little she supposed the idea would come to me that she should have decided to suggest it herself in that practical argumentative heroic way—with the timidity, however, so much more striking than the boldness, that her reasons appeared to come first and her feelings afterward.

As the day went on I grew to wish I had never heard of Aspern's relics, and I cursed the extravagant curiosity that had put John Cumnor on the scent of them. We had more than enough material without them, and my predicament was the just punishment of that most fatal of human follies, our not having known when to stop. It was very well to say it was no predicament, that the way out was simple, that I had only to leave Venice by the first train in the morning, after addressing Miss Tina a note which should be placed in her hand as soon as I got clear of the house; for it was strong proof of my quandary that when I tried to make up the note to my taste in advance—I would put it on paper as soon as I got home, before going to bed—I couldn't think of anything but "How can I thank you for the rare confidence you've placed in me?" That would never do; it sounded exactly as if an acceptance were to follow. Of course I might get off without writing at all, but that would be brutal, and my idea was still to exclude brutal solutions. As my confusion cooled I lost myself in wonder at the importance I had attached to Juliana's crumpled scraps; the thought of them became odious to me and I was as vexed with the old witch for the superstition that had prevented her from destroying them as I was with myself for having already spent more money than I could afford in attempting to control their fate. I forget what I did, where I went after leaving the Lido, and at what hour or with what recovery of composure I made my way back to my boat. I only know that in the afternoon, when the air was aglow with the sunset, I was standing before the church of Saints John and Paul and looking up at the small square-jawed face of Bartolommeo Colleoni, the terrible *condottiere* who sits so sturdily astride of his huge bronze horse on the high pedestal on which Venetian gratitude maintains him. The statue is incomparable, the finest of all mounted figures, unless that of Marcus Aurelius, who rides benignant before the Roman Capitol, be finer: but I was not thinking of that; I only found myself staring at the triumphant captain as if he had had an oracle on his lips. The western light shines into all his grimness at that hour and makes it wonderfully personal. But he continued to look far over my head, at the red immersion of another day—he had seen so many go down into the lagoon through the centuries—and if he were thinking of battles and stratagems they were of a different quality from any I had to tell him of. He couldn't direct me what to do, gaze up at him as I might. Was it before this or after that I wandered about for an hour in the small canals, to the continued stupefaction of my gondolier, who had never seen me so restless and yet so void of a purpose and could extract from me no order but "Go anywhere—everywhere—all over the place?" He reminded me that I had not lunched and expressed therefore respectfully the hope that I would dine earlier. He had had long periods of leisure during the day, when I had left the boat and rambled, so that I was not obliged to consider him, and I told him that till the morrow, for reasons, I should touch no meat. It was an effect of poor Miss Tina's proposal, not altogether auspicious, that I had quite lost my appetite. I don't know why it happened that on this occasion I was more than ever struck with that queer air of sociability, of cousinship and family life, which makes up half the expression of Venice. Without streets and vehicles, the uproar of wheels, the brutality of horses, and with its little winding ways where people crowd together, where voices sound as in the corridors of a house, where the human step circulates as if it skirted the angles of furniture and shoes never wear out, the place has the character of an immense collective apartment, in which Piazza San Marco is the most ornamented corner and palaces and churches, for the rest, play the part of great divans of repose, tables of entertainment, expanses of decoration. And somehow the splendid common domicile, familiar domestic and resonant, also resembles a theatre with its actors clicking over bridges and, in straggling processions, tripping along fondamentas. As you sit in your gondola the footways that in certain parts edge the canals assume to the eye the importance of a stage, meeting it at the same angle, and the Venetian figures, moving to and fro against the battered scenery of their little houses of comedy, strike you as members of an endless dramatic troupe.

I went to bed that night very tired and without being able to compose an address to Miss Tina. Was this failure the reason why I became conscious the next morning as soon as I awoke of a determination to see the poor lady again the first moment she would receive me? That had something to do with it, but what had still more was the fact that during my sleep the oddest revulsion had taken place in my spirit. I found myself aware of this almost as soon as I opened my eyes: it made me jump out of my bed with the movement of a man who remembers that he has left the house-door ajar or a candle burning under a shelf. Was I still in time to save my goods? That question was in my heart; for what had now come to pass was that in the unconscious cerebration of sleep I had swung back to a passionate appreciation of Juliana's treasure. The pieces composing it were now more precious than ever and a positive ferocity had come into my need to acquire them. The condition Miss Tina had attached to that act no longer appeared an obstacle worth thinking of, and for an hour this morning my repentant imagination brushed it aside. It was absurd I should be able to invent nothing; absurd to renounce so easily and turn away helpless from the idea that the only way to become possessed was to unite myself to her for life. I mightn't unite myself, yet I might still have what she had. I must add that by the time I sent down to ask if she would see me I had invented no alternative, though in fact I drew out my dressing in the interest of my wit. This failure was humiliating, yet what could the alternative be?

Miss Tina sent back word I might come; and as I descended the stairs and crossed the sala to her door—this time she received me in her aunt's forlorn parlour—I hoped she wouldn't think my announcement was to be "favourable." She certainly would have understood my recoil of the day before.

As soon as I came into the room I saw that she had done so, but I also saw something which had not been in my forecast. Poor Miss Tina's sense of her failure had produced a rare alteration in her, but I had been too full of stratagems and spoils to think of that. Now I took it in; I can scarcely tell how it startled me. She stood in the middle of the room with a face of mildness bent upon me, and her look of forgiveness, of absolution, made her angelic. It beautified her; she was younger; she was not a ridiculous old woman. This trick of her expression, this magic of her spirit, transfigured her, and while I still noted it I heard a whisper somewhere in the depths of my conscience: "Why not, after all—why not?" It seemed to me I *could* pay the price. Still more distinctly however than the whisper I heard Miss Tina's own voice. I was so struck with the different effect she made on me that at first I wasn't clearly aware of what she was saying; then I recognised she had bade me good-bye—she said something about hoping I should be very happy.

"Good-bye—good-bye?" I repeated with an inflection interrogative and probably foolish.

I saw she didn't feel the interrogation, she only heard the words; she had strung herself up to accepting our separation and they fell upon her ear as a proof. "Are you going to-day?" she asked. "But it doesn't matter, for whenever you go I shall not see you again. I don't want to." And she smiled strangely, with an infinite gentleness. She had never doubted my having left her the day before in horror. How *could* she, since I hadn't come back before night to contradict, even as a simple form, even as an act of common humanity, such an idea? And now she had the force of soul—Miss Tina with force of soul was a new conception—to smile at me in her abjection.

"What shall you do—where shall you go?" I asked.

"Oh I don't know. I've done the great thing. I've destroyed the papers."

"Destroyed them?" I waited.

"Yes; what was I to keep them for? I burnt them last night, one by one, in the kitchen."

"One by one?" I coldly echoed it.

"It took a long time—there were so many." The room seemed to go round me as she said this and a real darkness for a moment descended on my eyes. When it passed, Miss Tina was there still, but the transfiguration was over and she had changed back to a plain dingy elderly person. It was in this character she spoke as she said "I can't stay with you longer, I can't;" and it was in this character she turned her back upon me, as I had turned mine upon her twenty-four hours before, and moved to the door of her room. Here she did what I hadn't done when I quitted her—she paused long enough to give me one look. I have never forgotten it and I sometimes still suffer from it, though it was not resentful. No, there was no resentment, nothing hard or vindictive in poor Miss Tina; for when, later, I sent her, as the price of the portrait of Jeffrey Aspern, a larger sum of money than I had hoped to be able to gather for her, writing to her that I had sold the picture, she kept it with thanks; she never sent it back. I wrote her that I had sold the picture, but I admitted to Mrs. Prest at the time—I met this other friend in London that autumn—that it hangs above my writing-table. When I look at it I can scarcely bear my loss—I mean of the precious papers.

The Pupil

The Pupil

THE PUPIL (1891) is characteristically a *nouvelle* both in theme and construction. It is not so well known as it deserves to be, probably because its plot is not quite so exciting or original as the plots of *The Aspern Papers* and *The Beast in the Jungle*. Yet it is one of James's best narratives, of which it can be said that it is converted by its rare measure of objectivity and insight into a piece of modern poetry pure and simple—a poetry not of the lyrical impulse but of the psychological faculty.

The objectivity is of a quality peculiar to James, which is quite unlike the objectivity of the naturalist school of fiction. It depends neither on exhaustive documentation nor on the author's assumption of an attitude of seemingly scientific detachment toward his material. For the Jamesian objectivity is not a calculated method but the result, rather, of an unusually concrete and close understanding of the characters and situation. So close and concrete is this understanding that it is transformed into a kind of self-contained irony which leaves us with no "problem" on our hands, no general issue or topic which we can extract from the work for purposes of discussion. Save for the work itself, there is nothing to discuss. As James tells it, the story of the worldly Moreen family and of their precocious son is an impression of life assimilated and criticized with such quiet intensity that it asks nothing of us except to experience it. And the experience and illumination are one.

Essentially this is what makes for the chief difference between James and novelists of like caliber whose writing is in the European tradition of deriving value directly from ideas, from ideological ferment and provocation. And for this reason, too, readers who are accustomed to judge literature by the ideological stimulus it provides, by the range and profundity of the questions raised, may be unable to appreciate the qualities of a *nouvelle* like *The Pupil*. T. S. Eliot once said that James's genius comes out "most tellingly in his mastery over, his baffling escape from, ideas; a mastery and an escape which are perhaps the last test of a superior intelligence. He had a mind so fine that no idea could violate it. . . ." This is a very shrewd observation, and, while it helps us to understand some Jamesian effects better than others, there can be no doubt of its relevance in the case of *The Pupil*.

As for the origin of this work, in the preface to the collected edition James recalled that the idea of it came to him all at once during a session with a friend in an Italian railway-carriage. The friend happened to speak of a migratory American family, with pretensions to worldliness, the most interesting member of which was a small boy of extraordinary intelligence who saw their life exactly for what it was. Then and there James grasped all the elements of the story—"to the last delicacy." It was a moment of absolute perception.

In *The Pupil* James again turns to account his method of presenting characters indirectly, through a perspective of the most careful design. His effort is to make us see the characters "through" those among them who possess the gift of consciousness, or, as the Jamesian phrase has it, "who are capable of a certain high lucidity." He believed that the human predicament dealt with in a work of fiction needs to be organized around a nucleus of "irrepressible appreciation," that is to say, that it needs a central intelligence to bring out its finer possibilities. Hence his emphasis on what seems like a purely technical issue—the issue of the "point of view" from which the action of a story is seen by the reader. For the choice of the "point of view" and its structural placing in the story are not only its available means of unity and coherence but also the means of securing for it the maximum amount of consciousness. Given this approach, it is obvious that a good deal of the drama of those who are conscious and who do "appreciate" what happens to them must consist of their relation to those who don't—the fools, as James called them. In *The Pupil* it is little Morgan Moreen and his tutor who stand at the post of observation and awareness, while the other figures are "the fools who minister to the free spirits engaged with them."

I

THE poor young man hesitated and procrastinated: it cost him such an effort to broach the subject of terms, to speak of money to a person who spoke only of feelings and, as it were, of the aristocracy. Yet he was unwilling to take leave, treating his engagement as settled, without some more conventional glance in that direction than he could find an opening for in the manner of the large, affable lady who sat there drawing a pair of soiled *gants de Suède* through a fat, jewelled hand and, at once pressing and gliding, repeated over and over everything but the thing he would have liked to hear. He would have liked to hear the figure of his salary; but just as he was nervously about to sound that note the little boy came back—the little boy Mrs. Moreen had sent out of the room to fetch her fan. He came back without the fan, only with the casual observation that he couldn't find it. As he dropped this cynical confession he looked straight and hard at the candidate for the honour of taking his education in hand. This personage reflected, somewhat grimly, that the first thing he should have to teach his little charge would be to appear to address himself to his mother when he spoke to her—especially not to make her such an improper answer as that.

When Mrs. Moreen bethought herself of this pretext for getting rid of their companion, Pemberton supposed it was precisely to approach the delicate subject of his remuneration. But it had been only to say some things about her son which it was better that a boy of eleven shouldn't catch. They were extravagantly to his advantage, save when she lowered her voice to sigh, tapping her left side familiarly: "And all overclouded by *this,* you know—all at the mercy of a weakness—!" Pemberton gathered that the weakness was in the region of the heart. He had known the poor child was not robust: this was the basis on which he had been invited to treat, through an English lady, an Oxford acquaintance, then at Nice, who happened to know both his needs and those of the amiable American family looking out for something really superior in the way of a resident tutor.

The young man's impression of his prospective pupil, who had first come into the room, as if to see for himself, as soon as Pemberton was admitted, was not quite the soft solicitation the visitor had taken for granted. Morgan Moreen was, somehow, sickly without being delicate, and that he looked intelligent (it is true Pemberton wouldn't have enjoyed his being stupid), only added to the suggestion that, as with his big mouth and big ears he really couldn't be called pretty, he might be unpleasant. Pemberton was modest—he was even timid; and the chance that his small scholar might prove cleverer than himself had quite figured, to his nervousness, among the dangers of an untried experiment. He reflected, however, that these were risks one had to run when one accepted a position, as it was called, in a private family; when as yet one's University honours had, pecuniarily speaking, remained barren. At any rate, when Mrs. Moreen got up as if to intimate that, since it was understood he would enter upon his duties within the weeks she would let him off now, he succeeded, in spite of the presence of the child, in squeezing out a phrase about the rate of payment. It was not the fault of the conscious smile which seemed a reference to the lady's expensive identity, if the allusion did not sound rather vulgar. This was exactly because she became still more gracious to reply: "Oh, I can assure you that all that will be quite regular."

Pemberton only wondered, while he took up his hat, what "all that" was to amount to—people had such different ideas. Mrs. Moreen's words, however, seemed to commit the family to a pledge definite enough to elicit from the child a strange little comment, in the shape of the mocking, foreign ejaculation, "Oh, là-là!"

Pemberton, in some confusion, glanced at him as he walked slowly to the window with his back turned, his hands in his pockets and the air in his elderly shoulders of a boy who didn't play. The young man wondered if he could teach him to play, though his mother had said it would never do and that this was why school was impossible. Mrs. Moreen exhibited no discomfiture; she only continued blandly: "Mr. Moreen will be delighted to meet your wishes. As I told you, he has been called to London for a week. As soon as he comes back you shall have it out with him."

This was so frank and friendly that the young man could only reply, laughing as his hostess laughed: "Oh! I don't imagine we shall have much of a battle."

"They'll give you anything you like," the boy remarked unexpectedly, returning from the window. "We don't mind what anything costs—we live awfully well."

"My darling, you're too quaint!" his mother exclaimed, putting out to caress him a practiced but ineffectual hand. He slipped out of it, but looked with intelligent, innocent eyes at Pemberton, who had already had time to notice that from one moment to the other his small satiric face seemed to change its time of life. At this moment it was infantine; yet it appeared also to be under the influence of curious intuitions and knowledges. Pemberton rather disliked precocity, and he was disappointed to find gleams of it in a disciple not yet in his teens. Nevertheless he divined on the spot that Morgan wouldn't prove a bore. He would prove on the contrary a kind of excitement. This idea held the young man, in spite of a certain repulsion.

"You pompous little person! We're not extravagant!" Mrs. Moreen gayly protested, making another unsuccessful attempt to draw the boy to her side. "You must know what to expect," she went on to Pemberton.

"The less you expect the better!" her companion interposed. "But we *are* people of fashion."

"Only so far as *you* make us so!" Mrs. Moreen mocked, tenderly. "Well, then, on Friday—don't tell me you're superstitious—and mind you don't fail us. Then you'll see us all. I'm so sorry the girls are out. I guess you'll like the girls. And, you know, I've another son, quite different from this one."

"He tries to imitate me," said Morgan to Pemberton.

"He tries? Why, he's twenty years old!" cried Mrs. Moreen.

"You're very witty," Pemberton remarked to the child—a proposition that his mother echoed with enthusiasm, declaring that Morgan's sallies were the delight of the house. The boy paid no heed to this; he only inquired abruptly of the visitor, who was surprised afterwards that he hadn't struck him as offensively forward: "Do you *want* very much to come?"

"Can you doubt it, after such a description of what I shall hear?" Pemberton replied. Yet he didn't want to come at all; he was coming because he had to go somewhere, thanks to the collapse of his fortune at the end of a year abroad, spent on the system of putting his tiny patrimony into a single full wave of experience. He had had his full wave, but he couldn't pay his hotel bill. Moreover, he had caught in the boy's eyes the glimpse of a far-off appeal.

"Well, I'll do the best I can for you," said Morgan; with which he turned away again. He passed out of one of the long windows; Pemberton saw him go and lean on the parapet of the terrace. He remained there while the young man took leave of his mother, who, on Pemberton's looking as if he expected a farewell from him, interposed with: "Leave him, leave him; he's so strange!" Pemberton suspected she was afraid of something he might say. "He's a genius—you'll love him," she added. "He's much the most interesting person in the family." And before he could invent some civility to oppose to this, she wound up with: "But we're all good, you know!"

"He's a genius—you'll love him!" were words that recurred to Pemberton before the Friday, suggesting, among other things that geniuses were not invariably lovable. However, it was all the better if there was an element that would make tutorship absorbing: he had perhaps taken too much for granted that it would be dreary. As he left the villa after his interview, he looked up at the balcony and saw the child leaning over it. "We shall have great larks!" he called up.

Morgan hesitated a moment; then he answered, laughing: "By the time you come back I shall have thought of something witty!"

This made Pemberton say to himself: "After all he's rather nice."

II

ON THE Friday he saw them all, as Mrs. Moreen had promised, for her husband had come back and the girls and the other son were at home. Mr. Moreen had a white moustache, a confiding manner and, in his buttonhole, the ribbon of a foreign order—bestowed, as Pemberton eventually learned, for services. For what services he never clearly ascertained: this was a point—one of a large number—that Mr. Moreen's manner never confided. What it emphatically did confide was that he was a man of the world. Ulick, the firstborn, was in visible training for the same profession—under the disadvantage as yet, however, of a buttonhole only feebly floral and a moustache with no pretensions to type. The girls had hair and figures and manners and small fat feet, but had never been out alone. As for Mrs. Moreen, Pemberton saw on a nearer view that her elegance was intermittent and her parts didn't always match. Her husband, as she had promised, met with enthusiasm Pemberton's ideas in regard to a salary. The young man had endeavoured to make them modest, and Mr. Moreen confided to him that *he* found them positively meagre. He further assured him that he aspired to be intimate with his children, to be their best friend, and that he was always looking out for them. That was what he went off for, to London and other places—to look out; and this vigilance was the theory of life, as well as the real occupation, of the whole family. They all looked out, for they were very frank on the subject of its being necessary. They desired it to be understood that they were earnest people, and also that their fortune, though quite adequate for earnest people, required the most careful administration. Mr. Moreen, as the parent bird, sought sustenance for the nest. Ulick found sustenance mainly at the club, where Pemberton guessed that it was usually served on green cloth. The girls used to do up their hair and their frocks themselves, and our young man felt appealed to to be glad, in regard to Morgan's education, that, though it must naturally be of the best, it didn't cost too much. After a little he *was* glad, forgetting at times his own needs in the interest inspired by the child's nature and education and the pleasure of making easy terms for him.

During the first weeks of their acquaintance Morgan had been as puzzling as a page in an unknown language—altogether different from the obvious little Anglo-Saxons who had misrepresented childhood to Pemberton. Indeed the whole mystic volume in which the boy had been bound demanded some practice in translation. To-day, after a considerable interval, there is something phantasmagoric, like a prismatic reflection or a serial novel, in Pemberton's memory of the queerness of the Moreens. If it were not for a few tangible tokens—a lock of Morgan's hair, cut by his own hand, and the half-dozen letters he got from him when they were separated—the whole episode and the figures peopling it would seem too inconsequent for anything but dreamland. The queerest thing about them was their success (as it appeared to him for a while at the time), for he had never seen a family so brilliantly equipped for failure. Wasn't it success to have kept him so hatefully long? Wasn't it success to have drawn him in that first morning at *déjeuner,* the Friday he came—it was enough to *make* one superstitious—so that he utterly committed himself, and this not by calculation or a *mot d'ordre,* but by a happy instinct which made them, like a band of gipsies, work so neatly together? They amused him as much as if they had really been a band of gipsies. He was still young and had not seen much of the world—his English years had been intensely usual; therefore the reversed conventions of the Moreens (for they had their standards), struck him as topsyturvy. He had encountered nothing like them at Oxford; still less had any such note been struck to his younger American ear during the four years at Yale in which he had richly supposed himself to be reacting against Puritanism. The reaction of the Moreens, at any rate, went ever so much further. He had thought himself very clever that first day in hitting them all off in his mind with the term "cosmopolite." Later, it seemed feeble and colourless enough—confessedly, helplessly provisional.

However, when he first applied it to them he had a degree of joy—for an instructor he was still empirical—as if from the apprehension that to live with them would really be to see life. Their sociable strangeness was an intimation of that—their chatter of tongues, their gaiety and good humour, their infinite dawdling (they were always getting themselves up, but it took forever, and Pemberton had once found Mr. Moreen shaving in the drawing-room), their French, their Italian and, in the spiced fluency, their cold, tough slices of American. They lived on macaroni and coffee (they had these articles prepared in perfection), but they knew recipes for a hundred other dishes. They overflowed with music and song, were always humming and catching each other up, and had a kind of professional acquaintance with continental cities. They talked of "good places" as if they had been strolling players. They had at Nice a villa, a carriage, a piano and a banjo, and they went to official parties. They were a perfect calendar of the "days" of their friends, which Pemberton knew them, when they were indisposed, to get out of bed to go to, and which made the week larger than life when Mrs. Moreen talked of them with Paula and Amy. Their romantic initiations gave their new inmate at first an almost dazzling sense of culture. Mrs. Moreen had translated something, at some former period—an author whom it made Pemberton feel *borné* never to have heard of. They could imitate Venetian and sing Neapolitan, and when they wanted to say something very particular they communicated with each other in an ingenious dialect of their own—a sort of spoken cipher, which Pemberton at first took for Volapuk, but which he learned to understand as he would not have understood Volapuk.

"It's the family language—Ultramoreen," Morgan explained to him drolly enough; but the boy rarely condescended to use it himself, though he attempted colloquial Latin as if he had been a little prelate.

Among all the "days" with which Mrs. Moreen's memory was taxed she managed to squeeze in one of her own, which her friends sometimes forgot. But the house derived a frequented air from the number of fine people who were freely named there and from several mysterious men with foreign titles and English clothes whom Morgan called the princes and who, on sofas with the girls, talked French very loud, as if to show they were saying nothing improper. Pemberton wondered how the princes could ever propose in that tone and so publicly: he took for granted cynically that this was what was desired of them. Then he acknowledged that even for the chance of such an advantage Mrs. Moreen would never allow Paula and Amy to receive alone. These young ladies were not at all timid, but it was just the safeguards that made them so graceful. It was a houseful of Bohemians who wanted tremendously to be Philistines.

In one respect, however, certainly, they achieved no rigour—they were wonderfully amiable and ecstatic about Morgan. It was a genuine tenderness, an artless admiration, equally strong in each. They even praised his beauty, which was small, and were rather afraid of him, as if they recognised that he was of a finer clay. They called him a little angel and a little prodigy and pitied his want of health effusively. Pemberton feared at first that their extravagance would make him hate the boy, but before this happened he had become extravagant himself. Later, when he had grown rather to hate the others, it was a bribe to patience for him that they were at any rate nice about Morgan, going on tiptoe if they fancied he was showing symptoms, and even giving up somebody's "day" to procure him a pleasure. But mixed with this was the oddest wish to make him independent, as if they felt that they were not good enough for him. They passed him over to Pemberton very much as if they wished to force a constructive adoption on the obliging bachelor and shirk altogether a responsibility. They were delighted when they perceived that Morgan liked his preceptor, and could think of no higher praise for the young man. It was strange how they contrived to reconcile the appearance, and indeed the essential fact, of adoring the child with their eagerness to wash their hands of him. Did they want to get rid of him before he should find them out? Pemberton was finding them out month by month. At any rate, the boy's relations turned their backs with exaggerated delicacy, as if to escape the charge of interfering. Seeing in time how little he had in common with them (it was by *them* he first observed it—they proclaimed it with complete humility), his preceptor was moved to speculate on the mysteries of transmission, the far jumps of heredity. Where his detachment from most of the things they represented had come from was more than an observer could say—it certainly had burrowed under two or three generations.

As for Pemberton's own estimate of his pupil, it was a good while before he got the point of view, so little had he been prepared for it by the smug young barbarians to whom the tradition of tutorship, as hitherto revealed to him, had been adjusted. Morgan was scrappy and surprising, deficient in many properties supposed common to the *genus* and abounding in others that were the portion only of the supernaturally clever. One day Pemberton made a great stride: it cleared up the question to perceive that Morgan *was* supernaturally clever and that, though the formula was temporarily meagre, this would be the only assumption on which one could successfully deal with him. He had the general quality of a child for whom life had not been simplified by school, a kind of homebred sensibility which might have been bad for himself but was charming for others, and a whole range of refinement and perception—little musical vibrations as taking as picked-up airs—begotten by wandering about Europe at the tail of his migratory tribe. This might not have been an education to recommend in advance, but its results with Morgan were as palpable as a fine texture. At the same time he had in his composition a sharp spice of stoicism, doubtless the fruit of having had to begin early to bear pain, which produced the impression of pluck and made it of less consequence that he might have been thought at school rather a polyglot little beast. Pemberton indeed quickly found himself rejoicing that school was out of the question: in any million of boys it was probably good for all but one, and Morgan was that millionth. It would have made him comparative and superior—it might have made him priggish. Pemberton would try to be school himself—a bigger seminary than five hundred grazing donkeys; so that, winning no prizes, the boy would remain unconscious and irresponsible and amusing—amusing, because, though life was already intense in his childish nature, freshness still made there a strong draught for jokes. It turned out that even in the still air of Morgan's various disabilities jokes flourished greatly. He was a pale, lean, acute, undeveloped little cosmopolite, who liked intellectual gymnastics and who, also, as regards the behaviour of mankind, had noticed more things than you might suppose, but who nevertheless had his proper playroom of superstitions, where he smashed a dozen toys a day.

III

AT NICE once, towards evening, as the pair sat resting in the open air after a walk, looking over the sea at the pink western lights, Morgan said suddenly to his companion: "Do you like it—you know, being with us all in this intimate way?"

"My dear fellow, why should I stay if I didn't?"

"How do I know you will stay? I'm almost sure you won't, very long."

"I hope you don't mean to dismiss me," said Pemberton.

Morgan considered a moment, looking at the sunset. "I think if I did right I ought to."

"Well, I know I'm supposed to instruct you in virtue; but in that case don't do right."

"You're very young—fortunately," Morgan went on, turning to him again.

"Oh yes, compared with you!"

"Therefore, it won't matter so much if you do lose a lot of time."

"That's the way to look at it," said Pemberton accommodatingly.

They were silent a minute; after which the boy asked: "Do you like my father and mother very much?"

"Dear me, yes. They're charming people."

Morgan received this with another silence; then, unexpectedly, familiarly, but at the same time affectionately, he remarked: "You're a jolly old humbug!"

For a particular reason the words made Pemberton change colour. The boy noticed in an instant that he had turned red, whereupon he turned red himself and the pupil and the master exchanged a longish glance in which there was a consciousness of many more things than are usually touched upon, even tacitly, in such a relation. It produced for Pemberton an embarrassment; it raised, in a shadowy form, a question (this was the first glimpse of it), which was destined to play as singular and, as he imagined, owing to the altogether peculiar conditions, an unprecedented part in his intercourse with his little companion. Later, when he found himself talking with this small boy in a way in which few small boys could ever have been talked with, he thought of that clumsy moment on the bench at Nice as the dawn of an understanding that had broadened. What had added to the clumsiness then was that he thought it his duty to declare to Morgan that he might abuse him (Pemberton) as much as he liked, but must never abuse his parents. To this Morgan had the easy reply that he hadn't dreamed of abusing them; which appeared to be true: it put Pemberton in the wrong.

"Then why am I a humbug for saying *I* think them charming?" the young man asked, conscious of a certain rashness.

"Well—they're not *your* parents."

"They love you better than anything in the world—never forget that," said Pemberton.

"Is that why you like them so much?"

"They're very kind to me," Pemberton replied, evasively.

"You *are* a humbug!" laughed Morgan, passing an arm into his tutor's. He leaned against him, looking off at the sea again and swinging his long, thin legs.

"Don't kick my shins," said Pemberton, while he reflected: "Hang it, I can't complain of them to the child!"

"There's another reason, too," Morgan went on, keeping his legs still.

"Another reason for what?"

"Besides their not being your parents."

"I don't understand you," said Pemberton.

"Well, you will before long. All right!"

Pemberton did understand, fully, before long; but he made a fight even with himself before he confessed it. He thought it the oddest thing to have a struggle with the child about. He wondered he didn't detest the child for launching him in such a struggle. But by the time it began the resource of detesting the child was closed to him. Morgan was a special case, but to know him was to accept him on his own odd terms. Pemberton had spent his aversion to special cases before arriving at knowledge. When at last he did arrive he felt that he was in an extreme predicament. Against every interest he had attached himself. They would have to meet things together. Before they went home that evening, at Nice, the boy had said, clinging to his arm:

"Well, at any rate you'll hang on to the last."

"To the last?"

"Till you're fairly beaten."

"*You* ought to be fairly beaten!" cried the young man, drawing him closer.

IV

A YEAR after Pemberton had come to live with them Mr. and Mrs. Moreen suddenly gave up the villa at Nice. Pemberton had got used to suddenness, having seen it practiced on a considerable scale during two jerky little tours—one in Switzerland the first summer, and the other late in the winter, when they all ran down to Florence and then, at the end of ten days, liking it much less than they had intended, straggled back in mysterious depression. They had returned to Nice "for ever," as they said; but this didn't prevent them from squeezing, one rainy, muggy May night, into a second-class railway-carriage—you could never tell by which class they would travel—where Pemberton helped them to stow away a wonderful collection of bundles and bags. The explanation of this manœuvre was that they had determined to spend the summer "in some bracing place"; but in Paris they dropped into a small furnished apartment—a fourth floor in a third-rate avenue, where there was a smell on the staircase and the *portier* was hateful—and passed the next four months in blank indigence.

The better part of this baffled sojourn was for the preceptor and his pupil, who, visiting the Invalides and Notre Dame, the Conciergerie and all the museums, took a hundred remunerative rambles. They learned to know their Paris, which was useful, for they came back another year for a longer stay, the general character of which in Pemberton's memory to-day mixes pitiably and confusedly with that of the first. He sees Morgan's shabby knickerbockers—the everlasting pair that didn't match his blouse and that as he grew longer could only grow faded. He remembers the particular holes in his three or four pair of coloured stockings.

Morgan was dear to his mother, but he never was better dressed than was absolutely necessary—partly, no doubt, by his own fault, for he was as indifferent to his appearance as a German philosopher. "My dear fellow, you *are* coming to pieces," Pemberton would say to him in sceptical remonstrance; to which the child would reply, looking at him serenely up and down: "My dear fellow, so are you! I don't want to cast you in the shade." Pemberton could have no rejoinder for this—the assertion so closely represented the fact. If however the deficiencies of his own wardrobe were a chapter by themselves he didn't like his little charge to look too poor. Later he used to say: "Well, if we are poor, why, after all, shouldn't we look it?" and he consoled himself with thinking there was something rather elderly and gentlemanly in Morgan's seediness—it differed from the untidiness of the urchin who plays and spoils his things. He could trace perfectly the degrees by which, in proportion as her little son confined himself to his tutor for society, Mrs. Moreen shrewdly forbore to renew his garments. She did nothing that didn't show, neglected him because he escaped notice, and then, as he illustrated this clever policy, discouraged at home his public appearances. Her position was logical enough—those members of her family who did show had to be showy.

During this period and several others Pemberton was quite aware of how he and his comrade might strike people; wandering languidly through the Jardin des Plantes as if they had nowhere to go, sitting, on the winter days, in the galleries of the Louvre, so splendidly ironical to the homeless, as if for the advantage of the *calorifère*. They joked about it sometimes: it was the sort of joke that was perfectly within the boy's compass. They figured themselves as part of the vast, vague, hand-to-mouth multitude of the enormous city and pretended they were proud of their position in it—it showed them such a lot of life and made them conscious of a sort of democratic brotherhood. If Pemberton could not feel a sympathy in destitution with his small companion (for after all Morgan's fond parents would never have let him really suffer), the boy would at least feel it with him, so it came to the same thing. He used sometimes to wonder what people would think they were—fancy they were looked askance at, as if it might be a suspected case of kidnapping. Morgan wouldn't be taken for a young patrician with a preceptor—he wasn't smart enough; though he might pass for his companion's sickly little brother. Now and then he had a five-franc piece, and except once, when they bought a couple of lovely neckties, one of which he made Pemberton accept, they laid it out scientifically in old books. It was a great day, always spent on the quays, rummaging among the dusty boxes that garnish the parapets. These were occasions that helped them to live, for their books ran low very soon after the beginning of their acquaintance. Pemberton had a good many in England, but he was obliged to write to a friend and ask him kindly to get some fellow to give him something for them.

If the bracing climate was untasted that summer the young man had an idea that at the moment they were about to make a push the cup had been dashed from their lips by a movement of his own. It had been his first blow-out, as he called it, with his patrons; his first successful attempt (though there was little other success about it), to bring them to a consideration of his impossible position. As the ostensible eve of a costly journey the moment struck him as a good one to put in a signal protest—to present an ultimatum. Ridiculous as it sounded he had never yet been able to compass an uninterrupted private interview with the elder pair or with either of them singly. They were always flanked by their elder children, and poor Pemberton usually had his own little charge at his side. He was conscious of its being a house in which the surface of one's delicacy got rather smudged; nevertheless he had kept the bloom of his scruple against announcing to Mr. and Mrs. Moreen with publicity that he couldn't go on longer without a little money. He was still simple enough to suppose Ulick and Paula and Amy might not know that since his arrival he had only had a hundred and forty francs; and he was magnanimous enough to wish not to compromise their parents in their eyes. Mr. Moreen now listened to him, as he listened to every one and to everything, like a man of the world, and seemed to appeal to him—though not of course too grossly—to try and be a little more of one himself. Pemberton recognised the importance of the character from the advantage it gave Mr. Moreen. He was not even confused, whereas poor Pemberton was more so than there was any reason for. Neither was he surprised—at least any more than a gentleman had to be who freely confessed himself a little shocked, though not, strictly, at Pemberton.

"We must go into this, mustn't we, dear?" he said to his wife. He assured his young friend that the matter should have his very best attention; and he melted into space as elusively as if, at the door, he were taking an inevitable but deprecatory precedence. When, the next moment, Pemberton found himself alone with Mrs. Moreen it was to hear her say: "I see, I see," stroking the roundness of her chin and looking as if she were only hesitating between a dozen easy remedies. If they didn't make their push Mr. Moreen could at least disappear for several days. During his absence his wife took up the subject again spontaneously, but her contribution to it was merely that she had thought all the while they were getting on so beautifully. Pemberton's reply to this revelation was that unless they immediately handed him a substantial sum he would leave them for ever. He knew she would wonder how he would get away, and for a moment expected her to inquire. She didn't, for which he was almost grateful to her, so little was he in a position to tell.

"You won't, you know you won't—you're too interested," she said. "You *are* interested, you know you are, you dear, kind man!" She laughed, with almost condemnatory archness, as if it were a reproach (but she wouldn't insist), while she flirted a soiled pocket-handkerchief at him.

Pemberton's mind was fully made up to quit the house the following week. This would give him time to get an answer to a letter he had despatched to England. If he did nothing of the sort—that is, if he stayed another year and then went away only for three months—it was not merely because before the answer to his letter came (most unsatisfactory when it did arrive), Mr. Moreen generously presented him—again with all the precautions of a man of the world—three hundred francs. He was exasperated to find that Mrs. Moreen was right, that he couldn't bear to leave the child. This stood out clearer for the very reason that, the night of his desperate appeal to his patrons, he had seen fully for the first time where he was. Wasn't it another proof of the success with which those patrons practiced their arts that they had managed to avert for so long the illuminating flash? It descended upon Pemberton with a luridness which perhaps would have struck a spectator as comically excessive, after he had returned to his little servile room, which looked into a closed court where a bare, dirty opposite wall took, with the sound of shrill clatter, the reflection of lighted back-windows. He had simply given himself away to a band of adventurers. The idea, the word itself, had a sort of romantic horror for him—he had always lived on such safe lines. Later it assumed a more interesting, almost a soothing, sense: it pointed a moral, and Pemberton could enjoy a moral. The Moreens were adventurers not merely because they didn't pay their debts, because they lived on society, but because their whole view of life, dim and confused and instinctive, like that of clever colour-blind animals, was speculative and rapacious and mean. Oh! they were "respectable," and that only made them more *immondes*. The young man's analysis of them put it at last very simply—they were adventurers because they were abject snobs. That was the completest account of them—it was the law of their being. Even when this truth became vivid to their ingenious inmate he remained unconscious of how much his mind had been prepared for it by the extraordinary little boy who had now become such a complication in his life. Much less could he then calculate on the information he was still to owe to the extraordinary little boy.

V

BUT it was during the ensuing time that the real problem came up—the problem of how far it was excusable to discuss the turpitude of parents with a child of twelve, of thirteen, of fourteen. Absolutely inexcusable and quite impossible it of course at first appeared; and indeed the question didn't press for a while after Pemberton had received his three hundred francs. They produced a sort of lull, a relief from the sharpest pressure. Pemberton frugally amended his wardrobe and even had a few francs in his pocket. He thought the Moreens looked at him as if he were almost too smart, as if they ought to take care not to spoil him. If Mr. Moreen hadn't been such a man of the world he would perhaps have said something to him about his neckties. But Mr. Moreen was always enough a man of the world to let things pass—he had certainly shown that. It was singular how Pemberton guessed that Morgan, though saying nothing about it, knew something had happened. But three hundred francs, especially when one owed money, couldn't last for ever; and when they were gone—the boy knew when they were gone—Morgan did say something. The party had returned to Nice at the beginning of the winter, but not to the charming villa. They went to an hotel, where they stayed three months, and then they went to another hotel, explaining that they had left the first because they had waited and waited and couldn't get the rooms they wanted. These apartments, the rooms they wanted, were generally very splendid; but fortunately they never *could* get them—fortunately, I mean, for Pemberton, who reflected always that if they had got them there would have been still less for educational expenses. What Morgan said at last was said suddenly, irrelevantly, when the moment came, in the middle of a lesson, and consisted of the apparently unfeeling words: "You ought to *filer,* you know—you really ought."

Pemberton stared. He had learnt enough French slang from Morgan to know that to *filer* meant to go away. "Ah, my dear fellow, don't turn me off!"

Morgan pulled a Greek lexicon toward him (he used a Greek-German), to look out a word, instead of asking it of Pemberton. "You can't go on like this, you know."

"Like what, my boy?"

"You know they don't pay you up," said Morgan, blushing and turning his leaves.

"Don't pay me?" Pemberton stared again and feigned amazement. "What on earth put that into your head?"

"It has been there a long time," the boy replied, continuing his search.

Pemberton was silent, then he went on: "I say, what are you hunting for? They pay me beautifully."

"I'm hunting for the Greek for transparent fiction," Morgan dropped.

"Find that rather for gross impertinence, and disabuse your mind. What do I want of money?"

"Oh, that's another question!"

Pemberton hesitated—he was drawn in different ways. The severely correct thing would have been to tell the boy that such a matter was none of his business and bid him go on with his lines. But they were really too intimate for that; it was not the way he was in the habit of treating him; there had been no reason it should be. On the other hand Morgan had quite lighted on the truth—he really shouldn't be able to keep it up much longer; therefore why not let him know one's real motive for forsaking him? At the same time it wasn't decent to abuse to one's pupil the family of one's pupil; it was better to misrepresent than to do that. So in reply to Morgan's last exclamation he just declared, to dismiss the subject, that he had received several payments.

"I say—I say!" the boy ejaculated, laughing.

"That's all right," Pemberton insisted. "Give me your written rendering."

Morgan pushed a copybook across the table, and his companion began to read the page, but with something running in his head that made it no sense. Looking up after a minute or two he found the child's eyes fixed on him, and he saw something strange in them. Then Morgan said: "I'm not afraid of the reality."

"I haven't yet seen the thing that you *are* afraid of—I'll do you that justice!"

This came out with a jump (it was perfectly true), and evidently gave Morgan pleasure. "I've thought of it a long time," he presently resumed.

"Well, don't think of it any more."

The child appeared to comply, and they had a comfortable and even an amusing hour. They had a theory that they were very thorough, and yet they seemed always to be in the amusing part of lessons, the intervals between the tunnels, where there were waysides and views. Yet the morning was brought to a violent end by Morgan's suddenly leaning his arms on the table, burying his head in them and bursting into tears. Pemberton would have been startled at any rate; but he was doubly startled because, as it then occurred to him, it was the first time he had ever seen the boy cry. It was rather awful.

The next day, after much thought, he took a decision and, believing it to be just, immediately acted upon it. He cornered Mr. and Mrs. Moreen again and informed them that if, on the spot, they didn't pay him all they owed him, he would not only leave their house, but would tell Morgan exactly what had brought him to it.

"Oh, you *haven't* told him?" cried Mrs. Moreen, with a pacifying hand on her well-dressed bosom.

"Without warning you? For what do you take me?"

Mr. and Mrs. Moreen looked at each other, and Pemberton could see both that they were relieved and that there was a certain alarm in their relief. "My dear fellow," Mr. Moreen demanded, "what use *can* you have, leading the quiet life we all do, for such a lot of money?"—an inquiry to which Pemberton made no answer, occupied as he was in perceiving that what passed in the mind of his patrons was something like: "Oh, then, if we've felt that the child, dear little angel, has judged us and how he regards us, and we haven't been betrayed, he must have guessed—and, in short, it's *general*!" an idea that rather stirred up Mr. and Mrs. Moreen, as Pemberton had desired that it should. At the same time, if he had thought that his threat would do something towards bringing them round, he was disappointed to find they had taken for granted (how little they appreciated his delicacy!) that he had already given them away to his pupil. There was a mystic uneasiness in their parental breasts, and that was the way they had accounted for it. None the less his threat did touch them; for if they had escaped it was only to meet a new danger. Mr. Moreen appealed to Pemberton, as usual, as a man of the world; but his wife had recourse, for the first time since the arrival of their inmate, to a fine *hauteur*, reminding him that a devoted mother, with her child, had arts that protected her against gross misrepresentation.

"I should misrepresent you grossly if I accused you of common honesty!" the young man replied; but as he closed the door behind him sharply, thinking he had not done himself much good, while Mr. Moreen lighted another cigarette, he heard Mrs. Moreen shout after him, more touchingly:

"Oh, you do, you *do*, put the knife to one's throat!"

The next morning, very early, she came to his room. He recognized her knock, but he had no hope that she brought him money; as to which he was wrong, for she had fifty francs in her hand. She squeezed forward in her dressing-gown, and he received her in his own, between his bath-tub and his bed. He had been tolerably schooled by this time to the "foreign ways" of his hosts. Mrs. Moreen was zealous, and when she was zealous she didn't care what she did; so she now sat down on his bed, his clothes being on the chairs, and, in her preoccupation, forgot, as she glanced round, to be ashamed of giving him such a nasty room. What Mrs. Moreen was zealous about on this occasion was to persuade him that in the first place she was very good-natured to bring him fifty francs, and, in the second, if he would only see it, he was really too absurd to expect to be *paid*. Wasn't he paid enough, without perpetual money—

wasn't he paid by the comfortable, luxurious home that he enjoyed with them all, without a care, an anxiety, a solitary want? Wasn't he sure of his position, and wasn't that everything to a young man like him, quite unknown, with singularly little to show, the ground of whose exorbitant pretensions it was not easy to discover? Wasn't he paid, above all, by the delightful relation he had established with Morgan—quite ideal, as from master to pupil—and by the simple privilege of knowing and living with so amazingly gifted a child, than whom really—she meant literally what she said—there was no better company in Europe? Mrs. Moreen herself took to appealing to him as a man of the world; she said "Voyons, mon cher," and "My dear sir, look here now"; and urged him to be reasonable, putting it before him that it was really a chance for him. She spoke as if, according as he *should* be reasonable, he would prove himself worthy to be her son's tutor and of the extraordinary confidence they had placed in him.

After all, Pemberton reflected, it was only a difference of theory, and the theory didn't matter much. They had hitherto gone on that of remunerated, as now they would go on that of gratuitous, service; but why should they have so many words about it? Mrs. Moreen, however, continued to be convincing; sitting there with her fifty francs she talked and repeated, as women repeat, and bored and irritated him, while he leaned against the wall with his hands in the pockets of his wrapper, drawing it together round his legs and looking over the head of his visitor at the grey negations of his window. She wound up with saying: "You see I bring you a definite proposal."

"A definite proposal?"

"To make our relations regular, as it were—to put them on a comfortable footing."

"I see—it's a system," said Pemberton. "A kind of blackmail."

Mrs. Moreen bounded up, which was what the young man wanted.

"What do you mean by that?"

"You practice on one's fears—one's fears about the child if one should go away."

"And pray, what would happen to him in that event?" demanded Mrs. Moreen, with majesty.

"Why, he'd be alone with *you*."

"And pray, with whom *should* a child be but with those whom he loves most?"

"If you think that, why don't you dismiss me?"

"Do you pretend that he loves you more than he loves *us*?" cried Mrs. Moreen.

"I think he ought to. I make sacrifices for him. Though I've heard of those *you* make, I don't see them."

Mrs. Moreen stared a moment; then, with emotion, she grasped Pemberton's hand. "*Will* you make it—the sacrifice?"

Pemberton burst out laughing. "I'll see—I'll do what I can—I'll stay a little longer. Your calculation is just—I *do* hate intensely to give him up; I'm fond of him and he interests me deeply, in spite of the inconvenience I suffer. You know my situation perfectly; I haven't a penny in the world, and, occupied as I am with Morgan, I'm unable to earn money."

Mrs. Moreen tapped her undressed arm with her folded bank-note. "Can't you write articles? Can't you translate, as *I* do?"

"I don't know about translating; it's wretchedly paid."

"I am glad to earn what I can," said Mrs. Moreen virtuously, with her head high.

"You ought to tell me who you do it for." Pemberton paused a moment, and she said nothing; so he added: "I've tried to turn off some little sketches, but the magazines won't have them—they're declined with thanks."

"You see then you're not such a phœnix—to have such pretensions," smiled his interlocutress.

"I haven't time to do things properly," Pemberton went on. Then as it came over him that he was almost abjectly good-natured to give these explanations he added: "If I stay on longer it must be on one condition—that Morgan shall know distinctly on what footing I am."

Mrs. Moreen hesitated. "Surely you don't want to show off to a child?"

"To show *you* off, do you mean?"

Again Mrs. Moreen hesitated, but this time it was to produce a still finer flower. "And *you* talk of blackmail!"

"You can easily prevent it," said Pemberton.

"And *you* talk of practicing on fears," Mrs. Moreen continued.

"Yes, there's no doubt I'm a great scoundrel."

His visitor looked at him a moment—it was evident that she was sorely bothered. Then she thrust out her money at him. "Mr. Moreen desired me to give you this on account."

"I'm much obliged to Mr. Moreen; but we have no account."

"You won't take it?"

"That leaves me more free," said Pemberton.

"To poison my darling's mind?" groaned Mrs. Moreen.

"Oh, your darling's mind!" laughed the young man.

She fixed him a moment, and he thought she was going to break out tormentedly, pleadingly. "For God's sake, tell me what *is* in it!" But she checked this impulse—another was stronger. She pocketed the money—the crudity of the alternative was comical—and swept out of the room with the desperate concession: "You may tell him any horror you like!"

VI

A couple of days after this, during which Pemberton had delayed to profit by Mrs. Moreen's permission to tell her son any horror, the two had been for a quarter of an hour walking together in silence when the boy became sociable again with the remark: "I'll tell you how I know it; I know it through Zénobie."

"Zénobie? Who in the world is *she*?"

"A nurse I used to have—ever so many years ago. A charming woman. I liked her awfully, and she liked me."

"There's no accounting for tastes. What is it you know through her?"

"Why, what their idea is. She went away because they didn't pay her. She did like me awfully, and she stayed two years. She told me all about it—that at last she could never get her wages. As soon as they saw how much she liked me they stopped giving her anything. They thought she'd stay for nothing, out of devotion. And she did stay ever so long—as long as she could. She was only a poor girl. She used to send money to her mother. At last she couldn't afford it any longer, and she went away in a fearful rage one night—I mean of course in a rage against *them*. She cried over me tremendously, she hugged me nearly to death. She told me all about it," Morgan repeated. "She told me it was their idea. So I guessed, ever so long ago, that they have had the same idea with you."

"Zénobie was very shrewd," said Pemberton. "And she made you so."

"Oh, that wasn't Zénobie; that was nature. And experience!" Morgan laughed.

"Well, Zénobie was a part of your experience."

"Certainly I was a part of hers, poor dear!" the boy exclaimed. "And I'm a part of yours."

"A very important part. But I don't see how you know that I've been treated like Zénobie."

"Do you take me for an idiot?" Morgan asked. "Haven't I been conscious of what we've been through together?"

"What we've been through?"

"Our privations—our dark days."

"Oh, our days have been bright enough."

Morgan went on in silence for a moment. Then he said: "My dear fellow, you're a hero!"

"Well, you're another!" Pemberton retorted.

"No, I'm not; but I'm not a baby. I won't stand it any longer. You must get some occupation that pays. I'm ashamed, I'm ashamed!" quavered the boy in a little passionate voice that was very touching to Pemberton.

"We ought to go off and live somewhere together," said the young man.

"I'll go like a shot if you'll take me."

"I'd get some work that would keep us both afloat," Pemberton continued.

"So would I. Why shouldn't *I* work? I ain't such a *crétin*!"

"The difficulty is that your parents wouldn't hear of it," said Pemberton. "They would never part with you; they worship the ground you tread on. Don't you see the proof of it? They don't dislike me; they wish me no harm; they're very amiable people; but they're perfectly ready to treat me badly for your sake."

The silence in which Morgan received this graceful sophistry struck Pemberton somehow as expressive. After a moment Morgan repeated: "You *are* a hero!" Then he added: "They leave me with you altogether. You've all the responsibility. They put me off on you from morning till night. Why, then, should they object to my taking up with you completely? I'd help you."

"They're not particularly keen about my being helped, and they delight in thinking of you as *theirs*. They're tremendously proud of you."

"I'm not proud of them. But you know *that*," Morgan returned.

"Except for the little matter we speak of they're charming people," said Pemberton, not taking up the imputation of lucidity, but wondering greatly at the child's own, and especially at this fresh reminder of something he had been conscious of from the first—the strangest thing in the boy's large little composition, a temper, a sensibility, even a sort of ideal, which made him privately resent the general quality of his kinsfolk. Morgan had in secret a small loftiness which begot an element of reflection, a domestic scorn not imperceptible to his companion (though they never had any talk about it), and absolutely anomalous in a juvenile nature, especially when one noted that it had not made this nature "old-fashioned," as the word is of children—quaint or wizened or offensive. It was as if he had been a little gentleman and had paid the penalty by discovering that he was the only such person in the family. This comparison didn't make him vain; but it could make him melancholy and a trifle austere. When Pemberton guessed at these young dimnesses he saw him serious and gallant, and was partly drawn on and partly checked, as if with a scruple, by the charm of attempting to sound the little cool shallows which were quickly growing deeper. When he tried to figure to himself the morning twilight of childhood, so as to deal with it safely, he perceived that it was never fixed, never arrested, that ignorance, at the instant one touched it, was already flushing faintly into knowledge, that there was nothing that at a given moment you could say a clever child didn't know. It seemed to him that *he* both knew too much to imagine Morgan's simplicity and too little to disembroil his tangle.

The boy paid no heed to his last remark; he only went on: "I should have spoken to them about their idea, as I call it, long ago, if I hadn't been sure what they would say."

"And what would they say?"

"Just what they said about what poor Zénobie told me—that it was a horrid, dreadful story, that they had paid her every penny they owed her."

"Well, perhaps they had," said Pemberton.

"Perhaps they've paid you!"

"Let us pretend they have, and *n'en parlons plus.*"

"They accused her of lying and cheating," Morgan insisted perversely. "That's why I don't want to speak to them."

"Lest they should accuse me, too?"

To this Morgan made no answer, and his companion, looking down at him (the boy turned his eyes, which had filled, away), saw that he couldn't have trusted himself to utter.

"You're right. Don't squeeze them," Pemberton pursued. "Except for that, they *are* charming people."

"Except for *their* lying and *their* cheating?"

"I say—I say!" cried Pemberton, imitating a little tone of the lad's which was itself an imitation.

"We must be frank, at the last; we *must* come to an understanding," said Morgan, with the importance of the small boy who lets himself think he is arranging great affairs—almost playing at shipwreck or at Indians. "I know all about everything," he added.

"I daresay your father has his reasons," Pemberton observed, too vaguely, as he was aware.

"For lying and cheating?"

"For saving and managing and turning his means to the best account. He has plenty to do with his money. You're an expensive family."

"Yes, I'm very expensive," Morgan rejoined, in a manner which made his preceptor burst out laughing.

"He's saving for *you,*" said Pemberton. "They think of you in everything they do."

"He might save a little——" The boy paused. Pemberton waited to hear what. Then Morgan brought out oddly "A little reputation."

"Oh, there's plenty of that. That's all right!"

"Enough of it for the people they know, no doubt. The people they know are awful."

"Do you mean the princes? We mustn't abuse the princes."

"Why not? They haven't married Paula—they haven't married Amy. They only clean out Ulick."

"You *do* know everything!" Pemberton exclaimed.

"No, I don't, after all. I don't know what they live on, or how they live, or *why* they live! What have they got and how did they get it? Are they rich, are they poor, or have they a *modeste aisance*? Why are they always chiveying about—living one year like ambassadors and the next like paupers? Who are they, any way, and what are they? I've thought of all that—I've thought of a lot of things. They're so beastly worldly. That's what I hate most—oh, I've *seen* it! All they care about is to make an appearance and to pass for something or other. What do they want to pass for? What *do* they, Mr. Pemberton?"

"You pause for a reply," said Pemberton, treating the inquiry as a joke, yet wondering too, and greatly struck with the boy's intense, if imperfect, vision. "I haven't the least idea."

"And what good does it do? Haven't I seen the way people treat them—the 'nice' people, the ones they want to know? They'll take anything from them—they'll lie down and be trampled on. The nice ones hate that—they just sicken them. You're the only really nice person we know."

"Are you sure? They don't lie down for me!"

"Well, you shan't lie down for them. You've got to go—that's what you've got to do," said Morgan.

"And what will become of you?"

"Oh, I'm growing up. I shall get off before long. I'll see you later."

"You had better let me finish you," Pemberton urged, lending himself to the child's extraordinarily competent attitude.

Morgan stopped in their walk, looking up at him. He had to look up much less than a couple of years before—he had grown, in his loose leanness, so long and high. "Finish me?" he echoed.

"There are such a lot of jolly things we can do together yet. I want to turn you out—I want you to do me credit."

Morgan continued to look at him. "To give you credit—do you mean?"

"My dear fellow, you're too clever to live."

"That's just what I'm afraid you think. No, no; it isn't fair—I can't endure it. We'll part next week. The sooner it's over the sooner to sleep."

"If I hear of anything—any other chance, I promise to go," said Pemberton.

Morgan consented to consider this. "But you'll be honest," he demanded; "you won't pretend you haven't heard?"

"I'm much more likely to pretend I have."

"But what can you hear of, this way, stuck in a hole with us? You ought to be on the spot, to go to England—you ought to go to America."

"One would think you were *my* tutor!" said Pemberton.

Morgan walked on, and after a moment he began again: "Well, now that you know that I know and that we look at the facts and keep nothing back—it's much more comfortable, isn't it?"

"My dear boy, it's so amusing, so interesting, that it surely will be quite impossible for me to forego such hours as these."

This made Morgan stop once more. "You *do* keep something back. Oh, you're not straight—*I* am!"

"Why am I not straight?"

"Oh, you've got your idea!"

"My idea?"

"Why, that I probably sha'n't live, and that you can stick it out till I'm removed."

"You *are* too clever to live!" Pemberton repeated.

"I call it a mean idea," Morgan pursued. "But I shall punish you by the way I hang on."

"Look out or I'll poison you!" Pemberton laughed.

"I'm stronger and better every year. Haven't you noticed that there hasn't been a doctor near me since you came?"

"*I'm* your doctor," said the young man, taking his arm and drawing him on again.

Morgan proceeded, and after a few steps he gave a sigh of mingled weariness and relief. "Ah, now that we look at the facts, it's all right!"

VII

THEY looked at the facts a good deal after this; and one of the first consequences of their doing so was that Pemberton stuck it out, as it were, for the purpose. Morgan made the facts so vivid and so droll, and at the same time so bald and so ugly, that there was fascination in talking them over with him, just as there would have been heartlessness in leaving him alone with them. Now that they had such a number of perceptions in common it was useless for the pair to pretend that they didn't judge such people; but the very judgment, and the exchange of perceptions, created another tie. Morgan had never been so interesting as now that he himself was made plainer by the sidelight of these confidences. What came out in it most was the soreness of his characteristic pride. He had plenty of that, Pemberton felt—so much that it was perhaps well it should have had to take some early bruises. He would have liked his people to be gallant, and he had waked up too soon to the sense that they were perpetually swallowing humble-pie. His mother would consume any amount, and his father would consume even more than his mother. He had a theory that Ulick had wriggled out of an "affair" at Nice: there had once been a flurry at home, a regular panic, after which they all went to bed and took medicine, not to be accounted for on any other supposition. Morgan had a romantic imagination, fed by poetry and history, and he would have liked those who "bore his name" (as he used to say to Pemberton with the humour that made his sensitiveness manly), to have a proper spirit. But their one idea was to get in with people who didn't want them and to take snubs as if they were honourable scars. Why people didn't want them more he didn't know—that was people's own affair; after all they were not superficially repulsive—they were a hundred times cleverer than most of the dreary grandees, the "poor swells" they rushed about Europe to catch up with. "After all, they *are* amusing—they are!" Morgan used to say, with the wisdom of the ages. To which Pemberton always replied: "Amusing—the great Moreen troupe? Why, they're altogether delightful; and if it were not for the hitch that you and I (feeble performers!) make in the *ensemble,* they would carry everything before them."

What the boy couldn't get over was that this particular blight seemed, in a tradition of self-respect, so undeserved and so arbitrary. No doubt people had a right to take the line they liked; but why should *his* people have liked the line of pushing and toadying and lying and cheating? What had their forefathers—all decent folk, so far as he knew—done to them, or what had *he* done to them? Who had poisoned their blood with the fifth-rate social ideal, the fixed idea of making smart acquaintances and getting into the *monde chic,* especially when it was foredoomed to failure and exposure? They showed so what they were after; that was what made the people they wanted not want *them.* And never a movement of dignity, never a throb of shame at looking each other in the face, never any independence or resentment or disgust. If his father or his brother would only knock some one down once or twice a year! Clever as they were they never guessed how they appeared. They were good-natured, yes—as good-natured as Jews at the doors of clothing-shops! But was that the model one wanted one's family to follow? Morgan had dim memories of an old grandfather, the maternal, in New York, whom he had been taken across the ocean to see, at the age of five: a gentleman with a high neckcloth and a good deal of pronunciation, who wore a dress-coat in the morning, which made one wonder what he wore in the evening, and had, or was supposed to have, "property" and something to do with the Bible Society. It couldn't have been but that *he* was a good type. Pemberton himself remembered Mrs. Clancy, a widowed sister of Mr. Moreen's, who was as irritating as a moral tale and had paid a fortnight's visit to the family at Nice shortly after he came to live with them. She was "pure and refined," as Amy said, over the banjo, and had the air of not knowing what they meant and of keeping something back. Pemberton judged that what she kept back was an approval of many of their ways; therefore it was to be supposed that she too was of a good type, and that Mr. and Mrs. Moreen and Ulick and Paula and Amy might easily have been better if they would.

But that they wouldn't was more and more perceptible from day to day. They continued to "chivey," as Morgan called it, and in due time became aware of a variety of reasons for proceeding to Venice. They mentioned a great many of them—they were always strikingly frank, and had the brightest friendly chatter, at the late foreign breakfast in especial, before the ladies had made up their faces, when they leaned their arms on the table, had something to follow the *demi-tasse*, and, in the heat of familiar discussion as to what they "really ought" to do, fell inevitably into the languages in which they could *tutoyer*. Even Pemberton liked them, then; he could endure even Ulick when he heard him give his little flat voice for the "sweet sea-city." That was what made him have a sneaking kindness for them—that they were so out of the workaday world and kept him so out of it. The summer had waned when, with cries of ecstasy, they all passed out on the balcony that overhung the Grand Canal; the sunsets were splendid—the Dorringtons had arrived. The Dorringtons were the only reason they had not talked of at breakfast; but the reasons that they didn't talk of at breakfast always came out in the end. The Dorringtons, on the other hand, came out very little; or else, when they did, they stayed—as was natural—for hours, during which periods Mrs. Moreen and the girls sometimes called at their hotel (to see if they had returned) as many as three times running. The gondola was for the ladies; for in Venice too there were "days," which Mrs. Moreen knew in their order an hour after she arrived. She immediately took one herself, to which the Dorringtons never came, though on a certain occasion when Pemberton and his pupil were together at St. Mark's—where, taking the best walks they had ever had and haunting a hundred churches, they spent a great deal of time—they saw the old lord turn up with Mr. Moreen and Ulick, who showed him the dim basilica as if it belonged to them. Pemberton noted how much less, among its curiosities, Lord Dorrington carried himself as a man of the world; wondering too whether, for such services, his companions took a fee from him. The autumn, at any rate, waned, the Dorringtons departed, and Lord Verschoyle, the eldest son, had proposed neither for Amy nor for Paula.

One sad November day, while the wind roared round the old palace and the rain lashed the lagoon, Pemberton, for exercise and even somewhat for warmth (the Moreens were horribly frugal about fires—it was a cause of suffering to their inmate), walked up and down the big bare *sala* with his pupil. The scagliola floor was cold, the high battered casements shook in the storm, and the stately decay of the place was unrelieved by a particle of furniture. Pemberton's spirits were low, and it came over him that the fortune of the Moreens was now even lower. A blast of desolation, a prophecy of disaster and disgrace, seemed to draw through the comfortless hall. Mr. Moreen and Ulick were in the Piazza, looking out for something, strolling drearily, in mackintoshes, under the arcades; but still, in spite of mackintoshes unmistakable men of the world. Paula and Amy were in bed—it might have been thought they were staying there to keep warm. Pemberton looked askance at the boy at his side, to see to what extent he was conscious of these portents. But Morgan, luckily for him, was now mainly conscious of growing taller and stronger and indeed of being in his fifteenth year. This fact was intensely interesting to him—it was the basis of a private theory (which, however, he had imparted to his tutor) that in a little while he should stand on his own feet. He considered that the situation would change—that, in short, he should be "finished," grown up, producible in the world of affairs and ready to prove himself of sterling ability. Sharply as he was capable, at times, of questioning his circumstances, there were happy hours when he was as superficial as a child; the proof of which was his fundamental assumption that he should presently go to Oxford, to Pemberton's college, and, aided and abetted by Pemberton, do the most wonderful things. It vexed Pemberton to see how little, in such a project, he took account of ways and means: on other matters he was so sceptical about them. Pemberton tried to imagine the Moreens at

Oxford, and fortunately failed; yet unless they were to remove there as a family there would be no *modus vivendi* for Morgan. How could he live without an allowance, and where was the allowance to come from? He (Pemberton) might live on Morgan; but how could Morgan live on him? What was to become of him anyhow? Somehow, the fact that he was a big boy now, with better prospects of health, made the question of his future more difficult. So long as he was frail the consideration that he inspired seemed enough of an answer to it. But at the bottom of Pemberton's heart was the recognition of his probably being strong enough to live and not strong enough to thrive. He himself, at any rate, was in a period of natural, boyish rosiness about all this, so that the beating of the tempest seemed to him only the voice of life and the challenge of fate. He had on his shabby little overcoat, with the collar up, but he was enjoying his walk.

It was interrupted at last by the appearance of his mother at the end of the *sala*. She beckoned to Morgan to come to her, and while Pemberton saw him, complacent, pass down the long vista, over the damp false marble, he wondered what was in the air. Mrs. Moreen said a word to the boy and made him go into the room she had quitted. Then, having closed the door after him, she directed her steps swiftly to Pemberton. There *was* something in the air, but his wildest flight of fancy wouldn't have suggested what it proved to be. She signified that she had made a pretext to get Morgan out of the way, and then she inquired—without hesitation—if the young man could lend her sixty francs. While, before bursting into a laugh, he stared at her with surprise, she declared that she was awfully pressed for the money; she was desperate for it—it would save her life.

"Dear lady, *c'est trop fort!*" Pemberton laughed. "Where in the world do you suppose I should get sixty francs, *du train dont vous allez?*"

"I thought you worked—wrote things; don't they pay you?"

"Not a penny."

"Are you such a fool as to work for nothing?"

"You ought surely to know that."

Mrs. Moreen stared an instant, then she coloured a little. Pemberton saw she had quite forgotten the terms—if "terms" they could be called—that he had ended by accepting from herself; they had burdened her memory as little as her conscience. "Oh, yes, I see what you mean—you have been very nice about that; but why go back to it so often?" She had been perfectly urbane with him ever since the rough scene of explanation in his room, the morning he made her accept *his* "terms"—the necessity of his making his case known to Morgan. She had felt no resentment, after seeing that there was no danger of Morgan's taking the matter up with her. Indeed, attributing this immunity to the good taste of his influence with the boy, she had once said to Pemberton: "My dear fellow; it's an immense comfort you're a gentleman." She repeated this, in substance, now. "Of course you're a gentleman—that's a bother the less!" Pemberton reminded her that he had not "gone back" to anything; and she also repeated her prayer that, somewhere and somehow, he would find her sixty francs. He took the liberty of declaring that if he could find them it wouldn't be to lend them to *her*—as to which he consciously did himself injustice, knowing that if he had them he would certainly place them in her hand. He accused himself, at bottom and with some truth, of a fantastic, demoralised sympathy with her. If misery made strange bedfellows it also made strange sentiments. It was moreover a part of the demoralisation and of the general bad effect of living with such people that one had to make rough retorts, quite out of the tradition of good manners. "Morgan, Morgan, to what pass have I come for you?" he privately exclaimed, while Mrs. Moreen floated voluminously down the *sala* again, to liberate the boy; groaning, as she went, that everything was too odious.

Before the boy was liberated there came a thump at the door communicating with the staircase, followed by the apparition of a dripping youth who poked in his head. Pemberton recognised him as the bearer of a telegram and recognised the telegram as addressed to himself. Morgan came back as, after glancing at the signature (that of a friend in London), he was reading the words: "Found jolly job for you—engagement to coach opulent youth on own terms. Come immediately." The answer, happily, was paid, and the messenger waited. Morgan, who had drawn near, waited too, and looked hard at Pemberton; and Pemberton, after a moment, having met his look, handed him the telegram. It was really by wise looks (they knew each other so well), that, while the telegraph-boy, in his waterproof cape, made a great puddle on the floor, the thing was settled between them. Pemberton wrote the answer with a pencil against the frescoed wall, and the messenger departed. When he had gone Pemberton said to Morgan:

"I'll make a tremendous charge; I'll earn a lot of money in a short time, and we'll live on it."

"Well, I hope the opulent youth will be stupid—he probably will—" Morgan parenthesised, "and keep you a long time."

"Of course, the longer he keeps me the more we shall have for our old age."

"But suppose *they* don't pay you!" Morgan awfully suggested.

"Oh, there are not two such—!" Pemberton paused, he was on the point of using an invidious term. Instead of this he said "two such chances."

Morgan flushed—the tears came to his eyes. "*Dites toujours*, two such rascally crews!" Then, in a different tone, he added: "Happy opulent youth!"

"Not if he's stupid!"

"Oh, they're happier then. But you can't have everything, can you?" the boy smiled.

Pemberton held him, his hands on his shoulders. "What will become of *you*, what will you do?" He thought of Mrs. Moreen, desperate for sixty francs.

"I shall turn into a man." And then, as if he recognised all the bearings of Pemberton's allusion: "I shall get on with them better when you're not here."

"Ah, don't say that—it sounds as if I set you against them!"

"You do—the sight of you. It's all right; you know what I mean. I shall be beautiful. I'll take their affairs in hand; I'll marry my sisters."

"You'll marry yourself!" joked Pemberton; as high, rather tense pleasantry would evidently be the right, or the safest, tone for their separation.

It was, however, not purely in this strain that Morgan suddenly asked: "But I say—how will you get to your jolly job? You'll have to telegraph to the opulent youth for money to come on."

Pemberton bethought himself. "They won't like that, will they?"

"Oh, look out for them!"

Then Pemberton brought out his remedy. "I'll go to the American Consul; I'll borrow some money of him—just for the few days, on the strength of the telegram."

Morgan was hilarious. "Show him the telegram—then stay and keep the money!"

Pemberton entered into the joke enough to reply that, for Morgan, he was really capable of that; but the boy, growing more serious, and to prove that he hadn't meant what he said, not only hurried him off to the Consulate (since he was to start that evening, as he had wired to his friend), but insisted on going with him. They splashed through the tortuous perforations and over the humpbacked bridges, and they passed through the Piazza, where they saw Mr. Moreen and Ulick go into a jeweller's shop. The Consul proved accommodating (Pemberton said it wasn't the letter, but Morgan's grand air), and on their way back they went into St. Mark's for a hushed ten minutes. Later they took up and kept up the fun of it to the very end; and it seemed to Pemberton a part of that fun that Mrs. Moreen, who was very angry when he had announced to her his intention, should charge him, grotesquely and vulgarly, and in reference to the loan she had vainly endeavoured to effect, with bolting lest they should "get something out" of him. On the other hand he had to do Mr. Moreen and Ulick the justice to recognise that when, on coming in, *they* heard the cruel news, they took it like perfect men of the world.

VIII

WHEN Pemberton got at work with the opulent youth, who was to be taken in hand for Balliol, he found himself unable to say whether he was really an idiot or it was only, on his own part, the long association with an intensely living little mind that made him seem so. From Morgan he heard half-a-dozen times: the boy wrote charming young letters, a patchwork of tongues, with indulgent postscripts in the family Volapuk and, in little squares and rounds and crannies of the text, the drollest illustrations—letters that he was divided between the impulse to show his present disciple, as a kind of wasted incentive, and the sense of something in them that was profanable by publicity. The opulent youth went up, in due course, and failed to pass; but it seemed to add to the presumption that brilliancy was not expected of him all at once that his parents, condoning the lapse, which they good-naturedly treated as little as possible as if it were Pemberton's, should have sounded the rally again, begged the young coach to keep his pupil in hand another year.

The young coach was now in a position to lend Mrs. Moreen sixty francs, and he sent her a post-office order for the amount. In return for this favour he received a frantic, scribbled line from her: "Implore you to come back instantly—Morgan dreadfully ill." They were on the rebound, once more in Paris—often as Pemberton had seen them depressed he had never seen them crushed—and communication was therefore rapid. He wrote to the boy to ascertain the state of his health, but he received no answer to his letter. Accordingly he took an abrupt leave of the opulent youth and, crossing the Channel, alighted at the small hotel, in the quarter of the Champs Elysées, of which Mrs. Moreen had given him the address. A deep if dumb dissatisfaction with this lady and her companions bore him company: they couldn't be vulgarly honest, but they could live at hotels, in velvety *entresols,* amid a smell of burnt pastilles, in the most expensive city in Europe. When he had left them, in Venice, it was with an irrepressible suspicion that something was going to happen; but the only thing that had happened was that they succeeded in getting away. "How is he? where is he?" he asked of Mrs. Moreen; but before she could speak, these questions were answered by the pressure round his neck of a pair of arms, in shrunken sleeves, which were perfectly capable of an effusive young foreign squeeze.

"Dreadfully ill—I don't see it!" the young man cried. And then, to Morgan: "Why on earth didn't you relieve me? Why didn't you answer my letter?"

Mrs. Moreen declared that when she wrote he was very bad, and Pemberton learned at the same time from the boy that he had answered every letter he had received. This led to the demonstration that Pemberton's note had been intercepted. Mrs. Moreen was prepared to see the fact exposed, as Pemberton perceived, the moment he faced her, that she was prepared for a good many other things. She was prepared above all to maintain that she had acted from a sense of duty, that she was enchanted she had got him over, whatever they might say; and that it was useless of him to pretend that he didn't *know,* in all his bones, that his place at such a time was with Morgan. He had taken the boy away from them, and now he had no right to abandon him. He had created for himself the gravest responsibilities; he must at least abide by what he had done.

"Taken him away from you?" Pemberton exclaimed indignantly.

"Do it—do it, for pity's sake; that's just what I want. I can't stand *this*—and such scenes. They're treacherous!" These words broke from Morgan, who had intermitted his embrace, in a key which made Pemberton turn quickly to him, to see that he had suddenly seated himself, was breathing with evident difficulty and was very pale.

"Now do you say he's not ill—my precious pet?" shouted his mother, dropping on her knees before him with clasped hands, but touching him no more than if he had been a gilded idol. "It will pass—it's only for an instant; but don't say such dreadful things!"

"I'm all right—all right," Morgan panted to Pemberton, whom he sat looking up at with a strange smile, his hands resting on either side on the sofa.

"Now do you pretend I've been treacherous—that I've deceived?" Mrs. Moreen flashed at Pemberton as she got up.

"It isn't *he* says it, it's I!" the boy returned, apparently easier, but sinking back against the wall; while Pemberton, who had sat down beside him, taking his hand, bent over him.

"Darling child, one does what one can; there are so many things to consider," urged Mrs. Moreen. "It's his *place*—his only place. You see *you* think it is now."

"Take me away—take me away," Morgan went on, smiling to Pemberton from his white face.

"Where shall I take you, and how—oh, *how*, my boy?" the young man stammered, thinking of the rude way in which his friends in London held that, for his convenience, and without a pledge of instantaneous return, he had thrown them over; of the just resentment with which they would already have called in a successor, and of the little help as regarded finding fresh employment that resided for him in the flatness of his having failed to pass his pupil.

"Oh, we'll settle that. You used to talk about it," said Morgan. "If we can only go, all the rest's a detail."

"Talk about it as much as you like, but don't think you can attempt it. Mr. Moreen would never consent—it would be so precarious," Pemberton's hostess explained to him. Then to Morgan she explained: "It would destroy our peace, it would break our hearts. Now that he's back it will be all the same again. You'll have your life, your work and your freedom, and we'll all be happy as we used to be. You'll bloom and grow perfectly well, and we won't have any more silly experiments, will we? They're too absurd. It's Mr. Pemberton's place—every one in his place. You in yours, your papa in his, me in mine—*n'est-ce pas, chéri?* We'll all forget how foolish we've been, and we'll have lovely times."

She continued to talk and to surge vaguely about the little draped, stuffy *salon,* while Pemberton sat with the boy, whose colour gradually came back; and she mixed up her reasons, dropping that there were going to be changes, that the other children might scatter (who knew?—Paula had her ideas), and that then it might be fancied how much the poor old parent-birds would want the little nestling. Morgan looked at Pemberton, who wouldn't let him move; and Pemberton knew exactly how he felt at hearing himself called a little nestling. He admitted that he had had one or two bad days, but he protested afresh against the iniquity of his mother's having made them the ground of an appeal to poor Pemberton. Poor Pemberton could laugh now, apart from the comicality of Mrs. Moreen's producing so much philosophy for her defense (she seemed to shake it out of her agitated petticoats, which knocked over the light gilt chairs), so little did the sick boy strike him as qualified to repudiate any advantage.

He himself was in for it, at any rate. He should have Morgan on his hands again indefinitely; though indeed he saw the lad had a private theory to produce which would be intended to smooth this down. He was obliged to him for it in advance; but the suggested amendment didn't keep his heart from sinking a little, any more than it prevented him from accepting the prospect on the spot, with some confidence moreover that he would do so even better if he could have a little supper. Mrs. Moreen threw out more hints about the changes that were to be looked for, but she was such a mixture of smiles and shudders (she confessed she was very nervous), that he couldn't tell whether she were in high feather or only in hysterics. If the family were really at last going to pieces why shouldn't she recognise the necessity of pitching Morgan into some sort of lifeboat? This presumption was fostered by the fact that they were established in luxurious quarters in the capital of pleasure; that was exactly where they naturally *would* be established in view of going to pieces. Moreover didn't she mention that Mr. Moreen and the others were enjoying themselves at the opera with Mr. Granger, and wasn't *that* also precisely where one would look for them on the eve of a smash? Pemberton gathered that Mr. Granger was a rich, vacant American—a big bill with a flourishy heading and no items; so that one of Paula's "ideas" was probably that this time she had really done it, which was indeed an unprecedented blow to the general cohesion. And if the cohesion was to terminate what was to become of poor Pemberton? He felt quite enough bound up with them to figure, to his alarm, as a floating spar in case of a wreck.

It was Morgan who eventually asked if no supper had been ordered for him; sitting with him below, later, at the dim, delayed meal, in the presence of a great deal of corded green plush, a plate of ornamental biscuit and a languor marked on the part of the waiter. Mrs. Moreen had explained that they had been obliged to secure a room for the visitor out of the house; and Morgan's consolation (he offered it while Pemberton reflected on the nastiness of lukewarm sauces), proved to be, largely, that this circumstance would facilitate their escape. He talked of their escape (recurring to it often afterwards), as if they were making up a "boy's book" together. But he likewise expressed his sense that there was something in the air, that the Moreens couldn't keep it up much longer. In point of fact, as Pemberton was to see, they kept it up for five or six months. All the while, however, Morgan's contention was designed to cheer him. Mr. Moreen and Ulick, whom he had met the day after his return, accepted that return like perfect men of the world. If Paula and Amy treated it even with less formality an allowance was to be made for them, inasmuch as Mr. Granger had not come to the opera after all. He had only placed his box at their service, with a bouquet for each of the party; there was even one apiece, embittering the thought of his profusion, for Mr. Moreen and Ulick. "They're all like that," was Morgan's comment; "at the very last, just when we think we've got them fast, we're chucked!"

Morgan's comments, in these days, were more and more free; they even included a large recognition of the extraordinary tenderness with which he had been treated while Pemberton was away. Oh, yes, they couldn't do enough to be nice to him, to show him they had him on their mind and make up for his loss. That was just what made the whole thing so sad, and him so glad, after all, of Pemberton's return—he had to keep thinking of their affection less, had less sense of obligation. Pemberton laughed out at this last reason, and Morgan blushed and said: "You know what I mean." Pemberton knew perfectly what he meant; but there were a good many things it didn't make any clearer. This episode of his second sojourn in Paris stretched itself out wearily, with their resumed readings and wanderings and maunderings, their potterings on the quays, their hauntings of the museums, their occasional lingerings in the Palais Royal, when the first sharp weather came on and there was a comfort in warm emanations, before Chevet's wonderful succulent window. Morgan wanted to hear a great deal about the opulent youth—he took an immense interest in him. Some of the details of his opulence—Pemberton could spare him none of them—evidently intensified the boy's appreciation of all his friend had given up to come back to him; but in addition to the greater reciprocity established by such a renunciation he had always his little brooding theory, in which there was a frivolous gaiety too, that their long probation was drawing to a close. Morgan's conviction that the Moreens couldn't go on much longer kept pace with the unexpended impetus with which, from month to month, they did go on. Three weeks after Pemberton had rejoined them they went on to another hotel, a dingier one than the first; but Morgan rejoiced that his tutor had at least still not sacrificed the advantage of a room outside. He clung to the romantic utility of this when the day, or rather the night, should arrive for their escape.

For the first time, in this complicated connection, Pemberton felt sore and exasperated. It was, as he had said to Mrs. Moreen in Venice, *trop fort*—everything was *trop fort*. He could neither really throw off his blighting burden nor find in it the benefit of a pacified conscience or of a rewarded affection. He had spent all the money that he had earned in England, and he felt that his youth was going and that he was getting nothing back for it. It was all very well for Morgan to seem to consider that he would make up to him for all inconveniences by settling himself upon him permanently—there was an irritating flaw in such a view. He saw what the boy had in his mind; the conception that as his friend had had the generosity to come back to him he must show his gratitude by giving him his life. But the poor friend didn't desire the gift—what could he do with Morgan's life? Of course at the same time that Pemberton was irritated he remembered the reason, which was very honourable to Morgan and which consisted simply of the fact that he was perpetually making one forget that he was after all only a child. If one dealt with him on a different basis one's misadventures were one's own fault. So Pemberton waited in a queer confusion of yearning and alarm for the catastrophe which was held to hang over the house of Moreen, of which he certainly at moments felt the symptoms brush his cheek and as to which he wondered much in what form it would come.

Perhaps it would take the form of dispersal—a frightened *sauve qui peut,* a scuttling into selfish corners. Certainly they were less elastic than of yore; they were evidently looking for something they didn't find. The Dorringtons hadn't reappeared, the princes had scattered; wasn't that the beginning of the end? Mrs. Moreen had lost her reckoning of the famous "days"; her social calendar was blurred—it had turned its face to the wall. Pemberton suspected that the great, the cruel, discomfiture had been the extraordinary behaviour of Mr. Granger, who seemed not to know what he wanted, or, what was much worse, what *they* wanted. He kept sending flowers, as if to bestrew the path of his retreat, which was never the path of return. Flowers were all very well, but—Pemberton could complete the proposition. It was now positively conspicuous that in the long run the Moreens were a failure; so that the young man was almost grateful the run had not been short. Mr. Moreen, indeed, was still occasionally able to get away on business, and, what was more surprising, he was also able to get back. Ulick had no club, but you could not have discovered it from his appearance, which was as much as ever that of a person looking at life from the window of such an institution; therefore Pemberton was doubly astonished at an answer he once heard him make to his mother, in the desperate tone of a man familiar with the worst privations. Her question Pemberton had not quite caught; it appeared to be an appeal for a suggestion as to whom they could get to take Amy. "Let the devil take her!" Ulick snapped; so that Pemberton could see that not only they had lost their amiability, but had ceased to believe in themselves. He could also see that if Mrs. Moreen was trying to get people to take her children she might be regarded as closing the hatches for the storm. But Morgan would be the last she would part with.

One winter afternoon—it was a Sunday—he and the boy walked far together in the Bois de Boulogne. The evening was so splendid, the cold lemon-coloured sunset so clear, the stream of carriages and pedestrians so amusing and the fascination of Paris so great, that they stayed out later than usual and became aware that they would have to hurry home to arrive in time for dinner. They hurried accordingly, arm-in-arm, good-humoured and hungry, agreeing that there was nothing like Paris after all and that after all, too, that had come and gone they were not yet sated with innocent pleasures. When they reached the hotel they found that, though scandalously late, they were in time for all the dinner they were likely to sit down to. Confusion reigned in the apartments of the Moreens (very shabby ones this time, but the best in the house), and before the interrupted service of the table (with objects displaced almost as if there had been a scuffle, and a great wine stain from an overturned bottle), Pemberton could not blink the fact that there had been a scene of proprietary mutiny. The storm had come—they were all seeking refuge. The hatches were down—Paula and Amy were invisible (they had never tried the most casual art upon Pemberton, but he felt that they had enough of an eye to him not to wish to meet him as young ladies whose frocks had been confiscated), and Ulick appeared to have jumped overboard. In a word, the host and his staff had ceased to "go on" at the pace of their guests, and the air of embarrassed detention, thanks to a pile of gaping trunks in the passage, was strangely commingled with the air of indignant withdrawal.

When Morgan took in all this—and he took it in very quickly—he blushed to the roots of his hair. He had walked, from his infancy, among difficulties and dangers, but he had never seen a public exposure. Pemberton noticed, in a second glance at him, that the tears had rushed into his eyes and that they were tears of bitter shame. He wondered for an instant, for the boy's sake, whether he might successfully pretend not to understand. Not successfully, he felt, as Mr. and Mrs. Moreen, dinnerless by their extinguished hearth, rose before him in their little dishonoured *salon*, considering apparently with much intensity what lively capital would be next on their list. They were not prostrate, but they were very pale, and Mrs. Moreen had evidently been crying. Pemberton quickly learned however that her grief was not for the loss of her dinner, much as she usually enjoyed it, but on account of a necessity much more tragic. She lost no time in laying this necessity bare, in telling him how the change had come, the bolt had fallen, and how they would all have to turn themselves about. Therefore cruel as it was to them to part with their darling she must look to him to carry a little further the influence he had so fortunately acquired with the boy—to induce his young charge to follow him into some modest retreat. They depended upon him, in a word, to take their delightful child temporarily under his protection—it would leave Mr. Moreen and herself so much more free to give the proper attention (too little, alas! had been given), to the readjustment of their affairs.

"We trust you—we feel that we can," said Mrs. Moreen, slowly rubbing her plump white hands and looking, with compunction, hard at Morgan, whose chin, not to take liberties, her husband stroked with a tentative paternal forefinger.

"Oh, yes; we feel that we can. We trust Mr. Pemberton fully, Morgan," Mr. Moreen conceded.

Pemberton wondered again if he might pretend not to understand; but the idea was painfully complicated by the immediate perception that Morgan had understood.

"Do you mean that he may take me to live with him—for ever and ever?" cried the boy. "Away, away, anywhere he likes?"

"For ever and ever? *Comme vous-y-allez!*" Mr. Moreen laughed indulgently. "For as long as Mr. Pemberton may be so good."

"We've struggled, we've suffered," his wife went on; "but you've made him so your own that we've already been through the worst of the sacrifice."

Morgan had turned away from his father—he stood looking at Pemberton with a light in his face. His blush had died out, but something had come that was brighter and more vivid. He had a moment of boyish joy, scarcely mitigated by the reflection that, with this unexpected consecration of his hope—too sudden and too violent; the thing was a good deal less like a boy's book—the "escape" was left on their hands. The boyish joy was there for an instant, and Pemberton was almost frightened at the revelation of gratitude and affection that shone through his humiliation. When Morgan stammered "My dear fellow, what do you say to *that*?" he felt that he should say something enthusiastic. But he was still more frightened at something else that immediately followed and that made the lad sit down quickly on the nearest chair. He had turned very white and had raised his hand to his left side. They were all three looking at him, but Mrs. Moreen was the first to bound forward. "Ah, his darling little heart!" she broke out; and this time, on her knees before him and without respect for the idol, she caught him ardently in her arms. "You walked him too far, you hurried him too fast!" she tossed over her shoulder at Pemberton. The boy made no protest, and the next instant his mother, still holding him, sprang up with her face convulsed and with the terrified cry "Help, help! he's going, he's gone!" Pemberton saw, with equal horror, by Morgan's own stricken face, that he *was* gone. He pulled him half out of his mother's hands, and for a moment, while they held him together, they looked, in their dismay, into each other's eyes. "He couldn't stand it, with his infirmity," said Pemberton—"the shock, the whole scene, the violent emotion."

"But I thought he *wanted* to go to you!" wailed Mrs. Moreen.

"I *told* you he didn't, my dear," argued Mr. Moreen. He was trembling all over, and he was, in his way, as deeply affected as his wife. But, after the first, he took his bereavement like a man of the world.

The Turn of the Screw

The Turn of the Screw

For sheer measureless evil and horror there are very few tales in world literature that can compare with *The Turn of the Screw.* Its plot was suggested to James by a story he had heard about a couple of small children in a remote place, to whom the "spirits of certain 'bad' servants, dead in the employ of the house, were believed to have appeared with the design of 'getting hold' of them." In his characteristic way he felt that more details would be superfluous, as he had heard quite enough to make the "vividest little note for sinister romance" he had ever jotted down.

In writing his bogey-tale James succeeded so well in conveying a sense of dreadful and unguessable things that upon its publication (1898) he found himself answering questions that apparently he preferred not to answer. Some readers determined to satisfy their curiosity by applying directly to the author, and to judge by the vagueness and coyness of his replies, James was deliberately trying to choke off the discussion. Thus he wrote to F. W. H. Myers (December 19, 1898) that *The Turn of the Screw* was a "very mechanical matter . . . an inferior, a merely *pictorial* subject and rather a shameless potboiler." But this dismissal of the story jibes not at all with its inclusion in the collected edition and the long and serious examination of it in the preface. One suspects that knowing as he did the prudishness of his Anglo-American public and its signal capacity to consider itself outraged, he was at first disposed to pass off his "designed horror" as a piece of mystification pure and simple. But so to read the story is to do it an injustice. Mystification in art is of the same order as naïveté, of which James once said that it is "like a zero in a number: its importance depends on the figure it is united with." And it is not difficult to see that in *The Turn of the Screw* the element of mystification is united with an element of morbid sexuality. It is the sexuality expressed through the machinery of the supernatural that makes for the overwhelming effect.

That the "badness" of the prowling demonic spirits is of an erotic nature is shown by everything we are allowed to learn about them. Mrs. Grose, the housekeeper, tells the governess that Peter Quint "did what he wished" not only with Miss Jessel but also with the children. He "played" with them, and altogether he was "much too free . . . there had been matters in his life—strange passages and perils, secret disorders, vices more than suspected. . . ." Thus to interpret the story, that is in terms of the *reality* of Peter Quint and Miss Jessel's "badness," enables us to take it *as given* and at the same time to take it as a study in abnormal psychology.

Attempts to explain away the ghosts are but a fallacy of rationalism. There is the theory, for example, propounded by Edna Kenton and Edmund Wilson, which places the governess in the center of the plot as a case of sex-repression; in this manner the ghosts are immediately accounted for as hallucinations, the products of her neurosis. For one thing, there is not quite enough evidence to support this theory; it glosses over the fact that Mrs. Grose confirms the governess's minute description of Peter Quint; for another, the Freudian insight which this theory puts into operation is so elementary as to make the story less rather than more interesting. It lets off, so to speak, too many of the agents—the servants and the children. Of course, there is no doubt that the story may be read that way, but that is by no means the same as saying that such a reading conforms with the author's intention.

So far as intention goes, we should keep in mind that in James we are always justified in assuming the maximum; and the trouble with the governess theory is that it reduces the intention to a minimum. In *The Turn of the Screw* James strove above all to expand the limits of suggestion. "What, in the last analysis," he remarks in the preface, "had I to give the sense of? Of their being, the haunting pair, capable, as the phrase is, of everything—that is of exerting, in respect to the children, the very worst action small victims so conditioned might be conceived as subject to. . . . Only make the reader's general vision intense, I said to myself . . . and his own experience, his own imagination . . . will supply him quite sufficiently with all the particulars. Make him *think* the evil, make him think it for himself. . . ."

THE story had held us, round the fire, sufficiently breathless, but except the obvious remark that it was gruesome, as, on Christmas eve in an old house, a strange tale should essentially be, I remember no comment uttered till somebody happened to say that it was the only case he had met in which such a visitation had fallen on a child. The case, I may mention, was that of an apparition in just such an old house as had gathered us for the occasion—an appearance, of a dreadful kind, to a little boy sleeping in the room with his mother and waking her up in the terror of it; waking her not to dissipate his dread and soothe him to sleep again, but to encounter also, herself, before she had succeeded in doing so, the same sight that had shaken him. It was this observation that drew from Douglas—not immediately, but later in the evening—a reply that had the interesting consequence to which I call attention. Someone else told a story not particularly effective, which I saw he was not following. This I took for a sign that he had himself something to produce and that we should only have to wait. We waited in fact till two nights later; but that same evening, before we scattered, he brought out what was in his mind.

"I quite agree—in regard to Griffin's ghost, or whatever it was—that its appearing first to the little boy, at so tender an age, adds a particular touch. But it's not the first occurrence of its charming kind that I know to have involved a child. If the child gives the effect another turn of the screw, what do you say to *two* children ——?"

"We say, of course," somebody exclaimed, "that they give two turns! Also that we want to hear about them."

I can see Douglas there before the fire, to which he had got up to present his back, looking down at his interlocutor with his hands in his pockets. "Nobody but me, till now, has ever heard. It's quite too horrible." This, naturally, was declared by several voices to give the thing the utmost price, and our friend, with quiet art, prepared his triumph by turning his eyes over the rest of us and going on: "It's beyond everything. Nothing at all that I know touches it."

"For sheer terror?" I remember asking.

He seemed to say it was not so simple as that; to be really at a loss how to qualify it. He passed his hand over his eyes, made a little wincing grimace. "For dreadful—dreadfulness!"

"Oh, how delicious!" cried one of the women.

He took no notice of her; he looked at me, but as if, instead of me, he saw what he spoke of. "For general uncanny ugliness and horror and pain."

"Well then," I said, "just sit right down and begin."

He turned round to the fire, gave a kick to a log, watched it an instant. Then as he faced us again: "I can't begin. I shall have to send to town." There was a unanimous groan at this, and much reproach; after which, in his preoccupied way, he explained. "The story's written. It's in a locked drawer—it has not been out for years. I could write to my man and enclose the key; he could send down the packet as he finds it." It was to me in particular that he appeared to propound this—appeared almost to appeal for aid not to hesitate. He had broken a thickness of ice, the formation of many a winter; had had his reasons for a long silence. The others resented postponement, but it was just his scruples that charmed me. I adjured him to write by the first post and to agree with us for an early hearing; then I asked him if the experience in question had been his own. To this his answer was prompt. "Oh, thank God, no!"

"And is the record yours? You took the thing down?"

"Nothing but the impression. I took that *here*"—he tapped his heart. "I've never lost it."

"Then your manuscript ——?"

"Is in old, faded ink, and in the most beautiful hand." He hung fire again. "A woman's. She has been dead these twenty years. She sent me the pages in question before she died." They were all listening now, and of course there was somebody to be arch, or at any rate to draw the inference. But if he put the inference by without a smile it was also without irritation. "She was a most charming person, but she was ten years older than I. She was my sister's governess," he quietly said. "She was the most agreeable woman I've ever known in her position; she would have been worthy of any whatever. It was long ago, and this episode was long before. I was at Trinity, and I found her at home on my coming down the second summer. I was much there that year—it was a beautiful one; and we had, in her off-hours, some strolls and talks in the garden—talks in which she struck me as awfully clever and nice. Oh yes; don't grin: I liked her extremely and am glad to this day to think she liked me too. If she hadn't she wouldn't have told me. She had never told anyone. It wasn't simply that she said so, but that I knew she hadn't. I was sure; I could see. You'll easily judge why when you hear."

"Because the thing had been such a scare?"

He continued to fix me. "You'll easily judge," he repeated: "*you* will."

I fixed him too. "I see. She was in love."

He laughed for the first time. "You *are* acute. Yes, she was in love. That is, she had been. That came out—she couldn't tell her story without its coming out. I saw it, and she saw I saw it; but neither of us spoke of it. I remember the time and the place—the corner of the lawn, the shade of the great beeches and the long, hot summer afternoon. It wasn't a scene for a shudder; but oh——!" He quitted the fire and dropped back into his chair.

"You'll receive the packet Thursday morning?" I inquired.

"Probably not till the second post."

"Well then; after dinner ——"

"You'll all meet me here?" He looked us round again. "Isn't anybody going?" It was almost the tone of hope.

"Everybody will stay!"

"*I* will—and *I* will!" cried the ladies whose departure had been fixed. Mrs. Griffin, however, expressed the need for a little more light. "Who was it she was in love with?"

"The story will tell," I took upon myself to reply.

"Oh, I can't wait for the story!"

"The story *won't* tell," said Douglas; "not in any literal, vulgar way."

"More's the pity, then. That's the only way I ever understand."

"Won't *you* tell, Douglas?" somebody else inquired.

He sprang to his feet again. "Yes—to-morrow. Now I must go to bed. Good-night." And quickly catching up a candlestick, he left us slightly bewildered. From our end of the great brown hall we heard his step on the stair; whereupon Mrs. Griffin spoke. "Well, if I don't know who she was in love with, I know who *he* was."

"She was ten years older," said her husband.

"*Raison de plus*—at that age! But it's rather nice, his long reticence."

"Forty years!" Griffin put in.

"With this outbreak at last."

"The outbreak," I returned, "will make a tremendous occasion of Thursday night"; and everyone so agreed with me that, in the light of it, we lost all attention for everything else. The last story, however incomplete and like the mere opening of a serial, had been told; we handshook and "candlestuck," as somebody said, and went to bed.

I knew the next day that a letter containing the key had, by the first post, gone off to his London apartments; but in spite of—or perhaps just on account of—the eventual diffusion of this knowledge we quite let him alone till after dinner, till such an hour of the evening, in fact, as might best accord with the kind of emotion on which our hopes were fixed. Then he became as communicative as we could desire and indeed gave us his best reason for being so. We had it from him again before the fire in the hall, as we had had our mild wonders of the previous night. It appeared that the narrative he had promised to read us really required for a proper intelligence a few words of prologue. Let me say here distinctly, to have done with it, that this narrative, from an exact transcript of my own made much later, is what I shall presently give. Poor Douglas, before his death—when it was in sight—committed to me the manuscript that reached him on the third of these days and that, on the same spot, with immense effect, he began to read to our hushed little circle on the night of the fourth. The departing ladies who had said they would stay didn't, of course, thank heaven, stay: they departed, in consequence of arrangements made, in a rage of curiosity, as they professed, produced by the touches with which he had already worked us up. But that only made his little final auditory more compact and select, kept it, round the hearth, subject to a common thrill.

The first of these touches conveyed that the written statement took up the tale at a point after it had, in a manner, begun. The fact to be in possession of was therefore that his old friend, the youngest of several daughters of a poor country parson, had, at the age of twenty, on taking service for the first time in the schoolroom, come up to London, in trepidation, to answer in person an advertisement that had already placed her in brief correspondence with the advertiser. This person proved, on her presenting herself, for judgment, at a house in Harley Street, that impressed her as vast and imposing—this prospective patron proved a gentleman, a bachelor in the prime of life, such a figure as had never risen, save in a dream or an old novel, before a fluttered, anxious girl out of a Hampshire vicarage. One could easily fix his type; it never, happily, dies out. He was handsome and bold and pleasant, off-hand and gay and kind. He struck her, inevitably, as gallant and splendid, but what took her most of all and gave her the courage she afterwards showed was that he put the whole thing to her as a kind of favour, an obligation he should gratefully incur. She conceived him as rich, but as fearfully extravagant—saw him all in a glow of high fashion, of good looks, of expensive habits, of charming ways with women. He had for his own town residence a big house filled with the spoils of travel and the trophies of the chase; but it was to his country home, an old family place in Essex, that he wished her immediately to proceed.

He had been left, by the death of their parents in India, guardian to a small nephew and a small niece, children of a younger, a military brother, whom he had lost two years before. These children were, by the strangest of chances for a man in his position,—a lone man without the right sort of experience or a grain of patience,—very heavily on his hands. It had all been a great worry and, on his own part doubtless, a series of blunders, but he immensely pitied the poor chicks and had done all he could; had in particular sent them down to his other house, the proper place for them being of course the country, and kept them there, from the first, with the best people he could find to look after them, parting even with his own servants to wait on them and going down himself, whenever he might, to see how they were doing. The awkward thing was that they had practically no other relations and that his own affairs took up all his time. He had put them in possession of Bly, which was healthy and secure, and had placed at the head of their little establishment—but below stairs only—an excellent woman, Mrs. Grose, whom he was sure his visitor would like and who had formerly been maid to his mother. She was now housekeeper and was also acting for the time as superintendent to the little girl, of whom, without children of her own, she was, by good luck, extremely fond. There were plenty of people to help, but of course the young lady who should go down as governess would be in supreme authority. She would also have, in holidays, to look after the small boy, who had been for a term at school—young as he was to be sent, but what else could be done?—and who, as the holidays were about to begin, would be back from one day to the other. There had been for the two children at first a young lady whom they had had the misfortune to lose. She had done for them quite beautifully—she was a most respectable person—till her death, the great awkwardness of which had, precisely, left no alternative but the school for little Miles. Mrs. Grose, since then, in the way of manners and things, had done as she could for Flora; and there were, further, a cook, a housemaid, a dairywoman, an old pony, an old groom, and an old gardener, all likewise thoroughly respectable.

So far had Douglas presented his picture when someone put a question. "And what did the former governess die of?—of so much respectability?"

Our friend's answer was prompt. "That will come out. I don't anticipate."

"Excuse me—I thought that was just what you *are* doing."

"In her successor's place," I suggested, "I should have wished to learn if the office brought with it ——"

"Necessary danger to life?" Douglas completed my thought. "She did wish to learn, and she did learn. You shall hear tomorrow what she learnt. Meanwhile, of course, the prospect struck her as slightly grim. She was young, untried, nervous: it was a vision of serious duties and little company, of really great loneliness. She hesitated—took a couple of days to consult and consider. But the salary offered much exceeded her modest measure, and on a second interview she faced the music, she engaged." And Douglas, with this, made a pause that, for the benefit of the company, moved me to throw in——

"The moral of which was of course the seduction exercised by the splendid young man. She succumbed to it."

He got up and, as he had done the night before, went to the fire, gave a stir to a log with his foot, then stood a moment with his back to us. "She saw him only twice."

"Yes, but that's just the beauty of her passion."

A little to my surprise, on this, Douglas turned round to me. "It *was* the beauty of it. There were others," he went on, "who hadn't succumbed. He told her frankly all his difficulty—that for several applicants the conditions had been prohibitive. They were, somehow, simply afraid. It sounded dull—it sounded strange; and all the more so because of his main condition."

"Which was——?"

"That she should never trouble him—but never, never: neither appeal nor complain nor write about anything; only meet all questions herself, receive all moneys from his solicitor, take the whole thing over and let him alone. She promised to do this, and she mentioned to me that when, for a moment, disburdened, delighted, he held her hand, thanking her for the sacrifice, she already felt rewarded."

"But was that all her reward?" one of the ladies asked.

"She never saw him again."

"Oh!" said the lady; which, as our friend immediately left us again, was the only other word of importance contributed to the subject till, the next night, by the corner of the hearth, in the best chair, he opened the faded red cover of a thin old-fashioned gilt-edged album. The whole thing took indeed more nights than one, but on the first occasion the same lady put another question. "What is your title?"

"I haven't one."

"Oh, *I* have!" I said. But Douglas, without heeding me, had begun to read with a fine clearness that was like a rendering to the ear of the beauty of his author's hand.

I

I REMEMBER the whole beginning as a succession of flights and drops, a little see-saw of the right throbs and the wrong. After rising, in town, to meet his appeal, I had at all events a couple of very bad days—found myself doubtful again, felt indeed sure I had made a mistake. In this state of mind I spent the long hours of a bumping, swinging coach that carried me to the stopping-place at which I was to be met by a vehicle from the house. This convenience, I was told, had been ordered, and I found, toward the close of the June afternoon, a commodious fly in waiting for me. Driving at that hour, on a lovely day, through a country to which the summer sweetness seemed to offer me a friendly welcome, my fortitude mounted afresh and, as we turned into the avenue, encountered a reprieve that was probably but a proof of the point to which it had sunk. I suppose I had expected, or had dreaded, something so melancholy that what greeted me was a good surprise. I remember as a most pleasant impression the broad, clear front, its open windows and fresh curtains and the pair of maids looking out; I remember the lawn and the bright flowers and the crunch of my wheels on the gravel and the clustered tree-tops over which the rooks circled and cawed in the golden sky. The scene had a greatness that made it a different affair from my own scant home, and there immediately appeared at the door, with a little girl in her hand, a civil person who dropped me as decent a curtsey as if I had been the mistress or a distinguished visitor. I had received in Harley Street a narrower notion of the place, and that, as I recalled it, made me think the proprietor still more of a gentleman, suggested that what I was to enjoy might be something beyond his promise.

I had no drop again till the next day, for I was carried triumphantly through the following hours by my introduction to the younger of my pupils. The little girl who accompanied Mrs. Grose appeared to me on the spot a creature so charming as to make it a great fortune to have to do with her. She was the most beautiful child I had ever seen, and I afterwards wondered that my employer had not told me more of her. I slept little that night—I was too much excited; and this astonished me too, I recollect, remained with me, adding to my sense of the liberality with which I was treated. The large, impressive room, one of the best in the house, the great state bed, as I almost felt it, the full, figured draperies, the long glasses in which, for the first time, I could see myself from head to foot, all struck me—like the extraordinary charm of my small charge—as so many things thrown in. It was thrown in as well, from the first moment, that I should get on with Mrs. Grose in a relation over which, on my way, in the coach, I fear I had rather brooded. The only thing indeed that in this early outlook might have made me shrink again was the clear circumstance of her being so glad to see me. I perceived within half an hour that she was so glad—stout, simple, plain, clean, wholesome woman—as to be positively on her guard against showing it too much. I wondered even then a little why she should wish not to show it, and that, with reflection, with suspicion, might of course have made me uneasy.

But it was a comfort that there could be no uneasiness in a connection with anything so beatific as the radiant image of my little girl, the vision of whose angelic beauty had probably more than anything else to do with the restlessness that, before morning, made me several times rise and wander about my room to take in the whole picture and prospect; to watch, from my open window, the faint summer dawn, to look at such portions of the rest of the house as I could catch, and to listen, while, in the fading dusk, the first birds began to twitter, for the possible recurrence of a sound or two, less natural and not without, but within, that I had fancied I heard. There had been a moment when I believed I recognised, faint and far, the cry of a child; there had been another when I found myself just consciously starting as at the passage, before my door, of a light footstep. But these fancies were not marked enough not to be thrown off, and it is only in the light, or the gloom, I should rather say, of other and subsequent matters that they now come back to me. To watch, teach, "form" little Flora would too evidently be the making of a happy and useful life. It had been agreed between us downstairs that after this first occasion I should have her as a matter of course at night, her small white bed being already arranged, to that end, in my room. What I had undertaken was the whole care of her, and she had remained, just this last time, with Mrs. Grose only as an effect of our consideration for my inevitable strangeness and her natural timidity. In spite of this timidity—which the child herself, in the oddest way in the world, had been perfectly frank and brave about, allowing it, without a sign of uncomfortable consciousness, with the deep, sweet serenity indeed of one of Raphael's holy infants, to be discussed, to be imputed to her and to determine us—I felt quite sure she would presently like me. It was part of what I already liked Mrs. Grose herself for, the pleasure I could see her feel in my admiration and wonder as I sat at supper with four tall candles and with my pupil, in a high chair and a bib, brightly facing me, between them, over bread and milk. There were naturally things that in Flora's presence could pass between us only as prodigious and gratified looks, obscure and roundabout allusions.

"And the little boy—does he look like her? Is he too so very remarkable?"

One wouldn't flatter a child. "Oh, Miss, *most* remarkable. If you think well of this one!"—and she stood there with a plate in her hand, beaming at our companion, who looked from one of us to the other with placid heavenly eyes that contained nothing to check us.

"Yes; if I do——?"

"You *will* be carried away by the little gentleman!"

"Well, that, I think, is what I came for—to be carried away. I'm afraid, however," I remember feeling the impulse to add, "I'm rather easily carried away. I was carried away in London!"

I can still see Mrs. Grose's broad face as she took this in. "In Harley Street?"

"In Harley Street."

"Well, Miss, you're not the first—and you won't be the last."

"Oh, I've no pretension," I could laugh, "to being the only one. My other pupil, at any rate, as I understand, comes back tomorrow?"

"Not tomorrow—Friday, Miss. He arrives, as you did, by the coach, under care of the guard, and is to be met by the same carriage."

I forthwith expressed that the proper as well as the pleasant and friendly thing would be therefore that on the arrival of the public conveyance I should be in waiting for him with his little sister; an idea in which Mrs. Grose concurred so heartily that I somehow took her manner as a kind of comforting pledge—never falsified, thank heaven!—that we should on every question be quite at one. Oh, she was glad I was there!

What I felt the next day was, I suppose, nothing that could be fairly called a reaction from the cheer of my arrival; it was probably at the most only a slight oppression produced by a fuller measure of the scale, as I walked round them, gazed up at them, took them in, of my new circumstances. They had, as it were, an extent and mass for which I had not been prepared and in the presence of which I found myself, freshly, a little scared as well as a little proud. Lessons, in this agitation, certainly suffered some delay; I reflected that my first duty was, by the gentlest arts I could contrive, to win the child into the sense of knowing me. I spent the day with her out of doors; I arranged with her, to her great satisfaction, that it should be she, she only, who might show me the place. She showed it step by step and room by room and secret by secret, with droll, delightful, childish talk about it and with the result, in half an hour, of our becoming immense friends. Young as she was, I was struck, throughout our little tour, with her confidence and courage with the way, in empty chambers and dull corridors, on crooked staircases that made me pause and even on the summit of an old machicolated square tower that made me dizzy, her morning music, her disposition to tell me so many more things than she asked, rang out and led me on. I have not seen Bly since the day I left it, and I dare say that to my older and more informed eyes it would now appear sufficiently contracted. But as my little conductress, with her hair of gold and her frock of blue, danced before me round corners and pattered down passages, I had the view of a castle of romance inhabited by a rosy sprite, such a place as would somehow, for diversion of the young idea, take all colour out of storybooks and fairy-tales. Wasn't it just a storybook over which I had fallen a-doze and a-dream? No; it was a big, ugly, antique, but convenient house, embodying a few features of a building still older, half replaced and half utilised, in which I had the fancy of our being almost as lost as a handful of passengers in a great drifting ship. Well, I was, strangely, at the helm!

II

THIS came home to me when, two days later, I drove over with Flora to meet, as Mrs. Grose said, the little gentleman; and all the more for an incident that, presenting itself the second evening, had deeply disconcerted me. The first day had been, on the whole, as I have expressed, reassuring; but I was to see it wind up in keen apprehension. The postbag, that evening,—it came late,—contained a letter for me, which, however, in the hand of my employer, I found to be composed but of a few words enclosing another, addressed to himself, with a seal still unbroken. "This, I recognise, is from the head-master, and the head-master's an awful bore. Read him, please; deal with him; but mind you don't report. Not a word. I'm off!" I broke the seal with a great effort—so great a one that I was a long time coming to it; took the unopened missive at last up to my room and only attacked it just before going to bed. I had better have let it wait till morning, for it gave me a second sleepless night. With no counsel to take, the next day, I was full of distress; and it finally got so the better of me that I determined to open myself at least to Mrs. Grose.

"What does it mean? The child's dismissed his school."

She gave me a look that I remarked at the moment; then, visibly, with a quick blankness, seemed to try to take it back. "But aren't they all ——?"

"Sent home—yes. But only for the holidays. Miles may never go back at all."

Consciously, under my attention, she reddened. "They won't take him?"

"They absolutely decline."

At this she raised her eyes, which she had turned from me; I saw them fill with good tears. "What has he done?"

I hesitated; then I judged best simply to hand her my letter—which, however, had the effect of making her, without taking it, simply put her hands behind her. She shook her head sadly. "Such things are not for me, Miss."

My counsellor couldn't read! I winced at my mistake, which I attenuated as I could, and opened my letter again to repeat it to her; then, faltering in the act and folding it up once more, I put it back in my pocket. "Is he really *bad*?"

The tears were still in her eyes. "Do the gentlemen say so?"

"They go into no particulars. They simply express their regret that it should be impossible to keep him. That can have only one meaning." Mrs. Grose listened with dumb emotion; she forbore to ask me what this meaning might be; so that, presently, to put the thing with some coherence and with the mere aid of her presence to my own mind, I went on: "That he's an injury to the others."

At this, with one of the quick turns of simple folk, she suddenly flamed up. "Master Miles! *him* an injury?"

There was such a flood of good faith in it that, though I had not yet seen the child, my very fears made me jump to the absurdity of the idea. I found myself, to meet my friend the better, offering it, on the spot, sarcastically. "To his poor little innocent mates!"

"It's too dreadful," cried Mrs. Grose, "to say such cruel things! Why, he's scarce ten years old."

"Yes, yes; it would be incredible."

She was evidently grateful for such a profession. "See him, Miss, first. *Then* believe it!" I felt forthwith a new impatience to see him; it was the beginning of a curiosity that, for all the next hours, was to deepen almost to pain. Mrs. Grose was aware, I could judge, of what she had produced in me, and she followed it up with assurance. "You might as well believe it of the little lady. Bless her," she added the next moment—"*look* at her!"

I turned and saw that Flora, whom, ten minutes before, I had established in the schoolroom with a sheet of white paper, a pencil, and a copy of nice "round O's," now presented herself to view at the open door. She expressed in her little way an extraordinary detachment from disagreeable duties, looking to me, however, with a great childish light that seemed to offer it as a mere result of the affection she had conceived for my person, which had rendered necessary that she should follow me. I needed nothing more than this to feel the full force of Mrs. Grose's comparison, and, catching my pupil in my arms, covered her with kisses in which there was a sob of atonement.

None the less, the rest of the day, I watched for further occasion to approach my colleague, especially as, toward evening, I began to fancy she rather sought to avoid me. I overtook her, I remember, on the staircase; we went down together, and at the bottom I detained her, holding her there with a hand on her arm. "I take what you said to me at noon as a declaration that *you've* never known him to be bad."

She threw back her head; she had clearly, by this time, and very honestly, adopted an attitude. "Oh, never known him—I don't pretend *that*!"

I was upset again. "Then you *have* known him ——?"

"Yes indeed, Miss, thank God!"

On reflection I accepted this. "You mean that a boy who never is ——?"

"Is no boy for *me*!"

I held her tighter. "You like them with the spirit to be naughty?" Then, keeping pace with her answer, "So do I!" I eagerly brought out. "But not to the degree to contaminate ——"

"To contaminate?"—my big word left her at a loss. I explained it. "To corrupt."

She stared, taking my meaning in; but it produced in her an odd laugh. "Are you afraid he'll corrupt *you*?" She put the question with such a fine bold humour that, with a laugh, a little silly doubtless, to match her own, I gave way for the time to the apprehension of ridicule.

But the next day, as the hour for my drive approached, I cropped up in another place. "What was the lady who was here before?"

"The last governess? She was also young and pretty—almost as young and almost as pretty, Miss, even as you."

"Ah, then, I hope her youth and her beauty helped her!" I recollect throwing off. "He seems to like us young and pretty!"

"Oh, he *did*," Mrs. Grose assented: "it was the way he liked everyone!" She had no sooner spoken indeed than she caught herself up. "I mean that's *his* way—the master's."

I was struck. "But of whom did you speak first?"

She looked blank, but she coloured. "Why, of *him*."

"Of the master?"

"Of who else?"

There was so obviously no one else that the next moment I had lost my impression of her having accidentally said more than she meant; and I merely asked what I wanted to know. "Did *she* see anything in the boy——?"

"That wasn't right? She never told me."

I had a scruple, but I overcame it. "Was she careful—particular?"

Mrs. Grose appeared to try to be conscientious. "About some things—yes."

"But not about all?"

Again she considered. "Well, Miss—she's gone. I won't tell tales."

"I quite understand your feeling," I hastened to reply; but I thought it, after an instant, not opposed to this concession to pursue: "Did she die here?"

"No—she went off."

I don't know what there was in this brevity of Mrs. Grose's that struck me as ambiguous. "Went off to die?" Mrs. Grose looked straight out of the window, but I felt that, hypothetically, I had a right to know what young persons engaged for Bly were expected to do. "She was taken ill, you mean, and went home?"

"She had not taken ill, so far as appeared, in this house. She left it, at the end of the year, to go home, as she said, for a short holiday, to which the time she had put in had certainly given her a right. We had then a young woman—a nurse-maid who had stayed on and who was a good girl and clever; and *she* took the children altogether for the interval. But our young lady never came back and at the very moment I was expecting her I heard from the master that she was dead."

I turned this over. "But of what?"

"He never told me! But please, Miss," said Mrs. Grose, "I must get to my work."

III

HER thus turning her back on me was fortunately not, for my just preoccupations, a snub that could check the growth of our mutual esteem. We met, after I had brought home little Miles, more intimately than ever on the ground of my stupefaction, my general emotion: so monstrous was I then ready to pronounce it that such a child as had now been revealed to me should be under an interdict. I was a little late on the scene, and I felt, as he stood wistfully looking out for me before the door of the inn at which the coach had put him down, that I had seen him, on the instant, without and within, in the great glow of freshness, the same positive fragrance of purity, in which I had, from the first moment, seen his little sister. He was incredibly beautiful, and Mrs. Grose had put her finger on it: everything but a sort of passion of tenderness for him was swept away by his presence. What I then and there took him to my heart for was something divine that I have never found to the same degree in any child—his indescribable little air of knowing nothing in the world but love. It would have been impossible to carry a bad name with a greater sweetness of innocence, and by the time I had got back to Bly with him I remained merely bewildered—so far, that is, as I was not outraged—by the sense of the horrible letter locked up in my room, in a drawer. As soon as I could compass a private word with Mrs. Grose I declared to her that it was grotesque.

She promptly understood me. "You mean the cruel charge——?"

"It doesn't live an instant. My dear woman, *look* at him!"

She smiled at my pretension to have discovered his charm. "I assure you, Miss, I do nothing else! What will you say, then?" she immediately added.

"In answer to the letter?" I had made up my mind. "Nothing."

"And to his uncle?"

I was incisive. "Nothing."

"And to the boy himself?"

I was wonderful. "Nothing."

She gave with her apron a great wipe to her mouth. "Then I'll stand by you. We'll see it out."

"We'll see it out!" I ardently echoed, giving her my hand to make it a vow.

She held me there a moment, then whisked up her apron again with her detached hand. "Would you mind, Miss, if I used the freedom——"

"To kiss me? No!" I took the good creature in my arms and, after we had embraced like sisters, felt still more fortified and indignant.

This, at all events, was for the time: a time so full that, as I recall the way it went, it reminds me of all the art I now need to make it a little distinct. What I look back at with amazement is the situation I accepted. I had undertaken, with my companion, to see it out, and I was under a charm, apparently, that could smooth away the extent and the far and difficult connections of such an effort. I was lifted aloft on a great wave of infatuation and pity. I found it simple, in my ignorance, my confusion, and perhaps my conceit, to assume that I could deal with a boy whose education for the world was all on the point of beginning. I am unable even to remember at this day what proposal I framed for the end of his holidays and the resumption of his studies. Lessons with me, indeed, that charming summer, we all had a theory that he was to have; but I now feel that, for weeks, the lessons must have been rather my own. I learnt something—at first certainly—that had not been one of the teachings of my small, smothered life; learnt to be amused, and even amusing, and not to think for the morrow. It was the first time, in a manner, that I had known space and air and freedom, all the music of summer and all the mystery of nature. And then there was consideration—and consideration was sweet. Oh, it was a trap—not designed, but deep—to my imagination, to my delicacy, perhaps to my vanity; to whatever, in me, was most excitable. The best way to picture it all is to say that I was off my guard. They gave me so little trouble—they were of a gentleness so extraordinary. I used to speculate—but even this with a dim disconnectedness—as to how the rough future (for all futures are rough!) would handle them and might bruise them. They had the bloom of health and happiness; and yet, as if I had been in charge of a pair of little grandees, of princes of the blood, for whom everything, to be right, would have to be enclosed and protected, the only form that, in my fancy, the after-years could take for them was that of a romantic, a really royal extension of the garden and the park. It may be, of course, above all, that what suddenly broke into this gives the previous time a charm of stillness—that hush in which something gathers or crouches. The change was actually like the spring of a beast.

In the first weeks the days were long; they often, at their finest, gave me what I used to call my own hour, the hour when, for my pupils, tea-time and bed-time having come and gone, I had, before my final retirement, a small interval alone. Much as I liked my companions, this hour was the thing in the day I liked most; and I liked it best of all when, as the light faded—or rather, I should say, the day lingered and the last calls of the last birds sounded, in a flushed sky, from the old trees—I could take a turn into the grounds and enjoy, almost with a sense of property that amused and flattered me, the beauty and dignity of the place. It was a pleasure at these moments to feel myself tranquil and justified; doubtless, perhaps, also to reflect that by my discretion, my quiet good sense and general high propriety, I was giving pleasure—if he ever thought of it!—to the person to whose pressure I had responded. What I was doing was what he had earnestly hoped and directly asked of me, and that I *could*, after all, do it proved even a greater joy than I had expected. I dare say I fancied myself, in short, a remarkable young woman and took comfort in the faith that this would more publicly appear. Well, I needed to be remarkable to offer a front to the remarkable things that presently gave their first sign.

It was plump, one afternoon, in the middle of my very hour: the children were tucked away and I had come out for my stroll. One of the thoughts that, as I don't in the least shrink now from noting, used to be with me in these wanderings was that it would be as charming as a charming story suddenly to meet someone. Someone would appear there at the turn of a path and would stand before me and smile and approve. I didn't ask more than that—I only asked that he should *know*; and the only way to be sure he knew would be to see it, and the kind light of it, in his handsome face. That was exactly present to me—by which I mean the face was—when, on the first of these occasions, at the end of a long June day, I stopped short on emerging from one of the plantations and coming into view of the house. What arrested me on the spot—and with a shock much greater than any vision had allowed for—was the sense that my imagination had, in a flash, turned real. He did stand there!—but high up, beyond the lawn and at the very top of the tower to which, on that first morning, little Flora had conducted me. This tower was one of a pair—square, incongruous, crenelated structures—that were distinguished, for some reason, though I could see little difference, as the new and the old. They flanked opposite ends of the house and were probably architectural absurdities, redeemed in a measure indeed by not being wholly disengaged nor of a height too pretentious, dating, in their gingerbread antiquity, from a romantic revival that was already a respectable past. I admired them, had fancies about them, for we could all profit in a degree, especially when they loomed through the dusk, by the grandeur of their actual battlements; yet it was not at such an elevation that the figure I had so often invoked seemed most in place.

It produced in me, this figure, in the clear twilight, I remember, two distinct gasps of emotion, which were, sharply, the shock of my first and that of my second surprise. My second was a violent perception of the mistake of my first: the man who met my eyes was not the person I had precipitately supposed. There came to me thus a bewilderment of vision of which, after these years, there is no living view that I can hope to give. An unknown man in a lonely place is a permitted object of fear to a young woman privately bred; and the figure that faced me was—a few more seconds assured me—as little anyone else I knew as it was the image that had been in my mind. I had not seen it in Harley Street—I had not seen it anywhere. The place, moreover, in the strangest way in the world, had, on the instant, and by the very fact of its appearance, become a solitude. To me at least, making my statement here with a deliberation with which I have never made it, the whole feeling of the moment returns. It was as if, while I took in—what I did take in—all the rest of the scene had been stricken with death. I can hear again, as I write, the intense hush in which the sounds of evening dropped. The rooks stopped cawing in the golden sky and the friendly hour lost, for the minute, all its voice. But there was no other change in nature, unless indeed it were a change that I saw with a stranger sharpness. The gold was still in the sky, the clearness in the air, and the man who looked at me over the battlements was as definite as a picture in a frame. That's how I thought, with extraordinary quickness, of each person that he might have been and that he was not. We were confronted across our distance quite long enough for me to ask myself with intensity who then he was and to feel, as an effect of my inability to say, a wonder that in a few instants more became intense.

The great question, or one of these, is, afterwards, I know, with regard to certain matters, the question of how long they have lasted. Well, this matter of mine, think what you will of it, lasted while I caught at a dozen possibilities, none of which made a difference for the better, that I could see, in there having been in the house—and for how long, above all?—a person of whom I was in ignorance. It lasted while I just bridled a little with the sense that my office demanded that there should be no such ignorance and no such person. It lasted while this visitant, at all events,—and there was a touch of the strange freedom, as I remember, in the sign of familiarity of his wearing no hat,—seemed to fix me, from his position, with just the question, just the scrutiny through the fading light, that his own presence provoked. We were too far apart to call to each other, but there was a moment at which, at shorter range, some challenge between us, breaking the hush, would have been the right result of our straight mutual stare. He was in one of the angles, the one away from the house, very erect, as it struck me, and with both hands on the ledge. So I saw him as I see the letters I form on this page; then, exactly, after a minute, as if to add to the spectacle, he slowly changed his place—passed, looking at me hard all the while, to the opposite corner of the platform. Yes, I had the sharpest sense that during this transit he never took his eyes from me, and I can see at this moment the way his hand, as he went, passed from one of the crenelations to the next. He stopped at the other corner, but less long, and even as he turned away still markedly fixed me. He turned away; that was all I knew.

IV

It was not that I didn't wait, on this occasion, for more, for I was rooted as deeply as I was shaken. Was there a "secret" at Bly—a mystery of Udolpho or an insane, an unmentionable relative kept in unsuspected confinement? I can't say how long I turned it over, or how long, in a confusion of curiosity and dread, I remained where I had had my collision; I only recall that when I re-entered the house darkness had quite closed in. Agitation, in the interval, certainly had held me and driven me, for I must, in circling about the place, have walked three miles; but I was to be, later on, so much more overwhelmed that this mere dawn of alarm was a comparatively human chill. The most singular part of it in fact—singular as the rest had been—was the part I became, in the hall, aware of in meeting Mrs. Grose. This picture comes back to me in the general train—the impression, as I received it on my return, of the wide white panelled space, bright in the lamplight and with its portraits and red carpet, and of the good surprised look of my friend, which immediately told me she had missed me. It came to me straightway, under her contact, that, with plain heartiness, mere relieved anxiety at my appearance, she knew nothing whatever that could bear upon the incident I had there ready for her. I had not suspected in advance that her comfortable face would pull me up, and I somehow measured the importance of what I had seen by my thus finding myself hesitate to mention it. Scarce anything in the whole history seems to me so odd as this fact that my real beginning of fear was one, as I may say, with the instinct of sparing my companion. On the spot, accordingly, in the pleasant hall and with her eyes on me, I, for a reason that I couldn't then have phrased, achieved an inward revolution—offered a vague pretext for my lateness and, with the plea of the beauty of the night and of the heavy dew and wet feet, went as soon as possible to my room.

Here it was another affair; here, for many days after, it was a queer affair enough. There were hours, from day to day,—or at least there were moments, snatched even from clear duties,—when I had to shut myself up to think. It was not so much yet that I was more nervous than I could bear to be as that I was remarkably afraid of becoming so; for the truth I had now to turn over was, simply and clearly, the truth that I could arrive at no account whatever of the visitor with whom I had been so inexplicably and yet, as it seemed to me, so intimately concerned. It took little time to see that I could sound without forms of inquiry and without exciting remark any domestic complication. The shock I had suffered must have sharpened all my senses; I felt sure, at the end of three days and as the result of mere closer attention, that I had not been practised upon by the servants nor made the object of any "game." Of whatever it was that I knew nothing was known around me. There was but one sane inference: someone had taken a liberty rather gross. That was what, repeatedly, I dipped into my room and locked the door to say to myself. We had been, collectively, subject to an intrusion; some unscrupulous traveller, curious in old houses, had made his way in unobserved, enjoyed the prospect from the best point of view, and then stolen out as he came. If he had given me such a bold hard stare, that was but a part of his indiscretion. The good thing, after all, was that we should surely see no more of him.

This was not so good a thing, I admit, as not to leave me to judge that what, essentially, made nothing else much signify was simply my charming work. My charming work was just my life with Miles and Flora, and through nothing could I so like it as through feeling that I could throw myself into it in trouble. The attraction of my small charges was a constant joy, leading me to wonder afresh at the vanity of my original fears, the distaste I had begun by entertaining for the probable grey prose of my office. There was to be no grey prose, it appeared, and no long grind; so how could work not be charming that presented itself as daily beauty? It was all the romance of the nursery and the poetry of the schoolroom. I don't mean by this, of course, that we studied only fiction and verse; I mean I can express no otherwise the sort of interest my companions inspired. How can I describe that except by saying that instead of growing used to them—and it's a marvel for a governess: I call the sisterhood to witness!—I made constant fresh discoveries. There was one direction, assuredly, in which these discoveries stopped: deep obscurity continued to cover the region of the boy's conduct at school. It had been promptly given me, I have noted, to face that mystery without a pang. Perhaps even it would be nearer the truth to say that—without a word—he himself had cleared it up. He had made the whole charge absurd. My conclusion bloomed there with the real rose-flush of his innocence: he was only too fine and fair for the little horrid, unclean school-world, and he had paid a price for it. I reflected acutely that the sense of such differences, such superiorities of quality, always, on the part of the majority—which could include even stupid, sordid head-masters—turns infallibly to the vindictive.

Both the children had a gentleness (it was their only fault, and it never made Miles a muff) that kept them—how shall I express it?—almost impersonal and certainly quite unpunishable. They were like the cherubs of the anecdote, who had—morally at any rate—nothing to whack! I remember feeling with Miles in especial as if he had had, as it were, no history. We expect of a small child a scant one, but there was in this beautiful little boy something extraordinarily sensitive, yet extraordinarily happy, that, more than in any creature of his age I have seen, struck me as beginning anew each day. He had never for a second suffered. I took this as a direct disproof of his having really been chastised. If he had been wicked he would have "caught" it, and I should have caught it by the rebound—I should have found the trace. I found nothing at all, and he was therefore an angel. He never spoke of his school, never mentioned a comrade or a master; and I, for my part, was quite too much disgusted to allude to them. Of course I was under the spell, and the wonderful part is that, even at the time, I perfectly knew I was. But I gave myself up to it; it was an antidote to any pain, and I had more pains than one. I was in receipt in these days of disturbing letters from home, where things were not going well. But with my children, what things in the world mattered? That was the question I used to put to my scrappy retirements. I was dazzled by their loveliness.

There was a Sunday—to get on—when it rained with such force and for so many hours that there could be no procession to church; in consequence of which, as the day declined, I had arranged with Mrs. Grose that, should the evening show improvement, we would attend together the late service. The rain happily stopped, and I prepared for our walk, which through the park and by the good road to the village, would be a matter of twenty minutes. Coming downstairs to meet my colleague in the hall, I remembered a pair of gloves that had required three stitches and that had received them—with a publicity perhaps not edifying—while I sat with the children at their tea, served on Sundays, by exception, in that cold, clean temple of mahogany and brass, the "grown-up" dining-room. The gloves had been dropped there, and I turned in to recover them. The day was grey enough, but the afternoon light still lingered, and it enabled me, on crossing the threshold, not only to recognise, on a chair near the wide window, then closed, the articles I wanted, but to become aware of a person on the other side of the window and looking straight in. One step into the room had sufficed; my vision was instantaneous; it was all there. The person looking straight in was the person who had already appeared to me. He appeared thus again with I won't say greater distinctness, for that was impossible, but with a nearness that represented a forward stride in our intercourse and made me, as I met him, catch my breath and turn cold. He was the same—he was the same, and seen, this time, as he had been seen before, from the waist up, the window, though the dining-room was on the ground-floor, not going down to the terrace on which he stood. His face was close to the glass, yet the effect of this better view was, strangely, only to show me how intense the former had been. He remained but a few seconds—long enough to convince me he also saw and recognised; but it was as if I had been looking at him for years and had known him always. Something, however, happened this time that had not happened before; his stare into my face, through the glass and across the room, was as deep and hard as then, but it quitted me for a moment during which I could still watch it, see it fix successively several other things. On the spot there came to me the added shock of a certitude that it was not for me he had come there. He had come for someone else.

The flash of this knowledge—for it was knowledge in the midst of dread—produced in me the most extraordinary effect, started, as I stood there, a sudden vibration of duty and courage. I say courage because I was beyond all doubt already far gone. I bounded straight out of the door again, reached that of the house, got, in an instant, upon the drive, and, passing along the terrace as fast as I could rush, turned a corner and came full in sight. But it was in sight of nothing now—my visitor had vanished. I stopped, I almost dropped, with the real relief of this; but I took in the whole scene—I gave him time to reappear. I call it time, but how long was it? I can't speak to the purpose today of the duration of these things. That kind of measure must have left me: they couldn't have lasted as they actually appeared to me to last. The terrace and the whole place, the lawn and the garden beyond it, all I could see of the park, were empty with a great emptiness. There were shrubberies and big trees, but I remember the clear assurance I felt that none of them concealed him. He was there or was not there: not there if I didn't see him. I got hold of this; then, instinctively, instead of returning as I had come, went to the window. It was confusedly present to me that I ought to place myself where he had stood. I did so; I applied my face to the pane and looked, as he had looked, into the room. As if, at this moment, to show me exactly what his range had been, Mrs. Grose, as I had done for himself just before, came in from the hall. With this I had the full image of a repetition of what had already occurred. She saw me as I had seen my own visitant; she pulled up short as I had done; I gave her something of the shock that I had received. She turned white, and this made me ask myself if I had blanched as much. She stared, in short, and retreated on just *my* lines, and I knew she had then passed out and come round to me and that I should presently meet her. I remained where I was, and while I waited I thought of more things than one. But there's only one I take space to mention. I wondered why *she* should be scared.

V

OH, SHE let me know as soon as, round the corner of the house, she loomed again into view. "What in the name of goodness is the matter ——?" She was now flushed and out of breath.

I said nothing till she came quite near. "With me?" I must have made a wonderful face. "Do I show it?"

"You're as white as a sheet. You look awful."

I considered; I could meet on this, without scruple, any innocence. My need to respect the bloom of Mrs. Grose's had dropped, without a rustle, from my shoulders, and if I wavered for the instant it was not with what I kept back. I put out my hand to her and she took it; I held her hard a little, liking to feel her close to me. There was a kind of support in the shy heave of her surprise. "You came for me for church, of course, but I can't go."

"Has anything happened?"

"Yes. You must know now. Did I look very queer?"

"Through this window? Dreadful!"

"Well," I said, "I've been frightened." Mrs. Grose's eyes expressed plainly that *she* had no wish to be, yet also that she knew too well her place not to be ready to share with me any marked inconvenience. Oh, it was quite settled that she *must* share! "Just what you saw from the dining-room a minute ago was the effect of that. What *I* saw—just before—was much worse."

Her hand tightened. "What was it?"

"An extraordinary man. Looking in."

"What extraordinary man?"

"I haven't the least idea."

Mrs. Grose gazed around us in vain. "Then where is he gone?"

"I know still less."

"Have you seen him before?"

"Yes—once. On the old tower."

She could only look at me harder. "Do you mean he's a stranger?"

"Oh, very much!"

"Yet you didn't tell me?"

"No—for reasons. But now that you've guessed——"

Mrs. Grose's round eyes encountered this charge. "Ah, I haven't guessed!" she said very simply. "How can I if *you* don't imagine?"

"I don't in the very least."

"You've seen him nowhere but on the tower?"

"And on this spot just now."

Mrs. Grose looked round again. "What was he doing on the tower?"

"Only standing there and looking down at me."

She thought a minute. "Was he a gentleman?"

I found I had no need to think. "No." She gazed in deeper wonder. "No."

"Then nobody about the place? Nobody from the village?"

"Nobody—nobody. I didn't tell you, but I made sure."

She breathed a vague relief: this was, oddly, so much to the good. It only went indeed a little way. "But if he isn't a gentleman——"

"What *is* he? He's a horror."

"A horror?"

"He's—God help me if I know *what* he is!"

Mrs. Grose looked round once more; she fixed her eyes on the duskier distance, then, pulling herself together, turned to me with abrupt inconsequence. "It's time we should be at church."

"Oh, I'm not fit for church!"

"Won't it do you good?"

"It won't do *them* ——!" I nodded at the house.

"The children?"

"I can't leave them now."

"You're afraid ——?"

I spoke boldly. "I'm afraid of *him.*"

Mrs. Grose's large face showed me, at this, for the first time, the far-away faint glimmer of a consciousness more acute: I somehow made out in it the delayed dawn of an idea I myself had not given her and that was as yet quite obscure to me. It comes back to me that I thought instantly of this as something I could get from her; and I felt it to be connected with the desire she presently showed to know more. "When was it—on the tower?"

"About the middle of the month. At this same hour."

"Almost at dark," said Mrs. Grose.

"Oh no, not nearly. I saw him as I see you."

"Then how did he get in?"

"And how did he get out?" I laughed. "I had no opportunity to ask him! This evening, you see," I pursued, "he has not been able to get in."

"He only peeps?"

"I hope it will be confined to that!" She had now let go my hand; she turned away a little. I waited an instant; then I brought out: "Go to church. Good-bye. I must watch."

Slowly she faced me again. "Do you fear for them?"

We met in another long look. "Don't *you*?" Instead of answering she came nearer to the window and, for a minute, applied her face to the glass. "You see how he could see," I meanwhile went on.

She didn't move. "How long was he here?"

"Till I came out. I came to meet him."

Mrs. Grose at last turned round, and there was still more in her face. "*I* couldn't have come out."

"Neither could I!" I laughed again. "But I did come. I have my duty."

"So have I mine," she replied; after which she added: "What is he like?"

"I've been dying to tell you. But he's like nobody."

"Nobody?" she echoed.

"He has no hat." Then seeing in her face that she already, in this, with a deeper dismay, found a touch of picture, I quickly added stroke to stroke. "He has red hair, very red, close-curling, and a pale face, long in shape, with straight, good features and little, rather queer whiskers that are as red as his hair. His eyebrows are, somehow, darker; they look particularly arched and as if they might move a good deal. His eyes are sharp, strange—awfully; but I only know clearly that they're rather small and very fixed. His mouth's wide, and his lips are thin, and except for his little whiskers he's quite clean-shaven. He gives me a sort of sense of looking like an actor."

"An actor!" It was impossible to resemble one less, at least, than Mrs. Grose at that moment.

"I've never seen one, but so I suppose them. He's tall, active, erect," I continued, "but never—no, never!—a gentleman."

My companion's face had blanched as I went on; her round eyes started and her mild mouth gaped. "A gentleman?" she gasped, confounded, stupefied: "a gentleman *he*?"

"You know him then?"

She visibly tried to hold herself. "But he *is* handsome?"

I saw the way to help her. "Remarkably!"

"And dressed ——?"

"In somebody's clothes. They're smart, but they're not his own."

She broke into a breathless affirmative groan. "They're the master's!"

I caught it up. "You *do* know him?"

She faltered but a second. "Quint!" she cried.

"Quint?"

"Peter Quint—his own man, his valet, when he was here!"

"When the master was?"

Gaping still, but meeting me, she pieced it all together. "He never wore his hat, but he did wear—well, there were waistcoats missed! They were both here—last year. Then the master went, and Quint was alone."

I followed, but halting a little. "Alone?"

"Alone with *us*." Then, as from a deeper depth, "In charge," she added.

"And what became of him?"

She hung fire so long that I was still more mystified. "He went too," she brought out at last.

"Went where?"

Her expression, at this, became extraordinary. "God knows where! He died."

"Died?" I almost shrieked.

She seemed fairly to square herself, plant herself more firmly to utter the wonder of it. "Yes. Mr. Quint is dead."

VI

It took of course more than that particular passage to place us together in presence of what we had now to live with as we could —my dreadful liability to impressions of the order so vividly exemplified, and my companion's knowledge, henceforth,—a knowledge half consternation and half compassion,—of that liability. There had been, this evening, after the revelation that left me, for an hour, so prostrate—there had been, for either of us, no attendance on any service but a little service of tears and vows, of prayers and promises, a climax to the series of mutual challenges and pledges that had straightway ensued on our retreating together to the schoolroom and shutting ourselves up there to have everything out. The result of our having everything out was simply to reduce our situation to the last rigour of its elements. She herself had seen nothing, not the shadow of a shadow, and nobody in the house but the governess was in the governess's plight; yet she accepted without directly impugning my sanity the truth as I gave it to her, and ended by showing me, on this ground, an awe-stricken tenderness, an expression of the sense of my more than questionable privilege, of which the very breath has remained with me as that of the sweetest of human charities.

What was settled between us, accordingly, that night, was that we thought we might bear things together; and I was not even sure that, in spite of her exemption, it was she who had the best of the burden. I knew at this hour, I think, as well as I knew later what I was capable of meeting to shelter my pupils; but it took me some time to be wholly sure of what my honest ally was prepared for to keep terms with so compromising a contract. I was queer company enough—quite as queer as the company I received; but as I trace over what we went through I see how much common ground we must have found in the one idea that, by good fortune, *could* steady us. It was the idea, the second movement, that led me straight out, as I may say, of the inner chamber of my dread. I could take the air in the court, at least, and there Mrs. Grose could join me. Perfectly can I recall now the particular way strength came to me before we separated for the night. We had gone over and over every feature of what I had seen.

"He was looking for someone else, you say—someone who was not you?"

"He was looking for little Miles." A portentous clearness now possessed me. "*That's* whom he was looking for."

"But how do you know?"

"I know, I know, I know!" My exaltation grew. "And *you* know, my dear!"

She didn't deny this, but I required, I felt, not even so much telling as that. She resumed in a moment, at any rate: "What if *he* should see him?"

"Little Miles? That's what he wants!"

She looked immensely scared again. "The child?"

"Heaven forbid! The man. He wants to appear to *them*." That he might was an awful conception, and yet, somehow, I could keep it at bay; which, moreover, as we lingered there, was what I succeeded in practically proving. I had an absolute certainty that I should see again what I had already seen, but something within me said that by offering myself bravely as the sole subject of such experience, by accepting, by inviting, by surmounting it all, I should serve as an expiatory victim and guard the tranquillity of my companions. The children, in especial, I should thus fence about and absolutely save. I recall one of the last things I said that night to Mrs. Grose.

"It does strike me that my pupils have never mentioned——"

She looked at me hard as I musingly pulled up. "His having been here and the time they were with him?"

"The time they were with him, and his name, his presence, his history, in any way."

"Oh, the little lady doesn't remember. She never heard or knew."

"The circumstances of his death?" I thought with some intensity. "Perhaps not. But Miles would remember—Miles would know."

"Ah, don't try him!" broke from Mrs. Grose.

I returned her the look she had given me. "Don't be afraid." I continued to think. "It *is* rather odd."

"That he has never spoken of him?"

"Never by the least allusion. And you tell me they were 'great friends'?"

"Oh, it wasn't *him*!" Mrs. Grose with emphasis declared. "It was Quint's own fancy. To play with him, I mean—to spoil him." She paused a moment; then she added: "Quint was much too free."

This gave me, straight from my vision of his face—*such* a face!—a sudden sickness of disgust. "Too free with *my* boy?"

"Too free with everyone!"

I forbore, for the moment, to analyse this description further than by the reflection that a part of it applied to several of the members of the household, of the half-dozen maids and men who were still of our small colony. But there was everything, for our apprehension, in the lucky fact that no discomfortable legend, no perturbation of scullions, had ever, within anyone's memory, attached to the kind old place. It had neither bad name nor ill fame, and Mrs. Grose, most apparently, only desired to cling to me and to quake in silence. I even put her, the very last thing of all, to the test. It was when, at midnight, she had her hand on the schoolroom door to take leave. "I have it from you then—for it's of great importance—that he was definitely and admittedly bad?"

"Oh, not admittedly. *I* knew it—but the master didn't."

"And you never told him?"

"Well, he didn't like tale-bearing—he hated complaints. He was terribly short with anything of that kind, and if people were all right to *him* ——"

"He wouldn't be bothered with more?" This squared well enough with my impression of him: he was not a trouble-loving gentleman, nor so very particular perhaps about some of the company *he* kept. All the same, I pressed my interlocutress. "I promise you *I* would have told!"

She felt my discrimination. "I dare say I was wrong. But, really, I was afraid."

"Afraid of what?"

"Of things that man could do. Quint was so clever—he was so deep."

I took this in still more than, probably, I showed. "You weren't afraid of anything else? Not of his effect ——?"

"His effect?" she repeated with a face of anguish and waiting while I faltered.

"On innocent little precious lives. They were in your charge."

"No, they were not in mine!" she roundly and distressfully returned. "The master believed in him and placed him here because he was supposed not to be well and the country air so good for him. So he had everything to say. Yes"—she let me have it—"even about *them*."

"Them—that creature?" I had to smother a kind of howl. "And you could bear it!"

"No. I couldn't—and I can't now!" And the poor woman burst into tears.

A rigid control, from the next day, was, as I have said, to follow them; yet how often and how passionately, for a week, we came back together to the subject! Much as we had discussed it that Sunday night, I was, in the immediate later hours in especial—for it may be imagined whether I slept—still haunted with the shadow of something she had not told me. I myself had kept back nothing, but there was a word Mrs. Grose had kept back. I was sure, moreover, by morning, that this was not from a failure of frankness, but because on every side there were fears. It seems to me indeed, in retrospect, that by the time the morrow's sun was high I had restlessly read into the facts before us almost all the meaning they were to receive from subsequent and more cruel occurrences. What they gave me above all was just the sinister figure of the living man—the dead one would keep awhile!—and of the months he had continuously passed at Bly, which, added up, made a formidable stretch. The limit of this evil time had arrived only when, on the dawn of a winter's morning, Peter Quint was found, by a labourer going to early work, stone dead on the road from the village: a catastrophe explained—superficially at least—by a visible wound to his head; such a wound as might have been produced—and as, on the final evidence, *had* been—by a fatal slip, in the dark and after leaving the public house, on the steepish icy slope, a wrong path altogether, at the bottom of which he lay. The icy slope, the turn mistaken at night and in liquor, accounted for much—practically, in the end and after the inquest and boundless chatter, for everything; but there had been matters in his life—strange passages and perils, secret disorders, vices more than suspected—that would have accounted for a good deal more.

I scarce know how to put my story into words that shall be a credible picture of my state of mind; but I was in these days literally able to find a joy in the extraordinary flight of heroism the occasion demanded of me. I now saw that I had been asked for a service admirable and difficult; and there would be a greatness in letting it be seen—oh, in the right quarter! that I could succeed where many another girl might have failed. It was an immense help to me—I confess I rather applaud myself as I look back!—that I saw my service so strongly and so simply. I was there to protect and defend the little creatures in the world the most bereaved and the most loveable, the appeal of whose helplessness had suddenly become only too explicit, a deep, constant ache of one's own committed heart. We were cut off, really, together; we were united in our danger. They had nothing but me, and I—well, I had *them*. It was in short a magnificent chance. This chance presented itself to me in an image richly material. I was a screen—I was to stand before them. The more I saw, the less they would. I began to watch them in a stifled suspense, a disguised excitement that might well, had it continued too long, have turned to something like madness. What saved me, as I now see, was that it turned to something else altogether. It didn't last as suspense—it was superseded by horrible proofs. Proofs, I say, yes—from the moment I really took hold.

This moment dated from an afternoon hour that I happened to spend in the grounds with the younger of my pupils alone. We had left Miles indoors, on the red cushion of a deep window-seat; he had wished to finish a book, and I had been glad to encourage a purpose so laudable in a young man whose only defect was an occasional excess of the restless. His sister, on the contrary, had been alert to come out, and I strolled with her half an hour, seeking the shade, for the sun was still high and the day exceptionally warm. I was aware afresh, with her, as we went, of how, like her brother, she contrived—it was the charming thing in both children—to let me alone without appearing to drop me and to accompany me without appearing to surround. They were never importunate and yet never listless. My attention to them all really went to seeing them amuse themselves immensely without me: this was a spectacle they seemed actively to prepare and that engaged me as an active admirer. I walked in a world of their invention—they had no occasion whatever to draw upon mine; so that my time was taken only with being, for them, some remarkable person or thing that the game of the moment required and that was merely, thanks to my superior, my exalted stamp, a happy and highly distinguished sinecure. I forget what I was on the present occasion; I only remember that I was something very important and very quiet and that Flora was playing very hard. We were on the edge of the lake, and, as we had lately begun geography, the lake was the Sea of Azof.

Suddenly, in these circumstances, I became aware that, on the other side of the Sea of Azof, we had an interested spectator. The way this knowledge gathered in me was the strangest thing in the world—the strangest, that is, except the very much stranger in which it quickly merged itself. I had sat down with a piece of work—for I was something or other that could sit—on the old stone bench which overlooked the pond; and in this position I began to take in with certitude, and yet without direct vision, the presence, at a distance, of a third person. The old trees, the thick shrubbery, made a great and pleasant shade, but it was all suffused with the brightness of the hot, still hour. There was no ambiguity in anything; none whatever, at least, in the conviction I from one moment to another found myself forming as to what I should see straight before me and across the lake as a consequence of raising my eyes. They were attached at this juncture to the stitching in which I was engaged, and I can feel once more the spasm of my effort not to move them till I should so have steadied myself as to be able to make up my mind what to do. There was an alien object in view—a figure whose right of presence I instantly, passionately questioned. I recollect counting over perfectly the possibilities, reminding myself that nothing was more natural, for instance, than the appearance of one of the men about the place, or even of a messenger, a postman or a tradesman's boy, from the village. That reminder had as little effect on my practical certitude as I was conscious—still even without looking—of its having upon the character and attitude of our visitor. Nothing was more natural than that these things should be the other things that they absolutely were not.

Of the positive identity of the apparition I would assure myself as soon as the small clock of my courage should have ticked out the right second; meanwhile, with an effort that was already sharp enough, I transferred my eyes straight to little Flora, who, at the moment, was about ten yards away. My heart had stood still for an instant with the wonder and terror of the question whether she too would see; and I held my breath while I waited for what a cry from her, what some sudden innocent sign either of interest or of alarm, would tell me. I waited, but nothing came; then, in the first place—and there is something more dire in this, I feel, than in anything I have to relate—I was determined by a sense that, within a minute, all sounds from her had previously dropped; and, in the second, by the circumstance that, also within the minute, she had, in her play, turned her back to the water. This was her attitude when I at last looked at her—looked with the confirmed conviction that we were still, together, under direct personal notice. She had picked up a small flat piece of wood, which happened to have in it a little hole that had evidently suggested to her the idea of sticking in another fragment that might figure as a mast and make the thing a boat. This second morsel, as I watched her, she was very markedly and intently attempting to tighten in its place. My apprehension of what she was doing sustained me so that after some seconds I felt I was ready for more. Then I again shifted my eyes—I faced what I had to face.

VII

I GOT hold of Mrs. Grose as soon after this as I could; and I can give no intelligible account of how I fought out the interval. Yet I still hear myself cry as I fairly threw myself into her arms: "They *know*—it's too monstrous: they know, they know!"

"And what on earth——?" I felt her incredulity as she held me.

"Why, all that *we* know—and heaven knows what else besides!" Then, as she released me, I made it out to her, made it out perhaps only now with full coherency even to myself. "Two hours ago, in the garden"—I could scarce articulate—"Flora *saw!*"

Mrs. Grose took it as she might have taken a blow in the stomach. "She has told you?" she panted.

"Not a word—that's the horror. She kept it to herself! The child of eight, *that* child!" Unutterable still, for me, was the stupefaction of it.

Mrs. Grose, of course, could only gape the wider. "Then how do you know?"

"I was there—I saw with my eyes: saw that she was perfectly aware."

"Do you mean aware of *him?*"

"No—of *her.*" I was conscious as I spoke that I looked prodigious things, for I got the slow reflection of them in my companion's face. "Another person—this time; but a figure of quite as unmistakeable horror and evil: a woman in black, pale and dreadful—with such an air also, and such a face!—on the other side of the lake. I was there with the child—quiet for the hour; and in the midst of it she came."

"Came how—from where?"

"From where they come from! She just appeared and stood there—but not so near."

"And without coming nearer?"

"Oh, for the effect and the feeling, she might have been as close as you!"

My friend, with an odd impulse, fell back a step. "Was she someone you've never seen?"

"Yes. But someone the child has. Someone *you* have." Then, to show how I had thought it all out: "My predecessor—the one who died."

"Miss Jessel?"

"Miss Jessel. You don't believe me?" I pressed.

She turned right and left in her distress. "How can you be sure?"

This drew from me, in the state of my nerves, a flash of impatience. "Then ask Flora—*she's* sure!" But I had no sooner spoken than I caught myself up. "No, for God's sake, *don't!* She'll say she isn't—she'll lie!"

Mrs. Grose was not too bewildered instinctively to protest. "Ah, how *can* you?"

"Because I'm clear. Flora doesn't want me to know."

"It's only then to spare you."

"No, no—there are depths, depths! The more I go over it, the more I see in it, and the more I see in it the more I fear. I don't know what I *don't* see—what I *don't* fear!"

Mrs. Grose tried to keep up with me. "You mean you're afraid of seeing her again?"

"Oh, no; that's nothing—now!" Then I explained. "It's of *not* seeing her."

But my companion only looked wan. "I don't understand you."

"Why, it's that the child may keep it up—and that the child assuredly *will*—without my knowing it."

At the image of this possibility Mrs. Grose for a moment collapsed, yet presently to pull herself together again, as if from the positive force of the sense of what, should we yield an inch, there would really be to give way to. "Dear, dear—we must keep our heads! And after all, if she doesn't mind it——!" She even tried a grim joke. "Perhaps she likes it!"

"Likes *such* things—a scrap of an infant!"

"Isn't it just a proof of her blessed innocence?" my friend bravely inquired.

She brought me, for the instant, almost round. "Oh, we must clutch at *that*—we must cling to it! If it isn't a proof of what you say, it's a proof of—God knows what! For the woman's a horror of horrors."

Mrs. Grose, at this, fixed her eyes a minute on the ground; then at last raising them, "Tell me how you know," she said.

"Then you admit it's what she was?" I cried.

"Tell me how you know," my friend simply repeated.

"Know? By seeing her! By the way she looked."

"At you, do you mean—so wickedly?"

"Dear me, no—I could have borne that. She gave me never a glance. She only fixed the child."

Mrs. Grose tried to see it. "Fixed her?"

"Ah, with such awful eyes!"

She stared at mine as if they might really have resembled them. "Do you mean of dislike?"

"God help us, no. Of something much worse."

"Worse than dislike?"—this left her indeed at a loss.

"With a determination—indescribable. With a kind of fury of intention."

I made her turn pale. "Intention?"

"To get hold of her." Mrs. Grose—her eyes just lingering on mine—gave a shudder and walked to the window; and while she stood there looking out I completed my statement. "*That's* what Flora knows."

After a little she turned round. "The person was in black, you say?"

"In mourning—rather poor, almost shabby. But—yes—with extraordinary beauty." I now recognised to what I had at last, stroke by stroke, brought the victim of my confidence, for she quite visibly weighed this. "Oh, handsome—very, very," I insisted; "wonderfully handsome. But infamous."

She slowly came back to me. "Miss Jessel—*was* infamous." She once more took my hand in both her own, holding it as tight as if to fortify me against the increase of alarm I might draw from this disclosure. "They were both infamous," she finally said.

So, for a little, we faced it once more together; and I found absolutely a degree of help in seeing it now so straight. "I appreciate," I said, "the great decency of your not having hitherto spoken; but the time has certainly come to give me the whole thing." She appeared to assent to this, but still only in silence; seeing which I went on: "I must have it now. Of what did she die? Come, there was something between them."

"There was everything."

"In spite of the difference——?"

"Oh, of their rank, their condition"—she brought it woefully out. "*She* was a lady."

I turned it over; I again saw. "Yes—she was a lady."

"And he so dreadfully below," said Mrs. Grose.

I felt that I doubtless needn't press too hard, in such company, on the place of a servant in the scale; but there was nothing to prevent an acceptance of my companion's own measure of my predecessor's abasement. There was a way to deal with that, and I dealt; the more readily for my full vision—on the evidence—of our employer's late clever, good-looking "own" man; impudent, assured, spoiled, depraved. "The fellow was a hound."

Mrs. Grose considered as if it were perhaps a little a case for a sense of shades. "I've never seen one like him. He did what he wished."

"With *her*?"

"With them all."

It was as if now in my friend's own eyes Miss Jessel had again appeared. I seemed at any rate, for an instant, to see their evocation of her as distinctly as I had seen her by the pond; and I brought out with decision: "It must have been also what *she* wished!"

Mrs. Grose's face signified that it had been indeed, but she said at the same time: "Poor woman—she paid for it!"

"Then you do know what she died of?" I asked.

"No—I know nothing. I wanted not to know; I was glad enough I didn't; and I thanked heaven she was well out of this!"

"Yet you had, then, your idea——"

"Of her real reason for leaving? Oh, yes—as to that. She couldn't have stayed. Fancy it here—for a governess! And afterwards I imagined—and I still imagine. And what I imagine is dreadful."

"Not so dreadful as what *I* do," I replied; on which I must have shown her—as I was indeed but too conscious—a front of miserable defeat. It brought out again all her compassion for me, and at the renewed touch of her kindness my power to resist broke down. I burst, as I had, the other time, made her burst, into tears; she took me to her motherly breast, and my lamentation overflowed. "I don't do it!" I sobbed in despair; "I don't save or shield them! It's far worse than I dreamed—they're lost!"

VIII

WHAT I had said to Mrs. Grose was true enough: there were in the matter I had put before her depths and possibilities that I lacked resolution to sound; so that when we met once more in the wonder of it we were of a common mind about the duty of resistance to extravagant fancies. We were to keep our heads if we should keep nothing else—difficult indeed as that might be in the face of what, in our prodigious experience, was least to be questioned. Late that night, while the house slept, we had another talk in my room, when she went all the way with me as to its being beyond doubt that I had seen exactly what I had seen. To hold her perfectly in the pinch of that, I found I had only to ask her how, if I had "made it up," I came to be able to give, of each of the persons appearing to me, a picture disclosing, to the last detail, their special marks—a portrait on the exhibition of which she had instantly recognised and named them. She wished, of course,—small blame to her!—to sink the whole subject; and I was quick to assure her that my own interest in it had now violently taken the form of a search for the way to escape from it. I encountered her on the ground of a probability that with recurrence—for recurrence we took for granted—I should get used to my danger, distinctly professing that my personal exposure had suddenly become the least of my discomforts. It was my new suspicion that was intolerable; and yet even to this complication the later hours of the day had brought a little ease.

On leaving her, after my first outbreak, I had of course returned to my pupils, associating the right remedy for my dismay with that sense of their charm which I had already found to be a thing I could positively cultivate and which had never failed me yet. I had simply, in other words, plunged afresh into Flora's special society and there become aware—it was almost a luxury!—that she could put her little conscious hand straight upon the spot that ached. She had looked at me in sweet speculation and then had accused me to my face of having "cried." I had supposed I had brushed away the ugly signs: but I could literally—for the time, at all events—rejoice, under this fathomless charity, that they had not entirely disappeared. To gaze into the depths of blue of the child's eyes and pronounce their loveliness a trick of premature cunning was to be guilty of a cynicism in preference to which I naturally preferred to abjure my judgment and, so far as might be, my agitation. I couldn't abjure for merely wanting to, but I could repeat to Mrs. Grose—as I did there, over and over, in the small hours—that with their voices in the air, their pressure on one's heart and their fragrant faces against one's cheek, everything fell to the ground but their incapacity and their beauty. It was a pity that, somehow, to settle this once for all, I had equally to re-enumerate the signs of subtlety that, in the afternoon, by the lake, had made a miracle of my show of self-possession. It was a pity to be obliged to re-investigate the certitude of the moment itself and repeat how it had come to me as a revelation that the inconceivable communion I then surprised was a matter, for either party, of habit. It was a pity that I should have had to quaver out again the reasons for my not having, in my delusion, so much as questioned that the little girl saw our visitant even as I actually saw Mrs. Grose herself, and that she wanted, by just so much as she did thus see, to make me suppose she didn't, and at the same time, without showing anything, arrive at a guess as to whether I myself did! It was a pity that I needed once more to describe the portentous little activity by which she sought to divert my attention—the perceptible increase of movement, the greater intensity of play, the singing, the gabbling of nonsense, and the invitation to romp.

Yet if I had not indulged, to prove there was nothing in it, in this review, I should have missed the two or three dim elements of comfort that still remained to me. I should not for instance have been able to asseverate to my friend that I was certain—which was so much to the good—that *I* at least had not betrayed myself. I should not have been prompted, by stress of need, by desperation of mind,—I scarce know what to call it,—to invoke such further aid to intelligence as might spring from pushing my colleague fairly to the wall. She had told me, bit by bit, under pressure, a great deal; but a small shifty spot on the wrong side of it all still sometimes brushed my brow like the wing of a bat; and I remember how on this occasion—for the sleeping house and the concentration alike of our danger and our watch seemed to help—I felt the importance of giving the last jerk to the curtain. "I don't believe anything so horrible," I recollect saying; "no, let us put it definitely, my dear, that I don't. But if I did, you know, there's a thing I should require now, just without sparing you the least bit more—oh, not a scrap, come!—to get out of you. What was it you had in mind when, in our distress, before Miles came back, over the letter from his school, you said, under my insistence, that you didn't pretend for him that he had not literally *ever* been 'bad'? He has *not* literally 'ever,' in these weeks that I myself have lived with him and so closely watched him; he has been an imperturbable little prodigy of delightful, loveable goodness. Therefore you might perfectly have made the claim for him if you had not, as it happened, seen an exception to take. What was your exception, and to what passage in your personal observation of him did you refer?"

It was a dreadfully austere inquiry, but levity was not our note, and, at any rate, before the grey dawn admonished us to separate I had got my answer. What my friend had had in mind proved to be immensely to the purpose. It was neither more nor less than the circumstance that for a period of several months Quint and the boy had been perpetually together. It was in fact the very appropriate truth that she had ventured to criticise the propriety, to hint at the incongruity, of so close an alliance, and even to go so far on the subject as a frank overture to Miss Jessel. Miss Jessel had, with a most strange manner, requested her to mind her business, and the good woman had, on this, directly approached little Miles. What she had said to him, since I pressed, was that *she* liked to see young gentlemen not forget their station.

I pressed again, of course, at this. "You reminded him that Quint was only a base menial?"

"As you might say! And it was his answer, for one thing, that was bad."

"And for another thing?" I waited. "He repeated your words to Quint?"

"No, not that. It's just what he *wouldn't!*" she could still impress upon me. "I was sure, at any rate," she added, "that he didn't. But he denied certain occasions."

"What occasions?"

"When they had been about together quite as if Quint were his tutor—and a very grand one—and Miss Jessel only for the little lady. When he had gone off with the fellow, I mean, and spent hours with him."

"He then prevaricated about it—he said he hadn't?" Her assent was clear enough to cause me to add in a moment: "I see. He lied."

"Oh!" Mrs. Grose mumbled. This was a suggestion that it didn't matter; which indeed she backed up by a further remark. "You see, after all, Miss Jessel didn't mind. She didn't forbid him."

I considered. "Did he put that to you as a justification?"

At this she dropped again. "No, he never spoke of it."

"Never mentioned her in connection with Quint?"

She saw, visibly flushing, where I was coming out. "Well, he didn't show anything. He denied," she repeated; "he denied."

Lord, how I pressed her now! "So that you could see he knew what was between the two wretches?"

"I don't know—I don't know!" the poor woman groaned.

"You do know, you dear thing," I replied; "only you haven't my dreadful boldness of mind, and you keep back, out of timidity and modesty and delicacy, even the impression that, in the past, when you had, without my aid, to flounder about in silence, most of all made you miserable. But I shall get it out of you yet! There was something in the boy that suggested to you," I continued, "that he covered and concealed their relation."

"Oh, he couldn't prevent——"

"Your learning the truth? I dare say! But, heavens," I fell, with vehemence, a-thinking, "what it shows that they must, to that extent, have succeeded in making of him!"

"Ah, nothing that's not nice *now*!" Mrs. Grose lugubriously pleaded.

"I don't wonder you looked queer," I persisted, "when I mentioned to you the letter from his school!"

"I doubt if I looked as queer as you!" she retorted with homely force. "And if he was so bad then as that comes to, how is he such an angel now?"

"Yes, indeed—and if he was a fiend at school! How, how, how? Well," I said in my torment, "you must put it to me again, but I shall not be able to tell you for some days. Only, put it to me again!" I cried in a way that made my friend stare. "There are directions in which I must not for the present let myself go." Meanwhile I returned to her first example—the one to which she had just previously referred—of the boy's happy capacity for an occasional slip. "If Quint—on your remonstrance at the time you speak of—was a base menial, one of the things Miles said to you, I find myself guessing, was that you were another." Again her admission was so adequate that I continued: "And you forgave him that?"

"Wouldn't *you*?"

"Oh, yes!" And we exchanged there, in the stillness, a sound of the oddest amusement. Then I went on: "At all events, while he was with the man——"

"Miss Flora was with the woman. It suited them all!"

It suited me too, I felt, only too well; by which I mean that it suited exactly the particularly deadly view I was in the very act of forbidding myself to entertain. But I so far succeeded in checking the expression of this view that I will throw, just here, no further light on it than may be offered by the mention of my final observation to Mrs. Grose. "His having lied and been impudent are, I confess, less engaging specimens than I had hoped to have from you of the outbreak in him of the little natural man. Still," I mused, "they must do, for they make me feel more than ever that I must watch."

It made me blush, the next minute, to see in my friend's face how much more unreservedly she had forgiven him than her anecdote struck me as presenting to my own tenderness an occasion for doing.

This came out when, at the schoolroom door, she quitted me. "Surely you don't accuse *him*——"

"Of carrying on an intercourse that he conceals from me? Ah, remember that, until further evidence, I now accuse nobody." Then, before shutting her out to go, by another passage, to her own place, "I must just wait," I wound up.

IX

I WAITED and waited, and the days, as they elapsed, took something from my consternation. A very few of them, in fact, passing, in constant sight of my pupils, without a fresh incident, sufficed to give to grievous fancies and even to odious memories a kind of brush of the sponge. I have spoken of the surrender to their extraordinary childish grace as a thing I could actively cultivate, and it may be imagined if I neglected now to address myself to this source for whatever it would yield. Stranger than I can express, certainly, was the effort to struggle against my new lights! it would doubtless have been, however, a greater tension still had it not been so frequently successful. I used to wonder how my little charges could help guessing that I thought strange things about them; and the circumstance that these things only made them more interesting was not by itself a direct aid to keeping them in the dark. I trembled lest they should see that they *were* so immensely more interesting. Putting things at the worst, at all events, as in meditation I so often did, any clouding of their innocence could only be—blameless and foredoomed as they were—a reason the more for taking risks. There were moments when, by an irresistible impulse, I found myself catching them up and pressing them to my heart. As soon as I had done so I used to say to myself: "What will they think of that? Doesn't it betray too much?" It would have been easy to get into a sad, wild tangle about how much I might betray; but the real account, I feel, of the hours of peace that I could still enjoy was that the immediate charm of my companions was a beguilement still effective even under the shadow of the possibility that it was studied. For if it occurred to me that I might occasionally excite suspicion by the little outbreaks of my sharper passion for them, so too I remember wondering if I mightn't see a queerness in the traceable increase of their own demonstrations.

They were at this period extravagantly and preternaturally fond of me; which, after all, I could reflect, was no more than a graceful response in children perpetually bowed over and hugged. The homage of which they were so lavish succeeded, in truth, for my nerves, quite as well as if I never appeared to myself, as I may say, literally to catch them at a purpose in it. They had never, I think, wanted to do so many things for their poor protectress; I mean—though they got their lessons better and better, which was naturally what would please her most—in the way of diverting, entertaining, surprising her; reading her passages, telling her stories, acting her charades, pouncing out at her, in disguises, as animals and historical characters, and above all astonishing her by the "pieces" they had secretly got by heart and could interminably recite. I should never get to the bottom—were I to let myself go even now—of the prodigious private commentary, all under still more private correction, with which, in these days, I overscored their full hours. They had shown me from the first a facility for everything, a general faculty which, taking a fresh start, achieved remarkable flights. They got their little tasks as if they loved them, and indulged, from the mere exuberance of the gift, in the most unimposed little miracles of memory. They not only popped out at me as tigers and as Romans, but as Shakespeareans, astronomers, and navigators. This was so singularly the case that it had presumably much to do with the fact as to which, at the present day, I am at a loss for a different explanation: I allude to my unnatural composure on the subject of another school for Miles. What I remember is that I was content not, for the time, to open the question, and that contentment must have sprung from the sense of his perpetually striking show of cleverness. He was too clever for a bad governess, for a parson's daughter, to spoil; and the strangest if not the brightest thread in the pensive embroidery I just spoke of was the impression I might have got, if I had dared to work it out, that he was under some influence operating in his small intellectual life as a tremendous incitement.

If it was easy to reflect, however, that such a boy could postpone school, it was at least as marked that for such a boy to have been "kicked out" by a school-master was a mystification without end. Let me add that in their company now—and I was careful almost never to be out of it—I could follow no scent very far. We lived in a cloud of music and love and success and private theatricals. The musical sense in each of the children was of the quickest, but the elder in especial had a marvellous knack of catching and repeating. The schoolroom piano broke into all gruesome fancies; and when that failed there were confabulations in corners, with a sequel of one of them going out in the highest spirits in order to "come in" as something new. I had had brothers myself, and it was no revelation to me that little girls could be slavish idolaters of little boys. What surpassed everything was that there was a little boy in the world who could have for the inferior age, sex, and intelligence so fine a consideration. They were extraordinarily at one, and to say that they never either quarrelled or complained is to make the note of praise coarse for their quality of sweetness. Sometimes, indeed, when I dropped into coarseness, I perhaps came across traces of little understandings between them by which one of them should keep me occupied while the other slipped away. There is a *naïf* side, I suppose, in all diplomacy; but if my pupils practiced upon me, it was surely with the minimum of grossness. It was all in the other quarter that, after a lull, the grossness broke out.

I find that I really hang back; but I must take my plunge. In going on with the record of what was hideous at Bly, I not only challenge the most liberal faith—for which I little care; but—and this is another matter—I renew what I myself suffered, I again push my way through it to the end. There came suddenly an hour after which, as I look back, the affair seems to me to have been all pure suffering; but I have at least reached the heart of it, and the straightest road out is doubtless to advance. One evening—with nothing to lead up or to prepare it—I felt the cold touch of the impression that had breathed on me the night of my arrival and which, much lighter than, as I have mentioned, I should probably have made little of in memory had my subsequent sojourn been less agitated. I had not gone to bed; I sat reading by a couple of candles. There was a roomful of old books at Bly—last-century fiction, some of it, which, to the extent of a distinctly deprecated renown, but never to so much as that of a stray specimen, had reached the sequestered home and appealed to the unavowed curiosity of my youth. I remember that the book I had in my hand was Fielding's *Amelia*; also that I was wholly awake. I recall further both a general conviction that it was horribly late and a particular objection to looking at my watch. I figure, finally, that the white curtain draping, in the fashion of those days, the head of Flora's little bed, shrouded, as I had assured myself long before, the perfection of childish rest. I recollect in short that, though I was deeply interested in my author, I found myself, at the turn of a page and with his spell all scattered, looking straight up from him and hard at the door of my room. There was a moment during which I listened, reminded of the faint sense I had had, the first night, of there being something undefineably astir in the house, and noted the soft breath of the open casement just move the half-drawn blind. Then, with all the marks of a deliberation that must have seemed magnificent had there been anyone to admire it, I laid down my book, rose to my feet, and, taking a candle, went straight out of the room and, from the passage, on which my light made little impression, noiselessly closed and locked the door.

I can say now neither what determined nor what guided me, but I went straight along the lobby, holding my candle high, till I came within sight of the tall window that presided over the great turn of the staircase. At this point I precipitately found myself aware of three things. They were practically simultaneous, yet they had flashes of succession. My candle, under a bold flourish, went out, and I perceived, by the uncovered window, that the yielding dusk of earliest morning rendered it unnecessary. Without it, the next instant, I saw that there was someone on the stair. I speak of sequences, but I required no lapse of seconds to stiffen myself for a third encounter with Quint. The apparition had reached the landing half-way up and was therefore on the spot nearest the window, where at sight of me, it stopped short and fixed me exactly as it had fixed me from the tower and from the garden. He knew me as well as I knew him; and so, in the cold, faint twilight, with a glimmer in the high glass and another on the polish of the oak stair below, we faced each other in our common intensity. He was absolutely, on this occasion, a living, detestable, dangerous presence. But that was not the wonder of wonders; I reserve this distinction for quite another circumstance: the circumstance that dread had unmistakeably quitted me and that there was nothing in me there that didn't meet and measure him.

I had plenty of anguish after that extraordinary moment, but I had, thank God, no terror. And he knew I had not—I found myself at the end of an instant magnificently aware of this. I felt, in a fierce rigour of confidence, that if I stood my ground a minute I should cease—for the time, at least—to have him to reckon with; and during the minute, accordingly, the thing was as human and hideous as a real interview: hideous just because it *was* human, as human as to have met alone, in the small hours, in a sleeping house, some enemy, some adventurer, some criminal. It was the dead silence of our long gaze at such close quarters that gave the whole horror, huge as it was, its only note of the unnatural. If I had met a murderer in such a place and at such an hour, we still at least would have spoken. Something would have passed in life, between us; if nothing had passed one of us would have moved. The moment was so prolonged that it would have taken but little more to make me doubt if even *I* were in life. I can't express what followed it save by saying that the silence itself—which was indeed in a manner an attestation of my strength—became the element into which I saw the figure disappear; in which I definitely saw it turn as I might have seen the low wretch to which it had once belonged turn on receipt of an order, and pass, with my eyes on the villainous back that no hunch could have more disfigured, straight down the staircase and into the darkness in which the next bend was lost.

X

I remained awhile at the top of the stair, but with the effect presently of understanding that when my visitor had gone, he had gone: then I returned to my room. The foremost thing I saw there by the light of the candle I had left burning was that Flora's little bed was empty; and on this I caught my breath with all the terror that, five minutes before, I had been able to resist. I dashed at the place in which I had left her lying and over which (for the small silk counterpane and the sheets were disarranged) the white curtains had been deceivingly pulled forward; then my step, to my unutterable relief, produced an answering sound: I perceived an agitation of the window-blind, and the child, ducking down, emerged rosily from the other side of it. She stood there in so much of her candour and so little of her nightgown, with her pink bare feet and the golden glow of her curls. She looked intensely grave, and I had never had such a sense of losing an advantage acquired (the thrill of which had just been so prodigious) as on my consciousness that she addressed me with a reproach. "You naughty: where *have* you been?"—instead of challenging her own irregularity I found myself arraigned and explaining. She herself explained, for that matter, with the loveliest, eagerest simplicity. She had known suddenly, as she lay there, that I was out of the room, and had jumped up to see what had become of me. I had dropped, with the joy of her reappearance, back into my chair—feeling then, and then only, a little faint; and she had pattered straight over to me, thrown herself upon my knee, given herself to be held with the flame of the candle full in the wonderful little face that was still flushed with sleep. I remember closing my eyes an instant, yieldingly, consciously, as before the excess of something beautiful that shone out of the blue of her own. "You were looking for me out of the window?" I said. "You thought I might be walking in the grounds?"

"Well, you know, I thought someone was"—she never blanched as she smiled out that at me.

Oh, how I looked at her now! "And did you see anyone?"

"Ah, *no*!" she returned, almost with the full privilege of childish inconsequence, resentfully, though with a long sweetness in her little drawl of the negative.

At that moment, in the state of my nerves, I absolutely believed she lied; and if I once more closed my eyes it was before the dazzle of the three or four possible ways in which I might take this up. One of these, for a moment, tempted me with such singular intensity that, to withstand it, I must have gripped my little girl with a spasm that, wonderfully, she submitted to without a cry or a sign of fright. Why not break out at her on the spot and have it all over? —give it to her straight in her lovely little lighted face? "You see, you see, you *know* that you do and that you already quite suspect I believe it; therefore why not frankly confess it to me, so that we may at least live with it together and learn perhaps, in the strangeness of our fate, where we are and what it means?" This solicitation dropped, alas, as it came: if I could immediately have succumbed to it I might have spared myself—well you'll see what. Instead of succumbing I sprang again to my feet, looked at her bed, and took a helpless middle way. "Why did you pull the curtain over the place to make me think you were still there?"

Flora luminously considered; after which, with her little divine smile: "Because I don't like to frighten you!"

"But if I had, by your idea, gone out——?"

She absolutely declined to be puzzled; she turned her eyes to the flame of the candle as if the question were as irrelevant, or at any rate as impersonal, as Mrs. Marcet or nine-times-nine. "Oh, but you know," she quite adequately answered, "that you might come back, you dear, and that you *have*!" And after a little, when she had got into bed, I had, for a long time, by almost sitting on her to hold her hand, to prove that I recognised the pertinence of my return.

You may imagine the general complexion, from that moment, of my nights. I repeatedly sat up till I didn't know when; I selected moments when my room-mate unmistakeably slept, and, stealing out, took noiseless turns in the passage and even pushed as far as to where I had last met Quint. But I never met him there again; and I may as well say at once that I on no other occasion saw him in the house. I just missed, on the staircase, on the other hand, a different adventure. Looking down it from the top I once recognised the presence of a woman seated on one of the lower steps with her back presented to me, her body half bowed and her head, in an attitude of woe, in her hands. I had been there but an instant, however, when she vanished without looking round at me. I knew, none the less, exactly what dreadful face she had to show; and I wondered whether, if instead of being above I had been below, I should have had, for going up, the same nerve I had lately shown Quint. Well, there continued to be plenty of chance for nerve. On the eleventh night after my latest encounter with that gentleman—they were all numbered now—I had an alarm that perilously skirted it and that indeed, from the particular quality of its unexpectedness, proved quite my sharpest shock. It was precisely the first night during this series that, weary with watching, I had felt that I might again without laxity lay myself down at my old hour. I slept immediately and, as I afterwards knew, till about one o'clock; but when I woke it was to sit straight up, as completely roused as if a hand had shook me. I had left a light burning, but it was now out, and I felt an instant certainty that Flora had extinguished it. This brought me to my feet and straight, in the darkness, to her bed, which I found she had left. A glance at the window enlightened me further, and the striking of a match completed the picture.

The child had again got up—this time blowing out the taper, and had again, for some purpose of observation or response, squeezed in behind the blind and was peering out into the night. That she now saw—as she had not, I had satisfied myself, the previous time—was proved to me by the fact that she was disturbed neither by my re-illumination nor by the haste I made to get into slippers and into a wrap. Hidden, protected, absorbed, she evidently rested on the sill—the casement opened forward—and gave herself up. There was a great still moon to help her, and this fact had counted in my quick decision. She was face to face with the apparition we had met at the lake, and could now communicate with it as she had not then been able to do. What I, on my side, had to care for was, without disturbing her, to reach, from the corridor, some other window in the same quarter. I got to the door without her hearing me; I got out of it, closed it and listened, from the other side, for some sound from her. While I stood in the passage I had my eyes on her brother's door, which was but ten steps off and which, indescribably, produced in me a renewal of the strange impulse that I lately spoke of as my temptation. What if I should go straight in and march to *his* window?—what if, by risking to his boyish bewilderment a revelation of my motive, I should throw across the rest of the mystery the long halter of my boldness?

This thought held me sufficiently to make me cross to his threshold and pause again. I preternaturally listened: I figured to myself what might portentously be; I wondered if his bed were also empty and he too were secretly at watch. It was a deep, soundless minute, at the end of which my impulse failed. He was quiet; he might be innocent; the risk was hideous; I turned away. There was a figure in the grounds—a figure prowling for a sight, the visitor with whom Flora was engaged; but it was not the visitor most concerned with my boy. I hesitated afresh, but on other grounds and only a few seconds; then I had made my choice. There were empty rooms at Bly, and it was only a question of choosing the right one. The right one suddenly presented itself to me as the lower one—though high above the gardens—in the solid corner of the house that I have spoken of as the old tower. This was a large, square chamber, arranged with some state as a bedroom, the extravagant size of which made it so inconvenient that it had not for years, though kept by Mrs. Grose in exemplary order, been occupied. I had often admired it and I knew my way about in it; I had only, after just faltering at the first chill gloom of its disuse, to pass across it and unbolt as quietly as I could one of the shutters. Achieving this transit, I uncovered the glass without a sound and, applying my face to the pane, was able, the darkness without being much less than within, to see that I commanded the right direction. Then I saw something more. The moon made the night extraordinarily penetrable and showed me on the lawn a person, diminished by distance, who stood there motionless and as if fascinated, looking up to where I had appeared—looking, that is, not so much straight at me as at something that was apparently above me. There was clearly another person above me—there was a person on the tower; but the presence on the lawn was not in the least what I had conceived and had confidently hurried to meet. The presence on the lawn—I felt sick as I made it out—was poor little Miles himself.

XI

It was not till late next day that I spoke to Mrs. Grose; the rigour with which I kept my pupils in sight making it often difficult to meet her privately, and the more as we each felt the importance of not provoking—on the part of the servants quite as much as on that of the children—any suspicion of a secret flurry or of a discussion of mysteries. I drew a great security in this particular from her mere smooth aspect. There was nothing in her fresh face to pass on to others my horrible confidences. She believed me, I was sure, absolutely: if she hadn't I don't know what would have become of me, for I couldn't have borne the business alone. But she was a magnificent monument to the blessing of a want of imagination, and if she could see in our little charges nothing but their beauty and amiability, their happiness and cleverness, she had no direct communication with the sources of my trouble. If they had been at all visibly blighted or battered, she would doubtless have grown, on tracing it back, haggard enough to match them; as matters stood, however, I could feel her, when she surveyed them, with her large white arms folded and the habit of serenity in all her look, thank the Lord's mercy that if they were ruined the pieces would still serve. Flights of fancy gave place, in her mind, to a steady fireside glow, and I had already begun to perceive how, with the development of the conviction that—as time went on without a public accident—our young things could, after all, look out for themselves, she addressed her greatest solicitude to the sad case presented by their instructress. That, for myself, was a sound simplification: I could engage that, to the world, my face should tell no tales, but it would have been, in the conditions, an immense added strain to find myself anxious about hers.

At the hour I now speak of she had joined me, under pressure, on the terrace, where, with the lapse of the season, the afternoon sun was now agreeable; and we sat there together while, before us, at a distance, but within call if we wished, the children strolled to and fro in one of their most manageable moods. They moved slowly, in unison, below us, over the lawn, the boy, as they went, reading aloud from a storybook and passing his arm round his sister to keep her quite in touch. Mrs. Grose watched them with positive placidity; then I caught the suppressed intellectual creak with which she conscientiously turned to take from me a view of the back of the tapestry. I had made her a receptacle of lurid things, but there was an odd recognition of my superiority—my accomplishments and my function—in her patience under my pain. She offered her mind to my disclosures as, had I wished to mix a witch's broth and proposed it with assurance, she would have held out a large saucepan. This had become thoroughly her attitude by the time that, in my recital of the events of the night, I reached the point of what Miles had said to me when, after seeing him, at such a monstrous hour, almost on the very spot where he happened now to be, I had gone down to bring him in; choosing then, at the window, with a concentrated need of not alarming the house, rather that method than a signal more resonant. I had left her meanwhile in little doubt of my small hope of representing with success even to her actual sympathy my sense of the real splendour of the little inspiration with which, after I had got him into the house, the boy met my final articulate challenge. As soon as I appeared in the moonlight on the terrace, he had come to me as straight as possible; on which I had taken his hand without a word and led him, through the dark spaces, up the staircase where Quint had so hungrily hovered for him, along the lobby where I had listened and trembled, and so to his forsaken room.

Not a sound, on the way, had passed between us, and I had wondered—oh, *how* I had wondered!—if he were groping about in his little mind for something plausible and not too grotesque. It would tax his invention, certainly, and I felt this time, over his real embarrassment, a curious thrill of triumph. It was a sharp trap for the inscrutable! He couldn't play any longer at innocence; so how the deuce would he get out of it? There beat in me indeed, with the passionate throb of this question, an equal dumb appeal as to how the deuce *I* should. I was confronted at last, as never yet, with all the risk attached even now to sounding my own horrid note. I remember in fact that as we pushed into his little chamber, where the bed had not been slept in at all and the window, uncovered to the moonlight, made the place so clear that there was no need of striking a match—I remember how I suddenly dropped, sank upon the edge of the bed from the force of the idea that he must know how he really, as they say, "had" me. He could do what he liked, with all his cleverness to help him, so long as I should continue to defer to the old tradition of the criminality of those caretakers of the young who minister to superstitions and fears. He "had" me indeed, and in a cleft stick; for who would ever absolve me, who would consent that I should go unhung, if, by the faintest tremor of an overture, I were the first to introduce into our perfect intercourse an element so dire? No, no: it was useless to attempt to convey to Mrs. Grose, just as it is scarcely less so to attempt to suggest here, how, in our short, stiff brush in the dark, he fairly shook me with admiration. I was of course thoroughly kind and merciful; never, never yet had I placed on his little shoulders hands of such tenderness as those with which, while I rested against the bed, I held him there well under fire. I had no alternative but, in form at least, to put it to him.

"You must tell me now— and all the truth. What did you go out for? What were you doing there?"

I can still see his wonderful smile, the whites of his beautiful eyes, and the uncovering of his little teeth shine to me in the dusk. "If I tell you why, will you understand?" My heart, at this, leaped into my mouth. *Would* he tell me why? I found no sound on my lips to press it, and I was aware of replying only with a vague, repeated, grimacing nod. He was gentleness itself, and while I wagged my head at him he stood there more than ever a little fairy prince. It was his brightness indeed that gave me a respite. Would it be so great if he were really going to tell me? "Well," he said at last, "just exactly in order that you should do this."

"Do what?"

"Think me—for a change—*bad!*" I shall never forget the sweetness and gaiety with which he brought out the word, nor how, on top of it, he bent forward and kissed me. It was practically the end of everything. I met his kiss and I had to make, while I folded him for a minute in my arms, the most stupendous effort not to cry. He had given exactly the account of himself that permitted least of my going behind it, and it was only with the effect of confirming my acceptance of it that, as I presently glanced about the room, I could say——

"Then you didn't undress at all?"

He fairly glittered in the gloom. "Not at all. I sat up and read."

"And when did you go down?"

"At midnight. When I'm bad I *am* bad!"

"I see, I see—it's charming. But how could you be sure I would know it?"

"Oh, I arranged that with Flora." His answers rang out with a readiness! "She was to get up and look out."

"Which is what she did do." It was I who fell into the trap!

"So she disturbed you, and, to see what she was looking at, you also looked—you saw."

"While you," I concurred, "caught your death in the night air!"

He literally bloomed so from this exploit that he could afford radiantly to assent. "How otherwise should I have been bad enough?" he asked. Then, after another embrace, the incident and our interview closed on my recognition of all the reserves of goodness that, for his joke, he had been able to draw upon.

XII

THE particular impression I had received proved in the morning light, I repeat, not quite successfully presentable to Mrs. Grose, though I reinforced it with the mention of still another remark that he had made before we separated. "It all lies in half-a-dozen words," I said to her, "words that really settle the matter. 'Think, you know, what I *might* do!' He threw that off to show me how good he is. He knows down to the ground what he 'might' do. That's what he gave them a taste of at school."

"Lord, you do change!" cried my friend.

"I don't change—I simply make it out. The four, depend upon it, perpetually meet. If on either of these last nights you had been with either child, you would clearly have understood. The more I've watched and waited the more I've felt that if there were nothing else to make it sure it would be made so by the systematic silence of each. *Never,* by a slip of the tongue, have they so much as alluded to either of their old friends, any more than Miles has alluded to his expulsion. Oh yes, we may sit here and look at them, and they may show off to us there to their fill; but even while they pretend to be lost in their fairy-tale they're steeped in their vision of the dead restored. He's not reading to her," I declared; "they're talking of *them*—they're talking horrors! I go on, I know, as if I were crazy; and it's a wonder I'm not. What I've seen would have made *you* so; but it has only made me more lucid, made me get hold of still other things."

My lucidity must have seemed awful, but the charming creatures who were victims of it, passing and repassing in their interlocked sweetness, gave my colleague something to hold on by; and I felt how tight she held as, without stirring in the breath of my passion, she covered them still with her eyes. "Of what other things have you got hold?"

"Why, of the very things that have delighted, fascinated, and yet, at bottom, as I now so strangely see, mystified and troubled me. Their more than earthly beauty, their absolutely unnatural goodness. It's a game," I went on; "it's a policy and a fraud!"

"On the part of little darlings——?"

"As yet mere lovely babies? Yes, mad as that seems!" The very act of bringing it out really helped me to trace it—follow it all up and piece it all together. "They haven't been good—they've only been absent. It has been easy to live with them, because they're simply leading a life of their own. They're not mine—they're not ours. They're his and they're hers!"

"Quint's and that woman's?"

"Quint's and that woman's. They want to get to them."

Oh, how, at this, poor Mrs. Grose appeared to study them! "But for what?"

"For the love of all the evil that, in those dreadful days, the pair put into them. And to ply them with that evil still, to keep up the work of demons, is what brings the others back."

"Laws!" said my friend under her breath. The exclamation was homely, but it revealed a real acceptance of my further proof of what, in the bad time—for there had been a worse even than this! —must have occurred. There could have been no such justification for me as the plain assent of her experience to whatever depth of depravity I found credible in our brace of scoundrels. It was in obvious submission of memory that she brought out after a moment: "They *were* rascals! But what can they now do?" she pursued.

"Do?" I echoed so loud that Miles and Flora, as they passed at their distance, paused an instant in their walk and looked at us. "Don't they do enough?" I demanded in a lower tone, while the children, having smiled and nodded and kissed hands to us, resumed their exhibition. We were held by it a minute; then I answered: "They can destroy them!" At this my companion did turn, but the inquiry she launched was a silent one, the effect of which was to make me more explicit. "They don't know, as yet, quite how—but they're trying hard. They're seen only across, as it were, and beyond—in strange places and on high places, the top of towers, the roof of houses, the outside of windows, the further edge of pools; but there's a deep design, on either side, to shorten the distance and overcome the obstacle; and the success of the tempters is only a question of time. They've only to keep to their suggestions of danger."

"For the children to come?"

"And perish in the attempt!" Mrs. Grose slowly got up, and I scrupulously added: "Unless, of course, we can prevent!"

Standing there before me while I kept my seat, she visibly turned things over. "Their uncle must do the preventing. He must take them away."

"And who's to make him?"

She had been scanning the distance, but she now dropped on me a foolish face. "You, Miss."

"By writing to him that his house is poisoned and his little nephew and niece mad?"

"But if they *are*, Miss?"

"And if I am myself, you mean? That's charming news to be sent him by a governess whose prime undertaking was to give him no worry."

Mrs. Grose considered, following the children again. "Yes, he do hate worry. That was the great reason——"

"Why those fiends took him in so long? No doubt, though his indifference must have been awful. As I'm not a fiend, at any rate, I shouldn't take him in."

My companion, after an instant and for all answer, sat down again and grasped my arm. "Make him at any rate come to you."

I stared. "To *me?*" I had a sudden fear of what she might do. " 'Him'?"

"He ought to *be* here—he ought to help."

I quickly rose, and I think I must have shown her a queerer face than ever yet. "You see me asking him for a visit?" No, with her eyes on my face she evidently couldn't. Instead of it even—as a woman reads another—she could see what I myself saw: his derision, his amusement, his contempt for the break-down of my resignation at being left alone and for the fine machinery I had set in motion to attract his attention to my slighted charms. She didn't know—no one knew—how proud I had been to serve him and to stick to our terms; yet she none the less took the measure, I think, of the warning I now gave her. "If you should so lose your head as to appeal to him for me——"

She was really frightened. "Yes, Miss?"

"I would leave, on the spot, both him and you."

XIII

It was all very well to join them, but speaking to them proved quite as much as ever an effort beyond my strength—offered, in close quarters, difficulties as insurmountable as before. This situation continued a month, and with new aggravations and particular notes, the note above all, sharper and sharper, of the small ironic consciousness on the part of my pupils. It was not, I am as sure today as I was sure then, my mere infernal imagination: it was absolutely traceable that they were aware of my predicament and that this strange relation made, in a manner, for a long time, the air in which we moved. I don't mean that they had their tongues in their cheeks or did anything vulgar, for that was not one of their dangers: I do mean, on the other hand, that the element of the unnamed and untouched became, between us, greater than any other, and that so much avoidance could not have been so successfully effected without a great deal of tacit arrangement. It was as if, at moments, we were perpetually coming into sight of subjects before which we must stop short, turning suddenly out of alleys that we perceived to be blind, closing with a little bang that made us look at each other—for, like all bangs, it was something louder than we had intended—the doors we had indiscreetly opened. All roads lead to Rome, and there were times when it might have struck us that almost every branch of study or subject of conversation skirted forbidden ground. Forbidden ground was the question of the return of the dead in general and of whatever, in especial, might survive, in memory, of the friends little children had lost. There were days when I could have sworn that one of them had, with a small invisible nudge, said to the other: "She thinks she'll do it this time—but she *won't!*" To "do it" would have been to indulge for instance—and for once in a way—in some direct reference to the lady who had prepared them for my discipline. They had a delightful endless appetite for passages in my own history, to which I had again and again treated them; they were in possession of everything that had ever happened to me, had had, with every circumstance the story of my smallest adventures and of those of my brothers and sisters and of the cat and the dog at home, as well as many particulars of the eccentric nature of my father, of the furniture and arrangement of our house, and of the conversation of the old women of our village. There were things enough, taking one with another, to chatter about, if one went very fast and knew by instinct when to go round. They pulled with an art of their own the strings of my invention and my memory; and nothing else perhaps, when I thought of such occasions afterwards, gave me so the suspicion of being watched from under cover. It was in any case over *my* life, *my* past, and *my* friends alone that we could take anything like our ease—a state of affairs that led them sometimes without the least pertinence to break out into sociable reminders. I was invited—with no visible connection—to repeat afresh Goody Gosling's celebrated *mot* or to confirm the details already supplied as to the cleverness of the vicarage pony.

It was partly at such junctures as these and partly at quite different ones that, with the turn my matters had now taken, my predicament, as I have called it, grew most sensible. The fact that the days passed for me without another encounter ought, it would have appeared, to have done something toward soothing my nerves. Since the light brush, that second night on the upper landing, of the presence of a woman at the foot of the stair, I had seen nothing, whether in or out of the house, that one had better not have seen. There was many a corner round which I expected to come upon

Quint, and many a situation that, in a merely sinister way, would have favoured the appearance of Miss Jessel. The summer had turned, the summer had gone; the autumn had dropped upon Bly and had blown out half our lights. The place, with its grey sky and withered garlands, its bared spaces and scattered dead leaves, was like a theatre after the performance—all strewn with crumpled play-bills. There were exactly states of the air, conditions of sound and of stillness, unspeakable impressions of the *kind* of ministering moment, that brought back to me, long enough to catch it, the feeling of the medium in which, that June evening out-of-doors, I had had my first sight of Quint, and in which, too, at those other instants, I had, after seeing him through the window, looked for him in vain in the circle of shrubbery. I recognised the signs, the portents—I recognised the moment, the spot. But they remained unaccompanied and empty, and I continued unmolested; if unmolested one could call a young woman whose sensibility had, in the most extraordinary fashion, not declined but deepened. I had said in my talk with Mrs. Grose on that horrid scene of Flora's by the lake—and had perplexed her by so saying—that it would from that moment distress me much more to lose my power than to keep it. I had then expressed what was vividly in my mind: the truth that, whether the children really saw or not—since, that is, it was not yet definitely proved—I greatly preferred, as a safeguard, the fulness of my own exposure. I was ready to know the very worst that was to be known. What I had then had an ugly glimpse of was that my eyes might be sealed just while theirs were most opened. Well, my eyes *were* sealed, it appeared, at present—a consummation for which it seemed blasphemous not to thank God. There was, alas, a difficulty about that: I would have thanked him with all my soul had I not had in a proportionate measure this conviction of the secret of my pupils.

How can I retrace today the strange steps of my obsession? There were times of our being together when I would have been ready to swear that, literally, in my presence, but with my direct sense of it closed, they had visitors who were known and were welcome. Then it was that, had I not been deterred by the very chance that such an injury might prove greater than the injury to be averted, my exultation would have broken out. "They're here, they're here, you little wretches," I would have cried, "and you can't deny it now!" The little wretches denied it with all the added volume of their sociability and their tenderness, in just the crystal depths of which—like the flash of a fish in a stream—the mockery of their advantage peeped up. The shock, in truth, had sunk into me still deeper than I knew on the night when, looking out to see either Quint or Miss Jessel under the stars, I had beheld the boy over whose rest I watched and who had immediately brought in with him—had straightway, there, turned it on me—the lovely upward look with which, from the battlements above me, the hideous apparition of Quint had played. If it was a question of a scare, my discovery on this occasion had scared me more than any other, and it was in the condition of nerves produced by it that I made my actual inductions. They harassed me so that sometimes, at odd moments, I shut myself up audibly to rehearse—it was at once a fantastic relief and a renewed despair—the manner in which I might come to the point. I approached it from one side and the other while, in my room, I flung myself about, but I always broke down in the monstrous utterance of names. As they died away on my lips, I said to myself that I should indeed help them to represent something infamous if, by pronouncing them, I should violate as rare a little case of instinctive delicacy as any schoolroom, probably, had ever known. When I said to myself: "*They* have the manners to be silent, and you, trusted as you are, the baseness to speak!" I felt myself crimson and I covered my face with my hands. After these secret scenes I chattered more than ever, going on volubly enough till one of our prodigious, palpable hushes occurred—I can call them nothing else—the strange, dizzy lift or swim (I try for terms!) into a stillness, a pause of all life, that had nothing to do with the more or less noise that at the moment we might be engaged in making and that I could hear through any deepened exhilaration or quickened recitation or louder strum of the piano. Then it was that the others, the outsiders, were there. Though they were not angels, they "passed," as the French say, causing me, while they stayed, to tremble with the fear of their addressing to their younger victims some yet more infernal message or more vivid image than they had thought good enough for myself.

What it was most impossible to get rid of was the cruel idea that, whatever I had seen, Miles and Flora saw *more*—things terrible and unguessable and that sprang from dreadful passages of intercourse in the past. Such things naturally left on the surface, for the time, a chill which we vociferously denied that we felt; and we had, all three, with repetition, got into such splendid training that we went, each time, almost automatically, to mark the close of the incident, through the very same movements. It was striking of the children, at all events, to kiss me inveterately with a kind of wild irrelevance and never to fail—one or the other—of the precious question that had helped us through many a peril. "When do you think he *will* come? Don't you think we *ought* to write?"—there was nothing like that inquiry, we found by experience, for carrying off an awkwardness. "He" of course was their uncle in Harley Street; and we lived in much profusion of theory that he might at any moment arrive to mingle in our circle. It was impossible to have given less encouragement than he had done to such a doctrine, but if we had not had the doctrine to fall back upon we should have deprived each other of some of our finest exhibitions. He never wrote to them—that may have been selfish, but it was a part of the flattery of his trust of me; for the way in which a man pays his highest tribute to a woman is apt to be but by the more festal celebration of one of the sacred laws of his comfort; and I held that I carried out the spirit of the pledge given not to appeal to him when I let my charges understand that their own letters were but charming literary exercises. They were too beautiful to be posted; I kept them myself; I have them all to this hour. This was a rule indeed which only added to the satiric effect of my being plied with the supposition that he might at any moment be among us. It was exactly as if my charges knew how almost more awkward than anything else that might be for me. There appears to me, moreover, as I look back, no note in all this more extraordinary than the mere fact that, in spite of my tension and of their triumph, I never lost patience with them. Adorable they must in truth have been, I now reflect, that I didn't in these days hate them! Would exasperation, however, if relief had longer been postponed, finally have betrayed me? It little matters, for relief arrived. I call it relief, though it was only the relief that a snap brings to a strain or the burst of a thunderstorm to a day of suffocation. It was at least change, and it came with a rush.

XIV

WALKING to church a certain Sunday morning, I had little Miles at my side and his sister, in advance of us and at Mrs. Grose's, well in sight. It was a crisp, clear day, the first of its order for some time; the night had brought a touch of frost, and the autumn air, bright and sharp, made the church-bells almost gay. It was an odd accident of thought that I should have happened at such a moment to be particularly and very gratefully struck with the obedience of my little charges. Why did they never resent my inexorable, my perpetual society? Something or other had brought nearer home to me that I had all but pinned the boy to my shawl and that, in the way our companions were marshalled before me, I might have appeared to provide against some danger of rebellion. I was like a gaoler with an eye to possible surprises and escapes. But all this belonged—I mean their magnificent little surrender—just to the special array of the facts that were most abysmal. Turned out for Sunday by his uncle's tailor, who had had a free hand and a notion of pretty waistcoats and of his grand little air, Miles's whole title to independence, the rights of his sex and situation, were so stamped upon him that if he had suddenly struck for freedom I should have had nothing to say. I was by the strangest of chances wondering how I should meet him when the revolution unmistakeably occurred. I call it a revolution because I now see how, with the word he spoke, the curtain rose on the last act of my dreadful drama and the catastrophe was precipitated. "Look here, my dear, you know," he charmingly said, "when in the world, please, am I going back to school?"

Transcribed here the speech sounds harmless enough, particularly as uttered in the sweet, high, casual pipe with which, at all interlocutors, but above all at his eternal governess, he threw off intonations as if he were tossing roses. There was something in them that always made one "catch," and I caught, at any rate, now so effectually that I stopped as short as if one of the trees of the park had fallen across the road. There was something new, on the spot, between us, and he was perfectly aware that I recognised it, though, to enable me to do so, he had no need to look a whit less candid and charming than usual. I could feel in him how he already, from my at first finding nothing to reply, perceived the advantage he had gained. I was so slow to find anything that he had plenty of time, after a minute, to continue with his suggestive but inconclusive smile: "You know, my dear, that for a fellow to be with a lady *always*——!" His "my dear" was constantly on his lips for me, and nothing could have expressed more the exact shade of the sentiment with which I desired to inspire my pupils than its fond familiarity. It was so respectfully easy.

But, oh, how I felt that at present I must pick my own phrases! I remember that, to gain time, I tried to laugh, and I seemed to see in the beautiful face with which he watched me how ugly and queer I looked. "And always with the same lady?" I returned.

He neither blenched nor winked. The whole thing was virtually out between us. "Ah, of course, she's a jolly, 'perfect' lady; but, after all, I'm a fellow, don't you see? that's—well, getting on."

I lingered there with him an instant ever so kindly. "Yes, you're getting on." Oh, but I felt helpless!

I have kept to this day the heartbreaking little idea of how he seemed to know that and to play with it. "And you can't say I've not been awfully good, can you?"

I laid my hand on his shoulder, for, though I felt how much

better it would have been to walk on, I was not yet quite able. "No, I can't say that, Miles."

"Except just that one night, you know——!"

"That one night?" I couldn't look as straight as he.

"Why, when I went down—went out of the house."

"Oh, yes. But I forget what you did it for."

"You forget?"—he spoke with the sweet extravagance of childish reproach. "Why, it was to show you I could!"

"Oh, yes, you could."

"And I can again."

I felt that I might, perhaps, after all, succeed in keeping my wits about me. "Certainly. But you won't."

"No, not *that* again. It was nothing."

"It was nothing," I said. "But we must go on."

He resumed our walk with me, passing his hand into my arm. "Then when *am* I going back?"

I wore, in turning it over, my most responsible air. "Were you very happy at school?"

He just considered. "Oh, I'm happy enough anywhere!"

"Well, then," I quavered, "if you're just as happy here——!"

"Ah, but that isn't everything! Of course *you* know a lot——"

"But you hint that you know almost as much?" I risked as he paused.

"Not half I want to!" Miles honestly professed. "But it isn't so much that."

"What is it, then?"

"Well—I want to see more life."

"I see; I see." We had arrived within sight of the church and of various persons, including several of the household of Bly, on their way to it and clustered about the door to see us go in. I quickened our step; I wanted to get there before the question between us opened up much further; I reflected hungrily that, for more than an hour, he would have to be silent; and I thought with envy of the comparative dusk of the pew and of the almost spiritual help of the hassock on which I might bend my knees. I seemed literally to be running a race with some confusion to which he was about to reduce me, but I felt that he had got in first when, before we had even entered the churchyard, he threw out——

"I want my own sort!"

It literally made me bound forward. "There are not many of your own sort, Miles!" I laughed. "Unless perhaps dear little Flora!"

"You really compare me to a baby girl?"

This found me singularly weak. "Don't you, then, *love* our sweet Flora?"

"If I didn't—and you too; if I didn't——!" he repeated as if retreating for a jump, yet leaving his thought so unfinished that, after we had come into the gate, another stop, which he imposed on me by the pressure of his arm, had become inevitable. Mrs. Grose and Flora had passed into the church, the other worshippers had followed, and we were, for the minute, alone among the old, thick graves. We had paused, on the path from the gate, by a low, oblong, tablelike tomb.

"Yes, if you didn't——?"

He looked, while I waited, about at the graves. "Well, you know what!" But he didn't move, and he presently produced something that made me drop straight down on the stone slab, as if suddenly to rest. "Does my uncle think what *you* think?"

I markedly rested. "How do you know what I think?"

"Ah, well, of course I don't; for it strikes me you never tell me. But I mean does *he* know?"

"Know what, Miles?"

"Why, the way I'm going on."

I perceived quickly enough that I could make, to this inquiry, no answer that would not involve something of a sacrifice of my employer. Yet it appeared to me that we were all, at Bly, sufficiently sacrificed to make that venial. "I don't think your uncle much cares."

Miles, on this, stood looking at me. "Then don't you think he can be made to?"

"In what way?"

"Why, by his coming down."

"But who'll get him to come down?"

"*I* will!" the boy said with extraordinary brightness and emphasis. He gave me another look charged with that expression and then marched off alone into church.

XV

THE business was practically settled from the moment I never followed him. It was a pitiful surrender to agitation, but my being aware of this had somehow no power to restore me. I only sat there on my tomb and read into what my little friend had said to me the fulness of its meaning; by the time I had grasped the whole of which I had also embraced, for absence, the pretext that I was ashamed to offer my pupils and the rest of the congregation such an example of delay. What I said to myself above all was that Miles had got something out of me and that the proof of it, for him, would be just this awkward collapse. He had got out of me that there was something I was much afraid of and that he should probably be able to make use of my fear to gain, for his own purpose, more freedom. My fear was of having to deal with the intolerable question of the grounds of his dismissal from school, for that was really but the question of the horrors gathered behind. That his uncle should arrive to treat with me of these things was a solution that, strictly speaking, I ought now to have desired to bring on; but I could so little face the ugliness and the pain of it that I simply procrastinated and lived from hand to mouth. The boy, to my deep discomposure, was immensely in the right, was in a position to say to me: "Either you clear up with my guardian the mystery of this interruption of my studies, or you cease to expect me to lead with you a life that's so unnatural for a boy." What was so unnatural for the particular boy I was concerned with was this sudden revelation of a consciousness and a plan.

That was what really overcame me, what prevented my going in. I walked round the church, hesitating, hovering; I reflected that I had already, with him, hurt myself beyond repair. Therefore I could patch up nothing, and it was too extreme an effort to squeeze beside him into the pew: he would be so much more sure than ever to pass his arm into mine and make me sit there for an hour in close, silent contact with his commentary on our talk. For the first minute since his arrival I wanted to get away from him. As I paused beneath the high east window and listened to the sounds of worship, I was taken with an impulse that might master me, I felt, completely should I give it the least encouragement. I might easily put an end to my predicament by getting away altogether. Here was my chance; there was no one to stop me; I could give the whole thing up—turn my back and retreat. It was only a question of hurrying again, for a few preparations, to the house which the attendance at church of so many of the servants would practically have left unoccupied. No one, in short, could blame me if I should just drive desperately off. What was it to get away if I got away only till dinner? That would be in a couple of hours, at the end of which—I had the acute prevision—my little pupils would play at innocent wonder about my non-appearance in their train.

"What *did* you do, you naughty, bad thing? Why in the world, to worry us so—and take our thoughts off too, don't you know?—did you desert us at the very door?" I couldn't meet such questions nor, as they asked them, their false little lovely eyes; yet it was all so exactly what I should have to meet that, as the prospect grew sharp to me, I at last let myself go.

I got, so far as the immediate moment was concerned, away; I came straight out of the churchyard and, thinking hard, retraced my steps through the park. It seemed to me that by the time I reached the house I had made up my mind I would fly. The Sunday stillness both of the approaches and of the interior, in which I met no one, fairly excited me with a sense of opportunity. Were I to get off quickly, this way, I should get off without a scene, without a word. My quickness would have to be remarkable, however; and the question of a conveyance was the great one to settle. Tormented, in the hall, with difficulties and obstacles, I remember sinking down at the foot of the staircase—suddenly collapsing there on the lowest step and then, with a revulsion, recalling that it was exactly where more than a month before, in the darkness of night and just so bowed with evil things, I had seen the spectre of the most horrible of women. At this I was able to straighten myself; I went the rest of the way up; I made, in my bewilderment, for the schoolroom, where there were objects belonging to me that I should have to take. But I opened the door to find again, in a flash, my eyes unsealed. In the presence of what I saw I reeled straight back upon my resistance.

Seated at my own table in clear noonday light I saw a person whom, without my previous experience, I should have taken at the first blush for some housemaid who might have stayed at home to look after the place and who, availing herself of rare relief from observation and of the schoolroom table and my pens, ink, and paper, had applied herself to the considerable effort of a letter to her sweetheart. There was an effort in the way that, while her arms rested on the table, her hands with evident weariness supported her head; but at the moment I took this in I had already become aware that, in spite of my entrance, her attitude strangely persisted. Then it was—with the very act of its announcing itself—that her identity flared up in a change of posture. She rose, not as if she had heard me, but with an indescribable grand melancholy of indifference and detachment, and, within a dozen feet of me, stood there as my vile predecessor. Dishonoured and tragic, she was all before me; but even as I fixed and, for memory, secured it, the awful image passed away. Dark as midnight in her black dress, her haggard beauty and her unutterable woe, she had looked at me long enough to appear to say that her right to sit at my table was as good as mine to sit at hers. While these instants lasted indeed I had the extraordinary chill of a feeling that it was I who was the intruder. It was as a wild protest against it that, actually addressing her—"You terrible, miserable woman!"—I heard myself break into a sound that, by the open door, rang through the long passage and the empty house. She looked at me as if she heard me, but I had recovered myself and cleared the air. There was nothing in the room the next minute but the sunshine and a sense that I must stay.

XVI

I HAD so perfectly expected that the return of my pupils would be marked by a demonstration that I was freshly upset at having to take into account that they were dumb about my absence. Instead of gaily denouncing and caressing me, they made no allusion to my having failed them, and I was left, for the time, on perceiving that she too said nothing, to study Mrs. Grose's odd face. I did this to such purpose that I made sure they had in some way bribed her to silence; a silence that, however, I would engage to break down on the first private opportunity. This opportunity came before tea: I secured five minutes with her in the housekeeper's room, where, in the twilight, amid a smell of lately-baked bread, but with the place all swept and garnished, I found her sitting in pained placidity before the fire. So I see her still, so I see her best: facing the flame from her straight chair in the dusky, shining room, a large clean image of the "put away"—of drawers closed and locked and rest without a remedy.

"Oh, yes, they asked me to say nothing; and to please them—so long as they were there—of course I promised. But what had happened to you?"

"I only went with you for the walk," I said. "I had then to come back to meet a friend."

She showed her surprise. "A friend—*you?*"

"Oh, yes, I have a couple!" I laughed. "But did the children give you a reason?"

"For not alluding to your leaving us? Yes; they said you would like it better. Do you like it better?"

My face had made her rueful. "No, I like it worse!" But after an instant I added: "Did they say why I should like it better?"

"No; Master Miles only said, 'We must do nothing but what she likes!' "

"I wish indeed he would! And what did Flora say?"

"Miss Flora was too sweet. She said, 'Oh, of course, of course!'—and I said the same."

I thought a moment. "You were too sweet too—I can hear you all. But none the less, between Miles and me, it's now all out."

"All out?" My companion stared. "But what, Miss?"

"Everything. It doesn't matter. I've made up my mind. I came home, my dear," I went on, "for a talk with Miss Jessel."

I had by this time formed the habit of having Mrs. Grose literally well in hand in advance of my sounding that note; so that even now, as she bravely blinked under the signal of my word, I could keep her comparatively firm. "A talk! Do you mean she spoke?"

"It came to that. I found her, on my return, in the schoolroom."

"And what did she say?" I can hear the good woman still, and the candour of her stupefaction.

"That she suffers the torments——!"

It was this, of a truth, that made her, as she filled out my picture, gape. "Do you mean," she faltered, "—of the lost?"

"Of the lost. Of the damned. And that's why, to share them——" I faltered myself with the horror of it.

But my companion, with less imagination, kept me up. "To share them——?"

"She wants Flora." Mrs. Grose might, as I gave it to her, fairly have fallen away from me had I not been prepared. I still held her there, to show I was. "As I've told you, however, it doesn't matter."

"Because you've made up your mind? But to what?"

"To everything."

"And what do you call 'everything'?"

"Why, sending for their uncle."

"Oh, Miss, in pity do," my friend broke out.

"Ah, but I will, I *will*! I see it's the only way. What's 'out,' as I told you, with Miles is that if he thinks I'm afraid to—and has ideas of what he gains by that—he shall see he's mistaken. Yes, yes; his uncle shall have it here from me on the spot (and before the boy himself if necessary) that if I'm to be reproached with having done nothing again about more school——"

"Yes, Miss—" my companion pressed me.

"Well, there's that awful reason."

There were now clearly so many of these for my poor colleague that she was excusable for being vague. "But—a—which?"

"Why, the letter from his old place."

"You'll show it to the master?"

"I ought to have done so on the instant."

"Oh, no!" said Mrs. Grose with decision.

"I'll put it before him," I went on inexorably, "that I can't undertake to work the question on behalf of a child who has been expelled——"

"For we've never in the least known what!" Mrs. Grose declared.

"For wickedness. For what else—when he's so clever and beautiful and perfect? Is he stupid? Is he untidy? Is he infirm? Is he ill-natured? He's exquisite—so it can be only *that*; and that would open up the whole thing. After all," I said, "it's their uncle's fault. If he left here such people——!"

"He didn't really in the least know them. The fault's mine." She had turned quite pale.

"Well, you shan't suffer," I answered.

"The children shan't!" she emphatically returned.

I was silent awhile; we looked at each other. "Then what am I to tell him?"

"You needn't tell him anything. *I'll* tell him."

I measured this. "Do you mean you'll write——?" Remembering she couldn't, I caught myself up. "How do you communicate?"

"I tell the bailiff. *He* writes."

"And should you like him to write our story?"

My question had a sarcastic force that I had not fully intended, and it made her, after a moment, inconsequently break down. The tears were again in her eyes. "Ah, Miss, *you* write!"

"Well—tonight," I at last answered; and on this we separated.

XVII

I went so far, in the evening, as to make a beginning. The weather had changed back, a great wind was abroad, and beneath the lamp, in my room, with Flora at peace beside me, I sat for a long time before a blank sheet of paper and listened to the lash of the rain and the batter of the gusts. Finally I went out, taking a candle; I crossed the passage and listened a minute at Miles's door. What, under my endless obsession, I had been impelled to listen for was some betrayal of his not being at rest, and I presently caught one, but not in the form I had expected. His voice tinkled out. "I say, you there—come in." It was a gaiety in the gloom!

I went in with my light and found him, in bed, very wide awake, but very much at his ease. "Well, what are *you* up to?" he asked with a grace of sociability in which it occurred to me that Mrs. Grose, had she been present, might have looked in vain for proof that anything was "out."

I stood over him with my candle. "How did you know I was there?"

"Why, of course I heard you. Did you fancy you made no noise? You're like a troop of cavalry!" he beautifully laughed.

"Then you weren't asleep?"

"Not much! I lie awake and think."

I had put my candle, designedly, a short way off, and then, as he held out his friendly old hand to me, had sat down on the edge of his bed. "What is it," I asked, "that you think of?"

"What in the world, my dear, but *you*?"

"Ah, the pride I take in your appreciation doesn't insist on that! I had so far rather you slept."

"Well, I think also, you know, of this queer business of ours."

I marked the coolness of his firm little hand. "Of what queer business, Miles?"

"Why, the way you bring me up. And all the rest!"

I fairly held my breath a minute, and even from my glimmering taper there was light enough to show how he smiled up at me from his pillow. "What do you mean by all the rest?"

"Oh, you know, you know!"

I could say nothing for a minute, though I felt, as I held his hand and our eyes continued to meet, that my silence had all the air of admitting his charge and that nothing in the whole world of reality was perhaps at that moment so fabulous as our actual relation. "Certainly you shall go back to school," I said, "if it be that that troubles you. But not to the old place—we must find another, a better. How could I know it did trouble you, this question, when you never told me so, never spoke of it at all?" His clear, listening face, framed in its smooth whiteness, made him for the minute as appealing as some wistful patient in a children's hospital; and I would have given, as the resemblance came to me, all I possessed on earth really to be the nurse or the sister of charity who might have helped to cure him. Well, even as it was, I perhaps might help! "Do you know you've never said a word to me about your school—I mean the old one; never mentioned it in any way?"

He seemed to wonder; he smiled with the same loveliness. But he clearly gained time; he waited, he called for guidance. "Haven't I?" It wasn't for *me* to help him—it was for the thing I had met!

Something in his tone and the expression of his face, as I got this from him, set my heart aching with such a pang as it had never yet known; so unutterably touching was it to see his little brain puzzled and his little resources taxed to play, under the spell laid on him, a part of innocence and consistency. "No, never—from the hour you came back. You've never mentioned to me one of your masters, one of your comrades, nor the least little thing that ever happened to you at school. Never, little Miles—no, never—have you given me an inkling of anything that *may* have happened there. Therefore you can fancy how much I'm in the dark. Until you came out, that way, this morning, you had, since the first hour I saw you, scarce even made a reference to anything in your previous life. You seemed so perfectly to accept the present." It was extraordinary how my absolute conviction of his secret precocity (or whatever I might call the poison of an influence that I dared but half to phrase) made him, in spite of the faint breath of his inward trouble, appear as accessible as an older person—imposed him almost as an intellectual equal. "I thought you wanted to go on as you are."

It struck me that at this he just faintly coloured. He gave, at any rate, like a convalescent slightly fatigued, a languid shake of his head. "I don't—I don't. I want to get away."

"You're tired of Bly?"

"Oh, no, I like Bly."

"Well, then——?"

"Oh, *you* know what a boy wants!"

I felt that I didn't know so well as Miles, and I took temporary refuge. "You want to go to your uncle?"

Again, at this, with his sweet ironic face, he made a movement on the pillow. "Ah, you can't get off with that!"

I was silent a little, and it was I, now, I think, who changed colour. "My dear, I don't want to get off!"

"You can't, even if you do. You can't, you can't!"—he lay beautifully staring. "My uncle must come down, and you must completely settle things."

"If we do," I returned with some spirit, "you may be sure it will be to take you quite away."

"Well, don't you understand that that's exactly what I'm working for? You'll have to tell him—about the way you've let it all drop: you'll have to tell him a tremendous lot!"

The exultation with which he uttered this helped me somehow, for the instant, to meet him rather more. "And how much will *you*, Miles, have to tell him? There are things he'll ask you!"

He turned it over. "Very likely. But what things?"

"The things you've never told me. To make up his mind what to do with you. He can't send you back——"

"Oh, I don't want to go back!" he broke in. "I want a new field."

He said it with admirable serenity, with positive unimpeachable gaiety; and doubtless it was that very note that most evoked for me the poignancy, the unnatural childish tragedy, of his probable reappearance at the end of three months with all this bravado and still more dishonour. It overwhelmed me now that I should never be able to bear that, and it made me let myself go. I threw myself upon him and in the tenderness of my pity I embraced him. "Dear little Miles, dear little Miles——!"

My face was close to his, and he let me kiss him, simply taking it with indulgent good-humour. "Well, old lady?"

"Is there nothing—nothing at all that you want to tell me?"

He turned off a little, facing round toward the wall and holding up his hand to look at as one had seen sick children look. "I've told you—I told you this morning."

Oh, I was sorry for him! "That you just want me not to worry you?"

He looked round at me now, as if in recognition of my understanding him; then ever so gently, "To let me alone," he replied.

There was even a singular little dignity in it, something that made me release him, yet, when I had slowly risen, linger beside him. God knows I never wished to harass him, but I felt that merely, at this, to turn my back on him was to abandon or, to put it more truly, to lose him. "I've just begun a letter to your uncle," I said.

"Well, then, finish it!"

I waited a minute. "What happened before?"

He gazed up at me again. "Before what?"

"Before you came back. And before you went away."

For some time he was silent, but he continued to meet my eyes. "What happened?"

It made me, the sound of the words, in which it seemed to me that I caught for the very first time a small faint quaver of consenting consciousness—it made me drop on my knees beside the bed and seize once more the chance of possessing him. "Dear little Miles, dear little Miles, if you *knew* how I want to help you! It's only that, it's nothing but that, and I'd rather die than give you a pain or do you a wrong—I'd rather die than hurt a hair of you.

Dear little Miles"—oh, I brought it out now even if I *should* go too far—"I just want you to help me to save you!" But I knew in a moment after this that I had gone too far. The answer to my appeal was instantaneous, but it came in the form of an extraordinary blast and chill, a gust of frozen air and a shake of the room as great as if, in the wild wind, the casement had crashed in. The boy gave a loud, high shriek, which, lost in the rest of the shock of sound, might have seemed, indistinctly, though I was so close to him, a note either of jubilation or of terror. I jumped to my feet again and was conscious of darkness. So for a moment we remained, while I stared about me and saw that the drawn curtains were unstirred and the window tight. "Why, the candle's out!" I then cried.

"It was I who blew it, dear!" said Miles.

XVIII

THE next day, after lessons, Mrs. Grose found a moment to say to me quietly: "Have you written, Miss?"

"Yes—I've written." But I didn't add—for the hour—that my letter, sealed and directed, was still in my pocket. There would be time enough to send it before the messenger should go to the village. Meanwhile there had been, on the part of my pupils, no more brilliant, more exemplary morning. It was exactly as if they had both had at heart to gloss over any recent little friction. They performed the dizziest feats of arithmetic, soaring quite out of *my* feeble range, and perpetrated, in higher spirits than ever, geographical and historical jokes. It was conspicuous of course in Miles in particular that he appeared to wish to show how easily he could let me down. This child, to my memory, really lives in a setting of beauty and misery that no words can translate; there was a distinction all his own in every impulse he revealed; never was a small natural creature, to the uninitiated eye all frankness and freedom, a more ingenious, a more extraordinary little gentleman. I had perpetually to guard against the wonder of contemplation into which my initiated view betrayed me; to check the irrelevant gaze and discouraged sigh in which I constantly both attacked and renounced the enigma of what such a little gentleman could have done that deserved a penalty. Say that, by the dark prodigy I knew, the imagination of all evil *had* been opened up to him: all the justice within me ached for the proof that it could ever have flowered into an act.

He had never, at any rate, been such a little gentleman as when, after our early dinner on this dreadful day, he came round to me and asked if I shouldn't like him, for half an hour, to play to me. David playing to Saul could never have shown a finer sense of the occasion. It was literally a charming exhibition of tact, of magnanimity, and quite tantamount to his saying outright: "The true knights we love to read about never push an advantage too far. I know what you mean now: you mean that—to be let alone yourself and not followed up—you'll cease to worry and spy upon me, won't keep me so close to you, will let me go and come. Well, I 'come,' you see—but I don't go! There'll be plenty of time for that. I do really delight in your society, and I only want to show you that I contended for a principle." It may be imagined whether I resisted this appeal or failed to accompany him again, hand in hand, to the schoolroom. He sat down at the old piano and played as he had never played, and if there are those who think he had better have been kicking a football I can only say that I wholly agree with them. For at the end of a time that under his influence I had quite ceased to measure I started up with a strange sense of having literally slept at my post. It was after luncheon, and by the schoolroom fire, and yet I hadn't really, in the least, slept: I had only done something much worse—I had forgotten. Where, all this time, was Flora? When I put the question to Miles he played on a minute before answering, and then could only say: "Why, my dear, how do *I* know?"—breaking moreover into a happy laugh which, immediately after, as if it were a vocal accompaniment, he prolonged into incoherent, extravagant song.

I went straight to my room, but his sister was not there; then, before going downstairs, I looked into several others. As she was nowhere about she would surely be with Mrs. Grose, whom, in the comfort of that theory, I accordingly proceeded in quest of. I found her where I had found her the evening before, but she met my quick challenge with blank, scared ignorance. She had only supposed that, after the repast, I had carried off both the children; as to which she was quite in her right, for it was the very first time I had allowed the little girl out of my sight without some special provision. Of course now indeed she might be with the maids, so that the immediate thing was to look for her without an air of alarm. This we promptly arranged between us; but when, ten minutes later and in pursuance of our arrangement, we met in the hall, it was only to report on either side that after guarded inquiries we had altogether failed to trace her. For a minute there, apart from observation, we exchanged mute alarms, and I could feel with what high interest my friend returned me all those I had from the first given her.

"She'll be above," she presently said—"in one of the rooms you haven't searched."

"No; she's at a distance." I had made up my mind. "She has gone out."

Mrs. Grose stared. "Without a hat?"

I naturally also looked volumes. "Isn't that woman always without one?"

"She's with *her*?"

"She's with *her*!" I declared. "We must find them."

My hand was on my friend's arm, but she failed for the moment, confronted with such an account of the matter, to respond to my pressure. She communed, on the contrary, on the spot, with her uneasiness. "And where's Master Miles?"

"Oh, *he's* with Quint. They're in the schoolroom."

"Lord, Miss!" My view, I was myself aware—and therefore I suppose my tone—had never yet reached so calm an assurance.

"The trick's played," I went on; "they've successfully worked their plan. He found the most divine little way to keep me quiet while she went off."

" 'Divine'?" Mrs. Grose bewilderedly echoed.

"Infernal, then!" I almost cheerfully rejoined. "He has provided for himself as well. But come!"

She had helplessly gloomed at the upper regions. "You leave him——?"

"So long with Quint? Yes—I don't mind that now."

She always ended, at these moments, by getting possession of my hand, and in this manner she could at present still stay me. But after gasping an instant at my sudden resignation, "Because of your letter?" she eagerly brought out.

I quickly, by way of answer, felt for my letter, drew it forth, held it up, and then, freeing myself, went and laid it on the great hall-table. "Luke will take it," I said as I came back. I reached the house-door and opened it; I was already on the steps.

My companion still demurred: the storm of the night and the early morning had dropped, but the afternoon was damp and grey. I came down to the drive while she stood in the doorway. "You go with nothing on?"

"What do I care when the child has nothing? I can't wait to dress," I cried, "and if you must do so, I leave you. Try meanwhile, yourself, upstairs."

"With *them*?" Oh, on this, the poor woman promptly joined me!

XIX

WE WENT straight to the lake, as it was called at Bly, and I dare say rightly called, though I reflect that it may in fact have been a sheet of water less remarkable than it appeared to my untravelled eyes. My acquaintance with sheets of water was small, and the pool of Bly, at all events on the few occasions of my consenting, under the protection of my pupils, to affront its surface in the old flat-bottomed boat moored there for our use, had impressed me both with its extent and its agitation. The usual place of embarkation was half a mile from the house, but I had an intimate conviction that, wherever Flora might be, she was not near home. She had not given me the slip for any small adventure, and, since the day of the very great one that I had shared with her by the pond, I had been aware, in our walks, of the quarter to which she most inclined. This was why I had now given to Mrs. Grose's steps so marked a direction —a direction that made her, when she perceived it, oppose a resistance that showed me she was freshly mystified. "You're going to the water, Miss?—you think she's *in*——?"

"She may be, though the depth is, I believe, nowhere very great.

But what I judge most likely is that she's on the spot from which, the other day, we saw together what I told you."

"When she pretended not to see——?"

"With that astounding self-possession! I've always been sure she wanted to go back alone. And now her brother has managed it for her."

Mrs. Grose still stood where she had stopped. "You suppose they really *talk* of them?"

I could meet this with a confidence! "They say things that, if we heard them, would simply appal us."

"And if she *is* there——?"

"Yes?"

"Then Miss Jessel is?"

"Beyond a doubt. You shall see."

"Oh, thank you!" my friend cried, planted so firm that, taking it in, I went straight on without her. By the time I reached the pool, however, she was close behind me, and I knew that, whatever, to her apprehension, might befall me, the exposure of my society struck her as her least danger. She exhaled a moan of relief as we at last came in sight of the greater part of the water without a sight of the child. There was no trace of Flora on that nearer side of the bank where my observation of her had been most startling, and none on the opposite edge, where, save for a margin of some twenty yards, a thick copse came down to the water. The pond, oblong in shape, had a width so scant compared to its length that, with its ends out of view, it might have been taken for a scant river. We looked at the empty expanse, and then I felt the suggestion of my friend's eyes. I knew what she meant and I replied with a negative headshake.

"No, no; wait! She has taken the boat."

My companion stared at the vacant mooring-place and then again across the lake. "Then where is it?"

"Our not seeing it is the strongest of proofs. She has used it to go over, and then has managed to hide it."

"All alone—that child?"

"She's not alone, and at such times she's not a child: she's an old, old woman." I scanned all the visible shore while Mrs. Grose took again, into the queer element I offered her, one of her plunges of submission; then I pointed out that the boat might perfectly be in a small refuge formed by one of the recesses of the pool, an indentation masked, for the hither side, by a projection of the bank and by a clump of trees growing close to the water.

"But if the boat's there, where on earth's *she*?" my colleague anxiously asked.

"That's exactly what we must learn." And I started to walk further.

"By going all the way round?"

"Certainly, far as it is. It will take us but ten minutes, but it's far enough to have made the child prefer not to walk. She went straight over."

"Laws!" cried my friend again; the chain of my logic was ever too much for her. It dragged her at my heels even now, and when we had got half-way round—a devious, tiresome process, on ground much broken and by a path choked with overgrowth—I paused to give her breath. I sustained her with a grateful arm, assuring her that she might hugely help me; and this started us afresh, so that in the course of but few minutes more we reached a point from which we found the boat to be where I had supposed it. It had been intentionally left as much as possible out of sight and was tied to one of the stakes of a fence that came, just there, down to the brink and that had been an assistance to disembarking. I recognised, as I looked at the pair of short, thick oars, quite safely drawn up, the prodigious character of the feat for a little girl; but I had lived, by this time, too long among wonders and had panted to too many livelier measures. There was a gate in the fence, through which we passed, and that brought us, after a trifling interval, more into the open. Then, "There she is!" we both exclaimed at once.

Flora, a short way off, stood before us on the grass and smiled as if her performance was now complete. The next thing she did, however, was to stoop straight down and pluck—quite as if it were all she was there for—a big, ugly spray of withered fern. I instantly became sure she had just come out of the copse. She waited for us, not herself taking a step, and I was conscious of the rare solemnity with which we presently approached her. She smiled and smiled, and we met; but it was all done in a silence by this time flagrantly ominous. Mrs. Grose was the first to break the spell: she threw herself on her knees and, drawing the child to her breast, clasped in a long embrace the little tender, yielding body. While this dumb convulsion lasted I could only watch it—which I did the more intently when I saw Flora's face peep at me over our companion's shoulder. It was serious now—the flicker had left it; but it strengthened the pang with which I at that moment envied Mrs. Grose the simplicity of *her* relation. Still, all this while, nothing more passed between us save that Flora had let her foolish fern again drop to the ground. What she and I had virtually said to each other was that pretexts were useless now. When Mrs. Grose finally got up she kept the child's hand, so that the two were still before me; and the singular reticence of our communion was even more marked in the frank look she launched me. "I'll be hanged," it said, "if *I'll* speak!"

It was Flora who, gazing all over me in candid wonder, was the first. She was struck with our bareheaded aspect. "Why, where are your things?"

"Where yours are, my dear!" I promptly returned.

She had already got back her gaiety, and appeared to take this as an answer quite sufficient. "And where's Miles?" she went on.

There was something in the small valour of it that quite finished me: these three words from her were, in a flash like the glitter of a drawn blade, the jostle of the cup that my hand, for weeks and weeks, had held high and full to the brim and that now, even before speaking, I felt overflow in a deluge. "I'll tell you if you'll tell *me*——" I heard myself say, then heard the tremor in which it broke.

"Well, what?"

Mrs. Grose's suspense blazed at me, but it was too late now, and I brought the thing out handsomely. "Where, my pet, is Miss Jessel?"

XX

JUST as in the churchyard with Miles, the whole thing was upon us. Much as I had made of the fact that this name had never once, between us, been sounded, the quick, smitten glare with which the child's face now received it fairly likened my breach of the silence to the smash of a pane of glass. It added to the interposing cry, as if to stay the blow, that Mrs. Grose, at the same instant, uttered over my violence—the shriek of a creature scared, or rather wounded, which, in turn, within a few seconds, was completed by a gasp of my own. I seized my colleague's arm. "She's there, she's there!"

Miss Jessel stood before us on the opposite bank exactly as she had stood the other time, and I remember, strangely, as the first feeling now produced in me, my thrill of joy at having brought on a proof. She was there, and I was justified; she was there, and I was neither cruel nor mad. She was there for poor scared Mrs. Grose, but she was there most for Flora; and no moment of my monstrous time was perhaps so extraordinary as that in which I consciously threw out to her—with the sense that, pale and ravenous demon as she was, she would catch and understand it—an inarticulate message of gratitude. She rose erect on the spot my friend and I had lately quitted, and there was not, in all the long reach of her desire, an inch of her evil that fell short. This first vividness of vision and emotion were things of a few seconds, during which Mrs. Grose's dazed blink across to where I pointed struck me as a sovereign sign that she too at last saw, just as it carried my own eyes precipitately to the child. The revelation then of the manner in which Flora was affected startled me, in truth, far more than it would have done to find her also merely agitated, for direct dismay was of course not what I had expected. Prepared and on her guard as our pursuit had actually made her, she would repress every betrayal; and I was therefore shaken, on the spot, by my first glimpse of the particular one for which I had not allowed. To see her, without a convulsion of her small pink face, not even feign to glance in the direction of the prodigy I announced, but only, instead of that, turn at *me* an expression of hard, still gravity, an expression absolutely new and unprecedented and that appeared to read and accuse and judge me—this was a stroke that somehow converted the little girl herself into the very presence that could make me quail. I quailed even though my certitude that she thoroughly saw was never greater than at that instant, and in the immediate need to defend myself I called it passionately to witness. "She's there, you little unhappy thing—there, there, *there*, and you see her as well as you see me!" I had said shortly before to Mrs. Grose that she was not at these times a child, but an old, old woman, and that description of her could not have been more strikingly confirmed than in the way in which, for all answer to this, she simply showed me, without a concession, an admission, of her eyes, a countenance of deeper and deeper, of indeed suddenly quite fixed, reprobation. I was by this time—if I can put the whole thing at all together—more appalled at what I may properly call her manner than at anything else, though it was simultaneously with this that I became aware of having Mrs. Grose also, and very formidably, to reckon with. My elder companion, the next moment, at any rate, blotted out everything but her own flushed face and her loud, shocked protest, a burst of high disapproval. "What a dreadful turn, to be sure, Miss! Where on earth do you see anything?"

I could only grasp her more quickly yet, for even while she spoke the hideous plain presence stood undimmed and undaunted. It had already lasted a minute, and it lasted while I continued, seizing my colleague, quite thrusting her at it and presenting her to it, to insist with my pointing hand. "You don't see her exactly as *we* see?—you mean to say you don't now—*now*? She's as big as a blazing fire! Only look, dearest woman, *look*——!" She looked, even as I did, and gave me, with her deep groan of negation, repulsion, compassion—the mixture with her pity of her relief at her exemption—a sense, touching to me even then, that she would have backed me up if she could. I might well have needed that, for with this hard blow of the proof that her eyes were hopelessly sealed I felt my own situation horribly crumble, I felt—I saw—my livid predecessor press, from her position, on my defeat, and I was conscious, more than all, of what I should have from this instant to deal with in the astounding little attitude of Flora. Into this attitude Mrs. Grose immediately and violently entered, breaking, even while there pierced through my sense of ruin a prodigious private triumph, into breathless reassurance.

"She isn't there, little lady, and nobody's there—and you never see nothing, my sweet! How can poor Miss Jessel—when poor Miss Jessel's dead and buried? *We* know, don't we, love?"—and she appealed, blundering in, to the child. "It's all a mere mistake and a worry and a joke—and we'll go home as fast as we can!"

Our companion, on this, had responded with a strange, quick primness of propriety, and they were again, with Mrs. Grose on her feet, united, as it were, in pained opposition to me. Flora continued to fix me with her small mask of reprobation, and even at that minute I prayed God to forgive me for seeming to see that, as she stood there holding tight to our friend's dress, her incomparable childish beauty had suddenly failed, had quite vanished. I've said it already—she was literally, she was hideously, hard; she had turned common and almost ugly. "I don't know what you mean. I see nobody. I see nothing. I never *have*. I think you're cruel. I don't like you!" Then, after this deliverance, which might have been that of a vulgarly pert little girl in the street, she hugged Mrs. Grose more closely and buried in her skirts the dreadful little face. In this position she produced an almost furious wail. "Take me away, take me away—oh, take me away from *her*!"

"From *me*?" I panted.

"From you—from you!" she cried.

Even Mrs. Grose looked across at me dismayed, while I had nothing to do but communicate again with the figure that, on the opposite bank, without a movement, as rigidly still as if catching, beyond the interval, our voices, was as vividly there for my disaster as it was not there for my service. The wretched child had spoken exactly as if she had got from some outside source each of her stabbing little words, and I could therefore, in the full despair of all I had to accept, but sadly shake my head at her. "If I had ever doubted, all my doubt would at present have gone. I've been living with the miserable truth, and now it has only too much closed round me. Of course I've lost you: I've interfered, and you've seen—under *her* dictation"—with which I faced, over the pool again, our infernal witness—"the easy and perfect way to meet it. I've done my best, but I've lost you. Good-bye." For Mrs. Grose I had an imperative, an almost frantic "Go, go!" before which, in infinite distress, but mutely possessed of the little girl and clearly convinced, in spite of her blindness, that something awful had occurred and some collapse engulfed us, she retreated, by the way we had come, as fast as she could move.

Of what first happened when I was left alone I had no subsequent memory. I only knew that at the end of, I suppose, a quarter of an hour, an odorous dampness and roughness, chilling and piercing my trouble, had made me understand that I must have thrown myself, on my face, on the ground and given way to a wildness of grief. I must have lain there long and cried and sobbed, for when I raised my head the day was almost done. I got up and looked a moment, through the twilight, at the grey pool and its blank, haunted edge, and then I took, back to the house, my dreary and difficult course. When I reached the gate in the fence the boat, to my surprise, was gone, so that I had a fresh reflection to make on Flora's extraordinary command of the situation. She passed that night, by the most tacit, and I should add, were not the word so grotesque a false note, the happiest of arrangements, with Mrs. Grose. I saw neither of them on my return, but, on the other hand as by an ambiguous compensation, I saw a great deal of Miles. I saw—I can use no other phrase—so much of him that it was as if it were more than it had ever been. No evening I had passed at Bly had the portentous quality of this one; in spite of which—and in spite also of the deeper depths of consternation that had opened beneath my feet—there was literally, in the ebbing actual, an extraordinarily sweet sadness. On reaching the house I had never so much as looked for the boy; I had simply gone straight to my room to change what I was wearing and to take in, at a glance, much material testimony to Flora's rupture. Her little belongings had all been removed. When later, by the schoolroom fire, I was served with tea by the usual maid, I indulged, on the article of my other pupil, in no inquiry whatever. He had his freedom now—he might have it to the end! Well, he did have it; and it consisted—in part at least—of his coming in at about eight o'clock and sitting down with me in silence. On the removal of the tea-things I had blown out the candles and drawn my chair closer: I was conscious of a mortal coldness and felt as if I should never again be warm. So, when he appeared, I was sitting in the glow with my thoughts. He paused a moment by the door as if to look at me; then—as if to share them—came to the other side of the hearth and sank into a chair. We sat there in absolute stillness; yet he wanted, I felt, to be with me.

XXI

BEFORE a new day, in my room, had fully broken, my eyes opened to Mrs. Grose, who had come to my bedside with worse news. Flora was so markedly feverish that an illness was perhaps at hand; she had passed a night of extreme unrest, a night agitated above all by fears that had for their subject not in the least her former, but wholly her present, governess. It was not against the possible re-entrance of Miss Jessel on the scene that she protested—it was conspicuously and passionately against mine. I was promptly on my feet of course, and with an immense deal to ask; the more that my friend had discernibly now girded her loins to meet me once more. This I felt as soon as I had put to her the question of her sense of the child's sincerity as against my own. "She persists in denying to you that she saw, or has ever seen, anything?"

My visitor's trouble, truly, was great. "Ah, Miss, it isn't a matter on which I can push her! Yet it isn't either, I must say, as if I much needed to. It has made her, every inch of her, quite old."

"Oh, I see her perfectly from here. She resents, for all the world like some high little personage, the imputation on her truthfulness and, as it were, her respectability. 'Miss Jessel indeed—*she*!' Ah, she's 'respectable,' the chit! The impression she gave me there yesterday was, I assure you, the very strangest of all; it was quite beyond any of the others. I *did* put my foot in it! She'll never speak to me again."

Hideous and obscure as it all was, it held Mrs. Grose briefly silent; then she granted my point with a frankness which, I made sure, had more behind it. "I think indeed, Miss, she never will. She do have a grand manner about it!"

"And that manner"—I summed it up—"is practically what's the matter with her now!"

Oh, that manner, I could see in my visitor's face, and not a little else besides! "She asks me every three minutes if I think you're coming in."

"I see—I see." I too, on my side, had so much more than worked it out. "Has she said to you since yesterday—except to repudiate her familiarity with anything so dreadful—a single other word about Miss Jessel?"

"Not one, Miss. And of course you know," my friend added, "I took it from her, by the lake, that, just then and there at least, there *was* nobody."

"Rather! And, naturally, you take it from her still."

"I don't contradict her. What else can I do?"

"Nothing in the world! You've the cleverest little person to deal with. They've made them—their two friends, I mean—still cleverer even than nature did; for it was wondrous material to play on! Flora has now her grievance, and she'll work it to the end."

"Yes, Miss; but to *what* end?"

"Why, that of dealing with me to her uncle. She'll make me out to him the lowest creature——!"

I winced at the fair show of the scene in Mrs. Grose's face; she looked for a minute as if she sharply saw them together. "And him who thinks so well of you!"

"He has an odd way—it comes over me now," I laughed, "—of proving it! But that doesn't matter. What Flora wants, of course, is to get rid of me."

My companion bravely concurred. "Never again to so much as look at you."

"So that what you've come to me now for," I asked, "is to speed me on my way?" Before she had time to reply, however, I had her in check. "I've a better idea—the result of my reflections. My going *would* seem the right thing, and on Sunday I was terribly near it. Yet that won't do. It's *you* who must go. You must take Flora."

My visitor, at this, did speculate. "But where in the world——?"

"Away from here. Away from *them*. Away, even most of all, now, from me. Straight to her uncle."

"Only to tell on you——?"

"No, not 'only'! To leave me, in addition, with my remedy."

She was still vague. "And what *is* your remedy?"

"Your loyalty, to begin with. And then Miles's."

She looked at me hard. "Do you think he——?"

"Won't if he has the chance, turn on me? Yes, I venture still to think it. At all events, I want to try. Get off with his sister as soon as possible and leave me with him alone." I was amazed, myself, at the spirit I had still in reserve, and therefore perhaps a trifle the more disconcerted at the way in which, in spite of this fine example of it, she hesitated. "There's one thing, of course," I went on: "they mustn't, before she goes, see each other for three seconds." Then it came over me that, in spite of Flora's presumable sequestration from the instant of her return from the pool, it might already be too late. "Do you mean," I anxiously asked, "that they *have* met?"

At this she quite flushed. "Ah, Miss, I'm not such a fool as that! If I've been obliged to leave her three or four times, it has been each time with one of the maids, and at present, though she's alone, she's locked in safe. And yet—and yet!" There were too many things.

"And yet what?"

"Well, are you so sure of the little gentleman?"

"I'm not sure of anything but *you*. But I have, since last evening, a new hope. I think he wants to give me an opening. I do believe that—poor little exquisite wretch!—he wants to speak. Last evening, in the firelight and the silence, he sat with me for two hours as if it were just coming."

Mrs. Grose looked hard, through the window, at the grey, gathering day. "And did it come?"

"No, though I waited and waited, I confess it didn't, and it was without a breach of the silence or so much as a faint allusion to his sister's condition and absence that we at last kissed for good-night. All the same," I continued, "I can't, if her uncle sees her, consent to his seeing her brother without my having given the boy—and most of all because things have got so bad—a little more time."

My friend appeared on this ground more reluctant than I could quite understand. "What do you mean by more time?"

"Well, a day or two—really to bring it out. He'll then be on *my* side—of which you see the importance. If nothing comes, I shall only fail, and you will, at the worst, have helped me by doing, on your arrival in town, whatever you may have found possible." So I put it before her, but she continued for a little so inscrutably embarrassed that I came again to her aid. "Unless, indeed," I wound up, "you really want *not* to go."

I could see it, in her face, at last clear itself; she put out her hand to me as a pledge. "I'll go—I'll go. I'll go this morning."

I wanted to be very just. "If you *should* wish still to wait, I would engage she shouldn't see me."

"No, no: it's the place itself. She must leave it." She held me a moment with heavy eyes, then brought out the rest. "Your idea's the right one. I myself, Miss——"

"Well?"

"I can't stay."

The look she gave me with it made me jump at possibilities. "You mean that, since yesterday, you *have* seen——?"

She shook her head with dignity. "I've *heard*——!"

"Heard?"

"From that child—horrors! There!" she sighed with tragic relief. "On my honour, Miss, she says things——!" But at this evocation she broke down; she dropped, with a sudden sob, upon my sofa and, as I had seen her do before, gave way to all the grief of it.

It was quite in another manner that I, for my part, let myself go. "Oh, thank God!"

She sprang up again at this, drying her eyes with a groan. " 'Thank God'?"

"It so justifies me!"

"It does that, Miss!"

I couldn't have desired more emphasis, but I just hesitated. "She's so horrible?"

I saw my colleague scarce knew how to put it. "Really shocking."

"And about me?"

"About you, Miss—since you must have it. It's beyond everything, for a young lady; and I can't think wherever she must have picked up——"

"The appalling language she applied to me? I can, then!" I broke in with a laugh that was doubtless significant enough.

It only, in truth, left my friend still more grave. "Well, perhaps I ought to also—since I've heard some of it before! Yet I can't bear it," the poor woman went on while, with the same movement, she glanced, on my dressing-table, at the face of my watch. "But I must go back."

I kept her, however. "Ah, if you can't bear it——!"

"How can I stop with her, you mean? Why, just *for* that: to get her away. Far from this," she pursued, "far from *them*——"

"She may be different? she may be free?" I seized her almost with joy. "Then, in spite of yesterday, you *believe*——"

"In such doings?" Her simple description of them required, in the light of her expression, to be carried no further, and she gave me the whole thing as she had never done. "I believe."

Yes, it was a joy, and we were still shoulder to shoulder: if I might continue sure of that I should care but little what else happened. My support in the presence of disaster would be the same as it had been in my early need of confidence, and if my friend would answer for my honesty, I would answer for all the rest. On the point of taking leave of her, none the less, I was to some extent embarrassed. "There's one thing of course—it occurs to me—to remember. My letter, giving the alarm, will have reached town before you."

I now perceived still more how she had been beating about the bush and how weary at last it had made her. "Your letter won't have got there. Your letter never went."

"What then became of it?"

"Goodness knows! Master Miles——"

"Do you mean *he* took it?" I gasped.

She hung fire, but she overcame her reluctance. "I mean that I saw yesterday, when I came back with Miss Flora, that it wasn't where you had put it. Later in the evening I had the chance to question Luke, and he declared that he had neither noticed nor touched it." We could only exchange, on this, one of our deeper mutual soundings, and it was Mrs. Grose who first brought up the plumb with an almost elate "You see!"

"Yes, I see that if Miles took it instead he probably will have read it and destroyed it."

"And don't you see anything else?"

I faced her a moment with a sad smile. "It strikes me that by this time your eyes are open even wider than mine."

They proved to be so indeed, but she could still blush, almost, to show it. "I make out now what he must have done at school." And she gave, in her simple sharpness, an almost droll disillusioned nod. "He stole!"

I turned it over—I tried to be more judicial. "Well—perhaps."

She looked as if she found me unexpectedly calm. "He stole *letters*!"

She couldn't know my reasons for a calmness after all pretty shallow; so I showed them off as I might. "I hope then it was to more purpose than in this case! The note, at any rate, that I put on the table yesterday," I pursued, "will have given him so scant an advantage—for it contained only the bare demand for an interview—that he is already much ashamed of having gone so far for so little, and that what he had on his mind last evening was precisely the need of confession." I seemed to myself, for the instant, to have mastered it, to see it all. "Leave us, leave us"—I was already, at the door, hurrying her off. "I'll get it out of him. He'll meet me—he'll confess. If he confesses, he's saved. And if he's saved——"

"Then *you* are?" The dear woman kissed me on this, and I took her farewell. "I'll save you without him!" she cried as she went.

XXII

Yet it was when she had got off—and I missed her on the spot—that the great pinch really came. If I had counted on what it would give me to find myself alone with Miles, I speedily perceived, at least, that it would give me a measure. No hour of my stay in fact was so assailed with apprehensions as that of my coming down to learn that the carriage containing Mrs. Grose and my younger pupil had already rolled out of the gates. Now I *was*, I said to myself, face to face with the elements, and for much of the rest of the day, while I fought my weakness, I could consider that I had been supremely rash. It was a tighter place still than I had yet turned round in; all the more that, for the first time, I could see in the aspect of others a confused reflection of the crisis. What had happened naturally caused them all to stare; there was too little of the explained, throw out whatever we might, in the suddenness of my colleague's act. The maids and the men looked blank; the effect of which on my nerves was an aggravation until I saw the necessity of making it a positive aid. It was precisely, in short, by just clutching the helm that I avoided total wreck; and I dare say that, to bear up at all, I became, that morning, very grand and very dry. I welcomed the consciousness that I was charged with much to do, and I caused it to be known as well that, left thus to myself, I was quite remarkably firm. I wandered with that manner, for the next hour or two, all over the place and looked, I have no doubt, as if I were ready for any onset. So, for the benefit of whom it might concern, I paraded with a sick heart.

The person it appeared least to concern proved to be, till dinner, little Miles himself. My perambulations had given me, meanwhile, no glimpse of him, but they had tended to make more public the change taking place in our relation as a consequence of his having at the piano, the day before, kept me, in Flora's interest, so beguiled and befooled. The stamp of publicity had of course been fully given by her confinement and departure, and the change itself was now ushered in by our non-observance of the regular custom of the schoolroom. He had already disappeared when, on my way down, I pushed open his door, and I learned below that he had breakfasted—in the presence of a couple of the maids—with Mrs. Grose and his sister. He had then gone out, as he said, for a stroll; than which nothing, I reflected, could better have expressed his frank view of the abrupt transformation of my office. What he would now permit this office to consist of was yet to be settled: there was a queer relief, at all events—I mean for myself in especial—in the renouncement of one pretension. If so much had sprung to the surface, I scarce put it too strongly in saying that what had perhaps sprung highest was the absurdity of our prolonging the fiction that I had anything more to teach him. It sufficiently stuck out that, by tacit little tricks in which even more than myself he carried out the care for my dignity, I had had to appeal to him to let me off straining to meet him on the ground of his true capacity. He had at any rate his freedom now; I was never to touch it again; as I had amply shown, moreover, when, on his joining me in the schoolroom the previous night, I had uttered, on the subject of the interval just concluded, neither challenge nor hint. I had too much, from this moment, my other ideas. Yet when he at last arrived the difficulty of applying them, the accumulations of my problem, were brought straight home to me by the beautiful little presence on which what had occurred had as yet, for the eye, dropped neither stain nor shadow.

To mark, for the house, the high state I cultivated I decreed that my meals with the boy should be served, as we called it, downstairs; so that I had been awaiting him in the ponderous pomp of the room outside of the window of which I had had from Mrs. Grose, that first scared Sunday, my flash of something it would scarce have done to call light. Here at present I felt afresh—for I had felt it again and again—how my equilibrium depended on the success of my rigid will, the will to shut my eyes as tight as possible to the truth that what I had to deal with was, revoltingly, against nature. I could only get on at all by taking "nature" into my confidence and my account, by treating my monstrous ordeal as a push in a direction unusual, of course, and unpleasant, but demanding, after all, for a fair front, only another turn of the screw of ordinary human virtue. No attempt, none the less, could well require more tact than just this attempt to supply, one's self, *all* the nature. How could I put even a little of that article into a suppression of reference to what had occurred? How, on the other hand, could I make a reference without a new plunge into the hideous obscure? Well, a sort of answer, after a time, had come to me, and it was so far confirmed as that I was met, incontestably, by the quickened vision of what was rare in my little companion. It was indeed as if he had found even now—as he had so often found at lessons—still some other delicate way to ease me off. Wasn't there light in the fact which, as we shared our solitude, broke out with a specious glitter it had never yet quite worn?—the fact that (opportunity aiding, precious opportunity which had now come) it would be preposterous, with a child so endowed, to forgo the help one might wrest from absolute intelligence? What had his intelligence been given him for but to save him? Mightn't one, to reach his mind, risk the stretch of an angular arm over his character? It was as if, when we were face to face in the dining-room, he had literally shown me the way. The roast mutton was on the table, and I had dispensed with attendance. Miles, before he sat down, stood a moment with his hands in his pockets and looked at the joint, on which he seemed on the point of passing some humorous judgment. But what he presently produced was: "I say, my dear, is she really very awfully ill?"

"Little Flora? Not so bad but that she'll presently be better. London will set her up. Bly had ceased to agree with her. Come here and take your mutton."

He alertly obeyed me, carried the plate carefully to his seat, and, when he was established, went on. "Did Bly disagree with her so terribly suddenly?"

"Not so suddenly as you might think. One had seen it coming on."

"Then why didn't you get her off before?"

"Before what?"

"Before she became too ill to travel."

I found myself prompt. "She's *not* too ill to travel: she only might have become so if she had stayed. This was just the moment to seize. The journey will dissipate the influence"—oh, I was grand! —"and carry it off."

"I see, I see"—Miles, for that matter, was grand too. He settled to his repast with the charming little "table manner" that, from the day of his arrival, had relieved me of all grossness of admonition. Whatever he had been driven from school for, it was not for ugly feeding. He was irreproachable, as always, to-day; but he was unmistakably more conscious. He was discernibly trying to take for granted more things than he found, without assistance, quite easy; and he dropped into peaceful silence while he felt his situation. Our meal was of the briefest—mine a vain pretence, and I had the things immediately removed. While this was done Miles stood again with his hands in his little pockets and his back to me—stood and looked out of the wide window through which, that other day, I had seen what pulled me up. We continued silent while the maid was with us—as silent, it whimsically occurred to me, as some young couple who, on their wedding-journey, at the inn, feel shy in the presence of the waiter. He turned round only when the waiter had left us. "Well—so we're alone!"

XXIII

"Oh, more or less." I fancy my smile was pale. "Not absolutely. We shouldn't like that!" I went on.

"No—I suppose we shouldn't. Of course we have the others."

"We have the others—we have indeed the others," I concurred.

"Yet even though we have them," he returned, still with his hands in his pockets and planted there in front of me, "they don't much count, do they?"

I made the best of it, but I felt wan. "It depends on what you call 'much'!"

"Yes"—with all accommodation—"everything depends!" On this, however, he faced to the window again and presently reached it with his vague, restless, cogitating step. He remained there awhile, with his forehead against the glass, in contemplation of the stupid shrubs I knew and the dull things of November. I had always my hyprocisy of "work," behind which, now, I gained the sofa. Steadying myself with it there as I had repeatedly done at those moments of torment that I have described as the moments of my knowing the children to be given to something from which I was barred, I sufficiently obeyed my habit of being prepared for the worst. But an extraordinary impression dropped on me as I extracted a meaning from the boy's embarrassed back—none other than the impression that I was not barred now. This inference grew in a few minutes to sharp intensity and seemed bound up with the direct perception that it was positively *he* who was. The frames and squares of the great window were a kind of image, for him, of a kind of failure. I felt that I saw him, at any rate, shut in or shut out. He was admirable, but not comfortable: I took it in with a throb of hope. Wasn't he looking, through the haunted pane, for something he couldn't see?—and wasn't it the first time in the whole business that he had known such a lapse? The first, the very first: I found it a splendid portent. It made him anxious, though he watched himself; he had been anxious all day and, even while in his usual sweet little manner he sat at table, had needed all his small strange genius to give it a gloss. When he at last turned round to meet me, it was almost as if this genius had succumbed. "Well, I think I'm glad Bly agrees with *me*!"

"You would certainly seem to have seen, these twenty-four hours, a good deal more of it than for some time before. I hope," I went on bravely, "that you've been enjoying yourself."

"Oh, yes, I've been ever so far; all round about—miles and miles away. I've never been so free."

He had really a manner of his own, and I could only try to keep up with him. "Well, do you like it?"

He stood there smiling; then at last he put into two words—"Do *you*?"—more discrimination than I had ever heard two words contain. Before I had time to deal with that, however, he continued as if with the sense that this was an impertinence to be softened. "Nothing could be more charming than the way you take it, for of course if we're alone together now it's you that are alone most. But I hope," he threw in, "you don't particularly mind!"

"Having to do with you?" I asked. "My dear child, how can I help minding? Though I've renounced all claim to your company,—you're so beyond me,—I at least greatly enjoy it. What else should I stay on for?"

He looked at me more directly, and the expression of his face, graver now, struck me as the most beautiful I had ever found in it. "You stay on just for *that*?"

"Certainly. I stay on as your friend and from the tremendous interest I take in you till something can be done for you that may be more worth your while. That needn't surprise you." My voice trembled so that I felt it impossible to suppress the shake. "Don't you remember how I told you, when I came and sat on your bed the night of the storm, that there was nothing in the world I wouldn't do for you?"

"Yes, yes!" He, on his side, more and more visibly nervous, had a tone to master; but he was so much more succesful than I that, laughing out through his gravity, he could pretend we were pleasantly jesting. "Only that, I think, was to get me to do something for *you*!"

"It was partly to get you to do something," I conceded. "But, you know, you didn't do it."

"Oh, yes," he said with the brightest superficial eagerness, "you wanted me to tell you something."

"That's it. Out, straight out. What you have on your mind, you know."

"Ah, then, is *that* what you've stayed over for?"

He spoke with a gaiety through which I could still catch the finest little quiver of resentful passion; but I can't begin to express the effect upon me of an implication of surrender even so faint. It was as if what I had yearned for had come at last only to astonish me. "Well, yes—I may as well make a clean breast of it. It was precisely for that."

He waited so long that I supposed it for the purpose of repudiating the assumption on which my action had been founded; but what he finally said was: "Do you mean now—here?"

"There couldn't be a beter place or time." He looked round him uneasily, and I had the rare—oh, the queer!—impression of the very first symptom I had seen in him of the approach of immediate fear. It was as if he were suddenly afraid of me—which struck me indeed as perhaps the best thing to make him. Yet in the very pang of the effort I felt it vain to try sternness, and I heard myself the next instant so gentle as to be almost grotesque. "You want so to go out again?"

"Awfully!" He smiled at me heroically, and the touching little bravery of it was enhanced by his actually flushing with pain. He had picked up his hat, which he had brought in, and stood twirling it in a way that gave me, even as I was just nearly reaching port, a perverse horror of what I was doing. To do it in *any* way was an act of violence, for what did it consist of but the obtrusion of the idea of grossness and guilt on a small helpless creature who had been for me a revelation of the possibilities of beautiful intercourse? Wasn't it base to create for a being so exquisite a mere alien awkwardness? I suppose I now read into our situation a clearness it couldn't have had at the time, for I seem to see our poor eyes already lighted with some spark of a prevision of the anguish that was to come. So we circled about, with terrors and scruples, like fighters not daring to close. But it was for each other we feared! That kept us a little longer suspended and unbruised. "I'll tell you everything," Miles said—"I mean I'll tell you anything you like. You'll stay on with me, and we shall both be all right and I *will* tell you—I *will*. But not now."

"Why not now?"

My insistence turned him from me and kept him once more at his window in a silence during which, between us, you might have heard a pin drop. Then he was before me again with the air of a person for whom, outside, someone who had frankly to be reckoned with was waiting. "I have to see Luke."

I had not yet reduced him to quite so vulgar a lie, and I felt proportionately ashamed. But, horrible as it was, his lies made up my truth. I achieved thoughtfully a few loops of my knitting. "Well, then, go to Luke, and I'll wait for what you promise. Only, in return for that, satisfy, before you leave me, one very much smaller request."

He looked as if he felt he had succeeded enough to be able still a little to bargain. "Very much smaller——?"

"Yes, a mere fraction of the whole. Tell me"—oh, my work preoccupied me, and I was offhand!—"if, yesterday afternoon, from the table in the hall, you took, you know, my letter."

XXIV

My sense of how he received this suffered for a minute from something that I can describe only as a fierce split of my attention—a stroke that at first, as I sprang straight up, reduced me to the mere blind movement of getting hold of him, drawing him close, and, while I just fell for support against the nearest piece of furniture, instinctively keeping him with his back to the window. The appearance was full upon us that I had already had to deal with here: Peter Quint had come into view like a sentinel before a prison. The next thing I saw was that, from outside, he had reached the window, and then I knew that, close to the glass and glaring in through it, he offered once more to the room his white face of damnation. It represents but grossly what took place within me at the sight to say that on the second my decision was made; yet I believe that no woman so overwhelmed ever in so short a time recovered her grasp of the *act*. It came to me in the very horror of the immediate presence that the act would be, seeing and facing what I saw and faced, to keep the boy himself unaware. The inspiration—I can call it by no other name—was that I felt how voluntarily, how transcendently, I *might.* It was like fighting with a demon for a human soul, and when I had fairly so appraised it I saw how the human soul—held out, in the tremor of my hands, at arm's length—had a perfect dew of sweat on a lovely childish forehead. The face that was close to mine was as white as the face against the glass, and out of it presently came a sound, not low nor weak, but as if from much further away, that I drank like a waft of fragrance.

"Yes—I took it."

At this, with a moan of joy, I enfolded, I drew him close; and while I held him to my breast, where I could feel in the sudden fever of his little body the tremendous pulse of his little heart, I kept my eyes on the thing at the window and saw it move and shift its posture. I have likened it to a sentinel, but its slow wheel, for a moment, was rather the prowl of a baffled beast. My present quickened courage, however, was such that, not too much to let it through, I had to shade, as it were, my flame. Meanwhile the glare of the face was again at the window, the scoundrel fixed as if to watch and wait. It was the very confidence that I might now defy him, as well as the positive certitude, by this time, of the child's unconsciousness, that made me go on. "What did you take it for?"

"To see what you said about me."

"You opened the letter?"

"I opened it."

My eyes were now, as I held him off a little again, on Miles's own face, in which the collapse of mockery showed me how complete was the ravage of uneasiness. What was prodigious was that at last, by my success, his sense was sealed and his communication stopped: he knew that he was in presence, but knew not of what, and knew still less that I also was and that I did know. And what did this strain of trouble matter when my eyes went back to the window only to see that the air was clear again and—by my personal triumph—the influence quenched? There was nothing there. I felt that the cause was mine and that I should surely get *all.* "And you found nothing!"—I let my elation out.

He gave the most mournful, thoughtful little headshake. "Nothing."

"Nothing, nothing!" I almost shouted in my joy.

"Nothing, nothing," he sadly repeated.

I kissed his forehead; it was drenched. "So what have you done with it?"

"I've burnt it."

"Burnt it?" It was now or never. "Is that what you did at school?"

Oh, what this brought up! "At school?"

"Did you take letters?—or other things?"

"Other things?" He appeared now to be thinking of something far off and that reached him only through the pressure of his anxiety. Yet it did reach him. "Did I *steal*?"

I felt myself redden to the roots of my hair as well as wonder if it were more strange to put to a gentleman such a question or to see him take it with allowances that gave the very distance of his fall in the world. "Was it for that you mightn't go back?"

The only thing he felt was rather a dreary little surprise. "Did you know I mightn't go back?"

"I know everything."

He gave me at this the longest and strangest look. "Everything?"

"Everything. Therefore *did* you——?" But I couldn't say it again.

Miles, could, very simply. "No. I didn't steal."

My face must have shown him I believed him utterly; yet my hands—but it was for pure tenderness—shook him as if to ask him why, if it was all for nothing, he had condemned me to months of torment. "What then did you do?"

He looked in vague pain all round the top of the room and drew his breath, two or three times over, as if with difficulty. He might have been standing at the bottom of the sea and raising his eyes to some faint green twilight. "Well—I said things."

"Only that?"

"They thought it was enough!"

"To turn you out for?"

Never, truly, had a person "turned out" shown so little to explain it as this little person! He appeared to weigh my question, but in a manner quite detached and almost helpless. "Well, I suppose I oughtn't."

"But to whom did you say them?"

He evidently tried to remember, but it dropped—he had lost it. "I don't know!"

He almost smiled at me in the desolation of his surrender, which was indeed practically, by this time, so complete that I ought to have left it there. But I was infatuated—I was blind with victory, though even then the very effect that was to have brought him so much nearer was already that of added separation. "Was it to everyone?" I asked.

"No; it was only to——" But he gave a sick little headshake. "I don't remember their names."

"Were they then so many?"

"No—only a few. Those I liked."

Those he liked? I seemed to float not into clearness, but into a darker obscure, and within a minute there had come to me out of my very pity the appalling alarm of his being perhaps innocent. It was for the instant confounding and bottomless, for if he *were* innocent, what then on earth was *I*? Paralysed, while it lasted, by the mere brush of the question, I let him go a little, so that, with a deep-drawn sigh, he turned away from me again; which, as he faced toward the clear window, I suffered, feeling that I had nothing now there to keep him from. "And did they repeat what you said?" I went on after a moment.

He was soon at some distance from me, still breathing hard and again with the air, though now without anger for it, of being confined against his will. Once more, as he had done before, he looked up at the dim day as if, of what had hitherto sustained him, nothing was left but an unspeakable anxiety. "Oh, yes," he nevertheless replied—"they must have repeated them. To those *they* liked," he added.

There was, somehow, less of it than I had expected; but I turned it over. "And these things came round——?"

"To the masters? Oh, yes!" he answered very simply. "But I didn't know they'd tell."

"The masters? They didn't—they've never told. That's why I ask you."

He turned to me again his little beautiful fevered face. "Yes, it was too bad."

"Too bad?"

"What I suppose I sometimes said. To write home."

I can't name the exquisite pathos of the contradiction given to such a speech by such a speaker; I only know that the next instant

I heard myself throw off with homely force: "Stuff and nonsense!" But the next after that I must have sounded stern enough. "What *were* these things?"

My sternness was all for his judge, his executioner; yet it made him avert himself again, and that movement made *me*, with a single bound and an irrepressible cry, spring straight upon him. For there again, against the glass, as if to blight his confession and stay his answer, was the hideous author of our woe—the white face of damnation. I felt a sick swim at the drop of my victory and all the return of my battle, so that the wildness of my veritable leap only served as a great betrayal. I saw him, from the midst of my act, meet it with a divination, and on the perception that even now he only guessed, and that the window was still to his own eyes free, I let the impulse flame up to convert the climax of his dismay into the very proof of his liberation. "No more, no more, no more!" I shrieked, as I tried to press him against me, to my visitant.

"Is she *here*?" Miles panted as he caught with his sealed eyes the direction of my words. Then as his strange "she" staggered me and, with a gasp, I echoed it, "Miss Jessel, Miss Jessel!" he with a sudden fury gave me back.

I seized, stupefied, his supposition—some sequel to what we had done to Flora, but this made me only want to show him that it was better still than that. "It's not Miss Jessel! But it's at the window—straight before us. It's *there*—the coward horror, there for the last time!"

At this, after a second in which his head made the movement of a baffled dog's on a scent and then gave a frantic little shake for air and light, he was at me in a white rage, bewildered, glaring vainly over the place and missing wholly, though it now, to my sense, filled the room like the taste of poison, the wide, overwhelming presence. "It's *he*?"

I was so determined to have all my proof that I flashed into ice to challenge him. "Whom do you mean by 'he'?"

"Peter Quint—you devil!" His face gave again, round the room, its convulsed supplication. "*Where*?"

They are in my ears still, his supreme surrender of the name and his tribute to my devotion. "What does he matter now, my own?—what will he *ever* matter? *I* have you," I launched at the beast, "but he has lost you for ever!" Then, for the demonstration of my work, "There, *there*!" I said to Miles.

But he had already jerked straight round, stared, glared again, and seen but the quiet day. With the stroke of the loss I was so proud of he uttered the cry of a creature hurled over an abyss, and the grasp with which I recovered him might have been that of catching him in his fall. I caught him, yes, I held him—it may be imagined with what a passion; but at the end of a minute I began to feel what it truly was that I held. We were alone with the quiet day, and his little heart, dispossessed, had stopped.

The Beast in the Jungle

The Beast in the Jungle

THE BEAST IN THE JUNGLE, which first came out in a volume of short fictions called *The Better Sort* (1903), is a very good example of the later and ultimate manner of Henry James. It is the story of a man who spends his life expecting some rare and prodigious stroke of fate only to discover in the end that he has indeed suffered his fate—which is precisely to have been "the man in the world to whom nothing whatever was to happen." The idea that haunts John Marcher of being singled out for an extraordinary visitation bears all the marks of a compulsive fantasy. It generates the powerful image of the crouching beast lying in wait for him amidst the turns and twists of his life—an image which in its perfect fusion of terror and desire brings to the surface the innermost Jamesian attitude toward experience. John Marcher, with his obsessive search of experience and equally obsessive withdrawal from it, is a "poor sensitive gentleman" of the type who appears again and again in James's writings; and it may be said that in his account of Marcher's doom James created the unifying fable summing up the predicament of all those figures of his imagination who forfeit their allotted share of experience through excessive pride or delicacy or rationality.

It is important to note that *The Beast in the Jungle* appeared in the same year as *The Ambassadors*. There is a clear connection between the two works. The central scene of *The Ambassadors* is the scene laid in Gloriani's Parisian garden, where Lambert Strether, another poor sensitive gentleman, proclaims his conversion to the doctrine of experience. The lesson drawn by Strether is that "it doesn't so much matter what you do in particular so long as you have your life. If you haven't had that what *have* you had? . . . Live, live!" The same lesson is drawn by Marcher when with the wane of his hopes he comes to realize that "it wouldn't have been failure to be bankrupt, dishonoured, pilloried, hanged; it was failure not to be anything. . . ." Nowhere in James is this lesson of the primary uses of life demonstrated with the concentration achieved in *The Beast in the Jungle.* It is entirely possible to read the story as an expression of the cult of experience in American writing, but it would be a mistake thus to limit its meaning, which is so all-inclusive as to refer to every conceivable failure of human energy.

I

WHAT determined the speech that startled him in the course of their encounter scarcely matters, being probably but some words spoken by himself quite without intention—spoken as they lingered and slowly moved together after their renewal of acquaintance. He had been conveyed by friends, an hour or two before, to the house at which she was staying; the party of visitors at the other house, of whom he was one, and thanks to whom it was his theory, as always, that he was lost in the crowd, had been invited over to luncheon. There had been after luncheon much dispersal, all in the interest of the original motive, a view of Weatherend itself and the fine things, intrinsic features, pictures, heirlooms, treasures of all the arts, that made the place almost famous; and the great rooms were so numerous that guests could wander at their will, hang back from the principal group, and, in cases where they took such matters with the last seriousness, give themselves up to mysterious appreciations and measurements. There were persons to be observed, singly or in couples, bending toward objects in out-of-the-way corners with their hands on their knees and their heads nodding quite as with the emphasis of an excited sense of smell. When they were two they either mingled their sounds of ecstasy or melted into silences of even deeper import, so that there were aspects of the occasion that gave it for Marcher much the air of the "look round," previous to a sale highly advertised, that excites or quenches, as may be, the dream of acquisition. The dream of acquisition at Weatherend would have had to be wild indeed, and John Marcher found himself, among such suggestions, disconcerted almost equally by the presence of those who knew too much and by that of those who knew nothing. The great rooms caused so much poetry and history to press upon him that he needed to wander apart to feel in a proper relation with them, though his doing so was not, as happened, like the gloating of some of his companions, to be compared to the movements of a dog sniffing a cupboard. It had an issue promptly enough in a direction that was not to have been calculated.

It led, in short, in the course of the October afternoon, to his closer meeting with May Bartram, whose face, a reminder, yet not quite a remembrance, as they sat, much separated, at a very long table, had begun merely by troubling him rather pleasantly. It affected him as the sequel of something of which he had lost the beginning. He knew it, and for the time quite welcomed it, as a continuation, but didn't know what it continued, which was an interest, or an amusement, the greater as he was also somehow aware—yet without a direct sign from her—that the young woman herself had not lost the thread. She had not lost it, but she wouldn't give it back to him, he saw, without some putting forth of his hand for it; and he not only saw that, but saw several things more, things odd enough in the light of the fact that at the moment some accident of grouping brought them face to face he was still merely fumbling with the idea that any contact between them in the past would have had no importance. If it had had no importance he scarcely knew why his actual impression of her should so seem to have so much; the answer to which, however, was that in such a life as they all appeared to be leading for the moment one could but take things as they came. He was satisfied, without in the least being able to say why, that this young lady might roughly have ranked in the house as a poor relation; satisfied also that she was not there on a brief visit, but was more or less a part of the establishment—almost a working, a remunerated part. Didn't she enjoy at periods a protection that she paid for by helping, among other services, to show the place and explain it, deal with the tiresome people, answer questions about the dates of the buildings, the styles of the furniture, the authorship of the pictures, the favourite haunts of the ghost? It wasn't that she looked as if you could have given her shillings—it was impossible to look less so. Yet when she finally drifted toward him, distinctly handsome, though ever so much older—older than when he had seen her before—it might have been as an effect of her guessing that he had, within the couple of hours, devoted more imagination to her than to all the others put together, and had thereby penetrated to a kind of truth that the others were too stupid for. She *was* there on harder terms than anyone; she was there as a consequence of things suffered, in one way and another, in the interval of years; and she remembered him very much as she was remembered—only a good deal better.

By the time they at last thus came to speech they were alone in one of the rooms—remarkable for a fine portrait over the chimney-place—out of which their friends had passed, and the charm of it was that even before they had spoken they had practically arranged with each other to stay behind for talk. The charm, happily, was in other things too; it was partly in there being scarce a spot at Weatherend without something to stay behind for. It was in the way the autumn day looked into the high windows as it waned; in the way the red light, breaking at the close from under a low, sombre sky, reached out in a long shaft and played over old wainscots, old tapestry, old gold, old colour. It was most of all perhaps in the way she came to him as if, since she had been turned on to deal with the simpler sort, he might, should he choose to keep the whole thing down, just take her mild attention for a part of her general business. As soon as he heard her voice, however, the gap was filled up and the missing link supplied; the slight irony he divined in her attitude lost its advantage. He almost jumped at it to get there before her. "I met you years and years ago in Rome. I remember all about it." She confessed to disappointment—she had been so sure he didn't; and to prove how well he did he began to pour forth the particular recollections that popped up as he called for them. Her face and her voice, all at his service now, worked the miracle—the impression operating like the torch of a lamplighter who touches into flame, one by one, a long row of gas jets. Marcher flattered himself that the illumination was brilliant, yet he was really still more pleased on her showing him, with amusement, that in his haste to make everything right he had got most things rather wrong. It hadn't been at Rome—it had been at Naples; and it hadn't been seven years before—it had been more nearly ten. She hadn't been either with her uncle and aunt, but with her mother and her brother; in addition to which it was not with the Pembles that *he* had been, but with the Boyers, coming down in their company from Rome—a point on which she insisted, a little to his confusion, and as to which she had her evidence in hand. The Boyers she had known, but she didn't know the Pembles, though she had heard of them, and it was the people he was with who had made them acquainted. The incident of the thunderstorm that had raged round them with such violence as to drive them for refuge into an excavation—this incident had not occurred at the Palace of the Caesars, but at Pompeii, on an occasion when they had been present there at an important find.

He accepted her amendments, he enjoyed her corrections, though the moral of them was, she pointed out, that he *really* didn't remember the least thing about her; and he only felt it as a drawback that when all was made comfortable to the truth there didn't appear much of anything left. They lingered together still, she neglecting her office—for from the moment he was so clever she had no proper right to him—and both neglecting the house, just waiting as to see if a memory or two more wouldn't again breathe upon them. It had not taken them many minutes, after all, to put down on the table, like the cards of a pack, those that constituted their respective hands; only what came out was that the pack was unfortunately not perfect—that the past, invoked, invited, encouraged, could give them, naturally, no more than it had. It had made them meet—her at twenty, him at twenty-five; but nothing was so strange, they seemed to say to each other, as that, while so occupied, it hadn't done a little more for them. They looked at each other as with the feeling of an occasion missed; the present one would have been so much better if the other, in the far distance, in the foreign land, hadn't been so stupidly meagre. There weren't, apparently, all counted, more than a dozen little old things that had succeeded in coming to pass between them; trivialities of youth, simplicities of freshness, stupidities of ignorance, small possible germs, but too deeply buried—too deeply (didn't it seem?) to sprout after so many years. Marcher said to himself that he ought to have rendered her some service—saved her from a capsized boat in the Bay, or at least recovered her dressing-bag, filched from her cab, in the streets of Naples, by a lazzarone with a stiletto. Or it would have been nice if he could have been taken with fever, alone, at his hotel, and she could have come to look after him, to write to his people, to drive him out in convalescence. *Then* they would be in possession of the something or other that their actual show seemed to lack. It yet somehow presented itself, this show, as too good to be spoiled; so that they were reduced for a few minutes more to wondering a little helplessly why—since they seemed to know a certain number of the same people—their reunion had been so long averted. They didn't use that name for it, but their delay from minute to minute to join the others was a kind of confession that they didn't quite want it to be a failure. Their attempted supposition of reasons for their not having met but showed how little they knew of each other. There came in fact a moment when Marcher felt a positive pang. It was vain to pretend she was an old friend, for all the communities were wanting, in spite of which it was as an old friend that he saw she would have suited him. He had new ones enough—was surrounded with them, for instance, at that hour at the other house; as a new one he probably wouldn't have so much as noticed her. He would have liked to invent something, get her to make-believe with him that some passage of a romantic or critical kind *had* originally occurred. He was really almost reaching out in imagination—as against time—for something that would do, and saying to himself that if it didn't come this new incident would simply and rather awkwardly close. They would separate, and now for no second or for no third chance. They would have tried and not succeeded. Then it was, just at the turn, as he afterwards made it out to himself, that, everything else failing, she herself decided to take up the case and, as it were, save the situation. He felt as soon as she spoke that she had been consciously keeping back what she said and hoping to get on without it; a scruple in her that immensely touched him when, by the end of three or four minutes more, he was able to measure it. What she brought out, at any rate, quite cleared the air and supplied the link—the link it was such a mystery he should frivolously have managed to lose.

"You know you told me something that I've never forgotten and that again and again has made me think of you since; it was that tremendously hot day when we went to Sorrento, across the bay, for the breeze. What I allude to was what you said to me, on the way back, as we sat, under the awning of the boat, enjoying the cool. Have you forgotten?"

He had forgotten, and he was even more surprised than ashamed. But the great thing was that he saw it was no vulgar reminder of any "sweet" speech. The vanity of women had long memories, but she was making no claim on him of a compliment or a mistake. With another woman, a totally different one, he might have feared the recall of possibly even some imbecile "offer." So, in having to say that he had indeed forgotten, he was conscious rather of a loss than of a gain; he already saw an interest in the matter of her reference. "I try to think—but I give it up. Yet I remember the Sorrento day."

"I'm not very sure you do," May Bartram after a moment said; "and I'm not very sure I ought to want you to. It's dreadful to bring a person back, at any time, to what he was ten years before. If you've lived away from it," she smiled, "so much the better."

"Ah, if *you* haven't why should I?" he asked.

"Lived away, you mean, from what I myself was?"

"From what *I* was. I was of course an ass," Marcher went on; "but I would rather know from you just the sort of ass I was than —from the moment you have something in your mind—not know anything."

Still, however, she hesitated. "But if you've completely ceased to be that sort——?"

"Why, I can then just so all the more bear to know. Besides, perhaps I haven't."

"Perhaps. Yet if you haven't," she added, "I should suppose you would remember. Not indeed that *I* in the least connect with my impression the invidious name you use. If I had only thought you foolish," she explained, "the thing I speak of wouldn't so have remained with me. It was about yourself." She waited, as if it might come to him; but as, only meeting her eyes in wonder, he gave no sign, she burnt her ships. "Has it ever happened?"

Then it was that, while he continued to stare, a light broke for him and the blood slowly came to his face, which began to burn with recognition. "Do you mean I told you——?" But he faltered, lest what came to him shouldn't be right, lest he should only give himself away.

"It was something about yourself that it was natural one shouldn't forget—that is if one remembered you at all. That's why I ask you," she smiled, "if the thing you then spoke of has ever come to pass?"

Oh, then he saw, but he was lost in wonder and found himself embarrassed. This, he also saw, made her sorry for him, as if her allusion had been a mistake. It took him but a moment, however, to feel that it had not been, much as it had been a surprise. After the first little shock of it her knowledge on the contrary began, even if rather strangely, to taste sweet to him. She was the only other person in the world then who would have it, and she had had it all these years, while the fact of his having so breathed his secret had unaccountably faded from him. No wonder they couldn't have met as if nothing had happened. "I judge," he finally said, "that I know what you mean. Only I had strangely enough lost the consciousness of having taken you so far into my confidence."

"Is it because you've taken so many others as well?"

"I've taken nobody. Not a creature since then."

"So that I'm the only person who knows?"

"The only person in the world."

"Well," she quickly replied, "I myself have never spoken. I've never, never repeated of you what you told me." She looked at him so that he perfectly believed her. Their eyes met over it in such a way that he was without a doubt. "And I never will."

She spoke with an earnestness that, as if almost excessive, put him at ease about her possible derision. Somehow the whole question was a new luxury to him—that is, from the moment she was in possession. If she didn't take the ironic view she clearly took the sympathetic, and that was what he had had, in all the long time, from no one whomsoever. What he felt was that he couldn't at present have begun to tell her and yet could profit perhaps exquisitely by the accident of having done so of old. "Please don't then. We're just right as it is."

"Oh, I am," she laughed, "if you are!" To which she added: "Then you do still feel in the same way?"

It was impossible to him not to take to himself that she was really interested, and it all kept coming as a sort of revelation. He had thought of himself so long as abominably alone, and, lo, he wasn't alone a bit. He hadn't been, it appeared, for an hour—since those moments on the Sorrento boat. It was *she* who had been, he seemed to see as he looked at her—she who had been made so by the graceless fact of his lapse of fidelity. To tell her what he had told her—what had it been but to ask something of her? something that she had given, in her charity, without his having, by a remembrance, by a return of the spirit, failing another encounter, so much as thanked her. What he had asked of her had been simply at first not to laugh at him. She had beautifully not done so for ten years, and she was not doing so now. So he had endless gratitude to make up. Only for that he must see just how he had figured to her. "What, exactly was the account I gave——?"

"Of the way you did feel? Well, it was very simple. You said you had had from your earliest time, as the deepest thing within you, the sense of being kept for something rare and strange, possibly prodigious and terrible, that was sooner or later to happen to you, that you had in your bones the foreboding and the conviction of, and that would perhaps overwhelm you."

"Do you call that very simple?" John Marcher asked.

She thought a moment. "It was perhaps because I seemed, as you spoke, to understand it."

"You do understand it?" he eagerly asked.

Again she kept her kind eyes on him. "You still have the belief?"

"Oh!" he exclaimed helplessly. There was too much to say.

"Whatever it is to be," she clearly made out, "it hasn't yet come."

He shook his head in complete surrender now. "It hasn't yet come. *Only*, you know, it isn't anything I'm to *do*, to achieve in the world, to be distinguished or admired for. I'm not such an ass as *that*. It would be much better, no doubt, if I were."

"It's to be something you're merely to suffer?"

"Well, say to wait for—to have to meet, to face, to see suddenly break out in my life; possibly destroying all further consciousness, possibly annihilating me; possibly, on the other hand, only altering everything, striking at the root of all my world and leaving me to the consequences, however they shape themselves."

She took this in, but the light in her eyes continued for him not to be that of mockery. "Isn't what you describe perhaps but the expectation—or, at any rate, the sense of danger, familiar to so many people—of falling in love?"

John Marcher thought. "Did you ask me that before?"

"No—I wasn't so free-and-easy then. But it's what strikes me now."

"Of course," he said after a moment, "it strikes you. Of course it strikes *me*. Of course what's in store for me may be no more than that. The only thing is," he went on, "that I think that if it had been that, I should by this time know."

"Do you mean because you've *been* in love?" And then as he but looked at her in silence: "You've been in love, and it hasn't meant such a cataclysm, hasn't proved the great affair?"

"Here I am, you see. It hasn't been overwhelming."

"Then it hasn't been love," said May Bartram.

"Well, I at least thought it was. I took it for that—I've taken it till now. It was agreeable, it was delightful, it was miserable," he explained. "But it wasn't strange. It wasn't what *my* affair's to be."

"You want something all to yourself—something that nobody else knows or *has* known?"

"It isn't a question of what I 'want'—God knows I don't want anything. It's only a question of the apprehension that haunts me—that *I* live with day by day."

He said this so lucidly and consistently that, visibly, it further imposed itself. If she had not been interested before she would have been interested now. "Is it a sense of coming violence?"

Evidently now too, again, he liked to talk of it. "I don't think of it as—when it does come—necessarily violent. I only think of it as natural and as of course, above all, unmistakable. I think of it simply as *the* thing. *The* thing will of itself appear natural."

"Then how will it appear strange?"

Marcher bethought himself. "It won't—to *me*."

"To whom then?"

"Well," he replied, smiling at last, "say to you."

"Oh then, I'm to be present?"

"Why, you *are* present—since you know."

"I see." She turned it over. "But I mean at the catastrophe."

At this, for a minute, their lightness gave way to their gravity; it was as if the long look they exchanged held them together. "It will only depend on yourself—if you'll watch with me."

"Are you afraid?" she asked.

"Don't leave me *now,*" he went on.

"Are you afraid?" she repeated.

"Do you think me simply out of my mind?" he pursued instead of answering. "Do I merely strike you as a harmless lunatic?"

"No," said May Bartram. "I understand you. I believe you."

"You mean you feel how my obsession—poor old thing!—may correspond to some possible reality?"

"To some possible reality."

"Then you *will* watch with me?"

She hesitated, then for the third time put her question. "Are you afraid?"

"Did I tell you I was—at Naples?"

"No, you said nothing about it."

"Then I don't know. And I should *like* to know," said John Marcher. "You'll tell me yourself whether you think so. If you'll watch with me you'll see."

"Very well then." They had been moving by this time across the room, and at the door, before passing out, they paused as if for the full wind-up of their understanding. "I'll watch with you," said May Bartram.

II

THE fact that she "knew"—knew and yet neither chaffed him nor betrayed him—had in a short time begun to constitute between them a sensible bond, which became more marked when, within the year that followed their afternoon at Weatherend, the opportunities for meeting multiplied. The event that thus promoted these occasions was the death of the ancient lady, her great-aunt, under whose wing, since losing her mother, she had to such an extent found shelter, and who, though but the widowed mother of the new successor to the property, had succeeded—thanks to a high tone and a high temper—in not forfeiting the supreme position at the great house. The deposition of this personage arrived but with her death, which, followed by many changes, made in particular a difference for the young woman in whom Marcher's expert attention had recognised from the first a dependent with a pride that might ache though it didn't bristle. Nothing for a long time had made him easier than the thought that the aching must have been much soothed by Miss Bartram's now finding herself able to set up a small home in London. She had acquired property, to an amount that made that luxury just possible, under her aunt's extremely complicated will, and when the whole matter began to be straightened out, which indeed took time, she let him know that the happy issue was at last in view. He had seen her again before that day, both because she had more than once accompanied the ancient lady to town and because he had paid another visit to the friends who so conveniently made of Weatherend one of the charms of their own hospitality. These friends had taken him back there; he had achieved there again with Miss Bartram some quiet detachment; and he had in London succeeded in persuading her to more than one brief absence from her aunt. They went together, on these latter occasions, to the National Gallery and the South Kensington Museum, where, among vivid reminders, they talked of Italy at large—not now attempting to recover, as at first, the taste of their youth and their ignorance. That recovery, the first day at Weatherend, had served its purpose well, had given them quite enough; so that they were, to Marcher's sense, no longer hovering about the head-waters of their stream, but had felt their boat pushed sharply off and down the current.

They were literally afloat together; for our gentleman this was marked, quite as marked as that the fortunate cause of it was just the buried treasure of her knowledge. He had with his own hands dug up this little hoard, brought to light—that is to within reach of the dim day constituted by their discretions and privacies—the object of value the hiding-place of which he had, after putting it into the ground himself, so strangely, so long forgotten. The exquisite luck of having again just stumbled on the spot made him indifferent to any other question; he would doubtless have devoted more time to the odd accident of his lapse of memory if he had not been moved to devote so much to the sweetness, the comfort, as he felt, for the future, that this accident itself had helped to keep fresh. It had never entered into his plan that anyone should "know," and mainly for the reason that it was not in him to tell anyone. That would have been impossible, since nothing but the amusement of a cold world would have waited on it. Since, however, a mysterious fate had opened his mouth in youth, in spite of him, he would count that a compensation and profit by it to the utmost. That the right person *should* know tempered the asperity of his secret more even than his shyness had permitted him to imagine; and May Bartram was clearly right, because—well, because there she was. Her knowledge simply settled it; he would have been sure enough by this time had she been wrong. There was that in his situation, no doubt, that disposed him too much to see her as a mere confidant, taking all her light for him from the fact—the fact only—of her interest in his predicament, from her mercy, sympathy, seriousness, her consent not to regard him as the funniest of the funny. Aware, in fine, that her price for him was just in her giving him this constant sense of his being admirably spared, he was careful to remember that she had, after all, also a life of her own, with things that might happen to *her*, things that in friendship one should likewise take account of. Something fairly remarkable came to pass with him, for that matter, in this connection—something represented by a certain passage of his consciousness, in the suddenest way, from one extreme to the other.

He had thought himself, so long as nobody knew, the most disinterested person in the world, carrying his concentrated burden, his perpetual suspense, ever so quietly, holding his tongue about it, giving others no glimpse of it nor of its effect upon his life, asking of them no allowance and only making on his side all those that were asked. He had disturbed nobody with the queerness of having to know a haunted man, though he had had moments of rather special temptation on hearing people say that they were "unsettled." If they were as unsettled as he was—he who had never been settled for an hour in his life—they would know what it meant. Yet it wasn't, all the same, for him to make them, and he listened to them civilly enough. This was why he had such good—though possibly such rather colourless—manners; this was why, above all, he could regard himself, in a greedy world, as decently—as, in fact, perhaps even a little sublimely—unselfish. Our point is accordingly that he valued this character quite sufficiently to measure his present danger of letting it lapse, against which he promised himself to be much on his guard. He was quite ready, none the less, to be selfish just a little, since, surely no more charming occasion for it had come to him. "Just a little," in a word, was just as much as Miss Bartram, taking one day with another, would let him. He never would be in the least coercive, and he would keep well before him the lines on which consideration for her—the very highest—ought to proceed He would thoroughly establish the heads under which her affairs, her requirements, her peculiarities—he went so far as to give them the latitude of that name—would come into their intercourse. All this naturally was a sign of how much he took the intercourse itself for granted. There was nothing more to be done about *that.* It simply existed; had sprung into being with her first penetrating question to him in the autumn light there at Weatherend. The real form it should have taken on the basis that stood out large was the form of their marrying. But the devil in this was that the very basis itself put marrying out of the question. His conviction, his apprehension, his obsession, in short, was not a condition he could invite a woman to share; and that consequence of it was precisely what was the matter with him. Something or other lay in wait for him, amid the twists and the turns of the months and the years, like a crouching beast in the jungle. It signified little whether the crouching beast were destined to slay him or to be slain. The definite point was the inevitable spring of the creature; and the definite lesson from that was that a man of feeling didn't cause himself to be accompanied by a lady on a tiger-hunt. Such was the image under which he had ended by figuring his life.

They had at first, none the less, in the scattered hours spent together, made no allusion to that view of it; which was a sign he was handsomely ready to give that he didn't expect, that he in fact didn't care always to be talking about it. Such a feature in one's outlook was really like a hump on one's back. The difference it made every minute of the day existed quite independently of discussion. One discussed, of course, *like* a hunchback, for there was always, if nothing else, the hunchback face. That remained, and she was watching him; but people watched best, as a general thing, in silence, so that such would be predominantly the manner of their vigil. Yet he didn't want, at the same time, to be solemn; solemn was what he imagined he too much tended to be with other people. The thing to be, with the one person who knew, was easy and natural—to make the reference rather than be seeming to avoid it, to avoid it rather than be seeming to make it, and to keep it, in any case, familiar, facetious even, rather than pedantic and portentous. Some such consideration as the latter was doubtless in his mind, for instance, when he wrote pleasantly to Miss Bartram that perhaps the great thing he had so long felt as in the lap of the gods was no more than this circumstance, which touched him so nearly, of her acquiring a house in London. It was the first allusion they had yet again made, needing any other hitherto so little; but when she replied, after having given him the news, that she was by no means satisfied with such a trifle, as the climax to so special a suspense, she almost set him wondering if she hadn't even a larger conception of singularity for him than he had for himself. He was at all events destined to become aware little by little, as time went by, that she was all the while looking at his life, judging it, measuring it, in the light of the thing she knew, which grew to be at last, with the consecration of the years, never mentioned between them save as "the real truth" about him. That had always been his own form of reference to it, but she adopted the form so quietly that, looking back at the end of a period, he knew there was no moment at which it was traceable that she had, as he might say, got inside his condition, or exchanged the attitude of beautifully indulging for that of still more beautifully believing him.

It was always open to him to accuse her of seeing him but as the most harmless of maniacs, and this, in the long run—since it covered so much ground—was his easiest description of their friendship. He had a screw loose for her, but she liked him in spite of it, and was practically, against the rest of the world, his kind, wise keeper, unremunerated, but fairly amused and, in the absence of other near ties, not disreputably occupied. The rest of the world of course thought him queer, but she, she only, knew how, and above all why, queer; which was precisely what enabled her to dispose the concealing veil in the right folds. She took his gaiety from him—since it had to pass with them for gaiety—as she took everything else; but she certainly so far justified by her unerring touch his finer sense of the degree to which he had ended by convincing her. *She* at least never spoke of the secret of his life except as "the real truth about you," and she had in fact a wonderful way of making it seem, as such, the secret of her own life too. That was in fine how he so constantly felt her as allowing for him; he couldn't on the whole call it anything else. He allowed for himself, but she, exactly, allowed still more; partly because, better placed for a sight of the matter, she traced his unhappy perversion through portions of its course into which he could scarce follow it. He knew how he felt, but, besides knowing that, she knew how he *looked* as well; he knew each of the things of importance he was insidiously kept from doing, but she could add up the amount they made, understand how much, with a lighter weight on his spirit, he might have done, and thereby establish how, clever as he was, he fell short. Above all she was in the secret of the difference between the forms he went through—those of his little office under Government, those of caring for his modest patrimony, for his library, for his garden in the country, for the people in London whose invitations he accepted and repaid—and the detachment that reigned beneath them and that made of all behaviour, all that could in the least be called behaviour, a long act of dissimulation. What it had come to was that he wore a mask painted with the social simper, out of the eye-holes of which there looked eyes of an expression not in the least matching the other features. This the stupid world, even after years, had never more than half discovered. It was only May Bartram who had, and she achieved, by an art indescribable, the feat of at once—or perhaps it was only alternately—meeting the eyes from in front and mingling her own vision, as from over his shoulder, with their peep through the apertures.

So, while they grew older together, she did watch with him, and so she let this association give shape and colour to her own existence. Beneath *her* forms as well detachment had learned to sit, and behaviour had become for her, in the social sense, a false account of herself. There was but one account of her that would have been true all the while, and that she could give, directly, to nobody, least of all to John Marcher. Her whole attitude was a virtual statement, but the perception of that only seemed destined to take its place for him as one of the many things necessarily crowded out of his consciousness. If she had, moreover, like himself, to make sacrifices to their real truth, it was to be granted that her compensation might have affected her as more prompt and more natural. They had long periods, in this London time, during which, when they were together, a stranger might have listened to them without in the least pricking up his ears; on the other hand, the real truth was equally liable at any moment to rise to the surface, and the auditor would then have wondered indeed what they were talking about. They had from an early time made up their mind that society was, luckily, unintelligent, and the margin that this gave them had fairly become one of their commonplaces. Yet there were still moments when the situation turned almost fresh—usually under the effect of some expression drawn from herself. Her expressions doubtless repeated themselves, but her intervals were generous. "What saves us, you know, is that we answer so completely to so usual an appearance: that of the man and woman whose friendship has become such a daily habit, or almost, as to be at last indispensable." That, for instance, was a remark she had frequently enough had occasion to make, though she had given it at different times different developments. What we are especially concerned with is the turn it happened to take from her one afternoon when he had come to see her in honour of her birthday. This anniversary had fallen on a Sunday, at a season of thick fog and general outward gloom; but he had brought her his customary offering, having known her now long enough to have established a hundred little customs. It was one of his proofs to himself, the present he made her on her birthday, that he had not sunk into real selfishness. It was mostly nothing more than a small trinket, but it was always fine of its kind, and he was regularly careful to pay for it more than he thought he could afford. "Our habit saves you, at least, don't you see? because it makes you, after all, for the vulgar, indistinguishable from other men. What's the most inveterate mark of men in general? Why, the capacity to spend endless time with dull women—to spend it, I won't say without being bored, but without minding that they are, without being driven off at a tangent by it; which comes to the same thing. I'm your dull woman, a part of the daily bread for which you pray at church. That covers your tracks more than anything."

"And what covers yours?" asked Marcher, whom his dull woman could mostly to this extent amuse. "I see of course what you mean by your saving me, in one way and another, so far as other people are concerned—I've seen it all along. Only, what is it that saves *you*? I often think, you know, of that."

She looked as if she sometimes thought of that too, but in rather a different way. "Where other people, you mean, are concerned?"

"Well, you're really so in with me, you know—as a sort of result of my being so in with yourself. I mean of my having such an immense regard for you, being so tremendously grateful for all you've done for me. I sometimes ask myself if it's quite fair. Fair I mean to have so involved and—since one may say it—interested you. I almost feel as if you hadn't really had time to do anything else."

"Anything else but be interested?" she asked. "Ah, what else does one ever want to be? If I've been 'watching' with you, as we long ago agreed that I was to do, watching is always in itself an absorption."

"Oh certainly," John Marcher said, "if you hadn't had your curiosity——! Only, doesn't it sometimes come to you, as time goes on, that your curiosity is not being particularly repaid?"

May Bartram had a pause. "Do you ask that, by any chance, because you feel at all that yours isn't? I mean because you have to wait so long."

Oh, he understood what she meant. "For the thing to happen that never does happen? For the beast to jump out? No, I'm just where I was about it. It isn't a matter as to which I can *choose,* I can decide for a change. It isn't one as to which there *can* be a change. It's in the lap of the gods. One's in the hands of one's law —there one is. As to the form the law will take, the way it will operate, that's its own affair."

"Yes," Miss Bartram replied; "of course one's fate is coming, of course it *has* come, in its own form and its own way, all the while. Only, you know, the form and the way in your case were to have been—well, something so exceptional and, as one may say, so particularly *your* own."

Something in this made him look at her with suspicion. "You say 'were to *have* been,' as if in your heart you had begun to doubt."

"Oh!" she vaguely protested.

"As if you believed," he went on, "that nothing will now take place."

She shook her head slowly, but rather inscrutably. "You're far from my thought."

He continued to look at her. "What then is the matter with you?"

"Well," she said after another wait, "the matter with me is simply that I'm more sure than ever my curiosity, as you call it, will be but too well repaid."

They were frankly grave now; he had got up from his seat, had turned once more about the little drawing-room to which, year after year, he brought his inevitable topic; in which he had, as he might have said, tasted their intimate community with every sauce, where every object was as familiar to him as the things of his own house and the very carpets were worn with his fitful walk very much as the desk in old counting-houses are worn by the elbows of generations of clerks. The generations of his nervous moods had been at work there, and the place was the written history of his whole middle life. Under the impression of what his friend had just said he knew himself, for some reason, more aware of these things, which made him, after a moment, stop again before her. "It is, possibly, that you've grown afraid?"

"Afraid?" He thought, as she repeated the word, that his question had made her, a little, change colour; so that, lest he should have touched on a truth, he explained very kindly, "You remember that that was what you asked *me* long ago—that first day at Weatherend."

"Oh yes, and you told me you didn't know—that I was to see for myself. We've said little about it since, even in so long a time."

"Precisely," Marcher interposed—"quite as if it were too delicate a matter for us to make free with. Quite as if we might find, on pressure, that I *am* afraid. For then," he said, "we shouldn't, should we? quite know what to do."

She had for the time no answer to this question. "There have been days when I thought you were. Only, of course," she added, "there have been days when we have thought almost anything."

"Everything. Oh!" Marcher softly groaned as with a gasp, half spent, at the face, more uncovered just then than it had been for a long while, of the imagination always with them. It had always had its incalculable moments of glaring out, quite as with the very eyes of the very Beast, and, used as he was to them, they could still draw from him the tribute of a sigh that rose from the depths of his being. All that they had thought, first and last, rolled over him; the past seemed to have been reduced to mere barren speculation. This in fact was what the place had just struck him as so full of—the simplification of everything but the state of suspense. That remained only by seeming to hang in the void surrounding it. Even his original fear, if fear it had been, had lost itself in the desert. "I judge, however," he continued, "that you see I'm not afraid now."

"What I see is, as I make it out, that you've achieved something almost unprecedented in the way of getting used to danger. Living with it so long and so closely, you've lost your sense of it; you know it's there, but you're indifferent, and you cease even, as of old, to have to whistle in the dark. Considering what the danger is," May Bartram wound up, "I'm bound to say that I don't think your attitude could well be surpassed."

John Marcher faintly smiled. "It's heroic?"

"Certainly—call it that."

He considered. "I *am*, then, a man of courage?"

"That's what you were to show me."

He still, however, wondered. "But doesn't the man of courage know what he's afraid of—or *not* afraid of? I don't know *that*, you see. I don't focus it. I can't name it. I only know I'm exposed."

"Yes, but exposed—how shall I say?—so directly. So intimately. That's surely enough."

"Enough to make you feel, then—at what we may call the end of our watch—that I'm not afraid?"

"You're not afraid. But it isn't," she said, "the end of our watch. That is it isn't the end of yours. You've everything still to see."

"Then why haven't *you*?" he asked. He had had, all along, to-day, the sense of her keeping something back, and he still had it. As this was his first impression of that, it made a kind of date. The case was the more marked as she didn't at first answer; which in turn made him go on. "You know something I don't." Then his voice, for that of a man of courage, trembled a little. "You know what's to happen." Her silence, with the face she showed, was almost a confession—it made him sure. "You know, and you're afraid to tell me. It's so bad that you're afraid I'll find out."

All this might be true, for she did look as if, unexpectedly to her, he had crossed some mystic line that she had secretly drawn round her. Yet she might, after all, not have worried; and the real upshot was that he himself, at all events, needn't. "You'll never find out."

III

IT WAS all to have made, none the less, as I have said, a date; as came out in the fact that again and again, even after long intervals, other things that passed between them wore, in relation to this hour, but the character of recalls and results. Its immediate effect had been indeed rather to lighten insistence—almost to provoke a reaction; as if their topic had dropped by its own weight and as if moreover, for that matter, Marcher had been visited by one of his occasional warnings against egotism. He had kept up, he felt, and very decently on the whole, his consciousness of the importance of not being selfish, and it was true he had never sinned in that direction without promptly enough trying to press the scales the other way. He often repaired his fault, the season permitting, by inviting his friend to accompany him to the opera; and it not infrequently thus happened that, to show he didn't wish her to have but one sort of food for her mind, he was the cause of her appearing there with him a dozen nights in the month. It even happened that, seeing her home at such times, he occasionally went in with her to finish, as he called it, the evening, and, the better to make his point, sat down to the frugal but always careful little supper that awaited his pleasure. His point was made, he thought, by his not eternally insisting with her on himself; made for instance, at such hours, when it befell that, her piano at hand and each of them familiar with it, they went over passages of the opera together. It chanced to be on one of these occasions, however, that he reminded her of her not having answered a certain question he had put to her during the talk that had taken place between them on her last birthday. "What is it that saves *you*?"—saved her, he meant, from that appearance of variation from the usual human type. If he had practically escaped remark, as she pretended, by doing, in the most important particular, what most men do—find the answer to life in patching up an alliance of a sort with a woman no better than himself—how had she escaped it, and how could the alliance, such as it was, since they must suppose it had been more or less noticed, have failed to make her rather positively talked about?

"I never said," May Bartram replied, "that it hadn't made me talked about."

"Ah well then, you're not 'saved.' "

"It has not been a question for me. If you've had your woman, I've had," she said, "my man."

"And you mean that makes you all right?"

She hesitated. "I don't know why it shouldn't make me—humanly, which is what we're speaking of—as right as it makes you."

"I see," Marcher returned. " 'Humanly,' no doubt, as showing that you're living for something. Not, that is, just for me and my secret."

May Bartram smiled. "I don't pretend it exactly shows that I'm not living for you. It's my intimacy with you that's in question."

He laughed as he saw what she meant. "Yes, but since, as you say, I'm only, so far as people make out, ordinary, you're—aren't you?—no more than ordinary either. You help me to pass for a man like another. So if I *am*, as I understand you, you're not compromised. Is that it?"

She had another hesitation, but she spoke clearly enough. "That's it. It's all that concerns me—to help you to pass for a man like another."

He was careful to acknowledge the remark handsomely. "How

kind, how beautiful, you are to me! How shall I ever repay you?"

She had her last grave pause, as if there might be a choice of ways. But she chose. "By going on as you are."

It was into this going on as he was that they relapsed, and really for so long a time that the day inevitably came for a further sounding of their depths. It was as if these depths, constantly bridged over by a structure that was firm enough in spite of its lightness and of its occasional oscillation in the somewhat vertiginous air, invited on occasion, in the interest of their nerves, a dropping of the plummet and a measurement of the abyss. A difference had been made moreover, once for all, by the fact that she had, all the while, not appeared to feel the need of rebutting his charge of an idea within her that she didn't dare to express, uttered just before one of the fullest of their later discussions ended. It had come up for him then that she "knew" something and that what she knew was bad—too bad to tell him. When he had spoken of it as visibly so bad that she was afraid he might find it out, her reply had left the matter too equivocal to be let alone and yet, for Marcher's special sensibility, almost too formidable again to touch. He circled about it at a distance that alternately narrowed and widened and that yet was not much affected by the consciousness in him that there was nothing she could "know," after all, any better than he did. She had no source of knowledge that he hadn't equally—except of course that she might have finer nerves. That was what women had where they were interested; they made out things, where people were concerned, that the people often couldn't have made out for themselves. Their nerves, their sensibility, their imagination, were conductors and revealers, and the beauty of May Bartram was in particular that she had given herself so to his case. He felt in these days what, oddly enough, he had never felt before, the growth of a dread of losing her by some catastrophe—some catastrophe that yet wouldn't at all be *the* catastrophe: partly because she had, almost of a sudden, begun to strike him as useful to him as never yet, and partly by reason of an appearance of uncertainty in her health, coincident and equally new. It was characteristic of the inner detachment he had hitherto so successfully cultivated and to which our whole account of him is a reference, it was characteristic that his complications, such as they were, had never yet seemed so as at this crisis to thicken about him, even to the point of making him ask himself if he were, by any chance, of a truth, within sight or sound, within touch or reach, within the immediate jurisdiction of the thing that waited.

When the day came, as come it had to, that his friend confessed to him her fear of a deep disorder in her blood, he felt somehow the shadow of a change and the chill of a shock. He immediately began to imagine aggravations and disasters, and above all to think of her peril as the direct menace for himself of personal privation. This indeed gave him one of those partial recoveries of equanimity that were agreeable to him—it showed him that what was still first in his mind was the loss she herself might suffer. "What if she should have to die before knowing, before seeing——?" It would have been brutal, in the early stages of her trouble, to put that question to her; but it had immediately sounded for him to his own concern, and the possibility was what most made him sorry for her. If she did "know," moreover, in the sense of her having had some—what should he think?—mystical, irresistible light, this would make the matter not better, but worse, inasmuch as her original adoption of his own curiosity had quite become the basis of her life. She had been living to see what would *be* to be seen, and it would be cruel to her to have to give up before the accomplishment of the vision. These reflections, as I say, refreshed his generosity; yet, make them as he might, he saw himself, with the lapse of the period, more and more disconcerted. It lapsed for him with a strange, steady sweep, and the oddest oddity was that it gave him, independently of the threat of much inconvenience, almost the only positive surprise his career, if career it could be called, had yet offered him. She kept the house as she had never done; he had to go to her to see her—she could meet him nowhere now, though there was scarce a corner of their loved old London in which she had not in the past, at one time or another, done so; and he found her always seated by her fire in the deep, old-fashioned chair she was less and less able to leave. He had been struck one day, after an absence exceeding his usual measure, with her suddenly looking much older to him than he had ever thought of her being; then he recognised that the suddenness was all on his side—he had just been suddenly struck. She looked older because inevitably, after so many years, she *was* old, or almost; which was of course true in still greater measure of her companion.

If she was old, or almost, John Marcher assuredly was, and yet it was her showing of the lesson, not his own, that brought the truth home to him. His surprises began here; when once they had begun they multiplied; they came rather with a rush: it was as if, in the oddest way in the world, they had all been kept back, sown in a thick cluster, for the late afternoon of life, the time at which, for people in general, the unexpected has died out.

One of them was that he should have caught himself—for he *had* so done—*really* wondering if the great accident would take form now as nothing more than his being condemned to see this charming woman, this admirable friend, pass away from him. He had never so unreservedly qualified her as while confronted in thought with such a possibility; in spite of which there was small doubt for him that as an answer to his long riddle the mere effacement of even so fine a feature of his situation would be an abject anticlimax. It would represent, as connected with his past attitude, a drop of dignity under the shadow of which his existence could only become the most grotesque of failures. He had been far from holding it a failure—long as he had waited for the appearance that was to make it a success. He had waited for a quite other thing, not for such a one as that. The breath of his good faith came short, however, as he recognised how long he had waited, or how long, at least, his companion had. That she, at all events, might be recorded as having waited in vain—this affected him sharply, and all the more because of his at first having done little more than amuse himself with the idea. It grew more grave as the gravity of her condition grew, and the state of mind it produced in him, which he ended by watching, himself, as if it had been some definite disfigurement of his outer person, may pass for another of his surprises. This conjoined itself still with another, the really stupefying consciousness of a question that he would have allowed to shape itself had he dared. What did everything mean—what, that is, did *she* mean, she and her vain waiting and her probable death and the soundless admonition of it all—unless that, at this time of day, it was simply, it was overwhelmingly too late? He had never, at any stage of his queer consciousness, admitted the whisper of such a correction; he had never, till within these last few months, been so false to his conviction as not to hold that what was to come to him had time, whether *he* struck himself as having it or not. That at last, at last, he certainly hadn't it, to speak of, or had it but in the scantiest measure—such, soon enough, as things went with him, became the inference with which his old obsession had to reckon: and this it was not helped to do by the more and more confirmed appearance that the great vagueness casting the long shadow in which he had lived had, to attest itself, almost no margin left. Since it was in Time that he was to have met his fate, so it was in Time that this fate was to have acted; and as he waked up to the sense of no longer being young, which was exactly the sense of being stale, just as that, in turn, was the sense of being weak, he waked up to another matter beside. It all hung together; they were subject, he and the great vagueness, to an equal and indivisible law. When the possibilities themselves had, accordingly, turned stale, when the secret of the gods had grown faint, had perhaps even quite evaporated, that, and that only, was failure. It wouldn't have been failure to be bankrupt, dishonoured, pilloried, hanged; it was failure not to be anything. And so, in the dark valley into which his path had taken its unlooked-for twist, he wondered not a little as he groped. He didn't care what awful crash might overtake him, with what ignominy or what monstrosity he might yet be associated—since he wasn't, after all, too utterly old to suffer—if it would only be decently proportionate to the posture he had kept, all his life, in the promised presence of it. He had but one desire left—that he shouldn't have been "sold."

IV

THEN it was that one afternoon, while the spring of the year was young and new, she met, all in her own way, his frankest betrayal of these alarms. He had gone in late to see her, but evening had not settled, and she was presented to him in that long, fresh light of waning April days which affects us often with a sadness sharper than the greyest hours of autumn. The week had been warm, the spring was supposed to have begun early, and May Bartram sat, for the first time in the year, without a fire, a fact that, to Marcher's sense, gave the scene of which she formed part a smooth and ultimate look, an air of knowing, in its immaculate order and its cold, meaningless cheer, that it would never see a fire again. Her own aspect—he could scarce have said why—intensified this note. Almost as white as wax, with the marks and signs in her face as numerous and as fine as if they had been etched by a needle, with soft white draperies relieved by a faded green scarf, the delicate tone of which had been consecrated by the years, she was the picture of a serene, exquisite, but impenetrable sphinx, whose head, or indeed all whose person, might have been powdered with silver. She was a sphinx, yet with her white petals and green fronds she might have been a lily too—only an artificial lily, wonderfully imitated and constantly kept, without dust or stain, though not exempt from a slight droop and a complexity of faint creases, under some clear glass bell. The perfection of household care, of high polish and finish, always reigned in her rooms, but they especially looked to Marcher at present as if everything had been wound up, tucked in, put away, so that she might sit with folded hands and with nothing more to do. She was "out of it," to his vision; her work was over; she communicated with him as across some gulf, or from some island of rest that she had already reached, and it made him feel strangely abandoned. Was it—or, rather, wasn't it—that if for so long she had been watching with him the answer to their question had swum into her ken and taken on its name, so that her occupation was verily gone? He had as much as charged her with this in saying to her, many months before, that she even then knew something she was keeping from him. It was a point he had never since ventured to press vaguely fearing, as he did, that it might become a difference, perhaps a disagreement, between them. He had in short, in this later time, turned nervous, which was what, in all the other years, he had never been; and the oddity was that his nervousness should have waited till he had begun to doubt, should have held off so long as he was sure. There was something, it seemed to him, that the wrong word would bring down on his head, something that would so at least put an end to his suspense. But he wanted not to speak the wrong word; that would make everything ugly. He wanted the knowledge he lacked to drop on him, if drop it could, by its own august weight. If she was to forsake him it was surely for her to take leave. This was why he didn't ask her again, directly, what she knew; but it was also why, approaching the matter from another side, he said to her in the course of his visit: "What do you regard as the very worst that, at this time of day, *can* happen to me?"

He had asked her that in the past often enough; they had, with the odd, irregular rhythm of their intensities and avoidances, exchanged ideas about it and then had seen the ideas washed away by cool intervals, washed like figures traced in sea-sand. It had ever been the mark of their talk that the oldest allusions in it required but a little dismissal and reaction to come out again, sounding for the hour as new. She could thus at present meet his inquiry quite freshly and patiently. "Oh yes, I've repeatedly thought, only it always seemed to me of old that I couldn't quite make up my mind. I thought of dreadful things, between which it was difficult to choose; and so must you have done."

"Rather! I feel now as if I had scarce done anything else. I appear to myself to have spent my life in thinking of nothing *but* dreadful things. A great many of them I've at different times named to you, but there were others I couldn't name."

"They were too, too dreadful?"

"Too, too dreadful—some of them."

She looked at him a minute, and there came to him as he met it an inconsequent sense that her eyes, when one got their full clearness, were still as beautiful as they had been in youth, only beautiful with a strange, cold light—a light that somehow was a part of the effect, if it wasn't rather a part of the cause, of the pale, hard sweetness of the season and the hour. "And yet," she said at last, "there are horrors we have mentioned."

It deepened the strangeness to see her, as such a figure in such a picture, talk of "horrors," but she was to do, in a few minutes, something stranger yet—though even of this he was to take the full measure but afterwards—and the note of it was already in the air. It was, for the matter of that, one of the signs that her eyes were having again such a high flicker of their prime. He had to admit, however, what she said. "Oh yes, there were times when we did go far." He caught himself in the act of speaking as if it all were over. Well, he wished it were; and the consummation depended, for him, clearly, more and more on his companion.

But she had now a soft smile. "Oh, far——!"

It was oddly ironic. "Do you mean you're prepared to go further?"

She was frail and ancient and charming as she continued to look at him, yet it was rather as if she had lost the thread. "Do you consider that we went so far?"

"Why, I thought in the point you were just making—that we *had* looked most things in the face."

"Including each other?" She still smiled. "But you're quite right. We've had together great imaginations, often great fears; but some of them have been unspoken."

"Then the worst—we haven't faced that. I *could* face it, I believe, if I knew what you think it. I feel," he explained, "as if I had lost my power to conceive such things." And he wondered if he looked as blank as he sounded. "It's spent."

"Then why do you assume," she asked, "that mine isn't?"

"Because you've given me signs to the contrary. It isn't a question for you of conceiving, imagining, comparing. It isn't a question now of choosing." At last he came out with it. "You know something that I don't. You've shown me that before."

These last words affected her, he could see in a moment, remarkably, and she spoke with firmness. "I've shown you, my dear, nothing."

He shook his head. "You can't hide it."

"Oh, oh!" May Bartram murmured over what she couldn't hide. It was almost a smothered groan.

"You admitted it months ago, when I spoke of it to you as of something you were afraid I would find out. Your answer was that I couldn't, that I wouldn't, and I don't pretend I have. But you had something therefore in mind, and I see now that it must have been, that it still is, the possibility that, of all possibilities, has settled itself for you as the worst. This," he went on, "is why I appeal to you. I'm only afraid of ignorance now—I'm not afraid of knowledge." And then as for a while she said nothing: "What makes me sure is that I see in your face and feel here, in this air and amid these appearances, that you're out of it. You've done. You've had your experience. You leave me to my fate."

Well, she listened, motionless and white in her chair, as if she had in fact a decision to make, so that her whole manner was a virtual confession, though still with a small, fine, inner stiffness, an imperfect surrender. "It *would* be the worst," she finally let herself say. "I mean the thing that I've never said."

It hushed him a moment. "More monstrous than all the monstrosities we've named?"

"More monstrous. Isn't that what you sufficiently express," she asked, "in calling it the worst?"

Marcher thought, "Assuredly—if you mean, as I do, something that includes all the loss and all the shame that are thinkable."

"It would if it *should* happen," said May Bartram. "What we're speaking of, remember, is only my idea."

"It's your belief," Marcher returned. "That's enough for me. I feel your beliefs are right. Therefore if, having this one, you give me no more light on it, you abandon me."

"No, no!" she repeated. "I'm with you—don't you see?—still." And as if to make it more vivid to him she rose from her chair—a movement she seldom made in these days—and showed herself, all draped and all soft, in her fairness and slimness. "I haven't forsaken you."

It was really, in its effort against weakness, a generous assurance, and had the success of the impulse not, happily, been great, it would have touched him to pain more than to pleasure. But the cold charm in her eyes had spread, as she hovered before him, to all the rest of her person, so that it was, for the minute, almost like a recovery of youth. He couldn't pity her for that; he could only take her as she showed—as capable still of helping him. It was as if, at the same time, her light might at any instant go out; wherefore he must make the most of it. There passed before him with intensity the three or four things he wanted most to know; but the question that came of itself to his lips really covered the others. "Then tell me if I shall consciously suffer."

She promptly shook her head. "Never!"

It confirmed the authority he imputed to her, and it produced on him an extraordinary effect. "Well, what's better than that? Do you call that the worst?"

"You think nothing is better?" she asked.

She seemed to mean something so special that he again sharply wondered, though still with the dawn of a prospect of relief. "Why not, if one doesn't *know*?" After which, as their eyes, over his question, met in a silence, the dawn deepened and something to his purpose came, prodigiously, out of her very face. His own, as he took it in, suddenly flushed to the forehead, and he gasped with the force of a perception to which, on the instant, everything fitted. The sound of his gasp filled the air; then he became articulate. "I see—if I don't suffer!"

In her own look, however, was doubt. "You see what?"

"Why, what you mean—what you've always meant."

She again shook her head. "What I mean isn't what I've always meant. It's different."

"It's something new?"

She hesitated. "Something new. It's not what you think. I see what you think."

His divination drew breath then; only her correction might be wrong. "It isn't that I *am* a donkey?" he asked between faintness and grimness. "It isn't that it's all a mistake?"

"A mistake?" she pityingly echoed. *That* possibility, for her, he saw, would be monstrous; and if she guaranteed him the immunity from pain it would accordingly not be what she had in mind. "Oh, no," she declared; "it's nothing of that sort. You've been right."

Yet he couldn't help asking himself if she weren't, thus pressed, speaking but to save him. It seemed to him he should be most lost if his history should prove all a platitude. "Are you telling me the truth, so that I sha'n't have been a bigger idiot than I can bear to know? I *haven't* lived with a vain imagination, in the most besotted illusion? I haven't waited but to see the door shut in my face?"

She shook her head again. "However the case stands *that* isn't the truth. Whatever the reality, it *is* a reality. The door isn't shut. The door's open," said May Bartram.

"Then something's to come?"

She waited once again, always with her cold, sweet eyes on him. "It's never too late." She had, with her gliding step, diminished the distance between them, and she stood nearer to him, close to him, a minute, as if still full of the unspoken. Her movement might have been for some finer emphasis of what she was at once hesitating and deciding to say. He had been standing by the chimney-piece, fireless and sparely adorned, a small, perfect old French clock and two morsels of rosy Dresden constituting all its furniture; and her hand grasped the shelf while she kept him waiting, grasped it a little as for support and encouragement. She only kept him waiting, however; that is he only waited. It had become suddenly, from her movement and attitude, beautiful and vivid to him that she had something more to give him; her wasted face delicately shone with it, and it glittered, almost as with the white lustre of silver, in her expression. She was right, incontestably, for what he saw in her face was the truth, and strangely, without consequence, while their talk of it as dreadful was still in the air, she appeared to present it as inordinately soft. This, prompting bewilderment, made him but gape the more gratefully for her revelation, so that they continued for some minutes silent, her face shining at him, her contact imponderably pressing, and his stare all kind, but all expectant. The end, none the less, was that what he had expected failed to sound. Something else took place instead, which seemed to consist at first in the mere closing of her eyes. She gave way at the same instant to a slow, fine shudder, and though he remained staring—though he stared, in fact, but the harder—she turned off and regained her chair. It was the end of what she had been intending, but it left him thinking only of that.

"Well, you don't say——?"

She had touched in her passage a bell near the chimney and had sunk back, strangely pale. "I'm afraid I'm too ill."

"Too ill to tell me?" It sprang up sharp to him, and almost to his lips, the fear that she would die without giving him light. He checked himself in time from so expressing his question, but she answered as if she had heard the words.

"Don't you know—now?"

" 'Now'——?" She had spoken as if something that had made a difference had come up within the moment. But her maid, quickly obedient to her bell, was already with them. "I know nothing." And he was afterwards to say to himself that he must have spoken with odious impatience, such an impatience as to show that, supremely disconcerted, he washed his hands of the whole question.

"Oh!" said May Bartram.

"Are you in pain?" he asked, as the woman went to her.

"No," said May Bartram.

Her maid, who had put an arm round her as if to take her to her room, fixed on him eyes that appealingly contradicted her; in spite of which, however, he showed once more his mystification. "What then has happened?"

She was once more, with her companion's help, on her feet, and, feeling withdrawal imposed on him, he had found, blankly, his hat and gloves and had reached the door. Yet he waited for her answer. "What *was* to," she said.

V

HE CAME back the next day, but she was then unable to see him, and as it was literally the first time this had occurred in the long stretch of their acquaintance he turned away, defeated and sore, almost angry—or feeling at least that such a break in their custom was really the beginning of the end—and wandered alone with his thoughts, especially with one of them that he was unable to keep down. She was dying, and he would lose her; she was dying, and his life would end. He stopped in the park, into which he had passed, and stared before him at his recurrent doubt. Away from her the doubt pressed again; in her presence he had believed her, but as he felt his forlornness he threw himself into the explanation that, nearest at hand, had most of a miserable warmth for him and least of a cold torment. She had deceived him to save him—to put him off with something in which he should be able to rest. What could the thing that was to happen to him be, after all, but just this thing that had begun to happen? Her dying, her death, his consequent solitude—*that* was what he had figured as the beast in the jungle, that was what had been in the lap of the gods. He had had her word for it as he left her; for what else, on earth, could she have meant? It wasn't a thing of a monstrous order; not a fate rare and distinguished; not a stroke of fortune that overwhelmed and immortalised; it had only the stamp of the common doom. But poor Marcher, at this hour, judged the common doom sufficient. It would serve his turn, and even as the consummation of infinite waiting he would bend his pride to accept it. He sat down on a bench in the twilight. He hadn't been a fool. Something had *been*, as she had said, to come. Before he rose indeed it had quite struck him that the final fact really matched with the long avenue through which he had had to reach it. As sharing his suspense, and as giving herself all, giving her life, to bring it to an end, she had come with him every step of the way. He had lived by her aid, and to leave her behind would be cruelly, damnably to miss her. What could be more overwhelming than that?

Well, he was to know within the week, for though she kept him a while at bay, left him restless and wretched during a series of days on each of which he asked about her only again to have to turn away, she ended his trial by receiving him where she had always received him. Yet she had been brought out at some hazard into the presence of so many of the things that were, consciously, vainly, half their past, and there was scant service left in the gentleness of her mere desire, all too visible, to check his obsession and wind up his long trouble. That was clearly what she wanted; the one thing more, for her own peace, while she could still put out her hand. He was so affected by her state that, once seated by her chair, he was moved to let everything go; it was she herself therefore who brought him back, took up again, before she dismissed him, her last word of the other time. She showed how she wished to leave their affair in order. "I'm not sure you understood. You've nothing to wait for more. It *has* come."

Oh, how he looked at her! "Really?"

"Really."

"The thing that, as you said, *was* to?"

"The thing that we began in our youth to watch for."

Face to face with her once more he believed her; it was a claim to which he had so abjectly little to oppose. "You mean that it has come as a positive, definite occurrence, with a name and a date?"

"Positive. Definite. I don't know about the 'name,' but, oh, with a date!"

He found himself again too helplessly at sea. "But come in the night—come and passed me by?"

May Bartram had her strange, faint smile. "Oh no, it hasn't passed you by!"

"But if I haven't been aware of it, and it hadn't touched me——?"

"Ah, your not being aware of it," and she seemed to hesitate an instant to deal with this—"your not being aware of it is the strangeness *in* the strangeness. It's the wonder *of* the wonder." She spoke as with the softness almost of a sick child, yet now at last, at the end of all, with the perfect straightness of a sibyl. She visibly knew that she knew, and the effect on him was of something co-ordinate, in its high character, with the law that had ruled him. It was the true voice of the law; so on her lips would the law itself have sounded. "It *has* touched you," she went on. "It has done its office. It has made you all its own."

"So utterly without my knowing it?"

"So utterly without your knowing it." His hand, as he leaned to her, was on the arm of her chair, and, dimly smiling always now, she placed her own on it. "It's enough if *I* know it."

"Oh!" he confusedly sounded, as she herself of late so often had done.

"What I long ago said is true. You'll never know now, and I think you ought to be content. You've *had* it," said May Bartram.

"But had what?"

"Why, what was to have marked you out. The proof of your law. It has acted. I'm too glad," she then bravely added, "to have been able to see what it's *not*."

He continued to attach his eyes to her, and with the sense that it was all beyond him, and that *she* was too, he would still have sharply challenged her, had he not felt it an abuse of her weakness to do more than take devoutly what she gave him, take it as hushed as to a revelation. If he did speak, it was out of foreknowledge of his loneliness to come. "If you're glad of what it's 'not,' it might then have been worse?"

She turned her eyes away, she looked straight before her with which, after a moment: "Well, you know our fears."

He wondered. "It's something then we never feared?"

On this, slowly, she turned to him. "Did we ever dream, with all our dreams, that we should sit and talk of it thus?"

He tried for a little to make out if they had; but it was as if their dreams, numberless enough, were in solution in some thick, cold mist, in which thought lost itself. "It might have been that we couldn't talk?"

"Well"—she did her best for him—"not from this side. This, you see," she said, "is the *other* side."

"I think," poor Marcher returned, "that all sides are the same to me." Then, however, as she softly shook her head in correction: "We mightn't, as it were, have got across——?"

"To where we are—no. We're *here*"—she made her weak emphasis.

"And much good does it do us!" was her friend's frank comment.

"It does us the good it can. It does us the good that *it* isn't here. It's past. It's behind," said May Bartram. "Before——" but her voice dropped.

He had got up, not to tire her, but it was hard to combat his yearning. She after all told him nothing but that his light had failed—which he knew well enough without her. "Before——?" he blankly echoed.

"Before, you see, it was always to *come*. That kept it present."

"Oh, I don't care what comes now! Besides," Marcher added, "it seems to me I liked it better present, as you say, than I can like it absent with *your* absence."

"Oh, mine!"—and her pale hands made light of it.

"With the absence of everything." He had a dreadful sense of standing there before her for—so far as anything but this proved, this bottomless drop was concerned—the last time of their life. It rested on him with a weight he felt he could scarce bear, and this weight it apparently was that still pressed out what remained in him of speakable protest. "I believe you; but I can't begin to pretend I understand. *Nothing*, for me, is past; nothing *will* pass until I pass myself, which I pray my stars may be as soon as possible. Say, however," he added, "that I've eaten my cake, as you contend, to the last crumb—how can the thing I've never felt at all be the thing I was marked out to feel?"

She met him, perhaps, less directly, but she met him unperturbed.

"You take your 'feelings' for granted. You were to suffer your fate. That was not necessarily to know it."

"How in the world—when what is such knowledge but suffering?"

She looked up at him a while, in silence. "No—you don't understand."

"I suffer," said John Marcher.

"Don't, don't!"

"How can I help at least *that*?"

"*Don't*!" May Bartram repeated.

She spoke it in a tone so special, in spite of her weakness, that he stared an instant—stared as if some light, hitherto hidden, had shimmered across his vision. Darkness again closed over it, but the gleam had already become for him an idea. "Because I haven't the right——?"

"Don't *know*—when you needn't," she mercifully urged. "You needn't—for we shouldn't."

"Shouldn't?" If he could but know what she meant!

"No—it's too much."

"Too much?" he still asked—but with a mystification that was the next moment, of a sudden, to give way. Her words, if they meant something, affected him in this light—the light also of her wasted face—as meaning *all*, and the sense of what knowledge had been for herself came over him with a rush which broke through into a question. "Is it of that, then, you're dying?"

She but watched him, gravely at first, as if to see, with this, where he was, and she might have seen something, or feared something, that moved her sympathy. "I would live for you still—if I could." Her eyes closed for a little, as if, withdrawn into herself, she were, for a last time, trying. "But I can't!" she said as she raised them again to take leave of him.

She couldn't indeed, as but too promptly and sharply appeared, and he had no vision of her after this that was anything but darkness and doom. They had parted forever in that strange talk; access to her chamber of pain, rigidly guarded, was almost wholly forbidden him; he was feeling now moreover, in the face of doctors, nurses, the two or three relatives attracted doubtless by the presumption of what she had to "leave," how few were the rights, as they were called in such cases, that he had to put forward, and how odd it might even seem that their intimacy shouldn't have given him more of them. The stupidest fourth cousin had more, even though she had been nothing in such a person's life. She had been a feature of features in *his*, for what else was it to have been so indispensable? Strange beyond saying were the ways of existence, baffling for him the anomaly of his lack, as he felt it to be, of producible claim. A woman might have been, as it were, everything to him, and it might yet present him in no connection that anyone appeared obliged to recognise. If this was the case in these closing weeks it was the case more sharply on the occasion of the last offices rendered, in the great grey London cemetery, to what had been mortal, to what had been precious, in his friend. The concourse at her grave was not numerous, but he saw himself treated as scarce more nearly concerned with it than if there had been a thousand others. He was in short from this moment face to face with the fact that he was to profit extraordinarily little by the interest May Bartram had taken in him. He couldn't quite have said what he expected, but he had somehow not expected this approach to a double privation. Not only had her interest failed him, but he seemed to feel himself unattended —and for a reason he couldn't sound—by the distinction, the dignity, the propriety, if nothing else, of the man markedly bereaved. It was as if, in the view of society, he had not *been markedly* bereaved, as if there still failed some sign or proof of it, and as if, none the less, his character could never be affirmed, nor the deficiency ever made up. There were moments, as the weeks went by, when he would have liked, by some almost aggressive act, to take his stand on the intimacy of his loss, in order that it *might* be questioned and his retort, to the relief of his spirit, so recorded; but the moments of an irritation more helpless followed fast on these, the moments during which, turning things over with a good conscience but with a bare horizon, he found himself wondering if he oughtn't to have begun, so to speak, further back.

He found himself wondering indeed at many things, and this last speculation had others to keep it company. What could he have done, after all, in her lifetime, without giving them both, as it were, away? He couldn't have made it known she was watching him, for that would have published the superstition of the Beast. This was what closed his mouth now—now that the Jungle had been threshed to vacancy and that the Beast had stolen away. It sounded too foolish and too flat; the difference for him in this particular, the extinction in his life of the element of suspense, was such in fact as to surprise him. He could scarce have said what the effect resembled; the abrupt cessation, the positive prohibition, of music perhaps, more than anything else, in some place all adjusted and all accustomed to sonority and to attention. If he could at any rate have conceived lifting the veil from his image at some moment of the past (what had he done, after all, if not lift it to *her?*), so to do this to-day, to talk to people at large of the jungle cleared and confide to them that he now felt it as safe, would have been not only to see them listen as to a goodwife's tale, but really to hear himself tell one. What it presently came to in truth was that poor Marcher waded through his beaten grass, where no life stirred, where no breath sounded, where no evil eye seemed to gleam from a possible lair, very much as if vaguely looking for the Beast, and still more as if missing it. He walked about in an existence that had grown strangely more spacious, and, stopping fitfully in places where the undergrowth of life struck him as closer, asked himself yearningly, wondered secretly and sorely, if it would have lurked here or there. It would have at all events *sprung;* what was at least complete was his belief in the truth itself of the assurance given him. The change from his old sense to his new was absolute and final: what was to happen *had* so absolutely and finally happened that he was as little able to know a fear for his future as to know a hope; so absent in short was any question of anything still to come. He was to live entirely with the other question, that of his unidentified past, that of his having to see his fortune impenetrably muffled and masked.

The torment of this vision became then his occupation; he couldn't perhaps have consented to live but for the possibility of guessing. She had told him, his friend, not to guess; she had forbidden him, so far as he might, to know, and she had even in a sort denied the power in him to learn: which were so many things, precisely, to deprive him of rest. It wasn't that he wanted, he argued for fairness, that anything that had happened to him should happen over again; it was only that he shouldn't, as an anticlimax, have been taken sleeping so sound as not to be able to win back by an effort of thought the lost stuff of consciousness. He declared to himself at moments that he would either win it back or have done with consciousness for ever; he made this idea his one motive, in fine, made it so much his passion that none other, to compare with it, seemed ever to have touched him. The lost stuff of consciousness became thus for him as a strayed or stolen child to an unappeasable father; he hunted it up and down very much as if he were knocking at doors and inquiring of the police. This was the spirit in which, inevitably, he set himself to travel; he started on a journey that was to be as long as he could make it; it danced before him that, as the other side of the globe couldn't possibly have less to say to him, it might, by a possibility of suggestion, have more. Before he quitted London, however, he made a pilgrimage to May Bartram's grave, took his way to it through the endless avenues of the grim suburban necropolis, sought it out in the wilderness of tombs, and, though he had come but for the renewal of the act of farewell, found himself, when he had at last stood by it, beguiled into long intensities. He stood for an hour, powerless to turn away and yet powerless to penetrate the darkness of death; fixing with his eyes her inscribed name and date, beating his forehead against the fact of the secret they kept, drawing his breath, while he waited as if, in pity of him, some sense would rise from the stones. He kneeled on the stones, however, in vain; they kept what they concealed; and if the face of the tomb did become a face for him it was because her two names were like a pair of eyes that didn't know him. He gave them a lost long look, but no palest light broke.

VI

He stayed away, after this, for a year; he visited the depths of Asia, spending himself on scenes of romantic interest, of superlative sanctity; but what was present to him everywhere was that for a man who had known what *he* had known the world was vulgar and vain. The state of mind in which he had lived for so many years shone out to him, in reflection, as a light that coloured and refined, a light beside which the glow of the East was garish, cheap and thin. The terrible truth was that he had lost—with everything else—a distinction as well; the things he saw couldn't help being common when he had become common to look at them. He was simply now one of them himself—he was in the dust, without a peg for the sense of difference; and there were hours when, before the temples of gods and the sepulchres of kings, his spirit turned, for nobleness of association, to the barely discriminated slab in the London suburb. That had become for him, and more intensely with time and distance, his one witness of a past glory. It was all that was left to him for proof or pride, yet the past glories of Pharaohs were nothing to him as he thought of it. Small wonder then that he came back to it on the morrow of his return. He was drawn there this time as irresistibly as the other, yet with a confidence, almost, that was doubtless the effect of the many months that had elapsed. He had lived, in spite of himself, into his change of feeling, and in wandering over the earth had wondered, as might be said, from the circumference to the centre of his desert. He had settled to his safety and accepted perforce his extinction; figuring to himself, with some colour, in the likeness of certain little old men he remembered to have seen, of whom, all meagre and wizened as they might look, it was related that they had in their time fought twenty duels or been loved by ten princesses. They indeed had been wondrous for others, while he was but wondrous for himself; which, however, was exactly the cause of his haste to renew the wonder by getting back, as he might put it, into his own presence. That had quickened his steps and checked his delay. If his visit was prompt it was because he had been separated so long from the part of himself that alone he now valued.

It is accordingly not false to say that he reached his goal with a certain elation and stood there again with a certain assurance. The creature beneath the sod *knew* of his rare experience, so that, strangely now, the place had lost for him its mere blankness of expression. It met him in mildness—not, as before, in mockery; it wore for him the air of conscious greeting that we find, after absence, in things that have closely belonged to us and which seem to confess of themselves to the connection. The plot of ground, the graven tablet, the tended flowers affected him so as belonging to him that he quite felt for the hour like a contented landlord reviewing a piece of property. Whatever had happened—well, had happened. He had not come back this time with the vanity of that question, his former worrying, "What, *what?*" now practically so spent. Yet he would, none the less, never again so cut himself off from the spot; he would come back to it every month, for if he did nothing else by its aid he at least held up his head. It thus grew for him, in the oddest way, a positive resource; he carried out his idea of periodical returns, which took their place at last among the most inveterate of his habits. What it all amounted to, oddly enough, was that, in his now so simplified world, this garden of death gave him the few square feet of earth on which he could still most live. It was as if, being nothing anywhere else for anyone, nothing even for himself, he were just everything here, and if not for a crowd of witnesses, or indeed for any witness but John Marcher, then by clear right of the register that he could scan like an open page. The open page was the tomb of his friend, and *there* were the facts of the past, there the truth of his life, there the backward reaches in which he could lose himself. He did this, from time to time, with such effect that he seemed to wonder through the old years with his hand in the arm of a companion who was, in the most extraordinary manner, his other, his younger self; and to wander, which was more extraordinary yet, round and round a third presence—not wandering she, but stationary, still, whose eyes, turning with his revolution, never ceased to follow him, and whose seat was his point, so to speak, of orientation. Thus in short he settled to live—feeding only on the sense that he once *had* lived, and dependent on it not only for a support but for an identity.

It sufficed him, in its way, for months, and the year elapsed; it would doubtless even have carried him further but for an accident, superficially slight, which moved him, in a quite other direction, with a force beyond any of his impressions of Egypt or of India. It was a thing of the merest chance—the turn, as he afterwards felt, of a hair, though he was indeed to live to believe that if light hadn't come to him in this particular fashion it would still have come in another. He was to live to believe this, I say, though he was not to live, I may not less definitely mention, to do much else. We allow him at any rate the benefit of the conviction, struggling up for him at the end, that, whatever might have happened or not happened, he would have come round of himself to the light. The incident of an autumn day had put the match to the train laid from of old by his misery. With the light before him he knew that even of late his ache had only been smothered. It was strangely drugged, but it throbbed; at the touch it began to bleed. And the touch, in the event, was the face of a fellow-mortal. This face, one grey afternoon when the leaves were thick in the alleys, looked into Marcher's own, at the cemetery, with an expression like the cut of a blade. He felt it, that is, so deep down that he winced at the steady thrust. The person who so mutely assaulted him was a figure he had noticed, on reaching his own goal, absorbed by a grave a short distance away, a grave apparently fresh, so that the emotion of the visitor would probably match it for frankness. This fact alone forbade further attention, though during the time he stayed he remained vaguely conscious of his neighbour, a middle-aged man apparently, in mourning, whose bowed back, among the clustered monuments and mortuary yews, was constantly presented. Marcher's theory that these were elements in contact with which he himself revived, had suffered, on this occasion, it may be granted, a sensible though inscrutable check. The autumn day was dire for him as none had recently been, and he rested with a heaviness he had not yet known on the low stone table that bore May Bartram's name. He rested without power to move, as if some spring in him, some spell vouchsafed, had suddenly been broken forever. If he could have done that moment as he wanted he would simply have stretched himself on the slab that was ready to take him, treating it as a place prepared to receive his last sleep. What in all the wide world had he now to keep awake for? He stared before him with the question, and it was then that, as one of the cemetery walks passed near him, he caught the shock of the face.

His neighbour at the other grave had withdrawn, as he himself, with force in him to move, would have done by now, and was advancing along the path on his way to one of the gates. This brought him near, and his pace was slow, so that—and all the more as there was a kind of hunger in his look—the two men were for a minute directly confronted. Marcher felt him on the spot as one of the deeply stricken—a perception so sharp that nothing else in the picture lived for it, neither his dress, his age, nor his presumable character and class; nothing lived but the deep ravage of the features that he showed. He *showed* them—that was the point; he was moved, as he passed, by some impulse that was either a signal for sympathy or, more possibly, a challenge to another sorrow. He might already have been aware of our friend, might, at some previous hour, have noticed in him the smooth habit of the scene, with which the state of his own senses so scantly consorted, and might thereby have been stirred as by a kind of overt discord. What Marcher was at all events conscious of was, in the first place, that the image of scarred passion presented to him was conscious too—of something that profaned the air; and, in the second, that, roused, startled, shocked, he was yet the next moment looking after it, as it went, with envy. The most extraordinary thing that had happened to him—though he had given that name to other matters as well—took place, after his immediate vague stare, as a consequence of this impression. The stranger passed, but the raw glare of his grief remained, making our friend wonder in pity what wrong, what wound it expressed, what injury not to be healed. What had the man *had* to make him, by the loss of it, so bleed and yet live?

Something—and this reached him with a pang—that *he,* John Marcher, hadn't; the proof of which was precisely John Marcher's arid end. No passion had ever touched him, for this was what passion meant; he had survived and maundered and pined, but where had been *his* deep ravage? The extraordinary thing we speak of was the sudden rush of the result of this question. The sight that had just met his eyes named to him, as in letters of quick flame, something he had utterly, insanely missed, and what he had missed made these things a train of fire, made them mark themselves in an anguish of inward throbs. He had seen *outside* of his life, not learned it within, the way a woman was mourned when she had been loved for herself; such was the force of his conviction of the meaning of the stranger's face, which still flared for him like a smoky torch. It had not come to him, the knowledge, on the wings of experience; it had brushed him, jostled him, upset him, with the disrespect of chance, the insolence of an accident. Now that the illumination had begun, however, it blazed to the zenith, and what he presently stood there gazing at was the sounded void of his life. He gazed, he drew breath, in pain; he turned in his dismay, and, turning, he had before him in sharper incision than ever the open page of his story. The name on the table smote him as the passage of his neighbour had done, and what it said to him, full in the face, was that *she* was what he had missed. This was the awful thought, the answer to all the past, the vision at the dread clearness of which he turned as cold as the stone beneath him. Everything fell together, confessed, explained, overwhelmed; leaving him most of all stupefied at the blindness he had cherished. The fate he had been marked for he had met with a vengeance—he had emptied the cup to the lees; he had been the man of his time, *the* man, to whom nothing on earth was to have happened. That was the rare stroke—that was his visitation. So he saw it, as we say, in pale horror, while the pieces fitted and fitted. So *she* had seen it, while he didn't, and so she served at this hour to drive the truth home. It was the truth, vivid and monstrous, that all the while he had waited the wait was itself his portion. This the companion of his vigil had at a given moment perceived, and she had then offered him the chance to baffle his doom. One's doom, however, was never baffled, and on the day she had told him that his own had come down she had seen him but stupidly stare at the escape she offered him.

The escape would have been to love her; then, *then* he would have lived. *She* had lived—who could say now with what passion?—since she had loved him for himself; whereas he had never thought of her (ah, how it hugely glared at him!) but in the chill of his egotism and the light of her use. Her spoken words came back to him, and the chain stretched and stretched. The beast had lurked indeed, and the beast, at its hour, had sprung; it had sprung in that twilight of the cold April when, pale, ill, wasted, but all beautiful, and perhaps even then recoverable, she had risen from her chair to stand before him and let him imaginably guess. It had sprung as he didn't guess; it had sprung as she hopelessly turned from him, and the mark, by the time he left her, had fallen where it *was* to fall. He had justified his fear and achieved his fate; he had failed, with the last exactitude, of all he was to fail of; and a moan now rose to his lips as he remembered she had prayed he mightn't know. This horror of waking—*this* was knowledge, knowledge under the breath of which the very tears in his eyes seemed to freeze. Through them, none the less, he tried to fix it and hold it; he kept it there before him so that he might feel the pain. That at least, belated and bitter, had something of the taste of life. But the bitterness suddenly sickened him, and it was as if, horribly, he saw, in the truth, in the cruelty of his image, what had been appointed and done. He saw the Jungle of his life and saw the lurking Beast; then, while he looked, perceived it, as by a stir of the air, rise, huge and hideous, for the leap that was to settle him. His eye darkened—it was close; and, instinctively turning, in his hallucination, to avoid it, he flung himself, on his face, on the tomb.

NOTE ON SELECTION AND TEXT

The selection of short novels for this volume is limited to narratives between twenty and fifty thousand words in length. The text is that of the original editions. James introduced quite a few verbal changes into the text of the collected edition, but these revisions produce an impression of stylistic uniformity the value of which has been questioned by a number of authorities on James, especially with regard to its effect on his early work. The use of the original editions enables the reader to gain a direct impression of the development of James's style.